Elizabeth Warne w ... moved north via Ox ... now lives with her husband in a Regency garden situated in the beautiful wooded valley of the Water of Girvan in south-west Scotland. She sold her first short story at the age of nine and has since written a number of historical novels under pseudonyms, as well as *Ragtime Girl*, a novel praised by *Books Magazine* as deserving 'top marks for a talented portrayal of the Depression years and the wonderful range of low and high brow characters,' and by the *Bristol Evening Post* as a 'red-blooded rag-trade romance'.

Also by Elizabeth Warne

Ragtime Girl

Wild Silk

Elizabeth Warne

KNIGHT

First published in 1991
by HEADLINE BOOK PUBLISHING PLC

First published in paperback in 1991
by HEADLINE BOOK PUBLISHING PLC

This edition published 2000 by
Knight an imprint of Caxton Publishing Group

10 9 8 7 6 5 4 3 2 1

ISBN 1 84067 270 6

Typeset by:
Colset Private Limited, Singapore

Printed and bound in Great Britain by
J. H. Haynes & Co. Ltd., Sparkford, Somerset

Caxton Publishing Group
20 Bloomsbury Street
London
WC1B 3QA

To my husband with my thanks for his invaluable practical help and unfailing moral support.

My thanks go again to the senior citizens of Bristol who once more shared their fascinating memories with me.

Chapter One

'Not the sapphires!' said Adela impatiently.

'But, Miss Adela, they go perfectly with that gown. That's why your father bought them for you. He'll be dreadfully disappointed. You know how much he's enjoyed buying you presents, ever since you were a little girl.'

'The fighting's stopped,' said Adela, 'but we're still supposed to be embracing austerity. It's patriotic.' The disloyal thought crossed her mind, as it had done before, that Father's expensive presents were always ones which other people would see. George Danby liked his women to remind others of his success in his textiles and clothing business and he particularly enjoyed decking out the beautiful one of his two daughters.

'The war's over!' protested Bertha. She was Mother's maid. Adela's maid, Sarah, had gone to work in a munitions factory and had been cheeky about it, pointing out when she left that, as well as regular hours, she'd be getting a much bigger wage. Adela had been outraged. After all, she had treated Sarah well, making her the customary gifts of discarded clothing and the odd piece of costume jewellery of which she had tired. She had told her exactly what she thought of her impudence, but during the war there had been plenty of jobs for women and no one had applied for the vacant position. Other servants had left, too, and made for bigger money.

'They'll be sorry in the end,' Mother had said. 'They'll all come crawling back when the men return and we'll have our pick.'

'The war's only *just* over,' Adela reminded Bertha. 'They only signed the Armistice last week.'

1

'But Mr Ralph's family know the master gave you sapphires. Leaving them up here won't impress them.'

Adela possessed a stubbornness which her parents had tried hard to eradicate. 'I won't wear the sapphires,' she insisted.

Bertha said grimly, 'Very well, Miss Adela, if you say so. I'm sure you know best.'

'You don't believe any such thing,' snapped Adela.

Bertha sighed but ignored the petulant remark.

Adela fought hard against nausea. So far it was controllable and it had better stay that way until Ralph returned. If Mother learned what had happened to her . . . At this point Adela's imagination failed her. And what would Father say? Ralph must come home, and soon, to make everything all right! It was all his fault!

The newspapers said that craftsmen were to be demobilised first but the only craft possessed by Ralph was the ability to obey his parents. He had been ready to go to university, then to join his brothers in the family business which, like Danby's, dealt in textiles and wholesale clothing, but the outbreak of war had sent him, along with many other enthusiastic young patriots, racing to the nearest recruitment centre. Some people said that the first in the army must be the first out. Ralph had joined up in 1914 when he was eighteen and Adela seventeen. If rumour was to be believed then Ralph would soon be home.

She and Ralph Somers had been friends since infancy. He had proposed to her when she was nineteen and, sheltered, unworldly, proud of him in his warrior's uniform, she had accepted. Both sets of parents approved of their engagement, though insisted that, since it would be a long one, word of it must be kept within the family. Adela was very fond of Ralph, though disappointed that she felt no grand passion for him. Sensibly she had assured herself it probably didn't exist but was simply the product of the fertile imaginations of novelists or, more recently, the makers of animated pictures. Mother assured her that she would be happy with her choice. Their families were congenial, their backgrounds matched which was, Mother said, so important. Adela and Ralph would continue to move among top Bristol society, as they had always done.

Adela fidgeted while Bertha fastened the row of tiny hooks and eyes in the back of her silk dress.

'Keep still, Miss Adela. I never knew anyone fidget like you.'

Adela tried to obey though she resented the way Bertha bossed her about. Mother gave her too much licence and Adela was thankful that soon she would have a maid of her own again, one who would obey her without question. If the impudent Sarah applied for her job back she would get short shrift!

Bertha said, 'There you are, Miss Adela. That dress is one of my favourites. You look lovely in it and the stitches I had to let out in the bodice don't show at all.' She stood back and gazed at Adela. 'I do believe you're getting a little plump. Well, it suits you and it's not to be wondered at with all the lovely food that Mr Smithers manages to find. I don't know how he's done it all through the dreadful war.'

Adela didn't answer. She was glad that Bertha's meanderings gave her time to collect herself. She had to watch herself now all the time, dreading that she would reveal her ghastly secret.

At any other time, Bertha's inference that she had been wearing a gown for more than a few months, and that it must be let out rather than discarded for a new one, would have been considered an impertinence, even from a longtime servant. Now it was a compliment. Essential supplies had to be imported at great cost to the sailors who were constantly harried and drowned by German submarines, and women wanted to prove that they were not extravagant. She had heard that most materials now had to be home-produced by women slaving long hours though Adela had no personal evidence of this. Father's workroom girls always looked all right to her. The rumours were probably put about by the dreadful socialists who continually ranted on the subject of extreme poverty and were the bane of the existence of anyone with claims to decent living; or maybe by the raucous suffragettes whom Father insisted were a disgrace to womanhood. He hadn't mentioned them lately. Apparently they had put aside their militant striving to gain the vote to help wherever possible in the war against Germany. It was odd that Mother expected her family

3

to wear their clothes for more than a year, when she didn't hesitate to buy extra, illicit supplies for the pantry and fireplace, as well as petrol for the cars.

Thank God Bertha had assumed that her increase in size was due to overeating. Adela looked at her mirrored image as she moved and watched the panels of pale blue chiffon float softly from her waist round the darker blue of the underdress. The graceful drape made her look taller than her five feet six inches; her dark stockings flattered her slender ankles and her black satin shoes revealed well-shaped feet.

'What jewellery will you wear, then?' asked Bertha.

'I don't know. Anything that matches.' A wave of sickness almost made Adela gag. 'But *not* the sapphires,' she said.

Bertha pressed her lips together. Lately Miss Adela's moods had swung up and down disconcertingly. But then, it was no wonder the poor young lady was on edge when her young man had been in such awful danger at the front for four whole years. Now the terrible war was over and the men would come back and things would return to normal and Miss Adela and Mr Ralph could get married.

'I'll wear the long blue beads.' Adela put them on. They fell almost to her hips. Bertha lifted a modest oriental style headdress with a single feather and placed it on Adela's rich brown hair which was secured into a gleaming, luxuriant coil in the nape of her neck.

'There, Miss Adela, you look perfect.' She stared at the beads and sighed. 'Though I still think the sapphires—' She stopped as Adela flashed her a furious look and said quickly, 'Now I must go to Miss Blanche. She came home half an hour ago in those dreadful clothes she wears for her conductress work. To think of a lady taking fares on a tramcar. I never thought the day would come!'

Adela took a long look at herself in the mirror. No one would guess at her inner turmoil. Her skin was as clear and softly cream and pink-toned as always, her amber eyes bright. She picked up a white wool wrap and went downstairs.

In the drawing room one of Ralph's brothers and his wife had already arrived. Giles was playing the piano and Sybil, his

4

plebeian wife, was singing in a tiny voice: *I was a good little girl, till I met you.*

Mrs Danby raised a protesting hand at the saucy words, but she was trying to smile. She always said she enjoyed having young people about her, but Adela believed she was merely pandering to convention. Mrs Danby had never been interested in young people, not even her own children. Not that Giles, at thirty-three, was all that young, thought Adela. Sybil stopped singing when Adela entered and greeted her warmly.

'Here she is. Our next bride. Oh, how I long for Ralph to come home, and you must be positively aching for him, you poor thing. I know if Giles had been at the war I should have been fearfully worried.' Sybil stopped, aware that her words could be considered tactless.

'Of course you would,' agreed Adela.

Sybil was ten years younger than Giles. She was not pretty, and rather gauche, but such small imperfections counted for nothing against her father's money which came abundantly from woollen mills in the north.

The eldest son, Desmond, arrived with Violet, his wife, a mousy creature who had little to say. Not that the bombastic Desmond gave her much chance. He was exactly like his father who walked in almost immediately after his son.

Sir Wilfred shook Adela's hand, and Lady Somers gave her a peck on the cheek.

'You'll soon be our daughter,' boomed Sir Wilfred, 'and Blanche will have a brother. That young rascal of mine had better hurry home before some other lucky man runs off with you.'

Mrs Danby raised her brows and looked down her thin nose. 'There can be small chance of that, Sir Wilfred. I know their engagement has not yet been announced, but it is well understood in our families.'

'Just my little joke! Just a joke!'

Mrs Danby smiled frostily. She had no sense of humour. Her values were strictly Victorian; her chief pride, the length of her family tree and the fact that her ancestors had refused elevation to the ranks of the aristocracy, insisting that to be a Sutton, Mrs

5

Danby's family name, was honour enough. 'How are the children?' she asked collectively of Sybil and Violet. She was reassured that Sybil's little daughter was well, and that Violet's daughter and two sons were, under Nanny's careful regime, recovering from a severe cold which had swept through her nursery, and that the terrible septic influenza epidemic was not a threat to them. They were not encouraged to say more to her on the subject, though Sir Wilfred stayed by his daughters-in-law to ask more questions. He was fond of his grandchildren, though he had little time to spare from business for them.

'Have you heard from Ralph?' asked Lady Somers in her soft voice, as she seated herself beside Adela.

'Not since he returned to the front. Only six weeks ago, and I suppose he hasn't time to write, but it seems an age. I'm sure I shall hear soon. Have you had any letters?'

'I'm sorry to say we have not. I'll tell you instantly if we do. I thought he looked peaky when he left. Chest injuries can be awfully serious and I don't think he was properly over his. He seemed quite melancholy during his convalescence, though I suppose that is not surprising after four years in the army.'

'Nonsense!' said Sir Wilfred, overhearing. 'Soldiers don't need any molly-coddling from their fond mamas. I'm proud of him. He's done well to reach the rank of captain.'

Lady Somers leaned back into her chair. She never could fight the overbearing ways of her bombastic husband.

'Yes, indeed,' agreed Mrs Danby. 'He's a good and conscientious boy.'

'And never a hint of fear,' said Sir Wilfred. 'Not that there was ever any danger of that.'

That's what you think, thought Adela. A devil sprang up in her, tempting her to voice the words aloud, but she couldn't be so disloyal as to betray her future husband's weakness.

Mrs Danby gave a welcome smile to the next arrivals. Clifford and Mildred Smithers would not have got their noses past the front door of Speede House, the big family home in Clifton, if there hadn't been a war. They were definitely 'not the thing'. That was Mrs Danby's rigid criterion for judging people. But Mr Smithers was exceedingly useful at the moment, being able to get his hands on such essentials as butter, tea, sugar, cheese and coal, among other things. The list was long. He had made a fortune as a profiteer and with his large paunch, his gold ring, and his self-satisfied air, he could have been the model for the caricatures depicted so satirically in *Punch*.

'Welcome to our small Armistice celebration,' said Mrs Danby, her distaste at seeing such undesirables in her drawing room well hidden. She shook hands with Clifford and bent to brush Mildred's cheek with hers.

Clara, the elderly parlour maid, brought in a tray of sherry.

'Where is Evans?' asked Mrs Danby, her eyebrows raised.

'He's supervising the dinner, ma'am,' said Clara.

Mrs Danby lifted her hands in a display of horror which was only partly assumed. 'I did not think I should see the day when my butler must hang over the ovens to supervise the kitchen staff. Please God, now the war is over we can quickly fill the vacancies and live decently again.'

'How many servants have you got now?' asked Mrs Smithers.

Mrs Danby stared coolly at her. 'I believe there are eight indoors, and a gardener – oh, and of course, the chauffeur, though he hated having to learn to drive a motor car. He was our coachman for many years. Some of the servants would normally have retired by now; others are young and positively untrainable. They would not, in peace time, have found a place here.'

'We've got nine indoor staff,' said Mrs Smithers, 'an' they're all good. I think we get folks to stay with us because we pay them a lot in wages.'

Lady Somers said, 'It has become the thing for domestic staff to go where the wages are highest. I suppose one cannot blame them but in the old days a family's quality attracted the best.'

'Is that a fact?' Mrs Smithers was indignant.

Mrs Danby drew back her chin, disdaining to speak, then raised her glass. 'To the final homecoming of our boys.'

The toast was drunk enthusiastically. Adela sipped at hers. She didn't really want it.

'Drink up, lass,' said Mr Smithers heartily. 'You're the one with the most cause to rejoice!'

'Yes,' said Adela with a wan smile, pretending to take another sip.

'Do not forget that Ralph is the son of Sir Wilfred and Lady Somers,' reminded Mrs Danby, her voice cool, her eyes hard.

'I haven't forgot,' said Mr Smithers. He had forgotten, and he was flustered, and his carefully acquired upper-class accent almost slipped.

Lady Somers said, 'Mr Smithers is perfectly correct. A wife must come before parents.' She sounded apologetic, as if she had no right to express herself.

Adela thought of her future in the family of a bully like Sir Wilfred and his scared little wife. She would insist that Ralph buy a house a few miles away from Bristol, in Bath, maybe. It was a nice place, and if they put ten miles between themselves and their families it should lessen the amount of time they could spend with them.

'Is your motor car running well, Mr Smithers?' asked Mrs Danby. Her interest in the Smithers' mode of transport was minimal, but she found it difficult to converse with someone who had risen from being a market trader.

Adela had once suggested that if her mother found the company of the Smithers so distasteful, she should give up their acquaintance.

Mrs Danby had gone red with annoyance. 'Unfortunately one is dependent upon such vulgar people these days for the necessities of life.'

'Does everyone accept their help?' asked Adela. She had been innocent of any malice.

'Do not ask impertinent questions!' her mother had snapped. 'Of course there are many who cannot afford to avail themselves of help, but that doesn't matter since most of them are accustomed to deprivation. Go and polish up your French. You'll need it when this ghastly war is over and one can visit darling Paris again.'

'I'm glad to say that our Rolls-Royce never lets me down,' said Mr Smithers now, his beaming smile embracing the whole

8

company. 'She's a beauty isn't she, Mildred?'

'Lovely. I always say there's no better car than a Silver Ghost. We had the hood up comin' here. It's gettin' colder, though we got to expect it in November.' Mrs Smithers' efforts at improving her diction and grammar had not proved successful.

Mrs Danby scarcely bothered to hide her smile of mocking superiority.

Mr Smithers said, 'I drive it myself these days. Our chauffeur was called to the front when they began to take married men, and was killed as soon as he got there. What a waste! He was a good driver and a clever mechanic and he'd have done a lot better to have stayed with me. I've had to set to and learn about looking after the motor car myself because it's impossible to find anyone these days who can look after a Rolls-Royce properly.'

'Yes, indeed,' agreed Desmond, gallantly assisting Mrs Danby in the conversation, 'but one has to make sacrifices when the country is at war.'

Adela almost laughed. When, in 1916, the government had stopped relying on volunteers and introduced conscription, Desmond had convinced the military that he couldn't be spared from the essential war work in the Somers's workrooms, where fashions had given way to the manufacture of uniforms. His brother, Giles, had had severe scarlet fever as a child and it had left him an invalid. The Somerses, in any case, considered they had done enough for Britain when Ralph had enlisted.

Violet, who was seated beside Adela on a couch, leaned forward and murmured, 'What ghastly people! Your mother's a saint to put up with them.'

Mrs Smithers looked up sharply and Adela wondered if she had heard, or if she was constantly on the watch for snubs from these rich folk whom she would never understand. Gold chains glinted on her large bosom, while diamonds flashed from a hair ornament and rings.

Like Adela, the other women present wore gowns at least a year old, with very little jewellery, though Father had frowned when she had appeared without the sapphires. She had

9

countered with a smile which he had rather reluctantly returned and now she felt even more glad that she wore her inexpensive blue beads.

'Is dear Blanche to be with us tonight?' asked Lady Somers.

'Yes, I can't think what is keeping her.' Mrs Danby glanced at the ormolu clock on the marble fireplace. 'We are also expecting another guest. Mr Bennett. I don't know how many of you have met him. Sir Wilfred has made his acquaintance in a business capacity.'

'Sander Bennett?' asked Desmond. 'I've met him a few times in my dealings. He's a shrewd man. Do you know him, Mr Smithers?'

Mr Smithers struggled for a while with the social dilemma he had been handed. Sander Bennett was not accepted everywhere. Yet he was a guest of the Danbys. 'I've met him,' he managed.

Mrs Danby said, 'He is an up and coming man. His interests are so like our own, chiefly textiles, though he owns a boot factory which was once his uncle's. Mr Danby believes he will go far and increase the trading opportunities in Bristol.' She paused. 'He can be quite charming.'

Adela listened without interest. She had met Sander Bennett who, in spite of his humble beginnings, was accepted at many society functions, though he was seldom met in small gatherings in really top-drawer homes. She thought him much too pushy and knew that Father disliked him, while Mother found his company almost as distasteful as that of the Smithers.

Blanche joined them, her wispy blonde hair, sallow complexion and angular figure not helped by an unadorned fawn gown. Her pale eyes slid over her sister, then moved to Mrs Smithers and Adela saw that she kept her lip from curling in contempt only with an effort.

'Ah, dear Blanche,' said Mrs Danby, a shade too enthusiastically. She was a little nervous of her unattractive, outspoken daughter. 'I believe you know everybody here.'

'I'm starving,' said Blanche loudly. 'The Armistice doesn't appear to have slowed up the factories. The tramcars are always full. I wonder when it will penetrate our leaders' skulls that we

10

'don't actually require guns and bullets any more.'

'Such a disrespectful way to speak!' said Mrs Danby, fluttering her long, bony fingers. 'I am quite sure that our wonderful Field-Marshal Haig will prevail soon upon Mr Lloyd George to halt the manufacture of arms. The factories must then turn to plough shares.'

Adela knew that her mother reckoned she'd scored a pertinent point in referring to plough shares. She wondered if Mother knew what they looked like, or even, with any accuracy, what they did. She then realised that she was equally ignorant. What did it matter? The beastly fighting had stopped, that was all that concerned her, and soon she and Ralph would marry and she could escape this terrible, lonely burden of fear and guilt.

Blanche asked, 'Why are we waiting dinner? It's past eight o'clock.'

'It is, indeed,' said Mr Danby, glancing at his watch. He hated unpunctuality.

Mr Smithers reached into the pocket of his waistcoat and withdrew a gold hunter. 'You're right, Mr Danby. This watch keeps perfect time. It was made in Switzerland before the war.'

'It's real gold,' said Mrs Smithers.

Blanche turned her cool gaze on her. 'Indeed! How gratifying!'

Mrs Smithers, unable to identify the tone of Blanche's voice yet feeling uneasy, subsided. Her husband, sensing his wife's distress, glared at Blanche, his bushy eyebrows drawn together in a frown.

'We're waiting for Mr Bennett, dear,' explained Lady Somers.

'Sander Bennett?' Blanche looked pleased. She sat down and accepted sherry from the maid. 'Will he be long?'

'I'm sure he will not,' said Mrs Danby. She turned her head to listen. 'I believe that was the front door.'

A moment later Evans, the butler, announced, 'Mr Alexander Bennett.'

Sander Bennett walked in, his head thrust forward aggressively, his hair slick with pomade. He shook hands with his hostess. 'Sorry I'm late, Mrs Danby. Spot of bother at the factory. One of the machines broke down and since we've had no directives to stop making army boots I must assume that they are still wanted, though heaven alone knows what for.' His voice had a tinge of accent which he had failed to iron out.

'Just what I was saying about munitions, Mr Bennett,' said Blanche.

She likes him, thought Adela, watching her sister gaze at Sander. She wondered if Blanche could be a little in love with him. It was possible. She wondered at her sister's taste. Perhaps Blanche was desperate. She had never had a boy friend. She wondered if her parents would allow a match between Sander Bennett and their elder daughter. Sander, as Mr Danby put it, was 'a man of the people'. Adela looked at him. His large head was planted firmly on a thick neck above wide shoulders. His cheeks were slightly hollowed beneath high cheek bones. He looked what he was – a plebeian – and in spite of his perfect clothes, he would never look anything else. Not that he ever pretended. He, like the Smithers, was made welcome in the Danby house only because he was increasingly rich and successful and could be of use. His boot factory in Kingswood had expanded hugely during the war and he had recently bought a small corset factory. Although aged thirty in 1914 he had tried to join the army, but had been refused because of his expertise in bootmaking. And, later, when conscription was introduced, he had again been rejected for the same reason.

Adela got up when Evans announced, with a slight air of censure because they had run past the eight o'clock dinner hour, 'Dinner is served.' He, like Bertha and the parlourmaid, had been with the family for years.

Sander obligingly took Blanche in to dinner and Adela was placed on his other side.

The food was delicious and plentiful, though Adela merely toyed with hers. The talk unavoidably turned to the war and the Armistice, subjects which, at present, her emotions surfeited by fear and anxiety, Adela found nerve-racking.

Sander said, 'I look forward to seeing Ralph home again,

Lady Somers. I thought he went back to the front very soon after being wounded.'

'It was not a serious wound!' said Sir Wilfred, his voice expressing his strong disapproval of Sander's implied criticism.

'A blighty wound!' said Mr Smithers. 'It brought the young chap home for a while.'

'We were fortunate that we were able to pamper him a little,' said Lady Somers. She stared at her husband defiantly. 'I, too, thought he looked quite poorly when he rejoined his regiment.'

'Mothers!' exclaimed Sir Wilfred, giving a hearty laugh in which the men joined, except Sander Bennett who didn't look amused.

Mrs Danby waggled an admonishing finger. 'It's a good job we women do give the brave boys a little tenderness. They deserve it after fighting so well.'

Blanche said, 'Had I been a man I would have signed up like a shot to be a soldier. I don't understand why women weren't permitted to go to the front.'

'There are some very courageous nurses near the front line, dear,' said Mrs Danby, 'and women have been helping our brave men in various ways quite close to the fighting. Some have been killed, or badly wounded.'

'Oh, yes, women are permitted to serve in quite menial capacities,' snapped Blanche, 'and many at their own expense. I should have gone if I'd been permitted to carry a weapon.'

'Blanche!' expostulated Mrs Danby.

Mrs Smithers said, 'I can't never get used to seeing girls in men's clothes. Trousers on a woman doesn't – don't seem right.'

'I wear them for work,' said Blanche, staring hard at Mrs Smithers who was immediately silenced.

Mrs Danby gave Blanche an angry glance. 'I know what you mean, Mrs Smithers,' she said, smoothing the prickly atmosphere, 'but, of course, they are most suitable for the brave girls who do such dreadful tasks. It would not be at all fitting for my daughter to climb the stairs of a tramcar in skirts.'

Mrs Smithers was indignant. 'I'm sure when I travelled on

tramcars I kept my modesty up an' down the stairs.'

Mrs Danby went on as if she had not spoken, 'Now at last we shall see our daughters in proper clothes again. What a treat that will be. And imagine being able to go once more to Paris to shop.'

Mrs Smithers blinked. 'It's a long way when there's plenty of good shops in Bristol.' She sounded annoyed. 'There's Taylor's an' Alexandra's for clothes an' you can get anythin' else you want in Jones's in Wine Street, and as for shoes, well, Lennard's suits me. I go to Jolly's in Bath, too. Do you know that they're silk mercers to Queen Mary? Mind you, I like shoppin' in London sometimes too and Harrods is nice, but the prices!' She raised protesting eyes to heaven.

'We can afford them, love,' said Mr Smithers expansively.

The atmosphere grew increasingly frosty as Mrs Smithers rambled on, her rather strident voice dominating the table.

Sander said loudly, 'I wonder if the day will come when men will travel abroad to study the fashions.'

The notion raised a general laugh. Mrs Danby glanced round the table. 'Ladies, we will leave the men to their port and cigars. They can discuss us poor females to their hearts' content when we are gone.'

'And I've no doubt you ladies will have plenty to say about us men!' said Mr Smithers, chuckling and taking a large gold case from his pocket and opening it to show it filled with expensive cigars.

In the drawing room Blanche flopped on to a chair near the leaping fire. There were always fires in every room.

No one seemed inclined to speak. 'Do tell us a little about your war work, Blanche,' suggested Lady Somers.

Mrs Danby frowned, but before she could speak Blanche snapped, 'It's boring as hell.'

'Blanche!' Mrs Danby glanced at her guests. 'I'm afraid some of our young ladies' language has suffered by mixing with – with—' Mrs Danby stuttered to a halt. She had been about to refer to 'the lower classes', then remembered that Mrs Smithers had been born somewhere unspeakably low. In a Bedminster slum, she had heard.

Adela had managed to make quite a good dinner and felt much better. She was suddenly sorry for her mother who, after all, was enduring the company of these vulgar outsiders simply so that she could succour her family.

'I've heard girls using quite bad language, Mother,' she said, 'I think it's getting fashionable.'

'It is not a fashion I wish to encourage,' snapped Mrs Danby.

'No, indeed,' said Lady Somers. 'One would sink to the level of servants and people of that class. Their behaviour is inexplicable at times. Only yesterday I had occasion to dismiss a parlour maid. The foolish girl has got herself into trouble and Sir Wilfred cannot abide lax morals. Neither can I, of course. I only hope that her soldier friend returns in time to marry her. As Sir Wilfred said, "One is not surprised when a scullery girl lands herself in a predicament", but my maid was quite superior and from a respectable family. I have no doubt they will cast her off.'

Adela's stomach churned. She picked up a magazine and pretended to be riffling through it. Ralph, Ralph, come home soon, she prayed.

'That's really mean!' protested Mrs Smithers.

'What?' Lady Somers looked startled.

'Oh, not you, Lady Somers, though *I* wouldn't have—' Mrs Smithers paused, her face growing more florid. 'But if her own family throw a girl out! I mean, what'll she do? Where will she go?'

'Sir Wilfred says that is no concern of ours.'

'Well, I wouldn't do it to any daughter of mine,' declared Mrs Smithers.

'Fortunately you have no children to worry you,' said Mrs Danby coldly.

Mrs Smithers flushed a deeper red. 'That's by no wish of ours, I can tell you! I would have liked kiddies, but they never come along.'

Mrs Danby and Lady Somers exchanged scandalised glances.

Blanche said loudly, 'She'll probably be all right. A woman can go out to work and look after herself these days, thank God.'

'Maybe,' said Mrs Smithers, 'but it isn't easy for a girl who's got herself caught. I've seen some of it in my time, I can tell you.'

Mrs Danby looked up thankfully as coffee was brought by the butler, accompanied by a very young footman whose uniform, having been fashioned for his predecessor who had been called up, was a bad fit.

'Ah, coffee,' she said, unnecessarily.

'And such delicious coffee,' said Lady Somers, sipping at the cup carried to her by the footman.

'Thanks to my hubby,' said Mrs Smithers aggressively. She might be a bit slow on the uptake sometimes, but she knew that, at certain points in the evening, these upper-class folk had insulted her and Clifford.

'As you say, Mrs Smithers,' agreed Mrs Danby, managing to produce a tepid smile.

The men joined them quickly and Sander Bennett walked straight to Adela where she sat in an armchair. He drew up a chair and seated himself beside her. Adela could feel the annoyance directed at her by Blanche who had kept a place beside her on a sofa, hoping, perhaps expecting, Sander to join her. Adela couldn't help but feel that if her sister had more sense she would have dressed herself better, but then she looked down on women who pandered to men; and since going out to work she had taken on a number of opinions which worried her parents.

'It's the fault of the war,' Mrs Danby often declared. 'Mixing with all types of women has been the ruin of many of our girls.'

'You haven't touched your coffee,' observed Sander.

'I don't want it,' said Adela emphatically. What business was it of his?

Her voice had carried and Mrs Danby called across the wide drawing room, 'What's that? You should know better than to waste good coffee. We're very lucky to get it.'

'I read that the Germans are making theirs from dandelion roots,' said Lady Somers.

'It's their own fault for starting the war,' said Blanche.

'Charity,' said Lady Somers. 'We've won. We can afford to be magnanimous.'

'I find it hard to forgive a nation who dropped bombs on our beloved country, and actually killed innocent women and children,' said Sir Wilfred.

16

'War is horrible,' said Sander, 'but now we have to win the peace.' He gained the entire attention of the room.

'Win the peace?' Mrs Smithers was baffled. 'How d'you do that?'

'Make sure that the Boche never gets hold of weapons again,' said Sir Wilfred.

'Keep them down until they squeak for mercy,' said Mr Danby.

'Those are bad policies,' Sander said.

'What do you mean, sir?' asked Sir Wilfred, his rubicund face going redder with anger. 'They were the aggressors. Are you suggesting we should pat their heads and forgive them, as if they were naughty children? We've lost the flower of our youth to them!'

Sander said, 'No one regrets more than I do the terrible toll the war has taken of our young men, but the Germans are now suffering horrifying privations. To grind their faces even further into the dirt will make them hate us.'

'They already hate us!' exclaimed Mr Smithers.

'Not irrevocably. If we helped them rebuild their economy it would benefit us and, in the end, the whole world. Unfortunately,' he continued, regarding the outraged faces around him with a scowl, 'I have no hope that the government will see it that way.'

'I should think not!' said Sir Wilfred. 'By God, sir, if the war were not over I believe you could be interned as a traitor.'

'Shot even,' said Sander, acerbically.

The other men glared at him, then began to talk about the rising prices caused, they had no doubt, at least partly by irresponsible strike action.

'Though I daresay Mr Bennett doesn't condemn strikes, even in wartime.' Desmond's attack was sudden. 'I've been told, Mr Bennett, that you have socialist leanings.'

'You were correctly informed,' said Sander, 'though a man's politics is his own affair.'

Desmond flushed angrily.

'You follow the ideas of that dreadful man, Keir Hardy?' Mrs Danby's brows were raised in polite disbelief.

17

Sybil, always gauche, gave a shrill laugh and received a frown from her mother-in-law.

'Mr Hardy is dead,' said Sander, 'but his ideals live on in Arthur Henderson, among others. The miners are working men like ourselves.'

'Not like ourselves!' protested Sir Wilfred. 'We are the ones who get the contracts and bring in the work to pay our staff.'

Sander's face was thrust forward aggressively. 'And to pay ourselves. The miners only ask for a wage big enough to feed their wives and kids. People must eat, even in wartime.'

'I'm sure I pay my staff well,' said Mr Danby.

'I'm pleased to hear it,' said Sander.

Blanche said loudly, 'Thank God, that here in Britain a man's allowed to follow what politics he chooses. We're not a Bolshevik country. There's no revolution here. *We* wouldn't murder our royal family as the Bolsheviks murdered theirs.'

'Perhaps Mr Bennett thinks that dreadful act was deserved,' said Desmond.

Sander's eyes narrowed. 'No, I don't agree with murder, but the Czar could have taken his family to safety if he hadn't been so arrogant.'

'If there are enough men who think the same way as you, Mr Bennett, there may soon be a revolution here,' said Sir Wilfred.

'I don't think that Britons would ever go as far as the Bolsheviks,' said Sander, 'though if the extreme revolutionaries in Russia had listened to their political leaders, the bloodshed might have been avoided. Once the Czar had abdicated, there is no doubt that they would have won power through the ballot box. As surely as the socialists will one day win power in Britain.'

He turned to Adela, leaving the other men glaring malevolently at his back, and grinned. His strong teeth were white against his tanned skin. He was a big man and his clothes were faultless and fitted him perfectly. Too perfectly. He had none of the gentlemanly quality of wearing his clothes as if he'd been born in them. His dark eyes, as dark as his hair, roamed over her. He was so unspeakably boorish. 'What do you think of socialism?' he demanded.

'I don't know enough about it to give an opinion.'

'You should. Women have the vote now.'

'Not all of us. One must be over thirty and I shan't be that for many years.'

'But time goes by fast. You should start thinking about politics now.'

Adela said lightly, 'I read somewhere that men believe women will never vote because they'll refuse to tell their correct age.'

'Do you believe that?'

'I don't know.'

Sander looked intently at her. 'All young women should study the political situation, especially as it affects their poorer sisters. In that way the wealthy can bring influence for good to bear.'

'What have you done? You're much older than me.'

'I've been busy making a living, but now the war's over I intend to devote as much time as possible to politics.'

'How boring,' sighed Adela.

He was beyond her comprehension, such a contrast to Ralph, with his fair skin and hair, light brows and lashes, and the mild manners characteristic of so many Englishmen. And he was, naturally, a Conservative.

'You must be longing for your fiancé's return,' said Sander, changing the subject abruptly.

'How do you know he's my fiancé? It's supposed to be a family secret.'

'Your father mentioned it.'

'Did he? I wonder why? Of course I'm looking forward to Ralph's return. I agree with Lady Somers that he looked unfit to go back to fight. Besides he—' She stopped, horrified. She had almost revealed poor Ralph's terrible fear of the front line. If it hadn't been for that she wouldn't now be trying to control another wave of nausea as the smell of fresh coffee, brought her by Evans himself, assailed her nose.

'Now, Miss Adela,' said Evans, 'drink this fresh coffee. I'll take the cold cup to the kitchen and heat it for one of the under servants.'

'Who'll consider themselves lucky to get it,' said Sander Bennett, loudly enough to turn heads.

'Indeed they will, sir,' agreed Evans, failing to catch the sardonic note in Sander's voice.

Adela was not so slow. When Evans shuffled back to the coffee pot she said, 'I'm surprised at you! Mocking a poor old servant.'

'Who's been with the family, man and boy,' intoned Sander.

'Don't tell me you don't employ servants. I wouldn't believe you.'

'Then there's no point in my answering your question.'

'Don't be so provoking. I'm sure even you don't clean your own house.'

'Even me?'

Adela felt quite ill and she resented having to sit here trying to make small talk with a man who was incapable of it.

'I have a charwoman who comes in every day and a young man who cooks for me and looks after my clothes.'

'Only two servants!'

'I don't need more. My place isn't grand like this one.' Sander's eyes swept over the deep pile carpet, the antique furniture whose highly polished surfaces gleamed with lights from the dancing fire, the bone china cups, the Meissen ornaments, the masses of gold and rust-coloured chrysanthemums in cut-glass vases, the heavy silver coffee tray and cream jug and sugar bowl. 'My wants are quite modest.'

Adela felt that his manner was critical and wanted to strike out at him. 'Yet you keep a man from the front.'

She saw that she had angered the jumped-up parvenu and she was glad.

'Bill paid his blood money in the army. He was employed in my boot factory and one of the first to join up. Poor devil, he was injured badly. He's left with a limp and an eye missing.'

'Oh! I'm sorry.'

Sander looked her full in the face and grinned insolently and she was left without a reply. Ralph, she begged silently, come home soon. I need you so much.

Chapter Two

It was ten o'clock when Evans entered, looking troubled, and walking straight to Sir Wilfred, bent forward and murmured something. The butler's demeanour was ominous and Lady Somers looked up, her face anxious.

'What is it?' she asked.

'Probably nothing,' said Sir Wilfred. 'I'm wanted on the telephone.'

Lady Somers sank back into her seat as her husband left. He returned moments later.

'I told you it was nothing. Well, nothing we need worry too much about. The call was from London. Ralph is ill.'

'Wounded?' Lady Somers asked sharply.

Adela's fists clenched white.

'If he had been wounded I would have said so,' returned her husband irritably. 'He's ill. It seems he had a cold and it turned to a chill. He'll be fine soon, I am quite sure.'

'I knew his chest was still weak,' declared Lady Somers. 'You know, Mrs Danby, how he always had dreadful colds when he was little and several times contracted bronchitis. And now there's this frightful influenza killing people everywhere.'

'I didn't say he had influenza,' said Sir Wilfred. 'For heaven's sake, my dear, pull yourself together. He's a man, not a child.'

'I agree with Sir Wilfred, Lady Somers,' said Mr Danby heartily. 'He's young enough to shake off a mere chill.'

'How bad is he?' asked Adela, her voice breaking with nervousness. 'Surely they wouldn't have got in touch if the illness was trivial.'

'Oh, it's not official,' said Sir Wilfred. 'A fellow officer on

21

leave contacted the house and they suggested he telephone me here.'

Lady Somers said, 'You shouldn't have broken the news so abruptly, Wilfred. Adela looks quite ill herself.'

Mrs Danby frowned. 'My daughter is perfectly well able to sustain a small shock.'

Small shock! How unfeeling Mother was. Adela pressed her lips together to conceal their trembling. Sander Bennett watched her, his eyes curious. He said, 'He'll come back safe, I'm sure. A chill is nothing to a battle-hardened warrior like Ralph.'

Adela nodded. Maybe the illness would ensure Ralph's early return. She prayed that it would.

She awoke the following morning feeling more ill than ever. For the first two or three weeks after she had missed her monthly course she had tried to tell herself that her loss of appetite, her sickness, her general feeling of lethargy could be due to anxiety over Ralph. Now, she needed no doctor's examination to tell her that she was expecting a baby. Mother had explained certain facts to her when she was eighteen. Adela knew that beneath her impersonal manner she had been embarrassed and spoke simply of physical matters, not gilding her account with any notions of love. Her attitude had not encouraged questions. Adela lay still, dreading the moment when she had to move. Gathering her courage she sat up and was hit by a powerful wave of nausea. She fell back on the pillows. Oh, God, she prayed, don't let anyone come in yet. Not until I've got myself under control.

Her prayer was ignored. After a perfunctory tap on the door a housemaid entered carrying a cup of tea and a plate with thin bread and butter. No tray. Grace had taken the place of the proper housemaid who had gone to work in a factory. She was, declared Evans, an untrainable slut.

She plonked the cup and plate on Adela's bedside table. 'Your early mornin' tea, miss.' She then left without waiting for an acknowledgement, or for any further orders.

Once upon a time, Adela would have castigated a servant for such lax behaviour. Today she was grateful. As the smell of the

22

tea reached her she slid out of bed, grabbed her dressing gown and fled along the corridor on bare feet to the bathroom where she vomited. She leaned her head on the cold lavatory pan and moaned, 'Dear God, send Ralph home soon, *please*. Let him be just ill enough to come home.'

The nausea passed and she managed to eat a little of the bread and butter, washing it down with water from her jug. She threw the tea out of the window where it fell in a small shower on the garden. She dressed in tobacco brown, a colour which suited her though her choice was automatic. She brushed her hair until it shone, securing it in the usual coil, then stared at herself in the mirror. She was far too pale. Mother would be sure to notice. She wished she had pink powder to put on her face, but Mother said only actresses and a certain kind of woman painted themselves. She pinched her cheeks and bit her lips into colour. As she descended the wide stairway she hoped that her stomach would behave when confronted with food. She couldn't get out of appearing in the breakfast parlour. Father liked his womenfolk to eat with him at nine o'clock before he set off for his office, though Blanche often had to be excused. Her shift this week began at five o'clock. Although Father deplored her job, he was nevertheless in a good mood this morning. The war had been kind to him. The workrooms were never idle, though the delivery of khaki cloth was sometimes erratic.

He was reading the newspaper and greeted Adela with a routine smile before returning to it.

Her mother frowned. 'You are pallid, Adela. You mustn't let Ralph's illness upset you. I'm sure he will soon be quite well and on his return we will announce your engagement.'

'Do we have to go through all that formality?' asked Adela, trying to keep her desperate anxiety from her tone. 'Why don't we just get married as soon as he reaches home? We've waited long enough.'

Mr Danby lowered his paper and stared disbelievingly over his reading glasses at his daughter, while Mrs Danby gave a mirthless laugh. 'So far you have simply been unofficially engaged,' she said, 'and you only attained your twenty-first birthday in June. A year's public engagement is not too long, and before we can contemplate an engagement party we must hold one to celebrate your coming of age.'

'Oh, must we? And a year! That's absolutely ages!'

'It seems so to you, now, Adela,' said her mother, her tone hard. 'That is because the war years have been so dreary. I feel sorry for young girls nowadays. You have been denied so much pleasure, so many parties and outings with young men. Think of it. You'll enjoy catching up on the amusements you've missed. There will be time enough to settle down.'

'I've been to parties during the war!'

'Adela, I wish you would not take that stubborn tone with your mother,' said Mr Danby. 'It doesn't become you. And your wish to tumble head-long into marriage without a proper engagement does you no credit either.'

Adela subsided miserably. Father was indulgent towards her within the limit of his ideas of correct behaviour, but any attempt to flout his authority brought immediate reprimand. She had been an obedient daughter, preferring to bask in his approval, and felt a surge of pure terror at the thought of what he would say when he discovered her terrible lapse from grace. And as for Mother, whose rules of conduct were stringent! She tried to picture herself confessing to Mother and had to swallow hard. It would be bad enough when Ralph came home, but together they could face their families. She realised that Mother was speaking to her.

'Your wits are wandering again, Adela. You have grown inattentive lately. It must stop. The signing of the Armistice and the realisation that this dreadful war is over have excited you, but you must wait calmly for Ralph's return. Remember that he will need a period to adjust to civilian life. He went straight into the army from school. Now no more arguments, Adela. The functions you've attended have not been exactly thrilling, have they?'

Adela thought of the few parties she had attended with young women, older men, a few mature schoolboys and wounded officers, and when, all too often, she and her friends had had to struggle with the knowledge that yet another childhood companion was missing in action or dead. The atmosphere was always heavy with sorrow, yet the parties were held, as if the spurious gaiety would banish the reality of war.

Mrs Danby said, 'I want only what is best for you. I was married when I was twenty-three, after several enjoyable years out in society. Blanche was born less than a year later, so you see, once married, there is little time for play.'

'One's servants will be there to do the boring things,' said Adela.

Mrs Danby frowned. 'You are argumentative. It is most unseemly.'

Mr Danby lowered his paper again. 'Must there be this discord at my breakfast table? I am surprised at you, Adela.'

'Of course not, George,' said his wife, shaking her head at Adela.

The door opened and Evans entered. 'Mr Danby is required on the telephone,' he said in sombre tones.

Mr Danby swore beneath his breath. 'Is there no peace? Probably some small business problem. Why I employ over-seers, I don't know.'

He was gone for quite a time, during which Adela managed to eat enough toast to prevent her mother from scolding her. The parlourmaid came to Mrs Danby and said something quietly. Adela had daringly picked up her father's newspaper – he hated anyone to touch it before he'd finished it – and was engrossed in reading about the joyous celebrations which had broken out all through the kingdom, and scarcely noticed her mother's departure.

Then her parents returned and Mr Danby gently removed his paper from his daughter's grasp. This forbearance in itself was a surprise. Her mother took both her hands in hers and sat down beside her and Adela's pulse began to race.

'My poor unfortunate child,' said Mrs Danby, 'you must be very brave.'

An icy hand seemed to be squeezing the blood from Adela's heart.

'The telephone call was from Sir Wilfred. My dear, Ralph died yesterday of pneumonia.'

Adela sat stunned, unable to move, unable even to think. The words reverberated round her brain, blotting out everything else. Her parents were speaking. She could hear their voices, but couldn't understand what they were saying. She tried to get up and was pushed gently back into the chair. Father was putting a glass to her lips and urging her to drink. Brandy fumes wafted up her nostrils and her nausea grew and took possession of her entire body. She pushed her father aside and raced to the downstairs cloakroom where she was violently ill. Then she sank to the floor, shaking, while great dry sobs tore her apart.

Her mother had followed her and looked down at her. 'You must not give way so violently.'

Adela looked up at her mother. Her expression was calm, though Adela thought she detected sympathy and it brought tears welling to her eyes and trickling down her face.

Mrs Danby caught her daughter's arm and helped her to get up. 'It's back to bed for you, miss. You've sustained a severe shock. I'll call Nurse in to look after you.'

'No, Mother, there isn't any need.'

'I'll be the best judge of that.'

She helped Adela out of her dress with unaccustomed kindness and loosened her corset strings. 'There, now lie down for a while.'

'Please, don't trouble Nurse. She's far too old to look after me.'

'Nonsense! She's not much above sixty and she knows you better than anyone.'

Nurse had never worked for any family but Mrs Danby's. She had been given a retirement cottage quite near and arrived within the hour, delighted to have one of her nurslings in her charge again though she tutted in the old remembered way at the sight of Adela, white-faced, her eyes dark-ringed. 'There, there, my poor lamb. It's a dreadful thing for you. Poor Mr Ralph! To think of him dying right at the end of the war when he'd survived so long. It wasn't even a bullet. Fancy, pneumonia! I'm wondering if he shouldn't have convalesced longer after his wound.'

While she spoke she plumped pillows, straightened the tumbled sheets and trotted round the bedroom, tidying toilet articles, checking to see if the night-time skin cream was one of which she approved. She rang the bell and when Grace answered ordered more coal to be sent up. 'It should be done without my having to ask,' said Nurse. 'You can see how low the fire's got.'

'We let them run a bit low in the day,' said Grace perkily. 'It saves coal. There's a war on, you know. Well, there was,' she finished sheepishly, even her sauce collapsing beneath Nurse's stern gaze.

Nurse made up the fire herself, brought Adela a glass of iced lemon, and ordered her to rest, before sitting in an easy chair by the fire, knitting something in khaki.

In spite of herself, Adela fell asleep and woke to find Nurse watching her. 'You've been talking in your sleep, Miss Adela.'

'Oh! What did I say?'

'It was a bit of a jumble. You mentioned Mr Ralph's name and something about leaving you in the lurch.'

Adela sat up gingerly. It was all right. The sickness had gone. 'I'll get up,' she said.

'Now, my lamb, you've had a terrible shock losing your young man.' She sighed heavily. 'There won't be enough men to go round, but *you'll* get over it and soon find someone else, Miss Adela, you can be sure of that. With your family background and your looks—'

Adela found her sympathetic ramblings unbearable. She threw back the covers.

'Your mama said you were to stay in bed!'

'For how long? Anyway, I want to get up. Honestly, Nurse, I'm fine now.'

'Well, you've colour in your cheeks. You must change yourself. You can't wear the combinations you've slept in. I've got clean ones warming here.' She held up a pair of pretty cotton combinations trimmed with lace and ribbons. 'Put these on, then I'll help you into a nice afternoon gown.'

'One suitable for mourning,' said Adela, bitterness tinging her voice.

'It's not a bit of use being angry at what's happened,' chided Nurse. 'You're one of tens of thousands of young women who have lost their man. Some of them are in desperate straits, widows before they're thirty, with little ones to bring up.'

'Is that supposed to help me feel better?'

'Now, now, Miss Adela, that's no way to speak. I was just pointing out that things could be a lot worse. I've got lots of sympathy for you, but you've got to remember your place in life, keep your head up, set an example to lower-born young women.' Nurse had always assumed the mantle of her employer's station in life. She retied the corset strings and took a navy serge dress from the wardrobe. Adela stood patiently while it was slipped over her head.

'Goodness me!' exclaimed Nurse. 'Your bosoms are bigger than I would expect. Danby women don't have big bosoms. It must be the result of all that exercise you did at school. I always said it was no good for a girl. It's all very well to have proper bosoms, but they shouldn't be this big on a Danby lady.'

Adela turned her head away so that Nurse couldn't see the fear which she knew showed in her eyes. 'You're probably right, Nursie darling.'

The use of her old nursery pet name diverted Nurse's attention from Adela's bosoms. She thought breasts a vulgar word.

'You can wear your pearl earrings and necklace,' said Nurse. 'They're suitable for a young lady in mourning.'

A young lady in mourning, thought Adela. I suppose that's what I am. She realised with shock that although she was, of course, sorry that Ralph had been killed, she had no sense of overwhelming grief. In fact, she was more angry than anything at the way he had used her body, then left her to carry the consequences.

She felt hypocritical when she was treated as a figure of tragedy. Even Blanche was quite nice to her. The Somerses had Ralph's body brought home and he was given a family burial service. Adela stood by the graveside, looking down at the coffin with its simple brass plate, Lady Somers beside her, calm and dignified. Everyone was calm and dignified and at the gathering later in Aston Lodge, the home of the Somers family

28

for generations, no one was weeping. There were no tears for Ralph. It occurred to Adela that the family seemed fulfilled at being able to boast of a son who had died a hero's death. Even his mother accepted commiserations with pride. Granted, Ralph had been killed by pneumonia, but it was virtually certain that it had stemmed from an improperly healed chest wound. During his son's wartime service Sir Wilfred had boasted freely about Ralph's prowess at school and his career in the war, both of which had been undistinguished. Sir Wilfred made the most of them, magnifying every incident into one which lifted his son to the role of grand sport and martyr.

Back at home Adela went to her room and changed into a grey silk suit with a cream blouse. Ralph was dead, buried, and if it hadn't been for the burden within her body, forgotten. He had been a friend, she had liked him, but she hadn't loved him, not ever. She felt horribly confused.

It was all very well for Sir Wilfred to say that his son had not known fear. He hadn't been there when Ralph had been permitted to use precious petrol to take Adela on a picnic in the family Daimler before he returned to the front. He had looked pale and anxious as he drove to Combe Dingle and stopped the car beneath the trees which were turning red and gold and brown with the onset of autumn.

The air was soft and warm and sweet-scented with the lingering gentleness of summer and Adela had enjoyed sitting on a rug beneath the trees, eating the dainty sandwiches and cakes, and drinking the pale gold wine. She had leaned back on a grassy bank, looking up into the canopy of branches, the sun dappling her face, enjoying the play of light and colour above her head, feeling peaceful. Ralph poured himself another glass of wine which he downed as if it were water. Adela watched him as he finished up the bottle, then produced a silver flask from the car.

'What's that?' she had asked lazily.

'Brandy.' Ralph had taken a long drink.

'You'll be too drunk to drive back,' Adela giggled.

'Maybe. Would that be so bad?'

'Why, what do you mean?'

'If I stayed here – if *we* stayed here – I shouldn't have to return to France.'

Adela had sat up so quickly her hat had tilted over one eye. 'You can't mean that?'

'I never meant anything more in my whole life.' His face changed abruptly, assuming a desperate expression which alarmed her. 'God, Adela, you don't know what it's like! All one hears at home are tales of heroism. No one mentions the trenches as they really are, the deep shell holes filled with mud and the way that wounded men slide down into them and drown. It's either unendurably hot or freezing cold. There are lice that drive one crazy with itching, and rats, huge things that eat dead human flesh, and there's plenty of that with men just lying where they fall because there are too many to give them a proper burial. And the horses! The screams of wounded horses! Sometimes they just drown in mud under their dead riders. Oh, God, it's all horrible! Unbearable!'

'Oh, Ralph, I had no idea!'

'No, that's the problem. Men get sent to these hellish places by other men who also have no idea.'

'But we must win the war.'

'So I'm told! I don't understand why there has to be a war at all. Once, in a quiet period near the beginning, I met German soldiers. They're quite ordinary chaps, like us.'

'That's fraternising with the enemy!'

'More old men's talk!'

'Is it? I hadn't thought about it. Oh, dear. All war is dreadful.' Adela was ashamed to realise that embarrassment at Ralph's sudden breakdown exceeded concern. She spoke in bracing tones. 'I know you'll acquit yourself like a man.'

'Like a man! When they sent me out there I was eighteen – a boy, Adela! I should have been enjoying life. I've lost my youth forever.'

'Oh, Ralph, not forever. When the war is over—'

She got no further because, to her horror, he had let out a sob. She had felt like running away but, instead, had put out her hand and touched his shoulder gently. 'You're brave,

Ralph. You'll do your duty by Britain and the Empire, as you've always done.'

'To hell with Britain and the Empire!'

'Ralph, you can't mean that! Everyone has to fight against Germany. They might invade us if we don't.'

'What do you mean "we"? It's the men who do the fighting.'

'Do you expect women to carry guns?'

'I've heard Blanche say often enough that she'd fight if she was allowed.'

'Oh, if you're going to quote Blanche at me—'

'Don't be cross with me, please. Darling Adela, I must tell someone the truth – I'm terrified of going back. For four years I've seen men dying, or wounded so horribly they'd be better off dead. And those fearful gas attacks when some poor devils get caught before they can use a gas mask. They choke; they're in such agony. And some live, but go blind. It's too ghastly. We're supposed to be the superior sex, strong and silent. Well, I have been. Silent, at any rate. Strong, no. I was glad when I was wounded. I hoped it was serious enough to keep me from going back to the front. I'm sure my former sergeant knew how afraid I was, but he was a good sort, a fatherly man who tried to ease my life. Now he's dead and I've got a man who despises me.'

'I'm sure you're imagining that,' said Adela desperately, glad to have some comment she could make. She hated the way Ralph was tearing down her image of him. She hated this explosion of raw emotion, the first she had ever encountered in him.

Ralph had turned his haggard face to her and she was shocked and suddenly pitying, realising for the first time, if only dimly, what it had meant to him to have faced, day and night, death or dreadful injury for four long years. To have to go back and risk his life again.

She had put her hands on his shoulders. 'Ralph, my dear, I'm so sorry—'

She had got no further. 'I knew you'd understand,' he had cried as he seized and kissed her. Not in the gentle boyish way she had come to expect, but roughly, like a man slaking his

31

thirst. The kiss had left her breathless and scared, and she began to protest, but his lips descended on hers again and his hands began to wander over her body. She had struggled and tried to pull away, but he kept his lips close to hers and murmured mad things, crazy words that frightened her. 'Let me love you, darling. Give yourself to me. Please, please, give me this taste of happiness before I go back. Let me love you.' He said it over and over like a chant, holding her down with his weight while his hands stroked her.

'Ralph, stop it! Oh, do, please, stop it!' she had begged.

He didn't hear her. 'I need you, darling Adela. I need you. Please let me love you.'

She had managed to stop him for a moment. 'For heaven's sake – soon the war will be over and we'll be married.'

'I can't wait until then! I won't! I want you. Now! I must have you. If you cared one jot for me you would give way. If you loved me as I love you you would willingly give me what I ask. Other chaps have girls who comfort them in the best way they can. I've heard them talking.'

'That's shocking!'

'To do it, or talk about it?' he cried harshly.

'Both.'

'They talk sometimes just before we go over the top, remembering aloud the best things they've had, knowing that some of them will never see another day. Maybe I'll never come back. Adela, stop arguing with me. Give me your dear, beautiful body, just this once. I won't ask again until we're married. Just this once.'

Adela protested again, then saw to her horror that Ralph was weeping. Tears were coursing down his face. She turned away, unable to endure the sight, her resistance crumbling under the power of Ralph's physical and emotional onslaught. He had seemed half crazy. There had followed rough, embarrassing fumbling, terror in case someone strayed into this part of the wood and caught them, then pain which knifed through her so badly she forgot all other considerations while Ralph thrust himself into her, gasping and groaning, holding her mouth with his. It was over quickly and it was followed by more embarrassment as she endeavoured to clean herself and shield her nakedness.

Ralph had kissed her gently. 'My beloved Adela, you're the only woman I've ever made love to. It wasn't as good for you as it was for me, was it? I'm sorry I was rough. I needed you so much. It'll be better once we're married, I swear it. We'll have the rest of our lives to enjoy one another.'

'Of course,' she agreed, but she was resentful and extremely sore, and wished she could be back at home in an instant, stepping into a hot bath, ridding herself of all traces of Ralph's love-making. He hadn't sensed her mood at all, but continued to expound on the pleasures ahead of them. They had said their goodbyes that night and he had left Bristol at dawn the following day. And she was left here to face the consequences of his recklessness.

That afternoon Adela had planned to accompany her mother to a charity bazaar being held to raise money for servicemen's widows and was thankful that her mourning would permit her to stay at home.

At lunch Mrs Danby said, 'I should wear white today, Adela. It's so important for ladies to appear at their best and keep the atmosphere uplifting.'

She was shocked. 'Surely you don't expect me to come with you, Mother!'

Mrs Danby raised her brows. 'Not expect you? Of course I do. You are not officially in mourning and, even if you were, you will not be the only one there who has lost a loved one. There is scarcely a family who does not mourn someone. And Lady Somers is actually opening the bazaar.'

Adela gave up. It was easier than arguing. With her white wool dress she wore a small-brimmed grey hat with a feather tilted over one eye. The tops of her grey, high-laced shoes disappeared beneath her ankle-length skirt. No jewellery. She stared at herself in her mirror. Bridal white, she thought. White for purity. God, what was she going to do?

Mrs Danby approved of her ensemble. 'Absolutely correct, my dear. The car is at the door.'

At the Victoria Rooms their stall, which offered hand-made objects such as teacosies and table covers and rag dolls, was next to that of Lady Somers which held donated china. Lady Somers was in dark brown, her hat an out-of-date turban.

A three-piece band played softly as the doors were opened and people surged in. There was a brief pause while Lady Somers read out a stilted little speech for which she was applauded heartily, especially by those who knew of her recent loss, then the musicians struck up with cheerful tunes, *Peg o' My Heart*, and *When You Wore A Tulip*.

The room was filled with assumed gaiety until the musicians went into *Keep the Home Fires Burning*. The words ran through Adela's head: *While your hearts are yearning; Tho' your lads are far away* . . . The chatter became muted; women dressed in black, and there were so many, stopped buying. When the tune was followed with *Roses of Picardy* the atmosphere in the hall became charged with sorrow. *And the roses will die with the summertime* . . . The grief was almost tangible as women, both vendors and buyers, struggled against unbearable yearning for those who had gone.

Mrs Danby tutted. 'This will not do! People are leaving and we've sold barely half the goods.' She hurried to the stage and spoke to the pianist. The musicians swiftly changed to *There is a Tavern in the Town* and those who had been leaving were encouraged to return to purchase articles they didn't want, but which it was patriotic to buy.

Adela smiled, advised, took money and chattered, although her back ached and her head began to throb. She shouldn't be here. A woman in her condition should be reclining at home, fussed over, admired. It was all Ralph's fault. Anger was all that was keeping her going.

She finished selling a set of egg cosies to a woman, three of whose officer sons lay dead in France while the fourth had been repatriated with a leg missing, and watched the woman walk away, her head held high.

'Poor creature,' said a masculine voice.

She turned to see Sander Bennett. 'What on earth are you doing here?'

'Why shouldn't I be here?' His answer was belligerent and Adela wished she'd kept quiet.

She shrugged without replying.

'I'm spending my money like a good patriot.' He held up a carrier bag. 'In here I have an astonishing collection of gewgaws.'

His flippant tone irritated her and she said waspishly, 'All necessary to your well-being? Surely you would be of more use in your factories.'

'Chivvying on the men to work harder for the brave lads still at the front?'

'Are you making fun of our soldiers now?'

'God forbid! It's the world's leaders I despise.'

'It really is a wonder to me you haven't been shot as a traitor.'

'To me, also.'

He seemed impervious to criticism. He held up a lop-sided teacosy which clearly had been fashioned from odds and ends of coloured wools kept over years. 'A cosy of many colours. I'll buy it.'

'I hope you enjoy it.'

'I may give it to someone as a Christmas present. Would you care for it?'

'No. And, anyway, we won't be exchanging presents.'

'How sadly true. By the way, Miss Danby, I must offer my commiserations on the loss of your fiancé. Such a pleasant fellow, and so young.'

His tone was matter-of-fact and she realised that for several minutes she hadn't thought of Ralph, or even the problem he had bequeathed her.

'Thank you,' she said, her hands shaking as she wrapped up the teacosy. 'It's a tragedy.'

'One shared by too many.'

She nodded, and turned aside to serve another customer and Sander walked on to Lady Somers' stall.

Mrs Danby finished selling a pair of cushion covers and asked, 'What were you talking about with Mr Bennett.'

'He was giving me his sympathy.'

'He did not look overly sympathetic to me! The man's such an outsider.'

35

'Why was he told of my unofficial engagement?'

Mrs Danby concentrated on folding a small tablecloth. 'I'm sure Father had his reasons. Business, no doubt. Mr Bennett is an odd man. I don't understand him at all. When I was a girl one was not expected to meet such men in society. Times are changing for the worse.'

The afternoon seemed interminable to Adela, but it ended at last and a bevy of cleaning women brought tea to the ladies. Adela desperately wanted water, but to ask for it would draw her mother's attention so she pretended to sip the tea.

Thankfully, she returned home.

Chapter Three

Nurse called in just before dinner to ask after Miss Adela's health. As a privileged retired servant, she was ushered into the drawing room but did not sit down. That would not have been proper.

'I'm perfectly well, thank you,' said Adela.

Nurse peered closely at her. 'No, you're not. Perhaps you need a tonic. She might need a tonic,' she reiterated, turning to Mrs Danby.

Blanche stared at her sister. 'I can't imagine why Adela needs a tonic when I'm the one doing a man's job. She should get a bit more exercise.'

Mrs Danby frowned at her elder daughter. 'Thank you for your advice, Nurse, it was kind of you to call.'

Adela went to bed early and was lying wide-eyed, staring into the darkness, when a tap on the door was followed by the appearance of Blanche who snapped on the light.

Adela blinked and rubbed her eyes. 'Honestly, Blanche, your manners don't improve. I might have been sleeping.'

'Well, you weren't.'

'I never will if I'm disturbed like this.'

'What's the matter with you?'

'Nothing. What do you mean?'

'You are behaving very oddly lately.'

'I am not! I'm just tired, that's all.'

'All? Aren't you grieving over your poor deceased fiancé?'

'Blanche, you're rotten, you really are! Of course I'm grieving, but a lady doesn't allow her emotions to dominate her. Mother always says so, you know that.'

'Oh, not in public, I agree.' Blanche stood by the bed, staring down at her sister. 'But you don't cry in private either, do you? I don't believe you cared a whit for Ralph.'

'A lot *you* could know about it!'

This oblique reference to Blanche's lack of suitors infuriated her. She bent over, staring deep into Adela's eyes. 'Has my little sister been up to something naughty?'

Adela had to force herself to remain calm, though inside she was cringing. 'What an idea,' she said. She even managed a light laugh. 'Can you imagine Ralph—?' She laughed again, allowing the question to linger in the air.

'Oh, I can imagine him, all right. Since I went to work on the tramcars I can imagine almost anything. I haven't spent the war protected like you. I've met all sorts, and the quiet ones are often the worst.'

'There are different kinds of war work. Mother needed me and I've done a lot for our fighting men through committees and bazaars. First there were the poor Belgian refugees to look after; there are the funds for widows of—'

'Oh, do be quiet!' Blanche's tone held contempt. 'You're Mother's obedient little girl, aren't you? And, of course, Father's ideal daughter. They didn't want me to go on the trams, but I did and so could you have done.'

'Well, the war's over now and you can come home.'

'God, you're so smug! You have absolutely no idea of what life is like outside your own small sphere. There are girls working with me who know more about the world at eighteen than you know at twenty-one.'

'That's not my fault.'

'Isn't it? You could have left the security of your home and learned just what life is like for others.'

Adela remained silent.

'Aren't you going to ask why I've come in to see you?'

'To vent your temper on me for some reason?'

'You know that's not it! You're no little innocent, are you? You know more about men now, don't you?'

'Blanche, if you've got something to say, why don't you get it over with and we can both get some rest? I thought you were on

38

an early shift tomorrow. And why are you being so nasty to me, anyway?'

'Why?' Blanche straightened and walked to the window. She opened the curtain and stared down into the quiet garden. Then she turned and said with quiet menace, 'Nasty, am I? Because I'm interested in my little sister's welfare?'

'No you're not! You're jealous because Sander—'

'Yes? You were saying? Sander?' Blanche's tone became frigid and Adela wished she had held her tongue. 'Go on. What about Sander?'

'You like him, don't you, Blanche?' Adela's attempt to placate her sister was a disaster.

'That's none of your damn business!'

'Blanche, I sympathise with you, honestly I do, and I could help you look far more attractive. I know what colours you should wear and how you could do your hair better and—'

'Shut up! I don't want your advice! I'll not tart myself up for any man. But you will! You love them, don't you, and the way they flatter you?'

'No, not really. I mean, I haven't thought much about it.'

'You never *think* about anything.'

Adela felt abruptly exhausted. 'Please, leave, and let me get some sleep.'

'Not until you tell me what's ailing you.' Blanche bent over her. 'You vomited when Mother told you of Ralph's death.'

'That was shock.'

'Maybe, and maybe not! For some time you've often only pretended to drink and eat.'

'I haven't felt hungry lately.'

'A woman I work with hasn't felt hungry lately either and, funnily enough, she's gone off tea and coffee, though she used to drink quarts of it. With her there's a reason. She's expecting a child. She's married, of course. Always the best way to be when you start a family.'

Adela sat up with the intention of refuting Blanche's implied allegation, then slumped back on her pillows. Blanche had guessed the truth and she was implacable. There would be no more keeping of secrets. 'Why don't you say what you're thinking?' she asked wearily.

'All right, I will. You allowed Ralph to make love to you, didn't you?'

Adela stared at her sister, silent, her eyes wide.

'And now you're expecting his child.'

Adela took a deep breath. 'I think I must be. I feel so odd.'

'Don't try to act the innocent with me. We were both instructed in the facts of life.'

'Yes, I'm certain.'

'I knew it. What a disgrace! And you have the temerity to flirt with Sander Bennett, while inside you – God, you disgust me! How could you let yourself and the family down like this?'

'Ralph was—' Adela stopped.

'Father and Mother must be told!' Now Blanche had wormed the secret out she was suddenly calm.

Adela nodded miserably. 'I know.'

'Father's still out, but I'll tell Mother for you. It may help her get over the worst of the shock before she sees you, though I doubt it!' Her sister went out swiftly, an anticipatory gleam in her eyes. She was going to relish her task. Adela knew she should make her own confession. She hesitated, still fearful, then slid out of bed and was halfway to the chair where she'd thrown her dressing gown when her door opened and Mrs Danby hurried in, her dressing gown and her long hair in two plaits flying out behind her. Her face was white, her eyes starting in horror.

'Blanche has come to me with a dreadful accusation. Adela, tell me it is not true! You could not really sink so low?'

Adela's legs were shaking and she walked back to the bed and sat on it. 'I'm sorry, Mother,' she managed to gasp.

'Sorry? That means it is true. Oh, my God! What a filthy thing to happen! How could you demean yourself? What shall we do? What can we do?'

'I don't know. Mother, I'm sorry,' said Adela again.

'Sorry! Is that all you can say?'

'What else is there to say? Ralph—'

'Ralph what?'

'He was going back to the front. He loved me. He—'

'Be silent! Every word you say makes it worse. Ralph was a gentleman. He would never have taken advantage of you. You must have encouraged him.'

Adela remained silent. She was fuming with frustration, but how could she defile the memory of a dead soldier?

'I'm sorry,' she said yet again. Then in a shaking voice, 'Where's Father?'

'He's out.'

'When will he be home?' she asked fearfully.

'Late! He's at a meeting of prominent manufacturers. They are discussing their prospects now that the war has ended.' Mrs Danby stared at Adela as if she had become a different species of being. 'But what does that matter to you? Our position in society will be utterly compromised! Such a thing has never happened to us. To think that my daughter should be the one to debase a proud family. *Ladies* do not get themselves with babies before marriage. Housemaids, yes, scullery sluts, uneducated women. Not ladies!'

Adela leaned forward, elbows on knees, her head propped in her hands. 'Mother, I accept all you say. I've been very bad.'

Mrs Danby didn't speak for a while then she said abruptly, 'Maybe the damage can be undone. Yes, that's the solution.'

Adela looked up at her mother, hope springing in her. 'Undone? Can one undo a – thing like this?'

'There are ways. Get into bed.' Adela climbed into bed, hope rising within her. Mrs Danby spoke fast, spitting out the words as if she found them distasteful. 'A friend of mine once found herself in an embarrassing position. Her fiancé was killed on the hunting field. Her mother took her to France and when she returned her embarrassment was over.'

'Embarrassment?'

'Do not be obtuse!' Mrs Danby's anger boiled over again. 'She was in the same position as you find yourself.'

'How can I go to France now? It's in a dreadful state.'

'You can't, of course. We must find someone here. A medical man who will be co-operative. It will be expensive, of course,' she frowned angrily, 'but worth it. We shall all be discreet and this need not intrude upon your future.'

'What will happen to me?'

'A small operation. Quite quick.'

Adela lay back on her pillows looking up at her mother in inexpressible relief. She could rid herself of this horrible, unwanted encumbrance and everything would be all right. She wanted to pour out her gratitude but stayed silent, knowing that her mother found openly expressed emotion distasteful. 'What about Father?' she asked.

'I'll speak to him. He will be ready to fall in with our plans, never fear.'

'Thank you, Mother,' said Adela.

Mrs Danby made no response. After she had left, Adela wept in relief and for the first night in weeks she slept easily.

The next morning Mr Danby left the house at eight and Adela was thankful to be spared a confrontation until later in the day when she knew she would be able to deal with it better. She accompanied her mother on calls and to a meeting to plan another sale of work.

'Now the war is ended I thought you would no longer be holding bazaars,' said Adela. She longed for nothing more than to lie in bed in her large, airy room. On her seventeenth birthday she had been indulgently allowed to choose the redecorations. To soften the heavy walnut furniture bought by her grandfather she had chosen green, white and yellow wallpaper, curtains and woodwork, in the softly muted shades used to such good effect by the Art Nouveau designer, Beauclair. Father had bought her a beautiful carpet to match and Adela had never grown tired of the cool, clean result.

Mrs Danby said tartly, 'I do wish you would think sometimes. I have always worked for charity and now there are many wounded soldiers who need extra help, and thousands not yet back from the front. When they do arrive they will need financial aid to tide them over until they obtain work.'

Adela said in a burst of irritation, 'They're supposed to be going back to the jobs they left.'

'We have to get the women out of them first!' said Mrs

42

Danby grimly. 'I have already heard rumours that many of them are saying they like the freedom they've gained and won't be tied any longer to a house and children.'

'I dare say they'd like some pin money.'

'You know nothing about it. A woman's place is in her home and you will please refrain from arguing with me. You are so contentious lately and the last thing I want is for you to side with Blanche in her foolishness.'

'Does Blanche want to go on working on the tramcars?'

'She says so. I daresay she will eventually come to her senses.'

Adela's mind wandered as her mother and her friends discussed the sale of work then, thankfully, she returned home. She sat in her room working on her embroidery. She was usually soothed by the rhythmic movements of her needle, the mixing of the strands of silk to produce a picture. The patterns were originally ironed on to cloth from transparent paper, but Adela deviated from them, often quite dramatically, working out designs of her own. Today she couldn't concentrate. Mother insisted that she join her downstairs and Adela tried to read, but the words swam as her worries overwhelmed her.

Father returned home looking grim. It was dark and Adela and her mother were sitting in the light from table lamps. Adela switched hers off when she heard her father's voice in the hall and waited fearfully in comparative darkness.

Mr Danby poured himself a whisky and soda and stood by the fireplace glaring angrily at his wife.

'This country will go to the dogs,' he declaimed. 'I was called early to the warehouse because we were sent a large order of artificial silk which I intended to have made up into sets of pretty, inexpensive underwear, all ready for wives to buy to please their returning husbands. It is so full of faults it is useless and I have had to spend hours today telephoning. I may get some more; I may not. No one seems to know. Now, there's talk of a general election. Lloyd George is adamant that the Coalition will continue, but I've no such optimism.'

'It worked well during the war, dear,' said Mrs Danby soothingly.

'We're not at war now and we'll have the khaki vote to contend with. There's no telling which way returning soldiers will jump.'

'I'm sure you are worrying unnecessarily.'

'You are, are you? What would you say to a Labour Government? They are seriously considering disassociating themselves from the others and forming their own party.'

Mrs Danby looked at him in disbelief. 'Britain will never stand for it! After the dreadful Russian Revolution no one will want to give such people as the socialists a say in the government of Britain.'

'I wish I shared your conviction.' He swallowed his whisky and poured another. 'Where's Adela?'

The abrupt question brought bile into her throat. 'I'm here, Father.'

'Where? Why are you sitting in the dark?'

He switched on the overhead light and Adela had difficulty in not cringing beneath his angry, contemptuous gaze. In all her life he had never looked at her like that. 'You will know that your mother has spoken to me. I have spent a wretched day, and all through it I have had the burden of your appalling conduct on my mind. To think a daughter of mine should sink to such depths,' he grated. 'How could you?'

Adela sat in silent misery.

'It'll have to be got rid of, of course. I saw a man today, Caroline. Within a week Adela can go to London and be attended to in a small clinic. The cost will be heavy.'

He glared at Adela and she said, her voice quivering, 'Thank you.'

'Is that all you have to say?'

'I'm sorry it happened, Father, but I couldn't know that poor Ralph would die.'

'Couldn't know! Of course you couldn't, but you might just have suspected there was a chance.'

Adela hated it when her father used sarcasm to make a point. 'I know I should, Father,' she said miserably. 'But Ralph—' she coloured painfully 'he was so – persuasive – and—'

Her flush deepened as her father stared at her with

incredulity. 'I would prefer you to keep any details to yourself. You have not spoken of this to anyone, have you?'

'No, Father! As if I would!'

'I no longer have any certainty of your actions. Until yesterday I was under the impression that you were a chaste young woman whom I could trust.'

Dinner was eaten in gloomy silence in the presence of the servants. Afterwards Mrs Danby and Adela went to the drawing room and took up their work again, leaving Mr Danby to his cigar and port and a work session in the library.

Adela tried to sew, but the effort made her nauseous. She got up and went out quickly, pretending not to hear her mother's protest. In her room she sat as still as she could and sipped water. She couldn't blame her parents for being so angry. It was up to the woman always to say no. Her father had called the expected child 'it'. She supposed, at this stage, it was an 'it' yet, abruptly, she resented the word. Her strong chin, which precluded her claim to purely classical beauty, went up. Why should her baby be called an 'it' in such a derogatory tone, as if it were an unclean thing? Was it alive yet? Her ignorance of pregnancy was profound. Did it have limbs? A heart? A soul? She shivered. If it had a soul, surely the act of destruction would be murder and she would be condemned in the eyes of God? She and her family worshipped God in a very contained way every Sunday morning and she had never been encouraged to get on close terms with Him. But she could do no other than submit to her parents' decree. It simply was not possible for her to bear an illegitimate child. She shuddered. She couldn't face being an outcast in the only society she knew. Her mind veered this way and that, in a maze of doubt. The sooner the small operation was performed the better. She wondered if it would hurt. She looked down at herself. Only her breasts as yet showed early signs of pregnancy. She stared at her stomach and abruptly veered to her parents' point of view, hating what was growing there. It was an incubus, an unwanted parasite, the author of its existence dead. When it was gone she would never think of it again.

Mrs Danby sent a maid to summon her back to the drawing

room. Blanche had gone straight from her early shift to a meeting of militant women who were determined not to be ousted from their jobs.

'I cannot think where she gets such outrageous ideas from,' said Mrs Danby, as she and Adela were served by Evans with malted milk brought on a silver tray. Adela drank it, knowing that it would make her morning sickness worse, but that seemed preferable to another argument.

Mrs Danby looked at the door after it had closed silently. 'He suspects something is wrong.'

'Surely not, Mother.'

'He knows us too well to be fooled. However, he will not speak to anyone. He was reared in the old school. As were your father and I. Adela, how I wish you had shown proper self-control! It is dreadful to imagine one's servants finding out something so shameful.' Adela had no answer. There was another silence, then Mrs Danby said, 'I was disappointed when I had no sons, but Blanche was sturdy and independent and you were so beautiful I was reconciled by the certainty that you would bring honour to us through marriage. Honour!' The word scorched Adela. 'I was so pleased when I knew I would be welcoming Ralph as my son-in-law,' Mrs Danby continued inexorably. 'You have both let me down.'

'I can hardly be blamed for Ralph's death!'

'Don't be so ridiculous! You know I did not mean that.'

'I didn't mean to let you down, Mother.'

'Didn't mean to.' Mrs Danby's voice was low and bitter. There was a further short silence. 'I daresay Blanche will come to see reason and will eventually cease her involvement with her so-called work mates. I never liked the idea of girls of all classes mixing as equals. And you, Adela, should thank God that Father has such a strong fondness for you and feels a sense of responsibility towards you – some men would have cast you off – and that he has the money to buy what you need. I never thought to find myself in such a situation.'

It's I who am in the situation, thought Adela. She tried to conquer her rancour at the way her body had been taken over. She was helpless in the grip of the tiny organism planted in her womb, of her parents, of Ralph's lack of self-control, even of Blanche's vindictiveness. She had always felt secure as a favoured member of an old family of wealth and respectability, yet her safety had been so easily compromised by one mad act.

After the first wild rejoicing at the end of hostilities, parties held to celebrate the expected return of loved ones from the war exuded an air of forced jollity. In spite of all the patriotic speeches about victory for King and Country, an atmosphere of suffering and death could not fail to permeate the lives of the bereaved or those who waited in desperate hope for news of someone posted as missing. Mrs Danby insisted on Adela accepting invitations and she struggled with the nausea which sometimes afflicted her all day.

Blanche couldn't always control her acerbic tongue. Behind a façade of sympathy she was intensely gratified by the fall of her beautiful sister, the favourite daughter.

Adela grew more pale and silent as the days passed. She spent a lot of time in her room, hiding from the reproachful stares of her parents, sewing, and reading the several newspapers taken by Father; anything to take her mind from her nagging fears. Armistice fever had died and the papers contained surprisingly little post-war news but a great deal of speculation about the peace. Then Adela came upon a small item tucked into the corner of an inside page. The widow of a private in the army had lost her three-year-old son, her only child, killed before her eyes in a road accident and, straight after the funeral, had committed suicide. She was only twenty-five. Her note told the world that her boy was all that her beloved husband had left as a memorial, and that as she could no longer bring him up to honour his father she had no more purpose in life.

Adela let the paper fall to her lap, leaning her head on the back of her easy chair. She thought of the unknown woman receiving the news of her husband's death which had occurred near the beginning of the war when she was awaiting the birth of their child. She pictured her gallant struggle on a widow's pay, bearing her child in loneliness, taking care of him, only to end up with her head in a gas oven, gasping her life away. Adela picked up the paper again. Suicide was wicked, said a clergyman. Surely, thought Adela, God would allow that sometimes life became too harrowing to endure?

She took the paper downstairs and showed the sorrowful paragraph to her mother who read it and stared coldly, eyebrows raised, at Adela.

'What am I supposed to infer from this? That you are contemplating taking your life?'

Adela was horrified. 'Of course not, Mother. It's just that I think the poor woman was so brave in carrying on alone, only to have her purpose in existing snatched from her. Why do these things happen? Why do there have to be wars?'

'You are melancholy. You spend too much time alone. I can't tell you why the world is full of evil. No one can, not even the vicar. He says that there is a purpose behind everything and we must accept that.'

'What would he say if he knew about me?'

'I trust you have no intention of telling him!'

'No, of course not, but I was wondering if this baby was meant to be. If there truly is a grand purpose which shapes our destinies, maybe Ralph's child was given me to – to cherish.'

'Oh, my God!' With an effort Mrs Danby calmed herself. 'Adela, I was always full of fanciful notions when I was carrying a child. You'll forget such nonsense once it's over. It won't be long now and we can put it behind us for ever. You will have no problem in attracting another man. In fact, Sander Bennett admires you.'

'That boorish man? He's not one of us, and he's so old.'

'I suppose thirty-four does seem old to you, but whatever one thinks of him, Mr Bennett is successful. He is quite passable, even attractive to some, I dare say.'

'Not to me!'

'No, of course not. I used him simply to illustrate my point. Believe me, Adela, eventually you will forget your affection for Ralph.'

Adela, her mind on what lay ahead of her, said, 'Ralph's child—'

'Must *not* be born!' Mrs Danby said vehemently.

Adela tried again. 'Do you think we should consult Sir

Wilfred and Lady Somers? After all, the baby is their grandchild.'

'You stupid girl!' cried Mrs Danby. 'Do you imagine for one moment that they would want a child born outside of marriage? Do you think they would acknowledge a bastard?'

'Mother!'

'It's time you recognised how badly you've behaved. You appear to have forgotten how this could affect the rest of the family. Think of having to tell your Grandmother Sutton!'

Adela shrank from the idea. Grandmother Sutton lived in Cornwall and was visited by the whole family once a year. She seldom moved from home and her morals and manners seemed as rigid and strait-laced as her whaleboned Victorian corsets. She had little to say to her grand-daughters. Of late years, Adela felt that she was bored by the family.

'You see,' said Mrs Danby triumphantly. 'You see how impossible it all is.'

Adela was not normally a lachrymose person, but now she fought to hold back tears.

'Fetch your embroidery down here,' said Mrs Danby. 'We'll put some music on the gramophone. It will help to cheer us both.'

Adela shook her head. All the waltzes in the world could not soothe away her rising anxiety.

The day arrived when she was to go to London. Mr Danby drove, rather badly, and Mrs Danby sat in the back with Adela, holding her hand. Adela wished the touch arose only from compassion, but she had the strong impression that Mother's fingers were being used as emotional handcuffs.

They stayed overnight at the Connaught Hotel and were to go to the doctor's surgery in his private residence where, Adela had been told, the operation would be performed swiftly and, after a short rest, she would return to the hotel. In the morning she was actually at the door of her bedroom when all power seemed to leave her legs.

Mrs Danby, who had come to Adela's room to make sure she was ready on time, was irritably nervous. After all, what they were proposing to do was a serious offence. If news of it should leak out there would be the devil to pay. She gave Adela a small push. 'Go along, child. We shall be late.'

'Late for the murder, do you mean?'

Mr Danby had joined them and looked around hurriedly. 'You little fool! You could be overheard! Will you, for God's sake, shift yourself.'

Adela remained still. 'I – can't – move.'

'Can't move?' snapped her father. He pulled her arms roughly and she half fell against him. A passing chambermaid gave them a curious glance.

'Adela!' hissed Mr Danby.

'I can't! I can't!' Adela kept repeating, until her parents supported her back inside her room.

Mr Danby began to bluster and was silenced by his wife. 'You'll only make her worse. Adela, pull yourself together. Father has engaged a very good doctor for you. He'll give you a whiff of gas and it will be over almost before you can blink an eye.'

'I can't!'

'Will you stop saying that!' cried Mrs Danby, losing the remnants of her patience. 'Father has left his work, I have had to cancel three committee meetings, everything's arranged and you are behaving in this stubborn, ridiculous way!'

'I am not ridiculous. I am *not*! I just can't kill Ralph's baby!'

'Ralph's baby?' Mr Danby lifted his hand and for a horrifying moment it looked as if he might strike Adela. His hand fell to his side and he walked to a chair and sat down heavily.

'What are you trying to do to us, Adela?' asked Mrs Danby. 'You cannot say that we treat you unkindly, not even now, when you have disappointed us past bearing. For heaven's sake, be sensible. Father and I understand your scruples. You speak of Ralph's baby, but there is no baby. Not yet. It is only a very small piece of you that can come out as easily as drawing a tooth. Probably easier. Come now, Adela, let us go.' She glanced at her watch. 'We shall be late, but it probably won't matter.'

'No,' said Adela. 'No, no, no!'

Mr Danby got up. 'If you defy us, you must take the consequences. Understand this, my girl, there will be no bastards born beneath my roof. If you don't obey us, out you go.'

Mrs Danby turned angrily. 'George! You're making matters worse.'

'Am I, by God! I would not have thought they could be worse. Adela, what have I done to deserve this? Tell me! Where have I gone wrong? I've done my best to be a good father to you.'

'I know, but please try to understand. I can't kill this child.'

There was a whispered consultation between her parents, then Mrs Danby said, 'Adela, we will not force you to visit the doctor today. It is obvious that you are in too nervous a state. Father will telephone and make an appointment for tomorrow. I'm sure by then you will reach a more reasonable frame of mind.'

Adela's father was still angry. He left the room, not quite slamming the door.

'You mustn't blame him, Adela,' said her mother. 'Not only is he dreadfully worried about this, but he has business problems. He really should have remained in Bristol.'

'It was good of him to come,' said Adela, miserably.

'I'm glad you see it that way. He has decided to take the opportunity to look at some London fashion houses. Would you like to visit the shops? We'll go to Harrods. You love it there, don't you?'

Adela felt slightly hysterical with relief. 'Just like Mrs Smithers!'

'What?'

'Mrs Smithers likes Harrods, except for the prices.' She ended on a giggle which brought a frown to her mother's face.

'That dreadful creature! Don't compare yourself with her. How she'd crow over us if she knew what we are about.'

Adela's mirth died. She accompanied her mother obediently to Harrods, and then to Liberty's, where Adela pored over the lovely fabrics. For a short time she forgot her problems, but on the following morning, when the time came to visit the surgery, she reacted even more stubbornly than before.

In the end, with bitter reproaches, her parents had no choice but to drive home to Bristol. Adela sat alone in the back, struggling with sickness, frightened of the future.

When the car drew up before the smart front door of Speede House, her father said, 'To think we could have been coming home without worries! Instead of which—' He didn't finish, but got out and opened the car door for his wife, leaving Adela to follow. She went straight to her room where she lay on the bed and sobbed weakly.

At the weekend he called her to his study. Her mother sat in a deep leather armchair, her head up, her face coldly composed.

'Sit down,' said Mr Danby.

Adela sat and waited.

'Your mother and I have been discussing your future. As you refuse to do the wisest thing we have decided we must find you a husband.'

Adela's eyes opened wide in shock. 'A husband? I don't understand. How?'

'How, indeed?' said Mr Danby. 'It was difficult, but I have found someone.'

Adela stared at her father. 'You expect me to marry a stranger?'

'Don't be so stupid,' said Mr Danby angrily. 'We have spoken to a man well known to you, one who is respected for his business acumen. He knows your condition and is prepared to offer you the protection of his name. It is fortunate that your engagement to Ralph was never made public.'

'That is so,' said Mrs Danby. 'People will speculate, of course, especially when they realise you are in a delicate condition, but no one can prove anything. Yours will be a quiet post-war wedding.'

Adela hardly heard her. 'What kind of man would accept such an offer?'

'Sander Bennett,' said Mr Danby. 'He is coming here tonight so that we can arrange details. The wedding will take place as soon as is decently possible.'

Adela sat in her room, filled with horror. Sander Bennett! That man with his rough manners, his low background, to be her husband. At the thought of all it implied she had argued passionately with her parents, pleaded with them to let her go away to some place where she wasn't known and have her child in secret. They refused to countenance the suggestion.

'No,' Mother had said, 'it won't do. We should be hard put to explain your absence, and what of the child? You do not, I hope, imagine you can bring it here with you. Where would it go?'

'You could find a decent woman to look after it,' said Adela. 'I've read of that being done.'

'Where have you read it?' asked Mr Danby angrily. 'In some cheap novel, I suppose; or you've seen it in one of those idiotic animated pictures.'

'Father, I believe some quite famous people have managed to keep the birth of a child secret for many years. Often nothing was known until after their death.'

'Name me one,' thundered Mr Danby.

Adela couldn't. Beneath her father's ferocious scrutiny she was no longer sure if she had read it, dreamt it, or merely imagined it.

'You see,' he had said triumphantly. 'Decent people don't do that kind of thing.'

'Decent people don't try to kill babies,' retorted Adela.

She had thought her father would have an apoplectic fit, he went so red. Mrs Danby tried to cool the situation. 'Calm down, please, both of you. Adela, you are not thinking. If we did as you ask, what would eventually become of the child? And think of yourself. Do you wish to marry in the future? At what point could you confess you had borne a child out of wedlock? Or would you try to conceal the fact? Could you succeed in deceiving a man for the whole of your lives together?'

'I won't marry,' said Adela stubbornly. 'When I'm able to support my child I'll go away with it and wear a wedding ring.'

'When you can support a child!' Mr Danby gave a mirthless bark of laughter. 'You've never even had to mend your own clothes.'

'But I could if I had to. I can sew.'

'We're talking about enough money to keep yourself and a child,' said Mr Danby coldly.

Adela fell into a miserable silence.

Mrs Danby broke it. 'Adela, think! Married to Mr Bennett you would have all the comforts you are used to. Father has said many times that he is an up and coming business man and his manners could be polished by the right woman. You can live in style, sheltered from criticism, have your child and watch it grow, protected and cared for. You can't throw away such a chance.'

Adela asked dully, 'How have you persuaded him to marry me?'

'We offered him something he wants which he cannot obtain without help. In other words, a foothold in society.'

Adela was astonished. 'But surely he goes everywhere.'

'No, he does not,' said Mr Danby. 'By forming a connection with two of Bristol's oldest and most respected families, doors hitherto closed will open to him.'

Adela's face flamed. 'Did you ask him outright if he would marry me? Did you barter me?'

'You're being melodramatic again,' said Mr Danby, frowning. 'Of course we did no such thing. He once expressed his admiration of you, which is why I told him of your unofficial engagement to Ralph!'

'Adela!' said her mother. 'Mr Bennett is rather a rough diamond, but his case is not hopeless by any means. Just because his beginnings were humble—'

'How humble?' demanded Adela.

'His uncle owned a boot factory so evidently he doesn't come from the lowest end of society.'

'What a relief,' said Adela.

'Sarcasm, at a time like this, is out of place and trivial,' snapped Mr Danby.

'Does Mr Bennett profess to love me?'

Mrs Danby threw up her hands. 'What does it matter? He wants you. He's prepared to rescue you from your own folly.'

In the end Adela had been persuaded to meet the man and talk to him. He called early that evening. Mr Danby was still in his office so Mrs Danby dispensed sherry and tried to make small talk until Adela had got over her nervousness.

Adela couldn't meet Sander's eyes. He was dressed in a dark

suit which was stretched across his heavy body. His complexion was swarthy, she noticed, and he looked as if he might need to shave twice a day. The general impression he gave was one of power and Adela disliked it. She tried to concentrate on the advantages of marriage to him, the chance to buy safety for Ralph's child, but her mind kept sliding to visions of herself in Sander's arms, held as Ralph had held her, giving her pain and embarrassment. The intimacy had been bad enough with Ralph, a gentleman. God knew how Sander Bennett would behave.

Mrs Danby got up. 'I'll leave you two together,' she said. 'I shall be in the morning room if you need me.'

Adela put out a hand, opened her mouth ready to make a desperate plea for her mother to stay. She let her hand fall and watched the door as it closed, keeping her eyes upon it.

Sander stayed where he was, sitting several feet away. 'Adela, you're nervous. I can't blame you.'

His normally rough voice was quite gentle which surprised her. He walked across the room and seated himself beside her, though not touching her.

'Your father has explained the unhappy position you are in,' he said. 'I'm sure we shall do well together.'

Some of Adela's nervousness evaporated. He sounded quite reasonable.

'Adela, look at me.' Slowly she raised her head and stared at him. He said, 'I met Ralph a few times when he was still at school. He was a nice boy and I'm sure his child will be lovable.'

Adela felt her whole body grow hot with shame. 'I daresay it will,' she muttered. 'People will think it's yours,' she added.

'Does that matter?'

'There's bound to be speculation when the birth is early.'

'We'll face that together.'

'Together,' repeated Adela. Sander Bennett was not proving quite so unpleasant as she had feared, and the prospect of carrying and bearing Ralph's child within the protection of marriage was a relief.

'Let the wedding be soon,' she said abruptly.

'Do you care for me at all, Adela?'

'No!' she said vehemently.

Sander frowned, the lines on his face deep.

'I'm sorry, Mr Bennett – Sander – but you wouldn't want me to tell you lies, would you?'

'Sometimes there is a place for a thoughtful lie.'

Adela clasped her hands awkwardly. 'I may learn to care for you – in time.'

'Then I must rest content with that.' He looked anything but content.

Chapter Four

The wedding was arranged. Soon Adela would become Sander's wife. The idea often terrified her; then she had to concentrate on the fact that the baby would be safe. There were frequent dark times when she wondered why she was putting herself through such misery on behalf of the child of a man whom she had never loved. She saw Sander every day. At first, he spent only short times with her in Speede House, or strolling with her round the garden, Adela in her furs, Sander in a wool tweed overcoat and soft grey hat.

Their conversation was limited to uncontroversial subjects. Sander spoke of his plans. 'I aim to be one of the most successful men in Bristol, Adela, *and* one of the richest.'

She responded awkwardly. Sander should talk to her father about money, not to her, she thought. It was always an unpleasant jolt to remember that her future husband wasn't among top-drawer society. Sander read her expression correctly and said, 'Surely I can mention money to my bride-to-be?'

His unexpected percipience gave Adela such a shock she said almost nothing more during the visit.

After establishing himself a little with Adela, Sander took her for a drive in a large grey car with yellow wheels and a black hood. 'Do you like it?' he asked.

It hadn't occurred to Adela to give any thought to his mode of transport, but she said, 'Yes,' adding, 'it's very pretty,' feeling her answer to be inadequate.

'*Pretty*? I hadn't exactly viewed it that way.'

Adela stole a sidelong glance at him before she pulled aside her motoring veil to get all the air she could.

'I believe the nausea disappears after a few weeks,' he said.

57

Adela was overcome with embarrassment at Sander's plain speaking on such a subject. She wished he would ignore her condition. Perhaps if she hid all physical evidence as long as possible he would forget the pregnancy, as she longed to do.

She bought new corsets and commanded Bertha to pull the strings tighter and tighter until she gagged. Bertha was the only servant in the Danbys' confidence. She lived in such close proximity to her employers it would have been virtually impossible to deceive her, and she was completely trustworthy. She obeyed Adela over the corset, but she was angry. 'You'll hurt yourself, and the little mite, if you're not careful.'

'Oh, blast the little mite! I wish I'd done what Father and Mother wanted in the first place.'

The maid looked sharply at her and Adela controlled herself. No one could be told about the planned abortion. Not even Bertha. 'Sorry. I don't know what I'm saying half the time.'

'Is it to be wondered at, you poor lamb! War is dreadful. If it hadn't been for that you and Mr Ralph would have got wed and everything would be wonderful for you, instead of the way it is now.' The maid recollected herself. 'Of course, Mr Bennett will be able to keep you in your proper station in life, and I'm sure you'll get to understand him in time. All men are the same underneath.'

Adela laughed more naturally than she had for a long time. 'Bertha!'

'Nothing saucy intended, Miss Adela. I meant, they all respond to a bit of flattery. They want their homes well run, their food on the table at the right time, properly cooked, and outward obedience from their wives.'

'How do you know so much? You aren't married.'

'I've got married sisters and I've watched plenty of folk in my time. The best marriages are the ones where the woman gets her own way by flattery and persuasion. That's what you use – flattery and persuasion.' Adela found the prospect unwelcome. Bertha tied the corset laces. 'There, that's enough. I've given you a good shape without lacing you so tight you can't breathe properly. You won't show. Luckily skirts are quite full at present, but you'll need to get one of those new sort of chest supporters – I forget what they're called, it's some foreign name. Anyway, Mr Bennett knows the truth about you which is what matters. I've heard of girls marrying without telling their husbands that they were expecting by someone else and you'd never believe the havoc that causes.'

'Yes, I would,' said Adela fervently. 'And the chest supporters are called brassières, Bertha. *The Lady* says that French and American women wear them and so must we. *Friends and Allies must stand together*, they say.'

Bertha sniffed. 'The war's over now and we don't have to do what foreigners tell us.'

Sander escorted Adela to the Clare Street Picture House where they watched a murder film which had been adapted from a play. It was followed by a humorous turn and Adela felt slightly more comfortable in his company after they had laughed together. Afterwards he took her for supper to a small, exclusive restaurant. An attendant took Adela's coat and she sat opposite Sander at a table for two, beneath muted light which rendered the atmosphere intimate. She looked round quickly, but saw no one she recognised. That was a relief. Their official engagement, and the wedding date, had been announced in all the leading newspapers and gifts had been arriving every day, but she was sensitive on the subject. Friends who, knowing of her former attachment, had made an attempt to discuss Ralph, had been courteously but firmly silenced. Others, less charitable, had uttered sly remarks about Sander Bennett. Adela had deflected, or ignored, them.

The Somerses had been the most difficult to deal with. 'Marrying!' gasped Lady Somers. 'And Ralph not yet cold in the ground. I cannot understand you, Adela.'

'And marrying *such* a man, after looking forward to Ralph as your husband,' said Sir Wilfred. 'The contrast between the two couldn't be greater.'

Mrs Danby had stared at him, keeping her anger under control. She said evenly, 'Adela discovered she had mistaken her affection for Ralph and that she cared for him in a sisterly fashion.'

'Sisterly!' Sir Wilfred reddened with anger. 'They were engaged to be married!'

Mrs Danby had maintained her calm. 'Unofficially,

remember? My daughter accepted Ralph's proposal because he was a soldier fighting a war. She wanted him to be happy. As soon as he had returned home and settled down she intended to ask for a year or so in which to discover if she had mistaken her sentiments.'

'Is that so?' Sir Wilfred snapped. 'How very condescending of her!'

Lady Somers said timidly, 'Wilfred, Adela did what she believed was right, and if she made our son content before he died, we should thank her.'

'Should we? Ralph was extremely fond of Adela. I am positive he would have wished to marry her, had he lived!'

'Probably you are right,' Mrs Danby said diplomatically. 'In fact, I believe that Adela and Ralph would have married and I do not doubt that two such nice young people would have settled together.'

'I'm sure they would,' sighed Lady Somers. 'Adela, I must wish you and Mr Bennett happiness.' She sounded doubtful.

Mr Danby had firmly turned the conversation to politics and Adela listened to their talk, still hearing nothing in their tone to indicate any depth of sorrow. Ralph's mother must be suffering but, true to her code of conduct, she would conceal it.

She herself could scarcely remember what Ralph looked like. He had left no clear impression, except for the child he had planted in her. Adela had come close to telling Lady Somers the truth, but she would feel nothing but intense shock, embarrassment and revulsion towards a woman of breeding expecting a child outside marriage. Adela must hold her tongue. Words, once spoken, could never be retracted and could ruin lives. Poor Ralph, to have lived an undistinguished short span, and died so young, and for what? For a land fit for heroes? Already fierce conflict had begun between the government and non-combatants on one side and, on the other, the fighting men who wanted the world reconstructed to a pattern in which they held safe jobs and earned good money.

Seeing only strangers in the restaurant relaxed her. She smiled uncertainly at Sander.

'Welcome back,' he said.

'Sorry, I was thinking.'

'Of me? Of our bright future together?'

'No! As a matter of fact I was wondering why Ralph, and so many others, had to die. What have we gained?'

Sander's brows rose. 'You surprise me.'

'Do I? I was engaged to Ralph, remember?'

'I haven't forgotten,' said Sander, 'though when you are with me I would prefer you to concentrate only on me.'

'Isn't that a little selfish?'

'Possibly, but it's the way I feel. Now, shall we order? The waiter has been hovering for some time. The poor devil looks so ancient and shaky I fear he may collapse.'

Adela smiled, properly this time, and some of her tension dissolved. She actually enjoyed the food, and drank wine chosen by Sander. She leaned back, replete and slightly hazy.

'Is your health improving?' he asked.

'My health? I feel well this evening.' His question brought back her situation. 'We had better go home.'

'Are you tired?'

'Not really, but you have to be up early for work tomorrow, don't you?'

'I'm the boss, remember? I can allow myself time off.'

'Yes, of course. May I have more wine, please?'

'Is that good for you?'

'For heaven's sake, stop treating me as if I were a child!'

'I apologise. I know very little about your condition.'

Adela's fragile calm broke. The wine had loosened her tongue to danger point. 'I wish you'd stop referring to it. Didn't your mother have other children? I've always believed that women in poor circumstances were forever having babies.'

Sander's eyes grew flint-hard and Adela shrank back.

'Don't act as if I was about to beat you,' he rasped.

'I'm so sorry.'

'Sit up and look as if you like being with me.'

'I am truly sorry for the way I spoke of your mother. I didn't mean to.'

'I'm aware of that. Your sort never mean to be insulting. It just happens.'

61

'My sort? What sort is that?'

'The sort who feel free to take the work their impoverished brothers and sisters do for them and toss them a few coins in return.'

'Is that what you think I'm like?'

'Aren't you?'

'I wonder you want to marry me!'

'Sometimes I wonder too.'

Adela began to stand and Sander seized her wrists and held her fast. He took a deep breath. 'Adela, it's stupid of us to quarrel.'

She sat down. 'I suppose it would be better if we waited until we're married before we do so,' she said, trying to lighten the atmosphere.

He said smoothly, 'We must hope that we have an amicable relationship.'

'I do hope so. Oh, Sander, I can't believe our marriage will be happy. I don't understand why you should want me at all. I'm damaged goods!'

'Don't say that!'

'But I am! What have I to offer you.'

'What did your father tell you?' Sander watched her keenly.

'He said— Oh, does it matter what he said?'

'Certainly it does.'

'Even if it's a bit insulting?'

'I'm not very easy to insult.'

'He said you wanted to become attached to a high-class family. Apparently you have great earning power, but no background.' Adela had spoken with downcast eyes, but now she looked up. 'You don't like the truth. I knew you wouldn't.'

'I don't fear the truth,' he said harshly.

'But you didn't like it. I'm afraid you are much easier to insult than you think.'

He gave her a long, unfathomable stare. 'I will amend my claim. Usually I'm not easy to insult, but you, Adela, seem to have the power to get under my skin.'

'Have I? Are you truly willing to spend the rest of your life with a woman who irritates you and who is carrying another

62

man's baby, just so that you can swan around in upper-class drawing rooms?'

'It may seem odd to you, Adela,' Sander had himself well under control again, 'but that has meaning to a man who has climbed from the depths of poverty.'

'Depths of poverty? Hardly that! I understood that you inherited a boot factory from your uncle.'

Sander stared at her, then took out his cigarette case. His hands were broad, his fingers thick. An artisan's hands, thought Adela. He offered the case to her.

'I don't smoke and certainly not in public. No lady does.'

Sander's brows rose. 'Is that so? I've seen ladies smoking in restaurants.'

'Oh, maybe profiteers' wives, actresses, and that sort.'

After a brief silence, he said, 'Do you mind if I enjoy a cigarette?'

She shook her head.

Sander blew out a stream of smoke and smiled a trifle acerbically. 'Adela, you have a lot to learn and I'll begin now with lesson number one. My father was killed in an accident at work. The bosses found a lawyer to say that it was his own fault so my mother got no compensation. She was expecting a baby and died giving birth. I realise now that she hadn't eaten properly, though she'd made sure I was well nourished. I was six and was taken in by my uncle and aunt.'

'The uncle who left you the factory?'

Sander's heavy black brows drew together. 'People believe that I inherited the factory and I've allowed the lie to stand because the truth is so ugly.'

There was a look on his face which disturbed her. She hoped he wouldn't go on, but he said, 'My uncle was a swine. He beat me. So did my aunt. I wanted desperately to stay on at school. I won a scholarship which should have led me eventually to university but, at thirteen, I was put to work in my uncle's boot factory without wages. I was told that I was now to pay for my keep over the years.'

Adela was truly shocked. 'How dreadful! Fancy treating a young boy like that!'

'I left as soon as possible, worked at anything I could get and saved every penny I could. I also read when I had the chance – books, newspapers, magazines, anything. By the time I was nineteen I was an overseer in a cotton mill in the north and helping a pal who ran a second-hand furniture business. I was reasonably well educated and had a good bank account and when I heard that my uncle was rapidly heading towards bankruptcy, I got someone to act for me and borrowed enough money to put a large down payment on the boot factory. My uncle had let it get into a poor state and there was little competition.' Sander paused. 'That was gratifying. I have long since paid off the mortgage and turned the business into a large, profitable organisation.'

'What happened to your relatives?'

Sander stared. 'How should I know? I never saw them again. I hope they suffered some of what they put me though.'

Adela's nervousness increased. Admittedly Sander's uncle and aunt had behaved disgracefully towards him but, if they still lived, they must be quite old and maybe in need of help. There was such a thing as forgiveness. She was beginning to see for herself just what being ruthless meant. And she would be absolutely in this man's power.

To her relief Sander had little time to spare for her in the final run up to the hastily called December general election. She knew he was canvassing for the socialists. Her parents, who would once have despised him vociferously, remained mute on the subject, but when Lloyd George's coalition government was returned with a huge Conservative majority, ousting many of the socialist leaders and leaving Labour with only sixty members, they had a hard task to hide their jubilation from him.

'I'd much prefer them to be open about their beliefs,' Sander said to Adela later. His tone was acerbic and she flushed with annoyance.

'They are only trying to be polite. After all, you'll be their son-in-law.'

'That's true,' he said with such satisfaction that Adela wanted to deflate him a little.

She hesitated. He had a way of turning the tables which unnerved her. 'It's not like you to be on the side of losers,' she finally said.

'They'll get their turn. There will be a Labour Government.'

'Never!'

'And I say there will.'

'Lots of people insisted that the khaki vote would defeat the Coalition, but they were wrong. The troops didn't stand up for the socialists.'

'The troops!' Sander was angry. 'The poor devils hate their masters more than they hate Germans. They were given a proxy vote, then were unable to use it because their names weren't yet on the register. It was just another ploy by the government to make it look as if it cared, while getting what it wanted.'

Adela was nonplussed. 'I suppose you see yourself as a political expert, maybe even a member of Parliament.'

'Maybe. It's in my mind, but I've enough to contend with at present when men like Somers and your father are competing with me in business, though Sir Wilfred isn't such a threat as your father.'

'Father, a threat?'

'His workrooms used to produce well-made clothes at competitive prices. Of course, making uniforms has curtailed much of his usual trade, but I don't doubt he will make fashion garments again.'

'Yes, his girls do make lovely things, don't they?' said Adela eagerly, forgetting their discord in her enthusiasm. 'Father used to take me to the workroom when I was little because I adored the different fabrics. The overseers kept bits for me and I made clothes for my dolls. Whole outfits, from underwear to evening gowns. Before the war Father was talking of looking for outlets in London. Maybe he will now. He has this woman working for him, have you met her? Elsa Maitland is her name. Father says she has a genius for design. She's just devised a new line in artificial silk underwear. Father believes it will become all the go among women with limited incomes.'

'Is that so?'

Adela glanced sharply at Sander. There was something in his

voice she couldn't comprehend, something she didn't care for. 'It's a secret actually. I suppose I shouldn't have mentioned it, but you won't tell anyone, will you?'

He smiled and touched her nose lightly with a forefinger. 'Of course not, you silly girl. Why should I hurt the goose that's about to lay such golden eggs?'

A few days before the wedding, when the final arrangements were being made, he took Adela to a restaurant near Bath. She was feeling much better and dined almost as liberally as he. They both partook freely of excellent wines which the proprietor kept for his more affluent customers.

After the meal Sander guided Adela to his car. The night was cold and clear and filled with stars and Adela, feeling replete and content, tied her motoring veil over her hat and snuggled herself into the fur rug Sander had placed gently over her. They drove past houses whose occupants, inspired by the lifting of the blackout, had placed illuminated Christmas trees in their windows.

'Christmas,' said Adela. 'We'll be married before then.'

'So we will, my love.'

His reply jolted her. It was the first endearment he had used and it brought back all her feelings of vulnerability.

He broke the awkward silence. 'Don't you like being called "my love"?'

'I don't know! It sounds odd coming from you.'

'Odd! Coming from your future husband? Only a few days now. My love,' he repeated.

She retreated deeper into the fur rug and wrapped the collar of her beaver coat around her ears. Then Sander stopped the car.

'Where are we?' she asked. 'Why have we stopped?'

'We're nowhere in particular, and we've stopped because—' he leaned across and kissed her softly on her lips '—because I wanted to do that.'

'To kiss me! You could have waited until I got home.'

'No, I couldn't. I want to kiss you properly.'

He tugged the car rug aside and pulled her to him. His hands slid beneath her coat, and up and down her spine in a tingling caress. His breath was hot on her face. Then his lips descended on hers again, but this time in a way that startled her. She struggled for a moment before an unfamiliar excitement quickened in her. She found herself returning his kiss. His tongue pushed its way into her mouth and a frisson rippled through her, part pleasure but mostly fear. It restored the memory of what had followed Ralph's kisses. The shocking pain, the embarrassment, the dreadful consequences.

She tried to turn her head and Sander let her. 'My dear Adela! I always knew you had a fire in you.'

'I haven't! I don't care for such kisses.'

'Liar,' he said softly. 'You do and I shall make you want them even more.'

'You seem to forget I'm expecting a baby.' She immediately wished the words unsaid.

Sander laughed in the darkness. 'I thought you didn't like talking about it, and I've yet to learn that kissing hurt a baby.'

'Maybe not, but—' She couldn't continue. Even in the darkness she couldn't talk of taboo subjects.

'You are thinking of what I will expect of you after marriage?'

'Yes,' she managed.

'Don't worry, Adela, I shall take great care of you.'

'What does that mean?'

For answer he kissed her again and this time the kiss went on until she was breathless.

'You enjoy it, don't you?' he said.

'Are you mocking me?'

'Of course not. I think too much of you to mock you at a time like this.'

'At a time like what?' Again she wished she'd held her tongue. She wished she could be whisked home and not have to sit here discussing intimate matters with a man who still seemed a stranger to her.

'At a time,' said Sander, 'when we're discovering what a responsive body you've got. I look forward to awakening it.'

'Ralph already did,' she flashed, resenting his superior attitude.

'Nonsense! I don't believe it! That young man's lips were still wet with mother's milk.'

'That's a pretty vulgar thing to say.'

Sander laughed. 'Vulgar, is it? It's natural, just as love-making is natural. The difference is that whereas a baby will suck its mother's breast in a purely instinctive way, men and women must learn how to make love to give each other maximum pleasure.'

Adela found it difficult to believe that this conversation was actually taking place. Surely her parents never talked to one another in such a way. 'I want to go home,' she said.

'And home you shall go, when we've done with talking, and when I've had another kiss.'

'You're drunk!'

'I most certainly am not. Though,' he added, reflectively, 'I have had more than my usual quota. We were on the subject of love.'

'*You* were. *I* want to go home.'

'Adela, you disappoint me. I asked you to marry me, believing I should get a passionate woman in my bed.'

'I suppose you got that impression because Ralph and I forgot ourselves!'

'Forgot yourselves?' Sander gave a shout of mirth. 'What an expression for an act which created a life.'

'It's what happened.'

'Nonsense! I'm quite sure Ralph knew exactly what he was doing. I'm not so sure about you. How did he get you to yield? Was it the old soldier's lament: "I'm off to the war. I may never return"?'

Adela burned with anger at this slight on Ralph's memory. She recalled his tears and sudden pity for her dead lover flooded her. 'You think it's *funny*!' she cried.

'No, my dear,' he replied gravely, 'I do not. Nothing about the war is funny, certainly not the death of a promising young man.'

'I don't want to continue this conversation.'

He went on as if she hadn't spoken. 'When I make love to you I shan't have forgotten myself. I shall be well aware of

68

everything I do. I look forward to leading you into the true delights of sex.'

Adela was silent for a while. Nothing seemed to pierce Sander's armour. She asked impulsively, regretting the question instantly, 'Do you love me?'

It was his turn to remain silent while she struggled with embarrassment, then he said without a trace of amusement, 'You value honesty, and you've told me you don't love me. I admire you, I desire you, I think I shall learn to love you.'

'Those are sufficient reasons for marrying me?'

'Can you doubt it? Many have married on less.'

'Even though I'm carrying Ralph's child?'

'Perhaps because you are carrying Ralph's child. Society is merciless towards those who transgress its laws.'

'You're sorry for me!'

'A little. And why not? My mother—' He stopped.

'Is Father paying you any money?' she burst out.

'Good God, Adela! *You* are actually speaking of money! How crude,' he taunted her.

She flushed. 'The idea of your being paid to marry me is crude, I agree. Is he?'

'Paying me money? No, he is not! I don't need his money.'

Adela sighed. Sander took her in his arms and kissed her again, but this time his lips were gentle as they traced a pattern over her brows, her eyelids, her well-shaped nose and down to her mouth.

The weather was cold, but remained crisp and clear. The wedding was to be a quiet affair because of wartime austerity which promised to continue for some time to come. Although the fighting was over, peace would not be officially declared until the provisions of the Armistice had been met, and the government had cautioned that all commodities would still be scarce.

'Of course,' said Mrs Danby to Adela, 'there is no lack of food and coal in this house and, if your circumstances had been different, we would have given you a proper wedding. As it is, we must be content with a hole-in-the-corner affair with a small reception.'

Adela was angry. 'Hole-in-the-corner! That sounds dreadful!'

'Make no mistake,' said Mrs Danby, coldly, 'it *is* dreadful. It's scarcely what I planned for you. I expected a good match for you, an alliance with a family like your own, with you dressed in a bridal gown by Poiret or Lanvin. However, we must be content with Mr Bennett who at least behaves outwardly like a gentleman. At least, most of the time.'

'Even if he isn't one! And when will you begin to call him Sander? That's his name, you know.'

Mrs Danby pressed her lips together angrily. 'Your gown is finished. Please try it on.'

Adela was to be married in white. She flinched from the idea, but her mother insisted. She would carry a small posy of Christmas roses and wintersweet, with its fragrant creamy wax-like bells.

Adela knew that gossip persisted among her acquaintances about her decision to marry Sander, but too many people were numbed by the effects of war to care much about the affairs of others. The peace celebrations had not lasted long and not everyone had rejoiced. Men were still dying in large numbers from terrible wounds, or from the agonising effects of mustard gas; families of soldiers reported missing were hoping desperately that they would receive good news; death had come close to nearly every family in the land and blotted out all but sorrow.

Blanche went about with a grim face, her animosity towards her sister reawakened by the engagement. 'So you're marrying Sander Bennett,' she had said, when the news was given her. 'You always land on your feet, don't you?'

'I wouldn't say that after what's happened to me,' protested Adela hotly.

'What happened to you was a result of your own folly. Now you're being given a prize for it.'

Two days before the wedding Mr Danby came home from the office with a request that Adela should visit the workrooms to receive a gift from the women there.

'They have a soft spot for you,' he said. 'Several of them remember you growing up.'

Adela was pleased. 'And I remember them, Father, especially Miss Maitland. She's so clever. No one will ever best you while she designs for you.'

Mr Danby muttered something and picked up his newspaper. Adela was surprised at his lack of response. Her father valued Elsa Maitland who had worked for Danby's since she was fifteen. She was now forty and appeared to have no interest in life apart from her job. Danby's owed much of its success to Miss Maitland's skilful hands and inventive brain.

When Adela walked through the workrooms she looked around and sniffed happily. True, the strong smell from the bolts of khaki cloth was not as pleasant as the smell of fine fabrics from looms and silk mills, and there were few colours to delight her eyes or different textures to satisfy her touch, but still the scent of the machines, of oil, of new cloth, of the hot irons, were a joy to her. The loud hum of many machines was stilled and the older women came to her, while their juniors and the apprentices watched, wide-eyed, as the rich Miss Danby was welcomed.

A box was produced and Adela unwrapped white tissue to find a pair of sheets and two pillow slips, all in the finest linen with lace insets, and hand worked with pink, green and white embroidery.

'They're beautiful!' exclaimed Adela. 'How very kind of you.' She looked closely at the intricate designs. 'Who made the patterns? Oh, it must have been Miss Maitland.'

'It was,' she was assured.

'Where is she? I do hope I haven't picked a day when she's away. I don't see her. She's not ill, is she?'

The women's eyes slid away from hers.

'Is she ill?' asked Adela.

'No, miss,' said a woman who had been with Danby's even longer than Elsa Maitland. 'She's left Mr Danby's employ.'

'But she can't have!' Adela spoke unthinkingly, then recollected herself. 'Well,' she smiled, 'if she's gone to better herself—' Her words held no conviction and died away. 'Thank you all once more for the gift. It is really beautiful.'

She walked up the stairs to the top of the building where her father had his office. His secretary, Miss Shawcross, was in the ante-room, busily typing. She looked up. 'Mr Danby is out,' she said briefly.

'How long will he be?'

'He said he'd be back in an hour, Miss Danby.' Miss Shawcross had known Adela since she was a baby, but she had not used her Christian name for many years. Adela always felt awkward with her and, in the face of the hostility which was clearly emanating from her, even more so today.

As Adela hesitated, Miss Shawcross asked frostily, 'Is it something I can help you with?'

'I expect you can. You are in Father's complete confidence.'

Adela's attempt at flattery didn't work. Miss Shawcross glanced down meaningfully at the pile of work awaiting her attention.

Adela said, 'Miss Maitland is a friend of yours, isn't she? I've just learned that she's left Father's employ. She always said she would never work for anyone else and I'm puzzled.'

The secretary pressed her lips together and typed an envelope.

'Do you know why she left?'

'I do, but it isn't my place to criticise. It's up to your father to give you an explanation.'

'Yes, of course. I feel quite hurt at her desertion. I never thought she'd be disloyal.'

Miss Shawcross went an unattractive shade of red. 'Miss Maitland was never disloyal! She wouldn't know how to be! She had no choice but to go!' She stopped abruptly and Adela felt afraid. There was something about the fixed way Miss Shawcross was staring at her which made her heart beat unpleasantly fast.

She tried to sound cool. 'You've said too much to stop there. You had better tell me.'

Miss Shawcross briskly removed the envelope and stared at her empty typewriter for a moment then said in a toneless voice, 'Her services were dispensed with because they were required elsewhere.'

'But where?'

'I should have thought he'd have told *you*. It's such a triumph for him.'

'For who? Will you stop hinting and come straight out with it?'

Miss Shawcross frowned. 'Miss Maitland has gone to design clothes for Mr Alexander Bennett, and what's more, she's taken the drawings for the new underwear collection with her. It's customary for work done in factory hours to belong to the boss.' Her cold eyes swept over Adela. 'But I suppose it's a kind of dowry. *I* think it's a disgrace. Miss Maitland was happy here. She respects your father as we all do and I'm sure she didn't really want to go. *I* wouldn't wish to work for an upstart like Mr Bennett.' Her flush grew deeper as she realised what she had said. 'I apologise, Miss Danby, that was extremely rude of me. I forgot he is your future husband.'

But Adela wasn't listening any more. Sander had assured her that he hadn't been paid money to marry her, and he hadn't. But he had demanded one of Father's best assets, a woman who had learned everything she knew in his employ, and who loved her place of work. Father had paid Sander to marry her by letting his chief designer go to him. She and Elsa Maitland had been bartered like a pair of slaves; like a pair of animals even. Adela felt sick humiliation.

'Miss Danby, are you all right?' Miss Shawcross actually sounded anxious. 'Sit down. I'll send for a cup of tea.'

'No, thank you, Miss Shawcross. Tell me, were you asked not to mention Miss Maitland's defection to me?'

'No. Mr Danby takes it for granted that I never discuss business matters with outsiders, but you're not an outsider, are you, Miss Danby?'

'No,' said Adela. She couldn't remember going downstairs, getting into the car and being driven home. Her mind was filled with images of her father and Sander Bennett making their deal.

Father must have said, "You give the child a name and save my daughter's reputation and you can take anything you want of mine."

Even unto half my kingdom, thought Adela, just like the old fairy tales which Nurse used to read. And Sander had chosen Elsa Maitland as his reward for marrying second-hand goods.

Chapter Five

Adela went straight to her room. She felt so deeply humiliated and angry she couldn't think clearly. Bought and sold! Her mother was at a committee meeting, and was to go on to another, this time to help fallen women. She should be home helping the fallen woman closest to her, trying to soothe away the unbearable ache of betrayal.

Adela tried to picture herself walking down the aisle of the church on Father's arm, then married to Sander Bennett, a man who had to be bribed to take her. No! every instinct screamed.

She spoke aloud, 'I can't! I won't!'

She refused to eat, sending away the maids who knocked on her door. In the end, Bertha walked in without knocking.

'How dare you!' stormed Adela.

Bertha ignored her bad temper. 'Your mother isn't here to guard you against yourself, Miss Adela. Now, either you must come downstairs and eat, or I shall bring something up.'

'You can do what you like! I won't eat. I'm not hungry!'

Bertha set her lips and shortly afterwards reappeared with a tray. She removed the snowy napkin and said, 'Look, your favourites. Consommé, chicken breast and a salad. Do eat it.'

Adela turned away without answering and Bertha sighed. 'I'll leave it. Don't forget,' she said before she left, her voice sinking conspiratorially, 'you have to eat for two now.'

Far from helping, her remarks inflamed Adela. Eating for two! She was expected to sublimate her whole existence to this being which had taken root in her against her wishes. Looking at the food, she realised she was hungry and felt even angrier as, despite herself, she sat down, drank the soup and ate the chicken, all the time raging at the circumstances which had led to her helplessness and humiliating treatment by her parents, in league with Sander Bennett. After she had eaten she grew a little calmer and began to think. The idea of marrying Sander Bennett was now totally repellent. She must try again to persuade her parents that the problem should be tackled in a different way.

In the library Mrs Danby stared at Adela in disbelieving horror. 'Are you mad? Everything is arranged. Cars, flowers, clothes, food, invitations – even though they are few.'

'Is that all my wedding means to you?' Adela almost yelled. 'Where do *I* fit in?'

'But it is all for you! Why do you think Father and I have been planning it? It's not for Blanche or us! It's for you, can't you understand?'

'But it isn't just for me, Mother! It's because my family are afraid to face people if they learn the truth about me.'

'Is that so dreadful of us? I would have thought you could understand that.'

'The world is different from when you were a girl, Mother. The war has changed things. Lots of unmarried girls have given birth after their men have been killed. I've read accounts which sound quite sympathetic.'

'Some newspaper reporter, or magazine editor, anxious to sell his wares, pretends sympathy. They call it romance, I suppose. The unfortunate girls will find true life very different, and their children will fare even worse. There will be no romance for them! As for a girl of your background, you would be an outcast, no one would receive you, your life would be ruined.'

'I'm willing to take the chance,' said Adela.

'You! You have been protected all your life. You have never had a single independent thought. You have no conception of what the world would do to you.'

'If you really cared about me, you wouldn't want to get rid of me this way.'

'Must you exaggerate? Of course I don't want to get rid of you, and neither does Father. When you are married you will always be welcome in our home. That's why Father—' She stopped and took a deep breath. 'Adela, as a married woman you will be acceptable – and so will he – with your background and his money—'

'His name's Sander. You don't even like him, do you? And you mean I'll be acceptable to you, don't you?'

'Acceptable to everyone,' said Mrs Danby wearily. 'To your friends, to their parents, even to Their Majesties' Court.'

'If I married Sander the child would be born too early.'

'People will turn a blind eye as long as you are protected by a husband.'

'What a hypocritical thing to say! Mother, I can't help feeling this way. I'm not going on with this charade.'

Mrs Danby looked furiously at her daughter. 'God knows what your father will say!'

'It doesn't matter what he says,' cried Adela.

'Doesn't matter! How can you speak like that when he's forgiven the disgusting way you've behaved? Though I can tell you it goes very much against the grain with either of us to condone, or appear to condone, such licentious behaviour as yours.'

'Licentious? All I did was give way once to—'

'Be quiet! I don't want to hear—'

The library door opened and Mr Danby hurried in, closing it behind him. 'For heaven's sake, what's going on in here? Your voices are audible through the door.'

Mrs Danby said anxiously, 'You couldn't hear what we said, could you?'

'No, fortunately. What are you arguing about?'

His wife gestured towards Adela. 'She says she won't get married.'

Mr Danby was bereft of speech for a moment. His face paled, then flushed, and Adela took a step towards him. 'Father?'

'Won't marry?' he asked, bewildered. 'But, Adela, you must! You promised! It's been in the newspapers. Everything has been organised. You can't back out now. Think of our humiliation and imagine what it would do to Bennett! He'll never forgive you. And, if our public humiliation does not move you, consider the situation you'll be in, unmarried, with Bennett knowing about the child and resenting you. You're overwrought. You'll feel differently tomorrow.'

'No, I won't!'

Mr Danby turned on his wife. 'What kind of an upbringing have you given her? She's lost to all decency!'

'How dare you blame me! I've always done my best. It is you who have pampered her and made her so wilful, or else there is bad blood in her and it is most certainly not from my side of the family.'

Adela's parents glared at one another, then Mrs Danby said, 'You see, Adela, you have caused a rift between us. This affair will ruin us all.'

'I'm sorry, truly sorry, but I can't marry that man.'

'What can we tell him?' cried Mr Danby.

'You can tell him,' said Adela deliberately, 'that he can't buy me.'

'What in hell are you talking about?'

'You know very well, Father. I went to the workroom today.'

'Yes, so Miss Shawcross said. I'm sorry I missed you. I was busy.'

'Busy arranging another staff transfer to Sander Bennett's employment?'

'So that's it. You are speaking, I suppose, of Elsa Maitland.'

'You suppose right.'

'She went freely. Mr Bennett made her strong inducements.'

'I don't believe you,' said Adela. 'She loves Danby's. You let her go to get me married to Sander. Who thought of it? Did you, or was it he who saw a fine chance to steal one of the best designers in Bristol? One thing puzzles me. What did you tell her to get her to cooperate?'

Mrs Danby intervened. 'That is not important. She cooperated and you'll have a husband.'

'I shall not! I refuse absolutely to marry Sander Bennett.'

'Adela, you fool!' cried Mrs Danby.

'Silence,' said Mr Danby. He spoke in low, icy tones. 'Adela, you are dismissing every plan we have made to assist you. Understand this: unless you marry Bennett you will leave this house. Your mother and I have always held our heads high in Bristol. There has never been a breath of scandal in either of our families and I will not countenance one now. If you persist in your wilful behaviour, you must make your way elsewhere.'

'That's exactly what I suggested. You have money. You could so easily let me hide somewhere and—'

'Don't talk arrant rubbish,' said Mr Danby. 'Your wedding *will* take place and I want to hear no more of this idiocy.'

'I won't marry him! Why don't you listen?'

Mrs Danby struggled to speak calmly. 'Adela, my dear, I was dreadfully nervous when my wedding day approached. All brides have an attack of fright. Marriage is such a big step.'

'Especially when you discover from an outsider that the man you are to marry cares so little for you he has to be bought before he'll stand in front of the altar with you.'

'You're impossible!' Mrs Danby's voice was shrill. 'Impossible! What is wrong with giving a dowry? You need a husband, he needs something from us. For hundreds of years settlements have been made when rich people marry!'

'So Elsa Maitland is a settlement, is she? I ask you again, what did you tell her to make her leave?'

'The truth,' burst out the goaded Mr Danby. 'We told her the truth.'

'She knows? She *knows* and she will be working for Mr Bennett for years and years, all the time *knowing* that she and I were part of a shameful bargain.' Adela put her hands to her burning cheeks. 'How could you? How could you do this?'

'How could I not?' asked Mr Danby in low, angry tones. 'What does one do with a daughter who gets herself a baby and no husband?'

'I'll have to face her knowing that she sees me as a bit of merchandise, bought and sold like a prize pig. I could put up with anything if my family would support me. This clandestine deal is degrading.'

'Do you have to be so vulgar?' said Mr Danby.

Mrs Danby said, 'Miss Maitland was shocked and upset only on your behalf, Adela. She wanted to help. She would never take a mean advantage.'

79

'Oh, my God.' Tears filled Adela's eyes and rolled down her cheeks. 'Oh, my God. This is horrible. I'd be better off dead.'

'Don't say such a wicked thing,' rasped her mother.

'I can't go through with the wedding. Mother, can't you understand? You're a woman. I don't know if I even like Sander Bennett.'

After dinner that evening, Adela waited for Sander in the morning room. Her heart was beating so hard it seemed to shake her. Just being with him made her nervous, and the taste she had had of his love-making terrified even while it excited her. She wouldn't think about it. For a woman sex was suffering, and only led to more suffering. She still had attacks of nausea; her back ached as did her head. She was a keen, competitive tennis player, a promising golfer and a good swimmer, but all her athleticism was as nothing against these alien sensations. She heard Sander's voice as Evans let him in and she wanted to run away, but Mother had insisted that she tell him her decision herself.

Sander walked in, his hands out to take hers. 'Not long now.'

If Adela had not known better she might have mistaken the warmth of his greeting for affection, the gleam in his eyes for pleasure, instead of the avaricious greed which it undoubtedly was.

When she kept her hands in her lap, Sander frowned. 'Not feeling so well?'

'No, I am not.'

His thick eyebrows went up. 'What's made you so cross?'

'Sit down, please.'

He sat, looking faintly amused.

'I am not going to marry you.'

He stared at her. 'What did you say?'

'It was perfectly clear. I have absolutely no intention of marrying you.'

Sander said, 'Your mother mentioned that you were very nervous. It's apparently quite natural for prospective brides, though not having really known any, I wouldn't know.'

'Will you stop being so – so damned condescending?'

'Would you prefer me to chastise you?'

80

Adela, close to hysteria, almost laughed.

'That's better. Now let's talk over what's worrying you.'

'There's nothing to talk over. The wedding is off!'

'By God, you're serious! Have I done something to upset you? Was it my kisses? You mustn't worry, I shall be very gentle with you.'

Adela flushed. 'I can't imagine why you should want to make love to me at all when I'm carrying another man's child.'

'But isn't that why I'm marrying you?'

She gasped.

'I don't mean to be derogatory,' said Sander, 'but you have told me you don't love me. I'll make you content, I promise.'

'And we might even end up in love?'

'We might at that.'

'Hypocrite! You and my parents are such hypocrites! When did you decide to use me? Was it when you heard about the new underwear collection? No, I'm sure you've had your eyes on Miss Maitland for ages. You must have seen this as a heaven-sent opportunity to steal her.'

'So that's it. You're angry about Elsa.'

'Elsa? You're on first-name terms already? How cosy! Perhaps you expect me to entertain her, and we can make a jolly threesome discussing your cleverness and my sin.' Sander tried to speak, but Adela talked him down. 'Perhaps you look forward to my entertaining *all* your workers. After all, you have the same background. It's probably easier for you to mix with them than with people born so far above you.'

'You little bitch!'

Adela gasped. 'You see! No man of true standing would speak to me like that.'

'Is that what you believe? My God, but you're naive, Adela.'

'Not so naive that I intend to let you bargain for me. Go away! I never want to see you again. Do I make myself clear?'

'Very clear. Very clear indeed. I really thought you were beginning to like me. I had no idea you looked down on me from such a superior height. What an arrant snob you are, Adela.'

'I am not a snob. I can't help being born in better circumstances than yours.'

'No, and I didn't choose my birthplace either.' He paused, then said, 'If you don't marry me, what will you do?'

'That's my affair. I'll tell you this and don't ever forget it – I would rather starve than marry you. I despise you!'

Sander stood up, his face pale. 'Would you? Would you actually starve? You, who have never even known what it is to be really hungry? You have no idea of what life can do to people, especially women who have no money.'

'I have money, thank you. My grandmother left me some.'

'Then you have nothing to worry about.' Sander turned abruptly and walked out.

Adela remained where she was, exhilarated by the luxury of telling that upstart that she rejected him. Her mother hurried in. 'So you've burnt your bridges. Mr Bennett is angry, very angry.'

'I don't care. I'm glad!'

'Glad, are you? You've made a business enemy for Father!'

Adela said nothing, but her resentment grew.

'I told Mr Bennett that I would make a fresh announcement in the newspapers and send back the presents. He scarcely spoke to me.'

'He's not the first person to be jilted,' Adela said, almost jauntily, still buoyed up by defiance.

'No, but it will strike him deeper than most. There will be many who will sneer at him. He will not forgive you.'

'No one seems to consider me in this at all.'

Mrs Danby stared in helpless fury at her daughter. 'You! Considering it's all your fault, I think we have been very considerate.'

Mrs Danby left and Adela sat thinking. She did not for one moment believe that Father would keep to his threat to disown her. All her life he had cherished her, if a little distantly of late years. He was trying to frighten her. Maybe she should give him a bigger fright, big enough to force him to a realisation of his responsibility and affection for his daughter. A year ago Grandmother Danby had left her three hundred pounds to spend as she pleased. Father had tutted at this licence to waste money, but Adela had enjoyed using her own bank account.

She had a hundred pounds left. She would leave the house and hide herself for a while until Father was so worried about her safety he would be glad to help her. She would write them a note, but first she must pack.

From a big cupboard in her bedroom she pulled out one large suitcase and one small, then put the large one back. She wouldn't need it. Father would soon capitulate. She chose two wool dresses, a serge skirt and two blouses, underwear, night-gowns and a dressing gown. A few trinkets, her embroidery, and she was ready to compose her note.

> Dear Father and Mother,
>   I am truly repentant for the unhappiness I have caused you. I am going away to think. If you will not fall in with my wishes, I must face the world on my own. Don't look for me. I shall be well hidden, but will soon contact you.

She read the note through. It sounded over-dramatic but she hadn't the patience to try again. When should she go? Not tonight. Very early in the morning would be best when she would have the whole day to look for a suitable lodging. The weight of anxiety that had been pressing on her for so long lifted after she had made her decision and she became almost gleeful. When the house was quiet she crept downstairs and picked up the two latest copies of the *Western Daily Press* and pored over them, writing down addresses and rents.

She slept lightly, troubled by vague, oppressive dreams, and got up at six o'clock. At the last moment she remembered her ration cards and crept down to the kitchen and rummaged through the drawers until she found them. She didn't stop to eat. Very soon now the maids would be about. As soon as she had settled she would go shopping. She had a couple of pounds in her purse and could get more when the bank opened. She paused. Perhaps she should send her note to her parents through the post. She didn't want to find Father waiting for her when she withdrew her money. Yes, that would be best.

She walked to the tram stop, and paid for her ticket, enjoying the novelty. Her enjoyment wore off when she discovered how the tram jumped and jolted and she was glad when she reached her destination. There were several nice-sounding flats advertised near Clifton Down Railway Station, quite a good area and not far from home. One in particular had taken her fancy, a garden flat, with its own bathroom. She waited until eight o'clock and tried there first. A thin woman in black answered her knock.

'I've come about the flat,' said Adela.

'Oh, yes?'

'I won't be needing it for long.'

'Are you married?'

'Er, no.'

'Sorry, I don't let to single women.' The door closed, leaving Adela open-mouthed with amazement. At the second address which was several streets away she hardly had time to open her mouth before she was reminded that the advertisement stipulated a business gentleman only. By this time she was very hungry and found a small tea room. After eating an indifferent bun and drinking a cup of tea she continued her quest. By the time she had withdrawn her money and rented a bed-sitting room in Eastville, a district on the other side of town, she was exhausted. The rent was five shillings and sixpence a week, said the landlady, Mrs Gardiner, whose tight lips let out her words grudgingly then shut like a trap behind them. Adela was learning. She had bought a gold ring and now said she was married to a soldier, a corporal.

'No children here, mind,' snapped the landlady.

'No, of course not,' agreed Adela. She would have agreed to anything to find a private place to sit down and rest her back.

'And no men in your room – except your husband, of course.'

Adela held on to her temper with difficulty. She thought longingly of home where she could have rung for refreshments to be brought. Instead, she must make her way to a shop. Thank goodness this wouldn't last long! Father and Mother would soon realise that they couldn't allow her to cope with her problem alone and would agree to her wish to hide away and have her baby. She bought a few groceries and returned to her temporary home. Home? The servants at Speede House would have scorned to stay here. The room contained a chest, a dining chair, an easy chair, a table with one leg shorter than the others, a small square of carpet and a bed which, she discovered later, had a lumpy flock mattress. The upper half of the walls was painted an acid yellow; the lower, dark brown. Everything was shabby with long use and grubby with the grime of years. Tomorrow she would buy polish and a duster and washrag. She had watched the maids and thought it might be fun to try her hand at housework. It would help to pass the time. There were other rooms let in the house and she had to wait for some while to use the lavatory and the small washbasin with a cold water tap. It, too, was dirty, and she was disgusted. She ventured to complain to the landlady.

Mrs Gardiner stared belligerently at her. 'It's not my worry. I've got my own facilities downstairs and I'm not cleaning up after other people. My advertisement said "no attendance" and that's exactly what it meant. If you don't like it here you can go elsewhere. It's getting harder to find a place to live and it'll be harder still when all the troops come home. Tenants are easy enough to come by already.'

'Yes, of course,' agreed Adela, fearful at the thought of being ordered out. 'I should have thought.'

'Yes, you should!'

Adela walked away. What a ghastly woman! She had posted her letter so that her parents would receive it the next morning. Bertha would have discovered that one of her cases and some of her clothes were missing and they would know her disappearance was planned so would not be too worried. On reflection she was glad now that she had had to go into the suburbs to find a room. No one would think of looking for her here.

Unused to packing for herself, she had forgotten several things. Handkerchiefs, for instance. She had one in her pocket and another in her handbag. And she had only two pairs of stockings. It got dark early. In her room there was a single gas lamp on a wall bracket, but she had no matches. The idea of confronting the landlady again daunted her, so she knocked timidly on one of the tenant's doors. A man with a thin pimply face and greasy hair opened it and looked her up and down appreciatively. 'Well, now, missy, what brings you here? Not that I'm complainin' mind you. Come in.'

Adela remained firmly outside. 'I wonder, could you lend me a match?'

The man's eyes opened wide. 'My, ain't we posh! A match. Here you are, sweetheart, you can have two or three. An' come back any time. Anythin' Joe Bailey's got is yours. *Anythin'*, mind.' He roared with mirth.

Adela thanked him and walked back into her room, knowing he had remained outside his door, watching her. She felt hot with embarrassment. It was impossible to mistake his salacious meaning.

When she washed her underwear she discovered that drying facilities were exceedingly poor at Mrs Gardiner's. She was given access to the garden, but the December air was damp and there was no warm drying room or airing cupboard. She had to drape her washing on a chair in front of a small fire.

After an uncomfortable night she asked for more coal and was shocked to learn that fifteen pounds a day was the ration for one essential fireplace. 'Essential means you have to cook on it,' said Mrs Gardiner. 'And of course I charge extra for it.' At home Adela had smiled at wartime articles in the press, telling women not to be 'wasteful Cinderellas' by always poking the fire and losing bits of the precious black stuff through the grate. She didn't laugh now; and she had to buy a saucepan and kettle, as well as a teapot.

Food too was an unexpected problem. When she went shopping she found queues everywhere: for bread, margarine – butter was unobtainable – vegetables, meat, even bundles of firewood. And when she finally reached the counters and handed over her ration card the amounts allowed each person were tiny. She was amazed that the women around her could actually manage to make jokes about shortages.

Thank heaven she had remembered her embroidery, though she had to sit propped in bed with a hot water bottle at her feet to stay warm enough to work, and even then her fingers grew stiff with cold and the feeble gas light scarcely reached the bed.

Her spirits fell lower. She tried in a desultory way to find a better place to live, but nothing turned up and in the end she gave up. Soon, she would be home again, or at least in somewhere decent found for her by Father, where she could have a servant. The attraction of housework soon palled, and cleaning the communal lavatory and washbasin before she used them was a chore which sickened her. She yearned for a bath, and thought longingly of the big bathtubs at home with geysers gushing forth steaming water. Here she must make do with washing herself with a bowl of water in her room. She went for long walks, finding her way to a place called Snuffy Jacks, and sauntered by the river. It was chilly and she wished she had brought her furs from home. She shivered. The winter sun was setting and it was getting colder than ever. She hurried through the lamplit streets, looking through windows where curtains had been left open, permitting a glimpse of Christmas festoons. Christmas was almost upon them. Surely she would be home for the festival and Father would find her a safe place to have her baby?

In the newspapers she saw the announcement which told the world that the wedding which had been arranged between Miss Adela Danby and Mr Alexander Bennett would not now take place, but nothing appeared which she could remotely connect with a plea for her to return home. They must be waiting for her to make contact. Should she write or telephone? She would telephone. It was so much quicker and, having decided on a course of action, she was eager to call her parents and go home again, leaving this ghastly house for ever.

She put five pounds in her purse. The remaining money, eighty-five pounds, was well hidden beneath the tea leaves inside her tea caddy. She had never used a coin-operated callbox, but it wasn't difficult. She pictured the telephone bell ringing in the library and when she heard the voice of Evans announcing: 'The Danby residence. Who do you wish to speak to?' she could have cried at the welcome sound.

'May I speak to Mrs Danby, please?'

'Miss Adela! I'm sorry, but Mrs Danby is out. Miss Blanche is at home.'

Adela hesitated, doubting that she would receive any help or sympathy from her sister, then Blanche's voice asked, 'What do you want?'

'To speak to Mother.'

'She's out.'

'You had no need to come to the phone to tell me something I already know.'

'What an idiotic note you sent! What message shall I give Mother?'

'I'd prefer to speak to her.'

'You won't get any joy from her. She's really angry at you for sloping off like that.'

'Nevertheless, I would prefer to speak to her, or Father.'

There was a pause, a slight bustle then, to Adela's relief, Blanche said, 'Mother's just arrived home.'

Mrs Danby said, 'I am pleased you have telephoned, Adela. You should not have left the house the way you did. Your father and I have been most concerned.'

Adela was cold and nervous and her voice shook as she said, 'I'm sorry.'

'Are you? Are you really?' There was an eager tone to her mother's voice which made Adela feel hopeful.

'Yes, truly. I shouldn't have given you more worry by running away.'

'Is that all you are apologising for?'

'Oh, no, no, I'm sorry for everything, Mother.'

'I am relieved – happy to hear it and Father will be, too. I take it that this means you are ready to fall in with our wishes.' Mrs Danby failed to keep a slightly triumphant note from her voice.

Adela was chastened by it, but she asked as calmly as her nerves would allow, 'What do you want me to do?'

'Adela, you are well aware of what we want.'

'To rid myself of the baby?' Adela's voice was a husky whisper.

'Hush! We cannot discuss this on the telephone. We had better meet.'

'I'd like that, Mother. Shall I come home?'

After a slight hesitation Mrs Danby said, 'Please do. In fact, you had better come tonight. Father will be here.'

Adela felt almost light-hearted that evening when Evans opened the front door of Speede House and beamed a welcome at her.

Mr Danby appeared at the library door. 'In here, Adela.' He held the door for her and her mother greeted her with a cool kiss.

They seated themselves and Mr Danby said, 'Your mother tells me that you are ready now to fall in with our wishes.'

'I didn't quite say that.'

'I understood you to mean it,' said Mrs Danby. 'Otherwise we are all wasting our time.'

'Please, I cannot agree to an abortion.'

Mrs Danby sighed and Mr Danby said with heightened colour, 'I don't know how a girl reared as carefully as you can talk so calmly about such a matter.'

'I'm not calm. The past weeks have been dreadful.' Adela's voice broke and Mr Danby half rose from his chair. His wife motioned to him to remain seated and he obeyed. For the first time it occurred to Adela that although her father was putative master of his house it was really her mother who ruled. 'I'm prepared to go to whatever place you choose,' continued Adela, speaking directly to her mother. 'I promise never to do anything to embarrass you.'

Mr Danby smiled. 'You see, Caroline, I told you she'd be amenable in the end.'

Mrs Danby said, 'You have decided wisely. Your father and I will see that you want for nothing, your health will be carefully watched and the child, if you must insist on going through with it, will be settled somewhere pleasant.'

Adela stared. 'What do you mean? It'll stay with me.'

'Adela!' cried Mrs Danby angrily, 'I understood that you were ready to accept our conditions. In return for all the help we shall give you we must have your sacred word that you will hand the child straight over to someone who will find adoptive parents for it. If it is done at birth you will soon forget.'

Adela stared, horrified. 'Forget? Forget my own baby? Is this your idea of helping me?'

'It is far more than most parents in our position would consider. Some would have disowned you.'

Adela knew this to be true, but pleaded, 'Mother, please don't try to force such a condition on me. I couldn't bear to suffer like that.'

'What else did you expect in your circumstances? Have you given a thought to the suffering your child will have to endure if you remain stubborn, and think of us. How do you imagine Father and I feel?'

'I'm truly sorry.'

'Apologies are useless unless they are followed by action. Do you agree to our terms?'

'Agree to let my baby go? Agree to abandon Ralph's child – Ralph is dead! It's all he left!'

'You are getting hysterical, Adela,' said Mrs Danby coldly. 'We mean to see that the child is brought up in a respectable home where we must hope it never learns of the disgrace attached to its birth.'

'Mother, I can't agree. Father, surely you—'

'Your father is at one with me in this.' Mrs Danby hesitated and her voice softened as she said, 'Adela, we don't want to lose you. We have such plans for you, such hopes. You are our daughter.'

'And this baby I'm carrying is my child. I'll never let it go.'

Mrs Danby was bitterly angry. 'I do not understand where you can have acquired such disgustingly low standards.'

'It's you who have low standards,' cried Adela. 'You talk of my flesh and blood – and *yours* – as if it were a carcase to be disposed of.'

'Control your tongue,' cried Mrs Danby. She glanced at her watch. 'I have to go now. I am sure when you have had time to think the matter over you will fall in with our wishes. You may telephone me tomorrow. I shall be in all day.'

She left and Mr Danby stood for a moment, hesitating, until his wife called from the hall, reminding him that he, too, had an engagement. Adela sat for a while, unwilling to move, conscious as she had never been before of the comfort and wealth with which she was surrounded. Her eyes roamed over the many leather-bound volumes, the upholstered furniture, the coal burning steadily in the big fireplace. Then she got up and left Speede House.

During that long, lonely, sleepless night her resolution to care for Ralph's child grew even firmer. She telephoned Speede House the next day to tell her mother and made one last plea for the kind of help she most wanted. It was refused.

'Then I must fend for myself,' said Adela.

'Remember that you did the choosing. We did not cast you off. Bertha tells me that you packed very little clothing. You will need your furs. The weather is cold.'

'Yes. Thank you. Should I fetch them?'

'No, Blanche can bring them to you, along with the rest of your clothes.'

'I would also like my jewellery.' Adela's mind leapt ahead to the possibility of selling her fine gems.

'I think not. I shall send a few trinkets, but the best pieces had better remain here. I must suppose that you will be living a secluded life and will not need them. Where can Blanche meet you?'

'On Temple Meads Station the day after tomorrow at eleven o'clock in the morning.'

'Very well. Blanche is on a late shift so it will be convenient. I take it that you intend to leave Bristol. That would be best. As soon as you arrive at your destination you should see a doctor. Be discreet. Mr Bennett has behaved well and has promised to keep your secret.'

'How helpful of him.'

'Sarcasm ill becomes you at such a time.'

'In your eyes nothing I do becomes me!'

'You have money,' said Mrs Danby. 'The hundred pounds you drew from your account is enough to see you through.'

'Mother, I may never see you again.'

There was silence for a moment, then Mrs Danby said in controlled tones, 'That must be your decision.'

Chapter Six

Adela returned to her lodgings. It was raining, cold winter rain that numbed her face and fingers. She realised now how much she had been kept going by the hope, the surety, that her parents would see reason and permit her to bear Ralph's child somewhere pleasant and keep her in the style she was used to. Her life had become circumscribed by the necessity to carry the baby to term and bear it in reasonable comfort and she had given no thought to anything else. She walked through a puddle she hadn't even noticed and icy water seeped into her shoes as she stamped along angrily. Well, she wouldn't leave Bristol to please them, and hide in some industrial town she had never heard of! She had been born here and felt at home here. At least, she had up to now. All the way back to her comfortless room she was buoyed up by resentment, but when she reached the dismal house and climbed the stairway, with its linoleum worn in places to the bare boards, her spirits drooped. Mr Bailey's door was wide open to reveal a smaller room even more sparsely and shabbily furnished than her own.

Mrs Gardiner came to his door. 'Oh, it's you. Mr Bailey's left. He went very sudden. Said he'd heard of a job in Scotland that would suit him. I didn't believe him for a minute. He's a very nasty man and I shouldn't be at all surprised if he wasn't in trouble with the police. I was sorry I let the room to him. If he hadn't gone I should have thrown him out. I run a respectable house and haven't never had no trouble with the law and I don't intend to start now. When you get policemen coming to your door, you lose your good name.'

She didn't bother to wait for a reply. She had needed someone to vent her annoyance on and Adela had served her purpose. Now she stumped downstairs and went into her own quarters.

Adela put her key in her lock, but the door opened before she could turn it. She gasped. Her few possessions were strewn about, the upholstery of the easy chair had been slashed, her milk jug lay broken on the floor and her cupboard door hung on one hinge. Then her heart jumped. On one of the shelves she saw a pile of tea leaves. She ran across the room and looked in the tea caddy. It was empty, of course. Her money had gone, undoubtedly with Mr Bailey. Shocked, trembling, she staggered downstairs and knocked on Mrs Gardiner's door. When she told her of the disappearance of her money the landlady's expression remained frigid.

'How foolish of you to leave so much money lying about. I always use a bank.'

'So do I, normally,' cried Adela, fighting down panic, 'but I withdrew it because—'

Mrs Gardiner stared at her, giving no help.

'Because I needed to buy something special.'

'Well, if you've that kind of money to play with you won't notice the loss of a few pounds.'

'Eighty-five pounds is more than a few – it's a small fortune! I must tell the police.'

Mrs Gardiner's hard eyes narrowed. 'I knew when I let you the room no good would come of it. You're different. You've probably got something to hide.'

'If I had something to hide, would I be going to the police for help?' flashed Adela.

'There's plenty of things a woman might want to hide that don't interest the police.' Mrs Gardiner's cold eyes raked up and down Adela's figure. 'You're the wrong sort to be living in a district like this!'

'*I'm* the wrong sort! What about Mr Bailey?'

'At least he didn't complain about the lavatory!'

Adela turned. 'I shall go to the police station,' she said angrily.

'They'll come poking and prying and I won't have it! You can take yourself off. I never had no scandal here before you came. Leaving all that money about to put temptation in folks' way!'

Adela didn't answer. If she approached the police, awkward questions would be asked. Her photograph had appeared in the papers when she had been gracing some society occasion. Her anonymity would be over. She returned to her room. Mrs Gardiner remained where she was and when Adela glanced nervously back the triumph in her face was unmistakable.

Adela sat thinking for a long time. The months ahead were going to be far more difficult than she had anticipated. She considered telling her parents what had happened to her money. Would they believe her, or would they think she was lying in order to gain help? She couldn't tell; she had lost her guidelines. Wearily, she tidied the room and went to bed.

On Temple Meads Station, Adela looked around her in horror and pity. The platforms were filled with wounded men, mostly on double-decker stretchers, a few hobbling on crutches, some with bandaged eyes and grey frightened faces. One or two men waved and grinned; others looked too ghastly for words, their faces white and exhausted, their bandages blood-stained. Nurses and volunteers did what they could to make the men more comfortable, tucking in blankets, holding a man's head while he took a drink, lighting a cigarette for another. The war had seemed far away, but this was close reality and it shocked her.

She was relieved to see Blanche. 'Well, you've done it now,' said her sister. 'What a fool you are!'

Her crowing stiffened Adela's resolve. 'Don't try to pretend you're sorry,' she said evenly.

'Have I said anything of the sort?'

'In fact, I dare say you're pleased,' continued Adela. 'I've left the field nicely open for you, haven't I?'

'What's that supposed to mean?'

'You want Sander Bennett, don't you? Now you can have him. But will he have you?' she ended, managing to produce a smile as malicious as Blanche's.

Her sister's sallow face turned an unattractive shade of red.

'It's not likely he'll ever want anything to do with any of us after the way you've treated him.'

'Well, that'll be a good excuse when he doesn't come courting you, won't it?'

Blanche stared at her sister furiously. 'I don't suppose you'll stay away. You've always been the pampered one. I give you three weeks or less on your own and then we'll see. You'll want to come crawling back!' Blanche's pale eyes swept over her sister. 'Your little bastard brat will have to go before you can come home.'

Adela's anger flared. 'I'll never crawl home! When I return it will be on my own terms.'

Blanche laughed mockingly. 'I'll believe that when I see it. If you had any sense at all you would have married Sander and been glad to. You're such a fool! You could have had your brat and a decent man to protect you.'

'I won't marry a man who doesn't care for me.'

'My God, you still believe in romance! How incredibly sweet.' Blanche gave her a calculating stare. 'You're a stupid, blinkered fool, and weak as well. You'll come back – on your knees.'

'I will *not*. You'll *never* see me crawl. When – if – I do return, it will be as a successful woman, able to stand on my own feet.' Adela took the big suitcase, threw her fox fur around her shoulders and folded her fur coat over her arm.

'Mother sent you twenty pounds,' said Blanche. 'With what you've got it should be ample. After all, you aren't likely to be going anywhere, are you? And the only clothes you'll want will be tents.' She looked round her at the cargo of human misery. 'God, what a mess. Some of these poor devils are done for, that's for sure.'

Adela watched Blanche hurry off and her defiance dwindled, leaving her cold and shaky. She had allowed her resentment the upper hand, and to what good? A successful woman able to stand on her own feet, she had said, and already she had foolishly lost her money in a lodging-house bedroom. She stood straight and drew a deep breath. She must manage. She would have her baby and keep it, no matter what the obstacles.

After a long tramp she found another room, this time in St Pauls. The area, once genteel, was now run down, but the Fudges' house was as clean as possible in such a place and the landlady had a careless kindness.

'The room's on the first floor so it's four and six. It's a bit dearer, but up there you don't get the damp an' the mice so bad. Mind you, I d'keep a few cats so the vermin bain't as bad as they might be. Rent in advance, no attendance, washhouse and lavatory in the yard. You can get as much water as you like from the scullery tap. Come in any time. You'll need a rent book. What's your name?'

'Mrs Danby,' said Adela. She had considered changing her name, but the difficulty of altering her ration cards daunted her. She handed over the first week's rent and Mrs Fudge led her up uncarpeted stairs. The room was smaller than the one at Mrs Gardiner's. It contained a narrow bed with a hard mattress – horsehair or straw, Adela guessed – a washstand with an unmatching china basin and cracked jug, a wooden chair, two easy chairs with sagging springs and rather greasy patches where many heads had rested, and a bare wooden table. A cupboard was set into the wall beside the small fireplace.

Mrs Fudge took a duster from her apron pocket and rubbed at the mark on the nearest chair. 'It's the grease the men d'put on their hair,' she said. 'If I was you I'd give them a scrub.'

'I'll put covers over the backs,' said Adela. 'I've just finished embroidering them.'

Mrs Fudge gave her a gap-toothed grin. 'Fancy! Are you good with your needle?'

'I am,' said Adela. 'Perhaps you can tell me if there is a call for such work hereabouts? Embroidery is about the only thing I can do well.' Except ride or play golf, tennis or bridge, she thought, and a lot of use those skills are going to be.

Mrs Fudge scratched her head, then wiped her fingers down her apron. 'I can't think of anythin' at the moment.'

'Is there any kind of work at all?'

Mrs Fudge shook her head. 'Not really. Most of the women are workin' while their men are at the front. They d'need the money an' jobs have been snapped up. 'Course, if you don't

97

mind travellin' up to the posh houses they d'always want maids or general servants, though a general bain't a job I'd do myself. They're nothin' but donkeys, with highfalutin women out to get all the work they can out of them.' Mrs Fudge looked doubtfully at Adela. 'You don't look the sort who's used to rough work.'

'No,' said Adela. 'But I'll need to look for something I can do.'

'Down on your luck, are you, missus? Hubby not sendin' you enough money to make up your army allowance?'

'What?'

'Hubby away at the front, is he? Some of them are real little buggers. No sooner than they d'get away from their homes than they d'forget who they left behind and take up with a mademoiselle from Armentières.'

'My husband—' Adela faltered over the unfamiliar phrase. Mrs Fudge took her hesitancy to be caused by a grief too great to express and her plump face creased into sympathetic lines. 'Lost him, have you? Dead, is he?'

'Yes.'

'Poor soul. Well, you're not alone. Far from it. Every family I d'know has lost someone. There's a woman up the street with eight kids and another on the way, and she's just been made a widow. An' there's many a woman won't never have a husband and babies because there's never goin' to be enough men to go round. The war was really terrible. An officer, was he, your hubby? I would have thought you'd get a big enough widow's pension without havin' to work. Where do your folks live?'

'Thank you for the room, Mrs Fudge. I had better fetch my luggage.'

Mrs Fudge laughed. 'That's tellin' me to mind my own business!'

'I'm sorry. I didn't mean to be impolite.'

'No more you were, my love. I'm a nosy parker.'

Adela felt comforted by the endearment even though she knew it to be a part of the Bristol vernacular. 'I'll go right away for my things,' she said.

She took a taxi to bring her suitcases from Mrs Gardiner's,

angrily ignoring the woman's heavy hint that damage had been done to her bed-sitter and *someone* ought to pay. She had decided not to flaunt her fur coat and had bundled it into a large brown paper parcel which she tied with string.

When she returned to St Pauls Mrs Fudge came out of her room. She was wearing a bright green loose dress which masked her heavy curves, a yellow cardigan and a black taffeta toque hat with two drooping feathers, which had clearly seen better times.

'Do you like my hat, missus? Got it cheap from one of the stalls in Old Market. Belonged to a lady, they said.'

'It's delightful,' managed Adela, turning her amused smile into one of admiration.

'Here's your key, missus, an' a key to the front door. Me and my hubby's goin' to the pub. We d'go most nights for a drink an' a chat with the neighbours. Like to come?'

Adela had never been in a public house. She shook her head.

'You definitely bain't the usual sort we d'get round here, missus.' Mrs Fudge paused for an answer and Adela almost wished she was back with Mrs Gardiner who, at least, didn't ask questions. She picked up the larger of her cases and began to haul it upstairs.

'Arthur,' shrieked Mrs Fudge, 'come out here an' help our new lodger.'

Arthur, a big man with a large, drooping, tobacco-stained moustache, looked sheepishly at Adela, picked up all her luggage and took it to her room. He wiped his hands on his trousers and held one out. 'I'm her downstairs's better half. Call me if you d'want anythin' heavy doin'. I'll be glad to oblige. I'll fetch up a bundle of wood an' a bucket of coal. I daresay you d'need newspaper too for a fire? It's perishin' cold. You can pay the wife later.'

Adela closed her door and sank on to the bed. In spite of her dismal surroundings she felt heartened by the rough kindness of the Fudges. She needed food and hurried out to the shops. This was one of the meatless days, and there were no eggs either, or any milk, but she joined a queue for bread and a small piece of cheese. She asked for butter and received an

99

incredulous glare from the shop keeper. 'Forgotten there's bin a war, have you? You're lucky I've got a bit of margarine.' He slapped a small piece into a paper and added it to her purchases.

Rather dispiritedly, Adela returned to her room, but when she opened her door a wave of welcoming warmth flowed out. One of the Fudges had taken the trouble to light her fire and her spirits were lifted. She sat toasting her feet, eating bread and cheese – she couldn't stomach the foul-tasting margarine – and drinking tea, and felt a sense of accomplishment.

In the days that followed her hopes were gradually whittled away. There was no work to be had; at least none that she could tackle. The only thing she was offered was a place in a brewery where girls with mannish muscles and wearing heavy wooden clogs were rolling barrels about as if they weighed nothing. She couldn't have stayed there anyway. The smell made her feel sick and she staggered away, white-faced. How odd it was that she had never before noticed that a pall of smoke lay over the town. Possibly it didn't reach the heights of Clifton in such a dense mass. She felt she could hardly breathe.

She woke on Christmas Day, remembering other times when she had gone downstairs to a blazing fire, a laden Christmas tree, costly gifts given with indulgent smiles. She was close to tears before she tore her mind from such useless imaginings and waited impatiently for the festival to finish so that she could search again for work. After more fruitless efforts she counted her money and apportioned it. She could exist for a while, but she must get an income from somewhere.

When she had almost given up hope she answered a knock on her door and Mrs Fudge came in, puffing after climbing the stairs. She looked round her. 'My goodness, but you're gettin' the place lookin' nice. The embroidery on those chairbacks d'look a treat. And what's this you'm doin'?'

'A tablecover to match,' said Adela, 'then I shall work a bedspread so that the room will have an overall theme.'

'A what?'

Adela smiled at the comical expression on Mrs Fudge's face. 'Sorry. I mean that everything will match. Of course, I can't do the bedspread until I get hold of more material. Everything is in such short supply.'

'It is that and not likely to get better for a long time, judgin' by the papers. You'd think the war was still on. An' there's still those horrible casualty lists, too. Have you thought of goin' to a second-hand shop for some stuff? Lots of folk are sellin' all sorts of things to make a bit of extra money. An' there's the stalls in Old Market. There's a nice chap there d'sell lovely material.'

'Thanks for the advice,' said Adela. It hadn't occurred to her to consider anything second-hand, leave alone something from a market stall.

'Well, it d'look grand in here, an' it'll be a deal grander when you'm finished. You haven't had luck with a job, have you?'

At Adela's shake of her head Mrs Fudge continued, 'Well, I got some cheery news because I've come about a bit of work that's right up your street. The local midwife, Lizzie Webb – everyone d'call her Lizzie, she hasn't got letters after her name or nothin', but she's a good 'un and she don't charge much – she's got a coat what she wants relined so she can give it to one of her patients. Remember that woman I spoke of who's lost her husband and was expectin' her ninth? She had the baby last night, another boy. She's got six now an' I d'think boys are harder to bring up than girls an' somehow they d'cost more. Lizzie's good that way. Could you do the job for her? It won't pay much 'cos nobody round here's got much, but it might set you off on somethin' useful when people d'know you can sew nice.'

'I'd be delighted, Mrs Fudge. Where must I go to get the coat?'

'Bless you, my hubby'll fetch it. It's enough to freeze a brass monkey's—' She stopped and laughed. 'I nearly said somethin' I shouldn't then.'

The brown cloth coat was well worn, especially about the elbows. Lizzie Webb had supplied lining material and thread and Adela laid the garment on her wooden table and set to work, measuring and cutting. It took her three full days to complete her task. She had never sewn clothes and the work was tiring and time-consuming, especially as the artificial silk

101

for the lining frayed easily. She rubbed her back which ached from the long hours of bending over, wondering if she'd get more jobs. She could never have imagined the poverty around her, but people needed clothes. She might even be able to buy a second-hand sewing machine. She kept up her spirits with dreams. Mrs Fudge lent her a flat-iron to steam the material as she progressed and round the corner, in Newfoundland Road, Adela found a small drapery shop where she bought a piece of matching cloth and reinforced the worn parts of the coat.

Mr Fudge took the coat to Lizzie who was delighted, and handed over one and sixpence. Adela looked at the two silver coins lying on the table. They were so small, so insignificant, yet they represented the first money she had ever earned and she felt a glow of achievement greater than any in her life before.

Adela received more commissions, always from women desperate for decent garments for their families, though there were too many who could barely afford a penny for a dress or a pair of worn shoes from the church jumble sales.

Mrs Fudge took a liking to her unusual tenant. Her garden backed on to the garden of a similar house in the road running parallel. The owner, who had several sons, kept ducks in a small dirt pond and Mrs Fudge negotiated eggs for Adela in return for her patching the boys' trousers. For the first time Adela realised the extent to which Clifford Smithers had assisted her family in keeping their larders stocked with food. In poor homes profiteers were hated and again, for the first time, Adela understood that he was virtually robbing the poor to supply the homes of the rich and felt ashamed of her past complacency when she saw war-weary wives and widows queuing endlessly for necessities. The issue of ration cards for some commodities, though late, had made for fairer conditions, but unrationed goods were scarce and had it not been for the kindness of Mrs Fudge whose sharp eyes had soon detected Adela's pregnancy she would be in those same queues.

'You should have said you were expectin',' said Mrs Fudge indignantly one day.

'How do you know?' Adela's eyes were big with apprehension. Was she about to be turned out to go tramping the streets looking for a place to stay? Landladies often stipulated 'no babies'.

'Lor' bless you, girl, I've had seven of my own. Lost four of them to the diphtheria, poor little mites. But I've got two good daughters left, an' the one son livin' at home, that's our Isaac, an' I've got grandchildren, an' anyone with eyes to see can tell you're gettin' fatter round the middle. How far gone are you?'

'The baby should be born in June,' said Adela, keeping her voice calm with an effort.

Mrs Fudge stared at her. 'You should have told me, really you should.'

'I suppose so,' said Adela wearily. She had been up half the night refurbishing a wedding dress a local girl had purchased from a pawn shop. 'I wasn't sure if – I mean, I wondered—'

'You thought I might tell you to go? Of course I won't. You can stay here as long as you d'want.' She hesitated, then said, 'Mrs Danby, it's not my place to speak, but you don't belong here. Surely your folks—'

'I don't wish to discuss it,' said Adela. In her distress her voice had taken on an autocratic tone and Mrs Fudge's face coloured. Adela was contrite. 'I'm sorry. Please forgive me. I've had such an anxious time.'

Mrs Fudge said slowly, 'Are you really married, my love?'

Adela looked away and stared through the window down at the street outside, where several small children were busy scooping up horse dung with which their parents would enrich the poor soil of their gardens and grow a few vegetables. That was another thing she had never considered before. Someone had to shovel away the tons of manure dropped in the streets. Not many people had motor cars.

She was suddenly tired of pretence. 'No,' she said flatly, 'I'm not married. My fiancé was killed.'

Mrs Fudge clasped her rough red hands. 'I'm sorry, really I am. You're doin' quite right to call yourself missus. Some folks are hard on girls who've got themselves into trouble.'

I've got myself into trouble, thought Adela, after Mrs Fudge had gone. It's as simple as that.

Nevertheless the admission of her pregnancy brought instant improvements. Mr Fudge carried up her fuel and water and she was forbidden to stand in queues by Mrs Fudge who took charge of her ration coupons and, Adela suspected, added a little something to the food she brought for her. In return Adela undertook Mrs Fudge's mending and eventually stopped protesting when she insisted on paying her. She was making a living, but it was frugal and she was forced to use her small nest-egg. She should be putting money aside towards the cost of bearing her child and for someone to help during her lying-in. Somehow she must increase her income. A sewing machine was what she needed, then she could buy cloth and make new garments for those who could afford them. Not everyone in St Pauls was desperately poor. The post war boom was proving quite beneficial to some and she could keep her prices low enough to compete easily with the shops.

The midwife had advised her to walk every day to keep up her strength and she was exploring places that had been only names on a map to her until now. Small shops, some of them merely a converted front room, were a revelation to her, and she was fascinated by the barrows in Old Market and Carey's Lane and the vendors who called their wares to the passing world. She lingered at one which sold material at cut prices. It was run by a man who looked taller than he was because he was cadaverously thin. He coughed a lot, coughs which came from deep inside his narrow chest and tore at his whole body, but didn't discourage him from smoking cigarettes. Adela moved along the front of his stall, taking off her glove to feel the fabrics; most were unexciting, but occasionally her fingers caressed satin or silk.

'If you don't want the goods, don't muck 'em about!'

Adela looked up and flushed. The stall holder was glaring at her with what looked frighteningly like hatred. She moved back fearfully, almost stepping into the path of a bicycle ridden dangerously fast by a small messenger boy. She turned her ankle. Pain shot up her leg and she gasped. For a moment the world seemed to spin round her. She cursed beneath her breath at the pregnancy which so weakened her. She had never fainted and didn't intend to now.

The next thing she knew she was sitting on a wooden chair in front of the stall for every passer by to see and a gravelly voice was telling her to stop still while he fetched some water. She sipped at the water and opened her eyes to see the stall holder staring down at her with dark eyes that seemed to burn like coals in his narrow face. She tried to get up, but her legs betrayed her and she sank back.

'For heaven's sake, woman, sit still a minute,' said the man, 'you're like a flea in a bucket.'

Adela took a few deep breaths. 'Thank you,' she said. 'I can't think what happened to me.'

The man continued to stare at her, his eyes travelling over the fur coat which she wore these days against the cold. She wore it even in her room where there was little or no coal to be had. Mr Fudge made endless trips upstairs to bring her wood, but it didn't give out the same heat and the room was often damp with condensation.

'I feel better now,' she said. 'May I get up?'

'No.'

Adela looked helplessly at the man. 'I can't sit here all day.'

'No one's askin' you to, but you look too pale to walk yet. What are you doin' down here, anyway? You don't belong here.'

'I most certainly do,' said Adela, in a haughty tone, then subsided. 'I live here. At least, I live in St Pauls.'

'Who do you think you're havin' on?'

'Don't believe me then! I don't care!'

'Why were you fingerin' the materials?'

Adela blinked. He jumped from subject to subject like a grasshopper. 'I'm interested in them.'

'Want to make yourself somethin', do you? A new party frock, or an outfit for Windsor or Sandown Park? I should have thought Jolly's was more up your street.' His tone was bitterly sarcastic and she flushed.

'I'm thinking of setting up as a dressmaker.'

'You!'

'Yes, me! And why are you so belligerent?'

He surprised her with a grin which relieved his thin features and crinkled the skin around his eyes. 'Belligerent, am I? A dressmaker, you say?'

'Yes.'

He eyed her coat and his gaze travelled down to her silk stockings and expensive boots and she had the feeling that he was pricing everything to a penny.

'All right,' she conceded, 'I don't look the part, but I'm telling you the truth. Believe it or not, as you choose.'

'You must admit it sounds unlikely.'

'My whole life is unlikely these days!' To her disgust her eyes felt prickly with unshed tears which might trickle down her cheeks at any moment. She looked down at her hands.

'I believe you do mean it,' he said. 'Down on your luck?'

'Yes,' she managed shakily.

'You don't go in much for conversation, do you?'

His acerbic tones stiffened her backbone. 'Not unless I've something to say.'

'You're a novelty then. For a woman, that is.'

Adela fumed.

The man grinned again. 'You're better now.' It was a statement.

'Yes.' She felt that more was needed. 'Thanks to you. Can I get up now?'

He took her hand, helped her to her feet, and carried the chair back behind the stall. 'What can I sell you?'

'Nothing today.'

'You can have anythin' you like on credit.'

'But you've never seen me before!'

'I reckon I'm a good judge of character.'

Adela felt warmed by his words, though the hoarse voice gave no intimation of sentiment.

'I would like to take up your offer, but just at present—' Adela stopped.

'I'll wait for payment till you get on your feet.'

'You're very kind.'

'What d'you most like to sew?'

Adela thought. 'If I could choose, something to do with interior decorating. Maybe one day I will, but I should need a

106

sewing machine for that. In fact, I need one now, but that's impossible.'

'Well, don't sound so mournful.'

Adela was suddenly angry. 'Why not? You'd sound mournful if you needed something as badly as I need a sewing machine and hadn't the money to pay for it.'

'Would you like me to find one for you?'

'You!'

'Yes, me. I've got friends in every trade you could mention. Can you afford any money at all?'

Adela made a quick calculation in her head. 'No, not if I'm to eat.'

'You're a stubborn female. I wasn't talkin' of a new one. How much can you give for a second-hand model?'

'I can scrape up a pound.'

'Is that all?'

'I told you I couldn't afford one.'

'I know where there's a machine for one pound ten. I'll pay the difference an' you can add it to my bill.'

'I can't permit you to do that. What bill?'

'The one for the materials you'll need.'

Adela made a quick decision. She'd never get a better offer. 'All right,' she said. 'It's a bargain.'

He came round to the front of the stall and stuck out his hand. It was as bony as the rest of him, but his handshake was strong. 'I'm Jack Webster. I was invalided out of the army. Got a dose of trench lung and a few whiffs of mustard gas. Not as bad as a lot of my mates. They died of it. Mine was enough to get me out of the army. Bloody Boche! And bloody government, sendin' men into conditions they wouldn't put a dog!'

'I'm Adela Danby. Widow. I'm expecting a baby.'

'That's bad luck.' Jack's eyebrows rose. 'Your first,' he said confidently.

'How do you know?'

He sighed. 'You're like an open book. Your hands are soft so you haven't been washin' nappies, you're livin' in St Pauls an' you're short of cash so you haven't got a nursemaid.'

'Proper Sherlock Holmes, aren't you?' Adela half expected Jack Webster to ask who he was. He didn't.

'An' you're like Dr Watson.'

She laughed.

'That's much better. You're very good lookin' when you laugh. You're pretty when you don't, but a scowl spoils any woman's looks.'

Adela marvelled. In about fifteen minutes she was having a conversation with a man on a level it would have taken weeks for one of her own class to reach.

'Select the stuff you want,' said Jack, then turned to serve a large woman with a length of calico.

Adela plunged her hands into the massed materials. The silks and satins were of inferior quality, but she saw possibilities in them. Women expecting their menfolk home from the front would want to greet them in something special. There was also artificial silk and, marvel of marvels, crepe de Chine!

Jack had finished with his customer and was watching her. 'Got hold of some ends of bolts and a whole bolt of flawed crepe de Chine. I'll put some aside for you.'

Adela's eyes glowed. She would make nightdresses and pretty underwear, too. The little shop in Newfoundland Road sold lace and ribbon by the yard and she had seen patterns on her latest visit. She felt a leap of excitement as she chose some cloth.

'I'll bring it all to you, along with the sewin' machine,' said Jack. 'What's your address?'

'My landlord will be glad to fetch the things for me.'

'I do my own work. Where do you live?'

Adela yielded to his aggression and told him. She wondered if she had been wise.

On her way home she bought three basic patterns: one for a nightgown which could be adapted to a petticoat; one for a blouse, and another for a skirt which she could fuse together for a gown.

Mrs Fudge looked at them critically. 'Can you do tricky stuff like that? Runnin' one pattern into another.'

108

'I have to admit I've never done it before, but I like sewing. I used to make doll's clothes. This is the same, only bigger.'

Mr Fudge, who had been sitting quietly by the fire, gave a shout of laughter then blushed. Mrs Fudge said, 'You'll do.'

Adela asked her about Jack. Mrs Fudge was reassuring. 'He's a good man. Had a lot of bad luck. Lost his wife when she wasn't yet thirty and had to bring up two girls and a boy on his own.'

'He had his mother's help,' said Mr Fudge.

Mrs Fudge grimaced. 'I suppose he did, though I wouldn't want Thora Webster helpin' me.' She turned to Adela. 'She's that bossy you'd never credit it. If you're goin' to have anythin' to do with Jack, you'd best watch out for her, though she bain't as much trouble as she used to be since the rheumatics got her and she can't get around so much.'

'Does Jack live near here?'

'St Philips. He does his best for his mother an' his girls are good to her, an' her own daughters do what they can, though it's little enough thanks any of them get. I've never known her when she wasn't bein' nasty to someone. Jack's son went away years ago. Some say to America, an' some say it was his gran that drove him away, but I don't know.'

'Well,' said Adela comfortably, 'my dealings with Jack Webster will only be business ones, so the question of his mother won't arise.'

Chapter Seven

Adela placed an old cotton sheet on the floor then unrolled upon it a length of shimmering white satin. She paused to look down at it, delighting in its soft sheen before, kneeling, she pinned a pattern to it. A wedding dress! The soldiers were coming home and excited girls talked of little else. Except those who would never welcome home their young man who had gone to the front, his heart overflowing with patriotism, his head filled with ideas of glory and honour, only to die in the mud and blood of France. There had always been more women in the country than men; now that one in every seven men had been killed, the proportion of spinsters to bachelors was frightening. Adela superstitiously pushed such thoughts aside in case they should communicate themselves to the gleaming material which awaited her skill. This was for one girl who had been lucky.

Jack Webster had kept his promise and had arrived at her door, puffing after the stairs, his breath harsh in his throat, in his arms a hand sewing machine. Strapped to his back was a brown paper parcel which, when opened, made Adela gasp with delight.

She had touched the materials disclosed with a tender, almost loving finger. 'Satin,' she had breathed, 'and pink chiffon, silver lamé, white crêpe de Chine – and cream *silk*. Real silk. They're so beautiful. Thank you! Thank you so much. It's very good of you.'

Jack sank into a chair, still short of breath. 'I like to see a woman ready to work for herself. All women should have a chance of doing it, an' they should all have equal opportunities with men.'

111

Adela had blinked. 'You really believe that?'

'I don't say things I don't believe.' His thin face was stern and Adela had not pressed him further.

'I can't think how you manage to buy such lovely materials so inexpensively,' she had said.

'They're seconds, flawed, but I dare say a clever girl like you can hide the faults.'

Adela had felt warmed by his compliment. She had given him a cup of tea before he left, promising to look out for more pretty cloth. 'Do you want any serge or other plain stuff?' he had asked.

When Adela said no he had frowned. 'Are you only goin' to make fancy things for better-off folk?'

'I have to,' she said simply. 'At least, to begin with. I must sell to live. Some girls are in good jobs, and anyway the war's over and what girl wants to get married or go to parties in the same ugly materials she's been forced to wear all through the past four years?'

She waited for an explosion of wrath, but none came. Jack smiled. 'I reckon you're right. It makes good commercial sense, too. I'll be seein' you, then.'

She had listened to his footsteps on the stairs, quick, light, always in a hurry. But he was a man who kept his promises and had brought her material whenever he could. Mrs Fudge had shown her how to work the sewing machine and she was making a living; only just, but she paid her rent and ate. Now she sat back on her heels and looked down at the satin. Her swelling stomach got in the way and her shoulder ached from turning the machine handle and her back from bending over her work. Darn baby, she thought, then felt guilty. Ralph's child. His legacy. The reason she had put herself in this unbelievable position. 'Ralph's legacy!' She said the words aloud to convince herself of their importance. Sometimes, lately, when she was desperately tired, uncomfortable and lonely, she was afraid because she felt no emotion towards her child.

She asked Mrs Fudge tentatively if she had loved her babies before they were born. Mrs Fudge gave her a speculative look. 'I suppose I felt somethin', though I can't really remember.

Child bearin's hard on a woman.' It was an unsatisfactory reply which didn't help.

She pinned patterns to the cloth and carefully applied her scissors. This was the only piece of decent white satin Jack had got hold of for ages and there was no room for mistakes. On the floor beside her lay a copy of *Vogue*, the American fashion magazine that had first been published in Britain halfway through the war. Adela used it constantly to keep up to date, copying designs as best she could within the bounds of her material and her knowledge. Making doll's clothes was very different from this, yet the memory helped her and she was finding in herself an unexpected flair for copying expensive garments in ways that were both pretty and practical.

There was a tiny miaow and a marmalade kitten which had attached itself to her reached out a playful paw for the scissors. 'No!' cried Adela. 'Sorry, Tibs, but you'll have to stay outside until this is finished. We can't have a wedding gown with paw marks.' The kitten suddenly became apparently boneless and hung over her hand. Adela laughed, kissed its soft head, and dropped it unceremoniously outside the door where it cried. When she had finished the cutting Adela let it back in and cuddled it. It was warm and loving, and purred happily.

Esther Allen, the girl who had ordered the wedding dress, came round for a fitting late that afternoon. Esther's parents believed in education for girls. She learned fast and had stayed at school until she was sixteen, pursuing her favourite subjects, English language and literature. Adela had tacked the pieces together and Esther looked at herself in the long, damp-stained mirror discovered by Mr Fudge in a local junk shop. Adela placed a short veil wreathed with white satin flowers on her head and Esther sighed with pleasure.

'It's all so beautiful,' she breathed. 'Exactly what I dreamed of.' She twisted this way and that, trying to see herself from all angles.

'I've pouched the bodice a little and made the skirt quite full,' said Adela.

'Yes, I see you have. I don't look as skinny as usual.'

'Slender,' protested Adela, 'and you'll be in fashion. Women

113

are dieting to lose weight. They say it's a declaration of their independence after so many years of doing a man's job through the war.'

'Well, I won't need to diet,' said Esther. 'I've got hardly any bust! And I can only wait and see if my Bert agrees with women's independence, though I don't hold out much hope. His dad was master in his own house and I bet Bert will be the same.' She grinned. 'To be honest, I'll be glad to see the back of the bloody munitions factory and just be a housewife. Oops, sorry, love! I forgot you don't like swearing.'

'I'm getting used to it,' said Adela calmly. 'Apparently that's getting fashionable, too, though I can't imagine Mother—' She stopped. She didn't want to think of home and family. After the first wave of rebellion had passed, she had had to struggle against the depression of homesickness, of being left alone, disregarded.

Esther stared at her for a moment, frowned, then turned back to the mirror. She held out her skirt and wafted it about, watching the material catch the light. 'It's really grand, Adela. I'll tell everyone you made it and you'll get lots of orders and make your fortune. Then you can go back—' It was Esther's turn to pause.

'Yes?'

'To where you belong. I'm sorry, Adela, I shouldn't say that, but it's obvious you come from the nobs. You don't belong here.'

'I've done my best to try.' Her voice sounded bleak.

Esther said hastily, 'And you've done really well, love. I wasn't meaning to criticise. I just thought that you might not be happy here. Oh, hell and damnation! Oh, sorry!' She broke into a peal of laughter in which Adela joined.

'Esther, you're a tonic.'

'Thank God for that. I thought you might tell me I'm a nuisance.'

'Never!' Adela said. 'Look, I've made a satin band to tie in a bow round your going-away hat, and I bought these.' She produced some pearl buttons and a narrow length of white fur. 'I'll sew the buttons right down the front of the wedding dress and I thought a fur trimming to the neck and cuffs would look pretty.'

'You're an angel! I'll have the best wedding dress ever seen in our street! And it'll be gorgeous as a party frock.'

After Esther had gone Adela sat still for a while. She must move herself and pull the tiny chain to bring the gas light up high enough to begin the machining. She was tired and drifted into a doze in which she heard the voices of her parents, of Blanche, and of Sander Bennett whose angry eyes suddenly appeared out of the dream mists and glared at her. She jerked awake, her heart thumping. Since her meeting with Blanche on Temple Meads Station she hadn't seen any of her family, but she had glimpsed Sander as he drove along Newfoundland Road in his powerful car on his way to his house in Fishponds. Now she always looked carefully each way before she crossed the road on her way to Jack's stall. She wondered if Blanche had made any headway with him.

That evening Adela heard familiar footsteps on the stairs and called, 'Come in,' at Jack's knock. He was carrying a bundle.

'Got some artificial silk today with hardly any flaws.'

'Wonderful! I can make some less expensive underwear. That'll make you happy, won't it?'

'Won't it make you happy?' he growled.

'Of course, I'm only teasing, Jack. I don't know what I'd do without you. Stay for a cup of tea.'

Adela bent to the hob in the grate and moved the kettle nearer the small fire.

'It's not very warm in here,' he said, frowning.

'No, the coal shortage seems worse than when the war was on.'

'Yes. Those stupid advertisements that tell housewives not to be wasteful Cinderellas an' lose the clinkers in the grate must be directed at rich folk because everyone knows that poor folk collect clinkers an' use them again. They always have.'

'Yes, I learned that from Mrs Fudge.'

'I don't suppose you ever lit a fire before you came here.'

Jack's slightly derisory tone rasped on her nerves. 'What if I hadn't! What's it to you?'

'Fiery little devil, aren't you?'

'Look who's talking!'

Jack smiled. 'I like you when you're riled. Your eyes glow.'

Adela poured boiling water into her small brown earthenware teapot. 'We'll wait a moment until it's brewed,' she said, pointedly ignoring his last comment, then fetched cups and saucers and a plate of cakes.

'Who baked those?'

'Oh, not me, naturally.' Her tone was as cutting as his had been, but he only grinned. 'Mrs Fudge made them. She's good like that. I buy the ingredients, of course, and before you say anything else, I help her with her mending, and she says it's no trouble or expense to her to bake because the range has to be lit anyway.'

She stopped for lack of breath and Jack gave her a humorous grimace. 'All right, you needn't go on. I know that Mrs Fudge is a good sort who'd rather do anyone a good turn than have one done for her. You were lucky to find her.'

'I consider I've been lucky all along,' said Adela. 'The Fudges, and you, and my customers. Everyone is so kind, even when—'

'When what?'

'When they pass remarks about my way of speaking, my way of doing things. They mock me, but in a nice way. I never knew working-class people could be like that!'

Adela knew as soon as the words passed her lips that they should have remained unspoken.

Jack fired up instantly. 'You thought workin'-class people were a bunch of idiots only fit to be your servants and fight your bloody wars for you! If it weren't for us the whole bloody country would have sunk into the shit that the so-called upper classes made of life. That's bloody typical of the daughter of George Danby.'

Shock drove out Adela's indignation at his bad language. 'You know who I am!'

'Yes, I recognised you the first time I saw you. Your picture's been in the paper several times when you've attended a party or weddin' or some big society do.'

'Then you know the truth about me?'

'That you're not married? Yes.'

116

'Oh! Does everyone hereabouts know who I am – that I'm single?'

Jack spoke soothingly. 'No. Newspaper photographs aren't all that clear, an' most folk have more than enough to do keepin' body and soul together to study them – even when they can afford to buy them.'

'But you knew me from them!'

'Well, no, to be honest I've seen you in person more than once. I sometimes walk about the better parts of Bristol to see how the bloated plutocrats live.'

'My family are *not* bloated plutocrats!'

'Well, they aren't exactly humble washerwomen or street cleaners.'

'You sound like a Bolshevist!' It was the worst insult Adela could think of and would have sent most society men into paroxysms of fury.

'I admire the Russians,' said Jack.

Adela was astonished. 'They murdered their royal family.'

'They asked for it. Many of the peasants were serfs. Slaves, Adela! Used in any way their masters decreed, treated like filth, their women defiled if it suited their exploiters. You talk of murder. Who was there to protect the serfs from murder? If a white Russian killed a servant, nobody cared.'

Jack was short and thin and the strain of his poor health showed in his face, but his eyes, alight with fervour, betrayed an indomitable spirit. He went on, 'I suppose you think a revolutionary has a black beard, a big black hat an' cape, an' carries a sizzlin' bomb in each hand!'

'That's stupid! I don't at all. You don't have to be so unpleasant about me, or my friends.' She was vehement because he had described the image she did have of Bolshevists.

'You've still got friends among the nobs?'

Adela pressed her lips together in irritation at his disbelieving tone, then said: 'Of course, though I haven't seen any of them lately.'

'They don't know the mess you're in, do they? And you're afraid to tell them. Some friends they are!'

'I am *not* afraid! My parents – my parents thought it best for me to – to—' Adela's words were lost in strangled tears that brought a lump to her throat. She picked up the teapot, carried it to the table, and poured two cups of tea. 'It's none of your bloody business,' she said deliberately.

'Language! What would Mumsie say?'

'If I was with my mother I wouldn't dream of swearing, but you obviously don't care. There's no milk, I'm afraid,' she finished coldly, 'but I've got a bit of sugar put away.'

'Keep your sugar!' Jack reacted to her coldness.

'Very well,' she said provocatively, knowing how much he liked his tea sweet. 'If you insist.'

Adela handed him his tea and he sipped it. It was scalding hot and he gasped, then ate three little cakes rapidly, every movement displaying his annoyance. Finally he let out a sigh.

'Adela, you'll have to be more careful what you say if you're goin' to stay in these parts, though I don't suppose you will.'

'Watch what I say, or stay in these parts?'

'Both. I'm sorry I yelled at you.'

'Did I actually hear you say you're sorry?'

'Yes.'

'That's kind of you.'

'Kind, be damned! I've never had a captive member of the nobs to indoctrinate before. I don't want to lose her.'

'I see. It may surprise you to know that some quite important *nobs* actually vote Labour.'

Jack smiled at her use of the slang word, but then his forehead creased in a frown. 'Who does?' he asked belligerently.

Adela frowned. She could think of only one person. 'Sander Bennett,' she said.

'Sander Bennett? Of course he does. He's workin'-class.'

'Is he? Do you mean that someone born in lowly circumstances remains working-class for ever and always votes socialist?'

'No, I damned well don't mean that! I know there are plenty of profiteers, such as the Smithers with their airs and graces, who've made money out of people's misery an' will vote Conservative so that they can hang on to it. But Sander's a good sort. He looks after his people, keeps jobs open if someone falls

118

sick, is interested in their families. Sander Bennett won't ever be a toffee-nosed bastard like—'

'Like who?' she asked acidly.

Jack sipped his tea and reached out automatically for the sugar which Adela, relenting, had thoughtfully placed within his reach. He spooned some into his cup and stirred his tea.

'Like who?' repeated Adela. 'My father, perhaps?'

'Your father's not bad.'

'Thank you so much.'

'He's not especially good, either. He refuses to recognise the need for a workers' union, though his people seem reasonably content with him. But there are others, like Sir Wilfred Somers, who wring the last ounce out of their staff, then kick them out when they fall ill.'

'Sir Wilfred is a very close friend of my family,' flared Adela, 'and, furthermore, his son, Ralph—' She stopped, appalled. She had been about to divulge who had fathered her child.

'I know that Somers is friendly with your father,' Jack said. He finished his tea and got up to go. 'Don't stay up half the night sewin', Adela. It's bad for you.'

'Mind your own business!' she snapped.

He saluted, grinning infuriatingly. 'Yes, madam! But someone has to tell you to take care.'

Adela stared at the closed door and listened to Jack descending the stairs, shouting a cheery farewell to the Fudges before he left. He was a tonic, a real friend.

As the weeks passed she felt as if she had spent most of her life sitting at a table, turning the handle of her sewing machine, measuring, tacking, finishing garments, going out to buy lace and threads, buttons and ribbons, dealing with the people in the small shops around her. Some had lost their initial hostility and treated her with friendliness; others were still suspicious.

No matter how tired she became, how hungry for a better diet, how dispirited she was, the baby went on growing, kicking inside her as if it couldn't wait to get out. She had let out her dresses and made one for best in amber wool. The colour of her eyes, Jack said, when he brought the cloth to her. She wore the dress to Esther's wedding. Until then she hadn't met the bride-groom, Bert Rawbone, and when she saw him in the church she was startled. Somehow she had expected Esther to choose a man like herself, one with whom she could share her zest for life, her enjoyment of each day. Bert Rawbone had an angry look. His short black hair was coarse and just beginning to grow out of the shorn army style. He was stocky, though Esther said he had lost weight as had so many of the returning soldiers, and his suit was ill-cut and brashly new compared with his neigh-bours' shabby garments.

Esther entered the chapel on her father's arm, looking so beautiful that some of the men as well as the women gasped. She had only one bridesmaid for whom Adela had made a dress of pale pink chiffon over white satin.

She smiled brilliantly at Adela as she passed her and joined Bert at the altar. Afterwards there was to be a proper shindig at the pub, Esther had said, to which Adela was invited. The large room upstairs in the public house had been decorated with flowers and streamers and there was a table laden with food. Everyone in the district must have helped provide it. They were good, generous people, thought Adela.

She was eyed with great curiosity when she walked in, accompanied by Mr and Mrs Fudge. Spring this year was bitterly cold, with heavy snow storms and a bitter east wind, and she was wearing her fur coat. She had embellished her brown velvet hat with a long curling feather and a diamanté hat pin. She smiled and greeted those who had not met her before, and managed not to blink when she saw that one lady was flaunting her fox fur which she had sold locally. She had intended to buy a large size cloth coat, but had been sickened by the stale smell in the cramped shop with its shelves crammed with cast-off clothing and worn-down shoes and boots, and hurried away.

Many of the wedding guests were seated on benches, but she was directed to a comfortable chair quite near the bride. She ate greedily, in a way that would once have horrified her, but she grew ravenously hungry very quickly these days. There was beer and wine and she was thirsty and drank quite deeply. A woman sitting near leaned over and said sympathetically, 'Eatin' for two, ain't you, ducky? Mine always took me that way. I've had eight kids and brought up six. I lost two to the diphtheria when they was babies. Three of my boys went to France. One came back whole. One lost both legs below the knee. And the third was blown up and they never found the bits of 'im. Terrible it was.'

In the face of such appalling disasters Adela was utterly lost for an answer so it was fortunate that the woman had decided to drown her sorrows in beer and demanded another pint.

Speeches were made, Bert's being short and confined to thanks; toasts were drunk; then Esther went into a side room to change and she and her new husband were waved off on a tram to get the train for a short honeymoon in nearby Clevedon on the Bristol Channel.

In Esther's luggage was a white cotton bag containing a crêpe de Chine nightdress with daring lace inserts over the breasts. She had received Adela's gift with a beaming smile. 'I've never seen anything so gorgeous. My Bert's going to love it.'

At weddings which Adela had attended in the past the atmosphere went flat as soon as the bride and groom had departed, but not here. There was still a quantity of alcohol to be drunk and the guests applied themselves to it. She was warm, full of good food, slightly hazy in a nice way from the wine, and she remained seated in the smoky fog from the many cigarettes, watching and listening and occasionally laughing at the banter, some of it quite crude, as she continued to sip at her glass which was constantly refilled. She wondered what her parents would say if they could see her now. What did it matter? She, Adela Danby, was weathering the storm. She'd show them all they couldn't buy and sell her. They'd respect her and take her back and admire her. She'd show them.

Help! She was more tipsy than she had realised. She doubted if she could get home without the support of Mr Fudge's arm so it was lucky that she and the Fudges had arranged to return together. Jack couldn't afford to close his stall on Saturday, his most lucrative day, and he arrived after nine and seated himself near Adela, grabbing a few forgotten sandwiches and accepting some beer.

'Enjoyin' yourself, Adela?'

'I am. I am, indeed. I really am. Yes, I think you can say that I'm enjoying myself.'

'My God, you're drunk!'

'I am no such thing, Jack Webster, so don't you slander me.'

He grinned and downed his beer. 'I'll wait an' see you home.'

'N— no need. Mr Fudge will do that, and Mrs Fudge o' course. It's all got to be very respectable. Very respectable indeed.'

'Of course,' agreed Jack equably.

'You know something, Jack Webster? You can be nice when you want to. Very, very nice. But sometimes you're quite—' Adela wanted to say 'obnoxious', but her tongue wouldn't curl around the word '—nasty,' she finished.

Jack gave her a humorous sideways glance. 'Definitely drunk,' he said, as he drank his beer.

The party finished when the drink ran out, and the guests made their way home, warmed and cheered. No wonder they took advantage of the occasion, thought Adela. Many of them lived immeasurably hard lives in primitive, overcrowded conditions.

Mr Fudge took one of her arms and Jack the other. Mrs Fudge reeled happily along, singing to herself. The sky was heavy and dark with snow, but the street lamps were lit again, the flickering gas flames dancing on the revellers. They arrived at Newfoundland Road and stopped in a yellow pool of gaslight as they saw a car approaching. Other guests were with them and a boy, evading the restraining hand of his mother, ran out into the road. There was a hiss of wheels on the snow as brakes were applied and the car just missed the boy, but skidded and crashed into a lamp post.

For a moment there was silence, then the air was filled with a burst of profanity from the child's father as he cursed the nob who had nearly run over his son.

'That's not fair,' protested Adela.

'Hush,' warned Jack. 'Keep out of it. The kid's not hurt and whoever owns that fancy car can afford to get it mended.'

As the driver climbed down he revealed himself to be a large man and the boy and his family faded into the darkness of the road opposite. The man removed his goggles.

Adela leaned forward to see the angry face of the driver. 'It's Sander Bennett,' she said to Jack.

'Sander Bennett.' Others caught the name and their hostility vanished. 'Sander, remember me? My dad worked for your uncle?'

'Hey, Sander, how's life treatin' you? All right, I reckon, judgin' by your car.'

Sander looked at the large dent in the front of his car. 'What's the celebration?' he asked.

'A weddin'. A lovely weddin',' said a large woman in a hat decorated with flowers that bobbed and swayed with her every move. 'We're on our way home now.'

'So I gather.'

The crowd began to cross the road, leaving Adela and her escorts visible. Sander caught sight of her and his eyes widened. 'You? Here?'

'Yes, me! Here!' Adela was belligerent. 'And why not?'

'You're drunk!'

'No I'm not, and what if I am?'

'I thought you had left Bristol.'

'Well, you thought wrong, didn't you? Come on,' she said to her companions, 'let's go home. Home, sweet home. Home with my friends. My chums! They don't buy and sell women!' She hiccuped, but it didn't seem to matter. 'When they get married, they do it for love.'

Even through her tipsy mist Adela saw the fury in Sander's eyes.

Her knees buckled and Mr Fudge and Jack caught her. 'Come on, my love,' Jack said. 'I'll get you back, and the sooner the better.'

Esther returned from her honeymoon and came to see Adela.

'How was the nightdress received?' Adela asked, smiling.

Esther coloured, hesitated. 'It looked lovely.'

'But?' asked Adela gently.

'Sorry, Adela, but my Bert didn't care for it. He prefers something plainer. It – got a bit torn. I've mended it and, I wonder, would you mind very much if I sold it?'

Adela looked at Esther's troubled face, sensing something more than a disagreement over a nightdress. 'Get what you can for it,' she said. 'It doesn't matter in the least. Would you like me to make a plain one for you? Perhaps with just a bit of lace round the neck.'

Esther shook her head and her colour deepened. 'It's awful good of you, love, but—' Again she stopped. Then she said slowly, 'Bert wanted to know where you got your hat and the diamond pin. He was a bit annoyed by it.'

'But it isn't diamond, it's only imitation.'

'Oh, I didn't know that.'

'Why should he mind?'

'He's different, Adela. He's come back from the war changed. He hates the government and anyone with money.'

'I haven't any money.'

'No, but you're from the ruling classes. That's what Bert says. I don't know what happened to him out there in France. I only know that when my Bert left he was a cheerful man, and he's come back angry and bitter.'

'Maybe he'll get better,' said Adela. 'It was dreadful in the trenches. I knew a soldier who told me about it.' Poor Ralph, she thought. She felt an upsurge of gratitude that she had protected his baby.

'I hope Bert's temper improves,' said Esther, 'because he's not very easy to live with, especially as we have to stay with Mum and Dad and the kids. We've only got a tiny upstairs back room to ourselves and we're lucky to have that. Bert gets into such rages. He says *they* promised the soldiers homes for all but no one cares about the promise any more and the men who fought for their country are looked on as nuisances.'

In the following weeks Adela heard more and more about what Bert said and Esther looked more and more unhappy. One night she came round and begged to stay until morning. Bert had upset the whole family and her father, unable to stand any more, had asked them to leave. Mr Fudge dragged an old mattress upstairs and Esther lay on it in front of the dwindling fire, covered by a blanket from Adela's bed, and her coat. She left early in the morning and returned later looking relieved. 'Dad's forgiven us this time, but says if Bert throws any more tantrums we're out for good. Oh, Adela, my Bert flares up like a lunatic for nothing! I think I fell in love with him because he made me laugh, but now I'm walking on eggshells all the time and I've just found out I'm expecting and God knows what'll happen to me and the kid if Dad throws us out.'

'A baby! Are you happy about it, Esther?'

'Of course I am. Any woman's glad to have a baby with the man she loves. You should know that, Adela.'

'Yes, I do,' she said quickly. 'Has Bert got a job yet?'

'No! He was a tram conductor and the women won't come off the tramcars. The firm promised him his old job back and they've broke their promise. They're glad to have the women because they needn't pay them as much as the men.'

Adela felt guilty, remembering Blanche, but she said comfortingly, 'I'm sure things will improve. No one can deny a man a job for long, especially a returning soldier.'

Chapter Eight

Adela awoke one morning feeling too hot and threw off the bedclothes. Overnight the weather had turned warm and the snow had thawed. She sat up, sniffing distastefully, wondering what on earth was making the smell which was wafting through the open window. She closed the window, dressed and went out to investigate. The stench was worse outside and invaded every corner. She asked Mrs Fudge about it.

Her landlady gave her a speculative look. 'Have you had any breakfast?'

Adela shook her head. 'I don't think I want to eat until the smell goes away.'

Mrs Fudge wiped her hands on her apron and poured Adela a cup of tea. 'Then I'm afraid you'll starve, love. Now get that down you.'

'Starve? What do you mean?'

Mrs Fudge sat at the kitchen table and poured some tea for herself. 'It's unusual for the weather to turn this fast. Usually you d'get a chance to get used to the smell.'

'Used to it? Won't it disperse?'

'Go away, d'you mean? I'm afraid not, my love. It's always like this in the warm months. There aren't enough lavatories for everyone to have one an' they have to share. Haven't you noticed?'

Adela had and thought it hateful, but the cold had kept the worst from her. 'It's disgusting!'

'It isn't our fault! We got no money to make our places better. We're lucky we've got one of our own an' don't have to share.'

'No. I'm sorry, I didn't mean to sound critical.'

'It's all right. I know you didn't mean to be rude.' She sipped her tea. 'Then, o' course, there's the horses and the dung. People d'still spread it on their bits o' garden.'

'But surely that's unhygienic in the summer! And what about the flies?'

'There's always been flies, an' a bit o' horse manure never hurt anyone. We collect it from the road an' it d'make the vegetables grow, though they don't ever do really well, not round here. But mothers need them to feed the kids. An' there's the butchers' shops where the men d'slaughter their own beasts. Gawd, you'll know when they're guttin' them to make chitterlings!'

'Chitterlings?'

'You never tasted them? You're in for a treat.'

'But what are they?'

'Pigs' innards. Mmmm, cold with vinegar they d'go down a treat. Fancy you never heard of chitterlings! There's the smells from the factories, too. Them as lives up on the hills in the posh places don't know the half of what we d'have to put up with from the factory stinks, an' the breweries, an' if the wind's in the right direction, the smells from Fry's Chocolates. You'd think that'd be nice, but it's a funny, sickly sort of smell. You'll get used to it all in time.'

To be polite Adela forced down some dry toast then returned to her room. She must move house! But move where? She was making money here, just enough for her daily expenses. Without it she would be destitute. Prices had risen horrifically during the war and although some families had an increased income to match, Adela was now one of the many thousands who didn't. And, oddly enough, she found she was reluctant to leave her new friends whom she valued. Mother's eyebrows would vanish into her hair if she knew the kind of people her daughter cared about.

The weather grew warmer and Adela felt lethargic, but there could be no let up in her work. Thank God her reputation was spreading and she was able to begin buying what she needed for her lying-in and necessities for the baby. A new spirit took root in her. She had bragged defiantly to Blanche that she was able to look after herself and now, to her surprise, she discovered that she had spoken the truth.

But her resolve was severely tried when she discovered that Tibs was scratching frantically and she found him to be infested by fleas.

Jack arrived and stared at her stricken expression. 'What's up?'

'Fleas,' she said dramatically, pointing to Tibs.

Jack grinned. 'That all? We can soon get rid of those. Anythin' else?'

'I don't know. What could there be? I'm itching myself, but I suppose it's from the fleas.'

Jack dragged the bedclothes from her bed and, to her horror, revealed some flat brown beetles.

'Oh, my God! What are those?'

'Bedbugs,' he said.

Adela shuddered uncontrollably. She had read a report which Mother had brought home from one of her charity meetings. It dealt with poverty-stricken homes and mentioned infestations of all kinds of insects of which bedbugs were considered the worst. She burst into tears. 'I'll have to leave here. I can't bear it!'

Jack laughed loudly at her which made her furious. 'It's all right for you! I suppose you're used to them, just like Mrs Fudge is used to the stinks.'

'Calm down, my love. Nobody likes to share their bed. Not with bugs, anyway.' He destroyed them, a smelly and messy business which made Adela feel ill. 'I'm afraid you'll never be completely free of them. They live behind the wallpaper, or in any crack they can find, an' there's cracks in plenty in these houses. But I'll protect your bed for you.' He went away and returned with a feather and some turpentine and meticulously painted the wooden bed frame with them. 'There! That'll keep them away from you, and the turps smells better than the slaughter houses and privies. Now for the cat!'

He put Tibs on a newspaper and produced a fine-toothed comb which he drew through the soft coat. 'Do this every day, Adela, an' he should stay free. Here, I bought another comb for you in case you've picked up fleas, too.'

'Oh, God, I *can't* bear it!'

129

'Of course you can. You're tough. Much tougher than I suspected when we met. Now, forget bugs and fleas and look at this.'

'This' turned out to be a length of material which made Adela gasp with delight. It carried a simple design of pale blue periwinkles with soft ochre centres. The flowers had been outlined in the same ochre and nestled among grey-green leaves decorated with darker green spots and stripes.

'Art Nouveau,' she breathed. 'It's by Eugene Grasset.'

Jack laughed delightedly. 'I had a feeling you'd know that.'

Adela turned to him. 'Did you know the designer?'

Jack was solemn as he replied, 'I did, ma'am. Some of us humble street traders aren't completely ignorant.'

Adela flushed. 'I didn't mean – well, all right, I did wonder. Do you often sell stuff like this from your barrow?'

'No, it's mostly cottons, velveteens and artificial silk in summer, wool mixtures in the winter, and serge all year round. They're all rejects that the factories have chucked out. Folk round these parts can't afford to be fussy.'

'Is this a reject?'

'No, I bought it just for you.'

Adela looked at him gratefully. 'You shouldn't have, but it's the nicest thing that's happened to me for ages.' She touched the material again. 'I shall use it for decorative cushions when I've time. I've got a bag of feathers, but I haven't seen anything I fancied. Nothing I could afford anyway. You must let me pay for it. How much?' she asked, suddenly anxious.

'To you, nothin'.'

Adela's hand left the material as if it were a poisonous snake. 'I can't accept.'

Jack looked amused. 'Mustn't take presents from a gentleman? It's a house-warmin' gift. A bit late, I know, but you can't refuse that.'

Adela smoothed the beautiful cloth again, then looked up, 'Thank you, Jack.' She paused. 'I'm always saying thank you to you. I don't know how I would have got on without you.'

'You'd have managed, love. You're a fighter.'

Adela said slowly, 'Maybe I am. I've surprised myself, but

you've eased everything wonderfully for me.'

She had spoken affectionately, and Jack smiled. 'Adela,' he said, 'I'd do anythin' for you.'

'I believe you would,' she said.

As she passed hours turning the handle of the sewing machine and putting in finishing stitches by hand to a crêpe de Chine blouse, or a velveteen jacket, or a bridal dress, she dreamed of the future. She would be an independent woman of means. She saw herself in a proper workplace, in a real shop, the head of a thriving concern. She wouldn't make clothes. She preferred to make beautiful things to cover furniture, to hang on walls, to grace floors. She had always had an ambition to work in some way with fabrics, and her secret dream had been to join the family business. She had known, deep down, that her parents would never allow it but, all the same, she had tested their reaction by asking if she could study drawing and textile design seriously. They had refused; Father smiling indulgently at the foolish aspirations of a daughter, Mother speaking for both, her voice crisp, brooking no disagreement.

'Your needlework will always be a delightful hobby for you, though when you are married you will find, as I have, that there is little time to spare after running a home and fulfilling social obligations.' Adela's mild protests had been easily over-ridden and she had returned to the boredom which had so often afflicted her.

She had read in the paper that Sander Bennett had bought a couple of failing textiles businesses and a place in Park Street where wealthy people shopped, and was infusing them with life. One morning, at a time when fashionable folk would still be at home preparing for the day's activities, she was unable to resist the temptation to see what Sander's Park Street shop was like. Everything in it would be up-to-date and could help her in her work. The double windows of the newly opened shop impressed her. In one, materials were draped; in the other were daytime and evening gowns clearly intended for the rich.

Fashions were changing. Though hems were still well below the knee the lines were simpler, more flowing. There was an evening dress she ached to wear. She studied the pale green gossamer chiffon with its darker green under-dress and could feel the way the material would caress her skin. Then she leaned nearer, peering. In one corner, almost hidden, displayed discreetly against a silky grey backcloth, were two petticoats which made her gasp. Their silken folds gave her the glow of the particular kind of pleasure she always got from rich materials and imaginative designs. Her hands itched to touch them. She gazed at them, awareness breaking in on her. The designs were Elsa Maitland's. Hadn't Elsa returned to Father? It suddenly seemed a matter of urgency to find out.

She glanced around. Park Street was still empty. She caught herself up guiltily at the thought. Park Street was empty only of the moneyed folk. Workers were hurrying to offices and shops, some faces anxious because they were late. She looked again at the window display and made up her mind. She hurried through the ground floor, looking quickly about her at the tempting bolts of cloth displayed on many stands, at the cabinets filled with threads and needles and scissors, and marched up the wide flight of stairs to the fashion floor. It was carpeted thickly and a sense of cathedral-like quiet permeated the atmosphere. She wanted to stop and examine the luscious clothes, but forced herself to hurry on, past the gowns and through an archway into an alcove marked 'Ladies' Underwear'.

It was partly curtained off and Adela found herself in a bower of beauty. Crêpe de Chine and satin pyjamas in heliotrope, soft pink, sky blue, black and white were arranged in a group with nightdresses, each of which had its matching boudoir cap. Knickers with lace-trimmed legs, and camisoles, sleeved and unsleeved; ribbon-trimmed Milanese silk combinations, and the new-fashioned wisps of underslips with fine pleating and ribbon shoulder straps, waited for the lucky woman who could afford them. Adela gazed around her, her mouth actually watering at the sight of so much loveliness. Every garment had clearly been influenced by Elsa Maitland's eye for design.

Her attention was caught by a small display of stockings and she leaned forward to see them better. They weren't woollen, nor the hideous lisle she was now forced to wear, but cobwebs of silk. A footfall sounded on the carpet behind her and she turned, anger giving her courage.

A saleswoman in black asked, 'May I be of service, madam?'

Adela knew the tone of voice. It was reserved for shabbily dressed customers and was designed to embarrass them and to send them scurrying from the sight of ladies who would spend liberally.

'Tell me, is Miss Elsa Maitland still working for Mr Bennett? Did she design this collection?'

Surprise at both Adela's cultured tones and her question brought a swift answer from the girl. 'Yes, madam. She is our chief lingerie designer.'

Adela was bewildered. She had freed her parents from all obligation to Sander so why hadn't Elsa returned to Danby's? She caught sight of herself in a mirror. God, was that really her? Her hat was decidedly the worse for wear, having been exposed to the storms of winter. Necessity, and the warmth of spring, had tempted her to pawn her fur coat and although her replacement was of good quality, it was dusty. However hard one tried to brush clothes in St Pauls it never quite seemed to be successful. And worst of all, her pregnancy was straining the buttons. She wished now she had yielded to the temptation to make herself a new coat or a cape, but her time was so precious and she was often so damned tired. She stared down at her stockings full of darns, her much mended gloves, and lost her nerve. She hurried from the underwear department, unexpected tears, born partly of fury and partly of regret, blinding her. Clumsily, she bumped into someone who caught her and held her still. It was Sander Bennett.

She blinked hard and tried to shake herself free to stride on.

'Good Lord, you! What's your hurry?'

'I have work to do,' she said coldly.

She forced herself to look into his eyes. They were hard, holding a spark of – contempt, was it? Dislike? She had, after all, made him an object of amusement, or worse, pity. 'Release me!' she demanded and he let her go.

She began to walk away, but he followed and put a detaining hand on her arm.

133

'Won't you visit my little restaurant for coffee? Or are you still off coffee?'

As he spoke his eyes flickered over her bulging stomach. She gritted her teeth. She wouldn't give him the satisfaction of driving her away.

'I am still not taking coffee,' she said, in tones as crisp as she could manage, 'but I'll take tea.'

'Allow me?' His arm was extended for her hand.

Adela caught a swift glimpse of the underwear salesgirl who was watching, open-mouthed, before she walked off, her fingertips on Sander's dark-coated arm.

He escorted her to the tiny restaurant, but she stopped at the entrance and he said in mock apology, 'I know it isn't very big yet, but it gives my customers an opportunity to rest their weary feet. Society ladies often have weary feet. But, of course, you already know that.'

Adela inclined her head. She was concerned more with the fact that the restaurant was public than with its size and that two women, in spite of the earliness of the hour, were already sitting and chattering there. A girl dressed as a parlourmaid in a black dress with a white apron and cap emerged from the kitchen, carrying a tray of coffee and scones. Adela didn't recognise either woman, but others might come.

'I have changed my mind,' she said. 'I shall return home.'

'You disappoint me.'

'Nonsense!'

Before she could say more he asked, 'Is the restaurant too public for you? We could take tea in my office.'

He opened a heavy door at the rear of the fashion department and ushered her into a large airy room where a girl was busy at a typewriter, while at a large desk sat a man who stood up at their entrance.

'Mr Trevor, the store manager,' Sander introduced him. 'And this is Miss Lloyd, his secretary.'

Adela nodded to them as Sander led her through another door into a small room beyond. It contained a desk, two identical chairs, a filing cabinet and a small table on which stood bottles of whisky, gin and wine.

'I didn't give them your name, Adela, because I'm not sure what you are calling yourself. Mrs something, I suppose.'

'You suppose right.'

Sander waited, but she refused to volunteer further information.

He shrugged. 'Will you take something stronger than tea?'

Adela shook her head. 'Tea will be enough, thank you.' She looked around her. 'This isn't a very grand office.'

'I'm not a very grand person, as you know.' The words came out as a challenge. He waited, but Adela remained silent. 'It's enough for me,' he said. 'My headquarters are at my textiles warehouse. Trevor is eminently suitable to run this place in my absence.'

Adela seated herself on one of the chairs. It was hard, straightbacked, and not at all comfortable. Tea was brought.

'Will you pour?' asked Sander.

Adela did so, feeling as if she were caught up in a mad dream. 'Milk? Sugar?' she asked, managing to keep her voice almost as easy as if she were in her parents' drawing room.

'Just milk, please.'

Adela sipped her tea, then blurted out, 'Does Miss Maitland still work for you?'

'Now she's no longer needed as the sacrificial lamb, do you mean?'

Adela flushed and glared at him angrily, and he said, 'Do you wish to see Elsa and ask her for yourself?'

'Certainly not!'

'Then I will inform you that she found her salary and working conditions so much better with me that she decided to stay.'

'That's immoral – of both of you.'

'Is it? I thought it good business. Your father would do the same. He has since approached Elsa several times in an effort to take her from me. She insists that she made a bargain and must stick to it. I guessed she was loyal from the moment I met her, but I like to make certain so I put her under contract to me. I daresay she's enjoying the extra money.'

'Danby's was her life!'

'Which she now devotes to me. Will you have a scone?'

Adela wanted to refuse, but she was always ravenously hungry and took one, sinking her teeth into the buttery, fruity mixture and chewing, trying not to eat too fast.

'I see it no longer affects your appetite.'

The abrupt reference to her condition disconcerted her and she pushed her plate away.

'You haven't finished.'

'Yes, I have. I don't know why I came in here with you at all.'

'I wondered myself.'

'Well, I shall leave and it'll be many a long day before we meet again.'

'Are you here on a visit?'

His question made her pause. 'A visit?'

'From your Grandmother Sutton's house in Cornwall.'

'Is that what Mother—?'

'How is Lady Sutton?'

'Quite well, thank you.'

'Indeed! Your presence must be good for her. Your father says that her health has been precarious and that's why you have gone to stay.'

'Oh.' Adela felt a surge of resentment against her parents, against Sander, against a world which could put a woman in such a position as hers. 'Yes, I'm here on a visit.' She rose and Sander stood up too.

'You left St Pauls then? If you recall we met there during the winter. You were with a group of very jolly friends.'

In her agitation Adela had forgotten that meeting. She ground her teeth. 'Yes,' she grated, 'I've left.'

'Good. It wasn't a suitable place for you to live.'

'How snobbish of you!'

His face darkened. She had scored a hit and it gave her fiendish satisfaction. A moment later, when she realised she must ask a favour of him, she wished she had curbed her tongue. 'Mr Bennett—' his eyebrows rose mockingly '—I would be obliged if you did not tell my parents, or anyone, of your having seen me. I should not have come.'

'To the shop, do you mean?' He was being deliberately obtuse.

'I mean to Bristol, as you damn well know!'

'Heavens! Your language has taken a turn for the worse. Surely Lady Sutton doesn't swear.'

'All right, have fun,' said Adela, wearily.

The amusement died from Sander's eyes. 'Have fun? I find *nothing* funny about my connection with you and your family.'

She made an inarticulate sound and hurried away, through the outer office, the showrooms, down the stairs and outside, cursing the impulse that had sent her into the store. She turned for a last look and saw, for the first time, the sign over the wide doors: 'Bennett's'. Just that. It was typical of the arrogant attitude of the man.

As she sewed in her room in St Pauls, or fitted her growing number of customers, kneeling on the floor, pins held in her mouth, or wielded her iron over damp cloth which sent steam pouring out, thickening the already pungent atmosphere, she dreamed even more of her own business. Her mind soared. She'd show everyone. She would also sell underwear. She might not have Elsa Maitland but she had ideas of her own which had blossomed while she worked. She had incorporated some of them into the garments she everlastingly fashioned.

Adela's euphoria didn't last. May was abnormally hot and dry and her body felt impossibly heavy and cumbersome. As the temperature rose the smell of the sketchily washed bodies of her customers combined with the stink from outside. Every night she stood at her wash-stand, cleaning herself from head to toe, trying not to think of the luxury of a bath. Mr Fudge had been genuinely astonished when Adela asked him to carry so much more water upstairs.

'Whatever do you do with it all? You d'come down to the wash house to do your washin'.'

'I need a lot to steam the sewing,' she muttered. She couldn't tell the truth, when it was obvious from the aura surrounding him and his wife that they were none too particular themselves.

Thank heavens Jack was better groomed. A mutual respect was growing between them, and their arguments about politics and the poor and the bloated aristocrats were conducted amicably. At least, most of the time, though Adela sometimes took a wicked delight in teasing Jack until his fiery spirit could take no more and he flared up in rage. Then she laughed at him and, instead of growing more angry, he disarmed her by calming down.

He arrived early one morning with a bundle containing the usual assortment of cloth. He also produced a bottle of lavender water. 'Mum says that lavender's good to keep clean with. It's antiseptic, she says. You can put it in your water.'

Adela took the bottle and unscrewed the top. The scent was crude, nothing like the delicious ones she had used at home, but it was a delight.

'Thank you, Jack, and please thank your mother.'

'She doesn't know about it. I've not mentioned our friendship. She's a suspicious old body an' she'd think somethin' funny was goin' on between us.'

'Something funny?'

'Don't try to pretend with me! I'm not one of your society chaps. You know what I mean.'

Adela flushed. 'But nothing is going on.'

'No, of course not.'

He picked up a reel of cotton from the floor. 'You spend too much time stuck in this room. You hardly ever leave it now.'

'I've no alternative. I must keep up with the sewing.'

'You should be takin' exercise. I remember when my wife, God rest her soul, was expectin' our kids, the midwife told her to walk every day.'

'Is that so! Well, I'm not your wife and I'll do as I wish.'

'And your wish is to hide yourself here. When the baby's bein' born you'll need strength in your muscles. Yours must be goin' soft.'

Adela was silenced.

Jack said gently, 'I'm not tryin' to worry you, Adela, that's the last thing I'd do, but honestly you should take more exercise. How about comin' along on Saturday to watch the barrow race? The walk to Old Market will do you good.'

'The barrow race? What's that?'

'Do you mean to say no one's ever told you about it?'

'I've never heard of it. Why didn't you tell me?'

'I thought you'd know. You've a treat in store, but you'll need to be there in time. We start at nine in the mornin'.'

'But why do you race?'

'To get the best pitches. There used to be a lot of fightin' but now the race settles it. Everyone wants the best side of Old Market. If we lose there are other streets we can go to; but on a Saturday Castle Street's where we all want to be an' the pace gets cruel sometimes because there isn't room for us all. Castle Street's narrow an' closed to traffic on a Saturday night and folk come there in their thousands. All the shops stay open and you can do more trade there than the rest of the week.'

'It sounds interesting. What time do the shops there shut?'

'Some of them stay open 'til midnight. Do you mean to tell me you've never seen Castle Street on a Saturday night?'

'No, never.'

'What were your folks thinkin' of? It's one of the sights of Bristol.'

'I don't think they would care much for it.'

'No. I forgot. I don't suppose they would. Well, I thought I'd ask you.'

Adela awoke early to a hot sunny day. Tibs was scratching himself. More tooth-combing. It was amazing how one became accustomed to even the most revolting things. She had even got used to visiting the outside privy, though she would always hate it. One day she would have the most marvellous bathroom in the world. One day.

A woman across the narrow street yelled and shattered Adela's daydreams. Her neighbour was even poorer than the other inhabitants of St Pauls and steered herself, her lazy husband and her over-large family through their nightmare days of poverty by constantly shrieking.

Adela arrived in Old Market as the men were lined up with their hand barrows. Old Market was wide, with several sets of tramlines and room left over for other vehicles. It was lined with shops and pubs. Jack had an outside place; the materials were tied down for security. The atmosphere was tense, and the air filled with advice yelled by onlookers, much of it ribald. A

139

policeman blew a whistle and the men began to run. The thunderous noise of the barrows over the cobbles, the shouts and curses as men got in one another's way, the shrieks of the crowd – some of whom, it was clear, had bets on the racers – created an excited din. Adela hurried along with the crowd, keeping Jack in sight, willing him to move faster. As he steered his teetering barrow she felt a sudden anxiety for him. Surely he was in no state to be undertaking such a task? Some of the other men were much younger and bigger. He was lost to her sight for a while in the jostling throng, then he reappeared and dropped the handles of his barrow with a grunt of relief, taking out a red-spotted handkerchief and wiping his red and streaming face.

Adela hurried to him. 'Jack, you were marvellous! Is this where you wanted to be?'

'You came.' He grinned delightedly. 'I haven't got the best place, but it's good enough.'

'You must be much stronger than you look.'

He smiled again, flexing his arm muscles, and she laughed. He began to untie the strings holding the bundles of cloth.

'Here, let me help you.' Adela saw that his hands were shaking with effort.

'That's nice of you.'

After a few moments he stood back and let her carry on alone. She draped great swathes of colour over a rack; vermilion on mauve, mauve on primrose, primrose on sky-blue, sky-blue on orange, orange on emerald, creating the effect of a collection of jewels. She unrolled a piece of net curtaining and displayed it over a piece of crimson satin. The dark bolts of serge lay on the barrow floor and added substance to the design. The barrow wasn't large and there was little scope for artistry, but when she had finished she stood back and was quite pleased. Others admired her work.

'That your new assistant, Jack?' someone called. 'She's a bloody sight better'n you at window dressing.'

'That's poncy women's stuff!' retorted the biggest of the street traders. His stall held bread and cakes and a few groceries which, to judge by the size of his belly, too often found their way down his throat.

'That's Fred Withycombe,' muttered Jack. 'He sells any food

140

he can get hold of. He's done it all through the war. Most of it's under the counter an' women with a bit of spare cash flock to him and pay what he asks. He does it with rationed stuff. It's illegal, but no one ever splits on him. They're all too busy buyin' his food. Them that can afford it, that is. The government's to blame. They should have brought in rationin' much earlier an' made sure that there was enough to go round. Do you know, Adela, that food is a hundred and thirty-three per cent dearer than it was when the war began?'

'I didn't know. How could I? I never knew what it cost before.'

'No, you wouldn't! You were pampered. All right, it wasn't your fault.'

'What about the ones that can't afford Mr Withycombe's extras. Don't they ever tell on him?'

'He's not daft. He makes sure that the poor women get a bargain now and then, or even a present, an' it's always kept them from going to the law.'

'What a horrible man!'

'He's bad enough when he's sober, but a bugger when he's not, as his family knows only too well. Steer clear of him, Adela.'

She was astonished to think that Jack should believe she had any intention of even speaking to such a man, but his face held such genuine concern for her safety that she could only thank him for his warning.

'I'll be getting back now,' she said.

'Still plenty of work?'

'Lots, thank goodness.'

'You ought not to have to slave over sewin' for such long hours.'

'I'm only one of thousands.'

'But you're not used to it. Sometimes lately – you've not looked well. Are you all right?'

'I'm perfectly well, thank you.' She managed to sound indignant. She had felt ill quite often recently, but she'd be fine when the baby came. It wouldn't be long now.

Mrs Fudge spent a precious penny a week on a magazine,

Woman's World, and passed it on to Adela who read it, seeking advice. There were articles on food for the nursing mother, and on how to grow more hair; offers of reducing pills, complexion creams, cough medicine, but nothing for an expectant mother. The magazine's columnists addressed all women as 'sister'.

'Sister!' snorted Adela aloud, throwing the magazine on the table.

She grew more and more lethargic and unwilling to move. Even getting up in the mornings was difficult.

Jack was anxious. 'You ought to see a doctor, my dear.'

'Doctors cost money.'

'Are you eatin' properly?'

'Yes. I'm not a fool, you know.'

Adela instantly regretted her snappy reply, but Jack refused to take umbrage. He brought her fruit and wouldn't let her pay him for it. 'I got it real cheap. It's pinky fruit, a bit bruised, see?'

It wasn't, but Adela was too weary to argue. She could no longer work long hours and had to turn away customers. They were understanding, but if this went on her income would fall dangerously low.

'Why not write to your folks and ask for help?' Jack suggested.

'No, never! I'll get through this somehow. I'll prove that I can look after myself.'

He sighed.

'Don't worry about me, Jack. You've problems of your own.'

'They don't mean as much to me as yours,' he said in a matter-of-fact way that astonished her.

'You really mean that, don't you? It's wonderful to have your friendship.'

Jack laughed. 'Yes, we're friends all right, though I feel more like your father.'

He sent Lizzie Webb, the midwife, round to visit her. 'Pull yourself together, dearie,' she advised. 'Women often get tired when they're expectin'. It's all to do with the blood goin' to the baby. You must eat lots of liver.'

'But it's practically unobtainable!'

'I know, but weaker women than you have to queue for it.'

Jack was furious when he heard. He paced Adela's room, his face dark with anger. 'Bloody cheek! Who does she think she is?'

'Stop stamping round,' said Adela, smiling. 'You're terrifying Tibs.'

Jack grinned and sat on the bed. 'Sorry, my love, but I get so furious when medical people treat us like ignorant fools. I never thought Lizzie Webb was like that.'

'She's not a medical person really, and have you had much experience of her services?'

Jack's grin grew wider. 'Not so as you'd notice. I'll see what I can do.'

What he did was somehow procure liver which Adela ate reluctantly, as she had never cared for offal.

'You're goin' to see a doctor if I have to drag you there,' he said.

Adela was too tired to argue. The doctor was thin and elderly. His surgery was in the heart of St Pauls and as dismal as the houses of many of his patients, but he was kind as he examined and questioned her.

Afterwards she dressed herself and sat opposite him. 'You have a special kind of anaemia which sometimes afflicts pregnant women,' he said. 'It will get better when baby is born. Meanwhile I'll have a tonic made up for you. Call back later today for it. Baby's due soon, isn't he? Mind you finish the bottle. That will be two and sixpence, please.'

The tonic was bitter and Adela grimaced over it, but it brought a resurgence of strength and enabled her to stick at her work.

One evening Esther called. Adela had been working by the light of the setting sun, aided by a street light placed conveniently near the house.

'Esther, I'm so glad you came. I'll turn up the gas and we'll have a cup of tea.'

'No!' Esther's sharp voice startled Adela. 'Sorry, I didn't mean to yell. Don't put on the light. But I would like the tea.' She walked to an easy chair which was made bright by covers

Adela had sewn. The material was patterned with a sharp green willow design on a pale lemon background. In spite of her long hours at the sewing machine, Adela had found it impossible to live in dreary surroundings and had sat up late to create a cheerful decor. The weather had turned cool and wet and there was a small but welcome fire in the grate on which a kettle sang drowsily. She stirred the coals and fetched cups and saucers, pouring boiling water into the teapot and pulling a knitted cosy over it. She poured Esther's tea and the girl took it with murmured thanks.

They sipped in silence until Adela said, 'Aren't you well?'

'Sorry, love, I'm not very good company, am I? I suppose you could say I'm not too well, though I shouldn't be bothering you. The baby's due, isn't it?'

'I think I've a week or two to go. Esther, what is it?'

'Nothing, love.' Her friend got to her feet. 'Thanks for the tea. I must be getting home.'

On the word 'home' her voice broke and Adela walked swiftly to the door and tugged the small chain which brought up the gas light. Esther kept her face turned to the fire, but Adela waited and eventually the other girl was forced to move. She turned and Adela gasped. Livid bruises darkened her olive skin. One eye was purple and black.

'So now you know,' she said flatly.

'But who did it? Were you attacked? Shouldn't you go to the police?' Adela stopped as Esther stared at her helplessly, her face a grimace of misery, then shook her head.

'Do you know the person who did it?'

Esther nodded. 'Forget it, please. I shouldn't have come. He didn't mean it.'

'Not your husband!' cried Adela. 'Surely not Bert?'

Esther sank back into the chair. 'Yes, Bert,' she said flatly. 'Adela, it's not his fault!' Her words came out in a rush. 'He's ill, poor man. I told you he came back from the war different. He used to be ever so gentle and kind, but now every little thing upsets him. Sometimes he acts like a madman. Sometimes—' a sob broke from her '—sometimes, I think he's mad.'

'Oh, Esther, my dear, how dreadful!'

'I could tell you terrible things – about the pigs that sent men like my Bert to fight when they weren't much more than boys, then ignored them when they were desperate and sick with the awfulness of it all. There are lots like him. They look all right from the outside, but inside – inside they're slowly going crazy!'

'Esther, no!'

'If we had a place of our own it might be better, but there's no chance of that. A land fit for heroes, they promised us. That was when they needed our men. Now, even when they bother to build a few houses, the prices are too high for us. And Bert's had a fit of temper and got sacked from his job and we can't afford to rent a place.'

'Doesn't anyone understand? Doesn't anyone care? They know what the men went though in France.'

'Well, if they do, they're keeping it pretty dark,' said Esther bitterly. 'Oh, God, I can't face going home. Can I stay here tonight?'

'Does your family know where you are?'

'Mum does. She won't tell.'

'What about his family? What do they think?'

'That I should put up with everything Bert does. A wife's supposed to knuckle under to her husband, no matter what. I expect I'll get another good hiding when I go back tomorrow, but for tonight, Adela, let me stay. Please.'

'Of course you can. I only wish—'

'So do I,' interrupted Esther harshly. Then her voice broke again and tears rolled down her face.

'How could Bert attack you when you're carrying his child?'

'I don't know. We used to talk about when we were married and how we'd have our own home and children. When I reminded him about the baby it just made him crazier. I don't think he can bear the idea of someone else depending on him. Poor Bert. My poor husband.'

Mr Fudge brought up a mattress and Mrs Fudge followed with a rug. She tutted and muttered at the sight of Esther's face.

Adela tucked her friend up and dropped a kiss on her bruised face. 'Try to sleep.'

'I'll do my best. I think perhaps I shall. It's the first time for weeks I've been at peace.'

Esther did sleep. But Adela lay awake for a long time.

Chapter Nine

Adela's time was near. Still she worked, reaching over her huge bulk to sew. Jack visited every day and the Fudges kept an eye on her. It was Mrs Fudge who had pointed out the advertisement in the *Western Daily Press* for a second-hand cot and a crib and Mr Fudge who had fetched them for her.

'A bargain at three pounds the two,' said Mrs Fudge. 'You can put the crib inside the cot for the first few weeks and when the little one gets bigger you'll have the cot all ready.' She insisted on taking them into the yard and giving them a good scrub and now they stood in a corner of Adela's room, waiting. Jack had brought her the frame of a screen still with tattered remnants of brocade adhering. She had re-covered it in a design of her own, of pink apple blossom and green leaves embroidered on blue cloth.

'It'll be suitable for a boy or girl,' she said, surveying her work with satisfaction.

'What's the green for?' asked Jack mischievously.

'Don't be silly. Whoever heard of an apple tree without leaves?'

Jack grinned. He made sure that Adela had a good supply of the doctor's tonic and that she took it regularly, and he had insisted on escorting her on walks. The hot streets were filled with children playing among the dirt, too many showing the clear evidence of rickets, who watched enviously as their friends danced to the music of a barrel organ, holding out their ragged skirts, their feet bare or in shabby, high-buttoned boots. The air rang with the sounds of the laughing, quarrelling and fighting of both children and adults. It was a world totally alien to Adela, yet a respect, a sense of admiration, gradually grew in her when she saw how the women coped with grime, plain food they had to buy every day because nothing would keep here, too many babies, and hardly ever enough money. The increasing number of unemployed men leaned against walls in their overalls or worn suits, hands in empty pockets, talking, forever talking. They had nothing else to do. Most newspapers reported prosperity; they preferred to ignore the growing canker of failed businesses caused by foolish speculation, and the lack of a firm reconstruction policy on the government's part. The textile industry was the worst hit. Men who had sold their businesses at the right time had made enormous profits out of inexperienced speculators, but others were ruined.

Esther continued to visit her for, as she put it, a few minutes of peace and quiet. One evening, as the two girls sat quietly sewing baby clothes, there was a thunderous knocking on the door of Adela's room, before it was kicked open.

Bert stood there. Adela hadn't seen him since the wedding and was shocked at his gaunt and haggard face. 'There you are,' he rasped, peering round Adela and glaring at his wife. 'You think you can hide from me, do you? I'll show you who's boss in our family! As for you, you bitch—' he turned on Adela '— I'll thank you to keep your bloody meddlin' nose out of my business.'

'Oh, my God!' Esther jumped up, her face pale. 'I'm coming, Bert.'

He thrust her aside and continued to glare at Adela. His eyes were bloodshot and wild and his voice became a yell. 'Comin' between husband an' wife! That shouldn't surprise no one, you an' your misbegotten baby. You've never had a husband, have you? You shouldn't mix with decent women! You deserve a thrashin' an' I've a good mind to give it to you!'

'No, Bert, please—' Esther leapt in front of Adela and Bert threw her aside. She tripped and fell heavily.

Adela was incensed. 'You wicked man! How dare you treat her like that! Have you forgotten she's carrying your baby?'

'Don't, Adela,' begged Esther, climbing to her feet. 'He's not himself.'

'What!' Bert's eyes bulged and his face crimsoned with fury.

'Not myself, eh? Who am I then? I'm your husband, that's who I am, an' you an' this bitch here had better bloody well remember it.'

He took a step towards Adela, then was pinioned by a pair of strong arms.

'Mr Fudge, thank God!' Adela cried.

'Let me go, you bastard!' Bert was struggling violently when Jack walked through the door. He glanced at the terrified women and, drawing back his arm, hit the raging man once, hard. Bert slumped to the floor.

Esther screamed: 'You didn't have to do that! He's out of his wits. He doesn't mean any harm.'

Jack said, 'I haven't hurt him, love. Just put him out for the count. We'll carry him downstairs an' he'll come round in a minute.'

Later Jack returned to Adela. 'I walked them home,' he said sombrely. 'Bert was pretty quiet. The crack on the jaw did him good. Poor devil, it's shell-shock. It took some of the men like that.'

'Will he get better?'

'May do. Some don't.'

'What happens to the ones who don't?'

Jack was silent for a moment, then said in low tones, 'They join the other poor devils in some mental asylum; the ones who went crazy even before the war ended.'

'That's horrible! Horrible! He seemed well when he married Esther. How can he have changed so much?'

'Everythin's been boilin' up inside him, all the filthy business of the trenches. He kept it hidden for as long as he could, but now it's comin' out.'

'But what about Esther? She can't go on like that. She's covered in bruises.'

'It's no business of ours, Adela.'

'She's my friend!'

'An' she's his wife.'

'I'm surprised at you, I thought you believed women were equal to men, yet you condone Bert's brutality!'

Jack looked angry. 'You've no right to say such a thing to me.

I've never condoned brutality, an' I do believe in equality, an' that's why I say that Esther must decide what's best for herself. No one else has the right.'

'What can she do?' Adela voice was low and bitter. She had slumped in an easy chair, her hands palms up in her lap. 'Women are dependent on men; either on their fathers, or brothers, or husbands. No matter how hard they struggle to get free, some damn man orders them about.'

Jack's anger died as swiftly as it had arisen. He grinned. 'Well, this damn man says you've had enough excitement an' arguin' for one night. It's still light outside. Let's go walkin'.'

She shook her head. 'I don't feel well enough to walk.'

Jack looked anxiously at her. 'Has anythin' happened? I mean, have you had any pain?'

'A little. A few times today in my back.'

'Is it the baby?'

'How should I know?' Adela was petulant.

Jack laughed. 'I bet it is the baby. My wife always got really tetchy when it was about to begin.'

Adela couldn't answer as her body was suddenly gripped in a vice of pain. She gasped, rocking herself back and forth until it was over.

'I'm goin' for the midwife,' said Jack.

She listened to him running down the stairs and heard his voice as he spoke to someone. For a while she was alone. She looked round her room, almost in disbelief that she, Miss Adela Danby, educated at one of the best girls' schools in Britain, who would have graced a finishing school in Switzerland had it not been for the war, was about to give birth in this inadequate room, in the middle of a district her parents would have described as a slum. Then pain seized her again and she forgot everything as she fought to contain it.

Mrs Fudge came hurrying in. 'I've put lots of water on to boil, my love, an' I'll air the baby's clothes. Ah, is it bad? Never mind. When it's over and you d'hold your little one, you'll forget.'

Adela got up and staggered to the bed where she hung on to the rail. 'I hope it won't take long! God, I hope it comes soon. Will it be long, Mrs Fudge?'

'It'll come when it's ready. Come on, I'll help you undress. That's the way.'

No one, not even the midwife, had seen Adela completely nude. Even now she felt bashful, then the agony gripped her again and she no longer cared what she looked like.

'On with your nightie, that's the ticket, dearie.' That was Lizzie Webb's voice and it was surprisingly kind as she lifted Adela's legs and settled her on the bed.

Mrs Fudge made up the fire and put a large kettle on to boil. 'I've plenty of water,' she said to Lizzie. 'Just call when you want some. An' there's tea in the pot over there, an' milk an' sugar in the cupboard.'

Adela thanked them both politely for their kindness, then she was lost again in a tempest of agony which grew deeper and harder until her senses were mazed in its brutal domination. Time lost all meaning. It seemed as if she had laboured on this bed forever. She saw faces: Lizzie, Mrs Fudge, a couple of neighbours who stared at her with anxious eyes.

Lizzie was saying something. Something about the doctor. What was going wrong? No one in these parts had a doctor for childbirth unless there was something wrong. No one could afford him. She heard his voice, tried to speak to him, then something was pressed to her mouth and nose and she was told to breathe deeply. There was a sickly smell – a dentist's smell – and she felt as if she was suffocating. She tried to tell them that there was nothing wrong with her teeth and began to struggle against the hand that held the pad inexorably over her face. Then, mercifully, she floated above pain into the darkness.

She surfaced feeling a little sick, to hear the cry of a newborn baby. What was a baby doing here? Where was Bertha? She must ask her. Then memory returned, and with it pain again, but different. It had lost its agonising edge and resolved itself into soreness and aching, bearable if she didn't move.

'You've got a boy,' said Lizzie. 'A lovely little fellow.'

The doctor leaned over her. 'You've had a bad time, my dear, but your son is perfect.'

Lizzie placed Adela's son in her arms and she looked down,

horrified, at the blood and bruises on his mis-shapen head.

'Don't worry,' said the doctor. 'They'll go away and he'll soon be all right. I had to use instruments. It's lucky you're a strong woman.'

The baby opened its mouth and cried, showing its pink tongue and toothless gums. It was so small and helpless. Adela felt a surge of love, but she was unutterably weary and wished she could hand him to a nursemaid and just sleep.

Mrs Fudge took him gently from her. 'Lizzie will clean you up now, love, and I'll bathe the little fellow. I've bought some lovely scented baby powder for him. He'll look beautiful in one of his new nightgowns.'

Adela looked down at her son. She felt refreshed after a long sleep. What should she name him? She had never given a thought to names. The prospect of her child had never seemed real enough to think of a name for it. He should be called Ralph, she supposed. She looked into his face for a long time. He was asleep and his pale eyelashes, beneath pale brows, touched his cheeks. His hair was almost white. He looked like his father.

Mrs Fudge opened the door. 'You've got a visitor, love.'

Esther walked in on tiptoe, as if the ground was hallowed. She put a small pair of blue bootees on the bed. 'For – what is his name?'

'Harold,' Adela suddenly decided. 'That was my Grandfather Danby's name – he was always called Harry. I like that, I'll call my baby Harry. Thank you for the bootees. Though you shouldn't have. You've enough knitting to do for yourself.'

'You must give a present to a newborn child,' said Esther. She peered down at him. 'What horrible bruises. Mrs Fudge said the doctor had to come and use instruments. Was it awful?'

Adela looked into her friend's anxious eyes. 'It did hurt,' she admitted, trying to keep a tremor from her voice. The memory was still vivid. 'But you already know that, Esther.'

'Yes, I suppose I do. I try not to think about it too much, but it must be worth it when you hold your baby.' She looked at

Harry yearningly. 'I'm longing for mine. If only Bert—' She stopped.

'How are you?' asked Adela quickly.

'I'm well enough.'

'And Bert?'

Esther flushed. 'He's not had an outburst since the one you saw.'

'I'm glad. Perhaps he'll get better now.'

'Perhaps.' Esther stood up. 'Adela, he's forbidden me to visit you again, so I may not see you often, but I'll come when I can. I won't allow him to part us.'

'I don't want to be the cause of your getting beaten.'

'You won't be.' Esther bent and kissed her. 'I'll not be a slave to any man. Bert's ill, you know, Adela. He has terrible nightmares. He wakes screaming and only I can soothe him.'

'Esther, how did he guess I haven't a husband?'

Her friend looked embarrassed. 'It's what people say. I don't know how they know. You don't somehow seem married.'

Adela was ordered to stay in bed for two weeks and enjoyed the enforced rest, during which she hand-made a pair of cushion covers. Jack also brought her something to read.

She picked up the two books. '*Pride and Prejudice*. Jane Austen! Jack, how did you guess?'

'I didn't,' he confessed. 'I told the library woman what you were like and she suggested it.'

'Oh, and what am I like?'

'I said you were a highly educated, erudite woman,' he said.

'Thanks,' said Adela drily. 'That makes me sound like a dried-up old female.' She looked at the second book. 'What's this? *A Vindication of the Rights of Women*, by Mary Wollstonecraft.'

'It's grand,' said Jack. 'It was published in 1792 an' its truth is the same now as it was then. You're always sayin' that you're goin' to be an independent woman. I thought you'd enjoy it.'

Adela laughed. 'Thanks for the thought. And what's in this bag. *Vogue*! Oh, Jack, thank you. I do so like it! But it's so expensive!'

'I've left fruit and other stuff with Mrs Fudge.' He got up,

153

bent and kissed her forehead. 'Get better soon, love.'

Later Mrs Fudge brought up a newspaper. It was slightly greasy and damp, and had probably been used as a table-cover, but Adela read it avidly. Mother was often in the news as an active worker for charity and she half expected to see her name, but when she did she jumped. 'Mrs Danby is pictured here at a charity bazaar in aid of our gallant war wounded.' In the photograph Mother was smiling. In the background stood Lady Somers and Mrs Smithers. The sight of them brought back hurtful memories. Adela quickly turned the page and was alarmed by the next item she read.

Outrage In Old Market

Angry men set fire to a tramcar in Old Market today. They said that they were ex-soldiers protesting against the keeping on of women in jobs they had been told would be kept open for them.

There was another disgraceful incident when Miss Blanche Danby, one of our gallant young ladies who have been acting as conductresses on the trams all through the war, was struck in the face by a stone thrown by a cowardly man who ran away before he could be apprehended. It is understandable that our returning soldiers want their jobs back, but there can be no excuse for this sort of violence. There are far too many incidents of this nature. Miss Danby, who is the daughter of Mr George Danby, the well-known Bristol businessman, is recovering well and insists that she will return to her job within a few days.

Adela put the paper down, shaken by the reference to Blanche. She had read of the stoning of women, but knowing that one's sister had been attacked made it more personal and frightening.

Esther came in with a tray on which was a glass of milk and a piece of fruit cake. 'Here, Mrs Fudge said Jack left these for you. There's a tin of malted milk powder too.'

'That man!' said Adela.

'He's good, and he thinks a lot of you.'

Esther idly picked up the paper. 'Women actually stoned. In Bristol! It's unbelievable! Mind you, they're asking for it. Women like that have got no right to hang on to men's jobs, especially if they don't need the wages. If my Bert could get back on the trams, I'm sure he'd be well again. Having nothing to do is driving him frantic.' She paused and saw Adela's face. 'Danby! Is she related to you?'

'My sister.'

'Oh, I didn't know – I wouldn't have—'

'It's all right, Esther. The man shouldn't have hurt her, but he was probably desperate. Since coming here I see things very differently.'

Two weeks passed and Adela got up. At first she felt shaky, but the soreness had improved. Mrs Fudge brought her a large box of bicarbonate of soda. 'Shake a good dollop into warm water in a bowl an' sit in it,' she advised. 'It d'help the sore bits really well.'

Adela laughed. 'I'll do that.' She thought again of the big bathtubs at home, of the gush of hot water from polished geysers, of hot, fluffy towels warmed by a maid.

'What are you thinkin' of, love?' asked Mrs Fudge. 'You look kind of sad.'

'No, I'm not sad,' said Adela briskly. 'I'm thinking of work. I've been told I mustn't do any machining for another four weeks, but I can't wait that long.'

Anxiously Mrs Fudge said, 'Don't overdo it, my girl. You'll only store up trouble for yourself when you have your next.'

'Good heavens, I've no husband. And if I had—'

'If you had, you're thinkin' you'd never have another baby.' Mrs Fudge laughed. 'We all say that, but you will, one day.'

Two weeks later Adela was back at her sewing machine. Her back ached at the end of a long day, but otherwise she felt quite well. Well in her body, but not at peace. Harry was a baby who slept little and wailed a lot. His whining seemed unending. She fed him herself, holding him to her breasts, watching him as he sucked sustenance from her. Did babies usually cry so much? No one in her previous circle of friends would know the answer. Their babies were handed to a nanny who only brought them to their mother when required.

She asked Mrs Fudge about it. 'He wants lovin',' was her solution. 'He needs a lot of cuddlin'.'

'But I haven't time!'

'No, I know. That's the problem with a lot of women. They're so busy tryin' to make ends meet they can't cuddle their babies, and before they can look round they're expectin' again.'

Adela shuddered at the idea.

Jack visited her often. He'd sit holding Harry who would stare up at him with big, wondering blue eyes, and forget to cry.

'He's a nice kid, Adela.'

'He's driving me crazy with his wailing. He never stops.'

'He's not cryin' now.'

'No. Have you found the white cotton material I asked for?'

'It'll be with you tomorrow.'

'Good. I've no time to waste. Esther's got an order for me for maids' aprons and caps. She's brought me patterns.'

Jack was silent and Adela, after a few moments' rapid machining, looked round at him. 'Why don't you say something?'

'It's not easy to talk to your back, especially when I know you're not interested in what I've got to say.'

'What?'

Jack laid Harry in his crib where, thankfully, he didn't cry, and walked over to her, negotiating the material on the floor where she had been cutting out petticoats, and turned her to face him, his hands on her shoulders.

'Adela, what's happenin' to you?'

She shook herself free. 'Nothing. I don't know what you mean.'

'Yes, you do. You think only of makin' money now. We used to have fun. You used to laugh.'

She looked over at the crib from which was beginning the usual nerve-racking wail. '*That's* why I need money,' she said desperately. 'I must find a bigger place to live. He'll drive me mad with his incessant crying. What in hell's the matter with him?'

'Some kids bawl more than others.'

'Well, I can't stand it! If I don't get a place where he can have another room, I shall go crazy.'

156

She returned to her work and scarcely noticed that Jack had left.

The following night, when there was a brief tap on the door, she called for her visitor to come in and it opened. She didn't look round. 'That you, Jack? Have you brought the stuff?'

'No,' said a woman's voice, 'he hasn't.'

Adela whirled round to see two women, strangers, standing in her room.

'Who are you?'

The two stared at her for a moment. Both were in their twenties, one well built, the other thin. The thin one said, 'We're Jack Webster's daughters.'

Adela was quite shocked. She knew that Jack had married daughters, grandchildren even, but they had been mentioned only in passing, something to be pushed to the back of her mind. Jack was so young in outlook, but these two women, standing stolidly in her room, filling it with their unfriendly presence, were reminders of his years before she met him.

She got up. 'How do you do?' she said politely. 'If you wait one moment while I pick my things up from the floor, I'll make you a cup of tea. Or would you prefer coffee?'

She was pleased to see that the women were a little taken aback by her cool attitude. She wondered what they had been expecting. 'Do you know if Jack will be bringing the cotton to me today? I'm almost at the end of my supply and I have orders to fill.'

As she talked she cleared the floor and plumped up the cushions in the easy chairs. 'Do sit down. The kettle's already boiling.'

'We didn't come here—' began the plump one of the sisters.

The other nudged her. 'We'll have tea, Miss, er—?'

'It's Mrs,' said Adela. 'Mrs Danby.'

There was an unnerving silence as she fetched teacups and saucers and poured. 'Sugar?' she asked, as formally as if she were entertaining ladies in her mother's drawing room.

Both women helped themselves liberally. 'I daresay our dad brings you plenty of sugar from Withycombe's stall. We get stuff there,' remarked the well-built one.

'He brings me sugar sometimes,' agreed Adela. 'He likes it in his tea.'

The women sipped their tea, little fingers crooked daintily.

'May I know your names?' asked Adela.

The thin one spoke. 'I'm Mrs Florrie Harris an' my sister's Mrs Annie Black.'

'Jack has spoken of you. I'm delighted to meet you.' The social lie rose smoothly to Adela's lips. She loathed the sight of them, sitting there, their feet in shiny black button boots planted firmly on the rug, their large, unbecoming hats pinned on with huge hat pins.

As they made no move to continue the conversation, Adela poured more tea.

After ten minutes had passed practically in silence, she said, 'I'm gratified that you decided to visit me but, if you'll excuse me, I really must get back to work.'

At that moment Harry decided to cry. His all-too-familiar wail rose from behind the embroidered screen.

'Is that our dad's?' asked Florrie belligerently.

Adela looked at her scornfully. 'Most certainly not! What an outrageous suggestion!'

Florrie lost none of her belligerence. 'He's spent enough time with you to make us wonder.'

Adela stood up. 'If you've come here merely to insult me, you have succeeded.'

'We didn't come to do nothin' of the sort,' said Annie. 'We just wanted to see who our dad was spendin' so much time with. He's our father and since Mum died we've tried to look after him. We don't want him gettin' into any entanglements.'

'I am not an entanglement! Jack and I are business acquaintances.'

'That's not what we were told,' snapped Florrie.

'Oh? You've been gossiping about me?' The contempt in her voice brought a tinge of colour to Annie's cheeks. She plonked her cup and saucer down hard on the table and raised her voice to speak over Harry's wails which were increasing in volume.

'We were told by a friend that Dad had a woman.'

'How kind of her.'

158

'It wasn't a her,' said Florrie. 'It was Bert Rawbone. And he should know. You're pals with his wife, aren't you?'

'With Esther? Yes. I'm astonished that you should give credence to Bert's accusation. He's not himself these days.'

'Are you sayin' Bert Rawbone's out of his head?' cried Florrie.

'She never said that,' reproved Annie, unexpectedly. 'An' if she did, she'd be right. Can't you stop that child yellin'? Pick him up, do!'

'Jack's a friend, that's all,' said Adela loudly from behind the screen.

Harry's face was wet and bright red with temper, and judging from the obnoxious smell, he needed a clean napkin. She picked him up, wrapping him in his top sheet to protect her clothes, and carried him round the screen.

Annie and Florrie stood up to see him. 'He's got no eyelashes,' said Florrie.

'He's got some, but they're very light,' said Annie. 'I hope he don't grow up like that. I like a dark man myself. Is he anythin' like his father?'

'Oh, so you've decided he isn't Jack's, have you?'

'Our dad could never father a kid who looks like that!' said Florrie.

'He's still cryin',' said Annie unnecessarily.

Adela felt suddenly weary and angry. 'Perhaps you'd go and I could feed him?'

Annie wrinkled her nose. 'He'll need changin' first.'

The two women took themselves off, leaving behind them a faint scent of carbolic soap and mothballs, and Adela settled herself to the unpleasant task of cleaning Harry, and the time-consuming one of feeding him. Her mind was occupied by the visit from Jack's daughters. If they suspected that Jack had fathered her child, might not others? She decided to ask Mrs Fudge who couldn't quite meet her eye when she replied.

'There's a bit o' talk goin' round,' she admitted.

'But that's so unreasonable! When I came here I was several weeks into my pregnancy before ever I met Jack.'

'People d'know that, my love, but they still say that he brought his bit o' muslin here.'

Adela flushed. 'That's terrible! Dreadful!'

'Ah, don't worry about it. They d'say worse things about others.'

'That's hardly the point. Mrs Fudge, did you tell anyone I'm not married?'

'No, love, cross my heart.'

'They seem to know anyway.'

'Yes. Things d'get about somehow. Don't worry, love. You're not the only one, not by a long chalk.'

Jack arrived soon after with the cotton. She took it from him with a muttered word of thanks and he looked quizzically at her. 'Somethin' upset you?'

'Yes. Your daughters have been here.'

'What? Why?'

'You'd best ask them. It's quite a delicate subject.'

Adela had begun to speak angrily, but ended in embarrassed tones.

Jack gave a deep sigh. 'I see. I can guess what they said.'

'Then you know there's talk about us.'

'There's always talk about someone.'

'So Mrs Fudge tells me. It's as bad as—'

'As bad as what?'

'As bad as being back in society.'

'We're society too, Adela.'

'You know what I mean.'

'Oh, yes, I know what you mean. You think that because we're poor an' not well educated, we don't care about morals.'

'Jack!' Adela sat down heavily. 'I didn't mean to imply any such thing.'

'No, I know you didn't mean to but, just the same, it's what you think.'

'You'd better not come to my room again.'

'I see. Do you still want material from me?'

'Of course I do. But we'll have to reach a different arrangement.'

160

'I'd better speak to Arthur Fudge. He's a good 'un. He'll pick up the stuff from the stall.'

'The Fudges have already done so much for me. How can I ask more?'

'I'll ask and he'll not refuse. I suppose it's beyond you to understand that the lower orders, as we're known in social reports, don't weigh up every little thing we do to help our neighbours. We just do it without makin' a song an' dance about it.' Jack moved restlessly about the room. 'When I was just startin' up and my wife was expectin' our first, I lost my job. Every mornin', until I got another, I'd find somethin' left outside our door by one of the undeservin' poor. A bit o' bacon, a loaf, a sixpence. An' I knew that whoever had left it would have to go without somethin'. I've read of *your* kind of society. If some poor bugger's business goes down the drain, nobody wants to know about it. He's expected to disappear from the sight of upper-class eyes.'

'I can't help the way they're made,' cried Adela. 'I can't help the way I was brought up.'

'I never said you could, and I thought you were a real good 'un, the way you helped Esther, but you're no different from the other buggers.'

'I wish you'd stop swearing at me!'

'You're enough to make a saint swear!'

'If I disgust you so much, perhaps you'd better stop seeing me at all.'

Jack stopped his pacing and stared at her angrily, then his expression changed, 'Adela, don't let's quarrel. We've got a good friendship. Let's hang on to it.' He put his arm round her shoulder and gave her a hug and she leaned into him, enjoying the comfort of being close to another human being.

'I'm sorry,' she said.

'Don't be sorry, my love. You've got a tough fight on your hands an' it's bound to get on your nerves at times.'

'Jack, I don't know what I would have done without you. Your friendship means so much to me.'

'No more than yours does to me. My daughters are good women an' I'm real fond of them, but they don't take any

161

interest in the things I care about. If they read, it's trashy magazines an' their heads are full of the animated pictures. They hardly know one politician from another.'

Adela decided not to confess that until recently she had taken no interest whatsoever in politics and had she the right to vote would have gone to the polls and obediently put her cross beside her father's choice. However, she was learning.

'Your daughters said that they look after you. They really resent me, especially Florrie.'

'She was always the bitter one. Annie's got a much softer heart.'

'Perhaps they're afraid we might become—' Adela paused, blushing.

'More than friends?' asked Jack, grinning. 'No, there's no chance of that. My wife was the only woman I've ever wanted as a wife. I expect Mum's heard of you an' she's been passin' a few comments to them about you. She's suspicious of any woman I've talked to since my Jessica died.'

'Didn't she ever think you might be lonely?'

'Not her. She'd have kept us all at home if she could, workin' for her an' clusterin' round her. The only one she succeeded with is my sister, Ida.'

'I wonder you knuckle under to her!'

'Who says I do? I've had a few lady friends she doesn't know about, but I'd never replace my Jess. I've told Mum that, but she's a suspicious old body.

'Neither of my girls is artistic, like you,' mused Jack. 'I'd have liked at least one kid with a bit of imagination. I had hopes for my boy.'

'The son who left home?'

'Michael, yes. He was different from the others, much livelier, an' he laughed a lot an' was ready to chance his arm. He wasn't half bad at drawin' when he was at school.' Jack delved into his breast pocket. 'Here's the latest photo I've got of him. He sent it to me just before the war started. He's about eighteen there. I haven't had a word since.'

Adela saw a tall boy with dark hair, smiling out of the fading photograph.

'You miss him, don't you?'

'You never stop missin' someone you love.'

'No, I suppose not.'

'Don't you miss anyone?'

Adela thought. 'It's an awful thing to say, but I don't seem to very much. My family has never been openly affectionate. Father showed his feelings when I was younger, but lately he's clammed up, too.'

'Poor kid.'

'Oh, my life wasn't that bad. In fact, it was good. I miss the luxury I left. I suppose you despise me for that.'

'Of course not! If anythin' I admire you the more for givin' it up for your baby.'

'So we go on as before?' she asked anxiously.

'As before,' agreed Jack. His voice grew brisk. 'I'm hungry, are you?'

She laughed. 'I'll see what I can find.'

'No. You make us a pot of tea an' I'll slip over to Old Market and get some food from Owen's.'

He returned with steaming faggots and peas wrapped in newspaper. Adela had a fleeting thought of her parents' re-action if they were offered this working-class delicacy, before she plunged in and devoured the savoury balls of meat and onion and the satisfyingly thick peas.

Jack watched her with satisfaction as she drank a second cup of tea. She sighed dreamily and he said, 'What are you thinkin'?'

'I'm thinking how damned lucky I was to meet you! You're the kindest man I've ever met.'

'That doesn't say much for the other men you've known. What about Harry's father?'

'I suppose he was kind. Yes, he was. When we were children he always looked after stray animals or wounded birds, but in those days I never gave much thought to simple kindness. I had all I wanted in life. At least, at the time I believed I had. Now I realise I missed affection. Most of what I received was from our nurse.'

'Where's your boy friend now?'

'Dead. He died of pneumonia in France.'

'A soldier?'

'Yes, a soldier.'

'How old?'

'Twenty-one.'

'Just a lad. You did a good thing to give him happiness before he died.'

'You're the only one who thinks so! Because of it I'm an outcast in my kind of society, though it would be all right, apparently, if I gave Harry away and returned with a respectable excuse.'

'Your society needs radical changes an' the socialists will change it, too, when they get the chance. A fallen woman.' He grinned. 'That's what you're known as in some of the magazines my daughters read. Load of bloody rubbish! The socialists won't crucify women.'

'They'll condone free love, will they?'

'Good Lord, where did you learn about that?'

'In articles in magazines my sister, Blanche, brought home. She has leanings towards your precious socialism.'

'Good for her. Does she believe in free love?'

'I think she believes in any sort of love,' said Adela. 'She's not pretty and refuses to dress nicely, yet she wants a man. I think she wants Sander Bennett.'

'He's a great man, is Sander.'

'I forgot he's so well known round these parts.'

'Stop frowning. Don't you like him?'

'I detest him!'

'Yet you were goin' to marry him.'

'My God, are there no secrets? I suppose you read that in the newspapers, too.'

'Yes. Why was the weddin' called off?'

'Must we discuss him? He's a brash, pushy man who thinks everything and everyone has a price.'

'I see. What price did he put on you?'

'One I found too high.'

'Which is why you cancelled the marriage?'

'Yes. Oh, I suppose that's how people round here guessed about me. They made quite a to-do of it in the papers. And that's my last word on the subject.'

164

Jack shrugged. 'Are you feelin' well again after your ordeal?'

Adela shuddered. 'How did your wife endure having to go through childbirth three times?'

'Four. We lost a baby, stillborn.'

'It's awful for women. Some of the poor creatures round here look half dead. If only men realised, they'd stop—' Adela hesitated.

'Stop makin' love, you were goin' to say. There's ways of preventin' babies at source, as you might say.'

'Then why do they go on having them?'

'All sorts of reasons. Perhaps they can't afford to buy the necessary, but it's often sheer ignorance. Doctors won't tell them what to do an' priests think stoppin' babies is evil.'

'Perhaps the men should exercise self-control.'

Jack frowned. 'That's the kind of advice they get shoved at them. Makin' love is free an' it's a great comfort.' He stood up. 'I must go. I've got a promise of a consignment of goods an' have to be at the warehouse to pick them up. I'm borrowin' the baker's horse and cart. Actually it's Sander who's supplyin' them. The material, not the horse and cart.' He bent and kissed Adela's cheek. Then he was gone.

Chapter Ten

Adela threw down her sewing and walked across the room to pick up Harry, trying to not to feel irritable. She had fed him only an hour before, but he hadn't settled. She rocked him in her arms, put him over her shoulder and patted his back, changed him and gave him a drink, but still he went on crying. He was six weeks old and wailed by day and night. Adela, in despair, had taken him to the doctor who examined him and pronounced him perfectly fit.

'It's probably infant colic. Usually lasts for about three months, then he'll be as right as rain, you'll see. Do you feed him yourself?'

Adela nodded, hating his smugness, wanting to ask him if he had ever had a child who never stopped yelling.

'Good. Very good. Mother's milk is always best for a baby.'

'I wondered if he was fretful because of me. I'm rather nervous lately. I wondered if I should put him on to artificial feeding.'

The doctor looked at her closely and sighed, 'Why not use what Mother Nature intended? It's easier and cheaper.'

'He looked tired,' she said later to Jack. 'I suppose it must be difficult to run a practice when so many of your patients are too poor to buy medicine.'

He smiled. 'You're growin' up, Adela. You'd never have thought of that when you first arrived in St Pauls.'

'Wouldn't I? No, I dare say you're right. Was I really so selfish?'

'No, just indoctrinated.'

She was indignant. 'I wouldn't call the way my parents brought me up indoctrination exactly!'

'I don't suppose you would.'

167

'And what about you, and the way you're always going around telling people that the upper classes don't care about the workers?'

'It's true, they don't.'

'But *that's* indoctrination.'

'I'm just tryin' to teach them that they don't have to live in rooms crawlin' with lice and bugs, that they don't have to work long hours for poor pay, that there's enough money in the country to make their lives better if justice was done.'

'I suppose you'd like to see everyone toiling on the same level.'

'I'm not stupid, I know that some men lead and others prefer to follow, but I wish the leaders would show a bit of compassion to the followers. Adela,' he said, changing the subject abruptly, 'you need a change. Harry's old enough to be left with Mrs Fudge. How about comin' out with me?'

'Out?'

'Don't look so daft, my love. Out! You know, puttin' on the glad rags and enjoyin' yourself for a change. All you've done for months is work.'

'Not quite all I've done,' said Adela desperately as the familiar wailing began again. 'Oh God, Jack, I sometimes feel like throwing him out of the window.'

He laughed. 'No, you don't.'

'Don't I?' She looked down into the yard where children played in the dirt, heedless of the stinks that permeated the place all through the summer. There were so many children! A man walked by with a tray of matches round his neck, displaying a sign on which Adela could make out the words 'Ex-soldier'.

'Jack, I'm frightened,' she said.

'Frightened? What of?'

'Of everything. I get so tired and discouraged. There is so much poverty. Why should I imagine I'll ever climb out of it? And there are times when I don't think I like my Harry. There, I've told you, and I suppose you're shocked. You certainly should be.'

Jack said calmly, 'I'm not shocked. You're not the only over-burdened woman whose nerves are raw from the demands of their kids. You love him, really, don't you?'

'Oh, yes, I do love him, but sometimes it's mixed up with bad feelings. I have nasty dreams, too.'

'I know. My wife was the same. Our Florrie was always grizzlin'.'

'Was she? What happened in the end?'

'Oh, in the end, she stopped grizzlin'. Mind you she started again when she got married. Her husband doesn't earn enough to satisfy her an' she goes out to work an' hates it. I don't know how the poor devil puts up with her naggin'.'

Adela laughed and felt better.

'Now, will you come out with me? It'd do you no end of good.'

'Perhaps it would! Perhaps a few hours away from Harry and the sewing would help me to achieve a proper perspective. Yes, I'd like to come out.'

'I'm glad you managed to talk yourself into it,' said Jack, grinning. 'Tonight then.'

Mrs Fudge was delighted. 'Of course I'll have the little chap. You go an' enjoy yourself, my love. Harry will be fine with me. An' I won't forget to put the net over his crib to keep off the cats.'

Tibs had quickly discovered the warmth of Harry's cot and one day Adela had been horrified to find the kitten curled up beside his head. She had picked up the cat and run down to Mrs Fudge. 'I'll have to get rid of him,' she said.

'No need,' explained Mrs Fudge, and she had produced a net which she had used to protect her own babies.

Adela put on one of the dresses her mother had packed for her. It was totally unsuitable for everyday wear, but when Mother ordered the packing of her case she wouldn't have given that a thought, unable to imagine her daughter living under the present conditions. The afternoon dress was a dream of rose georgette with a large pale pink collar, a pink satin hem and a dull gold cord round her waist which had, Adela noted with satisfaction, returned to its original size. According to *Vogue* the dress was now out-of-date with its ankle-length skirt, but it would have to do. She had no time to turn it up. It had, she recalled, cost six and a half guineas. At the time the sum had meant nothing to her. In fact, Mother had called it 'quite a bargain'. The same sum would provide food for weeks for herself or even for a whole poor family. It was another of the flashes of insight she was gaining into Jack's way of thinking.

He arrived in his dark suit. 'Adela! You look real pretty.'

'And you're so smart,' she said. 'I'd pass you in the street and not realise it was you.'

'Liar,' laughed Jack. 'The suit only fits where it touches, but it's the most decent thing I've got.'

Adela grinned. 'Where are we going?'

'To Old Market, the Kingsley Hall.'

Adela was outraged. 'That's a socialist place! Do you mean I've dressed up like this, arranged for Harry to be looked after, just to attend a damn political meeting?'

'Calm down. Lots of things go on there besides politics. You'll see. What shoes are you wearin'?'

Adela held out a foot to display a black patent leather shoe with a grosgrain bow. 'Will these do?'

'No need for sarcasm! They're the same as mine. Well, almost.' He pulled up a trouser leg and revealed black patent leather laceups.

'Jack! Don't tell me we're actually going dancing?'

'That's right. Tonight we'll whirl about an enchanted ballroom to the strains of music.'

'Quite poetical, aren't you?'

'I can be,' returned Jack, in faraway tones. 'On the other hand, my hair's not long enough.'

'Fool!' said Adela.

The evening was warm and Jack took her coat over his arm and escorted her down the stairs.

'My, aren't you pretty!' exclaimed Mrs Fudge. 'Come out here, our Arthur, and see Mrs Danby.'

Arthur Fudge looked down at her gawkily, and grinned.

'He's gone all tongue-tied!' said his wife.

Adela and Jack made their way through the hot, narrow streets where women sat on their doorsteps in the evening sun, their aprons bunched in their arms, their hands still for once, and talked. Many of them knew Adela and waved, gazing at her slender figure in its elegant dress. The eyes of some of the young ones were envious, some resentful; but the older women were too tired to care about anything save this brief respite from back-breaking toil.

As Jack and Adela entered the hall they were greeted vociferously; everyone seemed to know Jack. The sound of a waltz drifted through to the foyer and set Adela's feet tapping, her heart beating harder. Until this moment she hadn't realised how much she had missed dancing. The wartime parties had produced partners, more often than not a convalescing soldier. She and Ralph had danced, too, but it seemed an age ago. They had taken their first dance together when they had been members of a house party before the war, before all the horror had begun, when the future had stretched brightly before them, planned and approved, and they had nothing to do but follow their elders' advice. And now Ralph was dead, and she was here with Jack, and at home was Ralph's bawling, unhappy baby.

'You're supposed to look pleased,' said Jack in her ear. 'With that expression, people will wonder if I've upset you.'

'Sorry. I was thinking.'

'Of times gone by?'

'Yes. Mostly.'

'That's no good to you. No good at all. The future is all that counts.'

The small band struck up a polka and Jack put his arm round Adela's waist, clasped her hand and they moved off in unison. Adela threw her head back and laughed her delight and Jack beamed. 'I knew I was right to bring you here.'

'Oh, you were. You were.'

They danced on, Adela exhilarated, her problems forgotten; Jack delighted to be guiding the prettiest, and certainly the best dressed, woman in the room. Some people had been ready to despise a woman whom they believed was amusing herself by slumming, but the news soon got about that she was down on her luck, and earned her own living, and didn't whine, and

Adela was smiled at by perfect strangers. At home, a formal introduction would have been obligatory.

They rested when Jack's breath gave out. Adela wasn't sorry. Since Harry's birth she had been troubled by backache, severe sometimes. She assumed it was the natural result of child-bearing since so many of the women around her complained of it. Jack insisted on fetching her a lemonade and Adela sat on a small wooden chair and looked round for something she could use as a fan. She picked up a stray leaflet and read: 'About one half of the land in the United Kingdom is owned by seven thousand, four hundred persons. Labour fights to secure for the producers by hand or brain the full fruits of their work.'

'Good for them,' she muttered, and folded the leaflet into a fan which she wafted lazily, disturbing small tendrils of her hair. She had coiled it, as usual, and added a simple band of blue velvet round her forehead, finishing off with a ribbon rose she had made herself. Then, at the last minute, she had pulled some strands of hair free, cut them and curled them with Mrs Fudge's curling iron.

'Would you care to dance?'

She looked up, surprised to see Mr Trevor, Sander Bennett's office manager.

'What are you doing here?' she asked, then smiled. 'Why shouldn't you be here? I won't dance just now, thank you. I came with someone who's getting me a lemonade.'

'I came with my boss,' said Mr Trevor.

'Sander Bennet?'

'Mr Bennett, yes. He's got me interested in politics.'

'Where is he?' Adela looked nervously round her, but the dancers obscured her view.

'He's chatting in the refreshment room with an old friend. A Mr Webster.'

'I see.' If Sander saw her it would provoke him into more sarcasm, more pointed remarks about Grandmother Sutton and Cornwall. To hell with him! He shouldn't drive her away. 'Then it doesn't look as if I'll get my lemonade for a while,' she said.

'May I—?'

'No. No, thank you. I'll wait. I'm sure Jack won't be long.'

He wasn't, and when he returned Sander came with him. 'Adela,' said Jack, 'I've got to see someone about a rally we're gettin' up. Sander'll keep you company.'

Mr Trevor said his goodbyes and went home and Sander said, 'Care to dance?'

She hesitated, but if they danced it would ease the awkward minutes away.

Sander took her slender hand in his big artisan's fingers which reminded her that much of his life had been passed in manual labour. 'Are you well?' he asked formally.

'Perfectly, thank you. Why should I not be?'

'Sometimes a woman ails after childbirth.'

'You seem to know a lot about it.'

'I remember my mother – you recall we spoke of her, Adela?' She had to make a conscious effort not to flinch. 'And I see the women who live in the poor parts of Bristol. I also watch the statistics.'

'Statistics!'

Sander frowned. 'They tell you a lot. For instance, that more mothers and babies die in poor homes than in rich and that poor mothers suffer more from the effects of childbed.'

'It doesn't take a statistic to tell me that,' said Adela scornfully. 'It's pretty obvious.'

'Was it obvious before you went to live in St Pauls?'

'No, it wasn't.'

'Staying there must be proving an education.'

'Yes, it is.'

'You're not very talkative.'

'No.'

She was thankful when the dance ended. 'Please excuse me,' she said. 'I'm going to find Jack.'

'He'll be back when he's ready. At the moment he's having an argument with one of his friends.'

'Quarrelling?'

'No, I said "arguing". His friend insists that women should stay in the home where they belong, while Jack thinks they should work if they want to. A forward thinker, is Jack.'

'Jack's the kindest man I've ever met,' she said.

'I don't doubt it. Come on, Adela, they're playing a waltz.'

'Don't they dance anything modern here?'

'No, this is the place for old-time dancing. If you want to tango or one-step or shimmy, you'll have to go to the Drill Hall.'

'Mother forbade me to learn the tango.'

'Well, your mother isn't here! Go to the Drill Hall and tango if you like, and shake yourself in the Turkey Trot, but here it's old-time or nothing.'

'Thank you but I'd rather not,' she said. Her back was troubling her again and it was an effort not to press her hand to the source of the pain.

When Sander returned her to her seat, Jack was waiting with the lemonade.

'I'm sorry I kept you waitin',' he said. 'I've been arrangin' a rally. We're tryin' to get men to join trade unions so they'll always have their rights. D'you know, Adela, we've got over six million members now, an' we're gettin' prepared for the Municipal Elections later this year. Isn't that right, Sander?' Jack turned to Adela again. 'We've been tryin' to persuade Sander here to stand.'

'I'm not ready yet,' said Sander, 'but the time will come.'

'I had a look round your Park Street store,' said Jack. 'It's great.'

'Thanks. I'm about to open a shoe department. I've turned my factory over to fashion footwear. I'm going to stock as varied a collection of fashion goods as possible.'

'Including exclusive underwear?' said Adela.

Sander frowned but Jack said proudly, 'Adela's in the fashion line herself now.'

Sander turned his dark eyes on her. 'Is she, indeed? I heard you were dressmaking, but I wasn't aware that you were in fashions.'

'The people I work for can't afford high fashion prices,' she said hotly. 'You claim to care about the poor, yet your store is expensive.'

'Sander's very generous towards party funds,' protested

174

Jack. 'The more money he makes, the more he gives.'

'Am I supposed to swoon with admiration? What good are party funds to starving children?'

Sander said roughly, 'The only way really to help the poor is to get a strong opposition in Parliament. Men who will expose all the wretchedness that others prefer to forget. Money can help.'

'He's right,' said Jack.

'Oh, men will always stick together. Please excuse me.'

She went to the ladies' cloakroom, a shabby room with peeling paint and an ancient mirror in which she could only view her head and shoulders. Her face was pink with heat and indignation. In dressmaking, but not in fashion! Implying that she was unable to cope with both! She took out her powder compact – Mother had permitted powder – and dabbed at her shiny nose then patted a little lavender water on the base of her throat. There were two other girls there who chattered in between making faces into the mirror while they renewed their lipstick and creamed their cheeks, adding plenty of powder and rouge. Mother would have been disgusted by the heavy make-up. 'Sweetness of temper and good health are all that is needed by a lady.' Adela could hear her saying it. She returned to the ballroom, hoping that Sander would have left. He hadn't.

'How's the little chap?' he asked.

'Who? Oh, the baby.'

'Yes, your son, Harry.'

'If your spies have told you his name, they must have told you he's healthy.'

'I'd hardly call Jack a spy. Besides, he says that Harry yells a lot.'

'Some babies do,' she muttered. 'Jack appears to have vanished again.'

'Another argument, perhaps?'

Some partner he turned out to be, thought Adela. She wouldn't criticise him aloud.

Sander glanced at his watch. 'I must be on my way soon.'

'Please don't let me detain you.'

'I won't, but I've time for a dance. That is, if you'll accept my offer?'

The band's repetoire seemed limited, but it was so long since she had enjoyed dancing and she felt pretty tonight and there was no wailing baby to try her nerves. 'All right,' she said, rather ungraciously.

The waltz was a slow one and they swayed to the rhythm, their steps matching well. Sander began to sing a little harshly, *After the ball is over, After the break of day, Many a heart is broken* . . . Her worries drifted away and she lost herself in the music and the movement. She came to abruptly. Sander was holding her too close, she decided.

'Don't clutch at me like that. I can scarcely breathe!'

'Sorry.' His answer was laconic. She felt indignant at his casual attitude and annoyed with herself for minding anything he did or said. The dance ended.

'I'm going to find Jack,' she said. 'He's supposed to be looking after me.' Sander followed her and she was even more annoyed to see Jack still deep in conversation with a couple of men.

'Please take me home,' she demanded.

Jack looked at Sander and asked half humorously, 'What's upset her?'

'Me, perhaps.'

'You?' Jack looked at Adela's angry face.

'Just joking,' said Sander. 'I have to be going. I've work to do.' He swung round and walked away.

'What have you been up to then, Mrs Danby?' said a man standing nearby. 'You can't afford to make an enemy of Sander Bennett.' The man was big, with a thatch of red hair, and Adela recognised Fred Withycombe. He looked at her with a mixture of lasciviousness and contempt. She stared him out, feeling a crazy desire to slap him. She was shocked at herself. The lady-like upbringing seemed to be slipping from her, leaving her with nothing but primitive urges.

Jack walked her home.

'Why did you leave me with Sander Bennett?' she demanded. 'You know I can't stand him.'

'You should forget the past. I'm sure he has.'

Adela pressed her lips together angrily as they walked on,

then Jack said, 'Fred Withycombe was right about not upsetting Sander Bennett. He wields a lot of power in Bristol.'

Adela, still burning with indignation, said, 'Does he really? Who can he hurt?'

'Me, for one.'

Adela stopped. 'You? Jack, I'm surprised at you. I never thought you'd humble yourself to anyone. I thought you were independent. You're always going on about independence.'

'An' I mean every word, but it doesn't follow that you can afford to be unpleasant to business people. An' I know Fred Withycombe's a bad lot, but you didn't need to look at him as if he was dirt.'

Adela strode on. 'Well, excuse *me*! I'll practise a few more becoming looks when I get home.'

'It's not your fault. You were brought up to look down on folk like us. It'll take longer yet for you to unlearn those lessons.'

'Actually, my parents never taught me any such thing.'

'It's been instilled in you. You've been listenin' to them an' their friends all your life. You still listen to them in your head.'

'I don't! I don't!'

Jack slid his arm through hers and, hating to be on bad terms with him, she held it close to her side. She had been foolish, she knew it. Sander Bennett could very well make life impossible for Jack if he chose to.

'I'm sorry I've put you and Sander on bad terms.'

'Forget it. He will, an' so shall I.'

'How did he come to be at the dance?'

'He often visits Kingsley Hall for political reasons, an' sometimes he turns up on a social evenin'. He's a good man. Dependable.'

'So you say, but he's not above a few dirty tricks in business.'

'Dirty tricks to one is good business to another.'

'That's more or less what he once said. Men stick together.'

'So do women, but unfortunately not enough of them in a political way. If they took the trouble they could rule the world. There's more of you than us. An' one day you'll all get the vote, then we men had better watch out.'

'Chance would be a fine thing!' said Adela. 'Women are always tied to babies.'

They arrived back at her room to find Harry asleep. Mrs Fudge tiptoed out, smiling, and Adela put the kettle on. They kept their voices low.

Adela's spirits had been buoyed up by the dance, but back in her cramped room she felt suddenly tired and dispirited.

'You're not happy,' Jack said worriedly. 'I wish I could help you.'

'You do enough,' said Adela. She knew she sounded abrupt.

'How's the dressmakin' goin'?'

'I've got plenty of work, but I don't make much money.'

'Folk round here haven't got much to give.'

'Well, you'd think they would pay me a fair sum.'

'They pay what they can. They give you what you ask for.'

'I don't ask for much because it wouldn't be any use and I'd lose trade.'

'We all have to cope with that kind of thing.'

'And that's good enough? You surprise me. I thought one of your chief principles was a fair day's wage for a fair day's work.'

'So it is. It's a shame, but sewin' has always been badly paid.'

'And you're content to leave it at that?'

'Of course not, but we can't do everythin' at once.'

'So you concentrate on men's wages!'

Jack glared at her. 'They're the main breadwinners.'

Adela was furious. 'They used to be! What about the thousands of war widows and the women who'll never have a man of their own? Are they supposed to starve?'

'We'll get to them all in time. At least they get unemployment benefit now.'

'Lower than the men's, and only for fifteen weeks in any year.'

'Their contributions are lower, an' the rules are the same for men. I admit we've got a lot to do, but we're fightin' every inch of the way for workers' rights. It's like the war over again, without the mud and blood.'

Jack sounded tired and Adela capitulated. She was venting all her confused feelings on the one person who didn't deserve it.

'Sorry, Jack,' she said. 'I'm being rotten to you.'

'It's all right, my dear. I can't imagine what it's like to be catapulted from your rich life to St Pauls an' havin' to keep yourself an' the baby. You're doin' well.'

Jack visited Adela most days. He was a welcome visitor and she always put the kettle on.

Seeing her rubbing her back again he said worriedly, 'Adela, you keep doin' that. I think you should see the doctor.'

'I'm all right, and I'm in damn sight better health than many of my customers.'

'That's not sayin' much!'

'No. Babies and pain go together, I've learned that much.'

'It can't be right, though. My Jessica always ailed after our first. Maybe if she'd had proper care she would have lived longer.'

Adela said gently, 'Jack, I haven't money for a doctor, especially when there's nothing really wrong with me. I'll get stronger in time.' She spooned tea into the pot and poured on boiling water. 'I'm not ill, Jack, honestly.'

'I hope not. Have you got plenty of orders?'

'More than I can cope with.'

'That's good. You should get someone to help.'

'I don't make enough money to pay wages.'

They drank their tea in companionable silence, but when Jack had left her depression settled on Adela like a grey smothering cloud. It was getting worse every day and her back was only comfortable when she was lying down. There were some mornings when she wished she could just stay in bed and fade away into nothingness. Then Harry's bawling would tell her that he needed attention.

Later that night, as she was about to climb into bed after a long day's work, Harry woke up and began to yell. Wearily she picked him up and held him to her breast. She looked down at him. His hair was longer, but still almost white and completely straight. His complexion was as fair as a girl's and his blue eyes were Ralph's. He still had no noticeable eyebrows. Amazing to think of him growing up into a man like his father, good looking, splendid at cricket and tennis, a steady golf player; in fact, a jolly good all-rounder. It gave her a jolt to remember that unless there was a miracle her son was more likely to resemble the cheaply dressed, short, under-nourished boys who ran about constantly seeking work, acting as messengers or playing games to pass the time. Harry pulled impatiently at her breast. He must have emptied it and she picked him up, burped him over her shoulder and put him to the other side where he settled down to suck greedily again. He was always hungry. He paused for a moment and looked up at her. What did he see when he looked into her eyes? Did he see the love he had a right to expect?

'Harry,' she whispered, 'I love you, but why must you cry so much?' If only life wasn't so difficult. He resumed feeding, keeping his eyes wonderingly on her face.

Adela was producing all sorts of clothes, from a Viyella petticoat for a chilly old lady to slumber suits for young women. Garments in this new style resembled men's pyjamas but were made from silky material. Her prices were ridiculously low, but it would be useless to raise them when she had to compete with big stores or, more often in this district, second-hand shops or pawn shops and, however hard she worked, she was able to save only a little money.

On one of her rare visits Esther said, 'You've got style, and that's something all women recognise.'

Adela laughed. 'You wouldn't say that if you could see my sister.'

'Your sister? That's the one who was hit by the stone, isn't it? Have you met her lately?'

'No,' said Adela briefly. 'How are you these days? I haven't seen you for such a long time.'

'I'm well now, thank goodness, though I fainted twice at work and had to leave.'

'Has Bert got a job yet?'

'He had one.' Esther paused, then went on miserably, 'He had one, Adela. He went back on the trams, but he got sacked after only three weeks.'

Adela stopped her hand-stitching on a maroon blouse and gave Esther her full attention.

180

'He was over the moon at first,' said Esther, 'but then he began to complain about the passengers. When he was sacked I went to see his boss – Bert would kill me if he ever found out – and he said that Bert objected to people jumping on the tram between stops. Well, of course, they're not supposed to but everyone does. Only Bert began to try to push them off and he shoved one chap so hard he fell and hurt his arm badly. The chap didn't get anywhere with his complaints because he shouldn't have been jumping, but then Bert began ringing the driver's bell before folk were properly on and off the tram and, of course, there were genuine complaints and he got sacked. He's still not well.'

'Is there any chance of getting his job back when he's recovered?'

'None. He punched the boss in the face. And he's not getting better. In fact, he's worse.'

Esther's baby was showing now. She looked pale and had dark rings under her eyes. 'Dad and Mum are letting us stay on because of the baby, so we've got a roof over our heads. They've been real good to us. We're having to live off the dole and that's not enough and will soon run out, then it'll be the Guardians and a kick in the teeth whenever we ask for help. And food's gone up again. I paid ninepence-halfpenny for a loaf yesterday.'

'But surely the government gave the returning soldiers quite a good allowance?'

'Yes, and it should be enough with care, but Bert – Adela, he's taken to drink. Not like Jack or normal people drink, but all the time. He says it's the only way to keep the terrible memories out of his head.'

'I'm so sorry, Esther.'

'You should hear the way he talks. About the stinking mud, and the shell holes filled with green water, and rotting tree stumps. He says it was like one huge grave and—'

'Please don't!' said Adela, putting out her hand.

'I'm sorry, but we ought to know what our menfolk suffered.'

'I do. I remember my – man. I've never told a soul, but he cried in my arms because he was so afraid to go back.'

181

'Oh, Adela, and he didn't come back! I'm being selfish.'

'No, not you,' said Adela. 'Has Bert – has he hurt you since you stayed here?'

'Once he laid about me, but my dad threatened to leather him if he beat me again. He just talks at me now, on and on, all night sometimes, just going on about the trenches. I'm beginning to get terrible dreams myself – that's when I can sleep, that is – and I'm afraid for the baby. All that rottenness being fed to me.'

'It'll be as sweet as its mother,' said Adela shakily.

She was wrong. No one would ever know how Esther's baby would have turned out because its father wrecked its chances of being born alive. Jack brought the news.

'Bert went off his head. Esther's mum and dad were out an' Bert came home in a filthy temper. He'd just been turned down for another job. He laid about her and the baby came early.'

'Oh, how terrible! Is Esther all right?'

'She is, but the baby was born dead. A boy. That's bad enough, but now the doctor says that Bert may have to be shut away for his own good, not to mention Esther's.'

'An asylum!'

'That's what it'll come to. Esther still loves him and she won't report him to the law. Lizzie Webb attended her an' saw the bruises on her body, but she won't talk either. I reckon she sees a lot of brutality in her job. Men go crazy with frustration, but they're not often as vicious as Bert. It seems he actually kicked Esther in the stomach.'

'Oh, no.' Adela laid her hands over her own stomach, remembering when Harry lay there, protected and safe. 'He really should be put away before he does any more harm.'

'It's not for us to judge him. We must leave it to Esther.'

She came to see Adela, looking thin and white. Adela made tea and Esther sank into a chair in front of the fire.

'I'm so sorry about the baby,' said Adela.

'It's probably for the best.' Esther's voice was harsh, her eyes bleak.

'You don't mean that!'

'Not the way it sounds, no, but Lizzie Webb said if the boy

had lived he'd have been a lunatic. He was injured inside me.'

Adela was silent for a while as the horror washed over her. 'How is Bert?' she whispered.

'Ill. Adela, life is hard on poor people. You should go back to your parents. Maybe they'll take you home. Maybe they're sorry for what's happened. It'll be Christmas soon. The time for good will.'

'That won't move my parents.'

Esther sighed. 'Are you ready for Christmas?'

'No, I've no time to spare.'

'And you're not really interested, are you?'

'Not this year. Harry's a bit too young to understand. Next year it'll be different.'

'Christmas has always been such a special time in our family.' Esther's voice sounded unbearably bleak.

'In mine, too,' said Adela. 'In the hall there was always a huge tree smelling of pine and covered with lights, and presents under it. We came down from the nursery to see Mother and Father on Christmas Eve and they pretended not to notice the way we felt the parcels and tried to rattle them. Then Nurse would take us upstairs and sit knitting by the fire with her door slightly ajar so that she could hear if we whispered. It seemed to take ages to get to sleep. In the morning our stockings were always filled with wonderful gifts and there were more after breakfast.' Adela stopped as her voice broke.

'You miss your folks.' Esther's words were a statement. Adela came back from the dream-world of yesterday. Her friend said, 'Your childhood was very different from most people's round these parts.'

'I didn't intend to boast.'

'No, love, I know. We all have our memories. Mine hold some lean Christmases, but even those were good. So full of love. That's the most important thing.'

Esther had known a great deal of love in her life. For Adela there had been total security in Speede House, but emotion had always been smothered. Mother had smelled sweet, her hands were soft and gentle; Father had been expansive, eaten heartily, puffed away at his cigar with a twinkle in his eyes while he watched his daughters opening their costly gifts.

'Are you still getting plenty of orders?'

'Yes, thank goodness.'

After Esther had left Adela sat on in the firelight, lacking the will to move. Harry had recently been fed and was quiet, though not asleep. She could hear him moving and gurgling to himself behind the screen. If he cried she was sure she'd go mad. A sense of oppression smothered her; the days and nights were clouding into one, a long tunnel of darkness without a light at the end. She recalled the time in London when she could have rid herself of her child and hurried guiltily to Harry's cot and bent over it. He smiled up at her, his first teeth shining white in the firelight. 'Harry,' she said, 'what have you done to deserve your fate? No wonder you're so miserable.'

He twisted around, then opened his mouth and the familiar wailing began. She picked him up and paced up and down while he continued to yell. How long could she stand living in one room with him? She put him down and lay on her bed. The tears began to flow; silent, hopeless tears that slid from beneath her lids and streamed down her face.

Jack found her there. He asked no questions; simply sat beside her and held her hand until the tears stopped. Then he brought out his handkerchief and wiped her face as she remembered Grandmother Danby doing once when she had fallen.

'Feel better now, Adela?'

'Not really. Jack, I'd be in a bad way without you. I feel so rotten, I often feel I can't go on.'

'You can, an' you will. You're a lot tougher than you know. For Harry's sake, if nothin' else, you'll pull through, but you need more support. I've been thinkin' about it for a long time an' wonderin' how I could help. I've got a plan to put to you.'

Chapter Eleven

Adela stared at Jack. 'You have a plan for me? Something good, I hope.'

He grinned. 'I hope so, too. How about taking lodgings with me?'

'Lodgings? With you?'

'Well, don't look so shocked! I won't charge more rent than you pay now, an' you'd have more room.'

'Jack, you're so kind.'

'Kind, be blowed. I'm very fond of you.'

'I know, and I am of you, but it wouldn't do. Surely there would be gossip? A widower with a widow under his roof. At least, I hope that's what most people think I am.'

'I thought you'd be above worryin' about gossip. It wouldn't bother me. An', anyway, who's to say people will talk? I've made no secret of the fact that no one can ever take Jessica's place, an' I'm old enough to be your father.'

'I wish you had been!'

'You don't mean that.'

'No, I suppose not.' Adela paused. 'Father changed as Blanche and I grew up. He seemed awkward with us.'

'I'd never have turned out one of my girls if she'd been in trouble,' said Jack.

'No, I don't suppose you would.'

'Adela, we're gettin' off the subject. Will you take lodgin's with me? Just think – you could put Harry to bed upstairs an' be free in the livin' room to spread your sewin' round and make as much noise as you wanted. He'd probably sleep better an' your health would improve.'

185

'What would your family say? Your mother lives next door, doesn't she?'

'At my time of life, I do as I please. Say you'll come.'

'No, I'd far better not, but thank you. It's like you to think of it.'

They had been sitting side by side on the bed. Now Jack got up and walked to the fireplace. The fire had burned low and he carefully placed a few small coals on it.

'Not too many,' said Adela, nervousness making her sharp. 'I'm almost out of coal.'

'I'm not a fool,' said Jack. 'I know that fuel is still in short supply. I'm the bloke that brings you logs, remember?'

Adela said contritely, 'Of course I do. I'm sorry, Jack. I'm not myself.'

'Who are you then?'

Adela smiled at his faintly humorous tone. 'I'm a woman who doesn't recognise herself.'

Harry had given up protesting and gone to sleep and, as usual, Adela's depression faded when she was in the company of friends. And Jack was a friend, such a good one.

He sat down by the fire and Adela seated herself opposite him.

'How's the little fellow these days?'

'Bawling most of the time.'

'Poor kid. You work too hard.'

'What's that got to do with Harry's temper? It's for him I'm doing all this. If it weren't for him—' She stopped, biting her lip.

'You wouldn't be here at all,' he finished. 'I still can't understand how your family could just throw you out.'

'They didn't. I left.'

'They must have made things damnably unpleasant, then. They've got money. Didn't anyone suggest an abortion?'

Adela gasped. 'What an idea!' But she knew she sounded unconvincing.

'They did, didn't they? An' you refused.'

She felt too weary to argue. 'Yes, I refused.'

'Why did you go on with it when you must have known you'd be an outcast in society? Your kind, anyway.'

Adela shrugged. 'I don't know. Yes, I do. It was because of Ralph, because of Harry's father.' She found herself telling Jack what had happened that day in the woods in Combe Dingle. He listened, a variety of expressions chasing across his thin face. Admiration, anger, pity . . . Pity for whom? wondered Adela. Her? Ralph? 'So now you know,' she finished.

'I respect you all the more,' he said simply.

'Thank you for that. My family certainly didn't.'

'Did you love Ralph?'

Adela flushed. 'I was very fond of him. I believed I loved him when I agreed to marry him. Our families expected it and it was comfortable to bask in their approval. But when he died—' Adela stopped, then continued, '—when he died I found I couldn't really mourn him, not as a lover. I was very sorry he lost his life. He was so young, and he had been my friend since we were babies.'

'You can't force love.'

Adela turned to Jack eagerly. 'No, you can't, can you? I get worried sometimes in case I don't love Harry enough. He makes my life so difficult.'

'You wouldn't be human if you didn't resent a child who behaves like he does, so that you're always tired. You're dejected a lot of the time.'

'Oh, Jack, I am!' It was wonderful that she needn't explain everything to him. 'There are times when I feel I just can't go on.'

He sat by her again and held her hand. 'Poor little kid! You had a bad time at the birth, an' you've had to work so hard. You're not cut out for a life like this.'

Adela almost surrendered. The thought of living in Jack's house, having him around to help carry her burdens was a sweet one but it wouldn't do. It just wouldn't do.

'Are you positive you won't move into my house?'

'Positive. I love you for asking, though.'

He grinned ruefully. 'I see. Well, that's somethin'.'

★   ★   ★

Jack took her to dance again at the Kingsley Hall. Adela was suffering through a dark time, trying to fight off the melancholy which was growing insidiously worse. At the hall she found herself looking round rather fearfully for Sander Bennett. She was astonished when Blanche walked in. Her sister wore an unbecoming brown jersey suit which drooped slightly at the hem. They came face to face and Blanche's eyes travelled over Adela.

'My goodness, aren't we all dolled up! You haven't changed, have you?'

'And neither have you,' retorted Adela. 'Still wearing the same ghastly clothes.'

Blanche smiled thinly. 'Got an admirer here, or did you come on your own?'

'I brought her.' Jack had approached unnoticed. 'Hello, Blanche. Sander not with you?'

Adela stared at him. He had greeted her sister like an old friend.

Blanche's eyes were on Adela as she said, 'He can't be here tonight. A problem at the corset factory. Some idiotic girl got a needle through her finger. You know how Sander is. He's organising a doctor for her and making sure she's not going to starve while she's off work.'

'Ah, he's a good bloke,' said Jack. 'If all bosses were like him, the world really would be a fit place for heroes.'

'Wouldn't it?' agreed Blanche.

Adela wondered if she and Sander wĕre now considered a twosome. They would make a good pair – both dogmatic, self-seeking, egotistical and belligerent! She danced with Jack and with others who were introduced by him and who entertained her while he held long conversations on his favourite topic, the progress of the Labour Party. Her partners were mostly tongue-tied as they guided this well-dressed woman with her cool, cultivated accent around the floor.

She stopped dancing when the pain started up in her back and sat as near the door as she could get, where an occasional breath of refreshing air wafted through the outer entrance. She sipped a glass of lemonade while the band played a Military Two-step and couples marched vigorously up and down to its beat. Then someone came to stand in front of her.

'Esther!' she cried. 'How lovely to see you here. Is Bert with you?'

Esther's smile didn't reach her eyes. 'He is. I had a terrible job persuading him to come. He knows you're here and says I mustn't speak to you. Please understand.'

Adela took Esther's hand in hers. It was icy cold. Her friend was thinner than ever, and when she put up her hand to push back her hair Adela saw a purple bruise on her arm where her sleeve fell away. 'Of course,' she said quietly. 'Hurry away or he'll catch you.'

'He's in the foyer giving his old mates a piece of his mind. He reckons they should follow the Russians and have a revolution to overthrow the rich bastards. That's what he calls them. He'll be a while yet.'

'He's here,' said Adela quietly. 'Quick! Move away.'

It was too late. Bert directed a malevolent glare at the two girls. When Esther joined him he ignored her and continued to stare at Adela. Esther put up her arms to encourage her husband to join in the dancing, but he shoved her away and pushed between a couple of dancers, ignoring their indignant remarks, until he stood in front of Adela.

'I thought I told you to keep away from my wife, you bitch! If you won't listen to reason, I'll have to use somethin' else. I bet you've never had a good beltin'!'

'Bert! Come away, please, my love. Don't!' Esther tugged at her husband's arm. He swung round on her and she staggered and almost fell.

Bert turned back to glare at Adela from red-rimmed eyes. 'Watch out, that's all I've got to say at present. I may be visitin' you sometime.'

As he strode away, followed by his wife, Adela found that she was trembling. Jack came hurrying towards her. 'What's goin' on? Someone said you'd been bullied by Bert.'

'He doesn't mean it, I'm sure.' Adela tried to smile, but her face felt stiff.

Jack sat beside her. 'What did he say to you? Did he threaten you?'

'Yes,' said Adela, 'but he's not himself. Everyone knows that.'

'I don't like you livin' alone while Bert's around in that mood,' he said worriedly.

'I'm not alone,' said Adela, 'Mr and Mrs Fudge are downstairs. Mr Fudge helped me once before, remember?'

'He might not be there next time.'

'I'm sure there won't be a next time,' said Adela. 'It was all talk.'

On the way home she asked, 'Are Blanche and Sander a couple now?'

'A couple of what?'

'You know what I mean. Do they see much of each other?'

'Quite a bit. It's because of their shared interests. Blanche is becoming a really useful party member. She finally had to give up her job to a man and she's got lots of spare time.'

'I see.' Adela felt a moment of pity for her parents who had watched both daughters reject them and their principles.

Adela's rest was badly disturbed that night. Harry was more than usually fretful, and when she did sleep she had nightmares about Bert. In the morning she wanted to pull the covers over her head and stay in bed forever. But Harry must be tended. The sewing must be done. With Christmas coming, she had orders for new clothes.

In October the government decontrolled meat, butter and sugar, but the shops were sparsely stocked and Jack railed about the way the government was taking so long adjusting to peace-time conditions. Adela listened to him, and occasionally leafed through the newspapers he left for her, but her chief interest was in the materials he brought her, and in sewing for money and trying to cope with Harry.

December was unseasonably warm and muggy. It kept on raining and Adela left Harry with Mrs Fudge while she did some Christmas shopping. The thought of the approaching festival irritated her, but the Fudges had asked her to share their Christmas Day dinner and she wanted to give them presents. Jack had brought her a particularly fine piece of pure silk in brilliant scarlet and Adela had hand-hemmed it into a scarf for Mrs Fudge, but she needed something for the others.

Walking in the rain, alone, brought an unexpected lift to her spirits and she actually enjoyed her outing. She bought tobacco for Mr Fudge and cigarettes for their son, Isaac, who was on shift work in a chocolate factory. Adela had seen little of him, but she had benefited by the fact that he could bring home cheap, mis-shapen chocolate. She bought a small teddy bear with a growly noise inside for Harry and then turned her mind to Jack. He deserved something special. After much thought she splashed out fifteen shillings on a bottle of whisky. Her purchases in a bag, she wandered through the streets which were filled with hurrying shoppers and found herself thinking about home. Not the room in Mrs Fudge's, but her lovely bedroom in Clifton and all the luxurious surroundings she had thrown away so recklessly. Depression settled on her again and for a moment she failed to see the man who had stepped out in front of her. When she did her heart seemed to contract. Bert stood there, barring her way.

She kept her voice even and managed a smile. 'Hello, Bert. Are you ready for Christmas yet?'

'Bugger Christmas!'

'Please let me pass. I must get home to my son.'

'Whore!'

'How dare you? How *dare* you!'

'Whore, I said, and whore I meant. You're not married, are you? I know who you are, an' any woman who has a baby without gettin' married is a whore in my book. Keep away from my wife. She's unsullied.'

'Perhaps you should keep away from her. She could do without all those bruises,' snapped Adela.

She regretted the words instantly. Bert took a step towards her and she dodged round him and ran. She thought he was following her and kept going until her breath sobbed in her throat and her chest hurt. She had to stop. She clung to some railings and looked behind her. Bert was gone. She hurried on, taking deep breaths, and before she arrived back at the Fudges'

191

paused to wipe her face, damp with rain and perspiration.

That night when she went to pull her curtains a figure in the street opposite, standing beneath a lamp post, made a sudden movement and she recognised Bert. He was staring up at her window.

She sat down, her legs shaky, and considered her position. Should she go to the police? Nobody round these parts dragged in the police. They preferred to solve their own problems. And there was Esther to consider. And Bert was ill, not wicked.

Wearily she bathed and fed Harry, wrapped up the presents and labelled them, before settling down to finish a pleated skirt. It was a fiddly job. She had first pinned then tacked the pleats, and now she knelt on the floor with the skirt on a piece of sheeting over an old blanket and began the difficult task of damp pressing before she used the sewing machine. She was tired and dispirited about the fact that her customer would be paying a ridiculously small amount for the hours of work. One day, she vowed, she would make real money, doing something she truly enjoyed. Harry was asleep and she had become absorbed in her task when the calm of the room was shattered as her door flew open.

She looked up, horrified to see Bert standing there. She knew the three Fudges were at the local pub and she was alone in the house. He glared down at her, his face suffused with blood. 'Over the top!' he yelled. 'Over the top!'

'What?'

'Over the top, lads. Get the Boche. Kill the bastards before they kill us!'

Adela stood up shakily and put out her hands. 'Bert,' she said steadily, 'it's over now. The war's over. There will be no more killing.'

'Over the top!' he repeated in a mindless fashion which terrified her. 'If you run out of bullets it's hand-to-hand fighting, lads. Use your bayonets. If your bayonets break, use your hands.'

He moved swiftly and his hands were at her throat. She fell back on the bed with Bert's weight on her. She couldn't scream, she couldn't breathe. She heard a ghastly gurgling sound and knew it was coming from herself. She was going to die, here in this room.

With piercing suddenness Harry began to cry and the hands at her throat were loosened as Bert lifted himself off her. She slid off the bed to the floor, her legs refusing to support her.

Bert was watching her, his face a mask of bewilderment, his hands to his head. 'Over the top,' he whispered, staring at Adela, wild-eyed and uncomprehending.

Her terror was replaced by an immense pity. She understood now why Esther stayed with him and refused to complain about the beatings he gave her. But he was dangerous and she remained absolutely still, not knowing if this was a temporary lull in the tortured man's attack on her. She watched in horror as he staggered across the room and went behind the screen. She heard the rustle of bedclothes, then Bert reappeared carrying the baby. Her baby. Her son. A protective instinct far more powerful than fear shot through her, giving her instant strength and forgetfulness of her own safety.

She got to her feet and walked to Bert. Fighting for calm, she held out her arms. Somehow she managed to smile and sound normal. 'Give him to me,' she said.

'Is he yours?'

'He's mine.'

'Why won't he stop yellin'?'

'I dare say he's hungry. He needs feeding.'

Bert handed over Harry and Adela clutched him to her in relief. 'I have to fetch a clean nappy for him,' she said, and walked steadily from the room and down the stairs. Once there she ran across the road where as usual she could hear the strident voice of her opposite neighbour.

She banged on the door. When it was opened a wave of fumes compounded of cabbage, cats and washing poured out. Mrs Hobbs' hair was pinned up in a skimpy knot. Her sacking apron was stained. Somewhere in the house children were quarrelling and someone was banging a tin drum.

Mrs Hobbs folded her arms beneath her apron. 'What do you want?' she asked belligerently.

'I'm sorry,' said Adela inadequately. Now the crisis was past

193

she felt ill. The long unhealthy hours bent over her sewing coupled with recent fear took a toll and she began to tremble violently.

Mrs Hobbs' shriek could have been heard in Old Market. 'Frank, Mabel, come here quick!'

Two of the older members of her brood arrived at the door. Mabel was halfway through applying heavy make-up; Frank was wearing an outfit of white tie inexpertly tied and a shabby tail coat with shiny lapels which had certainly come from a second-hand shop.

'Take the babby,' ordered Mrs Hobbs of Mabel, 'an' you help me in with Mrs Danby, our Frank.'

Mabel took Harry who, amazingly, stopped crying to stare up into her multi-coloured features. She held him slightly away from her. 'Ugh! He's wet, our Mam.'

'Wet!' mocked Mrs Hobbs. 'Anyone would think you didn't know nothin' about babies.'

'Fat chance,' retorted Mabel. 'Too many bloody kids round here not to know.'

Adela clung to the door post, wondering if she was about to be embroiled in a family argument until her shaky legs toppled her over.

'Better get her inside,' said Frank.

'You'm right there.' Mrs Hobbs put a hand which felt like a ham bone under Adela's arm, Frank held her on the other side, and together they guided her into the kitchen of the two-up, two-down house.

'Mam,' screamed Mabel, 'we'll be late for the display.'

'Then they'll just have to start without you,' said Mrs Hobbs.

'How can they do that when we're the bloody star turn?'

Mabel's piercing voice set Harry crying again and Mrs Hobbs took him impatiently out of her daughter's arms and handed him to a girl of about twelve who received him without a word, held him over her shoulder, and began to jiggle him and sing to him until his cries died away.

'That's the ticket,' said Mrs Hobbs. 'Our Mattie's good with kids, aren't you, girl?'

Mabel had disappeared through the door, followed by Frank, and Adela heard the clatter of their feet on the uncarpeted stairway.

'You'll have to excuse our Mabel,' said her mother. 'She an' Frank are partners. They d'give ballroom dancin' displays, old and modern dancin'. You should see them doin' jazz dancin'. It's a bloody marvel. They d'want to go on the stage, see?' Another child peered round the door and, scarcely taking breath, Mrs Hobbs bawled, 'Edith, fetch the teapot over here an' the sugar. What happened, my love?' She shot the question at Adela.

She had been given time to think. If she told the truth something awful might happen to Bert. He could even end up in prison and that would break Esther's heart.

'A man was trying to sell me something and pushed his way in. I got frightened.'

Mrs Hobbs took the enormous teapot from Edith, who couldn't have been more than nine, and began to pour the thick, dark brew into a chipped enamel mug. 'Ah, you don't belong in these parts. You don't understand the folks. I don't suppose he meant any harm. Probably some poor bugger out of the army – they can't find jobs, y'know – a land fit for heroes! Some bloody promise that was! He was probably desperate. Government don't care if folks like us d'live or die. Buggers!'

'That's not what our dad says,' interrupted Edith.

Mrs Hobbs' heavy hand swept out automatically and just as automatically Edith ducked. She stood out of reach. 'Our dad says the government d'want folks like us to live an' have lots of kids so there'll be factory fodder an' servants an' cannon fodder for the next war.'

'Well, he's doin' his best to keep up the supply of kids.' Mrs Hobbs' laugh was like a train hooter and Adela jumped.

She began to feel she was taking part in a farce. She had descended from fear into a situation she could never have envisaged. She took the enamel mug Mrs Hobbs handed her, after putting in three spoonsful of sugar, and sipped. The tea was acrid. It had probably been made hours if not days before and simply boiled up, and it was far too sweet, but as it went down it helped.

Edith was staring at her with large blue eyes. Beneath her grime she was pretty. 'You d'know the man who frightened you,' she stated.

'Well, of all the bloody sauce!' Mrs Hobbs lifted a long toasting fork from beside the fire and jabbed at Edith who dodged. 'Don't you go doubtin' Mrs Danby's words.'

'It was Bert Rawbone. Mrs Danby d'know Bert Rawbone. She was at his weddin'.'

Mrs Hobbs turned an enquiring glance on Adela who capitulated. She couldn't tell Mrs Hobbs that Edith was lying. 'Yes, it was Bert. I didn't want to get him into trouble.'

'That's real kind of you. Have more tea. Edith, fill Mrs Danby's mug.' Adela tried to refuse, but Edith picked up the pot and poured another stream of the strong liquid and spooned sugar into it. 'We ain't got no milk,' she said. 'Mam couldn't pay the milkman,' she added matter-of-factly.

Adela was embarrassed for her hostess, but Mrs Hobbs took no notice. 'I d'run out of money before pay day no matter how hard I d'try. The older kids d'bring in some now, but the food d'go so fast. Kids d'need a lot o' food.'

A cat jumped on to Adela's lap. She looked down at it and saw fleas crawling in its silky fur. She tried to put it down, but it dug its claws in.

'Poor bloody cat won't get no milk till payday. So it was Bert, was it? What did he do?'

Adela involuntarily put up her hand to her aching throat.

'Don't say he tried to throttle you? God, he's really gone off his chump! What's he got against you?'

'Nothing,' said Adela wearily, 'but he imagines he has.'

'Poor soul,' said Mrs Hobbs. Adela didn't know if her regret was for Bert or her visitor. 'Drink up the tea. Liquid'll do your throat good.' She had taken the news of an attempted strangulation as if it was an everyday occurrence. Perhaps it was in her world. Adela suddenly wanted to laugh.

She sat on in the Hobbs' house, while their family life surged about her, watching in amazement and admiration as Mrs Hobbs dealt with each minor crisis. The young dancers were sent off with wishes of good luck, and a couple of lads with brilliantined hair and three of their sisters in party finery left on their way to Christmas dances. Until today Mrs Hobbs had been no more than a strident voice, but as Adela watched her and heard her yells she understood. She was like a gallant sergeant major marshalling his forces and bringing order to their chaos.

Adela wondered where Bert was. She should go home, but she felt so lethargic. Mrs Hobbs worked round her, apparently unperturbed by her unexpected guest.

Edith and another young sister brought newspapers and laid them on the greasy table. Enamel mugs followed and dinner plates of different patterns and sizes and a few knives, forks and spoons.

'You'll stay an' have a bite with us,' said Mrs Hobbs. 'I've got a suet puddin' boilin' on the hob. It's got more vegetables in it than meat, but you'm welcome. Mattie'll nurse the baby 'til you'm ready.'

Adela finally moved. 'It's most awfully kind of you and I do appreciate your invitation, but I had better go home.'

'If you like,' said Mrs Hobbs amiably.

Edith said under her breath, ' "It's most awfully kind of you ..." Well, kiss my arse!' And she and her sisters burst into giggles.

'Shut your mouths,' yelled Mrs Hobbs. 'Behavin' that way to a lady.'

The door opened and Mr Hobbs walked in. He wore a torn tweed coat, a cap whose original colour was hidden by grease and grime, trousers tied under the knee with string and a pair of down-at-heel, very dusty boots.

'My hubby,' said Mrs Hobbs. 'He d'work on the roads. Digs holes in them. This here's Mrs Danby, Dad. She did have a spot of bother and come to me.'

Mr Hobbs removed his coat and cap and hung them on a peg behind the door. 'Nice to meet you,' he said. 'Couldn't have come to a better place. My ole woman's just the ticket when there's somethin' needin' seein' to. Give us a cup of tea, our Edith.'

Adela left the Hobbses reluctantly. Whatever else they

197

lacked in their home they had plenty of affection. She walked cautiously up the stairs to her room which, to her relief, was empty. She locked the door behind her. The fire had died down and she kissed the mercifully sleeping Harry and tucked him into his cot, put on some coal and resumed work, but her mind kept veering away to the memory of Bert's threats and his horrible attack. It could happen again. When there was a loud knock on her door, she hung back for a moment before calling, 'Who's there?'

'It's Jack. Can I come in?'

'Jack!' She hurried to unlock the door. Her relief was so immense that her self-control was shattered and she began to weep.

'What did he do to you?' rasped Jack.

'He tried to strangle me. Harry cried and that seemed to bring him to his senses and he let go of my neck. I never thought I'd be glad to hear my baby bawling. But how do you know about it?'

'I met one of the Hobbs kids. Adela, this can't go on. He's terrorisin' you.'

'What can I do about it? He hates me and I've done nothing to him.'

Jack sat on the bed. 'I've heard him ravin' on in the pub. He hates the government, an' everyone who had anything to do with sendin' men to fight.'

'But I had no part in that!'

'For him, you represent the ruling classes. You're the only one he can get at.'

'That's not fair.'

'Of course it isn't. And it wasn't fair to drive him crazy. Nor the other blokes who're sufferin' the same as him.'

'Surely the authorities realise what's happened? Can't they help these poor men? There are hospitals.'

'Asylums, you mean. Places to shut them up behind locked doors and barred windows.'

There was silence in the room, broken only by the slight hiss of the gaslight and a falling coal.

Jack said, 'Adela, you can't stay here alone. It isn't safe.'

She flopped into a chair. 'I'm sick and fed up with everything and everybody. All I want to do is get on with my work and keep Harry and me decently. Oh, Jack, I don't know which way to turn.'

He sighed. 'Poor kid. Poor little kid.'

'Harry, or me?'

'Both of you.'

She said slowly, 'If I wasn't so busy I could get to know Harry properly, and maybe he wouldn't be so miserable.'

'Maybe you could, but perhaps it's just his nature to grizzle a lot. It's a pity you couldn't ask Ralph's mother about his babyhood. Don't worry, he's sure to improve. Now sit down and listen to me, and don't argue. I've got a whole house to myself. Four whole rooms. You an' Harry *must* come an' live there. You can call yourself what you like, lodger or housekeeper, though of course I won't expect you to work for me.'

Adela pulled away from him and walked over to the window. Opposite, beneath the street lamp, she saw Bert watching her. Terrified she said, 'I'll come. I'll move now, tonight.'

'That's the ticket. I'll fetch the barrow and we'll load it with your stuff. The Fudges are back. I'll have a word with them.'

When Jack had left Mrs Fudge came bustling up, her bosom heaving beneath her best dress, a paste brooch which was pinned there tossing up and down like a boat on stormy water.

'Fancy Bert Rawbone goin' off his rocker like that! You could have been killed. Here, I've brought some string. Let me help tie up that bundle. I'll miss you and little Harry, but I think Jack's right. You'll be safer with him, an' his family's just next door so you'll have someone to watch out for you. Jack's sister Ida's a real nice woman.'

Watched by a glowering Bert, the Fudges helped Adela and Jack pile her possessions on to the barrow. There weren't many. Jack covered them with a tarpaulin, tied a cardboard box on top with Tibs inside, protesting, and grasped the two handles. The Fudges said goodbye, Mrs Fudge kissed Harry, and they began to trundle through the streets towards St Philips.

'I've never even seen your house,' said Adela.

'No more you have, my dear.'

Jack was breathing hard and Adela asked if she could help with the barrow. He laughed. 'It's not so heavy, and it isn't women's work.'

'Have you always done it?'

'Served off a barrow, d'you mean? Not always. I used to work at Fry's Chocolate. Dad owned the barrow and Mum helped him with the buyin' an' sellin'. Then Dad died an' Mum insisted on carryin' on and I couldn't leave her on her own so I left my job an' took over. Now Mum's rheumatics are too bad for her to work. When I came back from France I was glad I had an independent business, else I would have been out of a job like so many of the other poor sods.'

'An independent business.' How Father would laugh if he had heard Jack! Adela looked at him. His thin, lined face was damp with perspiration, his breath rasped and he coughed violently. She thought he was the finest man she had ever met.

They crossed Newfoundland Road and Old Market Street after which the streets grew narrower. They stopped outside a small house which looked exactly like twenty others in the row. 'Mine's the end one,' said Jack. 'Mum lives next door.'

Adela had forgotten Mrs Webster. Now she suddenly recalled Mrs Fudge's remarks about her.

She said, 'Does anyone know I'm coming? Your mother, for instance?'

Jack laughed. 'No fear! Do it first and tell Mum after is my policy. She can be a bit of a dragon, but you'll like her well enough when you get to know her.'

'But will she like me?'

'How could she fail?' said Jack, grinning.

He stopped and let the barrow rest on its supports, giving a sigh of relief. He opened the front door and ushered Adela in. There was a small lobby from which led steep stairs. Through the door on her left was the living room and she entered and stood with Harry in her arms, staring about her. It was dark and cold and even when Jack turned up the gas it was gloomy. There was a fireplace with paper, sticks and coal already laid, a sideboard, two easy chairs and a draw-leaf table and four chairs. In the front window there was a pot plant standing on a small table which was covered by a white lace cloth.

Jack said, 'It's not what you're used to, but it's clean. The girls see to that. An' they always have a dinner ready for me at night. One of them will be round later.'

'That's kind of them.'

She moved into the kitchen, the only other room on the ground floor. It contained a gas-stove, a low stone sink, a cupboard, a copper and a scrubbed deal table. The floor was stone. A few shelves held saucepans, a frying pan and some crockery. She pulled out a drawer in the table to reveal some cutlery and a tablecloth. She stared at the gas stove. At Mrs Fudge's she had managed to produce meals on the fire in her room, but often she had made do with bread and cheese or a tin of sardines.

Jack was unloading the barrow. He called, 'Have a look upstairs.'

She climbed the narrow stairway with Harry in her arms. The front bedroom was occupied by Jack. It was as sparsely furnished as the rooms downstairs, but the bed was made and the lino had been recently polished by, she supposed, 'the girls'. Along the landing was a slightly larger bedroom containing another double bed, a chest of drawers and a wardrobe. All the rooms were dark and dank and everything was cheap and shabby. Adela sat down on the bare mattress, hating it all.

Jack called and she went downstairs. 'Where would you like the sewing machine?' he asked. He looked happy which made her feel mean.

'Where will be convenient for you?'

'Anywhere. I'll fit round you.'

'Put it on the dresser for now. Perhaps we could get a small table for it.'

'What's wrong with the one we've got.' Jack moved the plant and stood it on the floor and put the machine in its place, rucking up the table cover. 'You'll be all right on your own for a bit, won't you?'

Adela was alarmed. 'Why? Where are you going?'

'I have to load the barrow again and get back to the market. With Christmas so close I can't afford to lose tonight's trade.'

'You left your work for me? Jack, I'm grateful to you.'

'No need to be. You'll find bedding stuff in the wardrobe in your room. I've carried up the cot. Help yourself to food. I'll see you later.

'Oh, by the way, there's a present for Harry in the garden shed. I was waitin' for Christmas, but you need it now. There's a Tilley lamp by the kitchen door if you want the privy. I'll tell Mum you're here.' Then he was gone.

Adela grasped the lamp gingerly and turned the large iron key in the kitchen door which led into the garden. It was narrow and there were still a few straggly cabbages and some brussels sprouts struggling for life in the chilly, sooty air. She pushed open the ramshackle shed door and stared. Jack had bought a pram. It was second-hand, but it had been cleaned and polished and she felt a wave of gratitude. Harry was getting heavy. She wheeled the pram into the kitchen and put two cushions into it. She sat Harry on them before she ran upstairs. She found a pillow and a small fluffy blanket and soon Harry was propped up in his pram, secured by the safety straps, and looking pleased with himself as he watched his mother light the fire. The contents of the kitchen cupboard were few, but she was used to that now. No one in these parts had money for extra stores or anywhere to keep them safe from rodents. She cut a couple of slices from a piece of bacon and took an egg. Carefully she lit the gas stove which popped alarmingly and put lard into the frying pan. When she added the bacon the lard spat and tiny prickles of pain dotted her arms. She turned the gas down. When she had finished the bacon was hard, the egg broken, but it was a meal and she was pleased with herself as she cleaned her plate with a slice of bread. No one would ever guess that she had never used a gas stove before. She cleared up and fed Harry, then went upstairs and prepared their bedroom. She heard the front door open.

'Is that you, Jack?'

A woman's voice said, 'No, it isn't Jack, an' what do you think you're doin' in my son's house?'

Chapter Twelve

Mrs Webster! Adela started nervously. After what she had heard, she had hoped to meet Jack's mother when he was there to give his support. She walked down the stairs, slowly enough to preserve her dignity but not so slowly as to annoy the older woman. She found not one but two women waiting for her. They were the same height, but one was almost hidden by the bulk of the other whom Adela took to be Mrs Webster. A first glance took in the stoutness of her figure, clearly well-corsetted, her large bosom firmly supported, her heavy stomach sternly controlled. She had a face which, in spite of its fleshy contours and a heavy frown, was still comely, and hair that was improbably black. The two women were standing in the tiny lobby, staring up at her.

They filled it and Adela was forced to stay on the stairs. She held out her hand. 'Mrs Webster? I've heard about you from Jack. I'm Adela Danby. Jack has kindly offered me lodgings with him.'

'Yes, I know.' Momentarily taken aback by Adela's cool reserve, Mrs Webster moved out of the way and, followed by the other woman, walked into the living room. Her sharp dark eyes darted around.

'You've moved the aspidistra!' she snapped.

'Yes. I'm sorry if you don't approve,' said Adela, 'but I needed somewhere for my sewing machine. I'm sure Jack will find another small table for the plant.'

'I bought him that! An' where's the lace cloth? His aunty crocheted it specially for him.'

'It was getting creased so I put it in the kitchen drawer.'

'Go an' fetch it, our Ida,' ordered Mrs Webster.

Adela felt a flash of annoyance which she quelled. If she began on bad terms with Mrs Webster it would rebound upon Jack as well as herself. There was a sound from upstairs.

'That your baby?' demanded Mrs Webster. 'I'm told he cries a lot.'

'Won't you sit down?' asked Adela, clinging to the rags of her temper.

Mrs Webster stared. 'I've never needed to be asked to sit down in my own son's house before.'

Adela said nothing and, after looking her up and down for a moment, Mrs Webster sat in an easy chair, stretched out her legs and put her feet on the fender. 'Not much of a fire.'

'I try to conserve fuel as much as possible.'

'We all do. We all know there's been a war.'

'Here's the cloth, Mum.' Ida came back.

'Give it here.' Mrs Webster examined the square of lace.

'I haven't damaged it,' said Adela.

'Who said you had? It needs a wash. Here, Ida, take hold of it. You can wash it tomorrow.'

'I intend to wash it as soon as I get settled,' said Adela, holding out her hand to Ida who looked nervously from one woman to the other.

'Ida will wash it,' said Mrs Webster, snapping her lips shut as if that was the end of the matter.

Adela suddenly felt stubbornly angry. 'Give it to me, Ida,' she said with deceptive calm, 'I am perfectly capable of washing the cloth. After all, I must wash every day because of my son.'

With trembling hands, Ida clutched the cloth to her sparse bosom. 'Mother, it would be more convenient for Mrs Danby to wash it. Tomorrow is when I do all the polishin'.'

'You'll have plenty of time to do some washin' as well. I want my ecru petticoat done. You can use the same water.'

Adela surrendered. She wished she hadn't argued and said to Ida, 'I'll leave it to you, then. Won't you sit down, too? I'll make us some tea.'

'No, she won't. She still has the washin' up to do. An' there's peas to put in soak for tomorrow.' Mrs Webster heaved her bulk out of the chair, groaning. 'I suffer with bad rheumatics. I can do without all these shocks.'

'Shocks, Mrs Webster?'

'Like our Jack bringin' a woman to live with him.'

'I'm not living with him!' protested Adela angrily.

'What do you call it then?'

'I'm a lodger.'

'That's what I meant,' snapped Mrs Webster. 'What did you think?'

She walked heavily to the door and Ida scuttled after her. 'Don't trouble yourself,' Mrs Webster called to Adela. 'We can find our own way out, thank you very much.'

As they left she was sure she caught a reference to dirty minds and dirty thoughts. She paced up and down, seething with rage. What a ghastly woman! She wished she hadn't come here. She couldn't live next door to that bullying old monster who had clearly loathed her on sight. Tomorrow she would ask Mrs Fudge if she could have her room back. She would have a strong lock fitted to her door and never open it unless she knew who was outside. But when she saw Mrs Fudge she discovered that the room had already been let to a young couple.

'Just out of the army, he is, and the two of them as pleased as punch to get away from livin' with his mother.'

Jack had laughed when Adela told him about her first meeting with his mother. 'She's a stubborn old cuss, but she's had to be to bring up four girls an' me an' help Dad with his work. You won't see much of my other sisters. They've got their own families to look after. Oh, but I nearly forgot, you will meet them quite soon. Christmas is comin' an' they'll all be visitin'. My girls an' their families will be there, too.'

'*All* in that tiny house!'

'Yes, why not? Christmas is a time to get together. The more we're squashed up the better the fun.' Again, Adela thought of Christmas in Speede House, of the leisurely breakfast, the long peaceful day, guests for dinner at night. Dinner here was at mid-day.

Jack brought home a small tree from the market and Adela

decorated it from a box of baubles he had stored in the shed. Harry clapped his hands at the sight.

'You'll enjoy Christmas with my family,' he said.

'I promised the Fudges I'd go to them.'

'They'll understand. I'll nip round now and tell them.'

Adela wanted to protest, but he had gone. She felt hemmed in, captured by his kindness, imprisoned by the animosity of the old woman next door. But, to her surprise, Christmas Day was enjoyable. There were so many people crammed into the small house that Adela never managed to count them. Children shrieked, blew whistles and banged tin drums; the grown-ups chattered and gossiped. One of Jack's sisters had brought a massive turkey, still hot, from her oven; another supplied a pudding, and yet another dozens of mince pies. Florrie and Annie contributed chocolates, the men brought beer and wine. No one came empty-handed.

Toasts were drunk.

Adela was asked to propose one. She lifted her glass: 'To Lady Astor, the first woman to take her seat in Parliament.'

After a moment of surprise there were cheers, mostly derisive from the men. 'May there soon be others,' said Jack, and the derisive cheers grew louder.

At dinner he stood up and proposed a toast. 'To absent friends and loved ones.' Everyone drank and Annie said, 'I wonder how our Michael is?'

'He's never sent a Christmas card since the day he left,' said Mrs Webster, 'not even to me after I helped bring him up.'

Jack said quietly, 'He'll be in touch when he's ready. He told me he was goin' to see the world an' make somethin' of himself, and he wouldn't write until he could give us good news. There's no call to criticise him for keepin' his word.'

'Bristol wasn't good enough for him,' sniffed Mrs Webster.

'Now, Mum, you know that's not right,' said Jack. 'I hope he's found what he went lookin' for.'

'How long is it since you heard?' an uncle asked.

'Not since before the war.'

A young boy's mother poked him with a stiff finger. 'Don't you go gettin' no funny ideas about leavin' home. You'll go into Wills' Tobacco like your father.'

The boy rubbed his sore rib. 'No need to poke so hard, Mum. I can't wait to leave school an' start work.'

'Michael must be twenty-three by now,' mused Mrs Webster. 'Old enough to know his father might worry, not to mention the rest of his family. After I helped bring him up, too,' she repeated stubbornly.

Jack began to look annoyed and Annie said soothingly, 'You've always been good to us, Gran.'

'That's true,' said Jack, giving Annie a grateful look and calming down. 'When my Jessie was ill, I knew I could count on you, Mum.'

'You still did until recently, son.' Mrs Webster's eyes slid towards Adela.

Annie jumped to her feet. 'Let's get this lot cleared away and play some games. Our Michael's sure to be all right. He's clever.'

After tea, Henry, Annie's husband, produced a mouth organ and her son a battered banjo, while Jack handed out nasal-sounding kazoos to the children. The adults joined in a sing-song and all the old favourites were laughed and sighed over. Then another son-in-law, Reg, stood up and began to sing in a fine baritone voice, deliberately exaggerating his gestures in Mrs Webster's direction as he sang: *Speak, speak, speak to me, Thora*— Mrs Webster's eyes swam with tears, partly of mirth at Reg's antics, partly at the sad fate of her namesake, Thora. She had sat through the day like an ancient Buddha, smiling, sometimes frowning if one of the children got out of hand, eating and drinking liberally of the special fare.

Harry was amazed and delighted by the children who held him, played with him and sang to him, and he didn't cry once. Everyone appeared to accept Adela, though she caught one or two exchanges of glances that made her wonder if the spirit of goodwill towards her would last.

At the end of the day, after she had put her son in his cot, Adela went downstairs.

Jack had cups of tea waiting. 'Well, Christmas with the Websters wasn't so bad, was it?'

'You should have told me there would be so many young children. I didn't have presents for them.'

'And they had none for you. It doesn't matter. Nobody minded.'

'Why are your sisters' children so young? There couldn't have been one over fourteen, yet your daughters are grown up with families of their own.'

Jack laughed. 'It is a bit muddlin' when there're aunties an' uncles younger than nieces an' nephews. I was the first born, and after me came Ida. Then Mum had several stillbirths. After that she didn't conceive for years, and when she did begin again she had my other sisters within about five years.'

'Your family looked me over as if I was a prize pig.'

Jack laughed. 'Nonsense! Of course they were interested in you, that's natural.'

'I suppose they all believe we're living in sin?'

Again Jack laughed. 'I've told them the truth, but I can't control their minds. Does it matter?'

Adela leaned back and sipped her tea. Jack was right. What did it matter what anyone thought?

'Mother loved the silk scarf you gave her.'

'Good,' said Adela. She'd had to stifle her guilt at transferring the gift of the scarf from Mrs Fudge to Mrs Webster. She had given the cigarettes and tobacco as her contribution to the party.

Jack reached down and picked up his bottle of whisky. 'An' I love this!' He opened it and poured a generous measure into his tea. 'This is better for my chest than all your doctor's medicines.' He stuck a cigarette between his lips and lit it. The first drag, as usual, made him cough.

'You shouldn't smoke. You cough too much and smoking makes it worse.'

'I've cut down, but a man can surely have a fag now an' then, an' there's nothing can be done about my cough. I'm a damn' sight more lucky than some of the men. Mustard gas is a killer, an' trench lung's never goin' to get better.'

Adela shuddered. 'Everything I hear about the war sounds terrible.'

Jack lay back in his chair and smoked for a few minutes. Adela watched the play of expressions across his face. 'It was worse than terrible. So much killin', an' for what? For a few yards of mud. Now the bloody politicians are playin' the same old games, apportionin' land that belongs to someone else, layin' up trouble for the future.'

'There can never be another war, can there? That's what everyone says.'

'We're still fightin' the Irish and there are British troops in Russia fightin' against the Bolsheviks.'

'I didn't think of that.'

'No, most people prefer to shut their eyes to it. An' there's the savage blockade of Germany.'

'But the Armistice—'

'There's goin' to be no let up until the terms are fulfilled and every last bit of paper is signed.'

'They started the war,' protested Adela.

'There's such a thing as mercy.'

'You and Sander Bennett seem to feel the same way.'

'I know. We discuss these things.'

'He brought them up at a party in my home,' mused Adela.

Jack grinned. 'An' what did the other guests say?'

'They were very annoyed.'

'I don't suppose that bothered him at all.'

Adela thought for a moment. 'I don't think so. I don't really know. He's a strange man. On the one hand he argues for the socialists; on the other he's anxious to get into top society. Even to the extent of being prepared to marry a woman he didn't love and who was—' Adela stopped. She had inadvertently revealed her bitter thoughts in words.

'He was usin' you? Is that why you refused to marry him?' asked Jack gently.

'Yes. I'm not something to be traded.'

'Good for you,' said Jack.

She turned to him, eyes shining with gratitude. 'You understand, don't you. No one else did.'

After Christmas Adela made tremendous efforts to settle in her new home. Jack hadn't wanted rent from her, but she insisted and in the end prevailed.

'All right,' he said, 'pay me what you paid Mrs Fudge.'

'I had only one room there.'

'You can cook me a nice dinner instead of payin' more money.'

Adela had looked doubtful. 'I don't seem to be much good at cooking.'

Jack laughed. 'You can go on practisin' on me. Earn your keep if that's what's worryin' you. Dust the furniture.'

Adela soon realised that in this district Jack's house was considered quite 'posh' when others lived three and four or more families to a house, with an outside privy shared by dozens and a cold water tap in the communal yard.

Esther came round to see her. 'It's because of Bert you've moved, isn't it, Adela?' she said.

She side-stepped the question. 'I'm better off here. Harry and I share a bedroom and I can work downstairs. Jack's bought me a big folding table to use to cut out clothes. It saves kneeling on the floor, and it's a plain wooden one so I can iron on it.'

'Jack's a good man.' Esther sounded wistful.

Adela was ashamed of her own evasiveness. 'How is Bert?' she forced herself to ask.

Esther said nothing for a moment. 'Worse,' she admitted finally. 'Often now he doesn't know where he is. Most of the time he thinks he's back at the front, either about to charge the enemy, or sitting in a filthy, freezing dugout trying to rest between battles. Sometimes I feel that if he says "over the top" once more I'll scream.'

'I'm so sorry, Esther.'

'I can't bear to think of what might have happened when he attacked you, Adela.'

She laid down her sewing, went to Esther and put her arms round her. 'He wasn't himself,' she said. 'Like you said, he thought he was back in the trenches. He mistook me for a Boche.' She managed a shaky laugh.

Esther clutched her. 'You're a good 'un, Adela, but what if he attacks someone else? A man perhaps who'll lay about him, or, worse, another woman who won't be as lucky as you were. He'd be a murderer. My Bert was so gentle. I can't let him become a murderer.'

Adela knelt beside her friend. 'What can you do about it?'

'I'm not sure, but something. Something.' Esther pushed back her hair and drew a deep breath, looking about her. 'Did you make the curtains?'

'Yes, do you like them?'

'They're beautiful. Lovely colours. All that yellow and orange makes the room really bright. And you've done cushion covers to match.'

'Yellow and orange?' Adela smiled. 'That makes them sound garish. To me the colours are buttercup, saffron and ochre; marigold, coral and russet.'

'Heavens, that's almost like poetry.'

'Colours *are* poetry to me. They have their own meanings, too. Some yellows are for joy, for the life-giving sun.'

'Are they? What about orange?'

'Oh, there are many different associations. Fruit, for instance, juicy and sweet, which is where the name came from originally. Oranges grow in warmth and sun. It isn't a primary colour so it contains a mixture of red and yellow.'

'I've never thought of colours in that way.'

'I always have, right from a child.'

'Do you like making clothes?'

'Not really, but how many people in these parts can afford to buy enough household furnishings to keep Harry and me? I've run up a bedspread for Jack and I'm going to make matching curtains. I shall tackle the rest of the house as I go along. By the time I've finished, it'll look like a garden.' She smiled faintly.

'You've been working so hard.'

'I had to. I couldn't bear such gloomy surroundings. Jack brings me the stuff and I stay up late to do the extra sewing. I really love making beautiful things that enhance a home. It seems the most worthwhile job in the world. Esther, there are people who earn a living doing just that. One day, I'll join them. I'll be an interior decorator, and the best of them all.'

Esther smiled. 'Nothing like having ambition! I hope you succeed. You deserve to. What does dear Mum next door think?'

'She snorts and grumbles and says that the house was fine

211

before and I've made it look cheap and common. Ida hardly ever speaks. I've never met such a poor down-trodden creature.'

'Mum says she was pretty in her youth and there were boys who wanted to walk out with her, but her mother kept her as a servant. When she was young Ida didn't have enough spirit to defy her, then her father died and she didn't have the heart. How do you get on with Jack's daughters?'

Adela sighed. 'They come round every day. They're like a pair of dreadful unmatched twins, poking and prying and dusting corners where I've already dusted and insisting on scrubbing the kitchen table.'

'Why don't you complain to Jack?'

'I did at first, but he couldn't understand why I should mind because he knows I dislike housework, so I try to be polite and let them get on with it. Actually, Annie is a bit nicer than Florrie. She's interested in my sewing and asked me to run up a pair of curtains for her. She says she'll pay proper rates. That left Florrie speechless. It's Mrs Webster who's the biggest problem. She's got a tongue like a viper. You should have heard her remarks when she found out I was making soup with a Gong's Soup Tablet!'

Esther laughed. 'Mum says Jack's wife couldn't get on with her easily.' She stood up. 'I must get home. They'll be wondering where I am. Dad and Mum have been so good to us, keeping us on when Bert's so difficult to live with. I'm lucky. I can't understand why your—' She stopped, reddening.

Adela said calmly, 'My family couldn't begin to cope with the kind of trouble that folk round here take in their stride. They could learn a lot from the poor.'

Esther gave her a quick kiss. 'You're a real good 'un, Adela. A real good 'un.'

Harry had decided that he disliked his teddy bear. Jack removed the growl and Adela sewed the toy together again, but still the baby flinched whenever he saw it.

'He's a mystery to me, Jack,' said Adela. 'I'll never understand him.'

'You can love people without understandin' them,' Jack pointed out.

'It's lucky you can, or we'd be in a fine state. His constant crying depresses me terribly.'

For once Jack failed to gauge the depth of her mood. Adela doubted if anyone could. Outwardly she was placid and calm as she went about her work, sewing, keeping the house tidy, biting her tongue when Jack's relatives intruded, looking after him and Harry as best she could; inwardly she was a seething storm of discontent. She now realised that Mrs Fudge had lived in a district which, compared with this one, was superior. In spite of the post-war economic boom and the fact that many wages were rising with the soaring prices, here there was still real, gruelling, bitter poverty among the families of unskilled men who couldn't find jobs, or widows with children. Here there were children who didn't know when they would get their next meal; who ran about the streets in shoes with flapping soles, or none at all; who, in desperation, took to petty pilfering only to bring the law down heavily on themselves and be despatched to a reformatory school or a Borstal institution for harsh corrective training.

'Why doesn't the government do something?' Adela demanded of Jack.

He was eating his meal at the time. He forked up a potato and examined it. 'You should completely cover potatoes with water before you boil them, my dear. That stops them goin' brown.'

'I will,' said Adela impatiently. She cooked with little interest and not much skill, and Mrs Webster and Jack's daughters were scathing. 'I asked you why the government doesn't help the people round here? They live like pigs.'

Jack looked up sharply. 'Not pigs!' He waved his fork at her. 'Like human beings who've been ground into the mud for most of their lives. Lots of them fought in the war. At the moment the ex-soldiers get non-contributory pensions. Such bloody generosity after they went through hell in France! Do you know that after some of them have paid their rent an' bought fuel and soap an' suchlike, their wives have only got twopence or threepence a day per head to feed their families? The high

213

rents are a sin. In some cases they represent a third of their income.'

'I didn't know,' said Adela. She wished she hadn't raised the subject. She couldn't do anything about it and it made her even more miserable, but trying to stop Jack in mid-flow would be futile. He was eating his meal at ten o'clock; she had eaten much earlier, and now picked up her sewing, pushing her needle in and out of the hem of a boring navy serge skirt. Now that the first rush of post-war marriages and demands for pretty wedding dresses had lessened, she took on any work she could get.

Jack paused from eating again. 'One good thing – the trade unions are gettin' stronger all the time. When we get all workin' men to join, we'll have the bloody bosses where we want them.'

'What about working women?' asked Adela, snipping off a thread.

Jack stared crossly at her. 'You're not takin' me seriously.'

'Yes, I am, but you used to profess to be in favour of women's independence and I haven't heard you saying much about it lately.'

Jack grinned. He could never be angry with Adela for more than a minute. 'No more I have. Women are joinin' unions, too, but I suppose my thoughts are mostly with the poor sods who have to keep goin' home to their wives without enough money to keep the family in food, leave alone clothes. An' there's the practice of makin' them sign on every day or holdin' back their dole. It's wicked, that's what it is. Wicked an' degradin'.'

He fell silent, brooding, and Adela continued to sew. At night, sitting in the warm room which she had made cheerful, she felt almost content; but tomorrow, when Jack had taken his barrow out and she was left with the usual heap of work, her fractious son and the derogatory remarks passed by Mrs Webster, she knew that her spirits would sink. Harry let out a piercing yell that jerked Jack's head up.

'God, what's that for?'

'I don't know,' said Adela wearily. 'Teeth, I suppose.'

Harry was bawling loudly by the time she went up to him. If

Jack had been out there would have been a loud banging on the party wall between her and Mrs Webster, but the old woman wouldn't irritate her son. Or, more likely, thought Adela grimly, she wouldn't let her son know about her persecution of his lodger. She lifted Harry, changed him and rubbed his gums where more teeth were pushing through. He continued to yell until her nerves jumped and she wanted to yell along with him.

She went downstairs. 'I'll wash the dishes and go to bed,' she said. 'If I rock his cradle he might settle down.'

Jack watched her as she piled dishes on to a tray. 'You're reasonably content, aren't you, my dear?' he said. 'Apart from having to cope with Harry's crying and too much work?' he added ruefully.

'Of course. Why should I be otherwise?' Adela knew her voice was bleak. She was so damned tired. She was always tired. Harry suddenly stopped crying and she felt weak with relief.

Jack got up and took the tray from her and carried it into the kitchen. When he returned he said, 'Leave it for the morning, for once.'

'My God, if your mother finds out I went to bed without washing up she'll blacken my name from here to Bath!'

Jack delved into the sacking bag which he used for everything, from his sandwiches to his takings on the stall, and drew out a bottle.

'Sherry, for you, my girl. It's good stuff. You're to drink a glass in the morning and one at night. It'll soothe you and help with the backache.'

'How do you know my back still hurts?'

'It does, doesn't it?'

'Yes. Your mother says that hers never stops hurting. She says it's something women have to put up with. She thinks I'm a weakling.'

'Then she's wrong.' Jack poured a generous glass of wine. 'Drink,' he ordered.

'Not unless you take some with me.'

Jack grinned and reached down for his whisky. 'I'd rather have this. The best Christmas present I've ever been given.'

'Surely not!'

'It beats socks and shirts into a cocked hat.'

They drank companionably together and Jack said, 'Try to forget the past and look forward to the future. Good times will come, you'll see. When the Labour Party get in—'

'Oh, damn the Labour Party! Can't we get through a conversation without you referring to socialism?'

Jack grinned again. 'Try not to shout that, my girl, or we'll get slaughtered. There aren't a lot of Conservatives or Liberals around these parts.'

Adela laughed. 'Jack, what would I do without you? You're so good to me.'

'Everyone should be good to you. You're a brave girl to walk out of a luxurious home for the sake of a dead soldier's child.'

'I don't feel very brave these days,' she sighed.

'Keep your chin up, my dear. One day you'll meet another chap an' this time you'll fall in love. I'm sure that a lot of your depression comes from knowing that you sacrificed yourself for a man you didn't really love.'

'I was very fond of him. I loved him in a way.'

'But not the way Esther loves Bert. The way thousands of women round here love their men. Half starved, poor souls, their bodies dragged down from child-bearin' an' sickness.'

Adela was suddenly tired of the tone of the conversation. 'Perhaps if they weren't so loving and giving, they wouldn't have so many children?'

'That's the remark of a bitch.'

'Indeed?'

'Yes, indeed. About the only pleasure they get in these parts is in bed. Snugglin' up to one another keeps them warm, an' not just their bodies, either.'

'I'm sorry,' said Adela. 'But how those poor women suffer!'

'Have you heard them complain?'

Adela had, many times, but only to other women. They didn't expect their menfolk to understand and the doctor had no remedies for the cruel aftermath of their constant pregnancies and miscarriages.

'You had a good marriage, didn't you, Jack?'

'The best.'

'I'm glad for you.' She got up. 'I think I had better wash up. I've a fitting first thing.'

'Damn the dishes! Go to bed.'

Adela managed a curtsey. 'I hear and obey, oh master, but I'll be sorry tomorrow, I know I will.'

Harry was sleeping peacefully and Adela undressed and slipped into her nightgown. The sherry had warmed and relaxed her and Harry didn't wake; for once she slept easily and dreamlessly.

In the morning she got up earlier than usual, boiled water and washed up quickly, and tidied ready for her first customer. Jack ate breakfast, then lit his first cigarette of the day, coughing even more harshly than usual, then he fetched his barrow from a nearby stable and carried out several new bolts of cloth and laid them on it. Adela watched him. He was undistinguished, too thin, someone she would once have passed in the street without noticing. Who could guess that he was so kind and wise? He kissed her goodbye. Harry began to cry and she sighed as she climbed the stairs to fetch her son, listening with fury to the banging on the next-door wall. Another day had begun.

There were times when Adela contemplated her present existence with disbelief. Life was an almost inflexible pattern of work, sleep and Harry.

Occasionally, Jack took her dancing, or to a film, or a theatre. Together they watched the film *God and the Man* at the Picture House in Clare Street, billed as 'a powerful drama of the futility of human hate'.

'Our wonderful leaders should come an' watch this several times a day,' said Jack. Together they thrilled to the music of *Maid of the Mountains* at the Princes Theatre, and laughed at the antics of comedians in Variety at the Hippodrome. They walked home together through the night, discussing the shows. After a particularly funny one Jack laughed again at the comic turns and Adela joined in, then suddenly her laughter turned to tears.

He stopped walking. 'What's up, my dear?'

She could only sob, 'I don't know. I don't know.'

217

'You're still melancholy. Havin' a baby affects some women that way. You'll get better in time. Just hang on.'

'I've been hanging on. Will it never end?'

'The sherry isn't enough. I'll buy you a pick-me-up.' He returned the next day with a bottle of Hall's Wine. 'Take this,' he ordered, 'it's a tonic for the nerves.'

They went to the Drill Hall in Old Market and watched men and women hurling themselves in a frenzy to the newest jazz dance, the Lindy Hop, and Adela saw that dance dresses were shorter than daytime wear and quite skimpy.

'Come on,' said Jack. 'I'm game, if you are.' And they joined the others as the musicians bashed out renditions of *At the Jazzband Ball* and *Tiger Rag*. They ended the evening breathless and laughing. Adela paid in pain the next day.

Mrs Webster didn't relax her disapproval. 'My son never gallivanted before you arrived,' she said acidly to Adela. 'The price of a cinema seat is one and ninepence and the theatres are five and nine.'

Adela preferred to keep the peace for Jack's sake, as much as for her own, but she couldn't let this pass. 'We go in the gods at the theatre, Mrs Webster, and it costs ninepence. It's the same price at the cinema.'

She could have told the old woman that she had offered to pay her share and been indignantly refused.

'An' then there's the dancin'! *Dancin'*, at his age. And not at the Kingsley Hall where they do proper dances, but at the Drill Hall.' She made it sound like the principal seat of Satan. 'Cavortin' about doin' dances with stupid names an' listenin' to stupid songs. From all I hear it's hullaballoo – not proper music at all.'

Gradually Adela felt her nerves giving way beneath the strain.

Once she heard Mrs Webster talking to a neighbour. 'She lets that baby cry its little heart out. A proper mother doesn't do that, but *she* never picks the mite up an' gives it a cuddle. Too busy, *she* says.'

Adela waited for Mrs Webster to get back indoors then picked up Harry and marched next door, banging thunderously on the door and walking straight in.

'Some people have got manners,' said Mrs Webster. 'Some people wait to be asked in.'

'I'm following the manners of *your* family,' said Adela furiously. 'Jack's daughters walk in and out of my place as if they own it.'

'It's their home. Well, it was till you came. What d'you want?'

Adela stared down at the old woman who sat near a roaring fire, her legs comfortably apart, bosom heaving with indignation. 'I heard what you said to your friend about me and Harry and you know damn well it's not true.'

'You heard that, our Ida! She swore at me.'

'You deserve it,' raged Adela. 'You know that my son is fractious. I give him all the attention I can. I have to earn my living.' She was pleased to see that this last statement left Mrs Webster disconcerted.

As Adela said later to Esther, 'She was in a cleft stick because if she blamed my work she'd have been implying that I could let Jack keep me.'

'That was a mean thing to say to her neighbour,' said Esther. 'Everyone knows that Harry cries a lot. It isn't your fault.'

Later, Adela thought about Esther's words as she bent over her sewing machine, back aching, stitching, forever stitching, at garments which she would have to sell for a song. In spite of her protests she felt guilty about her son. If she could cuddle him, take him for long walks in his pram, if she could only show him how much she loved him, maybe he would be different.

When the first warm days of spring arrived with more obnoxious smells she wilted again. The garden privy which they shared with Mrs Webster and Ida was smelly, but it was nothing compared with the local manure factory, the knacker's yards, the gas works, the cattle market, the soap works and many other busy industries. Often above them all the smell of the Feeder Canal, awash with ordure, floated like a miasma over St Philips. Harry was still cutting teeth and yelled louder. She had taken him to the doctor who had pronounced him perfectly normal.

'If he's normal, why does he cry so often?' demanded Adela.

'Some babies do. Maybe he gets a lot of wind. You should bring it all up before you put him back in his cot. Does he get enough fresh air?'

'Not where I live,' said Adela.

The doctor regarded her, his brows knitted. 'Walk him to Brandon Hill or the Downs. It would do you both good.'

'Pushing the pram hurts my back.'

The doctor looked at her over his glasses. 'You had a hard time at the birth.'

'You don't have to tell me that!' said Adela. 'What's that to do with constant backache?'

'Unfortunately you have displaced parts inside you. It often happens.'

'Displaced parts?' Adela was horrified. 'What can I do about it?'

'Nothing, I'm afraid, except rest with your feet up as much as possible.'

'I don't have time to rest.'

'Few women around here do and many have far worse medical problems than you.' He changed the subject briskly. 'You're looking peaky. I'll prescribe another tonic for you. Don't worry, Mother, Harry will stop grizzling one day.'

Adela was irritated at being addressed as 'Mother' and upset by his diagnosis. She didn't answer and the doctor called his next patient. She left his surgery with a feeling of hopelessness.

The following day, when spring had taken a backward step and freezing rain was sheeting down and Harry was more whiny than ever, she sat at the kitchen table which held her lunch of bread and cheese, and her head went down on to her arms. How long could she bear this life? She had set out with a confidence she now saw as foolhardiness. Her parents had been right all along. She couldn't cope. Was there nothing she could do to escape from this hideous rut?

Chapter Thirteen

On a fine, sunny spring day Adela rebelled against her punishing routine and decided to let the work go hang and comply with the doctor's advice. She dressed Harry in a blue pram set, a gift from Esther who had knitted it herself. She threaded his arms through the safety harness and they set off, Harry sitting up against his pillow, his eyes following the movements of passers by, of huge dray horses drawing heavy carts from the breweries and children playing in the gutters. Adela's guilt at the way she was rearing him grew with every chuckle or unintelligible word he uttered.

Nowadays he was perfectly happy as long as he was moving and had something else to look at besides the stunted tree in Jack's sparse garden or his mother's back; could hear sounds other than the whirring of her sewing machine. He was slow in walking, probably because he was heavy. She was afraid to let him play freely in the garden without someone to watch over him now he was beginning to get into everything. She was reduced to putting him in a safety harness on a length of rope just long enough to keep him from the fire and her machine. If he'd been born in different circumstances he would probably have been a much more tractable child.

As Adela pushed his pram past the mean houses in the mean streets, past women who gossiped in a moment's respite from their eternal work, wearing coarse sacking aprons and wornout men's caps, some turned back to front, she thought of how she had thrown away a chance of marriage without giving the welfare of the baby she was expecting a thought. She had believed, in the circumstances, that simply to bear it was enough.

'Afternoon, Mrs Danby.'

Adela turned to see a woman she had met in the Kingsley Hall eyeing her up and down.

'Don't recognise friends in the street?' the woman enquired sarcastically.

'I'm sorry,' said Adela. 'I was deep in thought.'

'That's as may be,' said the woman. 'Some of us got time to say hello.' She had deliberately raised her voice and there were answering murmurs, some of them hostile, from the other women. Adela smiled at them placatingly, but their faces were stony. Her clothes were shabby by her own early standards, but they were of good quality and immeasurably better than anything the local women could buy and they resented it.

She hurried on, across busy West Street, on through narrow streets of houses. She thought of the wide acres of Durdham Down, of Clifton Down, of Leigh Woods, and of golf courses with their beautifully shaved greens and spacious fairways. She used to walk miles without tiring, but she felt exhausted already and knew she couldn't reach any of them on foot.

When she arrived at St Pauls churchyard she walked through the gates to the patch of greenery in which it stood. Among the gravestones there was a bench, placed there in someone's memory. She sat on it and leaned back, closing her eyes, letting the sun warm her face. Harry put up with the abrupt lack of excitement for a few minutes, then began to grizzle, and then to cry. Adela opened her eyes and stared at him. Poor little thing. As far as he could tell, he had exchanged one ugly garden for another. Wearily she got up and lifted him out of his pram, pushing it up and down the paths while he clung to it. He laughed as a bird flew up into a tree.

'My son,' she said aloud. She owed him so much more than this. If only she could have a rest, just a short rest, she would have the energy to give him time.

As she pushed him back towards St Philips her whole being revolted against re-entering the warren of streets and houses. For once there was no traffic and no passers by. Then Adela heard footsteps behind her and, anxious not to offend another acquaintance, however unintentionally, turned, ready to smile.

Then she almost froze. She went on moving, but her legs

were shaking. Catching her up fast was Bert Rawbone. The expression on his face terrified her and brought back the ghastly memory of his attack. She walked faster and so did he.

He began to run and in panic she ran too, the heavy pram bumping up and down curbs, while Harry laughed loudly. Adela was stopped abruptly by a hand falling heavily on her shoulder. She turned and looked into Bert's tormented eyes.

'What's your hurry, *Mrs* Danby?'

'I have to return to my work,' said Adela, as pleasantly and calmly as fear and breathlessness would allow. 'I've been playing truant. My son needed a walk.'

'Did he really? That's a good one. From what I've heard you don't give a shit about him.'

'Then you've heard wrong. I care very much about him.'

'That's not what your neighbour says.'

'She's wrong.'

She tried to move away, but Bert grabbed both of her arms.

'Please, let me go,' she said.

'Please, let me go,' he mimicked. His eyes were wild.

Adela was silent, waiting, praying that Bert's attack of madness would wear off, or that someone would come along to help her.

'I really am busy,' she said.

'Busy? Busy turnin' wives against their husbands? Busy lookin' after your bastard? Busy bein' Jack Webster's whore?'

The sour, evil words beat upon Adela's consciousness. 'I am Jack's lodger, Bert, that's all,' she said, desperately trying to sound normal.

'That's what you say.'

'Let me go,' she begged hoarsely. Harry began to cry. 'Look, you're upsetting my baby.'

'What do you care?'

'I do care, I do truly, Bert. I'm his mother.'

'An' who's his father, eh? D'you know?'

'Of course I do. My former husband—'

'Husband!' Bert snarled. 'You aren't married. Never have been. If you had you wouldn't be livin' in a place like this, you

223

toffee-nosed cow! You don't belong here. Never did an' never will.' His words presaged a torrent which rambled over a variety of subjects, most connected with the war. His eyes began to glaze over and his grip on her arms tightened.

'Over the top,' he said tonelessly. 'Over the top.'

Harry began to whimper as he caught the atmosphere of hate and fear. Let someone come along, Adela prayed inwardly. Please, please, send someone to help me.

No one came. The people in the little houses were having their tea. She could hear voices inside, yelling, laughing, arguing. If she screamed someone might come, but what if they didn't hear and she exacerbated Bert's temper? Then the decision was taken from her as his fingers released her arms and moved as fast as striking snakes to her neck. Once again she felt the terrifying choking sensation and her senses began to whirl in the darkness that preceded unconsciousness. As she fought she could hear Harry. He was shrieking now. Bert's hands seemed made of steel and her frantic struggling and kicking had no effect upon him.

Her senses were all but gone when she thought she heard Esther's voice. It seemed to come from a long way off. Through suffused eyes she saw her desperately tugging at her husband's hands. Esther's lips were moving, but her voice was drowned in the rushing wave of sound in Adela's head. Then the dreadful pressure was removed and she sank to the pavement. When the mists cleared, Adela saw that Bert was in the grip of a policeman.

Esther knelt on the ground. 'Adela, I'm sorry, I'm so sorry. He's hurt you terribly.'

Adela tried to get up, but found she was helpless. At last front doors opened, there were shouts, and people poured into the street. A woman brought a drink of water and Adela swallowed a few mouthfuls painfully.

Esther was pleading with the policeman. 'Don't arrest him, please. He's an ex-soldier. He's ill, not violent.'

The policeman looked down at Adela sitting on the ground, her back against a wall, gasping. 'I'm sorry he's ill, missus, but you can't say he's not violent. If you hadn't come along and started screamin', an' if I hadn't happened along on my beat in time to hear you, there's no tellin' what might have happened. He could have been a murderer by now.'

'No,' moaned Esther. 'Please.'

'Sorry, but I'll have to take him in and charge him. I've got no choice.'

Adela croaked unintelligibly, then tried again. 'I won't press charges,' she managed.

'Now then, madam, that's not the way to act. This man's a danger to himself an' everyone around him.'

Adela shook her head. 'Please.'

'No, I can't let it go.' He looked at the assembled people. 'Can one of you help the lady up and bring her to the station? I'll need a statement.'

The eyes looking down at Adela were filled with curiosity, some sympathy, but mostly a prurient excitement. This was better than a picture show.

It was much later when Adela was able to leave the police station and return home. A kindly policeman accompanied her through the darkening streets. On their way, they met Jack.

'I heard what happened,' he said. 'Are you all right, Adela?'

She nodded. Speaking still hurt her throat and she had needed to do a lot in the police station.

'I'll take over from here,' said Jack.

The policeman looked doubtful. 'My orders are to see her home.'

'I'll take good care of her.'

The policeman looked at Adela, then at Jack. 'I know you, don't I? Jack Webster. You'll be all right with him, madam?'

Adela nodded and Jack slid his arm around her waist and tried to take the handle of the pram. At the police station Harry had been petted and given biscuits and milk and chocolate, and he was asleep, his mouth smeared with food.

'I need the handle to lean on,' croaked Adela.

When they reached home the street was lined with neighbours who had heard about the attack. There was no sign of life from next door.

Adela sank into a chair in front of the fire which Jack stirred into flames. She felt unutterably despondent and totally weary. Nothing Jack could do or say cheered her. He patted witch-hazel on her bruises and made her a drink of honey and lemon. When it was completely dark Mrs Webster walked in, followed by Ida, Florrie and Annie. The women sat or stood around Adela, looking at her.

'You've brought disgrace on my family name,' said Mrs Webster.

'Mum, stop it!' said Jack.

The old woman stared her son down. 'Disgrace, I said. That's what I mean, an' I'll go on sayin' it while you've got that woman livin' here.'

'My name is not the same as yours,' protested Adela hoarsely.

'Bert's crazy,' said Jack. 'Everyone knows that.'

'If he's so crazy why doesn't he attack anyone but her? Tell me that!'

Ida said, 'He doesn't like Adela's clothes, or her manners, or her way of speakin'.'

Mrs Webster couldn't have been more astonished if the aspidistra had suddenly joined the conversation. 'Who asked you for an opinion?'

'No one,' persisted Ida, 'but I'm sorry for Adela, the way you keep on at her an'—'

'Gran's right,' interrupted Florrie. 'An' it isn't only her clothes an' things Bert objects to – it's her morals. Them's what makes him the most angry.'

'It's none of your business,' Jack shouted angrily. 'Get out! Go on, all of you – get out!'

Mrs Webster snorted with angry indignation and tried to argue, but Jack refused to listen to her. When the women had gone he put his arms round Adela. 'Don't mind them,' he begged. 'They've got a crazy maggot eating their brains, all except our Ida.'

'They're right about Bert. It's obvious that everyone knows I'm not married. I shouldn't have come here.'

'Don't say that. It's my house and I want you here. You won't leave, will you?'

226

'No.' She managed a weak smile. 'All my customers are round here and I need them.'

Her hand went to her throat which was aching even more with tears which she was afraid to shed in case she couldn't stop crying. Jack put Harry to bed and carried the cot into his own room, then he tucked Adela in.

'I'll take care of the little fellow tonight. Sleep well, my dear.'

He blew out her candle and Adela heard him cross her room and open and close the door, then his feet descended the stairway and she was alone. Her pain and confusion drove rest from her. She dozed through the night, hearing Harry cry sometimes and Jack's soothing murmurs through the thin wall, her sleep disturbed as it was so often by nightmares in which the experiences of the past months were a ghastly jumble. In the morning she got up feeling more tired than ever. Her throat was sore and swollen and she couldn't eat. When Harry was in his pram under the tree in the garden, she sat down and began to work.

She stayed indoors for a week by which time the pain in her throat had almost gone, but the fear and humiliation of that day stayed with her and tormented her nerves. For Esther's sake she was determined not to speak against Bert, but no one had approached her about a court case. When she answered the door to Esther's knock she dreaded what her friend would say.

Esther was white, her eyes dark-shadowed. 'I've come to tell you not to be afraid any more, Adela. Bert can't hurt you again.'

'What? What's happened?'

'He's been put away.'

'Put away?'

'In an asylum for the insane.'

'No. Oh, no! It's what you dreaded. Esther, I didn't say anything against him.'

She slumped into a chair. 'I know and I'm grateful, but things couldn't go on as they were. I'm not prepared to leave you in such danger, and besides, he's getting worse and could attack anybody. Twice you've been saved, thank God, but someone else might not be so lucky, and a stranger wouldn't be as lenient as you. My Bert could have ended up in prison, or

227

worse. Our doctor spoke for him and managed to act quickly and get a couple of specialists to examine him. They agreed that he was not wicked, just unfortunate.' She paused painfully. 'I love him, Adela. I would have put up with anything. I love him. He's ill—' Her voice broke and Adela went to her and put her arms round her. Esther clung to her. 'My poor Bert. My poor husband. He was fine when he went to war. Why do we have to have wars, Adela? Why?'

'I don't know. Does anybody?'

'I thought I was so lucky when my Bert came home when so many others were killed. It might have been better if he had died, too.'

'No, don't say it. Don't even think it. He'll recover, I'm sure.'

'I can but hope.'

Adela made tea and they drank it together. 'I've managed to get a job,' said Esther. 'I'm starting on Monday in Sander Bennett's boot factory in Kingswood. It's quite a way to travel, but it was all I could get. Jobs for women aren't so plentiful now that the men are back.'

'I thought making boots was a man's occupation.'

Esther smiled wanly. 'No, there are plenty of women who do it. It's quite interesting where I'm going to work because it's been turned over to fashion shoes.'

After Esther had left Adela sat on, her hands in her lap, her mind in turmoil. Ralph's desperate plea to allow him to make love to her had ended by changing her life, but whatever decision she had made at that moment would have caused grief. If he had died after she had refused him the comfort of her body she would have been racked with guilt; perhaps that would have been better. As things were she was causing havoc in so many lives, not least in Jack's. She thought of Harry. Poor little creature, fatherless and with a mother whose emotions seemed to become more uncontrolled with every passing day.

Jack found her sitting in the dark and turned up the gaslight. 'What's up?'

'Everything,' she said miserably.

'Has Esther been to see you?'

'Yes. What made you ask?'

'I've heard about Bert, poor sod. He's one of the war's hidden victims. But Esther will manage. She's got guts.'

'Yes.'

Jack bent and kissed her forehead. 'You're so sad. Would you like to go to a music hall? We'd be in time for the last house. Ida will sit with Harry.'

'No thanks.' She got up. 'I haven't cooked anything for you. Will eggs and bacon do?'

'Don't you go to any trouble. I'll nip along and get some fish and chips.'

He returned with the steaming food, but Adela only toyed with hers. 'Sorry, I've no appetite.'

'You must eat.' Jack sounded almost angry. 'You're gettin' thinner by the day.'

'I can't help it.'

'Yes, you can. You've got a strong will, you've proved that. Let it work for you now.'

'It's a conscious effort to do anything.'

'Then make the effort and eat.'

'I can't.'

Jack stopped trying to persuade her, but later brought her a glass of milk which she drank because it was easier than refusing.

The following night she accompanied him to the Kingsley Hall. It had taken him a long time to coax her. Ida was going to look after Harry and had ensconced herself in front of the fire with a box of chocolates and a magazine, clearly happy to have this short time to herself. The evening was an occasion for socialising and discussing politics.

'There won't be any speeches,' promised Jack. 'An' you can try to make friends.'

'I don't think so. Most people round here seem to resent me.'

Jack said sternly, 'Can you wonder at it? You don't make any attempt to be pleasant. You were different in St Pauls.'

Adela felt a flash of anger which died as quickly. 'I know. I felt different there.'

'You must take folk as they are, not as you want them to be.'

'Really? I thought the whole idea of socialism was to give

229

them a better chance, not leave them as they are.'

'You know damn well what I mean. Adela, I wish you wouldn't provoke me into speakin' rough to you.'

She subsided and sat down in the hall which was busy with people, talking, laughing, arguing. Children ran about, dodging between legs, playing noisy games, occasionally reproved indulgently by their parents. Some mothers carried tiny infants.

Jack came and pulled her to her feet. 'Come on. I'll introduce you to people.'

'I don't feel like it.'

He refused to listen and she shook a lot of hands, smiled into a number of faces, all of which faded into obscurity as soon as she stopped looking at them.

'Are you absolutely determined to let me down?' asked Jack angrily.

'I told you I didn't want to come. I can't help it. I don't feel well.'

Jack was immediately contrite. 'Shall I take you home?'

'No. Stay here. I can go on my own.'

'I'd prefer to escort you. I brought you here an' I'll take you home.'

They had reached the door when it opened and Adela was confronted by her sister, Blanche.

She almost flinched, then held up her head, waiting for some scathing remark.

'My God, you look terrible!' said Blanche, right on cue.

'And you,' returned Adela, uplifted by a burst of indignant energy, 'look a great deal better than I've seen you for ages.'

It was true. Blanche was wearing a sage green suit with a paler blouse and a brilliant cerise scarf. Her hair had been cut short and permanently waved, her complexion was dusted with powder, and her lips were pink with lipstick. She looked attractive and animated.

'Hello, Jack,' Blanche said. 'Not going, are you? We're trying to get everyone together for a short meeting.'

'What kind of meeting?' asked Adela.

Blanche said, 'We want to set up a centre where we can

dispense food and clothes to children of the unemployed. The government has clearly got no intention of helping them.'

'That's true!' said Jack. 'And now they've invoked the Emergency Powers Act to force the miners back underground. It's a disgrace! It's industrial conscription an' allows the government to break any strike which involves anythin' they call essential services.'

'And if a man disobeys he can be sent to jail,' cried Blanche, 'or fined a hundred pounds, as if any poor working-class devil has got money like that.'

'Come down off your soapbox,' said Adela wearily. 'You don't have to yell at me.'

'Hasn't he told you what's going on? Haven't you told her, Jack? Don't you care about unfortunate people, Adela?'

'No, he hasn't told me.'

'I'm sure he must have tried.'

'I don't worry her more than I can help,' said Jack. 'She's got enough to do.'

'I do care about people,' protested Adela.

'Not the way Jack does! He suffers for the ones he's never even met. Adela, you should damn well know what's going on!'

'I don't read newspapers much,' said Adela. 'I never seem to have the time.'

'She's not at all well,' said Jack.

'I can see that.' Blanche was less belligerent as she noticed for the first time that her sister was pale and drawn. Her sudden, unexpected softening brought Adela near to tears. Too many things these days had her fighting tears.

'Come and talk to me,' said Blanche. 'Give Jack a chance to attend the meeting. I know he wants to. I'll follow later, Jack.'

Adela nodded and accompanied her sister into a small side room. Blanche shut the door and the voices and laughter beyond became muted. 'What's making you ill?' she asked.

'I can't seem to recover properly after the baby.'

'Have you seen a doctor?'

'He's useless. It seems that women are expected to suffer.'

Blanche shuddered. 'I'll never have a baby. Why don't you try a tonic?'

231

'Jack bought me one. It doesn't help. Blanche, do Mother and Father ever talk about me?'

'Not to me, at least Mother doesn't. Father's asked me a few times if I'd heard anything.'

'Will you tell them you've seen me?'

'Yes. Father, anyway. I'll sound Mother out first. She's a hard woman. I think she believes in death before dishonour.'

'That's terrible.'

'Unfortunately, it's the way she is.'

There was a burst of laughter from the hall and Blanche smiled. 'Salt of the earth, these people. But you must know that, living among them.'

'They don't really accept me,' said Adela bleakly.

'Have you tried to make friends?'

'I've told you, I've no time. I work such long hours.'

'What do you do?'

When Adela explained Blanche said, 'It sounds a hell of a lot. How's the baby?'

'He's well, but he cries so much.'

'That's a pity, but some kids are like that, I'm told. I dare say he'll grow out of it.'

There was a definite change in Blanche and it went further than her outward appearance. When they had been young they had shared most things and enjoyed life together, but their relationship had soured as they grew older.

'I can't give Harry the attention he needs,' said Adela.

'You look as if you could do with a rest,' said Blanche. 'I wish I could help, but I've no money to spare.' There was no need for Blanche to explain. Father had always paid their bills for them and allowed them only a small amount of pin money. 'I've even used the money Grandmother left me.'

'Mine was stolen almost as soon as I got it out of the bank.'

'Do you mean to tell me you've managed on your earnings alone?'

'Except for the twenty pounds you brought to Temple Meads.'

Blanche was silent for a moment. 'Adela, I used to think you were nothing but a spoiled butterfly, but you've got guts. By God, you have.'

'Thanks, but they don't pay bills.'

'Someone told me you were living with Jack.'

'I'm living in his house as a lodger.'

'And that's all?'

'That's all, though I'm very fond of him.'

'He's a splendid chap.'

'Yes, he is. Blanche, you're different,' said Adela. 'You look smart and pretty.'

'Thanks,' said Blanche drily.

Adela grimaced. 'Sorry, that sounded unkind. I didn't mean it to. Have you met someone nice?'

Blanche smiled, a small secretive smile. 'I most certainly have.'

'Do I know him?'

Blanche shook her head. 'Are you going home?' she asked in a tone which didn't encourage further questions.

'No, I've changed my mind. I'll stay.' The alteration in her sister had lifted Adela's depression and she began to enjoy herself.

Someone sat down at the rather tinny piano and began to play and people gathered round and sang spontaneously. Their voices blended into *Give Me a Little Cosy Corner* and *K-K-K-Katy*. A man in a shabby suit and down-at-heel shoes sang in a fine, tenor voice, *She Was One of the Early Birds; And I Was One of the Worms*, and a woman with a figure destroyed by child-bearing and with scarcely a tooth in her head sang *Love, Here Is My Heart* with a total absence of self-consciousness. She had lost her three eldest sons in the war and her husband had recently died from a wasting disease, leaving her with six children to rear alone, but she had no thought of giving up the struggle to survive. Adela remembered musical evenings at home, the guests surrounded by luxury, stomachs full of good food and wine, a perfect piano and well-schooled voices. It seemed a million miles away. During the singing Esther arrived, determinedly cheerful. She was asked many times about Bert and always parried the questions with a smile and the murmured assurance that he was improving.

She finally sat down beside Adela. 'I'm a liar,' she said. 'He doesn't even know me. It's all right, Adela, don't try to think of anything to say and don't offer me sympathy or I may cry.'

'How's the job at the boot factory?'

'It pays the bills. It's boring, but it's better than nothing.'

'What do you do?'

'Not much at the moment. I'm learning. I shall be working a machine that uses a sharp knife to cut the over-hanging leather after the soles are fixed.'

'Isn't that dangerous?'

'Not if it's done properly with the guard on. Sander Bennett tries to keep his employees safe, but some people are careless and lose fingers. Even then he does what he can for them.'

Adela changed the subject.

The cheerful evening made the next morning seem even more dismal. Adela was disturbed by the violent swing of her moods, and wondered if she would ever regain her natural optimism. Perhaps she would end up like Bert. The thought terrified her and she paced the living room, forgetting her sewing, delighting Harry who watched her and clapped his hands. She picked him up and held him so close he began to wriggle and whimper.

'My son,' she said over and over. 'My darling son.'

Two days later she was working on a wedding dress. The daughter of a local publican was getting married and, as the wedding had been arranged at short notice, Adela had been sewing frantically. It was rumoured that the girl was expecting, hence the rush.

She got up to answer a loud knocking on the front door and was astonished to find Blanche outside. Automatically she asked her in. Blanche looked round the living room and Adela saw it through her eyes. In spite of her improvements, it looked poor and shabby and, at the moment, none too clean. She had been too busy to cope with housework, and Annie and Florrie had finally understood that they were not to interfere in their father's household arrangements.

'What a dump,' said Blanche, seating herself by the fire and lighting a Turkish cigarette.

Adela chose to ignore her sister's frank criticism. 'Why are you here?'

'Not a very nice greeting,' said Blanche, staring at the antiquated sewing machine. 'Is that all you've got to work on?'

'I can't afford anything else. It does the job.'

'Are you comfortable here? It looks awfully dismal.'

'Jack makes up for a lot. He's like a father to me. He gives me a sense of security.'

'You certainly are different.'

'Of course I am. I've had a baby.'

'Where is the little blighter?'

'In his pram in the garden.'

Blanche blew out a stream of smoke. 'I told the parents I'd seen you and that you'd come safely through the birth. Father looked relieved.'

'And Mother?'

'She was angry at first. Said she didn't want to know. I told her you looked ill and she got up and walked to the door. Then she had a surprising change of mind. She wants you to come home.'

Adela stared. 'Do you mean she's willing to accept Harry?'

Blanche laughed mirthlessly. 'Of course not. She'll never relent where he's concerned. She suggests that he be left in a nursery somewhere, or with foster parents.'

'I'm not giving him up!'

'No one's asking you to. At least, not entirely. Mother promises that you won't lose touch with him. I think she misses you, Adela, in her way. She had such great hopes of your making a prestigious marriage.'

'I know. I've ruined that dream forever. I can't think why she wants me now.'

'The dream might still come true. Society has changed since the war. Young people are having fun without chaperones. The atmosphere would suit you.'

'Would it? Does it suit you?'

'God, no.' Blanche tossed her half-smoked cigarette into the fire and lit another. 'I enjoy an occasional social evening, but my interests are now completely different. I'm looking forward to seeing a socialist Britain and I'm doing everything I can to help it along.'

'I suppose your new friend has reformed you.'

Blanche evaded a reply. 'What shall I tell Mother?'

Adela sat still, her hands in her lap, wondering what to say.

'You look utterly frightful,' said Blanche.

'So you keep telling me.'

Blanche stood up. 'Well, will you be coming home?'

'I'm tempted,' admitted Adela. 'I should like to see Mother and Father, but I can never give up my son.'

'It's up to you. Actually Father needs cheering up. He doesn't like the way business is heading since the war. He's not looking too well, either.' Blanche opened her small purse. 'Here, he sent you this. He hopes you'll accept it.' She handed over two five pound notes. 'He's not such a bad old stick. He's obviously worried about you. If he was left to himself – if Mother'— She stopped and shrugged.

Adela stared down at the notes, half choked by emotion. 'Please – thank him for me.'

Jack came home late that night. 'I've had a good day,' he said, hanging his jacket and cap behind the kitchen door. 'I made more than usual. In a while I'll take you for a day trip to Weston an' you an' Harry can get some fresh air straight off the Channel. There's nothin' like Weston air to brace you up. What's for supper? I'm starvin'.'

Adela's culinary achievements were still limited, but she had improved and was able to give him a plate of savoury stew which he ate hungrily. 'Don't you want any?'

'I'm not hungry. Blanche came to see me today,' she hurried on before he could begin to lecture her.

'Did she?' Jack's face lit up. 'Good for her.'

'She thinks I look ill.'

'I'm not surprised.' Jack finished the last mouthful and sat down in an easy chair with the inevitable cigarette. 'What did she think of Harry?'

'She didn't look at him.'

Jack laughed. 'She'll never be domesticated.'

'She's got a new friend, but she won't tell me who he is.'

'She's entitled to her privacy.'

'Whoever it is has made a big difference to her. She's being quite nice to me.'

'Good.' Jack puffed and coughed.

'She brought a message from my mother. She wants me to go home for a rest.'

He said nothing for a moment. 'Do you want to go?'

Adela said slowly, 'In a way I should like to. I hate being on bad terms with my parents and I am very tired.'

'That means they're reconciled to Harry.'

'No, Blanche said he would have to go away to a nurse.'

'You won't accept that!'

'No, I couldn't leave him. But I'm so damned fed up with work and worry and feeling off colour, it would be wonderful to go home.'

Jack said quietly, 'I thought you looked upon here as home.'

'I do, I have, but my parents' house is home, too.'

'You'll go back to your pampered existence.'

'If I did it would only be for a little while.'

'Without Harry!'

Adela said, 'If circumstances had been different I would have had a nursemaid for my baby. I wouldn't have been responsible for his daily care, or need to get up at night to see to him.'

'You're tryin' to talk yourself into goin'. Once they get hold of you, you'll stay. Why should you throw away luxury and wealth for this place?'

'I did it before.'

'You didn't know what you were lettin' yourself in for that time.'

'Jack, I haven't made up my mind and whatever I do I'll come back, I promise I will.'

Adela thought of her mother's request while she continued to work. Her appetite grew smaller and Jack was angry with her.

'You've got a healthy, beautiful body an' you're ruinin' it.'

'I can't force feed myself!' snapped Adela. 'I'm looking after you and Harry properly, aren't I?'

'You cook for us. You make sure Harry's fed, but you don't give him much else. I cuddle him more than you do.'

'I'm too bloody tired all the time.'

'You stupid woman, it's because you don't eat.'

'Don't call me names!'

'Don't swear at me!'

'*Me* swear. What about you?'

'It's different for a man.'

'It's always different for a man! A man can do as he damn well pleases. He can get any woman he fancies and give her a baby and society ignores it, but let a woman transgress, no matter what the circumstances—'

Adela's voice broke and Jack put his arm round her shaking shoulders. 'Don't cry, my dear. Stick it out. Things will improve, an' when Harry's a bit older you might even get a chance to study interior decorating. You've told me so often how it fascinates you. An' don't forget, your parents won't take kindly to the idea of your takin' up a career.'

She shook herself free. 'Leave me alone! I must get on. Someone's coming round for a fitting in an hour.'

Jack looked hurt. He decided to go to a meeting at the Kingsley Hall. 'There's a good speaker on.' He didn't invite her to join him later and, although she knew she deserved it, Adela resented it.

About an hour after Adela's customer had left there was a knock on the door and she got up to answer it. Blanche walked past her into the living room.

'Father's ill,' she said baldly. 'You should come home. He wants to see you.'

'How ill?' Adela asked fearfully.

'The doctor says it's a heart attack. He'd like to see you.'

'The doctor?'

'No, you idiot! Father. Get ready quickly. The less he's worried, the better.'

Adela pulled on her coat and hat and picked up Harry.

'You can't bring him with you.'

Adela turned on her in sudden rage. 'Well, I sure as hell can't leave him here on his own!'

'Isn't there anyone to look after him? Where's Jack?'

'At the Kingsley Hall.'

'Oh, yes, I'd planned to go. Well, there must be someone. What about your next-door neighbour?'

'Jack's mother lives next door.'

'Fine. Take him round and we can go.'

'She dislikes me, but maybe she'd let Jack's sister have him.'

Mrs Webster glared at Adela when she walked in with Harry and asked for help, but Ida's longing to be of service made her reckless. 'Mum, we can't let Adela down, not when her dad's so ill. She must go an' see him. Give him here, Adela, I'll take care of him. Don't worry, he likes me.'

Harry held out his arms to Ida who took him happily and Adela waited no longer. She and Blanche hurried to the end of the street where Father's car waited. 'There's no one to drive it,' said Adela.

'Get in, I'm driving,' said Blanche.

'I didn't know you could.'

'No, and if Father had his way I wouldn't, but I got a friend to give me lessons.'

'Your new friend?'

'Yes!' Blanche lit a cigarette, stuck it between her reddened lips and pulled on driving gauntlets. Then she swung the starting handle. The big engine roared into life and with only a slight clash of gears she began the drive to Clifton.

Mr Danby was propped up in bed on a mass of pillows. A nurse whose clothes creaked with starch whenever she moved hovered beside him. 'Don't say anything to upset him,' she warned. 'He's been very ill.'

Adela bent over the bed. Mr Danby wore his pyjamas with the collar open and a tuft of greying hair was showing. Adela couldn't remember ever seeing him like that. Even on their holidays he had always been decorously dressed from his knife-creased trousers to his tie pin. 'Father,' she said softly.

He opened his eyes and smiled. 'Adela. I'm glad you came.'

'Of course I did. I'm so sorry you're ill, Father.'

'You've not been well yourself.'

'Don't worry about me.'

'But I do. When I pass on—'

'Oh, don't—'

The nurse interrupted swiftly. 'No more of that talk, Mr Danby. You're not going to "pass on" and we both know it.'

'She's a dreadful bully,' said Mr Danby.

'I need to be, with a stubborn man like you.'

'Well, you can take yourself off for a few minutes. I want to talk privately with my daughter.'

The nurse stalked out.

Mr Danby stared at Adela. 'You look worse than I do. You're so thin. Are you all right?'

'Yes, perfectly.'

'Adela, your mother's a good woman, a very good woman. I know I was angry with you at first, but if it had been left to me – but I couldn't flout her high principles.'

'You mustn't upset yourself, Father. It doesn't matter.'

'You didn't leave Bristol.'

'No.'

'We thought you had. You were on Temple Meads Station.'

'I didn't go away.'

'Your money must have run out by now. How are you managing?'

'I work. I'm doing well. I'm doing very well.'

'Good. Good. It's a comfort to know that before I die.'

'Please, Father—'

He continued feverishly, 'We told everyone you are with Grandmother Sutton.' He fell silent, breathing noisily. 'You'll come home now, won't you? Forget all that nonsense about being independent.'

Before she could answer the nurse swept in and Adela was shooed out, her emotions lacerated.

Mother was sitting in the drawing room and held up a cool cheek for Adela's kiss. They sat together in front of the blazing fire. Adela leaned back in the inexpressible comfort of a well-sprung, velvet-upholstered easy chair, her eyes roaming over the familiar beauty of the room, the polished wood and silver gleaming in the leaping firelight, and the softly shaded electric lamp above Mrs Danby's head.

'What do you think of Father?' asked Mrs Danby.

'He looks better than I expected after what Blanche said. Is he going to get really well, Mother?'

'You know what medical people are – always trying to soothe one, hiding the truth. I don't believe them half the time. You should have seen him when he had his attack. He was a dreadful colour, and in such pain! He was too ill even to move to a nursing home. I truly thought we had lost him.'

'Oh. Mother, don't! I can't bear it!'

'Is that so?' Mrs Danby was cool. 'Yet you appear to find it perfectly easy to bear being separated from him. We none of us know when our lives will be taken from us. Think how you would have felt if Father had died, especially as—' Mrs Danby paused. 'Especially as you were largely the cause of the attack.'

'Oh, no! No, that's too cruel!'

'Cruel, or not, it's the truth.'

Blanche sauntered into the room and lit a cigarette, ignoring her mother's dark frown. 'Like one?' she asked Adela.

'I don't smoke, thank you.'

'Of course you do not!' snapped Mrs Danby. 'No true lady smokes.'

'Actually, they do,' said Blanche, 'but I wouldn't care anyway. I shall do as I please.'

'That's nothing new.'

Adela sighed. She had forgotten the frequently acrimonious atmosphere in Speede House. She stood up. 'I must go back. I can't leave Harry any longer.'

'Harry!' said her mother in tones of deep bitterness. 'Harry. You think more of that fatherless child than you do of your own father.'

'I care a lot for Father. I never knew how much until—' Adela stopped, her throat constricted. 'I must go home,' she managed.

'Hang on, I'll run you there,' said Blanche. 'I promised I'd be at the meeting tonight.'

'Her disgusting socialist meeting,' said Mrs Danby. 'I have not said you may take the car.'

'You don't need it,' said Blanche rudely, 'and Father certainly doesn't. I'll bring it back when I've seen Adela home and finished at the meeting, then get a lift to my flat.'

'With your so-called friend, I suppose?'

'Yes, that's right. I shan't be long, Adela,' said Blanche. 'I'll just nip upstairs and get a few things I left behind.'

'What did Blanche mean when she said she would return to her flat?' Adela asked. 'Doesn't she live here now?'

Mrs Danby's face set in disapproving lines. 'She has taken accommodation elsewhere.'

'Where?'

'She has a bed-sitting room in Cotham Hill. She calls it a flat, but it's no more than a room and a minute kitchen and she actually *shares* a bathroom. Horrible!' Mrs Danby shuddered.

'You've been there?'

'No. Your cousin, Millie, has visited and she told her mother who told me.'

'How can Blanche afford to live away from home? She has no money?'

'Adela, I am tired of this subject. Please let it drop.'

Adela scarcely heard her. 'Has she got a job?' she persisted. 'She has no money of her own.'

Mrs Danby looked at her younger daughter warily. 'Your father allows her a small income. A *very* small one.'

'What! But you left me with only twenty pounds.'

'You had your grandmother's money.'

'You could have made my life so much easier! When I think of all I've suffered!'

Mrs Danby leaned forward. 'Come, sit by me.'

Adela resisted for a moment then, unwilling to provoke acrimony, she seated herself by her mother.

'You must know that Father and I did not want you to suffer,' said Mrs Danby stiffly. 'We talked the matter over and came to the conclusion that if we left you alone to realise the extent of your folly you would come to your senses quicker and return home.'

'Still expecting my child, I suppose!'

'There is no need to be sarcastic. We naturally would have found you a comfortable home until the child was born. Father's anxiety has cost him dear.'

Adela's feelings were bleak. 'I regret that, of course. I had no wish to hurt either of you, it's just that I knew I had to have Ralph's baby—'

'Be silent! Adela, can't you put what's happened behind you and come home? Father needs you. He must be nursed, not just by that harridan upstairs but with devotion by those who care for him. Surely he deserves a little of your time.'

Chapter Fourteen

Blanche drove her sister home. Jack was out and Adela fetched Harry from next door. 'He never cried once while he was here,' said Mrs Webster complacently. She sat in her usual place, close to the fire, her heavy body upright, legs slightly apart, showing her knee-length knickers.

Adela felt like slapping her for her smug self-satisfaction. 'I'm glad to hear it,' she said.

'I played with him all the time you were away,' said Ida.

'An' neglected her duties!' snapped Mrs Webster.

'I'll catch up now,' said Ida. 'It's not as if the ornaments are dirty.'

'They need washin' every week,' said Mrs Webster. She began to heave herself out of her chair, groaning a little, her corsets creaking slightly. 'Of course, if it's too much trouble I can do it. After all, I managed for years to work *an'* bring you all up. Bein' outside in all weathers is what brought on my rheumatics, but I can still get about if I don't get the help I should have.'

'Stay where you are, Mum,' said Ida with resignation. 'You know I'll do it. How was your father, Adela? I hope things weren't as bad as you feared.'

'It's difficult to tell. Mother says he's been extremely ill, but the nurse says he'll get well.'

'The nurse! Medical people!' Mrs Webster's voice crackled with contempt. 'I'm against the wicked rubbish they tell you. I never have anythin' to do with doctors or nurses. Nasty, evil lot!'

Adela was astonished by her outburst. 'Why would the nurse tell lies?'

'Because that's what they teach them to do.' Mrs Webster folded her arms over her large breasts and glared into the fire.

Ida ushered Adela outside. She laid a hand on her arm. 'You'll have to excuse Mum. A doctor persuaded her to have her first baby immunised against diphtheria. Well, Andy wasn't a baby by then, he was eight years old. Somethin' terrible went wrong an' he got a dreadful fever an' sickness an' head'aches that made him scream, then he went into a coma an' passed away.'

'That's dreadful! I had Harry immunised.' Adela shuddered. 'Thank God nothing awful happened to him.'

'Not many get a reaction like that, the doctor said, but Mother was heartbroken an' ordered him out. I was only little at the time, but I can remember she shut herself away for days. Dad tried to comfort her, but it was no use. She's never mentioned Andy's name since, but none of us was ever done an' I don't think Mum's ever been the same.'

Adela walked into Jack's house, sad over Mrs Webster's long-ago despair. She thought over her own last minutes with her mother.

'I want Father to get well as much as anybody,' she had pleaded, 'but he's got you and all the comfort he needs, and Harry is so small and totally dependent on me. He would be dreadfully upset if I changed his life now.'

Mrs Danby had said in a low voice, 'If you had married Sander Bennett—'

'Oh, please don't start that again.'

Mrs Danby had frowned. 'Adela, in normal circumstances you would have handed your baby straight to a nursemaid and only seen it at intervals. Father and I went away for weeks at a time when you and Blanche were small.'

Normal circumstances! Adela had thought of the people at the other end of the social scale. Her mind could never again shut out the sufferings of others.

'Adela, come home. Leave the rearing of the child to those who understand such matters. Take your rightful place in society.'

'Shouldn't Blanche be taking her rightful place? Or is Father hoping to starve her out, too?'

Mother had grown angry. 'Must you use such immoderate terms? We certainly do not wish to starve Blanche, any more than we wished to hurt you, though as a matter of fact, we would prefer her to stay away until her idiotic mania with socialist politics is past. She seems to care nothing for our standards, but mixes all the time with awful people. She has been a fearful embarrassment at society gatherings. She has a new *friend*.' Mrs Danby shuddered. 'I would prefer not to discuss your sister.'

'She looks more presentable than I've ever seen her,' said Adela.

'Oh, yes, she dresses up now. I once thought she had her sights fixed on Mr Bennett as a possible husband, but I know now how mistaken I was.' Mrs Danby paused. 'We do not receive him any more.'

'Don't you? And yet you can still reproach me for not marrying him.'

Mrs Danby's face coloured angrily. 'If you had done so he would have helped Father, instead of which he has behaved – is behaving – extremely badly towards him. Trade is very changeable, at present. There has been a post-war boom and it seems that Mr Bennett foresaw it some while ago and bought up all the small textiles firms he could get hold of. When they continued to come on to the market he outbid many other businessmen. Occasionally he lost, but never when your father was financially involved; then he gained his own ends by any means available.'

'But it sounds as if Father was trying to do the same.'

'I might have known you would be against Father.'

'I'm not. I'm just trying to make sense of what you're telling me.'

'You are simply not interested in Father's troubles.'

'I am, of course I am, but I can't do anything about them and I've so many of my own.'

'Of your own choosing!'

'Not exactly,' she had sighed. 'I must go home to Harry.' She had bent to Mother who again offered her cold cheek for a kiss.

'I assume that you will visit Father tomorrow.'

Adela had thought of the pile of sewing still to be done, of the many other tasks that awaited her. As she left she had remembered her beautiful bedroom, the serenity in which she had once lived. She stood with her feet in the soft, deep pile of the wool carpet, knowing that she had only to put out a hand to the bell pull to summon servants willing to carry out her every command. The room was warm and softly lit and every chair and couch had been chosen with care, for comfort as well as appearance. When Jack, and so many others like him, bought household furnishings it was nearly always because they were second-hand and cheap. It had taken an effort to leave Speede House. 'I'll be back,' she had said. 'I'll see you tomorrow.'

On the following day she worked fast to get the bride's gown finished and fitted it on to the delighted girl who paid her on the spot, then she left Harry with Ida again and caught a tram to Clifton. As she walked through the roads lined with large houses set in immaculate gardens she seemed to see them for the first time. How could she have been so blind as to take such wealth for granted when not far away there were people crammed into insanitary houses, many jobless, hungry and ill-clad? 'The salt of the earth', Blanche had called them and she was right.

Mrs Danby tutted at the state of Adela's clothes. 'I didn't notice them last night,' she said. 'Your hat! And that coat is shiny in the seat and very worn. It's so cold today. The garden has actually suffered frost damage and it will soon be summer. Why didn't you wear your fur coat?'

'I had to sell it.'

'What?' Mrs Danby looked as outraged as if Adela had said she had burned it. 'Your beautiful coat? Father chose it for you and loved to see you wearing it. He thought you looked lovely in it.'

'Did he?' Adela was amazed. 'He never said so.'

'Of course not, he's not a demonstrative man. Surely you could have hung on to it? It was expensive.'

'No, I'm sorry, I couldn't. I pawned it at first, but then I had to let it go.'

'*Pawned* it! That a daughter of mine should have entered such a place! I hope you got a good price for it?'

'No, I don't think I did, but I had to have money.'

'You must have spent your legacy fast.'

'It was stolen not long after I left home,' said Adela. 'Mother, must we go on with this catechism? How's Father?'

Mrs Danby ignored the question. 'What a good thing I kept your good jewellery here or I suppose you would have thrown that away, too. How have you been living? I trust you have not been doing anything shameful!'

Adela looked at her mother angrily. 'I resent any such suggestion!'

'You're as argumentative as ever!'

Adela sighed. 'I didn't come here to quarrel with you. I'll go and see Father.'

'Very well.' Mrs Danby's lips shut tight.

Adela paused. 'Mother, I'm really sorry you've had so much worry.'

Mrs Danby did not reply.

Adela went upstairs. Her father greeted her eagerly. 'I knew you would visit me again. Sit down and talk to me.'

Adela sat and talked. It was difficult. If her conversation ever strayed towards her recent experiences, and it was almost impossible to keep off them, he frowned at her worriedly, so she made her sewing sound almost as if it was a little hobby to pass the time and he nodded approvingly. 'I like to see young ladies with busy hands.'

Busy hands! He should come back with her to St Philips or St Pauls. Such saintly names for districts which encompassed so much human misery.

When she ran out of ideas and paused, her father half sat up and reached out and took her hand. His was hot and dry. 'You'll come home now, won't you, Adela? I need you here. Mother needs you. Blanche is hopeless – not at all like a real daughter – but you, you were always biddable and sweet. I miss you.'

Adela wondered how to combat a father whose customary stern manner had degenerated abruptly into maudlin appeals to

249

her compassion. She glanced at the nurse whose ears were almost flapping. 'I'll talk it over with Mother,' she prevaricated.

'Yes, do that. Mother will advise you.' He fell back on his pillows.

The nurse bustled over. 'You're letting yourself get agitated again. It won't do.' She glared at Adela. 'I cannot allow visitors who get him upset. He's still not out of the woods.' She marched to the door and flung it open. Adela followed her.

'I thought you said that my father is sure to recover?'

'He's had a comparatively mild attack, but he must have complete rest and calm if he's to get over it properly. If he's upset he could have another, worse attack. It's none of my business, but you should come home if he wants you to. It would do him a power of good. Might make all the difference to his recovery.'

Adela left Speede House seething with different emotions. She sat on the open top of the tram, the air cooling her hot face, and tried to calm down. Mother, Father and the nurse had all shamelessly used emotional blackmail to persuade her to return. To her parents Harry was an encumbrance, an embarrassment, to be forgotten as soon as possible. Mother had said it was Adela's fault that Father had had a heart attack. He could have died and then she would never have forgiven herself. By the time she walked wearily into Jack's house, her depression was stronger than ever.

Adela visited her father every day, and every day pressure was put on her to come home. It was insidious and wearing and she felt crushed beneath its weight. She began to make mistakes in her sewing. She managed to rectify them but then she cut out a whole dress wrong. The girl, only seventeen and proud of the first piece of beautiful material she had ever been able to afford, had brought the pale blue satin to her dressmaker with complete confidence and Adela had let her down.

'I'm deeply sorry. I'll replace it,' Adela promised.

'You can't. It was a remnant of a discontinued line. I've always dreamed of a dress in exactly that colour an' you've spoiled it.'

Adela had bought her a piece of the finest satin she could find, but the girl refused to trust her the second time and had taken it to a different dressmaker. Adela couldn't continue this way.

'I've something to tell you, Jack,' she said as soon as he walked through the door after the blue satin disaster. 'I've thought a lot about it, and I'm sorry, but I'll have to return home, at least until Father is well. It's my fault he's ill and the nurse says my presence there could help him to get well.'

Jack looked steadily at her. 'I don't believe it. He's like the others, cravin' more an' more money, jostlin' an' fightin' to buy up as many bankrupt businesses as they can find. The textiles market is boomin' at the moment. There have been cut-throat deals an' your father has been in the thick of them. I suppose the strain told on him.'

'Won't you support me in my duty?'

Jack sat down. He looked suddenly very tired. 'Your duty? Support you? What about your duty to Harry?' His face brightened and he asked eagerly, 'Did they ask you to bring him with you?'

Adela said flatly. 'No, but I'll make sure he's well cared for. And we'll be back – if you'll have us.'

'Need you ask?' He shook his head. 'But you'll get used to luxury again. You'll find a thousand reasons for staying.'

'No!'

'Your parents will trot out wealthy, eligible men.'

'I've already refused one of those! Wealthy, anyway.'

'Yes, and I respect you for your courage.' Jack paused, 'I can't understand how rich folk can marry off their daughters for money, or business reasons. We don't sell ours. We encourage them to marry for love.'

Adela felt sick. 'I told you the truth about me in confidence and now you're using it against me. That's cruel.'

Jack took her hand. 'Yes, it is. I'm sorry. Having you and Harry here is wonderful for me. And Ida worships you. You respect her and don't treat her like an unpaid slave.'

'Ida?' Adela was startled.

'Yes, I know she's like a timid mouse but she thinks the

world of you. Havin' you an' Harry next door has made a big difference to her.'

Adela sighed. 'I'm sorry, but Father needs me more. If I stay at home he'll get better. If I don't he could have another attack. They've all made it perfectly clear, and he looks so pathetically helpless. I just can't stand it any more.' Her voice broke.

Jack was defeated. 'I see. What will you do about Harry?'

'I don't know. Esther would have looked after him if she wasn't working. I don't know anyone round here who hasn't got her hands full. I shall have to leave it to Mother to decide.'

'Can you trust her?'

'Jack, what a question! Of course I can. She'll find a good nurse somewhere and Harry will be properly cared for until I can come back.'

Still Adela hesitated to take a step which would mean leaving her son to a stranger until on one of her visits she found that the doctor had been summoned urgently because her father had run a dangerously high temperature. Mother begged her to stay. 'At least until Father recovers properly. The doctor says he will if only he isn't worried, and he does so want you.'

Even Jack agreed then that her place was with her family.

Adela's fears for her father's life enabled her to say goodbye to Harry reasonably calmly. Her mother assured her that a good place had been found for him. She and Adela took him to a small hotel outside town and the elderly woman who arrived to collect him looked efficient and kind. She sat for a while, gaining the child's confidence, and when she finally took him, smiling, received a trusting smile in return.

'He's a dear little fellow,' said the woman. 'I can see he's going to get on very well.'

'I hope so, Miss—?' Adela paused.

'I'm Mrs Brown.'

'Are you a trained children's nurse?'

'Yes, and I've brought up several of my own, I've had no complaints.'

Adela looked at Harry who was sitting on Mrs Brown's lap, playing with her beads.

'I congratulate you,' Mrs Brown said. 'He's obviously healthy and happy, and good, too.'

'Where will he be living?'

'He's going to a fine place where he'll be well cared for.'

'Where?'

Mrs Danby looked anxiously at her watch. 'I told Father we would be back in fifteen minutes from now. We are going to be late and he'll fret.'

'My son tends to cry quite a lot,' said Adela anxiously to Mrs Brown.

The woman nodded. 'Some little ones do, but they often stop when a person other than their mother takes over. There isn't the emotional attachment, you see.'

Adela thought she saw, but said, 'You will be patient with him, won't you?'

'Of course. I love children.'

Again Adela would have said more, but Mrs Danby was seething with impatience. 'Adela, we *must* go home or Father will fret himself into another attack. Harry is going to be perfectly all right. You can trust me, can't you?'

'Yes, of course,' said Adela. She watched the nurse stepping into the back of a car with Harry in her arms. The car drove away and she wanted to run after it and snatch him back.

Her father gained strength, but so slowly. He suffered a few setbacks and always protested vehemently at the idea of Adela's leaving Speede House again. 'My heart almost gave out on me once,' he pleaded. 'You don't want it to happen again, do you?'

She assured him she would stay, but grew more and more anxious about Harry.

'Where exactly is my boy?' she asked her mother. 'I want to visit him.'

Mrs Danby looked round hastily. 'Adela, someone will hear you!'

They were sitting near the fire in the small breakfast room at the back of the house. Adela said calmly, 'No one is anywhere near. Where is Harry, Mother? You must tell me. He'll be missing me.'

'He is perfectly safe and happy, dear.'

'I'm sure he is, but I would like to know his address.'

'For what purpose?'

Adela looked at her mother incredulously. 'I want to know where he is! I've just told you, I want to see him. He's my *son*!'

'I have asked you to keep your voice down. Visiting him would be a foolish and a selfish thing to do. No doubt he has got over missing you by now and settled happily. Do you wish to upset him all over again?'

'No, of course not. Would he be so upset at seeing me?'

'He most certainly would.'

'I don't remember ever being disturbed by Father's and your many absences from home.'

'Of course you were not, because you always had Nurse. She was the main figure in your life.'

'Well, I'm the main figure in Harry's.'

'Please do not throw my words back at me. You must understand what I mean.'

Adela calmed down. 'I suppose I do,' she said miserably. 'You think I should wait?'

'Definitely.'

'Could you give me his address, please, and I'll write to Mrs Brown?'

'Of course. I have it in my writing case in the library.'

Adela got up. 'I'll fetch your case.'

'Not now, dear. I promised Father I would sit with him a while. He's recovering so well. Nothing must be allowed to upset him.'

Adela questioned her mother again later in the day and again was fobbed off. She made up her mind. This needed direct action. She went to the library and, without a qualm, searched every drawer in Father's big desk. There was no sign of Mother's writing case. Father was being nursed in a small room and Adela crept into her parents' big bedroom and tried to open her mother's small French escritoire. It was locked. She stood quite still for a moment. Her need to see and hold her son in her arms was probably leading her into quite erroneous fears. Harry was happy and well or she would have heard. She would have to be patient with her mother who had always been stubborn and was made even more so by anxiety.

In spite of the ache caused by Harry's absence, Adela had been able to appreciate many aspects of being back in Speede House, revelling in the luxury of hot baths, warmth, good food prepared by an expert cook and served with quiet efficiency by Evans and his minions, and fires always heaped with coal. The clothes she had left behind were still in her wardrobe and were inclined to hang loosely on her as well as being somewhat out of fashion. Mrs Danby sent her shopping and instructed her to charge as much as she liked to the Danby accounts. Some older women, notably Queen Mary, still wore their skirts long, but up-to-date women were buying shorter skirts and evening dresses were mid-calf length and flimsy, with the back and neckline cut astonishingly low. Blanche stayed with Father one day, leaving Mrs Danby free to shop with Adela, and she insisted on ordering several evening gowns. Adela protested. 'I shan't need them, Mother. I shall have no opportunity to wear them.'

'Nonsense!' Mrs Danby smiled frostily at the inquisitive saleswoman. 'See to the alterations as soon as possible and telephone me. You have my number.'

Adela had given up the argument. If Mother insisted on spending her money on something which would be useless nobody could prevent her, and the more harmonious she kept their relationship the better. Besides, Father enjoyed seeing her in the new clothes, insisting on her walking up and down his room so that he could admire her. He had never been so attentive before. It seemed he really did depend on her. Adela couldn't bring herself to make even a minor protest when her mother encouraged her to buy the delicious new-style underwear which everyone, down to the youngest salesgirl, now called *lingerie*. It was gossamer light, made of delicate silk voile, tulle and crêpe Georgette.

Adela spent a lot of time with her father, and his health began to pick up until he was allowed to sit out of bed. He liked Adela to read to him. It was as if his illness had reversed their roles, turning him into the dependent child and her into the figure of authority. She had never enjoyed such companionship with him and she valued it. He, as well as Mother, insisted that she accept the invitations which had poured in as soon as people realised she was back.

'Of course, you'll have to dissemble,' said Mrs Danby. 'They believe you've been with your grandmother. I must say I was very angry when I discovered that you had not left Bristol, but no one seems to know and you were near when Father needed you. Such a blessing! Without you, I am sure he would not have recovered so well. Perhaps not at all.'

Adela warded off questions, but there weren't many. Her friends seemed too intent on enjoying the new decade with frenetic enthusiasm to waste time talking about a temporary absence: dancing to jazz bands until the early hours with the young men who had come back from the war or were too young to have gone, smoking endless Egyptian and Turkish cigarettes which gave out a pungent, exotic aroma, drinking cocktails, and everlastingly chattering like a gaggle of brilliant cockatoos about the animated pictures and their star performers, or plays, or the newest drink. Many of the girls had had their hair cut quite short and when they danced their long earrings swung in time to the music.

To Adela it seemed unreal. Life at the bottom had marked her and underneath everything she did was a longing to get Harry back. The need to hold him, to kiss his face, to bury her nose in his soft neck and smell the sweetness of him, was growing into an unendurable pain. Again she broached the subject with her mother who reacted in a coldly angry way which reminded Adela of the past, when she had made some childish transgression.

Occasionally she saw Blanche; sometimes Sander Bennett who returned her look coolly, his head jutting aggressively forward, his mouth grim. There were plenty of women who welcomed his attentions and who danced with him, smiling.

The new fashions with their demand for extreme slenderness suited Blanche. Her clothes had definitely improved. Last time Adela saw her she had been wearing a crimson silk dress with only a hint of a waist, which was clearly Paris-inspired and flowed around her like liquid fire. She smoked expertly and incessantly, using a long holder. She didn't lack partners and treated them all with cool disdain.

No unpleasantness was permitted to sully the lives of the pleasure-seekers. Prices were still rising; many of the unemployed were ex-soldiers who were also without homes. There was a crime wave; wealthy profiteers were ignoring the Profiteering Act and getting away with it; and there was still fighting in Ireland and Russia. Worst of all in some eyes, society was being increasingly infiltrated by the vulgar new-rich.

The young weren't interested. Their lives were bounded by the newest fashion, by the craze to drive in cars packed with too many shrieking people from one rendezvous to another, by uninhibited drinking as they laughed at the foolish Americans who were suffering under Prohibition. No alcohol! No cocktails! It sounded like purgatory. Many of the revellers were Americans, sons and daughters of rich men who enjoyed the free-drinking life of Britain. Chaperones were declared redundant and restrictions on the lives of young women seemed to be abolished.

'Enjoying yourself?' Blanche asked her sister casually one evening as a noisy group of revellers left one party to go on to another.

'Not much,' said Adela. 'Not at all really.'

'That's a pity. Is Mother being particularly obnoxious?'

'I don't know where she's sent Harry. She keeps promising to give me his address, but never does. If I make the least fuss she gives Father's heart attack as an excuse.'

'She's a ruthless woman,' said Blanche, 'but even she can't keep your son from you forever.' She looked her sister up and down. 'I take it she's been shopping with you? Jade green suits you, but your hair is still quite long. That's quite out of fashion, you know.'

Adela shrugged. 'This is new for you, isn't it? Not long ago you didn't give a hang for fashion.'

'Well, I do now.'

'You've met someone, haven't you? Why are you so secretive? Who is he?'

Blanche sauntered off, saying over her shoulder, 'You'll find out when I'm ready.'

'Why do you go to so many parties?' Adela asked Blanche when she came to Speede House to visit their father. 'I thought you had grown too serious about politics to enjoy such frivolity.'

'I go to see if there are any likely recruits for the Labour Party,' answered her sister.

'You surely don't imagine you'll find them among today's society?'

'You never know. I'd have said you were the most unlikely person to sympathise with the poor, yet you do. How's the infant? Have you heard anything more?'

'He's well. At least that's what I'm told. Mother speaks of phone calls which always come when I'm not in. She says Harry is progressing satisfactorily.'

More than once Adela and Mrs Danby came close to quarrelling as Adela became increasingly aware of her mother's ruthless attempt to inveigle her back into society, leaving Harry behind, forgetting him. It didn't help to be told that her son didn't miss her at all. Her life was incomplete and there was a knot of desolation inside her which grew tighter day by day. 'He'll forget me,' she cried.

'Nonsense,' said Mrs Danby. 'Adela, we've been through this. When you and Blanche were small you lived entirely in the nursery. You didn't forget us.'

'It's not the same! We were brought to you every day.'

'No, you were not. There were times when we didn't see you from one week's end to another. It had no effect on you.'

'Are you sure?' burst out Adela.

'What is that supposed to mean? That you were neglected?'

'No, of course not.' Adela stopped. 'We're off the subject of Harry which, I suppose, is your objective. Does Father know how you are treating me? Is he a party to this?'

'Are you mad? As if I would worry your dear father!'

'You want me to come home for good?'

'Of course I do. We both do.'

'But I must forget my son's existence?'

258

'No, no, of course you cannot forget him, but you can put him to the back of your mind, take your proper place as our daughter again.'

'No, I can never do that! Never! I can't even begin to explain my reasons.'

Adela tried to go through the motions of enjoying life in society while hiding her heartache. The depression which had been suppressed when first she came back to Speede House attacked her with renewed intensity and she was hard put to it not to scream aloud her frustration and unhappiness to her friends who seemed to have turned into vapid, careless caricatures of women. Only a cousin, Millicent Penrose, remained close.

Millie was younger than Adela, but was quite mature for her nineteen years and they found shared amusement as they watched some rhythm-crazed acquaintance kicking up her legs on the dance floor, showing more of herself than she would have dreamed of only a year ago.

'How is Grandmother Sutton?' Millie had asked when she and Adela found themselves sitting out a dance.

'Well,' said Adela shortly.

'She's a jolly old stick, isn't she?'

Adela looked incredulously at her cousin. 'Are we speaking of the same woman? She's always struck me as being aloof. So unbending.'

Millie had given her a quick, curious look and changed the subject. 'They're nutty, aren't they?' she said, pointing with her cigarette to the cavorting couples.

'You're a little young to be so staid, aren't you?' said Adela teasingly.

'Hark at you, Granny Danby.'

Adela smiled and Millie said reflectively, 'You're very pretty. I remember you at school, two classes ahead of me. You were a bit of a heroine of mine. So good at all the sports and tall, and slim and clever. All the things I'm not.'

Adela looked at her cousin who was about five feet two in height, petite and dainty in every way. Her dark hair was short and adorned with a ribbon band studded with small pearls. Her ivory tulle dress was a perfect foil for her softly pink cheeks and lips.

'You can't deny you're good-looking,' said Adela. 'As for being good at sports, I don't know what use that ever was or will be.'

'You sound sad.'

'Sorry. I didn't mean to.'

'And you look sad as well. When you think you're not being watched, I'm afraid you may cry.'

'Good lord!' said Adela loudly, forcing a laugh. 'I had no idea I was being so closely observed.'

Millie blew out a stream of smoke. 'You can't fool me, you know. I'm an observer of the human species. One day I'm going to write a book.'

'Is that before or after you're married?' asked Adela, nodding towards Millie's left hand on which gleamed a ring with an impressively large ruby.

'Oh, it doesn't matter when. Algy is a darling. He'll let me do as I wish.'

'Algy Norton? You're marrying him?' Adela hastily tried to hide her surprise. Algernon Norton was a good-natured but rather brainless society adornment. She said quickly, 'He'll be a splendid husband, I'm sure. He's very well off and will be immensely rich one day, won't he? Of course, I'm not implying that that's why you're marrying him.'

Millie looked at her cousin through eyes narrowed by a broad smile. 'It's part of the reason, though I wouldn't have said yes if I hadn't liked the silly blighter. He's the kindest man I've ever met and he adores me.'

'And do you adore him?'

'Certainly not! I refuse to be a slave to love – that sounds like the title of a book, doesn't it? Or more likely a moving picture. Don't you just adore the animated pictures? Algy and I go to dozens. I know I can make a very good life with him.'

'I'm sure you'll be happy,' Adela said.

'I'm sure, too. Is there anyone on your horizon?'

'No, no one at all.'

Adela often had difficulty sleeping. As she lay awake, she was tormented by pictures in her mind. Of Ralph, poor Ralph; of Sander Bennett needing to be bribed to marry her; of Jack. She missed him and his rough kindness and felt guilty as she pictured him pushing his barrow through all weathers, coughing, arriving home cold and tired and lonely to an empty house. She smiled ruefully in the darkness. Fat chance! Jack's daughters would have taken over again as soon as she had left. Still, she saw herself there, tending Harry, working, cooking, cleaning. It was a picture so far removed from the glamorous scenes of the past few weeks that it seemed like a different world. It *was* a different world, and she *should* be there with her son. Father was much stronger now. In fact, she had a suspicion that he and Mother were using his illness, exaggerating his danger to keep Adela with them. Tomorrow she would demand to know Harry's whereabouts and refuse to be put off any longer. Then she would visit Jack and assure him that she and Harry were returning.

Every day Adela read the newspaper to her father, while often her mind was filled with her own problems. He always asked first for the financial page and today there was an article which spoke of the absurdly large sums which were being paid by megalomaniac men intent on buying out the opposition, especially in the metal and textiles industries.

Mr Danby grew restive. 'I should be out there competing, Adela.'

'Your health is far more important than money, Father. Leave the speculation to fitter people.'

'Like that blasted Bennett man, I suppose!'

His angry outburst made her jump. 'The doctor said you weren't to get over-excited.'

'Damn doctors! There are fortunes to be made. Huge stocks of surplus war garments are being sold at ridiculously low prices. All kinds of things. Bennett is always in there bidding. He's bought enough ex-army boots to kit out all the workmen in Bristol for years.'

The nurse, who hovered near, tutted and insisted that her patient should drink a calming potion.

Later Adela asked her mother, 'Has Father been worrying about business?'

Mrs Danby was surprised and quite gratified by her daughter's interest. 'Oh, yes, indeed he has. He cannot afford to be left behind and he has been borrowing money from the bank so that he, too, can buy up some of the many small thriving businesses now on the market. Mr Bennett positively persecutes Father. He hasn't forgiven the way you humiliated him.' She hurried on, not giving Adela a chance to speak. 'There is much reconstruction needed after the years of war and vast profits to be made by the shrewd.'

'What happens to the men who lose their businesses?' Adela asked.

Mrs Danby stared. 'How should I know? I leave all that kind of thing to Father.'

'It must be quite a strain for him.'

'Yes, of course it is. A dreadful strain.'

'So I am not entirely responsible for his heart attack.'

Mrs Danby sat up straight and shot her daughter a furious look. 'How dare you try to twist my meaning! Business is always a trial to a man, but he looks to his family to support him. He does not expect to have to contend with the kind of behaviour he's getting from his daughters at the moment. I think he could put up with Blanche – he always thought she was odd – but you, Adela, he had great hopes for you.'

'I'm sorry I disappointed him, but you know my reasons. Mother, I've had a word with the nurse and she assures me that Father is out of danger. I really must return home and—'

She got no further. Her mother cried, 'Return home? That is what you have done! This is your home and I won't listen to any more of your nonsense.'

Adela said doggedly, 'I can't live without my son. He needs me.'

'Nonsense! I am assured that he has a robust constitution.'

'That's true, but his nerves are not what they should be. He cries a great deal and needs a lot of love and understanding.'

'Which I suppose you can give him, hunched over a sewing machine? Blanche told me of the conditions in which she found

262

you. I was shocked. I am afraid I cannot countenance your returning to them.'

Adela stared at her mother. If the situation hadn't been so serious she might have laughed at the notion of her mother believing she had such power over her, especially in this new age of emancipation. 'You can't keep me here by force.'

'I am aware of that,' said Mrs Danby acidly, 'but surely there will be no need? Your place is with your parents until you marry a decent man of whom we can approve.'

'I thought you said that no decent man would want me after I'd borne a child out of wedlock.'

'Will you stop saying those dreadful things! You have no idea how much they wound me.'

'They wound your pride, that's all.'

'How wickedly untruthful.'

'So you care for me, do you?'

Mrs Danby flushed. 'It is easy to tell that you have been with people who allow their most private emotions to spill over into foolish talk. I am your mother. I have a mother's duty to you.'

'As I have to Harry.' Adela got up. 'There's no use in arguing. I must leave. Just give me Harry's address and I'll fetch him.'

'There will be a very large bill to settle.'

Adela stared at her mother angrily. 'I assume you will pay it.'

'I shall pay all monies connected with him so long as I have your co-operation.'

'Harry's address, please. I'll find a way of settling the debt.'

'I shall not give it to you.'

Adela sighed. 'You're acting very stubbornly, but it won't wash. Tell me where my child is.'

Adela's mother stood up and held herself rigid. Her eyes were flint-hard. 'I will not tell you. I will never tell you. I will not permit you to continue a wanton ruination of your life.'

'How can you be so wickedly heartless? I shall ask Father.'

'You really would risk his health? He has all his hopes pinned on your staying here. He won't help you to get away.'

'Then, if you care about him, you had better tell me what I need to know.'

'You would really agitate him at such a time? I find such wanton cruelty difficult to comprehend.'

'Mother, please—'

'You cannot weaken me. I know what I am doing is right. I shall not tell you the child's whereabouts, and it isn't any use going to your father because he doesn't know. No one knows except me. I have given the boy a new surname and I am the only person who can tell you what it is, and that I *never* will.'

'Mother,' cried Adela, 'you couldn't be so evil!'

'Evil! How dare you? I am thinking only of your good. And don't yell! Do you want the servants to hear you?'

'That's all you care about – what others think of us. I could be bleeding to death inside, but what would it matter as long as no one knew? You've never thought about me at all. You are determined to punish me. Well, I shall find my son and take him to a place where there is more love than you could ever understand.'

Mrs Danby glared at her daughter, opened her mouth to speak, changed her mind, and walked out of the room.

Chapter Fifteen

It was all very well for Adela to make bold, confident threats to her mother; being able to carry them out was another matter. She wondered what advice Jack would give her. He was shrewd enough to think of something. She decided to go and see him and, having once made up her mind, acted immediately. He would be on the barrow at this time of day and she would have preferred to wear her shabby coat and hat to Old Market, but discovered that her mother had consigned them, along with everything else she had brought home, to the dustbin.

'There are many poor people who would have been glad of a few clothes,' Adela protested.

Mrs Danby had set her lips. 'No doubt you number such among your friends?'

Adela didn't argue. What was the use? She had done her best to choose clothes which were as unobtrusive as possible, but her mother had insisted they shop in their usual places and, unwilling to provoke yet more acrimony, Adela had given in. Everything she now had spoke loudly of money. Her blue-grey gabardine suit and blue silk blouse were plain but beautifully tailored. Her buckled shoes, gloves and handbag were of fine leather, her stockings silk and her straw hat a poem of understated elegance. There was nothing she could do to make herself look less conspicuous. She left the house and caught a tram to Old Market.

The day was fine and the stall holders were in good voice, imploring passing folk to buy their wares. Adela hurried past the fruit and vegetable stalls, the man who sold seconds in underwear and hosiery, the old man with a small barrow of pinky fruit. She couldn't find Jack anywhere.

She saw Fred Withycombe at the same time as he caught sight of her. A flash of mutual antipathy passed between them as she walked up to his barrow. She was just in time to watch him weigh apples, a concealed thumb resting on the scales as he served a ragged woman, his face one big, beaming, confidential smile. 'You'll find no better stuff than mine, my love,' he assured her, 'an' no better value.' His eyes dared Adela to intervene.

The woman hurried away and before Adela could say a word Fred looked her up and down, 'My, my, aren't we all done up like a dog's dinner then? What you been up to, eh? Made yourself a fortune, have you? Doin' what?' His voice had got louder all the time and a couple of the nearest barrow boys sniggered.

Adela was no longer to be intimidated by the likes of Fred. He would know where Jack was. But before she could speak he went on, 'Found a richer bloke than Jack, I suppose?'

'You can suppose what the hell you like,' snapped Adela.

'Ooh, listen to her.' A customer who lived in the same rank of houses as the Websters threw up her hands. 'She's swearin' at you, Fred, an' all because you got her summed up proper. What would a fine lady like her be wantin' with Jack *now*?'

Adela was suddenly frightened by the woman's tone. She walked up to her and stood close, towering over her in a deliberately domineering way. 'What exactly do you mean?' she demanded.

The woman's bluster died down. 'You can't blame us for thinkin' you're a wrong 'un. As soon as Jack's cut down, as you might say, you run off an' leave him.'

'Cut down? What do you mean? Is Jack ill?'

'Are you pretendin' you don't know?' cried Fred Withycombe. 'That's a good one!'

'I asked you a question,' Adela said to the woman. 'Is Jack ill?'

'In a manner of speakin'. He's had an accident.'

'Oh, no! How bad?'

'Bad enough to keep him home. Probably for good.'

Adela waited no longer. She hurried away and took the well

remembered roads to Jack's house. She knocked on the front door. There was no movement inside. She knocked louder, and he answered. Her relief at hearing his voice almost made her weep. 'Come in, if you're comin'. The door's not locked.'

Adela went inside. The living room hadn't changed much, though she noticed the absence of her sewing machine. Then, as her eyes grew accusomed to the gloom, she saw that there was a bed in one corner in which Jack was lying, thinner than ever and pale, propped up by pillows.

'Jack!' She was with him in swift strides. 'What happened?'

'Adela!' For an instant his joy was reflected in his voice. Then it died away. 'Adela,' he said flatly, 'why have you come?'

'Why? What a question to ask. How long have you been lying here like this?'

'Too bloody long.'

Adela sat on the bed, leaned over and kissed his cheek gently. She thought for a moment he was going to pull away from her but at the last moment he didn't.

'Have you seen a doctor?' she asked.

'Of course I have. As a matter of fact, I've been in hospital. I haven't been out long.'

'It must have been a bad accident to send you there.'

'Bad enough, but I'll be all right soon. How are things in Speede House? How's your father?'

'A great deal better, thank you.'

'And your mother? Has she taken to Harry?'

'No, she scarcely looked at him.'

'Where is he?'

'I'll tell you about Harry later. Jack, you look so ill and you sound very weak.'

'It'll pass.'

'Would you like a cup of tea?'

'That I would.'

The place was clean – obviously Annie and Florrie had been busy again – and Adela found a tin containing a few small cakes which she took in along with the tea.

Jack sipped his and smiled at her. 'It's good to see you, my dear. You've been gone so long I thought you'd forgotten me.'

'Never! Oh, Jack, I assumed you'd be working as always. If only I'd known about the accident! How did it happen? You should have written.'

'What for? I've seen your photo in the papers again. You've been havin' a gay old time.'

'Whatever it looked like, I assure you I haven't been enjoying myself. I gather the terrible twins have been looking after you. Where's my sewing machine?'

'Out in the shed.'

'What? It'll get damp.'

'No, it won't, it's well covered. Mum wanted to sell it. She said it might as well go as it was obvious you'd never be back.'

'She would! Well, she was wrong.'

'I wouldn't let her get rid of the machine. I said—'

'Yes? You said?'

'I said that you might need it again.'

'So you didn't entirely give up hope of me?' Adela looked around her. 'At least the girls have left the curtains and cushions. I'm surprised they haven't replaced everything I did.'

'No, they're not that stupid. They've been good daughters.'

'Oh, I'm sorry. They must have been wonderful when you needed help so much. I'll thank them.'

Jack's eyebrows were raised. 'They'll not thank you for thanking them.'

'They'll get my gratitude anyway.'

Jack said slowly, 'You've changed.'

Adela looked intently at him, finding his cheeks sunken, his eyes ringed by dark shadows. 'So have you, me old love.'

Jack laughed again. 'You sound proper Bristol.'

'I am proper Bristol. And I'm going to be proper St Philips again, too.'

'No!'

'Don't you want me?'

'Wantin's got nothin' to do with it. It's a case of what's right an' proper, an' you can't live here now. I'm just a burden.'

'I've got used to burdens.'

'Not me! You'll not get used to me!'

'I'm only giving back what you gave me.'

268

'An' what's that?'

'Deep friendship and protection, care and trust, when they were most needed.'

'It's not the same. It's up to a man to look after a woman.'

'Nonsense! What about all your assertions that women are equal to men?'

Jack said ruefully, 'It doesn't seem the same when it's happenin' to me.'

'Well, it's the same to me. Jack, what happened? Tell me what happened, please.'

'It's simple, really. I was racin' with the barrow. The road was wet an' the wheels began to slide an' I almost got stuck in the tramlines. Then I got a fit of coughin' and lost my concentration. I tripped an' fell an' a motor car caught my legs. They tell me I was dragged along like a sack of coal for quite a way before the motor could stop. When I came to in hospital I was warned I might lose my legs altogether.'

'Oh, my God!'

'I'm lucky I didn't, though they're not much to look at any more. The doctors patched me up an' here I am. I've had to resign myself to never walkin' properly again.'

'And I wasn't here! I could have helped you, repaid you for all your goodness to me. Well, I'm here now and soon I'll be back for good.'

'No, Adela.'

'Yes, Jack.'

'You'd better listen to what I have to say before you make up your mind.' Jack sounded grim. 'I can never work the barrows again. I'll probably never get any work at all again. There are too many healthy young men lookin' for jobs for anyone to consider me. You thought you had a hard life before, but it'll be nothin' to what you'll get if you come back an' try to support me. *An'* I've always helped out Mum an' Ida.' He paused. 'Not that I'd expect anyone else to do that.'

Adela stared at his set face. 'I shall come back as soon as I get a few necessary things together, and I shall take care of you and make sure that your mother and Ida have things as easy as possible. I'm wiser than I was.'

269

'What's that supposed to mean?'

'It means that I shan't return empty-handed.'

He gave her a speculative look. 'Come into money, have you?'

'No, I'm bringing possessions of my own to sell, that's all.'

'Have your parents forgiven you?'

Adela considered. 'In a way. If you discount Harry, I suppose they have.'

'If you return here they might not forgive you again.'

'No, I don't suppose they will. I'm not at all sure my mother has anyway.'

'So there'll be no bridge back like there was before.'

'No, no bridge back.'

Jack handed her his cup and saucer. 'I know I should try to stop you. I had it all planned out that if you came here I'd be strong enough to send you away. There's nothin' here for you except work and worry, but I've missed you a hell of a lot. I've missed the little chap, too. Even his cryin'. I'm lookin' forward to seein' him again.' He was watching Adela's face. 'Why, what's wrong? Has somethin' happened to Harry?'

'I came here hoping for your advice. I didn't expect to find you so ill.'

'Not too ill to share your problems. Tell me.'

In a shaking voice Adela explained, and he swore. 'That woman! An' some people think *my* mother's a dragon. *Yours* could teach her a lot. What will you do?'

Adela said nothing for a while. Then: 'I shall find him.'

'I suppose you could threaten to make everythin' public if your mother doesn't give you Harry's address?'

'No. It would hurt everyone concerned, but Harry most of all. Illegitimacy is a burden which no one can ever throw off.' She paused. 'Jack, I've come to believe that money is power. In the past I've taken so much for granted. I never needed to think deeply or make decisions. Now, some way or other, I'm going to make money. Lots of it. And as soon as I have a few pounds together, I shall employ a private investigator to find my son. I'll get him back.'

Jack took her hand in his. 'That's my girl.'

His hand was thin and white, all the hard-working roughness smoothed away. 'Are you allowed out of bed?' she asked.

'Yes, I can get up whenever I want. I'm just havin' a rest. Move away, Adela, you'd best learn the whole truth before you finally decide on your future.'

She stood up and he threw aside the bedclothes. He was fully dressed and swung his feet to the floor. Then he reached for a pair of crutches that had been standing behind the bedhead, and grasped them. Easing himself off the bed he raised himself and began a slow, shambling walk to a chair by the fireplace. He sank into it with a grunt.

Adela watched in horror before running to him and seizing his hands. 'How you must have suffered! You should have told me, you really should.'

'You couldn't have left your father.'

'I could have visited you, talked to you. I might have been some comfort to you.'

'Well, you're with me now.' No one, hearing the joy in Jack's voice, could doubt that he had missed her.

She shivered. 'It's chilly in here.'

'Money's scarce and I have to save coal. I only light the fire in the evenings.'

'Well, we'll have a fire today.'

Calmly she put a match to the newspaper and sticks already prepared by Annie or Florrie.

Jack stretched out his hands to the warmth. 'I'm bein' selfish to take what you have to offer. Life with me could be too difficult even for you with your courage. My soldier's uncovenanted benefit ran out ages ago. Mum an' Ida miss my help. Mum's rheumatics are very bad lately an' she should have a doctor an' get medicine.'

'Ida told me your mother didn't trust doctors.'

'No, but she's in pain. If we got one to her I don't see how she could refuse to see him. Ida went to the Guardians for help an' they asked hundreds of questions an' then visited us. They told Mum that before she could get help she'd have to sell her ornaments. Even the pair of china dogs that were a weddin' present from her mother had to be sold, an' only when she had

271

nothin' left did they agree to give her somethin'. It's a bloody good job your sewin' machine was hidden! I told them my barrow had already gone. Bastards, they are, I hate them! Of course the girls are good, but they've got their own problems. None of us has much to spare. Now Ida gets food coupons an' soon I'll have to apply. I didn't tell them about the stuff I had left on the barrow, either. I've had to sell that.'

'Food coupons! Ration coupons, do you mean?'

'No, these are somethin' very different. They make you beg for these.'

'How do they work?'

Jack grimaced. 'You're allowed so much for meat, so much for bread, so much for all the needs the Guardians decide you have. They take a delight in humiliatin' you as much as possible. I hate them and their bloody charity, but we've got to have it to live. They strip a person of all their possessions an' don't leave them a shred of pride. Poor Mum loathes them. She's never got over havin' to have a means test when pensions started. She an' Ida have only got that to live on, an' half of it goes for rent an' burial insurance. By the time they've paid for gas an' coal they've got only two and six a week for everythin' else, plus the pittance that the Guardians dole out.'

'No one can exist on that!'

Jack sighed. 'You've still got a lot to learn. Some have to manage on less.'

There was a soft swift movement and Tibs jumped on to Adela's lap, purring and rubbing herself against her.

'Poor old Tibs,' said Jack. 'She's havin' to eat more bread than fish these days.'

'She's probably full of mice. God knows there are enough of them round here.'

Jack said, 'Mum's been thrifty, but she never had a chance to save. Annie's man brings coal to us from the wharf. It's a bit cheaper that way. He uses my barrow now I've got no use for it.'

'You didn't ever consider selling it?'

'No. I got so desperate one time I would have, but Mum was dead against it. It's all she's got left to remind herself of Dad an' days past when they got a fair livin' from it. She couldn't bear to see it go.'

'Poor soul. Who paid your hospital bills?'

'I was in a charity ward and another charity paid for doctor's visits an' medicine. That's finished now.'

'And yet you kept my sewing machine!'

'I couldn't sell it somehow, it's yours, though to be honest I don't think I could have held on to it much longer.'

Adela squeezed his hand and he said sadly, 'You'd do better to stay where you belong. Life here is bitter hard an' will get harder. An' do you know, Adela?' He went red with rage. 'The government, if you can call it that, has turned down a proposal for a levy on fortunes made during the war. Ex-soldiers have to beg in the streets, an' profiteers have got away with their dishonesty an' greed. The country's gone crazy.'

He had forgotten himself and his pain and she smiled to see the fire back in his eyes.

'It's not funny, Adela!'

'Of course it isn't. I'm just glad to see you yourself again.'

Jack fell sombre again. 'I don't know what use I'll be to the party now.'

'You'll think of something.'

'Do society nobs know anythin' about the hard lives of the poorest people?'

'Some do, and they care.'

'Your parents? Do they?'

'Mother only knows that business can be precarious. Father has been speculating.'

'I heard. In textiles, too. A lot of businesses are goin' down the drain.'

'Yes, but he's experienced.'

'So he may be, but there hasn't been anythin' like this before.'

'Sander Bennett is mixed up in it, too. I hope he gets his fingers burned.'

Jack raised his brows. 'Still on bad terms with him?'

'As far as I'm concerned we're not on any terms at all.'

'I see.' Jack watched her for a moment then said, 'Mum

wasn't the only reason I kept the barrow. I've been hopin' I'd get back to the market, but now I know I never will. Even if someone helped me, all the lyin' in bed an sittin' around has made my chest worse. The doctor says if I try to work outside again I won't last long.'

'Don't say that!' said Adela fiercely.

Someone banged on the front door and walked in. Florrie and Annie called out: 'It's only us, Dad. We've brought you your dinner.' They came into the living room.

'Well, look who's here!' cried Florrie. Her hostile eyes took in Adela's outfit. 'My, aren't we posh! Come to visit our dad, have you?'

'I should think that was obvious,' said Adela calmly. 'If you leave Jack's meal, I'll see to it.'

'*So* nice of you,' said Florrie, in a bad attempt to imitate Adela's accents.

'Give over, Florrie,' said Annie. 'Why didn't you come before, Adela? You must have known about Dad's accident? It was in the papers.' She had reproved her sister, but her manner was cool.

'Of course she knew,' cried Florrie. 'She reads the newspapers, doesn't she?'

'I didn't see the report,' said Adela. 'I read to my father, but he was only interested in business news.'

'He would be,' snapped Florrie.

Adela hung on to her temper. 'If I had known of Jack's accident, I would have been here much sooner.'

'An' what d'you think you're goin' to do now you *are* here?' asked Florrie. 'You're hardly dressed for work.' She peered around in the gloom. 'Where's Harry?'

'He's being properly cared for in a nursery,' said Adela. Her tone didn't invite comment and even Florrie was daunted by the look she received.

'Does it have to be so dark?' asked Adela. She pulled the gas chain and the gloomy room was illuminated by its feeble yellow glow.

'It's plain to see that you haven't heard of economy,' said Florrie.

Annie said, 'Dad has to be careful with everythin' now he's not earnin'. He can only afford enough light to read a short time every day. He uses candles a lot.'

Florrie, ignoring Adela's offer of help, went through to the kitchen and put her father's dinner to warm in the oven. 'Are you stayin' long?' she asked Adela pointedly when she returned.

'This is only a visit, but I'm coming back to live.'

Florrie gave her a furious look. 'Dad can't afford hangers-on any more.'

'I've never been a liability to him and I don't intend to be now.'

'Your customers go to a woman in the next street,' said Florrie in tones of malicious satisfaction. 'You'll not get them back. She's a trained tailoress an' *she* hasn't ruined any material. She's been left with six kids to bring up.'

'Then I had better not think of taking her trade away from her.'

'Goin' to the Guardians, are you?' Florrie sounded spitefully gleeful.

'Stop it, our Florrie,' said Jack wearily.

Annie bent over him. 'Aren't you so well today, Dad? You do look tired. How long have you been out of bed?'

'He looks exhausted!' snapped Florrie. 'I suppose he's been doin' the honours. Probably finds it hard to keep up with Lady Muck here.'

'He looks happier anyhow,' said Annie.

'Huh! I'm surprised at you, sidin' with *her*.' Florrie flounced out.

Annie said, 'What time are you leavin', Adela?'

'I'll wait to give Jack his dinner then I must get back. My parents will wonder where I am.'

'How is your father?'

'He's recovered, thank you. I needn't stay there any longer. I'll be returning for good tomorrow.'

'Will Harry be with you?'

'Not straight away, but I'll get him soon.' Soon, she repeated to herself. They can't keep my baby from me. They won't! I'll get him back!

* * *

Once in Speede House, Adela made careful plans. She gathered together several suitcases and packed all the clothes and shoes her mother had bought for her, filled several hat boxes with her new hats and put all her jewellery which wasn't in Father's safe into a capacious bag, including the costume pieces for which there was an increasing market. Underwear, dainty handkerchiefs, stockings, nightwear, expensive scent and toilet powder, were all collected and stowed away. It was hers and she was entitled to it. Then she went downstairs.

It was tea time and Mrs Danby was entertaining. Her guests greeted Adela with pleasure.

'You look prettier than ever,' whispered a blushing youth into her ear. Adela smiled at him, but made no answer, except to thank him for the tea he brought her.

'Will you have bread and butter? Cake?' asked Mother.

'I think I'll have everything,' said Adela. 'I'm ravenous.'

There was general laughter as she munched her way through as much as possible. It might be a long time before she could afford such delicacies again. Millie arrived and sat by her. 'Hello, Cousin Adela. How are you? You look like a cat who has swallowed a whole jug of cream.'

'Do I? I must try to modify my expression. How's Algy?'

'He's well. He's playing golf today.'

'Do you play?'

'Not really. I sometimes walk round with him. He's very grateful when I do. I prefer swimming, preferably in warm water. Thank God the war's over and we can visit the South of France again. Will you be taking a holiday abroad this year?'

'I think not.'

'What's that?' cried Mrs Danby. 'Why should you not go abroad, Adela? You've been so patient all through the war years. You deserve a little pleasure.'

Adela smiled. 'I must give it some thought.'

'Come with us,' said Millie. 'Our darling villa in Deauville wasn't even touched during the war.'

'I am sure that Adela will be delighted to accept your invitation, Millie. I'll telephone your mother and make it official.'

'Will you be at the Hendersons' dance?' asked the shy youth of Adela. 'It's sure to be one of the best of the season.'

'Do come,' said Millie, 'I've got the most marvellous Vionnet dress with simply blissful handkerchief points at the hem.'

'Thank heaven for Paris fashions,' said a languid girl in green. 'One almost died of frustration at times during the war.'

No one appeared to find her remark in the least bit incongruous and Adela stared round at them all. They seemed to have forgotten the agony, the carnage, and the incredible courage. They were unaware of, or they didn't care about, the state of the country outside their privileged circle.

She said so to her mother after everyone had gone. Mrs Danby's complacent smile turned to a frown. 'Just because people don't moan and groan over their losses does not mean that they do not feel them. You really must develop a sensible attitude to life and stop thinking of the ghastly people you've been living with.'

'Some of them are ghastly, many are extremely nice. It's the same in any society, I suppose.'

Mrs Danby set her lips, not deigning to answer. After the tea things were removed she said, 'I shall telephone Millie's mother now and accept your cousin's invitation to Deauville. The trip will do you good. You'll soon forget the past months.'

Adela put a detaining hand on her mother's arm. 'No, Mother, don't telephone. I shall not be going to France and I ask you once more, where is Harry?'

'Oh, no, not again! I thought you'd got over it!'

'Got over it! Got over losing my son!'

'*Will* you keep your voice down?'

'Will you tell me where Harry is to be found? What name he is living under? You can't mean to keep him from me. He means everything to me. He's my child. Can't you understand? My son. I want him with me. I need him. I must have him!' Adela was floundering in a welter of words, a quagmire of distress, but her mother watched her coldly.

'I refuse to discuss it. I have told you that I shall never reveal that – that *child's* whereabouts to you. I really must ask you to stop tormenting us!'

'What about my torment? Don't you care for me at all?'

'What I feel for you has nothing to do with what I feel about your astonishingly bad behaviour. I will go so far as to tell you that the child is perfectly safe and will never know want.'

Adela looked long at her mother who said, 'Don't look at me like that.'

'Like what?'

'As if – as if you hated me.'

'At this moment I do,' said Adela, and walked out of the drawing room and upstairs. Any reservations she might have had at taking everything she could legitimately lay her hands on completely vanished. She had meant to leave home later that night, or early in the morning, but she couldn't bear to spend another moment under the same roof as her mother. She finished her preparations and when Mrs Danby was dressing for dinner Adela telephoned for a taxi. She must get out of here. Later, from the vantage point of her own independence, she would take up the battle for Harry again. She knew that the servants would be in the kitchen quarters and Bertha with her mother, but her heart beat hard as a maid appeared. Fortunately she was a new young parlourmaid. Unfamiliar with the below-stairs routine she had no idea that she should be in the basement and was more than willing to help Adela who gave her a shilling for her pains.

Then Adela stood shivering with nerves on the front doorstep. She had left a note for her parents telling them briefly what she intended to do and giving them her address. After what seemed like hours a taxi arrived. The driver was loudly cheerful and Adela feared that someone would look out of a window and try to stop her. When the taxi pulled out into the road, she heaved a great sigh of relief.

'Where to, miss?'

Adela gave him the address and he said, 'I didn't quite catch the name, miss. I thought you said St Philips.'

'That's what I did say.'

'It's a rough place for a young lady such as yourself. You sure you've got the name right?'

'Quite sure.'

Her tone forbade further questioning and soon the taxi was driving through the narrow streets between the crowded little houses. People stopped to stare. A taxi was an almost unheard of luxury in these parts.

Adela paid the driver who left her on the doorstep of Jack's house surrounded by cases and boxes. The door opened and Jack himself appeared. He was very pale. He could do with a holiday in a darling villa in Deauville, if anybody could! He watched in obvious frustration as Adela herself carried everything through the front door and up to her bedroom. When she came down he had the kettle on and a plate of cold meat and bread on the kitchen table.

'Lovely,' said Adela, dismissing the thought of Welsh lamb with mint sauce and all the trimmings, or sirloin of beef with Yorkshire pudding so light it almost floated. She fetched a jar of pickles from the cupboard and spread some slices of bread with margarine. Then she and Jack sat at opposite ends of the table and ate, and as she saw the strain ebbing from his face Adela felt there was nowhere else she would rather be.

Jack's health improved under her care and his nerves grew stronger because she was there. He still felt the cold badly and on cool, wet summer days she kept up a bright fire.

He protested. 'Adela, we can't afford to have a fire goin' so often.'

'Lying in bed to keep warm is bad for you. And you shouldn't smoke.'

He blew a stream of smoke down his nostrils and coughed. 'It helps my lungs.'

'Helps make them worse, don't you mean?'

He sat back in the easy chair and dragged defensively on his cigarette. 'It's about my only occupation.'

Adela was kneeling at the grate where she had placed sticks over newspaper. 'When I get going with the work, I'll need you. I must learn all you can tell me about how to deal with customers, and how good are you at book-keeping?'

Jack couldn't help the gratified smile which spread across his face. 'Not bad. Arithmetic was my best subject at school.'

'That suits my plans very well.'

'What plans? Makin' more clothes? You were workin' flat out an' the money was slow enough in comin'. An' now some-one's taken your trade.'

'Not making clothes – interior decorating.'

'What?'

'Beautifying people's homes. Telling them the pattern of wallpaper they should have, the type of furniture, the colour of their carpets and curtains – oh, lots of things.'

'That's a good one! Surely people don't need tellin' things like that!'

'Not round here, they don't. They just have to buy anything they can get hold of.'

'An' how are you goin' to begin? How will you get well-off folk to ask you into their houses?'

Adela sat back on her heels as the fire took hold of the kindling and sent out a few sparks. She held her sooty hands clear of her clean apron. 'That will come later when I've some money put by. First I'll sell furnishing fabrics from the barrow.'

'You'll *what*?'

'There's no need to shout. You've still got the barrow, haven't you?'

'Yes, but—'

'Women do work on the barrows sometimes, don't they?'

'Yes, but—'

'Apart from backache, I'm healthy, aren't I?'

'Yes, but—'

'Can't you say anything else?' Adela's eyes were filled with laughter.

'I can if you'll give me half a chance. The only women I've seen on the barrows have been great, solid, tough women, an' few enough of those. You have to stand out in all weathers. You have to fight for the best places. My God, Adela, running with the barrow was how I got like this.' He gestured towards his legs.

'I don't intend to slip. If the truth be told I'm probably stronger than you with your poor old damaged lungs.'

'I shouldn't be surprised, though I've noticed you often rub your back when you think no one's lookin'. Does it still hurt bad?'

'It hurts,' she said, 'what of it? Most women have much worse to put up with.'

'Was it bad when you were with your parents?'

'Sometimes.'

'You could rest there if you wanted to, couldn't you?'

'You don't know my mother. She had me running here, there and everywhere.'

'Not runnin' with a barrow, though.'

'No, not that.' Adela smiled.

Jack didn't smile. 'Adela, even if you could manage to get a barrow full of stuff to a good place in the market—'

'Which I will.'

'Even *if* you could, where are you goin' to get the stuff in the first place? How will you pay for it?'

'I'm going to get the stuff from warehouses here and in London and anywhere else I find out about. And I'm getting money together to pay for the first lot by selling the things I brought with me.'

'You won't get much for second-hand clothes.'

'It depends on what they are and how second hand. Mine are brand new and expensive, some of them models. My mother insisted on taking me shopping. She spent a great deal of money. I think she thought she'd buy me back. It's odd,' reflected Adela, 'how people have thought they could buy me. First Sander Bennett and then my parents. You've never tried, Jack.'

'You're priceless,' he grinned.

'Thanks. I shall sell the real jewels to a second-hand dealer and advertise the clothes and costume jewellery in the newspapers. There are plenty of new-poor who want to look nice, as well as new-rich.'

'I see. And where will these fine ladies go to view the clothes?'

'I've thought of that, too. Blanche has a flat. It's bound to be presentable. I'll give a box number, of course.'

'Won't Blanche have somethin' to say?'

'She might, though she's a lot nicer to me than she used to be.

I'll offer her a cut of the sales. Unfortunately, Mother locked the best of my jewellery in Father's safe, but I expect I'll make a tidy sum from the rest.'

'You've got it all mapped out.'

'I certainly have.' Adela stared into the heart of the fire which was glowing now. 'All except finding my baby.' She paused, fighting down panic, hugging herself tight, forgetting her sooty hands, trying to contain the emptiness of her arms. 'I hardly know where to begin.'

Jack touched her hair gently. 'I suppose there's a list of nurseries somewhere. An' there are the orphanages.'

Adela stared in horror. 'Orphanages?'

'Don't look like that. They're not dens of iniquity.'

'But I've read about them. They do look after children, it's true, but in so regimented a way. Surely Mother wouldn't have put Harry in one? And how will I know who to ask for? She's given him a different name.'

Adela's newfound confidence drained from her and she slumped on the mat. 'Jack, nothing will be worth having unless I get him back.'

'I know. It's bad to lose your child. I suffer from not knowin' where my boy is. Or even if he's alive.'

'Your boy? Oh, I forgot. How awful of me!'

'Well, it's not the same as losin' a baby. He was a young man when he left.'

'He should write to you.'

'He did at first. Of course the war interfered a lot with the post, with so much shippin' bein' sunk.'

'Why did he go away?'

Jack seemed lost in thought then he said, 'He an' Mum had a terrible quarrel one day. She accused him of runnin' after girls, of smokin' an' gamblin' an' drinkin'.' He paused and smiled. 'Of course he was doin' all those things, but in a very small way. He was young, makin' good money for the first time, an' it was natural for him to swagger about a bit. He had a couple of brushes with the police, nothin' serious, just larkin' about. Mum said he was gettin' the family a bad name. She kept on an' on at him until he lost his temper, they had a blazin' row, an' in

282

the end she accused him of killin' his mother.'

'Jack!'

'I know. It was very wrong of her. My wife was never strong after his birth, she suffered quite cruelly at times with internal problems, an' died when he was eight. But you can't blame a kid for the way he was born. Florrie an' Annie were only kids an' Mum helped me with them all. I think she's always felt guilty about what she said to Michael.'

'I'm sure he'll get in touch some day. It wasn't your fault.'

'The trouble is he believed what his gran said, but it wasn't his fault that Jessica was never strong. She'd had scarlet fever when she was a child, but she wanted children so badly I gave in to her and ours were born one after the other. It was too much. I should have been firmer with her.'

'But she was happy. She must have been happy with you.'

'Yes, she had a sunny nature an' she loved her babies.' He reached into a cupboard that stood beside the fireplace and pulled out an envelope. 'Here's a photograph of my Jessica.'

Adela looked into the delicate smiling face of a woman with a mass of dark hair. Two little girls stood either side of her and in her arms she held a small boy. 'She was beautiful.'

'She was that! That's Michael in her arms. He grew up tall, like her, and favours her in looks. He was bigger than me when he was fourteen. He'll be twenty-four now.'

Jack took the photographs and studied them. 'Jessica really loved her babies.'

'As I love Harry. One day I'm going to have more children. I didn't think I'd want to, but now I know I do. I miss my baby so much—' Her voice broke.

'You'll get him back, my dear, I know you will. It strikes me you'll do anything you make up your mind to do. Nearly everything.' He shook his head. 'But you'll never manage the barrow. You'll be defeated there.'

Chapter Sixteen

Esther came hurrying round as soon as she heard the news of
Adela's return. Jack insisted that he could manage the stairs
now and his sons-in-law had shifted the big bed upstairs again.
He was resting when Esther called.

'I'm really glad you're back, Adela.'

She smiled gratefully at the welcome. Mrs Webster had
made the expected acid comments. 'I'm glad to be back.'

'Is your father well again?'

'Almost. The doctor says he can go back to work, though he
must take things easier.'

'He'll miss you. And so will your mother.'

'Miss me? Mother wants me to settle down at home as if
nothing had happened, as if Harry had never been, and I can't.'

'Perhaps she'll come round.'

'I don't think so. I've had a letter from her.' She didn't
enlarge upon the subject. Her mother's letter had been full of
recriminations, accusations that she would kill her father, that
she had purloined items from the house, and a reiteration that
she would never give way in a certain matter.

'How are you, Esther?' asked Adela. 'And how's Bert?'

Esther's face darkened. 'He's no better really, though
they've discovered that music helps him. They've got a gramophone and he listens to it for hours. They don't have many
records and I'm going to take some new ones as soon as I can
afford them.'

'Is your job all right? Can you manage the work?'

'Oh, yes, it's no problem at the moment, but it means a lot of
standing and I don't feel very well; I'm expecting again.'

'Oh, Esther! Did you mean it to happen?'

'I don't know. I think I did. Bert was so locked inside himself, he seemed so far away, and I love him and gave him all I could. I felt desperate. Yes, I really did want his child and nature did the rest. You see, Adela, the doctors say he might not get well for a long time and when he comes home to me I'll have a child all ready to begin our married life.' Esther's eyes were glowing at the picture.

'What do your parents say?'

'Mum was upset at first, thinking of me having to work and go through it all without a husband, but as I reminded her, thousands of women did the same in the war. Dad's always quiet, but I think he likes the idea of a grandchild and they both look after me like the good people they are. The trouble is, I don't feel fit like I did the first time. The doctor says it's worry. I get so horribly sick.'

'How far are you?'

'Oh, it's early days yet. Only a matter of weeks.'

'I was very sick with Harry, but it wore off.' Harry . . . Even the mention of his name hurt her, sharpened the pain of his loss.

'Harry's not with you,' said Esther.

'No. How did you hear that?'

Colour tinged Esther's cheeks. 'Mrs Webster is telling people that you're too busy to look after him so you've left him somewhere.'

'What a beast that woman is, Esther. Though I suppose she's entitled to think what she likes. I haven't explained. The truth is, though I'm ashamed for people to know it, that my mother has got him hidden away somewhere and won't give me his address. She's even changed his name.'

'Oh, Adela, how can she be so cruel?'

'She doesn't look at it the way we do. But I'll get him back.'

'I don't doubt it,' said Esther fervently. 'But I don't think Mrs Webster should spread gossip about you.'

Adela sighed. 'Gossip isn't confined to these parts. If my own circle found out they'd tear me to shreds. Mother's right about that.'

'Adela, I think all the time of my Bert. He should be sharing the baby with me. A child needs both parents right from the start.' She flushed. 'Oh, lord, Adela, I didn't mean – what a clumsy idiot I am.'

'It's all right, Esther. I agree with you.'

'But I've got a home and good parents, while you – Adela, you should kick me.'

'What? Attack an expectant mother? Do you want to get me arrested?' Adela stopped. 'Oh, hell, now *I've* let my tongue run loose.'

Both girls laughed and Adela made tea which they drank while talking over plans for the future.

'If there's ever anything I can do to help with the work, I will,' promised Esther.

'Thanks. I can't afford help at the moment,' said Adela, 'and you've enough to cope with without my imposing upon you.'

'You sound a bit grim.'

'I feel as if I've been playing at life until now.'

'Funny sort of playing! Having a baby and being a slave to a sewing machine.'

'You know what I mean. I only needed enough for Harry and me. Now there's Jack. And Mrs Webster and Ida need help, too.'

'It's good of you to feel responsible for them, especially when Mrs Webster is behaving so nastily to you. I hope she learns to appreciate you.'

'Do you think she will?'

Esther smiled. 'I don't know. She's a right old dragon. Ida's nice, though.'

'Whatever I do will be for Jack,' said Adela. She poured more tea. 'Tomorrow I'm going to the warehouses, ready to set myself up in business again.'

'You sound so confident.'

'I am,' said Adela, suppressing all doubts.

After Esther had gone Adela went on with her preparations. She had sold her gems for a ridiculously small sum, but it was enough to begin stocking the barrow, and she had written to Blanche asking for her help over selling the clothes and costume jewellery.

Jack came clumsily downstairs. It hurt Adela to hear his slow dragging tread, but when he appeared she smiled brightly. 'Had a good sleep?'

'I don't sleep much, but I'm rested. Did I hear Esther's voice?'

Adela gave him the gist of the conversation.

'A baby? My God, that girl's got guts.' He lit a cigarette and dragged on it. Adela said nothing as coughs racked his thin body.

When he had stopped coughing Adela said, 'I must begin to collect stock for the barrow. Which are the best wholesale houses for furnishing fabrics?'

Jack stared at her. 'You're serious. You really think you're goin' to wheel a barrow through the streets an' stand all day at a pitch. You can't do it!'

'Who's to stop me?'

'There's no need to get belligerent! No one will stop you, but you'll soon find that your strength isn't equal to it.'

'I asked for the name of the best warehouses, not a lecture.'

'There's your father, or Sir Wilfred Somers. Perhaps you'd get a discount.'

'Mock all you like, but if you won't help me I shall have to start from scratch and ask someone else.'

Jack said slowly, 'One of the best is owned by Sander Bennett.'

'Is there anything that man hasn't got a finger in?'

'Shouldn't think so.'

Adela was pensive. During her recent stay at Speede House she had been unable to avoid seeing Sander at social gatherings. He had behaved courteously to her, but there was still something implacably hard and unforgiving in his eyes. Still, she could cope with him if she had to, she assured herself.

'If I have to go to Bennett's warehouse, then I will,' she told Jack resolutely.

Adela paused outside the warehouse which stood on the wharf of the River Avon in the heart of Bristol. She had tried other wholesalers, but their top quality merchandise was beyond her pocket and their seconds were not at all what she was looking for. She needed something in between. She had telephoned this morning and eventually had reached Sander who had said he would see her. A man in a brown cotton coat directed her up a flight of steep stairs to the office where a couple of girls were typing busily. Adela knocked on a door marked 'Manager' and was told to come in.

Sander was standing at a big table with a tall woman in dark grey who turned and gave her a speculative look. 'That'll be all for now, Miss Anderson. Get the girls to type out the orders and send them off tonight. Now life is returning to normal we are bound to have a run on furnishing fabrics.' Miss Anderson left and Sander said, 'Obviously, Adela, you have the same idea.'

'I suppose I have.' Adela was wary. Although Sander was smiling at her, his eyes were hard and measuring. 'Jack tells me you deal in quality seconds,' she said. 'That you used to supply him.'

'How is he?'

'As cheerful as possible in the circumstances.'

'You've returned to St Philips, haven't you?'

'Have your spies been busy again?' Damn, this wasn't the way to get what she needed.

'Won't you sit down?' said Sander smoothly. 'So you're starting up a shop, are you?'

'In a way.'

Sander frowned, his heavy brows drawing together over his deepset eyes. 'Either you are or you aren't! Which is it?'

'That's my business,' she snapped. She cursed herself again. 'Sorry, my nerves are a bit frayed.'

'Poor you.' His tone mocked her. 'If you're going to found a business empire, you must learn to be polite to those who can help you.'

'A business empire?' Adela managed to speak coolly. 'At the moment I am making a very small beginning. Homes need refurbishing after the drabness of the war years.'

'I'm surprised you noticed any drabness. You certainly didn't see it at Speede House, or any of the houses of your rich acquaintances.'

'No,' said Adela, hanging on to her temper. He was being insufferable.

'And the folk in St Philips won't be going in for a lot of new furnishing,' said Sander.

'People there still get married. They still need to set up house.'

'As best they can. Where are your business premises?' He waited for her answer and when she didn't speak, handed her an order form. 'Give me your address. Someone will take you to see the textiles and make a note of your orders which we'll deliver to you.'

Adela hesitated, then wrote down Jack's address.

Sander looked down at the form. 'This is Jack Webster's house. You can't tell me you're setting up business there?'

'Why not?'

'Because we both know that everyone in that district is shockingly poor. There's scarcely one who would come to you to buy stuff for a house and you certainly won't attract the better off.'

'I don't intend to deal from there. I have a – a place in Old Market,' said Adela.

'That's better. Why not have the goods sent there?'

Adela's mind worked fast. If she told this arrogant man that her place was going to be a barrow she could imagine his scathing comments. 'I can't move there yet. Meanwhile I shall sort out the stuff I buy. I may make some curtains.' The idea sprang to life there and then and it was a good one. Her eyes shone.

'You look reasonably content,' said Sander. 'Blanche tells me you parted from your parents on bad terms.'

'Blanche should keep her mouth shut!'

'We're quite good friends. It's natural to talk to friends. *We* were friends once.'

Adela felt hot and her face burned. 'I should be obliged if you would ring for your assistant,' she said icily.

'Sorry, I don't have servants' bells here.' He yelled, making Adela jump, 'Nancy, come in here a minute, will you?'

One of the typists appeared. 'Show Mrs Danby round the

warehouse, please. She'll be giving you an order so take a notebook and pencil. She's interested in seconds only. That's right, isn't it, Mrs Danby?'

Adela nodded. 'Thank you.'

'No trouble,' said Sander, looking down at his desk, dismissing her as he would an inferior.

Adela thought she had developed a thicker skin but his attitude rankled. She forgot it when Nancy opened a door and led her into a large, cool, dry room where hundreds of bolts of cloth lay on slatted shelves that stretched from floor to high ceiling. From each collection hung a fat book of swatches. She must be crazy to think she could compete with a place like this. She imagined herself standing by a barrow, expecting women to pause and examine her wares, when Sander had such a massive stock, selling through outlets in warm, comfortable shops. She realised that Nancy was speaking to her.

'The seconds are at the other end, Mrs Danby.'

Adela followed her, feeling dejected, but when Nancy began to hand her the samples of imperfect goods her spirits were cheered. They might be seconds, but they had been carefully chosen and were good, and there was so much to choose from. She had a clear idea of what she wanted and decided quickly. She bought green with an abstract pattern in bright tango orange; a lighter green splashed with yellow flowers; blue-green that came startlingly alive with multi-coloured daises; sage green with a small leaf-green pattern. Nancy watched her open-mouthed as she continued to point to materials with a green background.

Unable to contain herself further she said, 'Mrs Danby, we've got lots of other colours.'

Adela smiled at her. 'I know, and I shall be back. I have ideas for – er – window-dressing.'

'I see.'

Nancy clearly didn't see at all and when the materials were delivered the next day Jack didn't see either. 'The customers won't have much of a choice there. Are you sure you know what you're doin'?'

'I hope so, and I shall soon find out. Tonight I'm going to

load up the barrow and tomorrow I'll be in Old Market and in Castle Street on Saturday night.'

Jack looked agonised. 'You'll never do it. You'll kill yourself. You don't know what you're talkin' about.'

'Maybe, but I'll learn, won't I? I'll learn, and you can tell the bloody Guardians to jump in a lake.'

'Adela, you shouldn't swear. It doesn't sound right coming from you.'

'That's too bad, I've quite taken to it. There's something oddly satisfying in a good round swear. From now on, my life is going to be very different. I'll succeed, never you fear, and I'll get my son back, too.'

Adela lay awake that night. Nancy had told her that she would receive an account and could pay then. Her heart beat faster when she thought of the tremendous gamble she was taking. She had gone to the dismal stables, lit only by an oil lamp, and loaded the barrow, arranging the cloth more by instinct than sight, but even there it wasn't too dark to see the predominance of green. Why hadn't she bought a conglomeration of colours that would probably please the kind of buyer she was trying to attract far more? Why had she tried to be so clever, so different? Jack had insisted on accompanying her to the stable. He had watched as she grasped the handles and lifted the barrow from the struts. It was heavy. Heavier than she had anticipated, and it pulled her sore back. Doubts had crowded in on her. She thought of Harry. Finding him would take money. Everything needed money. For his sake, if for no one else's, she must succeed. She tried desperately not to let herself despair, but her arms hurt from their emptiness and there was a bitter, grieving void in her heart. She finally slept and woke with a start, grabbing the clock. It was still only seven. At nine o'clock the barrow race for the best pitches in Old Market would begin and she would be there. For Jack, for Harry, even for old Mrs Webster and down-trodden Ida, she would be there. And also for herself, for her independence, for her future.

She trundled the barrow out of the stables and through the cobbled streets, thanking God for her athletic training, for her swimming and riding and walking miles round golf courses. Of course, this wasn't the same. A caddy had carried her clubs and when she returned home there had been others to perform the routine tasks: a maid to run a scented bath, a big warm towel, her clothes laid out, excellent food prepared. She shook herself free from useless memories. The sky was overcast and it was cool. She prayed it wouldn't rain. She found that it was easier to push the barrow once she had it moving and when she stopped to say goodbye to Jack she was in a more optimistic frame of mind. He was waiting in his coat and cap.

'What do you think you're doing?' she asked.

'Comin' with you. An' don't try to stop me. My God, Adela, you shouldn't have to do this.'

'Nonsense.' She spoke calmly, though her heart contracted with pity for his helplessness. 'I chose to come back to you and I'm choosing to do this.'

He was awkward on his crutches and it took all his breath to move so their journey was slow and silent. People stared at them as they passed. Adela tall and graceful in spite of her heavy task, looked incongruous against the barrow, and beside Jack, who swung himself along, looking even shorter because of the injuries to his legs. Adela took her place in the line of barrows that were waiting for the signal to go. Fred Withycombe arrived just after Adela and shoved his barrow aggressively between her and a fruit-seller who gave way nervously.

'Well, I never did!' said Fred Withycombe. 'Look who's joined us. Missus hoity-toity herself. Be careful, darlin', or you might trip up. Even good old Jack had an accident an' he's a man an' used to this.' He was a bully of the worst kind, decided Adela. Big of body, his mouth wide with full lips, his red hair coarse, growing thickly on his bare arms which showed beneath rolled-up shirt sleeves.

Adela turned aside from his jeering. Her outfit had been bought for her by her mother for the golf course. The skirt was warm and reached only to her calves and the matching jacket would keep her warm. She was wearing black wool stockings, button-up leather boots and riding gauntlets.

As she waited, she ignored Fred's Withycombe's constant

badgering and the jokes he made with other men, some of whom laughed while others glanced from Adela to Jack's angry frown then stared straight ahead.

A policeman appeared with a whistle and everyone gripped their barrow handles tightly. The whistle pierced the air and the race began. It was slightly downhill over rough cobbles and Adela's barrow gained an impetus of its own until she was barely controlling the steering. She had considered herself fit, but now realised that her cossetted sporting life had not been sufficient to harden her muscles for an ordeal like this. Her breathing was laboured, her chest hurt, her muscles ached horribly, but still she clung to the handles, her booted feet pounding the cobbles. She had dropped behind the leaders and now her race was to beat the slower men.

She saw an opening near Owen's faggot and peas shop and decided to stop there. It was quite a good pitch. The barrow carried on forward and she dug in her heels and was dragged the last few yards. At last she stopped and put the weight on the struts. She leaned on the barrow, wiping her face, almost choking in her need for breath, trying to cope with dizziness. She was still there when Jack arrived, paler than ever with exertion.

'You've done well,' he panted, 'but you shouldn't have run. Damn it, you shouldn't! But, by God, I'm proud of you.'

'I'll do better,' said Adela. 'I'll reach a prime position. Meanwhile the people who come to Owen's will have a chance to see my goods. Saturday will be the real test when we try for Castle Street.'

'You can't do that! You'll get killed in the rush. Look what's happened to me an' I'm a man.'

Adela, her heart still thumping uncomfortably, didn't answer as she removed the cover from her barrow and began to arrange the materials. From magazines she had cut out some coloured pictures of window curtains and bedspreads and stuck them to pieces of cardboard which she stood among the draped materials. She trailed the heavy sage green furnishing satin beside the linen with its splashes of tango orange abstract shapes and continued until the greens were graded from dark to light. All around her the other barrow holders were yelling their wares, each trying to outdo the other in noise. She made no attempt to compete in a contest she couldn't win.

Jack watched her for a while. 'I hope you get plenty of customers, my dear,' he said resignedly.

Adela said with a confidence which went no deeper than her smiling lips, 'I know I shall. Don't worry. Go home now and rest.'

'Why are you doin' this?'

Adela said humorously, 'It's a bit late to ask that, isn't it?'

'I mean you could probably get a job in an office as a clerk or somethin' an' make enough money, an' you've no call to work for me an' Mum an' Ida. You don't belong here. You don't even look as if you belong here.'

Adela raised her fine brows. 'Sorry. Perhaps I'd better tear a few holes in my clothes.'

Jack grinned in spite of himself. 'No, I wouldn't want that.'

Adela leaned towards him. 'I'm doing it for many reasons. Because you took me in when I was desperate and I owe you for that, and owing you means owing your mother and sister, too. To prove that I'm not a useless butterfly. To make money. To get Harry back.'

'You don't make much on the barrows,' said Jack sadly.

'Don't be so pessimistic. I don't intend to stop here forever. Quick, move off. I sense a potential customer.'

Jack swung himself away homewards and Adela waited while a young woman, her pregnancy just showing, hovered near the barrow. When she was within three feet Adela smiled and asked, 'Can I help you?'

The girl's eyes opened wide. 'Are you a customer?'

'No, I'm a seller. What can I do for you?'

'You're different from the others.'

'I know. I sell only furnishing fabrics.'

'I didn't mean that. You're just different.'

Adela waited, fearful of scaring off her first timid customer who fingered the various cloths. 'They're beautiful,' she breathed. 'An' the prices are reasonable. You should see what they're askin' in some of the shops. Everythin's dear these days and not everyone earns bigger money no matter what the news-papers say.' She returned to the green and orange linen. 'This is lovely. It'd look a treat made into curtains. An' only one an' six a yard. I've seen the self-same thing goin' for two an' six in the town.'

'There are flaws in the material,' said Adela, 'that's why it's cheaper.' Jack had warned her against even unintentional deception. 'How much do you need?'

'Not much. My hubby's blocked a few windows off.'

'Doesn't that make your house dark?'

'No, not really. Well, to tell you the truth we haven't got a house. It's an old railway carriage. Lots of them are bein' converted to homes because of the shortage. It's quite cosy when you get used to it. We've got oil lamps an' candles an' an oil heater, too.' The girl had begun humbly, but she ended proudly. 'So I only need a few yards. Here's the measurements. My hubby took them last night.'

Adela worked out the quantity of cloth needed and got out her scissors, but before she could begin to cut the girl said, 'I don't suppose you've got a pattern, have you? I've never sewed anythin' before. I don't want to make a mess of it. I've saved for ages to get the things we need.'

Adela said smoothly, 'Would you like me to make the curtains up for you?'

'Oh, could you?' The girl's eagerness died abruptly. 'But that'd cost a lot more.'

'For you I'll charge only ninepence a curtain. That'll be four at ninepence, just three shillings extra.'

'Three shillin's. That'd be fine. I can just about run to that.'

'Don't forget you'll need poles and curtain rings.'

'No, I know. My hubby has made some poles and rings don't cost much. Thank you ever so much, miss.'

Adela was so cheered and relieved that when Mrs Fudge paid her a friendly visit she said Adela's happy expression would be enough to draw people. Sales were quite good and Adela took another order for ready-made curtains.

'The woman chose the sage green with the little leaf pattern. I stopped off and bought some cotton to match the materials,'

Adela told Jack, flushed and tired after pushing the barrow back to the stable.

'What deposits did they pay on their orders?' he asked.

Adela looked blankly at him. 'Deposits? I didn't ask for any.'

'You should have. How do you know they'll come back?'

'Of course they will. They ordered the stuff.'

'Women have been known to change their minds before now.'

Adela, her euphoria fading, knowing Jack was right, snapped, 'And I suppose men never do!'

'Of course they do,' said Jack calmly. 'What's that got to do with it?'

'Nothing,' said Adela. She sat down heavily, suddenly bone weary.

Jack came to her and smoothed his hand over her hair. 'Never mind. I'm sure you're a good judge of character an' they'll be back. When did you promise to have the curtains ready?'

'Tomorrow.'

'What? You'll be up half the night.'

'No, I won't. It's just straightforward sewing. I'm even doing the hems on the machine. I said I couldn't manage hand-sewn hems.' She grinned, some of her dejection lifting. 'I told them my finisher was off sick.'

Jack laughed with her. Later he stayed up and made tea and encouraged her as she cut out the curtains and sewed them. She had brought brass rings home with her and she stitched them in by hand for the sage-green customer as the clock showed one. Then she got up, stretched her aching arms and back and went wearily to bed.

She had set off on this new venture with her spirits buoyed by hope and ambition, but the next day it was damp and chilly in the stable and it took all her resolution to push the barrow out into a cold mist. She had done well yesterday and she made straight for Owen's shop and settled there. Beside her was a small man who sold women's clothes. All day long he intoned his litany to passers-by. 'Black wool stockin's, missus, black lisle stockin's. Wool an' cotton vests, long or short sleeves, keep out the chills, missus, bodices, corsets, fleecy-lined knickers, missus, stop the draughts.'

At first he amused Adela, but then his monotonous voice and unchanging words got on her nerves until, finally, she no longer heard them at all and they became lost in the background yells of the other barrow boys.

Jack had prepared a signboard for her which read, 'Curtains made to order. No delay.' And, in smaller letters, 'Small deposit required.'

When, at midday, a group of laughing chattering young women passed in their clogs on their way back to their work in the brewery she dared to call out. 'Ready-made curtains, ladies. No extra charge.'

'Ooh, hark at her! "Ladies" she called us. We been promoted.'

They passed on, but their cheerful good humour was infectious and next time Adela called louder.

When the young pregnant woman appeared, clutching the exact money for her curtains, Adela could have kissed her. She wished she could give them away in celebration. She wrapped the curtains after the woman had inspected them. 'They'll look really nice,' she sighed. 'My hubby loves bright colours as much as I do.'

At the end of the day the second customer had not returned, and when Adela took another order she made sure that the deposit paid was big enough to matter.

That night she carefully unpicked the hems of the sage green curtains. 'I'll sell them unsewn,' she told Jack. 'Plenty of women will prefer to take up the hems by hand.'

Again she was proved right and the sage green went to a woman who obviously considered she was slumming by buying stuff in a market place. Adela didn't care what the woman thought as long as she handed over cash. The rent on both houses was due and Mrs Webster's rheumatics demanded immediate medical treatment.

On Friday night she stayed up almost until dawn cutting out curtains, hemming the tops and selvedges. She was gambling in earnest now with the notion that women would buy lengths of drapes ready to hem.

Saturday was the day she longed for, yet dreaded. This was when the real competition was rife for pitches. The vital run began at five o'clock and was for the best places in Castle Street which was narrow and couldn't accommodate many barrows.

She had made another visit to Bennett's warehouse. She loaded the barrow with the ready-mades and a selection of textiles and colours that she found mouth-watering and lined up with the others, her nerves jumping, already feeling tired, praying that she'd get a good place. Saturday night was the time for the best trading. It had drizzled through the day and the cobbles were gleaming wet in the gas lamps which were being lit by a man carrying a long, hooked pole which he balanced as he rode his bicycle. She wiped the barrow handles and took a firm grip, then the race began.

Everyone was determined but none more so than Adela who ran as if her life depended on it. She even kept up with Fred Withycombe who was beside her. He flashed her a dirty look and as she raced pell-mell he deliberately put out a foot to trip her. She slipped and skittered along the greasy cobbles and for an instant had a horrible vision of Jack falling under a car, being dragged along and left a cripple. The barrow was teetering out of control when suddenly it steadied and ran more easily. Some other hand was helping her and she looked round, amazed to see Annie, her face a mask of determination, shoving for all she was worth.

'Push, you stupid bitch,' yelled Annie, but she was laughing and Adela screamed, 'Thanks!' and the two women reached a good position in Castle Street, before the road was closed to traffic for the evening.

'Dad told me what you've been doin',' panted Annie. 'He's worried sick about you, but I think you got guts an' that's what counts in this world, especially for women.'

'He's no need to worry,' gasped Adela, gulping in breath. 'I'm capable of managing. Well, I have been all week. I thought I was finished back there. I can't thank you enough.'

'It's all right. I'll make sure I give you a hand when I can, certainly on a Saturday night. Got to get back now. You'll be all right?'

Adela assured her she would and turned to her task with a lift in her heart.

Castle Street on Saturday night was a shopper's paradise. The street was filled from end to end with people who drifted in and out of the brilliantly lit shops, some to buy, others to look, many came simply to enjoy the camaraderie, the companionship of their fellows in the knowledge that tomorrow was a day off, and tonight the show in Castle Street was free. Not until the last customer had gone would the weary sales girls be allowed to cover their counters and go home on the trams which waited obligingly. Adela had heard of Castle Street on a Saturday night, but had never seen it. No lady would go there, her mother insisted, there was no knowing how many germs were floating about to infiltrate the body. Adela was caught up in the excitement and called her wares as vigorously as anyone. 'Ready-made curtains, ladies. Take the work out of home-making!'

She doubted if anyone who knew her would see her here, except maybe servants and tradespeople. Servants gossiped, she remembered, then put it out of her head. What if they did? She wasn't ashamed of what she was doing.

Most of the ready-mades went and she took orders for cushion covers, curtains and a bedspread, each with a deposit, carefully writing the orders in an exercise book, and several women assured her that when they needed curtaining they would come to her. Many remarked on her low prices and a couple of times she caught sight of a black-coated floor walker checking for himself on the price undercutting that was going on in the street.

When Castle Street was almost empty she began to fold up the materials. Her money bag was pleasantly heavy, but she was extremely tired and in pain. How long could she keep up this kind of life? For as long as it takes, she decided grimly, shaking her head at negative thoughts.

'Got a headache, have you?'

She whirled round at the sound of a familiar voice.

'You!'

Sander Bennett came closer. 'So this is your Old Market business?'

She went on folding without replying. Damn the man! He waited, just watching her, and in the end she felt compelled to speak. 'I admire your perspicacity.' She shouldn't have embarked on so convoluted a word in her tired state and her tongue stumbled over it.

'Not been drinking again, have you?'

The sardonic humour he was directing at her got under her skin and she flared up. 'No, I haven't! I bloody well haven't!' she added for good measure.

'I'm glad to hear it. Who's coming to help you get the barrow back?'

'Mind your own business!'

'Careful, Adela, you need my warehouse, don't forget.'

She set her lips angrily and he said, 'It can't be Jack. Poor sod's no good for anything any more.'

'What a nasty thing to say. Just because he's down doesn't mean he's out. He's good for many things. He's my friend, my best friend.'

Sander was quiet for a moment before he said in reasonable tones, 'Someone is coming to help you, I suppose.'

'I can't stop you supposing.' She finished tying the cover on the barrow and pulled on her gloves before picking up the handles and beginning to push against the cobbles.

'My God,' Sander said, 'you haven't got anyone to help.'

She walked on and he strolled beside her. 'How long have you been selling off the barrow.'

'A week.'

'Who helps you in the race?'

'No one. I don't need anyone. Except today. I had a bit of help today. A swine called Fred Withycombe tried to trip me and Annie Black suddenly turned up and saved me.'

'Jack's daughter?'

'How many Annie Blacks do you know?'

'You really should be polite to me, Adela.'

She said in more moderate tones, 'Surely you aren't the only man in Bristol selling seconds?'

'No, but I'm the biggest and have the most choice.'

'I know.' The admission slipped out.

'You tried the others, did you? Before or after me?'

Adela didn't reply. She had reached a part of the road where workmen had been digging a hole. It was guarded by a fence and red oil lamps. She had to manoeuvre the barrow sideways and it almost tipped. Sander swiftly put out a hand and steadied it then helped her to push it over the roughened road.

'Thanks,' she muttered.

'No trouble.'

He kept his strong grip on the handle and they walked in a silence which Adela was beginning to find unbearable. 'Haven't you anything better to do?' she asked.

'Not for a while.'

'I wish you'd go away. Please! We've nothing to say to one another, outside of business.'

'I have things I'd like to say to you.'

'There's nothing!' she insisted fiercely. She let the barrow rest on the struts and wiped her gloved hand over her hot face. 'Do you want to quarrel with me? I must get home. Jack will wonder where I am. He worries.'

'Worries, does he? Are you lovers?'

'Certainly not! What a suggestion! How dare you question me in this way?'

'I find you quite interesting. After all, you did jilt me.'

Adela wanted to strike out at him. 'Was it dreadfully inconvenient for you?'

His hand shot out and he gripped her wrist hard. 'Inconvenient! Yes, it bloody well was.'

'For your self-esteem, or your social aspirations?'

He released her arm. 'You think I'm conceited?'

She was disconcerted by his sudden calm. 'Perhaps I spoke hastily.'

'You said what you thought. People who are angry often do.'

Adela leaned heavily on the barrow handles to lift it over an awkward dip in the road. This time Sander didn't help her.

302

'I have every right to be angry.'

'Because I tried to help you when you needed help?'

'That was not the aspect which occurred to me at the time.'

'Evidently not.'

'You tried to buy me.'

'That old refrain again. Thousands of women get "bought", as you call it, all the time. So do men. Money and property change hands and people along with them. What makes you so damn different?'

Adela wished she had never responded when he had provoked this conversation. She refused to continue with it.

Sander still walked beside her. They had reached the turning which would take Adela to St Philips. 'Are you coming all the way home with me?'

'Home? You really do look on Jack's house as home?'

'Certainly I do.'

Sander lifted his hat. 'I wish you joy of it.' He turned and strode off.

The encounter left Adela shaken. The feeling irritated her. She didn't want to believe that Sander had any effect on her at all. She tried to put him out of her mind but, infuriatingly, he wouldn't go. He had given her the freedom of his warehouse, extended her credit, and this evening had, a couple of times, sounded almost as if he cared what was happening to her.

Jack was waiting for her and something which smelt good was simmering in the oven. 'Annie brought a meat stew,' he said, kissing her. 'Sit down an' I'll be the waiter.'

'Annie cooked it for us? She's a real good sort. She helped me run with the barrow today.'

'Yes, so she said.'

He looked strained and ill and Adela found it difficult to remain seated while he waited on her. He was so eager to fuss round her, to show her that he was useful. The stew was simple but delicious, and warmed her.

'I met Sander today,' she said, annoyingly blurting out the thought that still occupied her.

Jack swallowed a mouthful of food and looked cautiously at her, struck by something in her voice.

'Where?'

'In the market. He walked part way home with me.'

'Does he still like you, then?'

'Still like me? What do you mean?'

'He must have liked you once to propose.'

'That was to get something for himself, not just a wife. It had nothing to do with feelings. I think he'd like to get under my skin after the way I jilted him.'

'I bet he can't understand it. Women have usually fallen for him before. Still do.'

'Women?' Adela was startled. 'How many has he had?'

'Plenty, though he was never serious about them. Until he met you, that is.'

'He wasn't serious about me. I told you, I was a business deal. Let's change the subject. I did well today. I've orders to fill and Sunday to do them. If it weren't for Annie it might have been a different story.'

'Yes. Good for her. She told me that bastard Withycombe almost tripped you.'

'He did it deliberately.'

'That's hard to believe.'

'Nevertheless, it's true.'

'That's what Annie said. Adela, my dear, you'll have to be careful. Try to stay away from him.'

'Don't worry, I will.'

Adela sat all day Sunday sewing. Mrs Webster came in at tea-time and tutted loudly at the state of the house.

'Dust,' she said, investing the word with the scorn merited by fornication. 'An' the stove's not been touched since our Florrie last did it.'

'I've no time,' said Adela. 'Will you have a cup of tea? And I've got a nice cake in the tin.'

'Shop cake!' said Mrs Webster when Adela handed her a slice.

'It's nice,' said Ida, taking another bite.

'Our Jack's not used to shop cake.'

'Our Jack's getting used to several different things these days,' said Adela. Mrs Webster's power to rile her was lessening.

Jack swung himself in from the garden where he had been

inspecting the rows of seedlings he had planted, bending himself awkwardly to reach the earth, once falling and grabbing at the barren branch of a sooty old apple tree to save himself. Adela had pretended not to notice.

'Hello, Mum. Ida.' He sat down and took the tea Adela poured, then cut a large slice of cake.

'I was just tellin' *her* that you aren't used to shop cake,' said Mrs Webster.

'She's got a name, Mum, an' I'm grateful for any cake at all. Adela's doin' great with the barrow.'

'Huh!' Mrs Webster glared. 'How long will that last?'

'As long as we need,' said Adela. 'And one day I'm going to open a shop.'

'That'll be the day,' snorted Mrs Webster, but her voice held a note of uncertainty. No one in her family had ever opened a shop.

Jack left, saying that he was going to check the barrow to make sure the wheels were running true.

'He shouldn't be doin' that,' said Mrs Webster.

'I'm afraid I'm not much good at mechanical things,' said Adela.

Mrs Webster glared at her. If she emphasised Jack's weakness, she also emphasised Adela's usefulness. 'Are you goin' to marry our Jack?' she asked belligerently.

Adela stared incredulously at her. 'Good heavens, no. He's like a father to me.'

'Better than what your own father's been lately,' said Mrs Webster smugly.

'Jack's a good man,' said Adela pacifically.

'He is that,' said Ida, 'an' you're a good woman, Adela.'

Mrs Webster glanced sideways. 'She hasn't always been so good,' she said slyly. 'An' she's got the proof of it somewhere. Where is Harry, by the way?'

Adela almost flinched. 'I shall be bringing him home soon,' she said. And prayed in her heart that she was speaking the truth.

Chapter Seventeen

Adela tipped up the old brown stone jar in which she saved her money and looked at the small pile of coins and bank notes. She had almost nothing to show for weeks of work. Mrs Webster's rheumatics had worsened and her medical bills had been heavy. Adela didn't grudge her the necessary treatment until she discovered that she had rejected the doctor's help, ignored his medicine, and was buying 'rheumatism tea' from an old woman in the next street.

'It won't do her any harm,' Jack had said, when Adela protested to him. 'It might even help.'

'It's a mixture of nettles and dandelion, among other things!'

'People have been curing themselves for years with herbs.'

'But why did she let Ida call the doctor and allow me to pay for bottles and pills?'

'Because we insisted on it, I suppose. I should have had more sense. She doesn't believe in doctors.'

'For heaven's sake!' Adela had cried. 'Doctors cured you.'

'She holds them responsible for my being crippled.'

'That's ridiculous.'

'She says that if doctors really knew their job, they'd have made me whole. Don't be hard on her,' Jack had pleaded, and Adela had stopped arguing. He was coughing more and grew tired far too quickly. He, too, must have regular medical checks and needed tablets for pain, though he had tried to do without them. He smoked more than ever and Adela had given up protesting. He seemed to need cigarettes. Then, unexpectedly, Ida had gone down with severe bronchitis. More medical bills. Adela had grown to love Jack's sister. She was sweet and hard

307

working, putting up with her mother's constant criticisms without complaint, caring for her with immense patience. Even in the most distressing stages of her illness, Ida had been apologetic over the trouble she was causing. During the crisis Florrie and Annie had come over regularly to keep the place clean. Florrie's animosity hadn't decreased, but Annie was proving a friend. She had too many commitments to be with Adela during the week but she turned up unfailingly on Saturdays to help get the barrow into the more lucrative Castle Street and she refused to join her sister in baiting Adela.

The capricious weather had produced frosts in summer and when Adela returned home she felt cold and so tired it was an effort to eat and wash herself with a rag dipped in a bowl of water. On Sundays she got the tin bath from the yard, and heated water in the copper and soaked herself. It was primitive, but these days it felt like luxury.

Although Adela's sales had meant she needed to buy more cloth, although she sat far into the night until her back and eyes ached, making up materials to her customers' requirements, the money had slipped away and she had barely enough in hand to cover a week's needs. At this rate she would never save enough to find Harry. He had passed his first birthday and she ached with longing to be with him.

She had written to her mother, a desperate plea for her to relent and divulge Harry's address, and received a reply so cold and unforgiving it seemed to strike her an almost physical blow. She could expect no help there, ever. Somehow, somewhere, she must get together enough money to employ someone to look for Harry.

Blanche had been helpful over the sale of the clothes, though she had raised her eyebrows at the idea. 'You've given my flat as an accommodation address, have you?'

'I had no choice. Say you don't mind.'

'It's all right. You're not the only woman trying to sell her wardrobe, though you stand more chance than most because your stuff's new. Lots of officers' widows are looking for ways of making money. Poor bitches! Most of them haven't been trained to do a thing except order around the servants. Their army pensions don't amount to much. Only two pounds a week and a bit more for children.'

Adela had stared. 'That's a fortune compared with what most people get. A private's widow gets a flat thirteen and ninepence.'

Blanche had given her a quizzical look. 'We've both changed, haven't we? If you stop to think you'll remember that Father allowed us nearly two pounds a week for pin money and paid our bills and we just took it for granted.'

'So we did.' Adela had fallen silent for a moment. 'What a selfish life I've led. I'll never go back to it.'

'Even if you get the chance! Mother's even more furious with you and Father's angry, too. They've heard about the barrow. Mother mentioned it once, then refused to discuss it again. They're terrified of someone bringing it up in public.'

'How are they? How's Father?'

'Mother is as usual. Father is a good deal better and seems extremely excited over business these days. He's still borrowing from the bank to bid for more small companies. Sander's sold him a couple.'

'Why isn't Sander hanging on to them if they're such good propositions?'

'He hasn't told me and I haven't asked. Business bores me.'

'Are you still friendly with him?'

'We're on reasonable terms. I get along with him as I do with others engaged in socialist work, and I meet him sometimes when I can't get out of some engagement.'

'I once thought you wanted him as a lover.'

'I thought I did for a while. That just shows how mistaken I was.'

'You've met someone else? Mother said you had a new friend.'

Blanche had given a small secretive smile. 'You could say so. Did Mother have a face like vinegar when she said it?'

'She didn't look happy.'

'I bet she didn't.'

Adela had waited, but Blanche refused to communicate further. 'I hope things work out well for you,' she said.

'Don't worry, they will,' Blanche had replied.

Adela replaced the money in the jar and went back to work on the sewing machine. She was making curtains, boring repetitive work which allowed her mind to roam. In spite of everything she now felt at home in St Philips, with Jack, with her new friends, and she was glad to have the opportunity to direct her own life, to strive for the distant goal of success which she meant to achieve. After she had found Harry. He must come first.

Jack was the one who couldn't completely accept her situation. He was hovering about her constantly. 'You shouldn't be here, workin' like a dog,' he had said only this morning as she loaded up the barrow. 'If you go back to your proper home you're bound to meet someone who'll love you so much he'll accept Harry.'

'I haven't got Harry back yet,' said Adela, heaving at a bolt of navy serge.

'No, but you will, an' when you do what's goin' to become of him? Are you goin' to let him grow up an' run in the streets with the other kids, joinin' gangs, gettin' into trouble the way they do? Remember my son? He was high-spirited. Poor kids can't escape the law by sayin' they're high-spirited, the way some high-up barrister says the rich kids are. Our lot get sent to reformatories for doin' a lot less than university students. I've heard about the so-called rags they get up to. Remember young Andy Barton? His mother's a widow with eleven children and he pinched some fruit off a barrow when they had nothin' to eat. Now he's in reform school an' he's only thirteen.'

'I know, it was Fred Withycombe's barrow,' said Adela.

'Fred's not got many friends these days. Harder times are comin', Adela, an' he'll wish he hadn't turned the kid in to the police. His mother's distracted. She can't get a pension because her husband died fallin' off an army lorry. They say he wasn't killed as a direct result of enemy action.'

'That's wicked,' said Adela. 'How can people be so heartless? Jack, how can you imagine I'd ever go back to live among them?'

'Not all the nobs are cruel,' he pointed out.

Adela had managed a small smile. 'I should be standing up for them, not you.'

'I try to be impartial.'

'Really? I'd not noticed! Who's the one who always speaks up for the exploited men and women against the bosses? I thought that was you!'

Jack had the grace to grin.

Esther was bitter over the prosecution of Andy Barton. 'Fred Withycombe's evil!' she raged. 'And he tried to trip you up.'

'How do you know that?'

'It's all over the neighbourhood. Did you know he was running next to Jack when he slipped under the car wheels? There are some who say he deliberately crowded him.'

'No one has ever said such a thing to me. Certainly not Jack.'

'He wouldn't. He doesn't like to believe evil of anyone, but he's furious about young Andy and about the near-disaster you had.'

'What a terrible man Withycombe must be. Why does he do these things?'

'He was brought up to hate the nobs, but not the way Jack does. Jack only gets angry with those who exploit their workers. He's ready enough to admit there are good people who treat their staff fairly. Fred just hates anyone who's got more money than himself, or comes from a privileged background, which explains his treatment of you. Now he's got an added grievance. He didn't see why he should go and fight for King and Country. He said they'd never done anything for him, and he got off army service somehow, and now he resents anyone who fought. He hates it when our men are called war heroes. That's what they call our returning boys, isn't it? War heroes!' Esther lost the thread of what she had been saying. 'There's Jack coughing his lungs up, and Bert, my Bert, shut away.' Her voice was bitter.

'How is he?' asked Adela.

'No better. The doctors have asked hundreds of questions about him, from right back in his childhood, and have decided that he had an unstable personality when he went into the army and his illness is a result of that and not due to the war and the shelling.'

'What?'

311

'Everyone who knows him says it's a lie, but there's nothing I can do about it.'

'Did Bert tell you?'

'No, he never says much, but the other patients told me. Bert's not the only one it's happened to.'

'Why should they do that?'

'It lets them off paying me a pension. They say I married him knowing of his disability.'

Adela said in low, angry tones, 'Is there nothing that the government won't sink to?'

'Apparently not. Adela, I've had to leave my job. I get terribly sick and have to take time off. I don't suppose you're making enough money to employ me yet, are you?'

'I'm sorry, I wish I could,' said Adela. 'There's no one I'd like more, but all my money is being swallowed. The price of coal seems to go up every week and Jack and his mother need warmth. These houses always seem so cold and damp.'

Esther nodded, sad but not surprised. 'I know. You're a real good woman to stick by Jack and his family the way you do, and I bet you don't get many thanks for it.'

Adela grinned. 'Not from Mrs Webster, anyway, but at least she's curing herself with potions.'

Esther laughed. 'Well, if you do need someone, will you let me know? Twelve shillings benefit doesn't go far and I shan't get even that for long. The trouble is that employers can pick and choose now and they won't settle for a woman expecting a baby, especially if she's not well.'

'I thought Sander Bennett was supposed to be different. Why have you left him?'

'He needs reliable people and, to tell you the truth, he made room for me in the first place. And when I'm sick I often feel giddy and he can't risk me falling on to one of the belts or knives.'

Adela shuddered. 'Couldn't he find you something else to do?'

'He hasn't got a single vacancy and he's not running a charity.'

The summer had been cool and wet and Adela often shivered as she waited behind her barrow. Once spring cleaning was over and women had refurbished their homes, trade slowed down. She had plenty of time to watch Fred Withycombe sell his fruit and groceries. People had to eat, though sometimes it seemed to Adela that an indifferent government failed to comprehend even this. She now understood only too well Jack's fervid adherence to a political party which promised help for the poor. Prices had begun to fall, but so had wages. A panicking government cut expenditure, creating more unemployment, and ex-soldiers were thrown on to parish relief and were to be found on the streets, busking cinema and theatre queues. Some were given soul-destroying work, such as stone-breaking, so that they might be seen to earn their benefit.

'As if they were bloody convicts,' raged Jack. Other men, frail still from wounds, amputees, the blind, gas victims, got along as best they could.

Jack was now constantly filled with anger which did nothing to help his own deteriorating health. 'The war heroes are now called lazy good-for-nothin's with revolutionary tendencies. Think of that, Adela! People who stayed at home in the war are now spurnin' the men who saved their way of livin'. And here, in Bristol, one workin'-class child in five comes from a home where the income's below the so-called poverty line. It's wicked. It's evil!'

Adela sympathised with him. She sympathised with the numbers of underfed, ragged people she saw daily. She would never again be impervious to sickness and want. Since she had returned to Jack she had begun to look around her properly. Before, she had regarded her situation as a temporary one which would eventually be relieved by her parents. There was no longer any hope of that. Yet, however much she was aware of the needs of others, she dared not identify with them. She must keep unclouded her determination to succeed.

Events which would once have thrilled her had no impact now. Since Alcock and Brown had flown across the Atlantic one could now fly easily to Paris. The city might as well be a million miles away as far as she was concerned. She had read of the Ladies' Golf Tournament; professional cricket had been restored; the rich were able to enjoy yachting at Cowes; there had been a record Derby; there were hunt-balls and operas. She scanned the newspaper sometimes, reading about society, and her first thought was always, how much did it cost? Money, or the lack of it, ruled her life.

One day when she entered the small house in St Philips after putting the barrow in the old stable she felt ill. Her back had been particularly bad that day and twice she had turned dizzy. Then a woman had spent an hour turning the materials over and over, had dropped a piece of silk brocade on the wet cobbles and shoved it back without a word of apology, saying only, 'It's not very good quality stuff, is it?' before going on her way towards Castle Street. It was a small thing but it had brought Adela's seething misery to a head. Jack took one look at her and got up from the table where he had been writing his latest pamphlet on the superiority of the Labour Party.

'What is there to eat?' demanded Adela.

Jack reached for his stick. 'Had a bad day, my dear?'

'A filthy day.' Adela knew she shouldn't punish Jack, but her nerves were quivering. 'A bloody awful filthy day. Some bitch dropped that special piece of brocade in the muck and it's ruined.'

'Did you ask her to pay for it?'

'Of course I did, but she just walked off. You know damn well there's nothing I could do about it. She'd have kicked up a fuss and a copper would have come along and probably moved me on.'

Jack put his arm round her shoulders and Adela was alarmed to realise that she could feel the pounding of his heart. It seemed to be shaking his whole frame. 'Sit down,' she muttered. 'I'm sorry.'

'It's not you who should be sorry,' said Jack, his voice cracking. 'My God, Adela, it was a bad day for you when you met me.'

Adela hated it when Jack fell into one of his self-denigrating moods. She usually coaxed him out of them but tonight she was too weary.

'I thought I saw Harry today,' she said abruptly, 'but it wasn't him. I think the woman with the push-chair thought I was mad. I left my stall and rushed over to have a closer look at her boy. I lost a sale over it, too. In fact, a woman took the opportunity to steal the bit of satin she was admiring.'

'That was mean!'

'I know, but the poor cow looked hungry and her shoes were in holes. I hope she enjoys her spoils.'

'You're a good girl.' Jack carried a brimming cup of tea to her.

She thanked him. 'I shouldn't take things out on you, Jack.'

'I don't mind. My back's still broad, even if my pins are a funny shape.'

That night they decided to go to the Kingsley Hall where there would be plenty of friendly warmth. Adela knew many of the other women now. What Blanche hadn't been able to sell had gone to cheaper second-hand dealers; her one coat was growing shabby, while her hat, a fur felt which gave warmth without fashion, had lost its original shape. The local people had assimilated her into their groups and she sat with other women holding an enamel mug filled with weak tea, enjoying the warmth on her fingers.

'Soddin' weather,' said one woman. 'It's not like summer at all.'

'An' it'll be winter again soon, an' the price of coal a disgrace,' said a thin woman in a tight green coat. 'An' bread's gone up again, an' butter three an' four a pound—'

There was a general outcry. 'Just listen to Sarah! Butter! Who can afford butter?'

'Not me,' she protested, 'but my ma-in-law d'live with us an' she won't eat margarine. Says she ate enough of the bloody stuff while the war was on. Poor old thing's not long for this world an' in her old age she says she d'want butter. She don't know she's dyin'. Worked all her days in a brewery an' it weakened her heart. How can I refuse her?'

The other women nodded understandingly and into Adela's mind came the memory of the dozens of pats of golden butter which had been so abundant in Speede House. Sometimes she saw Father's picture in the papers and, more often, Mother's, always to do with a big charity event. Blanche visited them occasionally, though she was no longer welcome. I'll never

315

treat my children like they treat us, vowed Adela, no matter what they do. My children. My child. Harry. Had someone ever made him a birthday cake? Had they put a candle on it? Had he enjoyed it? Did he still cry a lot? Did he cry even more? For her? Would she even know him now?

'Cheer up!' Adela turned and saw Esther. Someone fetched a chair for her.

'You d'look better, love,' said Sarah. 'How far gone are you now?'

'I feel much better. I'm expecting the baby before Christmas.'

'Have you found any work?'

Esther shook her head. 'No, it's impossible. I'm just a drain on Mum and Dad.'

'They won't grumble. How's Bert?'

'He's quietened down and been moved into a better ward. There's an old piano there and he's learning to play it. No one's teaching him. Seems he's musical.'

'That's good,' said Sarah. 'When he d'come out he'll be able to work on the stage.'

'Or in pubs,' said another woman, more realistically.

They nodded and no one pointed out that many shell-shocked men had been put into mental asylums and few had come out.

Adela went to fetch another mug of tea and saw Sander and Blanche talking earnestly to Jack.

Blanche strolled over to her sister. 'God, you're getting thinner! Well, it's fashionable these days, but a good figure is a bit wasted on you in those ghastly clothes.'

'To hell with my clothes,' said Adela.

'If you say so,' said Blanche amiably, 'though not long ago you seldom seemed to think of anything else.'

'Not long ago? It seems an age.'

Sander joined them and swiftly looked Adela up and down with measuring eyes which she resented.

Blanche said, 'I see someone I want to talk to.'

Adela and Sander watched her hurry to a large woman in a purple coat and hat.

'You look tired,' said Sander.

'That's because I am tired,' said Adela shortly.

'You work too hard.'

'How do you know what I do?'

'It isn't difficult to follow your progress. If progress it can be called.'

'No, I suppose not for the great Sander Bennett who has his spies.'

'Don't be childish.'

'Don't dare talk to me like that.'

'I respect you for the way you're coping,' said Sander unexpectedly. 'You've grown up, so don't act childishly. It spoils you.'

Adela fumed, wishing she could think of a relevant retort. 'You've put on weight,' she said.

'A little. You could do with some,' he said bluntly.

'I must return to my friends,' she said.

'Wait a moment,' said Sander. His tone made her pause. 'I've a proposition to put to you.'

'What?' She looked warily at him.

'A business proposition,' he said. 'I've just spoken to Jack and he's in favour.'

'So you spoke to Jack, did you? I suppose it didn't occur to you to speak to me first.'

'No, it didn't. My understanding is that you want to boost Jack's self-esteem whenever you can.'

'What proposition?' she asked baldly, recognising irritably that he had scored a point.

Sander glanced around. 'This is neither the time nor the place. We're likely to be interrupted.'

As if on cue Blanche returned with her friend. 'Meet Georgina Pitman. Georgie, my sister Adela.'

On closer inspection Georgie was very plain with nondescript wispy hair and no pretensions to following fashion, but she showed perfect teeth in an attractive smile which lit up her hazel eyes. Adela liked her and shook hands warmly.

'So you're Blanche's sister,' said Georgina in cultivated

317

accents, giving Adela an assessing look. 'A Danby, eh? You don't look like the other Danbys I've met.'

'I don't feel like them,' said Adela mildly.

Georgina laughed. 'She's a good 'un, Blanche, my dear.' She turned back to Adela. 'A group of us do our best to help poor kids. Blanche is joining us.'

Blanche was regarding Georgie with obvious affection, and the two women walked away, talking earnestly.

Sander watched them for a moment with an odd, quizzical expression. 'Now then, Adela, when can we meet?'

'What for? Oh, your proposition. I hope it's worth my time. I'm extremely busy.'

'It'll be worth it. How about coming to the warehouse tomorrow?'

'Tomorrow I'll be running my business.' Adela said the word proudly, daring him to mock.

'Can we meet on Sunday?'

'That's also a very busy day for me.'

'Doing housework?' asked Sander, unable to keep a hint of sarcasm from his voice.

'No.'

'What do you do on Sundays?'

'I make curtains and bedspreads. Also chair covers, the latest addition to my repertoire,' she finished flippantly.

'My God, you really do work hard. Are you making money?'

'Of course. You don't think I'd do it for nothing, do you?'

'You probably do it for little more.' He sounded angry.

'Am I undercutting you?'

'Undercutting me? How could your barrow affect me? I sell top-quality material in my store to women who can afford to have their furnishings made professionally.'

'My work is second to none!'

'I'm delighted to hear it. About our meeting – I have some accounts I want to check and I'll be in the office above the Park Street store on Sunday morning. If you want to hear what I have to say, call on me.'

Sander walked away. He was an odd man, thought Adela. His behaviour towards her seemed to veer abruptly between kindness and provocation. She might as well see what he had to say on Sunday. She couldn't afford to turn down anything which might mean more money, though it would mean she had to work late. At least it would give her a break. Besides, she had better remain on his good side or he might close his warehouse to her.

She was disappointed on Sunday when she arrived at Sander's store and discovered that she must use a side entrance and so wouldn't see his stock.

Sander answered the bell quickly. 'Come in,' he said briefly. He was informally dressed in an open-necked shirt which revealed his powerful neck.

He greeted her with a cool smile, though his words were welcoming. 'I'm glad you came. How did you get here?' he asked, peering past her as if he expected, she thought, to see a chauffeur-driven limousine.

'I walked.'

'Damn! I should have sent transport for you.'

'That really would have set tongues wagging! It's not so far to walk. Especially when I'm not pushing the barrow.'

He gestured to her to precede him up the stairs. For some reason she felt she had annoyed him by mentioning the barrow. He ushered her into a large room right at the top of the building. It was plainly furnished with a low couch, a couple of chairs, a cupboard and table. Various doors led off it.

'I've had it converted for my use,' said Sander. 'I find it easy to work when I'm here alone. The bathroom's through there—' he nodded towards one of the doors '—and the kitchen through here. I'll make some coffee. Sit down and relax.'

Adela wandered to the window and gasped at the view. From here she could see for miles. She could identify the church spires, the taller buildings, and away in the distance stretched the green and brown hills.

'What a lovely view,' she exclaimed, turning to Sander as he emerged from the kitchen carrying a tray.

'Glad you like it. I had the window put in. I can get to the roof itself from the kitchen. I sit there sometimes at night, just watching the lights. It's a marvellous treat after the darkness of the war years.'

319

'Everyone was so sure the war would end in a few weeks,' Adela recalled. ' "Peace before Christmas!" That's what everyone said. How blind we were! So many people suffered.'

'As you did,' said Sander.

'I? How?'

'Your fiancé died.'

'Yes. Poor Ralph.'

'And there was the aftermath for you.'

She flushed angrily. 'Must you refer to that? No gentleman would.'

It was Sander's turn to redden. He thrust his face aggressively forward. 'You forget I'm not a gentleman. Your parents make that only too plain.'

'They don't receive you any more?'

'Since you jilted me, no, they don't, and nor do some of their friends.'

Adela could imagine her mother's voice. 'A rank outsider, my dear. Adela almost married him. How thankful we were when she decided against it. Of course, he couldn't take it like a gentleman, but what can you expect? We don't receive him any more and would never go where he was expected.' And because the Danbys were top-drawer, others would not risk losing their acquaintance.

'Surely you still have plenty of friends?' Adela asked.

'You *almost* sound as if you care.'

Adela didn't reply and Sander poured two cups of coffee from an earthenware pot.

'That pot is a lovely shape,' said Adela.

'I had it made. I employ a potter in Devon and he brings me all his work. It's exclusive to Bennett's.'

'Like the underwear.'

'Exactly. Elsa gets better all the time.'

Was he being deliberately provocative?

'We were speaking of friends,' she said.

'Were we? Ah, yes. The Smithers invite me to all their functions, of course. Naturally your parents have dropped them. And there are other houses into which I can go.'

'Do you really want to know people who treat you so badly?'

Sander sat on the other end of the couch, leaned back and crossed his long legs. Adela felt his power. It wouldn't do to cross him, and she had to admit that at times he possessed a certain animal attraction. 'I suppose I despise them,' he said at last, 'but it irks me to be excluded.' He got out a silver cigarette case and offered it to her. 'Do you smoke yet?'

'I do sometimes. I have to in self-defence. Jack never stops.'

'It's the worst thing for his condition.'

'I know. I've told him often enough.'

For a few minutes they drank their coffee in silence. The clear air outside was rent by the sound of church bells and Adela pictured her parents leaving the house dressed in sombre Sunday clothes, being driven to church in their motor car for their weekly dose of worship.

'I can't stay long,' she said. 'Why did you ask me to come?'

'I've been watching you, Adela—'

'So I gather.'

'—and I can't help respecting your courage. I'm sure you'll succeed one day and I'd like to help you – and help myself at the same time. There's a small property coming up for rent in Castle Street. The lease has five years to run. I heard of it from a business acquaintance and asked him to hold back the advertisement. I think you should take it.'

Adela glared at him angrily. 'Are you crazy? Fancy getting me here for nothing when I'm so busy. I don't have that kind of money.'

'But I do.'

She jumped up. 'I won't take charity from you. You've deliberately wasted my time to offer me something you must have known I'd refuse. I suppose this is some kind of retaliation for past slights.'

'Past slights?' Sander growled. 'That's a novel way of describing a public jilting.'

'You can't forget it, can you?'

'No, I can't. Now sit down, for God's sake, and listen for once.' She was surprised into obedience by his commanding tone. 'I know you don't have fifteen hundred pounds, that's what's being asked for the lease, but what you do have is energy, flair, an ability to sell and sheer guts. Sorry if that's crude—'

'I hear cruder these days!'

'—but it's true. I'm asking you to come into partnership with me. Close your mouth, dear, your jaw is dropping. You'll have complete control and I'll undertake to keep the shop well stocked with the materials you choose and not to interfere with your method of working.'

Adela's mind was a whirl of emotions. She could stop heaving and shoving the heavy barrow and standing out in all weathers. Fred Withycombe would no longer have the opportunity to insult her. She could put into practice her ideas. It would be a step towards her ultimate goal of practising as an interior decorator. She looked at Sander who was watching her closely.

'Why are you doing this?' she asked.

'Because I think I can make money out of you.'

'I should have guessed.'

'Surely you didn't imagine I could have any other motive?'

Adela was angry. She got up. 'I'd like to think about it. How much time have I got?'

'My friend wants an answer by Wednesday.'

Adela walked back to St Philips not noticing anything around her. The sun was shining for once in this dismal autumn and she took off her coat and carried it. She was wearing a jumper suit lovingly knitted for her by Ida during her convalescence and she had refurbished her hat and added a gold silk rose. She caught sight of her reflection in a shop window and stood staring for a while. She really had got thin, but the suit fell in graceful folds around her. Her figure was good and if she worked indoors her hands would soon recover their softness and her complexion return to its smooth clarity. She thought of handling really beautiful cloth of the best kind which she saw in Sander's warehouse. Mother might not be so bitter towards her if she had a respectable shop. She might even soften and tell her where Harry was. Lots of officers' widows were setting up in business. Values were changing. It was even quite fashionable to marry an artisan, provided he had money.

322

Surely Mother must eventually accept the different standards brought by the war? Surely she would relent? Speculation ran round and round her brain as she walked home. Could she bear to be beholden to Sander? She had until Wednesday to make a decision which could never be rational, bound up as it was in so many ties of pain and humiliation and loss.

Chapter Eighteen

Jack had no doubts about the offer. 'Sander trusts you. He's got faith in your business sense, Adela, or he wouldn't want you to become his partner.'

'But can I trust him? I wouldn't want to see all my profits going into his pockets.'

Jack grinned. 'I'd back you against Sander any day where money's concerned.'

'Would you?' Adela wasn't sure she liked this view of herself. Then she laughed. 'You're right, of course. I think I'd kill him if he tried to cheat me. Oh, Jack, to have money! Enough to get my baby back, enough to keep him safe with me, enough to make sure that Harry and you and your mother and Ida never want for anythin' again.' Jack's face was a mixture of pride and chagrin and Adela said, 'Please don't mind. You gave your health for people like Sander Bennett. You're worth a thousand of him. I dislike him.'

'Are you sure?'

'Of course. Naturally I respect the way he's pulled himself up from humble beginnings, but it's turned him into a ruthless businessman, even a bit of a bully.'

Adela worked the next two days in a state of confusion. At one moment she saw herself moving into a shop of her own in Castle Street, attracting the crowds who flocked there; at the next she could see only that she would be indebted to Sander Bennett and remember that he had once humiliated her beyond bearing. How could such a partnership prosper? As she made her way home on Tuesday evening she knew she had to make up her mind and she realised that, however much she disliked

325

the idea of a close association with Sander, she had little choice. She must accept his offer. She pushed the barrow into the stable and wiped it. It had been drizzling most of the day. The barrow stayed dry under a raised tarpaulin, but she was cold and damp and depressed. She arrived at Jack's house and pushed open the front door.

'I'm home,' she called, as she did every night.

She walked through into the living room. 'What a day! My coat's wet and my hat is like a rag. Oh, good, you've lit the fire—' She stopped, staring, her heart in her mouth, unable to believe the evidence of her senses. Sitting in an armchair near the fire was Grandmother Sutton. Adela stood still, hanging on to her hat and coat as if they were life-lines. Lady Sutton! It was impossible! It couldn't be! Something had happened to her brain. It was as feasible as for the statue of King William in Queen's Square to descend from his horse and take possession of their living room.

Jack relieved her of her hat and coat. 'Your gran's come to visit you,' he said.

'Gran?' Adela repeated the word. No one had ever addressed Lady Sutton as 'Gran'.

She walked closer to the uncompromisingly stiff-backed figure in the chair. Lady Sutton, who had never relinquished her Edwardian way of dressing, was wearing a snuff brown poplin dress with a high-necked cream lace collar fastened at the throat with a brooch; her hair was dressed high and topped by a grey felt hat with grey ostrich plumes. Her black coat with its wide fur collar was hanging from a hook on the door, where it looked totally out of place.

'You may kiss me,' said Grandmother Sutton.

Adela breathed, 'It is you,' and bent automatically to place her cold cheek next to the old lady's. To her amazement her grandmother caught her and kissed her on the lips.

Adela sank into the chair opposite. The world had gone mad. 'I thought you were in Cornwall,' she said inadequately.

'Is that all you have to say to me after I've travelled so far to see you?'

'To see me?'

'Yes, my dear.'

326

'But why? How did you know I was here? What else do you know?'

'So many questions.' Lady Sutton grinned impishly and Adela remembered that Millie had told her she thought their grandmother was jolly. Adela hadn't been able to believe such an astonishing view of the stern old lady, but perhaps, in some inexplicable way, Millie was right.

'I have the Bristol newspapers sent to me,' said Lady Sutton, 'and saw the account of Blanche's injury on the trams, and realised that at least one grand-daughter was willing to venture out of her cosy world. I wrote to her and we discovered we had much in common.'

'You and Blanche?' Adela took the cup of tea Jack handed her as if she were in a trance.

'Yes, Blanche and me! She told me about you and Ralph and your son, and how cruelly your mother is behaving – not that it surprises me – and that you were actually working a barrow in Old Market. I very much wanted to help you to something better. Your mother doesn't yet know I'm in Bristol.' She paused, watching Adela. 'Well, say something, my dear.'

'I don't understand.'

'Understand which part?'

'Any of it,' said Adela. 'You're completely different from what I thought.'

'And so are you.'

'I've been tellin' her how brave you are, Adela,' said Jack who was sitting near Lady Sutton, listening with great satisfaction. 'More tea, your ladyship?'

Lady Sutton held out her cup and saucer and Adela refilled it and watched her grandmother take two spoonfuls of sugar which she stirred vigorously.

'You don't take sugar!' said Adela.

'Your mother says I don't, but actually I do. Your mother has built her own picture of me. It was once thought unfashionable to take sugar, therefore one did not take it.'

'I see,' said Adela, though she didn't see at all.

Lady Sutton sniffed the air. 'What's that? It smells delicious.'

327

'There's a shepherd's pie in the oven,' Jack said. 'My daughter, Annie, brought it over.'

'A fine daughter,' said Lady Sutton in tones of deep approval. 'I'm looking forward to the pie. I hope there's plenty of gravy to go with it.'

Jack assured her that there was and the old lady's eyes gleamed in anticipation. Then Jack went into the kitchen, leaving the two women to talk in privacy.

'I didn't know you liked shepherd's pie,' said Adela, feeling weakly that talk of meat pie seemed inadequate in the circumstances.

'Oh, yes, I do. I have a friend in Cornwall who makes it whenever I visit her cottage.'

'That sounds pleasant,' said Adela, knowing her comment to be inept but still too bemused to think of anything better. 'Have you seen Blanche?' she asked.

'No, she's expecting me tonight. I shall stay with her. In your mother's last letter she told me that Blanche was mixing with ghastly people and behaving outrageously. It seems that most of this is based on her activities in the political field.'

'And you're not shocked by us?'

'Shocked? Certainly not. Adela, I am very sorry that Ralph died and so much wish I had known what was happening. I would have assisted you as best I could. Your mother has built a myth around me, turning me into the kind of mother she feels that a woman in her station in life deserves. She has never told you that I was a suffragette?'

'A suffragette? You?'

'Yes, me. When I was eighteen I went to stay in Manchester with a friend I met in finishing school, the daughter of Dr Pankhurst. He had earlier tried to have women placed on the voters' register and he drafted a bill giving married women absolute control over their property and earnings, a bill which became law in 1882. That's when I met him.'

'*You* were a *suffragette*.' Adela was repeating herself as the artificial edifice of Grandmother Sutton's respectability crumbled before her.

'I was, indeed, and I'm proud of it.'

328

'But why have you never spoken of it? Why have you always been so aloof and unfriendly towards us?'

'You and Blanche came to visit once a year with your mother and sometimes your father – and two more proper, tedious children I never met.'

'We behaved as you expected us to!' retorted Adela indignantly.

'Not as *I* expected, as your mother did.'

'She told us you would be shocked and upset if we did anything unladylike.'

'I can imagine!'

'Why didn't you show us your proper self? Are you afraid of Mother?'

'No, damn it, I'm not! But she's held my purse strings for years. I worked for the movement until I was forty and then your grandfather, who was a charming man but a great gambler, died, leaving me almost penniless. In spite of my beliefs I unfortunately didn't take advantage of the Married Women's Property Act, and let him have access to my money which vanished with his own. I have to confess also that I kept him company and backed horses and wagered on card games. Your mother says that we were both exceedingly foolish, especially your grandfather, and I suppose the world would say that she is right, but I loved him and could deny him nothing. I do not suppose you remember him?'

'Not very well. I don't think I saw much of him.'

Lady Sutton sighed. 'No, I do not suppose you did. We were always in the thick of things. We went to every splendid race meeting and spent every season in London, then there were the country house parties – such grand affairs – and river regattas, yachting, Scotland for the shooting, and journeys abroad. How I missed it all when he died.'

'I'm so sorry,' said Adela.

'It was all a long time ago and I should repent all the gallivanting at my age. Though,' she said pensively, 'I do not seem to. At least I have my memories. No one can take those from me.'

'You said that Mother controls your money.'

Lady Sutton returned from her mental roving, smiling wryly. 'Your mother disapproved most strongly of my suffragette activities. In fact, she disapproved of almost everything I did – I cannot think how my dear husband and I ever got her – and she made me an allowance on condition that I behaved decorously and did not allow you and Blanche to learn the truth about me. She was afraid that I would contaminate you with my own rebellious nature. And now—' Lady Sutton paused to laugh '—here I find Blanche a socialist, living on her own, pleasing herself. And she told me about you and here I am, and I'd bet a pound to a penny your mother blames all your rebellion on a streak of recklessness inherited from your grandparents.'

Firelight shone on Lady Sutton's lined face; the lights and shadows danced on her high cheekbones and softened the wrinkles, and Adela saw that her grandmother must have been beautiful. She still was. A beautiful, wonderful, glorious surprise of a woman whose animation defied the years. Her rigidity had been only a defence.

'Where's Miss Anderson?' she asked. Miss Anderson was Grandmother's companion, a vinegary woman who had looked with disfavour upon the descent of her mistress's grandchildren in the summer.

'I slipped out of the house while she was walking on the sands.'

'She'll be frantic. She'll have telephoned Mother. They'll be worried to death about you. They may even get in touch with the police and when they find out where you've been, Mother and Father will be furious.'

Contradictory expressions chased across Lady Sutton's face. 'The police! I have had a good few brushes with them.' She leaned forward and said joyously, 'In fact, I once went to prison for throwing a brick through a shop window. I was so proud of what I had done, but your mother lives in dread that someone will bring up my past. I suppose I shall have to tell them I am all right though it has been lovely to be on my own for a while, except for meeting my unexpectedly wonderful granddaughter. And now I look forward to talking to Blanche. You need not worry about their contacting the police. My maid – another sour old witch chosen by your mother – will soon have discovered that I packed a small valise and the porter who mans our little rail halt saw me take the train.'

'Won't Mother make your life miserable over this? What about your allowance?'

Jack called Adela to the kitchen and she returned bearing a steaming dish which sent out savoury smells. Lady Sutton's eyes gleamed. 'Ah, the pie. Let us eat and then we will talk some more. I like to concentrate on my food.'

Lady Sutton tucked into the shepherd's pie with gusto, adding a large pool of tomato ketchup, something which Mother would have found inexpressibly vulgar. Adela ate slowly, watching her grandmother surreptitiously, still only half believing that this could really be the old dragon who had terrorised her holidays.

'Eat up,' said Lady Sutton. 'You're too damn thin.'

Adela laughed and Jack, who had been listening to Lady Sutton with amusement in his eyes, waved his fork in her direction. 'Just what I tell her, Lady Sutton. She works too hard an' eats too little.'

The plates were carried to the kitchen and left for later. Lady Sutton looked disappointed when informed there was no pudding, but she made up for it by accepting a cigarette from Jack. 'A Woodbine,' she said. She drew on it reflectively. 'A good smoke, if a little short.' Later she drew out a tortoiseshell case and offered a cigarette to Jack and Adela, and the room was scented by the aroma of Turkish cigarettes, reminding Adela of the life she had discarded.

'You smoke, too,' said Adela, feeling now that nothing her grandmother did could surprise her.

'Of course. Quite a few women of my day smoked, though not in public. That would have been too daring.'

Jack put a couple of pieces of wood on the fire. They crackled and sparked as the three of them puffed contentedly for a moment.

'Grandmother, I can't wait any longer,' said Adela. 'You must tell me how you propose to get out of this muddle you've got yourself into. Won't Mother stop your allowance?'

'Do not worry about me, my love. I shall make my explanation with a few small inexactitudes. I shall tell your mother that I had a sudden longing to revisit the places of my girlhood.'

Before Adela could answer, the front door opened and Adela heard the thump of Mrs Webster's stick and agonised pleas from Ida. 'They've got a visitor, Mum. They won't want us.'

Ida might have spared her protests. The reason that Mrs Webster was here was precisely because an unknown woman was visiting.

'How did you get here?' Adela whispered to her grandmother.

'By taxi, of course,' said Lady Sutton, making no attempt to lower her voice.

Mrs Webster opened the living-room door and hobbled in. She stopped on the threshold and stared. Lady Sutton stared back, smoke drifting from her nostrils. Adela half expected a bolt of lightning to pass between them.

Jack stood up, holding the back of his chair for support, shaky more from a longing to laugh than from his injured legs. 'Lady Sutton, my mother, Mrs Webster. Mum, this is Adela's gran.'

Mrs Webster continued to stand while Ida who couldn't get into the room peered from behind.

'Do come in,' said Lady Sutton, 'and please close the door. There is a draught. I am quite susceptible to draughts. And who is that poor soul whose passage you are preventing?'

No one had ever spoken quite like that to Mrs Webster. Speechless, she walked in and Ida scurried after her.

'My sister Ida,' said Jack, avoiding Adela's eyes, knowing that she, like himself, was close to laughter.

'I can't abide draughts neither,' said Mrs Webster.

'I am sure you cannot. At our age we must take care of ourselves. I see you walk with a stick. I do myself. I have rheumatism, don't you know?'

'Have you?' Mrs Webster sat heavily in Adela's vacated chair, frowning at Lady Sutton's cigarette.

Grandmother's sharp eyes missed nothing. 'Do you

disapprove of cigarettes, Mrs Webster? I am afraid I smoke. I find it a comfort. You should take it up.'

Ida's eyes opened wide as she waited for an explosion of indignation from her mother. None came. 'I dare say we're entitled to get what small comfort we can when we get old,' said Mrs Webster.

'Exactly! Whatever makes you feel happiest is best, of that I am sure.'

'I like a good strong cup of tea and *home-made* cake,' said Mrs Webster, giving Adela a scathing glance.

'Would you like a cup of tea now?' Adela asked.

'That'd be nice. I don't suppose you got any decent cake to go with it? Never makes cakes,' she said, leaning towards Lady Sutton confidentially, 'an' *boughten* cake's never the same.'

'I do so agree, though I must speak up on behalf of my grand-daughter. She has a business to run which takes up most of her time.'

Mrs Webster snorted, but mildly, and for once didn't argue. 'My Jack had a bad accident an' can't work,' she said, firmly sweeping away any doubt there might be about his qualities. 'An' that was *after* he gave his health for King and Country. He doesn't get enough money to live on.'

'A disgrace, indeed,' agreed Lady Sutton. 'There are far too many people existing in poverty caused by the war and things are getting worse.'

Mrs Webster peered suspiciously at Lady Sutton. 'Aren't you a Conservative?'

'Mum!' protested Jack.

Both old ladies looked at him in astonishment, then resumed their conversation.

'Down in Cornwall we are mostly Liberals,' said Lady Sutton.

'Well, that's a bit better, I dare say. *Her* family are all Conservatives. Grindin' the face of the poor.'

'Indeed, yes, Mrs Webster,' said Lady Sutton amicably. 'Some of our so-called leaders appear to be particularly adept at face-grinding.'

Jack and Adela went to the kitchen and carefully closed the

door before collapsing in mirth on one another's shoulders.

'I can't believe it,' gasped Adela.

'Nor me. I expected them to be at each other's throats an' they're gettin' on like a house afire. You'd think they'd known each other for years.'

When Adela carried in a tray of tea with a plate of biscuits which she had bought for Sunday, Lady Sutton was inviting Mrs Webster and Ida to Cornwall for a holiday and Jack's mother was graciously accepting.

'If I can scrape up the money for the fare, that is,' she said.

'Money is such a bore, isn't it?' said Lady Sutton.

Adela and Jack held their breaths, but Mrs Webster replied simply, ' 'Tis if you don't have any.'

Eventually Mrs Webster took a regretful leave and Lady Sutton settled back into her chair. 'What a splendid lady. Was she ever a suffragette?'

'Er, no,' said Jack. 'I think she was too busy lookin' after her family an' helpin' Dad with his business.'

'The barrow?'

'Yes. They'd just worked their way up to two barrows when Dad died an' we had to go back to the one.'

Lady Sutton looked pensive. 'I would so love to have had her freedom though I know my girlhood was privileged, at least where money was concerned. Your mother also had a happy marriage. We are two fortunate old ladies. Now I must come to the point. Adela, Blanche tells me that a man called Sander Bennett wishes to put some much-needed money into your business and that, for personal reasons, you would prefer not to accept. You caused him a great deal of embarrassment when you broke off your engagement, did you not?'

Adela agreed that she had.

'Why do you think he is anxious to invest in you?' asked Lady Sutton.

'Because he thinks he can make money out of me and it seems that Mr Bennett will stop at nothing which increases his fortune,' said Adela. 'I don't care for him at all.'

'Whose idea was your marriage? Oh, do not bother to answer, my dear. In the circumstances I am sure it was your

334

parents'. What courage you showed in the face of affliction. You are truly worthy of my help.'

'But, Grandmother, you yourself can't live without Mother's allowance—'

'Oh, I shall not forgo that; at least, not for the time being,' interrupted Lady Sutton. 'But, Adela, something quite extraordinary has happened. In our nearest village there is a little antique shop with a most delightful owner who cooperates with me in outwitting my guardian dragons. He has bought small items from me over the years – those which your dear grandfather did not consider worth the trouble of selling – with which I have supplemented my income. When I heard of your plight I searched around to see if there was something of real value I could sell. I knew it was hopeless from the start and could not discover a thing, but I am no expert.

'In the end I asked Edgar, my antique-dealer friend, to come and look for himself. He suggested going into the attics, though I assured him there was nothing to interest him there. We have, as you know, owned the Cornish house for generations to use for vacations, and the attics are dusty and hung with cobwebs. I went up with Edgar who rooted around for a while, then opened a couple of ancient chests of your great-grandfather's. I was almost choked on dust by this time, though Edgar was so excited he sneezed away indifferently.'

'What was in the chests?' breathed Adela.

'Only books, as I already knew, but I could not put up with the dust any longer and left him to it. My dear, when he came down he was delirious, absolutely babbling. He demanded a glass of whisky to wash away the dust, then explained. Apparently your great-grandfather was by way of being a discriminating book collector. I believe that the majority of his collection went to another branch of the family when he died, but somehow the chests came to us. Edgar said that all the books were worthy of auction, some much more so than others.' Lady Sutton delved into her handbag and drew out a piece of paper. 'Here is the list which Edgar gave me. It makes odd reading for one not well versed in ancient tomes. Many of them will fetch only smallish sums, ten pounds or a little more or less for such as those from the Kelmscott Press. But others – well! I am no more bookish than your grandfather was and would never have imagined that books could be so valuable. For instance, here is one called *Continental Key of the Liberties of America*, in three parts, which should fetch more than twenty pounds.'

'That much for a book!' exclaimed Jack.

'It is a first edition,' said Lady Sutton. She looked down her list. 'There are several foreign titles, some of which will net me quite substantial sums. Here is one which appears to be a French book about dissection, such a nasty subject, which Edgar has marked as a possible *four hundred pounds*. And so the list goes on, but the gem of them all is something called *The Cordyale, or the Four last things*, translated by Earl Rivers. The thing is that it was printed by Caxton of whom even I have heard and I am told it will go for something close to one thousand and nine hundred pounds!' She stopped talking and gazed appreciatively at their astonished faces. 'Amazing, is it not? And what a blessing that your dear grandfather never discovered such treasures or they would long ago have been gambled away. As it is, Adela, I can put some money aside for myself and invest in you.'

'What an incredible find!' said Adela, adding quickly, 'But, Grandmother, although it's wonderful of you to want to help me, it's far too great a risk. I might fail and you'd lose your money.'

'Nonsense! I was sure you would be a good proposition when I heard what you had done, and now I have met you I am even more sure. Watching your progress will be such an interest for me.'

'But to invest in me! To risk your windfall when you might use it to travel again and enjoy a season in London.'

'I am getting a little too old and tired for such diversions now and I do not think I would enjoy them very much without your dear grandfather. No, I shall lend you the money you need. Blanche told me that you have an original gift for home decorating.'

'Blanche did?'

'She was quite candid about her unpleasant attitude to you in the past, but now she admires you. She has evidently altered. It is my belief that she is in love.'

'In love? Do you know who with? Did she mention a name?'

'No! When I asked her she said she would tell me all in good time, but that your parents are disgusted with her.'

'It sounds intriguing,' said Adela. 'I hope she lets us in on her secret soon.' Adela still had the notion that Blanche's lover could be Sander Bennett. 'Grandmother, I don't think you realise how much money I need to set up in business. The Castle Street lease is being offered at fifteen hundred pounds and has only five years to run which means I may have a time limit on succeeding.'

'You probably won't get the Castle Street lease,' pointed out Jack. 'Sander has first refusal.'

'You must use cunning,' said Lady Sutton, 'but somehow, Adela, you have got to get that lease. Castle Street is in the heart of Bristol and people flock there. Do they still block the road on a Saturday night?'

When Adela assured her that they did, Lady Sutton looked wistful. 'Your grandfather and I sometimes used to creep off and mingle. When your mother discovered it she kept on interminably about germs spread by the lower orders. She is such a snob! You will have to stock the shop as well and I have to confess to ignorance in this respect. How much will you need altogether?'

Adela fetched pencil and paper and made some rapid calculations. 'On Monday I left the barrow in charge of someone I could trust and slipped up to Castle Street to look at the empty premises. The man next door told me about the accommodation. It's small in relation to the department stores, but big enough for my purposes. There's a good-sized front shop and a smaller room at the back. Upstairs there are two rooms and above them a couple of attics. It has electric lighting and is gas-heated, and there's a cold water tap in a tiny kitchen in the attic. There are two display windows and although they aren't very wide they go back at least six feet and I could make a good show of materials. Alternatively, I thought I could dispense with conventional windows and allow people to look right through to the shop floor and see much more than they normally would, and I'd have lights which would pick up the gleam from brilliant satins, the way they do it in theatres. The place isn't painted the way I want, but I could manage that myself. I reckon I could open up with two thousand pounds.'

Lady Sutton and Jack had listened in silence. When she had finished they both regarded her for a while, then Jack said solemnly, 'An' there's us thinkin' you were really serious about havin' a shop.'

Adela clasped her hands nervously. 'It's too important to me to joke about! I've thought of little else since Sunday.'

'You have convinced me even more that I am making a good investment,' said Lady Sutton. 'You will take my money, won't you, Adela my dear?'

Adela gave her grandmother an agonised look. 'Did you hear what I said I need? Two thousand pounds?'

'I heard. In fact, you will need more than two thousand if you are to compete with this man Bennett for the lease.'

'But what if you don't get as much as you hope for the books at the auction?'

'Edgar assures me that I will and may even get more, and if I need some extra cash I can sell a few bits of gold and diamond jewellery which were given to me by my mother-in-law – expensive, but too hideous to interest a buyer. I have not worn them since my mother-in-law died.' She laughed. 'Whenever she came to visit she expected to see me wearing the whole damn set. A necklace, earrings, brooch and hairpiece – ghastly! Now the splendid Edgar is going to reset the lot. The gems are good.'

'You'll be gambling on something unknown,' said Adela.

'Your grandfather gambled our fortunes away on "sure things". I believe my chances are one hundred per cent better with you. Now, how do you go about getting the lease?'

Jack insisted on escorting Lady Sutton to Blanche's flat. She left Adela a cheque for two thousand two hundred pounds. 'I have my bank manager's permission to overdraw on my account,' she explained. 'He has talked to Edgar and knows he can trust his judgement.'

A few days later Adela received a letter from Lady Sutton who said that she had telephoned Mrs Danby who had visited her in a very angry mood. Lady Sutton had placated her wrath with a tale that she had been possessed of a sudden longing to see the place where she had been happy with her deceased husband. Under her daughter's escort she was returned to Cornwall, ushered to the station like a naughty schoolgirl. 'I need hardly tell you, Adela,' she wrote, 'that I look forward keenly to the day when I am an independent woman again.'

Adela saw Sander the day after Lady Sutton's visit and told him she had decided against accepting his offer of a partnership.

He was angry. He paced the floor of his warehouse office where she had gone by appointment after work. 'You little fool! You could have your own business and yet you prefer to wallow in the muck of the open market.'

'Some of the barrow boys are my friends,' said Adela coldly. 'I don't consider I'm wallowing in muck.'

'I'm not talking of the barrow boys. I know those fellows and you know damn well what I mean. Trading in the open street is a poor proposition for you. You'll never get a better offer than mine.'

'Don't be so sure.'

Sander continued to pace the room then he stopped and seated himself behind his desk and spoke as calmly as he could. 'Things are happening behind the scenes, Adela. The textiles trade is ripe for a tremendous upheaval. Someone with your flair is bound to succeed. Take this chance now.'

'No.' She stood up. 'I don't need your money.'

'Is it because it's mine? Would you accept it from someone else?' he asked angrily.

'What business is that of yours?'

In a swift movement Sander came from behind his desk. 'Someone *has* made you an offer! Who is it? A man?'

'I'm leaving,' said Adela.

Sander stepped to the door and stood with his back to it.

'Let me pass!' she said angrily.

'Not until you tell me who's staked you!'

'Of all the damn cheek!'

'Why did you let me believe you were thinking over my offer?'

'I wasn't pretending—'

'Liar! You used this as another chance to watch me squirm.'

'You, squirm? That's funny.'

'Funny, is it?' Sander gripped her arms tightly.

'How dare you? Let me go! You're hurting me!'

'I'd like to hurt you more. By God, I'd like to beat you. Your behaviour to me is filthy.'

Pain and anger quickened Adela's tongue. 'I suppose with your antecedents you've had experience of violence towards women.'

He released her at once. 'What an extremely unpleasant remark,' he said.

She knew she had gone too far, but so had he. 'You're not the only one in the world with cash,' she said much more mildly.

'Maybe not. Maybe you have found another backer, but who do you know with my experience in business? Together we could have had a monopoly of high-class interior decorating in Bristol.'

'Just Bristol!' she scoffed. '*I* intend to take my skills further than Bristol. I shall make my name everywhere.'

'Modest, aren't you?'

Adela coloured slightly at his tone. 'What's the use of doing anything if you don't aim high?' she said jauntily.

'My God, Adela, but you had better be sure of what you're doing. No one will show you any mercy, or do you any favours, especially not me!'

'Why must you be so belligerent? Surely we can be in the same line of work and remain on reasonable business terms?' Her voice faltered as she encountered his furious stare and she decided to leave. She said goodbye as calmly as she could and hurried down the stairs, through the warehouse, past the hundreds of bolts of material, and out through the front door. She glanced back once. He stood at the head of the stairs watching her. On her way home, as her temper cooled, she wondered with trepidation where she would buy good material from in future.

Adela didn't get the Castle Street shop. She tried her best to persuade the estate agent to give her the lease, finally raising her offer to seventeen hundred pounds. Mr Addison looked regretful as he shook his head. 'It's just not possible, Mrs Danby. I have promised a businessman first refusal. Even if I forgot my ethics enough to yield, it wouldn't be good business sense. He's powerful enough to damage the reputation of the firm and, in this case, he would have justice on his side. I'm so sorry.'

'I see,' Adela surrendered. 'Have you got anything else in Castle Street, or Wine Street perhaps? Somewhere where there's plenty of passing trade?'

Again Mr Addison shook his head. 'The only place on our books around that district is a rather neglected property on the corner of Tower Hill and Castle Street. Unfortunately it is outside the area which is closed to traffic on Saturday nights, but lots of people must pass it. And, of course, it is not nearly as expensive as the Castle Street situation.'

'And there's absolutely nothing else?'

'Nothing. Would you like someone to take you to view it?'

Adela stepped through the front door of the empty premises and felt sick with disappointment. The place had been used to sell animal foods and there were overpowering smells of bone meal and other distasteful things she couldn't identify. The young man with her said, 'It doesn't seem much now, Mrs Danby, but it could be made good.'

Adela smiled at his enthusiasm. 'It needs an army of decorators, Mr Stanton.'

'I thought Mr Addison said that's the business you're thinking of setting up in.'

'Not that kind of decorator. I want to be an interior decorator, using beautiful materials to enhance homes.'

'That's marvellous. I'd love to do something artistic, but my parents are very much against it. They refused to let me study art.'

Adela looked more closely at him. He was young, about twenty, of medium height, with fair wavy hair and light blue eyes which were, at this moment, shining with exuberance. He reminded her a little of Ralph, in the days before the war. And of Harry. She mustn't think of Harry, not yet, not here. Longings for her baby must be kept for the long nights when she lay sleepless, wondering who had him and if they cared for him as they should. Here, she must plan for the future.

She recalled Mr Stanton's last remark. 'That's a pity,' she said, 'but parents have one's best interests at heart. At least, that's what they tell us.'

'Mine used to say it every day. You sound as if you've suffered, too. Are you related in any way to the Danbys of Clifton, the wealthy ones who deal in textiles and wholesale clothes?'

Adela turned away to examine a patch of crumbling wall plaster as she said as casually as she could, 'Distantly.' It was hardly a lie. Mother and Father could scarcely be more distant. She looked round her at the large room which would need a great deal of attention before she could think of moving in. 'What's the rest of the place like?'

The young man led her through into the back where there were two quite sizeable rooms, one equipped with a cold water tap and a gas ring. They climbed the stairs which took them to another large room and several small ones.

'That's it,' said Mr Stanton, 'except for a patch of rather sooty garden at the back.'

'A garden?' said Adela, thinking of the time when Harry would be back with her.

She stared at the patch behind the premises which was open to the sky. It was paved, but the paving stones had cracked beneath the onslaught of weeds which pushed their way towards what light there was. A few straggly bushes dripped the remnants of frost. 'It doesn't look nice now,' said Mr Stanton, 'but I'm sure you'd do wonders with it.'

Adela turned and looked him in the face. 'What makes you think that? You don't know me.'

He blushed. 'I do. There are some people you feel that you know right away.'

Adela raised her brows. 'Do you flatter all your female clients? If so, you must be a great asset to your company.'

'No, of course I don't! Most of our clients are self-satisfied, comfortably off stick-in-the-muds – just like my parents. You're not like that. You want to do something with your life.'

'Really, Mr Stanton—'

'My name's Frederick. My friends call me Freddy.'

Adela laughed. She couldn't imagine how Mr Addison kept Frederick Stanton in his place. The poor boy was bursting with creative longings. Then she sobered. The lease here was for seven years and was offered at twelve hundred pounds. The difference in cost between this and the other place would help to put it in order and still leave some for stock, though not enough to fill the huge open spaces. And here the possibility of failure would be greater. She told Freddy Stanton that she would give Mr Addison her answer tomorrow.

Jack was enthusiastic. So were Esther, who came calling, and Ida, who slipped out while Mrs Webster was dozing over the fire.

'I'll help,' promised Ida. 'I may not look much, but I'm wiry and I can paint. Doors, o' course, not pictures.'

'I'll come, too,' said Esther.

Adela glanced at her swollen stomach and Esther grinned. 'I'm perfectly well and I wield a nifty paint brush. Just try me.'

Jack kept his frustration under control. 'An' I can make tea an' heat soup an' keep the workers fed an' watered.'

Adela looked round at the eager faces of the three who were closer to her than ever her family had been and she had to fight back tears. 'I'll do it,' she decided. 'I'll take the damn place and I'll make money if it kills me.'

Jack produced a bottle of wine. 'We'll drink to that.'

'You had the wine all ready, Jack. How did you know I'd go ahead?' Adela demanded.

'I watched your face when Lady Sutton was talkin',' he said simply.

Adela had telephoned Lady Sutton with the latest news and had

343

been urged to go ahead. She had been in possession of the lease for a week.

Now she stood in the middle of the large room looking down at tins of paint, brushes and various tools. Jack had tracked down a consignment of paint put up for sale from a failed business and she had bought it for a song. The trouble was they had only white left. Jack had rounded up some out-of-work ex-soldier pals who were glad to earn a few extra shillings, provided it was paid in cash and kept secret. Just let the authorities get a whiff of illicit work and their inadequate subsistence allowances would be wiped out. Two of the walls were already painted and looked hideously garish in the unshaded electric light in the centre of the room.

Esther had gathered together several women also glad to earn something and the whole place, including the windows, had been scrubbed clean. Adela had bought a second-hand gas stove and kept a huge pot of soup simmering on it to feed the hungry workers. Even Mrs Webster, possibly won over by Lady Sutton's involvement, had hobbled over to view the operation.

'You'll have a terrible job fillin' a place this size with the money you've got,' she had snorted.

Adela suppressed a yell of rage. 'I know,' she said, endeavouring to sound pleasant. She failed.

'Don't take that tone with me, young woman! You'd best remember that that good lady, your gran, has got her money sunk in this.'

Adela had not answered. She had seized a paint brush and taken out her fury on the wall.

Late one night, there was a knock on the front door and she opened it to find Freddy standing there, holding a large canvas bag. 'Can I come in?'

Adela stood back. 'Why not?'

Freddy looked round him. 'What a great idea to use white. No one else would have thought of that, I'm sure, and it'll set the materials off perfectly.'

'If I've got enough material to look significant,' she said, thinking for the hundredth time of her last meeting with Sander. What a fool she had been to upset him!

344

'Don't be downhearted. Look, I've brought some paint, though it isn't white, I'm afraid. A friend bought it for his house, then his girl changed her mind about getting married and I got it dirt cheap.'

Adela looked at him. 'Not white?'

'No, I can take it away if—'

She bent and opened the bag and drew out one of the tins. 'Pale peach. Pale peach! And gloss paint! I could kiss you.'

Freddy smirked modestly, blushing slightly. 'You want it then.'

'It'll do for the doors and window frames. It couldn't be better. How much do I owe you?'

'Have it for an opening present.'

'I can't do that. You must let me pay.'

Freddy was wistful. 'I'd love to feel I had a hand in a place like this.'

Adela, catching his yearning tone, nodded. 'Well, all right. Thank you very much. Feel free to call at any time.'

'Thanks, I will.' Freddy left reluctantly, saying, 'Mother always serves cocoa and biscuits about now. She likes me to be there.'

By the time the premises were repaired and painted it was late November and Esther's baby was soon due. She was sad that the work had ended.

'You can come and help after the birth,' said Adela, 'if I can afford to pay you. Bring the baby, of course. Later I intend to do something with the back yard. It's not much of a place to leave a child at present.'

'It's no worse than many a garden I've seen,' said Esther. 'The baby will be fine there. Does it still smell painty inside?'

'A bit, but that's better than bone meal.'

While the decorating was in progress Adela had been looking round for sources to buy textiles. There were few who had stocks of the kind of thing she envisaged and she grew despondent.

'Go back to Sander,' advised Jack.

'I can't.'

'Why not? He's a businessman. He'll not pass up a chance to make money.'

'I can't,' she repeated. She hadn't told anyone of the scene in Sander's warehouse.

In the end she was forced to sink her pride and ask to see Sander Bennett. She was still selling from the barrow most days. It was a kind of life-line, something solid to cling to when so much else in her life was imponderable.

Sander received her in his Park Street flat one evening. A gas fire was glowing, warming the comfortable room, and Adela sank into the chair and put out her hands to the heat.

He watched her for a moment. 'How's the new place coming along?'

'Do you really care?' She was extremely tired and the words were out and instantly regretted.

'I gather you want something from me. You wouldn't be here otherwise, and if I were you I would be polite. Of course, you know your own business best but a man is much more likely to cooperate if a woman speaks softly and looks kindly.'

Adela was fuming inwardly as she smiled at him.

'You look like a boa-constrictor who can't quite see the joke,' remarked Sander.

'Shall I get to the point?' It was useless to try to pretend with him.

'Please do.'

'I have bought the lease of premises which I need to stock.'

'Ah, yes, the run-down property on the corner of Tower Hill and Castle Street. I'll soon be opening the place *in* Castle Street. That would have suited you much better, you know. I had a look at yours. It needs a hell of a lot of work done on it.'

'It's had a hell of a lot of work done,' she said. 'Now I need stock.'

'And I take it you want the run of my warehouse?'

'Yes.'

'Can't do that, my dear. Why should I give the opposition an advantage?'

'You've made it clear that I shall be in no position to compete fairly with you.'

'That's true.' He lit a cigarette and seated himself opposite

346

her, his dark eyes watchful. 'Do you smoke yet?'

'Yes, thank you.' Sander got up to light her cigarette, then sat down again.

They were silent for a while until Adela felt her nerves jumping. 'Well, will you?' she demanded.

'Will I what?'

'Will you let me have stuff from you?'

He raised his brows at her somewhat strident tone, appearing to consider the matter, and she felt herself reddening with frustration and anger. It was obvious he was merely amusing himself with her. 'I'll tell you what I'll do,' he said, 'I'll let you keep buying the seconds.'

'But I'm trying to open a high-class business!'

'And so am I. Do you want the stuff or not? It makes no difference to me one way or the other.'

Adela hated him. He had the power to ruin her before she began. She would need to go further afield for quality merchandise and that would take time and energy, neither of which she could spare. 'I'll take the seconds,' she said.

He looked surprised. 'In that case, feel free to go to the warehouse and buy all you want.' He looked at his gold watch. 'I'm sorry to throw you out, but I promised I'd attend a party.'

'A nice society party?' she asked. She cursed herself, wondering what inner demon incited her to provoke him.

Sander's face darkened but he said smoothly, 'Not high society, naturally. Merely a fund-raising event for the Socialist Party. I never see you at these things.'

'I've no time.'

'What about Jack? He used to be very active.'

'He's crippled, as well you know.'

'Of course I know. I merely wondered if you'd ever thought of giving him the kind of outing he enjoys. The Labour Party is going to win an election one day. Jack loves to be in the thick of things.'

Adela felt angrier than ever when she left Sander, but this time mostly at herself. She hadn't made any attempt to discover if Jack was feeling thwarted. She resolved to do better by him. Just let her get the shop open and she'd concentrate more time on him. And she'd start proceedings to find her baby.

Chapter Nineteen

Adela's well-meaning vow to give more time to Jack had gone the way of other promises she had made herself. She'd no time for anyone, working all day on the barrow and at nights in the shop, returning home so tired she could scarcely swallow soup.

Even Mrs Webster noticed. 'You'll be ill,' she pronounced with something that sounded almost like satisfaction. 'No one can go on long like that!'

Adela was too weary to answer.

Jack, worried about her, hating his helplessness, lashed out at his mother. 'If you can't say anythin' better than that, you'd best keep your mouth shut.'

Mrs Webster drew back her chin indignantly and left the house. They could hear her banging around next door and taking out her wrath on Ida.

Before Jack went to bed he went round to apologise. He returned looking amazed. 'She actually seemed sorry she'd criticised you. I think she's beginning to like you.'

That'll be the day, thought Adela as she climbed into bed and sank instantly into sleep.

She held a meeting to decide upon a name for the new shop. 'Adela's Stuff,' suggested Esther.

'Textiles Incorporated,' was Ida's contribution. When pressed for the meaning of 'Incorporated' she said, 'I don't know. I thought it sounded clever.'

'Housecraft,' suggested Freddy who now spent most of his free time in the shop.

'Homecraft,' said Esther 'How does that sound?'

'I think it should have Adela's name in it,' said Jack. 'She's worked like a demon for months. She deserves to have her name displayed.'

Adela waved the suggestion away, but Freddy said 'Adela *Fabriques*. It would look splendid on invoices.'

'It's foreign,' protested Esther. 'The ordinary people won't dare come in a shop that's got a foreign name.'

Blanche sat quietly chain-smoking, watching them with a slightly amused expression. She was taking much more pride in her appearance these days and wore a dark blue suit which flattered her.

'Have ordinary people got money to spend any more?' asked Georgie aggressively.

'Of course they have,' said Freddy. 'Not everyone is poor. Some people are doing better than ever.'

Georgina frowned at him. She was interested only in the labouring classes and regarded them from her haven of wealth with great indulgence and a supreme tenderness.

'Adela Fabrics' said Jack, and there was general approval. One of his pals made a large wooden sign, a white background with peacock blue wording, and fixed it over the front. The outside had also received a coat of white paint. There had been only enough for one coat and Adela prayed that they would get through the winter before it began to peel.

Blanche suggested an opening party.

'Can't be done,' said Adela. 'I've no money left. I've had to hire a couple of sewing machines and employ girls to use them and that's just about cleaned me out. At least, I do have a little money, but I'll need that for running expenses. Things will be very tight.' She fell silent, fear suddenly striking her. The renovations had cost far more than she had anticipated and she had been forced to go to a London warehouse for textiles and pay for them to be freighted back by train. She had made a vow to learn to drive and acquire a vehicle as soon as possible. Weariness almost overcame her and she swayed and put out a hand to support herself.

'Steady on,' said Blanche. 'Aren't you well?'

'I'm just tired and I get a lot of backache since Harry was born.'

'I'd be willing to pay towards a proper opening.'

'You? But you haven't any money.'

'Georgie has oodles of the stuff.'

'Your friend? Why should she help me? I don't know her.'

'She'll do it if I ask. She's very fond of me.'

Adela shook her head, but the temptation was too great, the need to succeed too urgent to be denied, and she let Blanche take charge. Invitations were sent to all the best houses as well as many of those whom the senior Danbys considered below them in the social scale. Cases of good wine were carried through to the back room and glasses hired, along with a bevy of young women to act as waitresses. Georgie was, as Blanche had promised, enthusiastic.

The opening was to be an evening event. 'Make it Monday,' advised Georgie. 'Not so many invitations on a Monday. People might be glad to have somewhere to go and it'll give you the rest of the week to consolidate.'

'Oh, God, I hope so,' said Adela, wrapping her arms round herself protectively. 'What if no one comes?'

'They'll come, if only out of curiosity.'

At the last moment Adela discovered that Blanche and Georgie had spread the word that Adela Fabrics was owned by George Danby's daughter – the one who had so mysteriously gone to live with her grandmother in Cornwall, but who had then been seen in the oddest places. 'She's set up in opposition to her father,' was the general opinion.

'It isn't true,' protested Adela. 'Father sells mostly dress materials and ready-made clothes.'

'Forget it,' advised Georgie. 'It was only something to catch the trade for you.'

Esther arrived, still shaky from childbed, having left her newborn daughter, Rose, with her mother. 'Nothing's going to keep me out of this, Adela.'

The doors were opened at seven, bottles and glasses stood on a table. It was just an old trestle but a cloth of shimmering green satin thrown carelessly over it transformed it. The 'carelessness' had been achieved by Adela in two nervous hours. There were plates of small savouries which Ida had baked, and silver baskets, lent by Georgie, of sugar-covered almonds and turkish delight. No one will come, Adela thought wildly. I must have been mad. Grandmother's savings! I'm almost down to my last penny.

Ida had said, 'You must have a new dress to wear for the opening, Adela.'

Adela had stared at her, stupefied to realise that she had been so concerned with the shop she hadn't given a thought to her clothes. 'My God, I've got nothing,' she said wildly. 'Not a thing. And Blanche is far too small to lend me anything.'

'And Georgie too big,' said Ida with a smile. 'Don't panic, Adela. Get some material you like and a pattern. I'm handy with a sewing machine. I'll make something for you.'

Georgie, hearing of the dilemma, offered further help which Adela refused. 'You've already given so much.' Georgie shrugged, stuck a cigarette in a corner of her mouth and leafed through *Vogue* which Ida had been studying. 'Load of bloody rubbish in it,' she said, puffing on her cigarette, her foot on the fire surround. She looked out of place in the little house in St Philips, in her excellent tweed suit and expensive leather brogues.

Ida gently but purposefully removed the magazine from Georgie's grasp and scurried off with it. Adela had time for only one fitting and received an impression of pale green silk which fell around her slender body in soft folds. 'It'll be gorgeous,' she said, but her mind was never far from the fact that so many livelihoods and futures were riding on her judgement.

On the morning of the opening Ida had carried the dress in and Adela tried it on, for once forgetting the shop in her amazement. 'Ida, it's beautiful,' she breathed. 'You're a genius. Fancy! You've been wasted all these years doing housework.'

'They call it an afternoon dress in *Vogue*,' said Ida, 'but I thought it was suitable for the opening.'

'Suitable! It's wonderful.' The dress was simple and flowed over Adela's form, caressing her slender body; it was lightly nipped in at the waist and had a deep V-neckline with a raised, stiffened collar which framed her face. She had washed her hair and Ida had brushed it until it gleamed.

'I made this, too,' said Ida, reaching up on tiptoes and placing a headdress of green silk and tiny yellow rosebuds on Adela's head. 'I got that from *Vogue* as well. It's a really lovely magazine, Adela.'

Adela kissed Ida, thanking her again, vowing that if ever she made money Ida would get her own copy and anything else she wanted. The wait dragged out interminably and when the first guests arrived she felt like kissing them.

'Trust the Smithers to get here before anyone else,' muttered Blanche, before greeting them effusively and even kissing Mrs Smithers on both cheeks, a manoeuvre that made the over-bejewelled lady preen.

'Welcome,' said Adela, shaking hands. 'Please do have a drink.'

'Don't mind if I do,' said Mrs Smithers, accepting a glass and wandering round, staring at the textiles which were draped over stands made by yet another of Jack's friends. Adela had discovered that Ida had once worked in a shop selling materials until her mother had decided that she was needed at home. Hoping to make a career in textiles, she had learned all she could about the trade.

'I've never forgot the elementary rules of drapin',' she told Adela proudly. 'The first thing to aim for is simplicity. Let the material fall in natural sweeps an' lines. Mushroom-top stands are good. Hang the stuff you're sellin', then rearrange it in graceful folds. Or pin it to the wall an' make pleats. It's all simple really, but it makes such a difference. Then there's the cylinder-top drape, or the tee-stand, an' the fancy-top stand, that's somethin' like an upside-down hanger. Oh, there's all sorts, an' when you've got enough money you can buy them an' I'll show you how to use them. Each has its own way of lettin' the material fall.' She had stopped abruptly, her face reddening. 'Sorry, Adela, I'm intrudin'. I expect you'll have experts to show you the way.'

Adela had given her a hug. 'It sounds as if I have an expert. I shall always be glad of your help, Ida.'

Adela had watched Ida trotting about, pulling out a swathe here, creating a fold there, her face absorbed, clearly happy, and wondered just how great a sacrifice she had made of her own aspirations.

Blanche had arrived with some tall, fancy baskets with handles, of the kind used in flower arranging. 'A cousin of Georgie's got married,' she said. 'She was going to throw these away.'

Adela had filled the baskets with cream lilies and brilliant scarlet amaryllis, all provided by Georgie, who always seemed to be with Blanche these days, and used them as a centre piece for the display of cool blue, vivid green and softly violet-based stuff she had used for pure decoration. Bit by bit the large shop had been filled with eye-catching pieces and stands of materials, some of them, the ones furthest from the single light hanging in the centre of the room, spot-lit. This miracle had been achieved by yet another unemployed ex-soldier who had promised to rewire the place as soon as Adela could afford it. Jack looked paler than usual. Nerves, Adela decided, though she thought worriedly he was getting frailer by the day. He kept in the background, watching, in his eyes a desperate longing that Adela should succeed.

Two more couples turned up, then a large party of young men and women who clearly thought they were slumming. Adela had met most of them casually at dances and house parties and didn't care if they thought they'd descended into hell as long as they were there, noisy, flirtatious, laughing, making a great play of declaiming over the materials. They said they adored the wall drapes.

'Just like being in an Eastern Potentate's tent,' exclaimed a girl called Vita.

'How would you know?' asked one of the young men, a question which brought shrieks of mirth.

'Bobbie, darling,' said Vita Wethered, 'this cretonne would make positively dreamy curtains for your sitting room.'

Bobbie darling agreed. 'It's lovely and all the rage, isn't it?'

'The Anna Martin nasturtium design,' said Adela. 'It *is* lovely, I agree, with its muted creams and blues and greens.'

'I see you make up materials, Adela,' Bobbie said. 'Have you any samples of your sewing for me to see? Though I don't suppose you do your own sewing, but have some little seam-stress beavering away somewhere. I'm getting married and have to decorate a whole house. At least, most of it is done, but I've been looking for something pretty for my own sitting room. So essential to have a place where one can be alone and it goes without saying that the decor must be restful.'

Adela thought of the cramped, overcrowded dwellings in St Philips and the hollow-eyed, over-burdened women who pre-sided over them, but she kept her professional smile bright and was only too thankful she had anticipated such a question and was able to satisfy Bobbie's demands. 'I have a set of chair covers and matching curtains on display over here, if you'd care to come and look.'

'Perfectly delicious,' pronounced Bobbie, and Freddy took her order and asked for a deposit.

'Heavens!' cried Bobbie. 'I haven't brought money with me. Look, my darling little purse isn't big enough to hold more than a comb and a handkerchief. Has anyone got any money? Gerard, you must have some!'

Her fiancé, obviously helplessly besotted by her and sweat-ing nervously, produced two beautiful, crackly five-pound notes and Adela Fabrics took its first order from a half-drunken society female and her lover.

'Do call on us again,' urged Freddy. 'Adela has such impec-cable taste.'

'Has she, indeed?' cried Bobbie, shrieking with mirth. 'I wonder what Daddy Danby thinks of her taste.'

Adela continued to smile, but she felt tempted to box Bobbie's ears.

'All the Jardines are vulgar,' she muttered to Esther. 'Mother only receives them because they're descended from earls.'

Esther stared at her and laughed, and suddenly seeing the situation from Esther's view, Adela laughed, too.

After that, people began to pour through the doors. Georgie and Blanche had, after all, been wise to spread the news of Adela's connections. Many came to stare and stayed to buy and the cash box was filling. Adela had only one glass of wine but she was feeling dizzy with weariness and triumph and when Sander Bennett walked in, just before they were due to close, greeted him expansively.

'My God,' he said, 'you're tipsy. How often do you drink too much?'

'Hardly ever,' cried Adela happily, then lowering her tone asked, 'How do you like the wall hangings?'

Sander looked at the pyramids of satin and silk draped from ceiling to floor, the apex vivid green, the slopes in pale violet and sky-blue. 'Very nice,' he said. 'What does the sign say?' He strolled over to look, followed by Adela, and his face darkened with anger.

'Wall hangings purchased from Bennett's. Seconds – for display only. All goods for purchase acquired from reliable London companies.'

'What's that supposed to mean?' he demanded, his face thrust aggressively towards her.

'Exactly what it says,' replied Adela chirpily, though to her annoyance his anger made her a little nervous. 'You refused to sell me anything but seconds and I can't use them here, not if I want to attract rich people and make money, which of course I do. The walls needed something to relieve the bare whiteness, so I've used them in the way you see.'

Sander glared at her so furiously she stepped back a pace. 'You want to compete with me, but you won't,' he said. 'My shop in Castle Street will get passing trade as well as high-class customers. You may be doing well tonight as a result of the help given you by Blanche and Georgie, but it'll soon tail off when the novelty goes.'

'Compete with you?' Adela trilled. 'How amusing. A shop in Castle Street? I really must pop over and have a look sometime.'

'Even if I hadn't told you myself, you know bloody well I'm opening there! I've discovered that you tried to bribe Addison into selling you the lease.'

They were standing facing the wall, apparently admiring the drapes, although a quick glance over her shoulder told Adela that Bobbie and some of her friends were watching them curiously. Sander's thick-muscled body was now taut with anger.

'Bribe?' she hissed. 'I did no such thing! It's fair in business to make a higher offer. And you told me you wanted the Castle Street property to go into partnership with *me*. I don't believe you had any intention of opening a place of your own until you knew I'd be trading. You've never forgiven me, have you?'

She wished the words unsaid. The wine was talking. She was glad when her sister interrupted them.

'Hello, Sander, you received my invitation, I see,' cried Blanche, raising her glass to him.

Sander looked irritable and when Georgie sauntered up he stared at her. 'You two, together as usual,' he said.

'Yes, we are, aren't we?' agreed Blanche, and Georgie laughed heartily.

Sander frowned at them and departed, leaving the two women still laughing.

'Good heavens, Blanche, old girl,' cried Georgie, 'how can you want such a bad-tempered bloke as a chum?'

'I don't but he has his uses. He's stinking rich and the party can do with all the funds available.'

'So true,' said Georgie. She tried to slide her arm round Blanche's waist, but Blanche moved away and Georgie looked disappointed.

My God, she's in love with Blanche, Adela realised. She wondered if her sister returned the love and decided that she probably did. No wonder she was so changed. Love had wrought the miracle, but it was no wonder that Mother was so outraged. This was flouting convention in a very determined way.

Adela had set aside some of her grandmother's money to hire a private detective to look for Harry. When Jack met Arnie Weekley he was unimpressed.

'I bet he's never done anythin' but spy on people wantin' to get divorced. I don't like his looks, he a right nasty character, I'd say.'

Adela argued, 'He's all I can afford, and surely it won't be beyond his capacity to find Harry? A child can't just disappear.'

Mr Weekley believed in keeping clients interested and twice Adela had been led to understand that he was on a warm trail, and twice he had to confess himself wrong.

The third time was different. 'I got a tip-off from a chum,' Arnie Weekley had said, 'about a kid that was supposedly adopted by a couple in Soundwell, but they've already got five of their own and they're not well-off so why should they take on another kid? I've been to look at the boy and I reckon we're on to a winner this time.'

Adela was shaking with excitement and hope when Mr Weekley drove her in his small, creaky car to a house in a quiet respectable street one afternoon. 'Every day about now either the woman or one of her daughters wheels the kid out for an airing. We'll just have to wait.'

Adela waited, her pulse hammering in her throat. The front door opened and the pram was propelled down the short garden path and out of the gate.

'Now,' said Mr Weekley, 'get out and pass, casual like, and have a look.'

Adela's legs would scarcely bear her weight as she walked as naturally as she could after the pram. She slowed her step as she reached it and looked eagerly at the child. With a sickening jolt of disappointment she saw that it wasn't Harry.

She hurried back to the car. 'How could you raise my hopes in such a way?' she stormed.

'I'm doing my best, Mrs Danby.'

'Your best! I told you exactly what my son looks like. That child has black curly hair and deep brown eyes. He's nothing like the description I gave you.'

'Well, I can't always be right,' said Mr Weekley, engaging the gears and driving them off. When Adela parted with him she handed him the remainder of what she owed and told him he was dismissed. He shrugged and drove away, whistling. Adela wondered how many others he had cheated. Of course, in a trade like his, there would be no redress. No one would want to admit employing such a man on personal matters. Jack was sympathetic. 'They're not all like that, my dear. We'll find a decent detective.'

'I've no more money left,' sobbed Adela. 'It'll take time to make enough to try again.' She worked harder than ever in an endeavour to relieve her sense of loss.

Sander was wrong about Adela's shop. Not only did it gain the passing trade of folk who were on their way to Castle Street, but its slightly shabby exterior didn't scare the less well-off shoppers who hesitated before Sander's high-flown establishments. And the speed and efficiency with which Bobbie's curtains and chair covers were made, and their reasonable cost, impressed many. Adela looked forward to a time when she could engage extra staff for serving, and more sewing women, and began to feel that her business could be made to thrive.

Christmas was again taken with the Websters, some of whom this year regarded Adela with admiration and a certain amount of awe. She tried hard to enjoy herself but she was now permanently tired and often quite irritable, more especially now when she saw the lights on the Christmas tree, and the many other children racing around gleefully. Pray God, someone was giving Harry a happy time. Pray God, that soon she could begin the search again.

Adela wrote a long letter to Grandmother Sutton and sent it with a card and a small gift of a silk scarf which she had sat up at nights to hand-hem herself, and photographs which Freddy had taken of the opening of Adela Fabrics.

She had received a gift with a note from her grandmother which brought loving tears to her eyes.

Dearest Adela,
I'm enclosing one of the few family heirlooms that your dear grandfather didn't manage to gamble away. I send it with my fondest love and deep appreciation of the new lease of life you've given me. It will replace the one your mother confiscated. The two dragons guard me closer than ever, but one day I shall escape them.

Adela had opened the scuffed red velvet case and drawn out a single strand of small, perfect pearls, and eardrops to match, much finer than the ones Mother had locked away from her. She had worn them to the party on Christmas Day. Only Jack knew their true value and Adela was amused when they were compared unfavourably with Florrie's enormous, glittering paste brooch, a gift from her husband.

Adela's cousin, Millie, arrived in the shop soon after Christmas and kissed her. 'Darling, I'm so sorry I haven't been before. Mummy discovered that I'd been away on a weekend with Algy when we told her we were going to a house party. So unfortunate that Daddy had a severe attack of influenza and Mummy telephoned and I wasn't where I was supposed to be. Now they say I must get married at once when I did so want to play a little longer. The dear old parents were so cross with us, mine and Algy's. I've been up to my eyes in preparations for the wedding.'

'Don't you want to get married?'

'Of course. I adore Algy, he's a sweet old dear,' cried Millie, 'but I've been having such a good time since the war ended, I wanted it to go on. However, I'm sure I shall be happy. Algy is such a *perfect* pet.'

Adela smiled at her cousin.

'The thing is, Adela,' said Millie confidentially, 'we're going to move in with Algy's parents because we can't get a house ready in time for the wedding. They've given us a whole floor to ourselves – did I tell you that they have oodles of the necessary?— and they're real darlings, but I want my own home. I've seen Bobbie's curtains and covers and they're *perfectly* divine. Would you consider having a look at the place we've bought with a view to taking over the decoration?'

Adela wanted to fling her arms around Millie's neck and shower kisses on her. She managed to contain herself enough to give her cousin a quick hug and a kiss, then she riffled through the order book and said, 'I can fit you in a week from now. Will that suit?'

'*Heavenly*, darling. I'll pick you up here, shall I?'

There had been a lull after the Christmas trade. Adela had expected it because she had nothing to put in a January sale and no money to buy in special sale goods, but still the actual lack of customers was frightening. The need for money was a constant worry. One of the sewing girls, installed upstairs, had had no real work for two weeks. Many employers would simply have dismissed her and re-engaged her later – it was done all the time – but Margery was the only breadwinner in her home and Adela understood now what that meant and couldn't do it.

Jack approved of her humanity, but was anxious. 'You can't carry everyone on your shoulders. You're looking really peaky these days. Why not go along and have a word with the doctor?'

'What's the use, Jack? He's already told me why I feel unwell all the time. Apparently women have to suffer and that's that.'

'I know,' said Jack sadly. 'It was just the same with my Jessica.'

'And your mother and most of the women I meet in the Kingsley Hall. I can't believe that doctors couldn't help us if only they would. If they had to put up with such misery, they'd soon find a way out.'

'You need to rest,' said Jack.

'How can I? The shop needs me there all the time if it's going to prosper.'

'I know, my dear. Well, at least you no longer have to work from the barrow.'

'If business doesn't buck up, I may have to go back to it.'

'That won't happen.' Jack sounded so confident it irritated Adela.

'Hark at Mr Fortune Teller!' she scoffed.

He raised his hand defensively. 'All right, don't get shirty with me. Why not ask Georgie for a loan? She'd hand over the necessary like a shot if you asked her.'

'Then I'd have to pay her back, with interest. She's obliging, but she doesn't encourage spongers.'

Blanche came up with the same idea. 'She'll do anything I ask,' she said.

'You seem to have a strong hold over her,' Adela said.

'Yes, that's because she's in love with me.'

'*In love* with you?'

'Yes, surely you've realised by now that she doesn't like men? She wants me to go and live with her. She's got an enormous house in Leigh Woods. Her parents have disowned her, but she inherited a fortune from an uncle. Apparently he had the same sexual proclivities and she was the only one of his relatives he liked.'

'I see. So that's why Mother sounded so disgusted. I take it that the new friend she was referring to was Georgie.'

'Of course.'

'What about you?' asked Adela.

'What about me?'

'You know what I mean. Are you – do you love Georgie?'

'Adore her,' said Blanche, lighting a cigarette. 'I understand now my ambivalent feelings towards men.'

Millie gave Adela a conducted tour over a large house in Westbury-on-Trym.

'It's rather a long way from the shops,' said Millie, 'but with my darling motor car I can get to them in no time. I just *adore* shopping, don't you? Oh, but I forgot. You've become one of the world's workers. I know I'm dreadfully frivolous, but I can't seem to be serious for more than ten minutes at a time.'

Adela didn't need to be reminded of Millie's frivolity, Mother and Father had always been voluble on the subject, but beneath her gaiety Millie was a dear girl. 'You're not as frivolous as you pretend,' she said.

Millie looked sideways at her. 'I don't suppose anyone could be quite that silly,' she grinned. 'But honestly, Adela, I could never cope with life as you do.'

She unlocked the big front door and the two girls inspected the hallway. 'It's very dusty,' said Millie. 'The previous owner has spent months in a nursing home and the house has been shut up. Now the poor soul is dead.'

There were a breakfast parlour, a drawing room and a study, four bedrooms, a kitchen and scullery, and servants' quarters.

'Fortunately,' said Millie, 'I don't anticipate any problems over servants. My *utterly* divine Algy is so rich that I shall be able to afford to outbid anybody. Don't be shocked, Adela darling. You know I couldn't possibly run a house without a housekeeper and lots of lovely maids and a butler and so forth.'

'Do you want the house furnished in a modern style?' asked Adela.

'Modern? Do you mean tub chairs and abstract upholstery?'

Adela gave her cousin a quizzical look. 'You seem to be quite up-to-date. Are you sure you need my services?'

'Oh, my *precious* Adela, I certainly do. You can't imagine how lazy I am. Mummy is forever chiding me for it. I begin something and end halfway through, and I could hardly live in a half-furnished house, now could I?'

'No, I suppose you couldn't,' agreed Adela, smiling. She was very fond of her scatter-brained cousin. 'What are your favourite colours?'

'Blue – all sorts of blues – and browns. Does that sound dreadfully dull?'

'Not at all. If that's what you want it's what you shall have. I'll plan the whole house. I'll begin right now and show you my suggestions, and if you approve my company will go ahead.'

'Absolutely *divine*, darling. When I tell Aunty Caroline and Uncle George how clever you are, surely they'll—'

Adela looked sharply at her cousin. 'Yes?'

'I don't know,' said Millie in a rush, 'but they are your parents and one can't help overhearing things said in the family. And I know you've quarrelled with them, though I don't know why, and I'm sure they miss you dreadfully.'

'Maybe,' said Adela.

Millie waited for more, but Adela remained silent and her cousin said, 'I must rush. I've a lunch appointment with Algy at one o'clock.'

Adela glanced at her watch. 'It's nearly two.'

'Oh, I know, I'm perfectly *dreadful* at keeping time, but Algy knows that and will probably have booked the table for one-thirty.' She paused. 'Don't be cross with me, please. I can't bear people to be cross with me.'

'It's all right, Millie. Don't worry. I'm not cross.'

Millie beamed and handed over the house keys and moments later Adela heard her car start up and drive away. She wandered round the empty rooms, her feet echoing, almost panicking as she realised what she was taking on. Her only concrete knowledge

363

of modern house interiors had been gleaned from books, magazines and museums, but she had ideas which she had always dreamed of incorporating into a place of her own. Years before, during the family's annual visit to their Scottish lodge, the Danbys' governess had taken her young charges to Glasgow and enthused over Charles Rennie Mackintosh, an architect and artist who was influenced by Japanese culture and had incorporated it into his own unique style. Blanche had been bored, but Adela had drunk in his unusual decors. The governess had taken them to see the Glasgow School of Art and to Miss Cranston's Tea Rooms, both places designed by Mackintosh in his brilliantly idiosyncratic style and, later, when she had grown up, Adela had gone back on her own.

She stood at the window of the master bedroom. If Ralph had survived she might have been living in just such a house as this, her mind on nothing more taxing than ensuring she didn't fall behind in fashion, with Harry safe in a nursery upstairs with his own nanny. Her baby, never really out of her thoughts, came vividly to mind. She seemed to feel the softness of his skin, the silk of his downy hair, to smell the clean scent of him when he was bathed and powdered. She leaned her head on the cool window pane and moaned aloud.

She scoured warehouses in Bristol and London for the right wallpaper and upholstery materials and ended by travelling to Scotland where she spent two days with notebook and pencil, adding up yardage and costs. In Bristol, she discovered the whereabouts, often through Jack, of unemployed men who were desperately trying to earn a living wage by using their creative skills, and commissioned stained glass from them, incorporating the Rennie Mackintosh rose, encased in abstract designs in turquoise and azure against browns ranging from muted gold to pale chocolate. She ordered furniture with high-back elegance, stencilled in complementary abstract shapes. In Glasgow she had seen delicate porcelain which would match the rest of the house, but Georgie came up with a young woman potter who desperately needed work and was pleased to throw vases and bowls to Adela's designs.

Her grinding, dragging backache had become so much a part of her everyday life she simply put up with it.

Sander had grown interested in her work, though their relationship remained cool. Once, when he walked into her shop, she greeted him sarcastically: 'I do hope you're not stealing my original ideas.'

'There's no copyright on ideas,' he answered caustically.

'Surely the great Mr Bennett would prefer to be first, not lagging behind a mere woman? A chattel, in your eyes.'

He flushed angrily. 'I don't look on women as chattels!'

'Have you forgotten so soon?'

'You are, I assume, harking back to our brief interlude of betrothal?'

His manner stung her. 'You know damn well I am, and especially to the terms of sale arranged between you and Father.'

'That's all past now. Why must you keep referring to it? We've both been hurt.'

'Oh! How were you hurt?'

'Are you ill?'

'What?' The question caught her completely off guard. 'That's impertinent!'

'You don't deny it.'

'I'm overworking, that's all.'

'You should visit a doctor.'

'I already have. Doctors!' She finished with enough venom in the word to rival Mrs Webster.

'I suppose you're suffering from some after effect of having Harry.'

'Really, Sander, I don't think it's a subject for us to discuss. And what do you know about it, anyway?' she added, undermining her own indignation.

'I employ a large number of women, remember? I also employ a full-time nurse.'

'Well, I'm quite capable of managing my own life.'

Sander shrugged and left, though she had clearly angered him again.

Adela didn't borrow from Georgie, but she was grateful to

her when she offered her name as guarantor for a bank loan. 'It'll only be until you get your shop going, old thing,' she said in her hearty way. 'You'll be a success. I can feel it in my bones.' Adela hugged her. She liked Georgie more each time she met her.

'She wouldn't be able to lead the kind of life she does if she wasn't so rich,' Jack pointed out. 'At least, not openly.'

'I suppose that's true. One day we'll be rich, too, and we'll do as we damned well please.'

'I thought you already did.'

Adela smiled sadly. 'No. If that were so I should send you to Switzerland, into the mountains, and the wonderful air would restore your health. Jack, I get so worried about you. You don't look well at all.'

'Neither do you. We're a right pair, aren't we?' He didn't sound bitter. Ill health was so prevalent among the poor it was expected.

Adela knew that the chance Millie had given her to display her talents wouldn't come again if she failed and she spent most of her time searching for the right artifacts to complement the decor. Consequently the shop takings dropped drastically. Esther did what she could, leaving her small daughter in an old pram in the sooty garden. In the end Blanche and Georgie came to the rescue, working when Esther couldn't, and the takings began to increase again.

Jack's life had taken on a new interest. In their desperation many former soldiers who found themselves without jobs or homes began to band together and march in orderly fours to fashionable shopping centres. They wanted to draw attention to the shocking plight of the many, but they frightened rich women shoppers and their activities were reported in the newspapers as if they were committing the most heinous of crimes.

'I'm not the only one on crutches,' said Jack, excitedly, 'there are even some fellows pushed in wheelbarrows. The poor devils have lost one or both legs and can't get a wheelchair. Their disablement allowance isn't enough to feed their families. I live for the day when this bloody government is out and we get the Labour Party in. We'll see some changes then.

They'll raise the old age pension, too. How can anybody be expected to survive on five shillin's a week?'

'They can't,' said Adela. She spoke almost automatically, busy with her notebook and measurements.

Jack watched her then said slowly, 'We're lucky to have you.'

Adela looked up. 'Don't sound so bloody humble!'

Jack grinned. 'Sorry, old thing,' he said in an accent passably like Georgie's. Adela paused in her frantic work to give him a proper look. He was getting more frail. His skin had lost its weather-beaten look and the blue veins stood out. When she had enough money, she vowed silently, when she had found Harry, she would concentrate on Jack and make sure he regained whatever health was possible, and she would take a rest herself and lie down for hours and days and cure her own cursed pain.

Adela met Millie at her house.

'Darling, you look rotten!' cried her cousin.

'Not you as well!'

'You know I don't mean it cattily. I think you're working too hard.'

'Never mind that, Millie. Just try to keep your mind on the subject and tell me if you approve of my suggestions. I've followed the designs of Charles Rennie Mackintosh—'

'Who?'

'A Scottish designer.'

Millie looked doubtful. 'I've never heard of him.'

'Few people south of the border have, darling, which is what will make your house different from any other. In England, anyway. He's appreciated abroad.'

Millie looked pleased. 'Show me your plans.'

Adela produced a folio and she and Millie pored over it.

'A *white* drawing room?' exclaimed Millie.

'It's difficult to make you see it in pen and water colour,' said Adela. 'Believe me, it will be beautiful.' She produced more drawings and colour swatches and Millie looked at them, her brow creased in unusual concentration.

'But it's all perfectly *lovely*, darling. You're so clever.'

'You haven't seen everything yet.'

'I know I shall adore it all. You tell me I shall be a leader of design fashion and I believe you.'

'Millie, you must pay attention!'

'Very well, cousin,' Millie sighed, 'if you insist.'

'I envisage a white dining-room table, and matching chairs with tall ladder backs, in part wood, part canvas, which will be stencilled in muted colours. For your drawing room, I suggest you have a mix of light and dark furniture. The chairs will be stained oak, tub-shaped with linen upholstery, and a sofa to match. You'll need low tables. I've suggested stained glass in the upper parts of the windows which face the south west and they'll throw tiny beams of colour across the rooms. The lamps are silver-plated brass with leaded glass, repeating the window design. One wall will be stencilled to match the chairs, and studded with small rectangles of mother-of-pearl.'

Even Millie's attention was caught. 'Darling, it's *very* different,' she said hesitantly, 'and there seem to be quite a lot of roses.'

'Yes, but not in the lush manner of Art Nouveau. They are bold yet simple shapes with the leaves creating contrasting diagonals. I see this continued in the curtains.'

'What about the rest of the house. Is it to be all white?'

'No, I've brought samples of wallpaper for you to see. Here, for instance, is Liberty's peacock feather print which seems right for the hall, stairways and landings. And here's my suggestion for cushions. A series of triangles from small to large, giving an impression of depth; those are after Dufy.'

'The painter?'

'Yes. He's also interested in textiles.'

'Do you think the styles really will mix?'

'I'm sure of it, and you can buy modern pictures and ornaments to continue the abstract theme. There are paintings by Mackintosh and others which will suit the rooms perfectly.'

'I wouldn't care to have white for our bedroom, Adela,' said Millie, looking worried. 'I think I'd find it too clinical and somewhat overpowering. Don't forget I have to live with what you do.'

'I'm only making suggestions,' said Adela, her heart

thumping. Surely Millie wasn't going to change her mind now? 'It's your house and you must have only what you want. And Algy, naturally.'

'Algy wants what I want,' said Millie. She riffled through the designs and fingered the swatches, then looked up with a smile. 'It's all perfectly *gorgeous*. You're such a brilliant old thing.'

Adela could have hugged her cousin in relief. 'I've emulated Mackintosh's designs in the whole house in your favourite colours. Oh, and the fireplaces will be painted oak with steel surrounds. Your home will be very distinctive.'

Millie giggled. 'Bobbie will be furious! She chose an old-fashioned flower print for her sitting room, didn't she?'

'I sold her a delightful material, and making Bobbie envious is not the main idea behind all this,' said Adela severely.

'But you're laughing, too! You'd love to score off Bobbie!'

'I can't afford to.'

'Oh, no, I forgot. Poor darling. But I'll invite everyone to my lovely new house and orders will positively flood in. How did you manage to collect all these precious things?'

'I've commissioned people and I've travelled to London, Manchester, and various other places.'

'Just so little me could have the best?'

'Of course. Also so that big me can have a living advertisement.'

Millie grinned. 'So we'll both be satisfied.'

'I certainly hope so. Of course, it's going to cost a great deal.'

'Oh, lovely. That'll make vicious Vita and boring Bobbie jealous. Of course,' Millie mused, 'Bobbie's fiancé is rich, though he hasn't as much money as Algy. Vita's got lots of money, too. I shouldn't be at all surprised if they both tried to copy my house. They may ask you to do it. You won't let them have anything like mine, will you?'

'Certainly not. Each one of my houses will be distinctive.'

'I just know you're going to be a success! It's all so *deliciously* exciting!' Millie grinned devilishly. 'And I'll be a part of it, won't I?'

Chapter Twenty

Millie had embraced the suggestion that plain, pale carpets would act as a mount for the decor and had promised to take Adela with her to buy Tiffany lamps and vases and other ornaments. Adela had suggested an ultra-modern bathroom, and at the end of a long morning left the house knowing that she had her showcase. Millie had dashed off to an appointment for which she was, as usual, late, and Adela sighed as she caught the tram back to Old Market. She was hot, sticky and tired, and she hadn't had what she called a proper bath since she had left home. Sitting in a tin bath in front of the fire once a week with Ida keeping guard was no treat; she was too tense to enjoy it.

Adela's anxiety, caused by the haste in which Millie's house must be completed, and the nagging fear of failure of her first expensive venture, took its toll on her health, but she ignored it as far as possible. Nevertheless it was difficult to cope with the lethargy which stole over her sometimes. After the cruel disappointment over Harry she was determined to engage a really reputable person to find her son as soon as she could afford to.

Jack's interest in marching around Bristol with other out-of-work and invalid ex-soldiers had grown to become the focal point of his life.

Blanche had spoken of it to Adela and laughed. 'You should hear what people are saying about them! They aim for the best shopping places and women clutching handbags stuffed with money, some of it ill-gained war profits which they're anxious to spend, refusing to see the misery practically on their doorsteps. They hate Jack and his pals for forcing them to look.'

'Did Father make a lot of money during the war?'

'Of course. You know his workrooms were turned over

371

almost entirely to uniforms, and he was only interested in the ones paid for by the government. The bespoke tailors who worked for officers lost oodles of money because so many of their customers were killed. Father did well, though he's looking a bit sick lately. He bought up some businesses due for liquidation and now he's found he can't make them pay. He's having to close them down at a loss and he's furious with Sander Bennett who sold some of them to him.'

'Father didn't have to buy.'

'Of course not. You can't blame Sander for making his own fortune where he can.'

'I don't,' said Adela.

'You sound very mild. There was a time not so long ago when you'd have flared up like a bonfire at the sound of Sander's name.'

Adela shrugged. 'I'm learning a lot about business methods and he lets me buy seconds from his warehouse. I have to be grateful for that.'

That evening Adela hurried about the house preparing a meal. Jack would soon be home, filled with stories of his comrades' rather pathetic triumphs, and would need hot soup and tea to warm his skinny body.

Ida, hearing her, came round. 'Now you sit down, Adela, an' leave the soup to me.'

She sank gladly into a chair by the fire which was heaped with coal. She was thankful for the rest and stared into the hot coals reflectively. They were lucky to have fuel, but Jack's sons-in-law continued to keep the coalhouse stocked in spite of the continuing shortages. She grew drowsy after a busy day, knowing that she must still balance the books and sketch new designs before she could go to bed. She would have a short rest, just a short one . . . She drifted into a doze.

She was awakened by Ida who was shaking her. Startled, Adela looked up. Ida's face was twisted and her eyes wild. 'Wake up, Adela. Wake up, love. Somethin' terrible has happened.'

'Something terrible?' Adela sat up. 'Is it Mrs Webster? Is she ill?'

'No. Oh, no!'

Adela stared, suddenly terrified.

'Not Jack?'

'Yes, our poor Jack.'

'What about him?' Adela's heart was pounding painfully.

'He's had an accident.'

Adela stood up so fast she felt giddy and steadied herself with a hand on the back of the chair. 'Is he badly hurt? Where is he? I'll go to him. I know he'll be looking for me.'

'Adela, he's hurt really bad.'

'Well, don't just stand there! Take me to him, or tell me where he is.'

Ida held her white knuckles to her face. 'It isn't any good, Adela.'

'What do you mean?' she cried, but she knew with horrible clarity what was coming, she could read it in Ida's face.

'Adela, you must be brave. Our Jack's dead.'

Adela sat down heavily. '*No!* I won't believe it! I can't!'

'It's true, my love.' Ida clasped her thin hands. 'I've sent for Florrie an' Annie. I'll have to go back to Mum. She looks fit to die herself.'

'Wait, please, wait a moment. Please tell me – how did it happen?'

Ida said, between painful sobs, 'He was marchin' with his pals. Today they decided they'd have a bigger show an' quite a lot of men joined them. There's so many of them now on parish relief, an' some are actually beggin' for food and pennies. They made placards about bein' unemployed soldiers, an' maimed an' sick an' nobody carin'. Some people took exception to them holdin' up the traffic. The police told them to disperse an' when they refused there was some fightin'. Jack was hittin' out with his crutch an' overbalanced, an' when he fell he bashed his head on a curbstone. He was bleedin' but still alive when they took him off to the hospital, but he was dead by the time they got him there. He had no stamina, you see?' There was an urgent banging on the wall and Ida said, 'I'm very sorry, Adela, but I must go to our Mum. Will you be all right on your own for a bit? I'll come back as soon as I can.'

'Yes, go. Go. I'll manage.'

Ida left with an anxious backward glance. Adela sank back into her chair. She couldn't believe in Jack's death, not really. Surely that fiery, courageous spirit hadn't been quenched forever? Her tears flowed. She had lost the best friend in the world. He had been father, brother, comforter to her but it had to be faced, Jack was dead. She had never felt so alone in her life.

Esther came in. 'Adela, I heard. What a terrible thing. That dear good man, to die like that after all he's suffered.'

Adela said, 'I can't think of going on without him. I never knew how much I depended on his strength.'

'I know what you mean.'

Esther's voice was quiet and Adela looked up at her. 'Of course you do. You've been so brave. You even had your baby without Bert.'

'You'll find the strength you need,' comforted Esther.

'I must. I have to make money to get my Harry back. He's growing up with strangers. Oh, Esther, I get so tired! Jack always bucked me up with his dry humour and his cheerful outlook. I shall miss him horribly.'

The entire street spent the next few days behind windows covered by blinds or drawn curtains in deference to the man laid out on his own bed. Jack's funeral was very well attended. Adela knew that he had been popular but she was surprised by the number and variety of people who came 'to pay their last respects', as Mrs Webster put it.

'What about his son?' asked Adela.

'I've written to the last address we had for him,' said Ida, 'but that was from before the war.'

Mr and Mrs Smithers were at the church and Mrs Smithers put her short fat arms round Adela and kissed her. 'My hubby worked with Jack's father on the barrows,' she said. 'I met Jack when he was young and as strong as a bull for all that he wasn't big. As if the war hadn't took away enough men without this happening.'

'The war took Jack away as surely as if he'd been shot in the

374

trenches,' said Adela bitterly. 'He just ran out of strength. If it hadn't been the knock on the head it would have been something else.'

'It's terrible.'

Sander was there and when Adela put out her hand to him he took it and held it a little longer than necessary. 'I'm more sorry than I can say, Adela. The world's a grimmer place without him. He was needed.' She had never heard him speak with such sad sincerity, and warmed to him.

After the interment, family and close friends went to Mrs Webster's house and when funeral meats had been consumed, the wine bottles emptied and the beer finished, Adela sat alone at the kitchen table in the small house in St Philips, a mug of tea cooling in front of her, and laid her head on her arms and wept. Ida found her there and tried to comfort her, though she too was weeping.

'How's your mother?' asked Adela.

'Ill with unhappiness. I gave her a potion I got from the herb woman an' she's asleep. Poor Mum! Our Jack was the only one of her boys to survive an' he's always been so good to her!' There was a brief pause and Ida said, 'I don't suppose you'll stay on here now.'

'Why not? Where else could I go?'

'I don't know. Mum seems to think you'll leave.'

'Has she said so?'

'Not in so many words, but just before she went to sleep she said somethin' about money.'

Adela was stricken with remorse. Jack would never have forgotten the financial plight of the two women. 'I'll come round tomorrow and talk to her.'

She found Mrs Webster sitting upright in her chair by the fire. Her eyes were red but her grief was well hidden. 'Adela,' she said uncompromisingly, 'it's you.'

'Sit down.' Ida fussed around, drawing a chair closer to the fire and plumping up the cushions, then went to the kitchen for the teapot. She poured two cups and returned to the washing up, much of it left from the night before.

'I'll help,' said Adela. 'Didn't Florrie or Annie offer?'

Mrs Webster scowled at her. 'Of course they did, but they got too much to do already an' I told them to go home. The neighbours have taken the plates they lent us, so it's not too much. Florrie an' Annie are worried sick. Their husbands have just lost their jobs. Businesses are closin' down all over the place. They got a week's pay each.'

'I know. Jack told me.'

'An' now they'll have to live on government charity.'

'It's not charity. The money is due to them.'

'Government charity,' insisted Mrs Webster. 'An' the money's not enough even for one, leave alone a family, an' they'll be shunted back an' forth between the dole money an' the Guardians.'

Adela knew she spoke only the truth.

Mrs Webster continued bitterly, 'An' our Annie's job's gone, too. They got a fifteen-year-old kid in who'll be glad of half Annie's wages. It's disgustin'! It's a disgrace! Our Florrie's the only one workin' and their men are out on the streets playin' music for pennies. It shouldn't be allowed.'

'No, it shouldn't,' said Adela.

'Why should you care?'

Adela looked into the unhappy face of Jack's mother and the angry retort died on her lips. 'I do care about the people around me,' she said. 'Surely you know that by now?'

'I don't know anythin' of the sort.'

'I wish I could help.'

'Could you give our Annie work?' Mrs Webster asked belligerently.

Adela knew she couldn't afford an unskilled worker, but she said, 'I'll try.'

Mrs Webster was taken aback. 'You will? Well, it'd do her a power of good.' She paused to wipe away a tear which had escaped. 'When will you be goin'?'

'Going where?'

'Well, you'll not want to stay in St Philips now our Jack's gone.' Mrs Webster's voice broke on her son's name and Adela almost rose to comfort her, but the old lady glared at her, daring her to feel pity.

'I have no plans for leaving,' Adela said gently. 'I'll stay here. I loved Jack, you know.'

'Did you?' For once, Mrs Webster didn't sound sarcastic. 'I suppose you did. But you've got to admit there's no love lost between you an' me. There's nothin' now for you to stay for.'

'I think of you as family,' said Adela.

'Think of us as family? You? We always used to manage without you.'

There was a world of fierce pride in Mrs Webster's voice but fear in her eyes. Adela understood that the old lady was looking into an abyss of humiliation and poverty in which she would be eternally at the mercy of cold bureaucracy.

Adela went through to the scullery. She picked up a teacloth. 'Ida,' she said softly, knowing that Mrs Webster's ears would be pricked, 'I want to help out with money and I know your mother won't accept charity from me. Can you work for me? I'll pay you well. You're worth it.'

'Oh, Adela, thank you!' Ida said. 'That's the thing I would like to do most of all. Mum *must* let me. I'll find a way.' She went on quietly with the washing up. 'Adela, our Mum's never been all that nice to you . . . I'm sorry for it.'

'Living with pain isn't easy.'

Ida glanced at her. 'An' you should know.'

'What?'

'You've not been out of pain since Harry was born, have you?'

'I'm young. I can cope with it.'

Ida lifted a plate carefully from the hot water. 'I thought I'd have to get short cleanin' jobs, well-off women are always wantin' servants, but I'll come to you all day if I can, Adela, even if it takes half my wages to employ someone to look after Mum while I'm out.' She smiled. 'It'll have to be a good-tempered woman who can put up with Mum's grumbles. Poor soul, she has days when she's nearly helpless now.'

She began to wash a large blue bowl. 'This is our Annie's. She must have forgot it. Mum respects you, you know.'

Adela raised her brows. 'She has an odd way of showing it.'

'I know. She's never been one to show her feelin's, but she

thinks you're clever. If she hadn't been struck down by illness, I think she'd have had a successful life herself. Perhaps she envies you a bit.'

'Do you think so? Maybe she does.' This was a new aspect of Mrs Webster. Ida, always quietly busy, often overlooked, evidently had the gift of insight.

By working long hours Adela got Millie's house finished in time. She received an invitation to the wedding and sent as her present a green, brown and gold Tiffany table lamp. She had not yet rendered her large bill.

The spring wedding was a grand affair. Millie wore a white crêpe de Chine dress with a beaded waist, and carried a bouquet of sweetly scented white clematis and blue hyacinths with delicate Japanese honeysuckle. The bridesmaids held posies of forget-me-nots. Adela wore the dress Ida had made for the opening of the shop, with a small cape and hat to match. At the reception she met many old friends, some of whom congratulated her on her brave new stand in running her own business, others of whom passed complimentary remarks yet somehow made them sound derogatory. The idea of a woman in her own business was still too new for many.

Blanche came, but not Georgie. 'Uncle Penrose is a stick-in-the-mud and refuses to speak to her,' said Blanche, 'though he still receives me.'

'I should think so!' Adela was indignant.

'Soon he may not. I'm going to move in with Georgie next week.'

'That's your business.'

'You've really changed,' said Blanche. 'You were once a prude.'

'Was I? Well, I've had that knocked out of me. Are Father and Mother here?'

'No. They heard you were invited and decided to have a pressing engagement in London. The fact that the wedding was arranged so quickly gave the excuse some credence.'

'I see.'

'Sander didn't get an invitation, either. The Penroses don't recognise him. I don't know how Millie ever came out of that family. She's not got a snobby bone in her body.'

Adela and her sister looked at one another and laughed. 'I don't know how *we* came out of our parents,' said Blanche.

That night as Adela lay in bed, tired but sleepless, she thought of the wedding. Algy was clearly in love and Millie so sweet-natured that she could never be unkind to him. They would have a tender honeymoon and a happy life together. Tonight Millie would lie in her husband's arms and probably feel as if nothing could ever hurt her. No one had ever given Adela complete emotional security. How she missed Jack! She had valued the reassurance of his presence in the next room, knowing he would always listen to her triumphs and disappointments when she needed a listener, sharing her sense of loss over Harry, imbuing her with optimism.

Lady Sutton had sent letters to Adela and Mrs Webster offering sincere condolences over Jack's death. Mrs Webster had read hers and tucked it into her pocket, giving the family only the gist of what was in it, but her eyes were moist when she read it and she carried the letter round with her.

Millie returned from her honeymoon looking radiant and sent out invitations for a party. It was to be limited to the young and Adela looked forward to it. The killing work, her sadness over Jack's death, her pain and the constant worry over Harry and the business, were all dragging her down.

'You'll need somethin' new for such a grand party,' said Ida. 'An' you should really have an escort, shouldn't you?'

'It doesn't matter. Society isn't nearly as starchy as it was before the war – at least, not among the young. As for a new dress, no, I don't think so. It'll have to be my one and only best dress again, and why not? It's beautiful, thanks to you.'

When Adela lifted the green dress from the wardrobe she discovered that Ida had been busy again. There were delicate diamanté decorations glittering at the waist and neck and the headdress sported pale green feathers and a small shiny brooch. Gloves need no longer be worn in the evening as they made holding a cigarette difficult. They had risen drastically in price and Adela was thankful. She felt a rush of love for Jack's sister.

When she was ready she went next door to thank her.

'You look lovely. She does, doesn't she, Mum?' said Ida.

Mrs Webster frowned. 'Very nice,' she commented, then set her lips. She was of the opinion that Adela should be dressed in black as she herself was, or at least not gallivanting off to parties.

A taxi arrived and was instantly surrounded by small boys and girls. The boys' attention was taken up by the car; the girls' by Adela. 'She d'look a real picture,' they agreed. Adela was ridiculously cheered by the opinion of the children, yet felt guilt she supposed she would always carry now that her eyes had been opened to the privations of the poor. Life in St Philips was getting worse than ever. The government appeared to have no plans to halt the rise of unemployment and hardships were increasing daily. Yet she couldn't help the lift in her spirits as she was driven to the big house in Westbury-on-Trym and heard the jazz music coming from the gramophone.

She joined a small queue at the front door and was welcomed in the hall by Millie. 'Lovely to see you, darling. I'm being formal for the one and only time tonight,' she cried. 'After this it'll be every man for himself.'

Adela looked round the hallway 'It's just as I pictured it,' she said. 'The oak settle looks splendid and the lights glow. What are people saying about the decor?'

Millie's eyes were shining. 'Some love it; a few are rather shocked because it's so different; one or two seem bewildered but daren't say much in case they are proved to be unfashionable. And Bobbie—' Millie paused to giggle '—is sick with envy. She's pretending that it's all *too* utterly outrageous for her, but underneath she hates me. I'm so happy. I'm sure you'll get other commissions.'

Adela couldn't help smiling at her cousin. 'I've brought you a house-warming present.'

Millie tore open the wrapping as eagerly as a child on Christmas morning and revealed a painting of a woman and child, executed in honey beige and softest pink, the elongated lines flowing like water.

'It's beautiful! Oh, thank you, Adela. It must hang here in the hall. It's perfect.'

380

'I'm so glad you think so. It's by Margaret, Rennie Mackintosh's wife.'

'How perfectly *heavenly*! Algy, darling, do be an angel and hang it straight away.'

Algy grinned and went to obey his wife.

If Adela's dress was noticed it would be only because it was so decorous compared with the others. Millie wore calf-length orange silk and chiffon with narrow shoulder straps which supported a deep V neckline and a plunge at the back. The other girls were similarly gowned. Male jokes in the *Bystander* about 'a conspiracy among women to leave as much of the spinal column uncovered as was compatible with a scanty bodice' cut no ice with the new woman in her black or white or flesh-coloured stockings. Dire warnings by doctors about uteral displacement failed to stop fashionable women from wearing high heels. Many of them had plumped for short hair. The Jazz Age was in full swing and the well-to-do meant to enjoy every minute of it.

As the evening progressed, opinion came down in favour of the new decor. Bobbie, escorted by Gerard, was furious. 'It's all very odd,' she snapped to Adela. 'I gather you are responsible for the whole thing.'

'I am. I thought you would like it. It's so *avant garde*.'

Bobbie immediately turned coat. 'Of course I realise that,' she snapped irritably. 'It's just that at first it strikes one as being so different. Millie,' she shrieked across the room, 'can I see the rest of the house?'

'Of course, darling. Everybody can. Help yourselves.'

'She means that metaphorically,' called Algy.

There was general laughter and pushing and shoving as the guests began an unguided tour. Bobbie returned first and cornered Adela. 'I've decided to have my house altered. Will you do it?'

'Of course, but you've only just had it decorated.'

'That's irrelevant. Gerard, you agree with me, don't you?'

He nodded. 'Of course, old thing. Though I rather care for your pretty sitting room.'

'That's still in fashion!' cried Bobbie. She sounded sure, but her eyes were anxious. 'It is, isn't it, Adela?'

'Certainly it is. When can I see the house?'

'Tomorrow. We're getting married soon and I'll expect to move in just like Millie has, with everything accomplished. I must have a new decor, like Millie's only completely original. And I want a bathroom as nice as hers only in different colours.'

'I'll do as you ask, I promise. How soon can I call on you for a consultation?' Adela was laughing inwardly at the note of authority in her voice.

Sander arrived and strolled round greeting people. He got to Adela. 'You look exhausted,' he said bluntly.

'Thank you. So very encouraging to my morale.'

'Morale, be damned! You're overdoing it. You'll make yourself ill.'

Adela was surprised by a note in his voice that actually sounded sincere. 'Nonsense!' she retorted. 'I'm as strong as a horse.'

They were sitting in Algy's study, as he and Millie called the room. It had two small bookshelves and a dainty writing desk and chair; the floor was of polished light oak which Millie declared to be perfect for dancing. Algy, who seldom did any writing that wasn't in a cheque book, was perfectly happy with the idea. Someone came in and wound the gramophone and the strains of jazz shattered the air. Millie called, 'Come on, chaps and chapesses, this is the Dixieland Jazz Band – *At the Jazz Band Ball*, don't you know?' And she and her guests threw themselves into the frenzied bodily activity of the Shimmy.

Adela remembered dancing with Jack and had to fight back tears. She must return home. This was no place for a mournful face.

'Would you like to dance?' asked Sander.

'How can you ask?' she snapped unjustly, turning an angry glare on him.

'What brought that on? I thought it might cheer you up.'

'You said I looked tired. How will dancing help?'

'I shouldn't be surprised if you were suffering from nervous exhaustion as much as anything. Often physical exercise helps.'

'My nerves are my own business!'

'You're determined to quarrel with me and I refuse to cooperate. Come, Adela, dance with me. Laugh a little.'

'Have you forgotten Jack already?'

'I know you mourn him sincerely. I also know that he wouldn't want you to shut yourself away from fun.'

'I can't forget him as if he'd never been.'

'Everyone who knew Jack feels the same way.'

'They don't miss him as I do.'

'Poor Adela. You haven't had much luck so far, have you?'

'Don't be absurd! I had a perfectly beautiful home and went to lots of parties and theatres and—'

'Childish things,' interrupted Sander. 'I meant since you've reached womanhood.'

'It isn't—'

'My business,' finished Sander. 'Why are you always so damned prickly?'

'I'm not.'

'Then it's just with me?'

Adela turned to look into his face and caught an expression which looked very much like sympathy. Algy's drinks were strong and she was getting foolish. She had better leave. But she lingered on in the warmth of Millie's house, watching how the leaping fire illuminated the touches of leaded glass and was reflected in the floor. 'Do you like the house?' she asked Sander.

'It's certainly different and I have no doubt it will become all the rage.'

'Do you truly think so?' Adela said eagerly.

'I'm sure,' he said. 'You'll make money out of the idle rich, Adela.'

'You forget I was one of them.'

'No, I don't, and *was* is the operative word. You've moved far away from your beginnings.'

A maid brought round a tray of drinks and Adela had another cocktail. Then someone put on a romantic melody. She hummed softly to it and when Sander stood up and reached for her, she agreed to dance and swayed to the music. She felt dreamily comforted. Tonight was unreal, everything was unreal, there was no pain or sorrow or ache of loneliness and she wished it could go on forever.

'This is too slow,' shouted Bobbie. 'Let's rumba.'

Adela left the floor and Sander followed her into the hall. She looked round for someone to fetch her coat. Sander said, 'I'm sorry you have to go. I look forward to our next meeting.'

Adela was feeling embarrassed by the past few minutes. 'We aren't likely to meet much. I scarcely go anywhere and I never see you at the warehouse.'

'Do you want to see more of me?'

Adela looked sharply at him, the gentle glow leaving her. 'Of course not,' she snapped.

'That's a pity.'

'If you feel that way, why won't you let me buy the good stuff from your warehouse?'

'I've decided you may in future.'

'Oh!'

'You're not often bereft of words.'

'No. Thank you,' she added.

A servant brought Adela's coat and Sander took it and held it for her to put on. 'Have you had any news of Harry?' he asked quietly.

'What? No, I haven't. Don't refer to him here. Someone might overhear.'

'They won't know who he is.'

'I don't want to discuss him. Not in public.'

'You're a free woman now. Why aren't you honest about him? Publicise what's happened and get professional help.'

'What do you mean?'

'Your son is being kept from you. Ask the police to search.'

'And have it plastered all over the newspapers! Are you crazy? Ruin his life for him before it's properly begun. Spoil my prospects of making the money I must have for him, just as my business is getting going.'

'Times are changing,' said Sander. 'I believe the new morality will eventually overcome false values and people will accept others for what they are, not censure them for things they can't help.'

384

There was a note in his voice which made Adela remember his early life and that her parents, and others like them, denied him access to their houses because of an accident of birth. But she feared he was wrong. 'I can't agree with you. It's all very well for society men and women to kick up their heels and pretend to have broadened their outlook, but the stigma for children like Harry remains and probably always will. They are ridiculed, despised. In the end, it's they who suffer most.'

'It's always seemed monstrous to me that children should be blamed for the sins of their parents.'

Adela said, 'I hadn't given it much thought before. In fact, I hadn't given it any at all.'

'Hardly surprising. It's not something you would think about, is it?'

Adela felt his manner to be critical. 'Is there any reason why I should have?'

'Calm down. I'm not accusing you.'

'Are you sure? And is that how you think of me? As a sinner?'

Sander gave her a long look which made her uncomfortable. 'No more than the rest of us,' he answered.

'I see.'

Sander lit Turkish cigarettes for them both and the fragrant smoke drifted around their heads. Adela said abruptly, 'I've made up my mind! I shall start another search for Harry as soon as Millie settles her bill. My creditors will have to wait.' She felt suddenly very weary. 'I must leave,' she said. 'I shan't be fit for work tomorrow.'

'You may delay payment of my bill,' said Sander blandly.

Adela flushed. She had forgotten he was her chief creditor and now felt grateful and angry at the same time. She wanted to refuse his offer, but her necessity was too pressing. 'I appreciate that,' she said. 'I shall insist on paying interest, of course.'

Sander shrugged. 'As you please.'

Adela wished now that she had driven to the party in her somewhat erratic car. A taxi had been called, but after fifteen minutes it still hadn't arrived. When a clock struck the quarter hour, she stood up quickly, feeling annoyed. The room swayed round her and she put out a hand to steady herself. Sander caught her and lowered her back on to her seat. 'Steady. You shouldn't leap about like that.'

He looked at the long-case hall clock, its face a perfect square with Roman numerals, embellished with the stained glass and abstract designs which were echoed throughout the house. 'I don't think you should wait any longer, Adela. You look all in. I'll take you home.'

'You're so bloody autocratic,' she retorted, but she felt absurdly weary and longed for sleep so allowed herself to be led outside. Sander tucked a rug around her and started the car. It was large and luxurious and Adela felt safe and relaxed. She closed her eyes. She had drifted into a doze when he next spoke.

'What do you intend to do about your predicament?'

She woke abruptly. 'My what?'

'You need medical help. Don't you?'

'If I had known you intended to ask me personal questions, I'd have walked home.'

'That hasn't answered me.'

'How do you know about my medical problem?'

'Esther mentioned it.'

Adela felt herself colour. 'What a subject for her to discuss with you! I'm surprised at her.'

'It wasn't a discussion. I asked after your health and she told me she was worried about you. She then explained a little of what you're suffering.'

'I see.'

'So what are you going to do about it?'

'What *can* I do? What can any woman do? We're just expected to suffer. Expected by men, that is.'

'We don't all feel the same.'

'Unfortunately, doctors are the ones who tell us to bear our burdens like good little women. They don't care.'

'Some do. There's some clever research going on in Manchester into female problems.'

'Female problems! I wish you'd shut up.'

'Aren't you interested in a possible cure?'

'A cure?' Adela couldn't keep the eagerness from her voice.

'You are interested,' he said.

'You don't even know what's the matter with me.'

'From what Esther told me, I've a very good idea.'

'What have the doctors been doing?' she asked cautiously.

'Two surgeons, Archibald Donald and William E. Fothergill, have devised an operation which has saved many women from constant pain and made future child-bearing a much safer proposition for them.'

'An operation! I might have known. It'll take me years to save for that. All my spare cash must go on finding Harry. That's the most important thing in my life.'

Sander slowed at a crossroads, then revved up again. 'I was only trying to help.'

'You can, by letting me have the run of your warehouse.'

'I've said I will, though I can't produce the Rennie Mackintosh stuff.'

'Not everyone will want to be that different and your cloth is good. Even the seconds,' she added.

'I was thinking of an entirely different kind of help,' said Sander. His tone was casual, yet Adela detected an underlying note of anxiety. 'I thought you might consider marrying me.'

She gasped. 'Marry *you*! My God!' She laughed hysterically. 'I don't understand you at all.'

'That's always been perfectly obvious.'

'I suppose you think you know all about me.'

'Not everything. I know that you're loyal, that you have courage, that you are capable of love, that you are creative and energetic. I know, of course, about your need for medical attention, and that most of the time you're frantic over Harry.'

'You're pretty clever, aren't you?' She was sarcastic, unwilling to lower her defences.

'I try to be. I've always had to scratch around wherever I can for a living. I've met a lot of different people and learned to read their characters. It's a great help in business.'

'Business! That's all you really care about.'

'No more than you, I think.'

She thought about it. 'I suppose you're right.'

Sander laughed. 'Well, don't sound so mournful about it.'

'I'm not.'

'Will you give me an answer, Adela? Will you marry me?'

'The idea is ridiculous.'

'Ridiculous?' Sander's voice was low and angry.

'No, that's wrong. It's just – just impossible. We don't care for each other.'

'You want romance, do you?'

'I suppose every woman has her dreams.'

'More than you want Harry and a return to full health for yourself?'

'Why do you twist things? Is it so wrong to want love?'

'No.'

'Don't *you* want it?'

'Perhaps we'll learn about it.'

'There's been too much between us in the past. We can't alter that.'

'I'm willing to try, if you are.'

'But why should you want me? What can I give you? Even a place in society is out now. I'm pretty much of an outcast myself.'

'That could be cured. If you marry and set up a respectable establishment – and don't forget it would be a wealthy one—'

'You still think you can buy anything you want!'

'I know that in the present climate of society you can buy most things. With my money and your antecedents we would go far. And the first thing I'd do is to find Harry for you, that I swear.'

The car drew up outside Jack's house and Adela made to get out.

'Not so fast,' said Sander. 'Give me my answer.'

She paused. 'Not now. I'm too tired to think straight.'

'Very well, but don't keep me waiting too long. Meanwhile, let's have something to remember each other by.' He pulled her close and his mouth came down on hers, but gently, caressingly. There was no force, she could have freed herself but didn't. The movement of his lips on hers was warm and exciting and she leaned forward and returned his kiss. A moment later she turned away. 'I must be more tired than I thought,' she said abruptly.

'Adela,' he breathed, 'I believe we could be happy.'

'There's more in life than sex,' she said, furious with her own lack of control. 'You don't love me at all, do you?'

'Does it matter? Do you love me?'

'No, I hate you!' she snapped, climbing out and slamming the car door.

She regretted it instantly as a baby in a house across the way began to wail. As Sander drove away she saw the upstairs curtain next door move slightly. Damn! Mrs Webster had been watching. She let herself in. The house was cold and she shivered. Later, in bed, clutching a hot water bottle, she thought about the evening and its surprising end. She visualised Sander. He was ruthless, overbearing, sarcastic, and he used his sexual power to try to win arguments. She hated him. But her body was giving out a different message.

Millie's house became a general topic of conversation and because of it social invitations began to arrive for Adela. She attended parties and dinners where she would meet potential clients.

The necessity to conserve money meant clothes were quite a problem. Ida had made her a plain brown dinner dress and a black crêpe de Chine for evening, both of which could be embellished with scarves or collars or small pieces of costume jewellery, designed to be smart but easily forgotten. Adela regretted the need to be so stringent with her money. Coco Chanel had startled the world with a chemise shape in jersey for daytime wear, and evening wear followed her style in chiffon, crêpe de Chine, georgette crêpe with intricate bead embroidery, metal brocade or lamé. Hems had stopped at calf level, but voluminous underwear was impossible beneath such delicate dresses and every girl had in her wardrobe a number of the new step-ins, a one-piece undergarment in crêpe de Chine with a startlingly small piece of material between the legs. Adela, annoyed by her own covetousness, wished she could buy the lovely garments.

Young people increasingly followed their own bent and laughed at the strictures of their elders. Sander was generally in great demand. Such a man as he, attractive and single, couldn't possibly be overlooked in a generation where eligible men were in short supply. The annoying thing about him was that he slid so easily out of any threatened romantic attachment. 'He's not a marrying man,' was the general opinion. Blanche said that some people attributed his wariness to Adela's public rejection of him. She however was all too aware of a different Sander. She often found herself sitting next to him at dinner parties, a situation she suspected he engineered, and he never failed to ask her to dance and frequently tried to monopolise her.

At a party thrown by Bobbie, she asked, 'Why don't you leave me alone? I don't give you any encouragement.'

He raised his dark brows and gave her a sardonic look. 'You surely don't mean that? After all, I'm very much in fashion and you'd hate to be a wallflower.'

'You're as insufferable as ever!'

'I face facts, Adela, which is something you should do.'

'Face facts? What in hell do you think I've been doing for the past years?'

'Keep your voice down, darling, people are looking.'

'Don't call me "darling", and if you stopped singling me out for attention, people wouldn't need to look.'

He grasped her hand. 'Come on, darling, let's shake a hoof.'

He made her laugh which, for a while, undermined her defences.

Bobbie's house was, as she had commanded, different from Millie's. She said that her favourite colours were violet and orange, and when Adela had tried to explain that Mackintosh's beautiful effects were gained by using colour in moderation on muted backgrounds, she had flown into one of her quick tempers.

'If you don't want the commission, you have only to say so,' she stormed.

'Of course I want it,' Adela had said, her heart thumping at the idea of incurring Bobbie's animosity. 'I'll put together a folio and you can be the judge of it.'

'All right, but it won't take long, will it? The wedding's almost upon us.'

390

Adela had sat far into the night to complete her plans and had called on Bobbie at noon. She was still in bed. She sat up and looked through the line and wash drawings.

'Not bad,' she said. She yawned, putting a hand to her mouth. 'God, I'm tired. I was up nearly all night at a party. Delightful, but in the mornings one wonders if it was worth all the effort. You're lucky to have an excuse to keep regular hours, Adela. You can't imagine how weary I get.'

Resisting the impulse to bang Bobbie over the head with her folio, Adela had smiled. 'I hope you feel better soon. Do you like the ideas for your house?'

'Mmm, not much colour, is there? I like things to be bright.'

If Adela had retained any doubts about the garishness of her suggestions for Bobbie's house they had been stilled after she walked into her bedroom which was a riot of colour in which violet and orange predominated. She wondered how on earth she would be able to decorate the newly-weds' house in a style which would impress others when she had to follow such gaudy ideas. The two women had talked for an hour, during which a maid brought Bobbie a tray of coffee and bread and butter. Bobbie didn't offer anything to Adela, but the maid asked if her friend would like coffee.

'Friend?' queried Bobbie absently. She looked at Adela. 'Oh, yes. Would you?'

Adela had accepted gratefully. She hadn't eaten or drunk since a seven o'clock breakfast.

Bobbie's house was ready for her wedding day. Adela had managed to get plain carpets, but Bobbie had set her face firmly against undecorated walls. She disliked everything shown her until Adela had produced a German collection of more exuberant designs.

'Why didn't you show me this first?' Bobbie had demanded. 'It's just what I like.'

Consequently, the wallpaper was bright with colour in both abstract and figurative patterns which contained flowers, fruit and even cherubs.

'And I want stained glass, only a lot more than Millie has,' Bobbie had insisted.

By this time Adela had given up trying to argue and Bobbie's house had leaded mirrors and glass in the larger designs and brighter hues of Daniel Cotter and Alex Walker. All this meant that Adela had to supply more materials to the small army of out-workers she now used which sent costs soaring, but when she presented her bill Bobbie scarcely glanced at it before tossing it into a bureau drawer. 'I'll give it to Gerard,' she had said. 'He'll pay.'

To Adela's relief Gerard proved to be a prompt payer and, when Millie also cleared her account, she set off round her workers to pay their wages. Her old car had broken down and she decided to travel on the tram. As she was getting off at Kingswood Terminus, about to walk down Warmley Hill to a small clock maker, a horn tooted behind her. She turned to see Sander leaning across, opening the passenger door of his car.

'Get in,' he said.

She was momentarily incensed by his autocratic attitude, then she climbed into the car and sank thankfully back into the seat.

'You look bloody awful,' he said.

'Oh, shut up!'

'You're working far too hard.'

'If I want criticism, I can get plenty from Jack's mother.'

'Still behaving like a tyrant, is she?'

Adela paused. It seemed disloyal to agree. 'She doesn't like being dependent on me. You can't blame her.'

'I don't. She's a game old thing.'

'You sound like Bobbie's set.'

'And why not? You and I have to make our living among these people. Oh, sorry, I forgot. They're your people, too.'

Adela glared at him, grateful and annoyed.

'For God's sake, Adela, stop glowering at me!'

'Have you seen Bobbie's house?' asked Adela gloomily.

He grinned. 'I have. It's a miracle that you managed to create harmony out of so many strident colours.'

'Have I created harmony?'

'Yes, didn't you know?'

'I couldn't see straight by the time I'd finished. You've taken a weight off my mind.'

'I'd like to take the weight off you for good. Marry me.'

'No,' she said automatically. She turned to look at him. He was staring in front of him, his head as always thrust slightly forward, giving him the look of a man who intended to win, his profile strong, hands firm on the wheel as he negotiated a rag-and-bone man's horse and cart and avoided a milk wagon on its slow way up the steep hill. 'You do realise – I mean, absolutely realise – that my chief object in life is to get back my son?'

Sander put his hand lightly over hers. 'You've been honest with me. I like that. Marry me and I'll get Harry back for you, and make sure that your health is restored.'

'You'll get little for yourself out of marrying me.'

'I should get all I want,' said Sander. 'In time.'

Chapter Twenty-One

Adela engaged Esther as a machinist as more orders came in. She would lighten the women's work by installing power machines as soon as possible, but the compulsion to build up her business had become second to her longing to hold her son in her arms once again. The pain of losing him was often so sharp that she lost concentration. She persuaded Esther to come with her on a guided tour around Muller's Orphanage.

'Adela, don't go,' Esther begged. 'There are two thousand children there. You'll only see a few.'

She persisted and was sickened by the regimentation, the drab uniforms and cropped hair, the subservient way the children were taught to behave. She stared into the faces of boys who were about Harry's age, wondering if she'd even know him now. Children changed so quickly in appearance and Harry had passed his second birthday in June. He would be walking well now. She had to close her mind to the agony of loss, take a respite from the pain of remembering him, or she'd go mad.

Afterwards Esther tried to comfort her. 'I'm sure he's safe and happy, Adela. Your mother wouldn't do anything to hurt her own grandson.'

'She doesn't recognise him as her grandson,' sobbed Adela. 'Her only consideration was to hide him.'

'Why not ask her again? She might feel differently now.'

Adela took Esther's advice. She arrived at Speede House, hoping that surprise tactics would get her to her mother. Evans said that she was not at home. His manner betrayed nothing and Adela had no means of knowing if this was true or false. She wrote a letter. It was returned unopened. She tried telephoning, but Evans recognised her voice and told her that madam was not at home. Blanche was still allowed in, reluctantly because of Georgie, but brought back the news that if the subject of Harry was broached, Mother got furious and refused to speak to anyone.

Adela pored over the shop accounts again and again but there was nowhere she could save money without having to dismiss staff, people who needed money to live. If she married Sander . . . The thought kept recurring to her. Each time she dismissed it, but it persisted. If only he would fall in love with her; if only she could fall in love with him. When she said as much to Blanche, her sister was derisive. 'What's love got to do with it? Half the women I know marry for security, and a good many take lovers afterwards.'

'That kind of life wouldn't suit me. I want a proper marriage.'

'You always did have fanciful ideas.'

'Would you live with Georgie if you weren't in love?' retorted Adela.

Blanche was silenced.

Adela found it difficult to look cheerful when she attended the social occasions where she met her friends and future clients. She thought of what Sander had said, that she should be open about Harry, and shuddered. People could be so cruel.

Vita Wethered made an appearance everywhere that promised to be fun, and part of her fun was engaging in scathing criticism of any lapse in conduct.

'Guess what?' she shrieked one evening at Bobbie's. 'Amy Howard is going to have a baby.'

'No!' cried Bobbie. 'I didn't know she was married. She kept that dark.'

'My dear, she *isn't*, that's what is so priceless. Her parents are about to hurry her up the aisle as soon as they can get a licence.'

'How do you know?' asked Millie, her small face pink with indignation. 'Are you making it up? Because if you are, I think it's rotten of you.'

Vita blew out a cloud of cigarette smoke. She was very pretty with chestnut hair and wide blue eyes which could look innocent of malice while her acid tongue burnt holes in her friends' self-esteem. She waved her long tortoiseshell holder at Millie. 'Thanks so much, *darling*, and no, I'm not making it up. My maid had it from one of the Howard servants. She told me this morning that a servant of the Howards stole something and they were unwise enough to dismiss her without finding out how much she knew of the big family scandal.'

'I heard about the theft,' said Bobbie. 'What did she take?'

Vita shrugged. 'Oh, something quite trivial, I believe.'

'It was a silver box,' said Vita's fiancé, Sir Claud Overton.

'But not at all costly,' she said.

'They treasured it for its sentimental value,' said Claud.

'Oh, I might have known you would consider that to be important,' snapped Vita.

Claud said mildly, 'It has its own importance, but my man told me that the kid who took it was only thirteen and money's short at home. They might have given her a second chance.'

'Once a thief, always a thief,' said Vita. 'Anyway, it doesn't matter when Amy gets married. Everyone knows all the circumstances around the baby.'

Adela was held by a ghastly fascination. If people like Vita were so obnoxious about Amy, what would they say about Harry? Sander, with his wealth, could help her to shield him. Maybe he could adopt him. There were times, lately, when she almost liked Sander. He had shown real magnanimity by allowing her access to his warehouse after she had treated him so badly . . . She brought herself up sharply. Her mind was running away with itself. There could be no question of their ever marrying.

'What's all the shrieking about?' asked a languid, monocled young man who had just sauntered through the door.

'Amy Howard's having a kid and she's not married,' explained Bobbie, getting in ahead of a furious Vita.

'What, here?'

'Don't be an ass, Charles, of course not here.'

Adela kept a smile pinned to her face and only Esther learned how angry she was inside. 'She's such a bitch, Esther. She's never had a worry in her life and she gets all her amusement from gossip.' Adela paused. 'Was I ever like that? It seems so long ago.'

'I don't expect so,' said Esther, 'though I think you've learned a lot about people since you left home. You'll never fit in with women like Vita Wethered. You can never go back.'

'No, never.'

'You sound so sad. Do you miss your old life so much?'

'No. I miss a life I'm not sure ever existed, and I wouldn't want to stop working now.'

'What if you get married?'

'I shall still work.'

'Your husband might not agree.'

'Then I wouldn't marry him.'

Esther laughed, then grew sober and said, 'Bert never wanted me to work. Poor man.'

'Is he any better?'

'No. Last time I visited the doctor warned me that he'll probably never quite recover. If he does begin getting well, it'll take years.'

'Esther, my poor girl, I'm so sorry.'

'Well, I've got his baby. She's such a comfort to me.'

'I'm so glad. If only I could find my boy.'

'Oh, Adela, Sander Bennett could let you have all the money you need for the search.'

'Why bring him into it?'

'He likes you a lot. I haven't seen you together much, but when you are he watches you all the time.'

'I think you're imagining it, Esther, but he is being good to me. He never presses for payment.'

'If all your customers paid up, you'd be a lot better off,' said Esther.

'That's for sure, but I daren't dun them. They'd take their custom elsewhere.'

'Are you sure? You're becoming all the rage now. "*Too*, too clever, my dear",' Esther said.

Adela laughed. 'That's enough cheek from my staff! Back to

398

your sewing machine, my girl. Is Rose asleep?'

'She is, and safe and happy, thanks to you.'

When Esther had gone upstairs Adela opened the back door. The sooty patch had been transformed into a garden room. It had taken too much of her money, but she felt they all needed a place of repose during the long day and Esther wasn't the only worker with a baby. The indoor garden had a ceiling of smoked glass which kept out the fiercest sun rays. Green plants in large terracotta pots lined the glass walls, and there were cane chairs where the girls could sit during their breaks. She peeped into the prams to see the sleeping babies, her heart contracting with the ache of wanting Harry. Her hurt was sharper since the day she thought she had found him. Somehow she must trace him. Sander had promised his help if she married him. The idea wouldn't go away.

When she returned home that night, Ida invited her in for a meal. 'It's steak an' kidney pie, with greens and gravy. It'll maybe put some flesh on your bones.'

'You can talk!'

Ida laughed. She was such a wisp of a woman, Adela sometimes thought that a strong wind would catch her and fling her into the air.

'You're late,' accused Mrs Webster, who hated waiting a minute for her food. She glared at Adela.

'Yes, I'm sorry. I had a last-minute customer who has asked me to redecorate her drawing room. I couldn't turn her away, could I?'

'Folks should finish their shoppin' in good time.'

'You should have started without me.'

'We couldn't do that,' snapped Mrs Webster, 'seein' as it's mostly your money that keeps us.'

Ida flushed.

Adela sighed. 'Ida earns the money. She keeps my house clean and comes into the shop to help with the draping. You know that.'

'I most certainly do! Neglectin' her mother to run round after you!'

Adela was silenced. No matter what she said she couldn't

win an argument with Mrs Webster. Not that she wished to. The old woman needed her aggression to keep going in the face of so much pain and sorrow.

After the meal Ida washed up while Adela sat on listlessly in front of the fire which Ida had lit against a sudden cold spell. She stared into the flames, seeing nothing but Harry's face.

'What's the matter?' asked Mrs Webster.

'I miss my son,' said Adela miserably.

'I suppose you do, but he's probably better bein' brought up where he is. Illegitimate children have a rough time of it. I should try to forget him if I was you.'

'Forget him! That's impossible.'

'Our Jack had to put his son out of his mind. Michael was always self-willed, but who'd have thought he'd go off like that an' disappear in America? Of course our Jack never sent him away, like you did your Harry.'

She had gone too far. 'Jack grieved over losing his son,' cried the goaded Adela. 'He didn't say much about it because he didn't want to hurt you.'

'Hurt me? What d'you mean? What have *I* got to do with it?' Mrs Webster grasped her stick and struggled up. She clung to the mantel-shelf and Ida came in in time to see the stick being shaken near Adela's head.

'Mum, whatever are you doin'? You nearly hit her.'

'I meant to. She's insinuatin' that our Michael left home because of me.'

'I didn't say that,' protested Adela, wishing she hadn't yielded to temper.

'No, but I know what you meant. Fancy badgerin' an old woman like me with your wickedness.'

'What happened, Adela?' asked Ida.

Adela explained briefly, ending, 'And I'm sorry I was unkind, Mrs Webster. I hope you'll forgive me.'

Mrs Webster sat down heavily in her chair. 'You insulted me in my own house. Tellin' lies about me like that. I don't think we should have her here again, our Ida. Tell her to go away an' stay away.'

Ida looked straight at her mother. 'It's no use you goin' on like that, Mum. You keep tryin' to provoke Adela into a row, an' you know you quarrelled with Michael an' after that he ran away.'

'He'll come back to see his gran who brought him up,' said Mrs Webster, 'though he's never written to me. Ungrateful boy!'

'Perhaps he can't,' said Ida. 'What with the war an' everythin', I sometimes wonder if he's dead.'

'No!' Mrs Webster's voice was a wail. 'Don't say he'll never see his old gran again.'

'Oh, Mum,' said Ida, 'don't go on like that. I'm sorry if I've upset you.'

'You never used to say nasty things to me. It's all the fault of that woman over there.'

Adela got up and stretched her aching shoulders. She had been cutting out all the afternoon. She looked as kindly as she could at Mrs Webster. 'Whatever I do for you and Ida is for Jack's sake. He helped me when I most needed help, so I hope you won't refuse anything I can give you.' Then she left. She was still annoyed and wished that the old woman didn't have the power to get under her skin. In fact, she realised, too many people had the power to provoke her these days. Her nerves were stretched almost to their limit. She sat for a long time in her cold living room, just thinking, until Ida came in.

'Are you all right? I couldn't hear you movin' about. I'm sorry for the way Mum behaves. She misses Jack somethin' terrible. He could always coax her out of her miseries.'

'I know. I'm just a handy target to lash out at.'

'You're very forgivin'.'

That night Adela ached even after she lay down. The pain lanced down her legs as far as her knees. The next morning she visited the doctor who examined her gently. 'I've told you what's the matter with you. Your womb is out of place and you'll never get well while you spend so much time on your feet. You should do nothing at all and give yourself a chance and this problem might ease.'

'*Might* ease!'

'I'm a doctor, not a magician.'

401

Adela said, 'A friend mentioned a certain operation. It seems that two researchers in Manchester have devised a way of helping women with my complaint.'

'I believe I did read something of the kind,' said the doctor. 'We must all hope that they succeed, though of course any operation is extremely expensive and quite hazardous. By the time you are successful in business, maybe a cure will have been found which you can afford.'

Adela felt irritated. 'If I have to lie around half my life, I shall never succeed.'

'You mothers,' said the doctor, smiling. 'So impatient with your little aches and pains.'

'Mine are not little,' said Adela. 'They threaten to incapacitate me.'

'Cheer up, my dear. I am not unsympathetic, you know.' The doctor's voice was bland but dismissive.

Adela walked back to St Philips in despair. How could she rest just as her business was getting off the ground? She couldn't let it go, she just couldn't! It meant far more to her to succeed than she had realised. And there was Harry. Always Harry.

A car pulled up beside her and Sander said, 'Are you all right?'

She turned and, too weary to dissemble, said, 'I'm feeling unwell.'

He got out and opened the door. 'Get in.'

Adela obeyed.

'Shall I take you home?'

'Yes, please.'

They pulled away from the curb. 'Where have you been?' he asked.

'To see the doctor. God, he was patronising.'

'What's the matter with you?'

'That's a very personal question to ask a lady.'

'Women's problems again.'

'They've never gone away,' said Adela, embarrassment keeping her flippant.

Sander stopped the car beneath some trees whose summer

402

leaves were struggling through the chimney grime. 'Why have you stopped?' she asked. 'I'm supposed to go straight home to rest. Some hope!'

'You won't obey the doctor, will you?'

'I can't! I must work. My business is beginning to pay and my order book is filling. I shall have to get in more staff.'

'Can you afford to?'

'I must.'

'And your health? It's the most precious thing you have.'

'As the doctor says, we mothers must learn to put up with our little aches and pains.'

'Yours aren't little.'

'No,' said Adela, flippancy dying in the face of his gravity.

'Adela, marry me. We can find someone reliable to take charge of the shop while you go into a nursing home and have the treatment you need. Give me the right to look after you.'

Adela stared at him. 'Marry you? And I thought you said the doctors were at the research stage.'

'They have performed the operation and found it completely successful.'

Adela thought of life without the constant nagging, dragging backache.

Sander sensed her indecision. 'And I'd undertake to find Harry, once you give me the authority of a husband.'

'Find Harry?' she repeated. 'What kind of marriage do you want?'

'Whatever you're prepared to give me.'

'I can't believe that. What will you get out of it?'

'A beautiful, clever wife with the right connections. A hostess, a companion. You must admit, when we're not actually yelling at each other we get along quite well. Won't you let me look after you?'

'You hated me once.'

'When you jilted me? Yes, I did for a while.'

'Do you love me?'

Sander was silent for a moment. 'I like you, I admire you, I think we could have a reasonable marriage. Do you love me?'

'No,' she said baldly.

'Well, that's telling me.'

'I'm sorry, I didn't mean to be abrupt. I don't love you, Sander, but I wish to heaven I did.'

'Will you marry me?'

'You're so damned insistent, like a dog worrying a bone! What's your real reason?'

'Perhaps because you don't have a name which can ever end in "ie".'

'What?'

'You can't be Bobbie, or Freddie, or Georgie, or—'

Adela managed a laugh. 'Don't you take marriage seriously?'

'I don't know, I've never been married, but I'm willing to give it a try. How about you?'

'I can't think of anything but my problems.'

Sander leaned back and got out his cigarette case. 'Can't you give me an answer?'

'I'm so damned tired and feel so ill and I so desperately want my son. Won't you lend me the money to look for Harry and have this operation, if it really does work?'

Sander was silent for a while. 'If you dislike the idea of marriage with me so much, I'll lend you what you need.'

'That's so generous of you! It might mean a hell of a lot of money. I wouldn't be able to pay you back for ages and ages.'

'I don't suppose you would.' His voice became coaxing. 'But if you married me you'd have all the money you need without the worry. Why not take the easiest way out? I'd do everything in my power to make you happy.'

'I believe you would. There would be conditions, though. One above all others.'

'This sounds serious.'

'Would you adopt Harry? Give him your name so that he can never be harmed by gossip?'

Sander sighed with relief. 'Of course. It would be a priority. What else?'

'I must have complete freedom to build my business.'

'Certainly. I could invest—'

'No! Adela Fabrics is mine.'

'Very well, I agree.'

Adela smoked quietly, turning over all the possibilities in her mind. 'All right,' she said finally, 'I'll marry you. It seems to be the best way out of the mess I'm in.'

'I'll try to be content with that and this time we'll keep it simple. No wedding gifts, no big reception. Just you and me and a couple of witnesses. Will you wear something pretty?'

'Only if you do.'

Sander laughed. 'I'll dress up, too.'

Mrs Webster received the news with astonishment. 'You're goin' to wed Sander Bennett? I thought you disliked him. If I've heard you say it once, I've heard it a dozen times.'

'Mum!' Ida protested. 'It's Adela's business. We should be glad she's got a nice man like Sander to look after her.'

'You're under her influence. It'll be a good thing when she's gone and we can live in peace again. I don't suppose you'll want our Jack's house any longer?' The note of fear was strong beneath the old woman's belligerence.

'No, I shan't need the house,' Adela said, 'but I shall pay Ida for her work.'

Mrs Webster, for once, didn't argue.

Adela wrote to tell her parents of her plans and ask them to the wedding. She received a short reply from her mother which said that Father was unwell again and they were not attending any social engagements. She was filled with a mixture of anxiety and regret.

Blanche said, 'Father's not so much ill as worried. His business is still not picking up. He really loathes Sander now. He seems to blame him for everything, though of course it was his own decision to dabble in stocks and shares. He got his fingers burnt.'

Adela asked anxiously, 'Do you mean they are short of money?'

'Heavens, no! They've got plenty, but they can't endure the idea that they've lost some. Father sees it as a personal failure and Mother's critical attitude doesn't help.'

*   *   *

Adela and Sander were married quietly. She wore a bouffant-skirted dress in pale primrose chiffon and a wisp of a hat with pale green feathers. She'd had her hair bobbed in the latest style which left a few curls over her ears, and carried a Victorian posy of primroses and forget-me-nots. Sander was smart in a grey gabardine suit with a white shirt and grey tie and Adela felt her worries ease and her spirits lift in the unexpected way they sometimes did when she was with him. Blanche and Georgie were the only guests and acted as witnesses.

'Well, I don't want marriage for myself,' said Blanche, 'but for once you've done something sensible. Sander's all right.'

'That's true,' agreed Georgie in her hearty way.

After a meal Sander drove Adela to his house in Fishponds. Neither had time or the inclination for a honeymoon. 'I'll make you as comfortable as I can,' Sander said as they drove. 'I'm negotiating for a place overlooking Clifton Down. It's large and stands in its own grounds. When you're well you can plan a beautiful garden for Harry – and our children.'

'Our children!'

'Of course. I want them, don't you?'

'I'm afraid I hadn't thought about it.'

'I see.'

Adela glanced at her husband. His face was expressionless, but she knew she had hurt or annoyed him. Which was it? She knew so little of him really. The stupendous reality of what she had done hit her. She was married to a man she didn't love, one who frequently annoyed her, one who was not of her own class and had unpredictable reactions. His big hands were tight on the steering wheel and she was suddenly nervous. They hadn't yet reached his house and already she had upset him.

She said tentatively, 'I'm sorry, Sander. I've not really been able to think of anything except getting through the work. One day, I know I shall welcome your children.'

The tension drained out of him and he said, 'I'm glad.'

His house in Fishponds was situated quite near the main road. It was not very large but the immaculate lawns and flower borders, and the freshly painted woodwork, gave it an air of prosperity.

A plump woman greeted them at the door. 'Welcome, Mrs Bennett,' she said, smiling. 'If you'll come with me, I'll take you to your room.'

Adela glanced at Sander who nodded. 'Go with Mrs Monkton, darling. Rest a while if you feel you need it.'

Adela was taken aback by the endearment. She was shown into a room overlooking the back garden. It was pleasantly decorated in pastel shades and contained a plain suite of furniture. She looked at the double bed and turned quickly away.

'It's not grand,' said the housekeeper, 'but it's comfortable. I understand we shall all be moving to a bigger place near the Downs.' She opened the door to a knock and a thin young man with a bad limp entered, carrying Adela's suitcase. He glanced at her awkwardly out of one eye. She thanked him and he touched his forehead to her and left.

'That's Mr Taylor – we all call him Bill,' said Mrs Monkton. 'He's often sick, poor lad, or so the charwoman tells me – I've only just been engaged – and Mr Bennett keeps him on and makes him rest whenever he needs it. Some employers wouldn't be so considerate, but Sander Bennett's one of us, for all his money.' She coloured. 'Beg pardon, Mrs Bennett, I shouldn't be talking like that to you. It's just that Mr Bennett never has any side on him. He cares about the workers, even if he is a boss.'

Adela hardly heard her. She wandered aimlessly round the room, looking at the pictures, touching the furniture, ending by the window and staring down at the rear garden which was as bright with flowers as the front.

'A man comes in to do the gardens,' said Mrs Monkton. 'Another of our wartime heroes. He's lost a lot of his stomach after being gassed. Mr Bennett prefers to employ ex-soldiers.'

'Are you the only female servant here?'

'Bless you, no. I've engaged a kitchen maid, a parlour maid and a cook. Mr Bennett said, quite rightly, that he couldn't go on living in his bachelor style, not now he was getting married. The parlour maid's called Mollie. You won't need to see the kitchen staff unless you've a mind to. I'll deal with them. Is there anything you want now, Mrs Bennett?'

Adela turned and smiled. 'No, thank you. I believe I'll take my husband's advice and rest.'

'It'll do you good. Marrying's very wearing an' I should know because I've had two husbands, both good men, both, sad to say, passed on.'

Adela lay on the counterpane still in her wedding dress. She stared up at the ceiling. Everything felt unreal. She closed her eyes and drifted into a doze. She was awakened by someone moving about the room. Sander was drawing the curtains. He sensed that she was awake and turned and smiled. 'Do you feel better? Mrs Monkton told me you were resting in accordance with my instructions. She's a trifle garrulous, but a good soul. She believes in wives being obedient to their husbands.'

'Oh, she does, does she?' Adela felt a surge of irritation. She sat up too quickly and felt giddy. She put a hand to her forehead.

Sander was swiftly at her side. 'You really must learn to take more care of yourself, my girl. The sooner we organise the necessary treatment the better.' He sat on the edge of the bed and Adela moved almost imperceptibly away. She saw by his heightened colour that he had noticed.

He took her hand. 'You're cold. You should have turned on the gas fire.'

Adela looked at the old fireplace. 'I didn't notice it. I've got used to bedrooms without heat.'

'That's going to end right here.' Sander went across and put a match to the fire and a bright, red glow began to give out welcome warmth. He frowned. 'Mrs Monkton should have thought of it. I'll have a word with her.'

'No! I'm the mistress here and I shall talk to my own servants. I'm quite used to it, you know. I have done it before, or had you forgotten?'

Sander had begun to smile, but at her last remark the smile died. 'No, I've forgotten nothing. Dinner will be in an hour. No need to change unless you want to.'

Adela and Sander sat opposite one another in the dining room while servants served an excellently cooked meal of chicken consommé, Dover sole, spring lamb, and fruit and cheese. When they had finished eating they sat in the drawing room over coffee. The rooms were clean and functional, but no real care had gone into their decoration. Already Adela's mind was busy with wallpaper patterns, carpets, furniture and ornaments.

'There's no need to redecorate this place, Adela. Save your energies for our new home.'

'How do you know what I was thinking?'

'It wasn't difficult. Will you have more coffee? No? How about some music?'

Adela leaned back in her comfortable chair as Sander wound the gramophone and the room filled with lovely sound. 'Mozart,' she said dreamily. 'I didn't know you liked classical music.'

'Yes, I do. Actually, quite a lot of the lower orders enjoy good music.'

Adela's calm was fractured. 'Must you be so – so damned sarcastic?'

'Must you be so damned patronising?'

'I wasn't! It's just that I know so little about you.'

He looked regretful. 'Sorry, it's a habit. I've been patronised so often that I tend to over-react. Please relax again. You looked lovely.' He stopped and bent unnecessarily to stir the fire. 'You're very beautiful, Adela.'

She leaned back again, though still ill at ease. Jack had admired her. His image came clearly to mind. She could see his thin, wounded body rigid with indignation as he told her of some new injustice against the poor and unemployed.

'What are you thinking of?' asked Sander.

'Nothing in particular.'

'That wouldn't make you look so sad.'

'All right, I was remembering Jack.'

'Goddamn it, Adela!' His furious exclamation made her jump. 'Why won't you think of me?'

'I thought you liked Jack. I thought you respected him.'

'I do! I did! But today we were married, remember?'

'I can hardly forget with you shouting at me every few minutes.'

409

'Adela, don't let's quarrel.'

'I have no wish to.'

The atmosphere in the room was prickly and both welcomed Mrs Monkton at eleven o'clock when she asked what they would like as a nightcap. Adela wanted a glass of hot milk, Sander said he'd pour himself a whisky and soda.

'I'll sit up to maid you until your own girl arrives, Mrs Bennett,' said the housekeeper. 'Mollie would do it, but she's had no experience. I was a lady's maid before I was married an' I've never forgotten the right way to go about things.'

'I can manage myself, thank you,' said Adela.

The housekeeper looked disappointed and Sander said, 'Mrs Monkton will help you, my dear.' His tone was soft, but there was a stern quality in his voice.

Adela said nothing and the housekeeper left.

'I'd prefer it if you didn't countermand my orders to the servants in front of them,' he said.

'Such a gentle contradiction would normally be perfectly acceptable.'

Sander stared at her, his dark eyes stormy. 'Not to me. I shall run my home as I see fit, whether you think it normal or not.'

'It's my home, too, remember?' she cried. 'And I thought I was to have jurisdiction over the servants.'

Sander walked to the sideboard and poured his drink. He sipped it, staring into the fire apparently lost in thought, and Adela was able to study him. She realised that he looked tired and for the first time appreciated that the situation must be as much of a strain on him as it was on her. Mrs Monkton arrived with her milk and left with scarcely a word.

Sander grinned. 'She's a quick learner. I think she understands that we don't want a lecture every time she comes in.'

Adela smiled, glad that his good humour was restored. She drank her milk. 'I'm sorry I was unpleasant, Sander. I'm so tired. I think I'll go to bed.'

He rang the bell, and got up and held out his hands. She took them nervously and stood up. A young woman entered.

'Ah, Mollie,' said Sander, 'Mrs Bennett wishes to retire. Please show her to her room.'

Adela laughed. 'I think I can find my own way. The house is quite small.'

She hadn't meant to be critical, but he immediately let go of her hands, frowning. 'I shall come up a little later,' he said.

Adela followed Mollie, wishing she hadn't annoyed Sander again. She recalled the account of his ghastly childhood and vowed she'd curb her tongue. She didn't want to hurt him. Also, she reflected ruefully, she preferred to be comfortable and there was no doubt that he could imbue any room with his powerful presence, pleasantly or otherwise.

Mrs Monkton had obeyed Sander and was waiting for her. 'I've run your bath, madam,' she said, clearly delighting in her role of personal maid. 'The bathroom's just along the landing. Here's your bath cap. I've unpacked your case. Will your other luggage be arriving soon?'

'I haven't any other. I shall be buying new things.'

Adela sank into a deep bath of lavender-scented water, breathing in the sweet, clearly expensive, aroma. Mrs Monkton picked up a sponge and soap. 'Would you like me to do your back, madam?'

Adela sat up breast deep in the hot water and revelled in the exquisite sensation of being cared for. 'That's wonderful,' she breathed. She finished bathing and stepped out into a huge white towel. 'Straight from the airing cupboard,' said the housekeeper, enveloping Adela in its warm folds. She towelled herself dry and used the talcum powder handed her by Mrs Monkton and soon she was in bed, a hot water bottle at her feet and one to cuddle.

'Mr Bennett doesn't have hot water bottles,' said the housekeeper. 'I suppose he'd think it was a bit cissy. Men like to be thought of as tough, don't they, madam? Are you perfectly comfortable? Do you want ice in your water jug? No?' Mrs Monkton wished her good night and left.

Adela sat up in bed. There were magazines on the bedside table, *Vogue* and *The Queen*. She hadn't had time to look at the current issues and opened them eagerly, but the facts that the Dolly Sisters had won a fancy dress contest and that the boning of corsets was growing less vicious, failed to interest her and in the end she put aside the magazines and lay back, waiting for Sander. He tapped and opened the door. She sat bolt upright as he walked in.

He stood looking at her for several long moments and she stirred uneasily. 'I'm not a prize pig,' she said.

'So romantic,' said Sander, and she smiled unwillingly. 'You're my prize,' he said.

'I'm your wife.'

'Yes. At last. I've waited long enough.' He bent over her and she couldn't prevent herself from shrinking back. 'Don't worry, I'm not going to make love to you.'

'I didn't suppose you were.'

'Liar! That's exactly what you thought.'

'All right, have it your way.'

'That's exactly what I won't have! Don't worry, I'm prepared to wait until your health has improved and then we'll make up for lost time.'

'Have you no delicacy?'

'I shouldn't think so. It was in short supply where I grew up. Oh, by the way, I have a girl working in my boot factory who used to be your maid. Sarah. Do you remember her?'

'I do, indeed. She was very cheeky when she gave me her notice.'

'Was she? The poor kid's had all the cheek knocked out of her. Would you consider employing her again? She's not suited to factory life, especially now.'

'Why especially now.'

'If you engage her, you can ask her yourself.'

'I'll see her.'

'Good.' He bent over and kissed her. 'I look forward to our proper wedding night,' he murmured.

Adela interviewed Sarah who was indeed very subdued. 'Mr Bennett tells me that factory life doesn't suit you.'

'No, Miss Adela. Sorry, I mean Mrs Bennett. I don't seem to pick up after the baby.'

'Baby?'

'Mr Bennett didn't tell you? I got married to a soldier an' had

412

a baby. He was killed and our daughter died of diphtheria.'

'I'm so very sorry.'

'Yes, the baby was a little pet. I was ill, too. Mr Bennett took me back afterwards. It was good of him. I needed the money.'

'But surely you got a widow's pension?'

'Yes, Mrs Bennett, but it's not enough. Besides, I'd like to work in a good house again. It's not so lonely. I'd have the other servants to talk to an' know where my next meal was comin' from without havin' to worry.'

'Are you strong enough for the duties involved? You know what they are and that they often entail quite late nights.'

'I haven't forgotten, but I'm sure I could manage. An' you were always kind to me, an' so's Mr Bennett.'

Adela engaged Sarah who began to pick up in health. The housekeeper had never had children of her own and she made up for it by treating everyone under her care as infants needing a lot of coddling.

'She's such a comfortable person to have around,' Adela said to Sander.

She was finding him unexpectedly pleasant to live with and they shared experiences and enjoyed jokes and only occasionally burst into arguments, though there were times when Adela caught him watching her as a cat might watch a mouse hole.

Sander wasted no time in arranging for Adela to go north for an operation. When he told her the date was fixed, she said, 'Harry must come first. I'll not be happy until I know someone is searching for him.'

'So you'll be pleased to know I've engaged a reliable and honest detective.'

Adela felt a deep sense of relief as she accompanied him to Manchester where the procedure called the 'Manchester Operation' was explained to them. The thought of being free from her crippling pain made Adela eager to enter hospital. She underwent the operation which left her feeling weak but well. Because of the demands of business, it was agreed that Sander should return to Bristol during Adela's recovery period. He visited as often as he could.

413

Always she asked, 'Is there any news of Harry?' and always the answer was 'No.'

When Adela was pronounced fit enough to travel, Sander fetched her home. Mrs Monkton welcomed her mistress with a glad smile. 'You look pounds better,' she exclaimed. 'Come in and rest yourself. You must be tired after such a long journey.'

Adela was glad to be settled on a daybed thoughtfully provided by Sander, with Mrs Monkton and Sarah anxious to attend to her needs, and for a while she was content to rest.

Sander had been so considerate and kind all through the uncomfortable and trying weeks, and he was so clearly interested in finding Harry, that Adela was warm with gratitude. She obeyed his dictates, knowing he had been primed by the Manchester doctors, but when she began to fret in her need to know what was happening at work, he eventually allowed Esther to visit and talk business.

'Adela, love,' said Esther as she entered carrying a large bunch of flowers, 'everyone sends best wishes and hopes you'll be back soon. The place isn't the same without you.'

'Why not?' Adela asked sharply.

Esther grinned. 'Sander said you were getting restless.'

'Oh, he did, did he?' Adela frowned, then laughed. 'I'm sorry I snapped at you. Esther, I'm so bored I could scream.'

'I remember when all you wanted was to lie down and sleep for days.'

'I know. We're never happy with our lot, are we? What's been happening at the shop?'

'We've kept going pretty well, taken good money and that kind of thing, but of course there isn't anyone who can go out to customers' houses and advise them.'

'Have we lost much trade?'

'Some weren't willing to delay, but others are only waiting for you to come back. Adela, you'll have to be careful for a while yet, won't you? You mustn't try to do everything at once.'

'Thank you, Doctor Esther.'

'I speak for your own good,' said Esther in a mock-solemn voice.

414

'I've had lectures from doctors, nurses and Sander. I'll try to remember them.'

Their conversation then roamed over many subjects as Esther caught Adela up with all the news. 'Ida's been wonderful,' she finished. 'I don't know how we'd have got on without her. She's so clever with the window dressing and draping.'

Grandmother Sutton wrote cheerfully to Adela, telling her not to return to work a moment too soon, and Blanche and Georgie visited, filling the room with talk and laughter and smoke. Georgie had taken to cigars.

Adela was able to thank Ida in person when she was able to visit. 'Mum is gettin' grumpier all the time,' she said, but her smile forgave her mother. 'Do you know, I think she misses you, Adela, though she'd die before she'd admit it.'

The last thing Adela had done before she left for Manchester was to engage Freddy Stanton as shop manager. He was spending so much time there and was so obviously capable and happy that she knew she could trust him, and he was over-joyed to throw off the yoke of the estate agent's office. His parents were furious, but still let him live at home.

'It's the most wonderful thing that's happened to me, Mrs Bennett,' he said happily when he made his first visit to her. By this time, Adela was strong enough to begin light work and Freddy brought the order book with measurements of potential clients' rooms. Adela spent hours poring over pattern books, making sketches and costing materials. It still wasn't enough to fill her active mind.

Sander bought her a gramophone of her own and as she grew stronger she played music and swayed to the sound of gentle waltzes, wondering when she'd get back to a dance floor again.

Sander came home one day filled with fury. 'We knew there'd be trouble when the government handed the mines back to private control,' he raged. 'What's the first thing the owners did?'

'Cut wages,' said Adela. No woman who had shared the lives of Jack and Sander could be unaware of the state of the workers.

'That's right, and when the poor devils refused the terms

415

they were locked out and let down by their own leader *and* other unions who withdrew the support they'd promised.'

'We knew all this,' said Adela gently. 'What's making you so angry today?'

'The miners have had to give in and go back to work on the bosses' terms.'

'I'm sorry,' said Adela. 'Those poor men! After they and their families have suffered all through summer, and the drought isn't making things easier for them. No one wants much coal.'

Sander gave her a warm approving look. 'You do care, don't you?'

'Since St Pauls and St Philips, yes, I care.'

Esther and Freddy had joined the others at the Kingsley Hall in the struggle to help the miners' families and so had Blanche and Georgie.

Millie called a couple of times and filled the room with laughter and gaiety as she recounted tales of parties and dances, fancy dress balls and endless shopping sprees.

'Do hurry and get well, Adela, darling,' she said. 'I can't tell you half of what you're missing. Oh, you have *Vogue*. Isn't it simply *splendid*? Didn't you adore the page of flame chiffon dresses which Ospovat designed for Lady Diana Cooper? Isn't she a beauty? And what about the restaurant hats? Positive cartwheels with *cascades* of feathers or flowers falling over the shoulder.'

Adela laughed at Millie, she couldn't help but respond to such bubbling enjoyment, but the contrast between her cousin's frenetic determination to enjoy herself and the bitter struggles of the poor tore Adela apart; she sympathised with the sufferers, yet she ached for some fun.

'It's quite natural to want to enjoy yourself,' said Sander when she confessed. 'There's nothing wrong in a little harmless fun. What I object to is the attitude of someone who can write an article which says that it's perfectly all right for the young to kick up their heels until they get married, then they must be encouraged to "replace those dear ones we have lost". There isn't a word about the million lame, blind or paralysed, or the sad, out-of-their-heads fellows like poor Bert Rawbone who still fill the mental asylums.' Sander's voice was bitter with anger. 'There are rich women who are raving about the first all-electric house shown in London. They see it as a release from drudgery. They've never known drudgery! All that will happen is they won't need so many servants so they'll sack them and a few more people will be thrown on to the labour market.'

'You sound like Jack.'

'It's a pity there aren't more of his quality and brains around.'

'I wish I could help.'

'So do I, Adela. We need your enthusiasm. But you understand my feelings, and won't mind my leaving you so often, and when you're completely well you can come along to the meetings too.' He glanced at his watch. 'As a matter of fact, I'm due at the Hall in twenty minutes. I'd better be off.' He gave her a quick kiss and left and Adela lay and listened to the sound of his car engine dying into the distance.

Chapter Twenty-Two

Adela didn't recover her strength as quickly as she had hoped. An attack of influenza had a far more adverse effect on her than it should have because she was still convalescing. For days she could eat nothing and Sander was anxious. When she felt a little better Mrs Monkton and Sarah brought all the delicacies they could think of to tempt her appetite. Her weakness made her helpless and gave her too much opportunity to worry about Harry. She had fearful nightmares: Harry was ill and crying for her; Harry was dead. She woke sobbing and sweating and there was no one to comfort her.

At first she had asked Sander daily for news of her son, but each time he had nothing good to report. 'I can't think what your mother has done with him,' he said. 'My man has followed every lead he can think of and there isn't a sign of the child. He's beginning to wonder if he's been spirited abroad. Do you think that's possible?'

Adela was horrified. 'Surely not! Where would she send him? Oh, Sander, he's so little. I want him back, I want him back.'

Her tears flowed too easily and Sander comforted her as best he could. 'We'll find him somehow, Adela.'

'You must! You promised!' she cried, knowing that she was being unfair.

When she next saw Sander she apologised.

'It's all right, my dear,' he said. 'I know you're feeling ill.'

'I just hope my baby's happy. I hope that the people who've got him bought him nice presents for his birthday. Do you know what I did?'

'No, what?'

'I bought him a present. I got one for his first birthday, too,

419

but he'll be too old for it now. This time I bought him a little wooden train with coaches. I hope he won't be too old for that as well by the time we find him. If we ever do.' Adela struggled again with her tears.

'We'll find him,' vowed Sander. 'He's somewhere and we'll get him back.'

Adela's convalescence seemed endless, but in the end her innate good health and young strength came to the rescue and as soon as the doctor gave her the word she was back in the shop.

Sander also was busy. In fact, she saw little of him and she still slept alone, as the Manchester doctors had advised. On the few occasions when they dined at home they found plenty to discuss. Sometimes she caught him watching her with a look which disturbed her. He was so aggressively masculine. She pushed her worries to the back of her mind. Creative work was the only true reality. No one could take that from her and she buried herself in it, pushing herself hard.

One evening over dinner Sander said, 'We have an invitation to a weekend house party in Dorset. The Fairfields. I take it you'd like to accept?'

'What? I've a load of designs to get through. Vita Wethered is getting married, though it amazes me that Claud wants the poisonous little beast, and she's asked me to make up a folio for decorating her house. It's huge, overlooking Durdham Down. She knows just about everyone and if I succeed in interesting her the advertising will be marvellous.'

'Vita's going to be there, and so will her fiancé, and Millie and Bobbie and their husbands, and a lot of other people. I thought you'd jump at the opportunity to get commissions and you may have a chance to show Vita your proposals there.'

'Get commissions at a house party? Imagine how our host and hostess would feel if I took my trade into their house! No, it's best to keep my negotiations strictly on a business footing. I'll stay here, thank you.'

'Don't be silly, Adela! If you don't accept you could offend the Fairfields as well as losing the opportunity to meet new clients.'

'I probably know everyone who's going, anyway.'

'I suppose that's likely, but if you wait for them to come to you, you may wait a long time.'

'You don't seem to realise that I can't do business in such a way.'

'I'm being impossibly vulgar, am I? I offend you?'

'No, of course not. It's just that I don't know anyone who's ever conducted such matters on a social occasion.'

'That's probably because you were never interested in the subject. Many men transact a great number of their financial deals over a glass of port or a game of golf.'

'I'd really rather not go.'

'I see. If that's your decision . . .' Sander looked disappointed and Adela asked, 'How many weekend house parties have you been to?'

'Not many.'

'You really want to go, don't you?'

'It might be amusing.'

'Amusing? I suppose so.' She paused. 'Ralph and I were guests there quite often before the war. Their son and daughter are about my age.'

Sander said gently, 'Would being there bring back hurtful memories?'

'I don't know. Maybe.'

'I see. I had better cancel the acceptance.'

'You've already accepted? Without consulting me?'

'I took it for granted that you'd appreciate a weekend in the country.'

'I prefer to do my own accepting! Perhaps you'd remember that in future.'

Sander frowned. 'I'll bear it in mind. Does that mean you will go?'

'Yes, all right.' Adela knew she was being ungracious. 'In fact, I'll go the whole way and take pattern books and colour swatches with me. I'll feel impossibly vulgar, but I'd better get over that.'

'If you'd let me invest in your business, you could stop worrying.'

'No! It's mine and it's going to stay that way! It's the only thing I have that is entirely mine and I value it above everything. Except my son, of course.'

'I see.'

'Oh, Sander, don't look like that.'

'Like what?'

'As if I'd just struck you.'

'Is that how I look?'

'Please try to understand. I've never done anything worthwhile before. I want to succeed alone.'

'You allowed your grandmother to lend you money.'

'That's different. She's family.'

The words hung in the air between them.

Adela said, 'Oh, lord, I didn't mean it to sound the way it does! My grandmother is in Cornwall and is content to leave all the decision-making to me. You'd be on the spot, watching me.'

'I see.'

'No, I don't think you do. Did you accept help in the beginning?'

'No one ever offered me any.'

'Oh! All the more credit to you.' There was an awkward silence. 'I wonder if I'll get new clients at the Fairfields'. Business is quite vulgar, really.'

'Is that what your mother taught you?'

'Yes. Well, it was true once. The war changed so much. Society is different now.'

'Lots of things are different. People's lives have been wrecked.'

'I don't need you to tell me that. My own life was ruined.'

'You consider marriage to me to be ruinous?'

'For heaven's sake, Sander, you know I didn't mean that! You are deliberately taking my words the wrong way.'

'Am I?' He glared at her. 'Are you feeling completely well now, Adela?'

'Yes, thanks.'

'I'm very glad to hear it.' He said more gently, 'The doctors who operated told me that I must wait several weeks before I approached you. That time was up some while back, but I've waited because of your attack of influenza.'

Adela flushed.

'Have you nothing to say?'

'I know you're right. The doctors spoke to me, too, but I thought—'

'You thought what?'

'That you were content as we were.'

'Do you expect me to be?'

'No, I suppose not.'

'Do you feel nothing for me?'

Adela had been enjoying a peach, but she pushed away her plate. 'I like you, if that's what you mean. Most of the time, anyway.'

'Nothing more?'

'No, not really. I'm sorry, Sander.'

'Have you finished eating?'

'Yes.'

He got up and pulled her to her feet. 'I think you feel more for me than you know. Sometimes I see more than liking in your eyes.'

'You're mistaken.' She freed herself. 'Sander, we're getting on so well. Why spoil it?'

'Do you think that sex will spoil our marriage?'

'Must you be so crude?'

'If you prefer, I'll call it love. Oh, but I forgot, you don't love me, do you?'

'Any more than you love me!'

His grasp tightened. 'No. All the same, Adela, I shall come to you tonight. Be ready for me.'

Adela lay in her bath while Sarah waited with a heated towel. When Adela stepped out, she wrapped the towel round her mistress. 'You're much thinner, madam. It's because you've been so ill. I reckon we've both been through the mill.'

Adela returned to her bedroom.

Sarah opened a drawer and drew out a flannel nightgown. 'This is too big for you now, madam.'

Adela looked at the nightgown with its high neck and long

423

sleeves and held up her arms for Sarah to slip it over her head. She tied the ribbons at the neck and sat down at her dressing table. Sarah stood behind her, brushing her hair.

She said, 'Your hair used to be so long. It seems a shame that we women have to cut our hair to suit the fashion. But yours is still very pretty.'

Adela put on her dressing gown and dismissed Sarah. The weather had turned wet and cold and she was glad of the fire. She sank into an easy chair beside it. She had bought herself some pretty nightdresses for hospital and hadn't been able to resist a transparent rose georgette nightgown which she had put away in tissue because it was not at all the kind of thing to flaunt to doctors. She went to the tallboy and took it out of its tissue paper. It slid silkily through her hands. She could see the glow of the fire through it. Sander would expect to find her dressed in something pretty. What would he say if he found her dressed in flannel? He had been so good to her.

She thought of wearing the georgette and excitement stirred in her. She was surprised. When had she begun to see him as an attractive man? She held the soft gown, smoothing it across her face, and knew that a part of her was glad that Sander wanted her. She dragged off the flannel monstrosity and put on the silk and stood looking at herself in the wardrobe mirror. God, she could see every curve of her body. Before she could move the door opened and Sander walked in, wearing a dark blue dressing gown. When he saw her, his breath caught on an involuntary gasp.

He snapped off the overhead light, leaving only the shaded lamp by her bed and the glow of the fire, and came to her swiftly, putting his hands on her shoulders. She remained still, waiting, and the memory of the pain which Ralph had caused her almost made her flinch. Sander's hands were gentle as they touched each breast and caressed them, squeezing the nipples as they peaked.

'Adela,' he murmured, 'you're so beautiful.'

He put his arm around her waist and together they walked to the bed where the covers had been turned down by Sarah. Sander dropped his dressing gown on the floor as Adela lay beneath the sheets and she saw that he was naked. His body was hard and muscular, the hair dark.

He pulled the bedclothes back. 'You won't be cold? The weather's so chill.'

Adela found her voice. 'Surely,' she said with a small laugh, 'you didn't come here to discuss the weather?'

He stopped moving and she wondered if she'd angered him. Then he laughed softly. 'No, I certainly did not.'

He gazed down at her, his eyes as they travelled over her a caress in themselves. 'You're the loveliest woman I've ever known, Adela.'

His hands moved, exploring her with slow deliberation, skilful as they stroked her, intimately, knowingly, and her body arched as unfamiliar sensations coursed through her. He kissed her, tenderly, then with passion. 'My wilful Adela,' he murmured on her mouth, 'my wife, my love.' He tugged down the straps of her nightgown and his lips found her breasts.

He entered her slowly, taking care not to hurt her in any way, and took his pleasure. Afterwards he lay beside her, leaning on one elbow, and looked into her face.

'You're happy, Adela?'

'You were gentle!' That sounded stilted and she added, 'Are you?'

'I certainly am. It's wonderful to make love to you.'

'Is it? I'm glad.'

'It'll get better for you, my dear, believe me. You're not properly awakened yet.'

The promise was similar to the one made by Ralph. At least Sander hadn't given her pain, and even if love-making had not proved very exciting she could appreciate his tender care.

'From the first moment I saw you I wanted to make love to you.'

'What? Is that all you thought when you saw me?'

Sander reached down and extracted cigarettes and matches from his dressing gown pocket. He lit one for himself and one for her. 'I suppose most men wonder what a girl's like in bed when they first meet her,' he said. 'That's no crime. It isn't all I thought about you.'

425

'No, I know. You saw me as a passport to society, someone who was available on the market.'

'Adela! Can't you forget that?'

'No. A woman could never forget such a thing.'

'She could if she—'

'If she what?'

'Nothing.' Sander sighed, then got up and pulled on his dressing gown. He bent and kissed her.

'Tomorrow Sarah can move your things into my room.'

She watched him go, anger filling her. So he'd give his orders to Sarah and they'd be obeyed! Then she remembered his lovemaking. It had been pleasant, something to look forward to again, and he had promised more joy in future encounters. She crushed out her cigarette and put out the light, but it was a long time before she slept.

Mrs Monkton and Sarah brought new hide suitcases to the bedroom. Adela had moved in with Sander and he made love to her most nights. She looked forward to it, love-making was becoming more of a pleasure, yet deep inside her there was still something which made her hold back. She tried to analyse it. She felt it was a kind of resentment of his power over her, the fact that he took her body when there was no love between them. She knew that he was disappointed by her reaction, and chagrined by his failure to arouse her to passion.

She looked at the suitcases and frowned. 'Don't you like them, madam?' asked Mrs Monkton. 'The master bought the best he could find.'

'They're very nice,' said Adela. She was wishing they didn't look so new. She wished she had the set of matching luggage which had once belonged to her grandfather. They also were leather, but bore the marks of years of travelling.

Sander came in. 'I'll be at the warehouse today if you need me. Oh, the new cases. Do you like them?'

He sounded anxious and Adela said, 'They're of the best quality, that's clear.'

He kissed her cheek decorously in front of Sarah and left. The discussion of what to take to the Fairfields' began.

Adela had no objection to spending her husband's money on clothes and she had enjoyed buying them. She had heaps of filmy underwear, a whole drawer full of pure silk stockings in beige and black and white, and had bought more clothes suitable for a country weekend.

Sander's advice had been to look as rich as possible as people were far more inclined to buy from someone who appeared not to need money. She had really splashed out on a Worth evening gown, the transparency of which needed quite substantial underwear beneath, and had acquired several of the new flattening bust bodices, just-on-the-market softly woven elastic corsets, and a long silk petticoat. She also needed crêpe de Chine cami-knickers with a fall which went just past her knees in handkerchief points to match the latest style of her gown. She intended to travel in her plain grey tailored suit without which, so Paris said, no woman's wardrobe was complete, and had also acquired a soft tweed coat and skirt and Oxford shoes for walking. She added a wool Paisley shawl to her luggage. Flimsy gowns were all very well, but the Fairfields' country house was as chilly as most British mansions.

Sarah held a sheer silk slip to her face. 'It's so pretty,' she breathed. 'It isn't long since everyone was wearing Wolsey combinations and vests.'

'No,' said Adela. 'It isn't long, though it seems an age.'

'Lots of things are different now.'

Adela nodded. 'Don't forget to pack all the shoes I'll need. And make sure you have plenty of clean caps and aprons and a smart afternoon dress.'

Adela left Sarah to it and got into the small, powerful, blue two-seater car which had been Sander's wedding gift. She enjoyed driving it and was almost sorry when she drew up outside Adela Fabrics. The exterior hadn't changed. She studied it and decided that it could wait a little longer for redecorating. Then she walked to the large window she had had installed.

The staff had been busy. Under Ida's instructions they had learned how to drape textiles to show them at their best and had grown to enjoy the Mackintosh designs as much as Adela, though her stock now encompassed many others. Ida had dressed the window, that was clear. The backdrop was blue and white striped material whose lines had been broken by fabrics of pale pink, orange, green and muted blue. She had positioned delicate frames of pink and green stained glass which reflected light on to the materials. Standing near the front was a round Royal Doulton vase painted with pale yellow plums and dark leaves, containing a single spray of cream magnolias. It could have been garish, but instead Ida had created a harmony of shape and colour which resembled an abstract painting.

When Adela went in Freddy was talking to a customer who was proclaiming loudly that she was looking for red velvet for her sitting room, but nothing gaudy.

'Of course not, madam,' he said, 'we at Adela Fabrics would not dream of stocking anything to offend the artistic sensibilities of ladies like yourself.' Adela turned her head to hide a smile. He was using an impossibly pretentious approach, but he had gauged his customer rightly and she preened herself; Freddy's eyes met Adela's humorously.

The showroom displayed the evidence of Ida's skill and Adela's taste and was satisfyingly filled with customers. Adela had never forgotten the Hobbses who had taken her in after Bert attacked her and she had taken on Mattie Hobbs whose rough manners and heavy accent had been keeping her out of the kind of job she wanted.

'See, Mrs Bennett,' she had explained earnestly, 'I know I got it in me to be a artistic person, but people d'listen to me talkin' an' they d'turn me down. An' my clothes are shabby, as well, but Mum can't afford to buy me new ones.' Adela liked her frankness and enthusiasm and with help Mattie was improving herself and worked in the showroom, though she took no part yet in the actual selling.

She was standing in a corner where materials of graded browns were draped from points which spilled them down in a rhythmic pattern. 'There's all kinds of browns, madam,' she was saying earnestly to a lady in a voile dress and a straw hat. 'There's burnt sienna an' sepia an' umber an' vandyke brown an' the ochres – they're a kind of yellow-brown – an' more that I haven't learnt yet, though Madam Adela d'know – knows –

them all and would be glad to talk to you. It's really better to come with a bit of stuff, I mean a swatch, an' let us match it up for you.'

Adela watched to see how the customer accepted this minor lecture and was relieved to see that she looked both pleased and amused. 'I think I'll take your advice, my dear, and return with something to match up.' Adela was content. She had taken a chance by putting Mattie into the showroom, but she had a special quality of friendly earnestness which appealed to most of the customers. She would do well.

Adela had taken on Jack's daughter, Annie, and having done so couldn't refuse Florrie, though she hadn't the right temperament for dealing with the public and was indignantly rude and dismissive when asked if she would work on the machines instead. Ida's well-earned wages brought money, with dignity, to Mrs Webster.

She climbed the stairs to the workroom where six girls were employed under the supervision of Esther who had become a full-time cutter, quickly mastering the intricacies of matching large curtain patterns with a view to ensuring the least possible wastage. Not that there was any, thought Adela, because Esther had decided that anything left over must be used for cushion covers, an idea which had pleased customers. Many now demanded cushions and curtains to match. She breathed in the familiar scent of materials, the faint odour from the gas burners kept going constantly beneath flat irons, the undertones of machine oil. To her it was sweeter than the sweetest perfume. It represented independence. Independence of a kind. Adela was still trapped in a miasma of misery over Harry. Each negative report dampened her inner hope. Even Sander was getting less optimistic.

Esther was bent over the large cutting table, her scissors busy with a heavy bottle green velvet. Adela kept quiet. When Esther had started she had once made a mistake and cut an expensive velvet so that the pile on one curtain ran the wrong way. She had been deeply shocked and mortified and begged to be permitted to make up the money, but Adela refused to allow this. Esther wasn't the sort who made the same mistake twice. Adela went to her small corner office which was really a partitioned area with a desk and a couple of chairs, thanking heaven for the day they had met. She settled down with the accounts and saw that she was making a respectable profit. She bought quite a lot of stuff from Sander and insisted on paying the full wholesale cost. He had shrugged. 'Please yourself.'

The figures wavered as she thought of her life with her husband. He was virile and skilful and she had begun to enjoy his body, but no words of love passed between them.

Esther came in and Adela smiled. 'You'll be in charge of the workroom this weekend,' she said. 'Mr Bennett and I are going to the country.'

Esther looked both pleased and scared. 'Oh, Adela, are you sure that I can manage?'

'Perfectly,' said Adela. 'You can run the workroom as well as I can, probably better.'

'I can't talk to the customers like you do.'

'That's because I'm already acquainted with so many of them. You have the practicalities of cutting and sewing at your fingertips. Freddy will support you and he'll be taking the cash away at night.'

'He's so clever, isn't he?'

'He is, indeed, and so are you, Esther, and I'll not be far away. If you need me you can telephone.'

Esther still regarded the brand new telephone which stood on Adela's desk with some suspicion, but she used it and coped well, as she had done with every situation in her life. They didn't discuss Bert any more. It seemed certain that he would never gain release from his personal hell. It was said that at least sixty-five thousand men were in the same position. To add to Esther's problems, Freddy Stanton clearly found her attractive. Esther repelled all his overtures, her devotion and faithfulness to Bert still paramount, but Freddy was persistent.

Sander drove them to the Fairfields' country house. Sarah sat in the back. Fairfield Grange had been built in the thirteenth century, wrecked by Parliamentarians during the Civil War and later rebuilt, and a succession of owners had altered and added to it since. Oddly enough it appeared to have overcome all that they could do to it and was still beautiful, a long low house in grey stone and red brick with an orangery at one end.

The front door was opened by Travers the butler who smiled genially at Adela. 'It's a long time since we had the pleasure of seeing you, Mrs Bennett. It's a pity about the damp weather, though it may be possible for you to get a game of tennis. Dinner will be at eight, as usual, and drinks will be served in the drawing room at seven-thirty. Your maid knows the way to the servants' quarters. Will Mr Bennett's valet be arriving soon?'

'Mr Bennett hasn't brought a valet,' said Adela. 'Please delegate a footman.'

'Certainly, madam.'

Adela smiled as Travers took Sander's coat and hat and ordered a couple of minions to take their luggage to their room. 'You're in the blue bedroom, Mrs Bennett. I remember you always preferred it.'

'You're a marvel, Travers. How can you recall so much?'

He looked pleased as he showed them upstairs.

In the bedroom Sander looked round. There was a fourposter bed, a couple of ancient chests, a large wardrobe and a tallboy. On either side of the bed were exquisite Regency tables on which stood candles in holders.

'Candles! In this day and age!'

'There's gas, too, and electricity downstairs. They can't afford to do the bedrooms yet.'

'A viscount, and he can't afford proper lighting!'

'He depends mostly on rents for his income and they're dwindling. Lots of country estates are having problems.'

'Are they? Poor things!' Sander sounded pleased.

'At least we've got a good fire,' she said.

'I should think so.'

'When we came here as children the rooms were always freezing. The aristocracy believe in breeding resistance to cold in their young.'

'A wise move if their houses are so primitive.'

'Don't you see any beauty here?'

'Fraying curtains and bed drapes, a practically threadbare

431

carpet, the walls needing repapering and the paintwork scuffed. Even the paintings need cleaning.'

Adela was surprised. 'Is that all you see?'

'No, it's got a certain beauty, I suppose, though I should think you'd be itching to get to work here to improve things.'

Again Adela was surprised. 'What an idea! I'm so used to its appearance that it hadn't occurred to me.'

'Maybe you can drop a few hints while you're here.'

'No!' Adela was horrified. 'That would be the height of bad manners.'

'I would have thought it was somewhat *infra dig* to chat to the butler.'

'It would have been if I didn't know him so well. He was born on the estate. It's difficult to be formal with a man who wiped my nose when I fell and hurt myself and cried, and who lent me a safety pin when my knicker elastic broke. I hasten to tell you that I was only six at the time. You'll get to know the protocol.'

Sander flushed. 'Be sure to tell me which knife and fork to use.'

Adela said coolly, 'Don't be ridiculous. You know perfectly well how to behave.'

'Sorry. Don't let's quarrel,' he said. 'I've been looking forward to having you to myself for a couple of days.'

'Hardly to yourself,' said Adela, stretching out a hand to ring for Sarah.

Sander grabbed her wrist. 'We don't have to dress for an hour. There's time to test the fourposter.'

'Not now!'

'Yes, now.' She had removed her costume and he ran his fingers up her arm to her neck. She protested again, but it was a token protest and they lay together in the large bed and made love.

Afterwards Adela made to get up at once and Sander held her back. 'Do you like making love to me?' he asked.

'Yes, of course.'

'Then why won't you let yourself go?'

'I don't know what you mean.'

'I think you do. Is it just shyness?'

'I suppose it must be. I've had no experience. Ralph—' She stopped.

'I understand about Ralph. A hurried coupling of a boy and girl. But you're a woman now.'

Adela tried again to get off the bed and this time he let her go. 'I'm sorry if you're not satisfied with me, Sander. I can't help it. I do my best.'

'No, Adela, you don't,' he said.

A few moments later Sarah knocked and the conversation had to end.

Adela bathed and Sarah helped her into a dinner dress of soft beige jersey to which Adela added amber beads and drop earrings.

'The kitchen's nearly the same as ever, madam,' said Sarah. 'They're still cookin' on the big range, though they've got a gas stove for the pastry an' cakes, an' it's lovely an' friendly like it always was.'

Sander was in a small dressing room where he had reluctantly accepted the services of a footman.

'I've dressed myself since I was three,' he'd protested to Adela. 'I feel a fool with a valet.'

They walked downstairs, past the paintings of Fairfield ancestors who peered through the gloom of grime. The drawing-room furniture was as varied in design as the house, but over the years a procession of housemaids had polished everything until the patina had grown to overall beauty. There was a huge stone fireplace filled with logs and red hot ash around which people were standing or sitting while the butler dispensed drinks. Adela sat in a carved mahogany velvet-upholstered Victorian chair. Sander joined the group of men, most of whom he appeared to know.

Vita Wethered was sprawled on a striped Regency sofa. Beside her, squashed to one end, sat her fiancé, Sir Claud, looking nervous.

Vita said stridently, 'Good heavens, Adela, don't tell me you've managed to tear yourself from that shop of yours!'

'We call it a showroom now,' said Adela calmly, though she felt like slapping the ill-mannered young woman.

'A showroom, eh?' Vita held out her glass for a refill. 'Another of your delicious cocktails, Travers.'

Lady Fairfield smiled at Adela. 'I'm so glad you could come, my dear. Several of your friends are here, and your cousin Millie and her charming husband. I asked Lady Diana, but she had another engagement.'

No one needed to be told that the person referred to was Lady Diana Cooper who, with her husband, Duff, was asked everywhere.

'It's marvellous how they manage to live so well on a small income,' said Millie.

'Darling, how naïve can you get?' cried Vita. 'Of course they don't need to live on their income. They're always guests in someone or other's place and Diana gets all her clothes free from couturiers, just for the advertising. It's not fair.'

'But you can buy all the clothes you want,' said Claud.

'I should hope so,' shrilled Vita, fitting a cigarette into her long holder. 'I don't need you to tell me something so obvious.'

Claud's pink face went pinker.

Douglas and Jane Fairfield joined the party with apologies. 'Sorry we're late, darlings,' cried Jane. 'Douglas and I have a tennis tournament going. At the moment it's a draw. *Lovely* to see you here, all of you.'

'It's lovely to be here,' said Vita. 'One is safe in this house from the ghastly profiteers who appear to infiltrate much of society these days. One even meets the gruesome Smitherses in some houses, though why anyone should still want them now the shortages are over I can't imagine. Or there are the equally ghastly nouveau riche. Oh!' Her hand went to her mouth in simulated horror. Her eyes met Bobbie's and they both glanced deliberately at Sander.

Jane was clearly embarrassed and made a point of welcoming him effusively, a gauche move which only made matters worse. Lady Fairfield barely hid her annoyance. Sander remained cool and polite.

Douglas Fairfield said, 'Society is vastly different from before the war. The diehards live in the past, but many people regard them as stuffy and one simply disregards their old rules. They'll be left behind in the grand new world we're going to create. It'll be just commerce and friendship and peace. Imagine it! All nations banded together forever. No more wars.'

Adela held her breath, waiting for Sander to say something about the ill-advised ruthlessness of the way the Germans were being treated. She was surprised when Lord Fairfield got in first.

'Europe will never achieve true peace while Germany is left out. They'll hate us even more and rise again.'

'We came to enjoy ourselves, not to take part in a political meeting,' screeched Vita who apparently didn't care whose toes she stepped on. She was invited everywhere, either for her blue blood or because she was so wealthy.

Dinner was announced. The food was appetising. Lady Fairfield served her guests plain English fare, prepared to perfection by her excellent cook. Afterwards the ladies adjourned and left the men to their port and cigars.

'They can discuss their damned politics while we're safely in here,' said Bobbie.

'How're the plans for my new house coming along?' demanded Vita, lighting a cigarette. She had smoked all through dinner, lighting up between courses and stubbing out almost whole cigarettes each time the food appeared. Adela had thought of the thousands of men who could barely scrape up the few pence for some Woodbines.

'They're ready for you to see,' she said.

'Fat lot of use that is if they're in Bristol and I'm here.'

'As a matter of fact,' said Adela, 'I brought them with me.'

'Darling, what a quaint idea! Do send for them and we can all have a look.'

A maid was despatched to the blue bedroom and Adela accepted a cigarette from a silver box, wishing she could slap Vita who had made her feel like a commercial traveller. Suppose she told Vita that she actually knew several commercial travellers by name and respected them? If it came to that, she could also claim acquaintance with a dustman. She almost laughed.

Vita carelessly ordered the maid to fetch her fiancé and stretched out her hand for the folio. She had reclaimed her seat on the sofa near the fire. She was expensively gowned in black, trimmed with silver and jet beads. Her back and arms were bare and her décolletage was low. She wore gold and pearl jewellery and round her shoulders was a silvery voile wrap.

Adela walked over to the sofa and smiled at Claud who made room for her.

Vita swung her legs to the floor, looking annoyed because she had to yield some space, and Adela forced herself to remember that Vita represented money and publicity.

'You remembered what I said, I hope,' said Vita. 'I want contrasts of light and dark.'

Adela opened the folio and began to turn the pages, pointing out the various designs.

'Is that a *black* room?' demanded Vita.

'It is, though of course you don't have to have it.'

'I should hope not.' Vita lit a cigarette and blew out a plume of smoke which wreathed round Adela's head. The others were smoking, too, but somehow Vita's smoke seemed more pervasive. She stared at the designs. 'Actually, black might not be so bad,' she said grudgingly. 'It'll certainly be different, unless someone copies it, but if they do everyone will know I thought of it first.' She sent Bobbie a challenging glare. 'I see you've put in chrome furniture and orange and blue curtains and cushions. Yes, I think it'll do very well.'

Claud coughed. 'Will chrome seats be comfortable?'

'How the hell should I know? I thought you might like to see what I've chosen. I certainly didn't expect criticism!' Vita glared at him and he subsided. Adela wondered if he considered the acquisition of the odious Vita worth it for the dowry she would bring. Adela herself would move back to St Philips before she'd marry someone like that.

Sander had been right and the folio was examined and exclaimed over by several ladies who promised that Adela Fabrics would be receiving a visit from them soon.

Millie kissed her that night as they retired. 'Well done, darling. It was brave of you to bring the folio.'

'That was Sander's idea.'

'He's a perfect poppet,' said Millie.

Chapter Twenty-Three

'Millie thinks you're a perfect poppet,' said Adela to Sander as they drove home on Sunday evening.

'I return the compliment.'

'Did you enjoy the weekend?'

'In parts,' said Sander. 'Sir Claud is completely different when he's not with Vita. He's fascinated by engineering and we talked about the attempts to make a helicopter.'

'A what?'

'A flying machine that will go straight up and down and not need a runway.'

'It sounds like a fantasy.'

'I think not, but we'll see.'

'I prefer to stay on the ground after reading about that dreadful crash of the R38.'

'That was tragic, but in my opinion air balloons will be replaced completely by aeroplanes. They're much safer.'

'I hope so. There are enough poor widows already. What else did you enjoy about the weekend?'

'Billiards, but I could have done without bridge. I'm not much good at it, as you probably noticed.'

'You made a few mistakes, but you have a feeling for cards. You must play more often.'

'Does that mean you're ready to accept more of the invitations we get?'

'When I decide I'm making enough money.'

Sander looked annoyed, but Sarah was listening in the back and he said no more.

When Adela arrived home she found a note which had been delivered by Esther.

Dear Adela,
A woman called on you at work. She said her name was
Bertha and that you know her. She wants you to get in
touch. She says it's important.

Adela stared at the note. The only Bertha she knew was her
mother's maid. Had something happened to Father? She telephoned Speede House and inquired and was told that Mr Danby
was a little indisposed. She asked Evans to give her father her
best wishes. He made a non-committal sound and Adela knew
that he would tell his mistress that her daughter had telephoned
and that Father would probably never get the message. Adela
wondered if, without his wife's intractable stance, Father might
have been won over. An hour later Bertha telephoned Adela.

'Mr Evans told me about your call. I must see you, Miss Adela,
but I can't get out until Mrs Danby retires.'

'Mother is usually in bed by eleven,' said Adela. 'I'll wait just
down the road. Come to me there.'

The wait seemed interminable. Sander had offered to accompany her, but Adela refused. 'I can't think what she wants, but if
you're there she might be inhibited.'

As a church clock was striking half-past eleven Bertha
appeared. She climbed into the car which Adela had parked
under a street lamp. She looked strained and uncomfortable.

'How are you?' asked Adela.

'I'm well, thank you. I'd better tell you quickly what I've come
for. Your mother doesn't sleep well lately and she might ring
for me.'

'She shouldn't do that. You need your rest.'

Bertha looked surprised. 'I'm her personal maid. It's always
been that way. You used to ring late at night sometimes.'

'I know, but now I see how inconsiderate it was.'

'You've changed, Miss Adela, and it's not to be wondered at
with all you've been through. But you're married now.'

'Yes.'

'Are you happy?'

'Quite, thank you.'

Bertha looked sharply at her, but made no comment.

438

Adela asked impatiently, 'What do you want to see me about?'

Bertha began hesitantly, 'Miss Adela, it's been on my conscience these past two years. I can't stand to think of you so unhappy about your son any longer.'

'You've news of Harry?' Adela went cold with nerves.

'I've news, yes. I believe I know where he is.'

'Oh, Bertha! How did you find him? Where is he? Did you say you've known for two years? Why haven't you come forward before?'

Bertha said sombrely, 'I wish now I had spoken earlier. He's living with a man and wife. They're not the kind of people I'd have chosen, but your mother was desperate. She sincerely believed she was acting for the best. Miss Adela, you've got to believe that. She was so sure you'd agree with her in time.' The maid sighed. 'I kept quiet because she's my mistress and I owe her my loyalty.'

'Even at the cost of me and my son?'

'I don't think that any longer.'

'Where is he? Please tell me.'

Bertha reached into her pocket and took out a piece of paper which she handed to Adela. It was a newspaper cutting and read: 'Advertiser wishes care of children or would adopt healthy baby. Premium. c/o 18 Opal Street'.

Adela stared down at the slip of paper in horror. 'My mother answered an advertisement in a newspaper?' Her voice was a hoarse whisper.

Bertha said, 'They seemed respectable people, Miss Adela.'

'*Seemed* respectable? Didn't you know?'

'For the first year, Mrs Danby got reports on his progress.'

'But he's over two years old now!'

'I know,' said Bertha miserably.

Adela read the advertisement again. 'It says "premium". Did they buy my son?'

'I believe a sum of money changed hands, but it wasn't your mother's fault. She didn't want to be paid. They insisted. They said it made him more theirs.'

'More theirs! Because they bought him? It seems that wives are not the only merchandise!'

439

'Don't, Miss Adela,' pleaded Bertha. 'It wasn't like it sounds.'

'Have they adopted him? Is that why the reports have stopped?'

'I don't know. Your mother hasn't any idea that I've kept the address. I'm ashamed of myself. I'm being deceitful all round. I read the early reports without her knowledge. All the time I've thought you should be told about your baby. I saw you searching for his address in your mother's desk and felt very bad. Then I heard how ill you've been, and all because of his birth, and it seemed so unfair that you should suffer so much and yet not have your baby with you.'

Adela sat still and quiet, the newspaper cutting clutched in her fingers, trying to control the waves of anger which were flooding her. 'You said they seemed respectable people. But not the kind I would choose to bring up my son?'

Bertha hesitated then said, 'I don't think so. No, I'm sure they're not. He's the son of gentlefolk and should be brought up as a gentleman, no matter what the circumstances of his birth.'

'How could she? How could his own grandmother do this?'

'I don't think she's ever felt as if he was her grandson. To her he was an outsider, just an encumbrance, to be hidden as quickly as possible. Don't be hard on her, Miss Adela. She can't help the way she is.'

'I'll go to the address. I'll go now!'

'No, Miss Adela, not now. Not when you're so full of anger. Go in the morning. I'll come with you.'

'That won't be necessary.'

'You're not thinking straight, and no wonder! The people who've got Harry know me.'

'How? A nurse came to fetch him. When did they see you?'

'The nurse was only a go-between. Mrs Danby sent me to see Mr and Mrs Prewett – that's the name of the couple who took your baby – a couple of times. The boy was well fed and seemed happy enough, though Mrs Prewett did grumble because he cried a lot. Your mother was satisfied that he was properly cared for and I wasn't sent again. I don't think she's checked since.'

'My God! He's been with strangers for two years and she hasn't even seen for herself?'

Bertha said nothing. Her breathing was laboured.

Adela said, 'If you come with me to the Prewetts, they're bound to tell Mother. What will happen to you? She'll be furious.'

'I'll have to take the risk, Miss Adela. I must. She'll be angry with me, I know, but I expect she'll get over it. We've been together since we were girls.'

Adela wasn't so sure. Her mother could hold a grudge for a very long time. She watched Bertha hurry along the street and disappear round a bend in the road, her figure slightly bent.

Sander was astonished when Adela told him. 'Your mother's a shocker! She's inhuman!'

'I suppose she thought she was doing her best for everyone.'

'Rubbish! She was doing her best for herself; she was concerned only for her own selfish pride.'

'She comes from a proud family.'

'Your Grandmother Sutton would have faced it out.'

'Mother isn't like her.'

'That's bloody obvious! Do you want me to come with you tomorrow? I'd be glad to help.'

Adela smiled warmly at him. 'Sander, that's good of you, but I think I'd better handle it. I'll have Bertha.'

'What do you mean to do if – when – you get him back?'

'I was going to bring him here. That's all right, isn't it? Then you can adopt him like we arranged.'

'Good girl,' he said. 'Are you sure you don't want me to come with you? I feel I should in case there's trouble.'

'I'm sure I'll be able to handle it,' said Adela. He looked at her grim expression and said no more.

That night Adela was restless and Sander made love to her, curbing his usual strength, trying to give her comfort rather than rousing passion, then holding her in his arms until she slept.

In the morning she drove to Clifton and picked up Bertha. 'I told your mother that my sister was ill and I wanted to go to her. I don't like telling her untruths.' Bertha sighed.

'Sometimes it's the best way,' said Adela, steering her car into the traffic on Blackboy Hill. Her fear was a tightening thread that constricted her throat. Nothing for a year! Nothing for a

441

year! Harry might be somewhere else and she'd never find him. He might be dead. She tried to control her thoughts. They reached Bedminster, passed Wills Tobacco Factory, and drove on through unfamiliar ways until they reached streets which reminded her of St Philips. She glanced down alleyways into courts surrounded by mean houses outside which played grubby children. The smells hung low and she gritted her teeth to stop herself from cursing. All this time she had honestly believed that Harry was in a good home somewhere, perhaps in health-giving hills, or woodland, or by the sea. Never could she have envisaged this.

Opal Lane consisted of two facing rows of redbrick houses. Adela wondered who had decided to call it by the name of a beautiful jewel, but at least Harry was not in one of the stinking courts. She stopped the car a couple of doors down from number eighteen.

'Shall I go first?' asked Bertha.

'No! If he's there I don't want to give them a chance to hide him. I'll try on my own. I'll pretend I'm inquiring about – about what? What can I say, Bertha? I should have had a story ready. I'm not usually so stupid.'

'You're not stupid, Miss Adela. It's terrible what's been done to you. You could say you were from the clinic.'

'What clinic?'

'It doesn't matter. The word will open doors. Say you're making a friendly check on the local children. Don't forget, the name's Prewett.'

Adela slid out of the car and stood looking towards the house, trying to stop the trembling in her knees. She walked up to the front door which opened straight on to the street and grasped the knocker. It sounded horribly loud and echoed through the small house. There was no sound or movement. Adela felt panicky. She knocked again, harder, and heard a door open somewhere and a voice yell, 'All right, I'm comin'. No need to bang the door down!'

The woman who answered was past her youth. She had greying hair twisted into an unbecoming knot on her head, her complexion was coarse and the hands she wiped on her apron were red and rough. None of this might have mattered since Adela knew that some of the roughest-looking women could be the most tender-hearted, but she disliked the woman on sight.

She managed to smile. 'I'm from the clinic, Mrs Prewett.' She waited for an answer, a denial of the name. None came and she continued, 'I've come to visit—' Oh, God, she didn't know what they called Harry.

'He's in the garden,' said Mrs Prewett. 'His dad's made him a little paddlin' pool. Daft idea, I call it, but his dad d'put him first. Puts him before me, I might tell you.' Her eyes were deep-set and dark and she frowned easily.

'May I come in?'

'I suppose so.' Mrs Prewett stood back and Adela walked into the living room. It was small and dark and smelled strongly of stale food. She followed the woman through the kitchen and out into the garden. It, too, was small with a few sparse plants round the outside privy. A large part of it was taken up by a shallow pool beside which a man was kneeling while a child sitting in the couple of inches of water was splashing and laughing. Adela held herself back. She mustn't rush this. First have a look at the boy. Be sure this time. Mr Prewett looked up as her shadow fell across him.

'Hello, then. Who's this, Mum?'

'From the clinic,' said Mrs Prewett. 'There he is, ma'am. There's our kid. You can see for yourself he's well.'

The boy looked at Adela. His pale gold hair was grubby, his lashes and brows were blond. Ralph looked at her through light blue, mildly curious eyes; looked at her as on a stranger. Harry! Her son! She ached to sweep him into her arms. She longed to kiss him.

'Well?' demanded Mrs Prewett. 'Had yer eyeful? I don't know what you're doin' here, anyway. I ain't brought him to the clinic for months.'

'I have a colleague outside,' said Adela. 'May she come in, too?'

'What for? What is this? A bloody inquisition?'

'Not in front of the child,' protested Mr Prewett.

'He'll hear a lot worse once he gets on the street with the other kids.'

Mr Prewett stood up. He was short and thick-set with a round, pink face and his red hair stuck up like a halo. He held out a hand to Adela who shook it. 'I admire you ladies what d'look after the mums and kids,' he said. 'You get your friend in if you've a mind to.'

Mrs Prewett's frown didn't seem to daunt him and Adela went to the front door and beckoned Bertha who immediately got out of the car and walked towards number eighteen. As soon as she had left the car a group of urchins swarmed over it, tooting the horn and pretending to drive. Bertha arrived and was inside before Mrs Prewett quite recognised her.

When she did her eyes opened wide with shock. 'You're a bloody liar!' she shrieked to Adela. 'You're not from the clinic! She's that woman's maid! What are you doin' here? She said no one would ever trouble me. Dad! Come here quick. These women are from the cow in Clifton.'

Mr Prewett came in with the boy in his arms. 'What d'you want with our Sidney?' he asked. He looked frightened.

'He's my son,' said Adela. 'Mrs Danby told me she was putting him in a nursery for a few weeks only. I've been searching for him ever since.' She swallowed hard and asked, 'Have you adopted him?'

Mr Prewett said, 'No,' as Mrs Prewett, quicker witted than her husband, said, 'Yes.'

'So you have no legal jurisdiction over him?'

'You an' your stupid mouth,' cried Mrs Prewett.

'None,' said Mr Prewett, 'but we d'love him, don't we, our Madge? He's like our own. We couldn't have none. We d'love him,' he repeated.

Adela looked from his anxious face to his wife's. 'Do you love him, too?' she asked.

'I wouldn't have bought him if I didn't want him,' said Mrs Prewett, 'but when I found out he grizzled from mornin' to night, I wished we hadn't.'

'You can't buy a child,' exclaimed Bertha. 'That's slavery.'

'Well, it's what we did, an' we couldn't do it on our own. Someone had to sell him. I should think she was glad to be rid of the miserable little devil.'

'He's got a sunny temper now,' said Mr Prewett.

'Only because I didn't listen to you. Soft-hearted fool. I smacked the nonsense out of him.'

Adela burned with rage. She wanted to strike this obnoxious woman. 'He was only a baby,' she managed.

'He was a noisy, bad-tempered brat!' snapped Mrs Prewett, 'but my husband wanted him an' he still does.' She turned her attention to Bertha. 'I'll have my own back on you!' she threatened. 'If you don't both get out of here this instant minute, I'll tell that stuck-up mistress of yours what you're up to. Sidney's our kid, an' you can take yourselves off.'

Mr Prewett sat down with Harry on his lap and wrapped him in a towel. 'Come on now, feller-me-lad, you d'need dryin'. Stop strugglin'. You can play in the water again's afternoon.'

'Dad,' said Harry, looking at Mr Prewett with love in his eyes. 'Play water.'

'I'm sorry, Mr Prewett,' said Adela. 'I've come to take my son home.'

'This is his home!' shouted Mrs Prewett.

Harry began to whimper and looked at the two strangers fearfully.

'Don't take him,' begged Mr Prewett. 'I d'love him more'n anythin' in the world. Don't take my kid away from me.'

'They won't, Alf, they got no right.'

'I've a mother's rights,' said Adela. 'He's my child and he was stolen from me and now I'm taking him back.' To Adela's horror tears began to seep from beneath Mr Prewett's lids. 'Please, please, don't cry,' she begged. 'If you love him so much, surely you can understand how I feel?'

'You ain't been nigh him the whole time he's been here,' snapped Mrs Prewett.

'That isn't her fault,' said Bertha. 'She was never a party to this.'

'If she'd really cared, she could have found him before now!'

Neither Adela nor Bertha answered.

'She couldn't, could she?' said Mr Prewett. 'He's got a different name.'

'Whose bloody side are you on?'

445

'Sidney's,' said Mr Prewett. He laid his cheek on Harry's head. The boy squirmed away, laughing. There was evidently a great rapport between the two.

'We're not good enough for him, I suppose!' snapped Mrs Prewett.

'That has no bearing on it,' said Adela. 'My son should be reared in his own home.'

'Huh!' Mrs Prewett's voice was scornful. 'Your son! I reckon that only part of what *she* said was the truth. The boy ain't got a father. At least here no one can point a finger at him. Did your lover leave you in the lurch, then?'

'My fiancé died in the war.'

'Is he a soldier's son?' asked Mr Prewett. 'I'm not surprised. He's a game little chap. Even when he was smacked—' He stopped, then continued, 'Is Mrs Danby a relation of yours?'

'Don't you know?'

Mrs Prewett said, '*She* said Sidney was a servant's kid an' she was doin' the girl a favour.'

'You're not a servant,' said Mr Prewett. 'I always knew there was somethin' special about our Sidney.'

'You! You think of nothin' but him!' Mrs Prewett turned to Adela. 'I got him because I couldn't have kids an' *he* wanted one.'

'You don't care about him at all, do you?'

''Course I do, but I got enough to do lookin' after the house an' workin' at Wills.'

'Who cares for him during the day?'

'He does.' Mrs Prewett nodded towards her husband. 'He's out of work. If we didn't have the allowance from *that woman's* lawyer—' Her tone suddenly altered. 'Tell you what,' she said confidentially, 'I can see you've got a right to the kid, but why not leave him here for now and visit him until he gets to know you? It'll be a shock if you d'take him away now.'

Adela knew she was right in theory, but she had caught the glint in Mrs Prewett's eyes. If she left Harry here she would telephone her mother who would intervene and whisk Harry away and this time he might never be traced.

She bent and caught Harry in her arms. She had pictured the moment so often. She would cradle him and kiss him and he would smile at her as he had once done. An immense satisfaction would fill her. Instead, Harry screamed and struggled to get out of her arms back to Mr Prewett. 'Dad, Dad, Dad,' he mouthed through his tears.

Mrs Prewett glared. 'You're upsettin' him,' she cried. 'How can you be so wicked?'

The towel slipped and Harry's naked body was difficult to hold. Adela was afraid of hurting him. Mr Prewett grabbed an old blanket from the back of a worn sofa and wrapped the child in it, holding him tight and kissing his mouth.

'My boy,' he murmured, 'my dear boy.'

Adela found it heart-rending to watch him. What she was about to do to him was what her mother had done to her.

Mr Prewett gave Harry a last kiss and handed him to Adela. 'If you're goin', for God's sake, go!' he pleaded.

Adela carried the struggling child out into the street. By some means or other word had spread and in nearly every doorway stood a woman watching the free show. Harry was strong and it was all Adela could do to hold on to him. Bertha got in the car and Adela handed the child to her and she spoke softly to him, managing to soothe him a little. He was interested in the car and his eyes opened wide when the engine sprang to life. He sat quietly in Bertha's arms, staring in wonder at the passing scenes.

'Motor,' he said. 'Motor.'

He stayed calm until they arrived at the house in Fishponds. When he understood that he was to be taken into a strange place he began to yell. 'Dad, Dad, Dad!' His voice was shrill and Adela recognised the tones which had so tormented her in his early babyhood. She was surprised to find Sander waiting.

'I cancelled my meetings,' he said.

When Harry saw him he held out his arms. Sander was surprised, but took him. The blanket slipped off and he held the small naked body carefully. Harry turned to glare at his mother and Bertha.

'He loves the man he's called Dad,' said Bertha.

'Dad,' said Harry, and Adela waited for more shrieks. Her nerves were stretched to their limit.

'I don't think Mrs Prewett gave him much love,' said Adela.

447

'It's Mr Prewett he wants. Sander, you can't spend the whole day holding Harry. I'd better take him.' She put out her arms and immediately Harry squirmed away, clutching Sander's hair with one small hand and his sleeve with the other.

'Don't look like that,' said Sander to Adela. 'He'll love you when he knows you. Poor little fellow. It's not his fault.'

'I know that!' snapped Adela, then was contrite.

Sander cut her apologies short. 'It's all right. I understand.'

Adela felt a rush of gratitude.

'I've an idea,' said Sander. He called Bill and said, almost casually, 'This is Harry. He's coming to live here. He's used to being looked after by a man. We're calling him Harry, though up to now he's been known as Sidney. Try to get him used to his new name. Would you take charge of him for now? We shall be adopting him.'

Adela hardly knew what to expect from Bill. An indignant refusal? Few men would be seen caring for a baby. Curiosity? Bill showed neither surprise nor reluctance. He held out his arms. Harry looked first at Sander, then at Bill whose sightless eye was surrounded by scars which gave him a slightly sinister aspect. But Harry, after studying him for a moment, appeared to like what he saw and went to him.

'Come on, lad,' said Bill. 'We'll go an' find somethin' to play with.'

'I should have brought his toys,' said Adela, stricken.

'That dreadful creature wouldn't have given them to you,' said Bertha. 'Shall I go out and get him some? And I'd better get clothes as well.'

Adela gave her money and Bertha left. Sander sat down and pulled Adela on to his lap. He had never done so before but she took comfort from the gesture. He held her close. 'Don't worry. Children get over things quickly. He'll forget the Prewetts and learn to love you in no time.'

Adela bent and impulsively pressed her lips to his abundant dark hair. He looked up into her eyes and for an instant there was harmony between them. Then the moment passed and Adela slid from his lap. 'I'll wait for Bertha's return and then get to work. I've several commissions I must complete. I hate to leave Harry,' she finished wistfully.

'You'll do no good by staying here,' said Sander. 'He's going to need a lot of patience and time to settle. Bill will take good care of him.'

'I know,' said Adela. 'I just wish my baby hadn't been away from me for so long.'

Sander bent and kissed her. 'Go to the showroom, darling. I must be off, too.'

Bertha returned with a good selection of toys, including a teddy bear which took Harry's fancy. 'Teddy,' he said. 'Sid's Teddy.'

'Will he ever get used to his proper name?' wondered Adela aloud.

'We'll just have to keep callin' him Harry,' said Bill. He picked up a small vest and began to dress the boy in his new clothes.

Adela found it difficult to keep her mind on her work when it kept sliding back to Harry. She told Esther about it.

'That Mrs Prewett sounds a dragon,' said Esther. 'Don't worry about Harry, though. He'll love you again in time.'

But Harry showed no sign of turning to Adela, or any other woman, and Adela cursed Mrs Prewett daily.

Harry had been back with her for three weeks when a woman who reminded Adela of Bertha was shown into her office. 'I'm Ellen,' she said, 'Bertha's sister.'

'She's spoken of you,' said Adela. 'Won't you sit down?'

Ellen sat, looking grim. 'I've come to tell you about our Bertha since she'd sooner cut out her tongue than beg.'

'What's happened?'

'Your mother sacked her without a reference, after more than thirty years' service. Bertha won't tell me why and Mrs Danby won't see me, so I thought I'd come to you. I wondered if you knew what's happened.'

'How could Mother do that? How could she?'

'Easy,' said Ellen. 'I'm sorry to say such a thing about your mother, but she's not renowned for her kindness.'

'Has Bertha tried to get her job back?'

449

'She went once and was refused entrance. Mr Evans said that madam was suited with another maid. I was wondering if you could maybe give her a position? She's been sending money for years to our brother in Devon. He's got eight children and only a labourer's job, and what savings she's got won't last long. She don't grumble, but she dreads the thought of going to the Guardians and ending up in the workhouse.'

'The very idea! I already have a maid, but I know I can find something for her. Please ask her to call here.'

'I'll ask her, but you might have to come to her. Proud? The queen's got nothing on her.'

Bertha arrived three days later. She looked pale and tired and Adela was angry with herself. 'I should have made sure you were all right,' she said. 'I get far too immersed in work.'

Bertha said, 'I'm not surprised. The showroom looks a treat – all the lovely materials, and ornaments and pictures and furniture, too.'

'They are recent additions. We've created "rooms" so that customers can see the finished effect. It's been very popular.'

'I always knew you were artistic. I thought your mother should have let you go to art school.'

'Did you, Bertha? You must have been the only one.'

'Oh, no, Mr Evans and Clara thought the same.'

'Fancy so much going on below stairs and I never knew.'

'Servants often know a lot. Employers forget we're there a lot of the time and we get to hear things.'

'Do the others know why you were dismissed?'

'Oh, no, of course not. Your mother will never speak of Harry.'

'It was Mrs Prewett, wasn't it?'

'Yes, she came to the house the same day. Mrs Danby was angrier than I've ever seen her. I had to get out, bag and baggage, immediately.'

'What makes Mother so callous?'

'She's just never seen further than her family. She's proud of her ancestry and can't abide anything by way of scandal.'

'Bertha, would you like to work in my house? We'll soon be shifting to a larger place. I'm doing the interior decorating myself. We would have moved by now were it not for my illness.'

'What kind of position could I have? You've got Sarah back and Mr Bennett's already got a good housekeeper.'

'How do you know?'

'I've been acquainted with Mrs Monkton a good many years.'

'Would you consider the position of nursemaid?'

Bertha shook her head. 'I don't know anything about babies. You need a properly trained woman and someone younger than me, too. Miss Adela, can I come and work here? I think it's wonderful. I can cut out and sew. A lady's maid has to have a lot of skills, as you know.'

'If that's what you want,' said Adela. When Bertha had left she scribbled down a few figures. The business wasn't ready to take on somebody new, but a living wage must be found for Bertha somehow.

The house overlooking Durdham Down had been thoroughly renovated. It had been built in Victorian times and needed attention which Sander had given it in good measure. All sources of damp had been eradicated, rotting window frames replaced, electric wiring installed, then Sander had given Adela a completely free hand. She revelled in the work, often finding it difficult to tear herself away to attend to customers' needs. She had great spending power and filled the house with beauty, pursuing the refinements of pure form and space, turning to Rennie Mackintosh and to abstract artists like Dufy, Chagall and Matisse for inspiration. The walls were hung with pastel paper; the floors were of polished oak over which were thrown rugs, mostly pale. The emphasis everywhere was on light.

'This will be the supreme showhouse for my work,' she told Sander. 'You won't mind?'

His brows went up in a sardonic look. 'Mind a showhouse? Not if that's what you want, but I hope you'll remember we have to live in it, too. Rich woods, new-style veneers, inlays, lacquers and stained glass are fine, but I like a bit of comfort.'

'There will be comfortable furniture as well!'

'I'm relieved to hear it. I saw the chaise longue in chrome, steel and leather when it was delivered.'

'The Le Corbusier? Oh, has it arrived? Did you try it?'

Sander pretended to look scared. 'No fear! I'm waiting for your permission.'

'Fool! Of course you may lie on it. I think you'll find it more comfortable than it looks.'

'It couldn't be less.'

Sander tried the chaise longue and was surprised. 'It's good,' he said.

'Now sit on one of the chairs in the small drawing room.'

'The steel and canvas ones, rather like chairs at the seaside?'

'All right, have a look at the library. You'll like that. I've incorporated easy chairs covered in blue-grey plush with modern tables and cupboards, and there's a window seat with cushions and two standard lamps. The fireplace is tiny mosaic tiles with inlays of pale blue and black.'

'I've seen it. I like it.'

'Well, why let me run on like that?'

'I'm enjoying your enthusiasm.'

Adela felt abruptly self-conscious. 'Are you making fun of me?'

'Of course not. Would I consent to move to a house I didn't like? I'd have refused my permission.'

'Oh, would you? It's my house, too, remember?'

'But my money.'

Adela flushed. 'Damn you, Sander, you told me to use what I needed. Why bring up money?'

'I never would have, but you began it.'

'I did not!'

'You did by refusing me a share in your shop.'

'I don't have a share in your business.'

'As a matter of fact, you do. I've instructed my solicitor to make a part over to you.'

'That's playing dirty. I haven't asked for anything and I don't want it. Now I suppose you'll expect me to reciprocate.'

'I expect nothing of you, Adela, beyond what you're prepared to give.'

The occasion which had begun so well had degenerated into one of the sharp quarrels which marred their relationship, each refusing to submit to the other. Adela had to remind herself that Sander had given Harry a secure home, had welcomed him without reservation and was in the process of quietly adopting him. To think of Harry was still to hurt. He turned to Sander or Bill, never to her. Bill was looking after him on a full-time basis with a young nursery maid to assist.

'Cheer up, it may never happen,' said Sander sardonically.

'Oh, go to hell!' Adela hurried to the front door and out to her car and moments later was driving towards her showroom, where she felt at home and serene in the only place which was truly hers. But today her serenity had forsaken her. Sander got under her skin like no one else. There were times when she wished she had held out against their marriage. Then she had to remind herself of all he had done for her and her son. She tried to think of life without Sander and realised she would miss his powerful personality.

The house move was accomplished and more servants engaged. Mrs Monkton, garrulous as ever, proved herself to be capable of controlling a large household. She was proud of her sitting room which was decorated in her favourite colours of pink and brown. 'You're a marvel, madam,' she said often to Adela. 'How you think up all the ideas I don't know.'

Harry was suspicious when he was taken to his new nursery at the top of the house. It held every luxury Adela could buy, but none of it would be of any use if he didn't settle. But he saw a rocking horse and ran to it, laughing, and after that seemed content.

Bill said, 'I've a suspicion that the boy wasn't all that happy before, Mrs Bennett. He flinched when Betsy lifted her hand over his head to reach something off a shelf.'

'Is he happy here?' Adela couldn't keep the wistfulness from her voice.

'He's blossoming. Don't worry, madam, he'll learn to trust women in time.'

Adela was startled that Bill had opinions. He was so quiet and unobtrusive that he was easily passed over. Sander had chosen wisely when he had assigned him to Harry. Sander was wise, she had to admit it. At first she tried to cope with all the running problems of the showroom without discussing them, but in the end she accepted his counsel which he gave only when asked. She was on sure ground when she was creative, but the financial side she found difficult.

They decided to give a house-warming party and settled down one evening to decide on the guest list.

'You'll ask your parents, of course,' said Sander.

'What? They won't come.'

'But you must still ask them. You can't snub them.'

'I feel I never want to see Mother again after the way she's behaved.'

'That's perfectly natural, but not clever. She may yet come round when she sees that you intend to be discreet about Harry. It's good for children to have grandparents.'

'I don't see why.' But Adela had caught the note of sadness in Sander's voice and knew he was thinking of his boyhood and she added them to the list.

'We must ask the Somerses, too,' said Sander.

'They won't come either. Why should we give them the chance to turn us down?'

'I think they'll accept if only out of curiosity. And Somers owes me a few business favours.'

'Oh! What sort of favours?'

'Financial ones,' said Sander. 'He needs to keep on my good side.'

'Do you really want them here?' asked Adela.

'Yes. I'd like to show off our new house to as many people as possible.' When Adela raised her eyebrows Sander actually looked quite sheepish and she said no more, but added the Somerses to the guest list, along with Ralph's brothers and their wives.

'I think you're crazy,' she said. 'They'll accept, then not turn up and have some perfectly valid excuse ready.'

'You may be surprised. You're becoming fashionable, and if I'm right Violet and Sybil won't miss a chance to look over the house.'

Adela chose a special dress for the occasion, a pale tangerine chiffon by Ospovat, with handkerchief points to the floor and the silk bodice beaded with crystal. Round her neck was a long string of topaz beads which reached to her hips and matching eardrops swung from her ears. Her shoes were studded with rhinestones and topaz, as was the orange velvet bandeau on her head.

Sarah stood back and clasped her hands. 'You'll be the belle of the ball!'

Adela studied her reflection, realising that she hadn't really looked at herself for a long time. She had lost all her curves and was as slender as the newest fashions demanded. Her hands were smooth once more, her hair expertly cut and curled.

Sander came in and Sarah left. 'By God, you're a lovely woman,' he said. 'It's a pity we have to go downstairs.' He held her close, his breathing quickening, and she pushed him away.

'Behave yourself. We've guests to entertain, and you're steaming up the crystal!'

Sander laughed. 'I'll see you later, wife.'

As Adela descended the stairs, Sander beside her, she felt the familiar tug between restrained enjoyment of Sander's caresses and irritation at being possessed by him. But there was no more time for thought. The guests began to arrive. Few had refused the invitation to look over the Bennetts' new house which, it was rumoured, was like nothing ever seen before. There were exclamations over the decor and promises that Adela would be receiving further commissions.

'Darling,' cried Vita, 'so many pale objets d'art. Aren't you worried that your dear little boy will mark things?'

'He's too young for that, surely?' said Bobbie loudly. 'Adela and Sander are so recently married.'

Adela glanced at Sander whose expression didn't change one iota. 'I've been Harry's guardian since his father was killed in the war,' he lied calmly to anyone within earshot. 'As soon as the necessary documents are ready he will be adopted and Adela and I don't care tuppence if he puts his sticky fingers on things. People, especially children, come before objects.'

Adela had the satisfaction of knowing that Sander had discomfited both Vita and Bobbie.

Bobbie leaned forward and peered at Adela's beads. 'How

quaint of you to wear inexpensive jewellery, darling. My husband gave me this.' She held out her arm and displayed a bracelet heavy with diamonds. 'And this.' She touched an emerald pendant on a gold chain. 'It's *so* wonderful to have a man who never grudges me anything I want.'

'I'm sure it is,' said Adela smoothly, 'and how brave of you to wear real jewels when Paris has decreed that costume jewellery is the thing. However, I do see that you'd want to display such pretty gems.'

Bobbie said grittily, 'Your gown, my dear . . . so *bright* it actually glitters.'

'Ospovat,' said Adela laconically. 'You must get yourself one.'

'Your round, I think,' murmured Sander in Adela's ear.

Esther arrived, escorted by Freddy Stanton, and Mr Trevor, from Sander's Park Street store, brought his wife.

'My dear, so original of you to invite the hired help!' said Vita.

'Original?' inquired Adela, with a slight lift of her brows. 'But, Vita, darling, we employ such superior people, don't you know, and we aim to keep them for years.'

Vita, whom everyone knew had constant servant trouble because of her bad temper, actually flushed.

'You're a perfect little bitch,' murmured Sander in Adela's ear as he took her in his arms to dance. The big drawing room had been cleared and a small band hired. The first dance was a waltz as Sander had ordered, and after that they were to play jazz. When the musicians swung into the new music, Adela danced the frenzied movements of the Cakewalk and the Shimmy as the band beat out the rhythm. They even played a hotted-up version of *It's a Long Way to Tipperary* and the guests kicked and swung to the music as if there had never been a time of slaughter. Adela ended by half falling into Sander's arms, laughing breathlessly.

It was a shock to look up and see Ralph's family watching from the door. She went to greet them, sobered by the disapproving look on Sir Wilfred Somers' face.

Chapter Twenty-Four

Adela kissed Lady Somers' cheek, greeted Sybil and Violet in the same way, and shook hands with Sir Wilfred and his two sons.

The family stood in a small group, gazing round the room and at the dancers until Adela feared that only a well-placed bomb would move them.

Then Sybil, true to form, said loudly, 'You've got black men in your band, Adela.'

'All the rage, my dear. I imported them from London for the evening. Charming fellows who live for their music.'

'Music!' snorted Sir Wilfred. 'It's a hellish racket.'

'I quite like it,' said Sybil.

'You would,' said her husband. 'It's typical of you to go against the rest of us.'

'Don't scold her, Giles,' said Adela. 'I want you all to enjoy the evening. Lady Somers, won't you let me take you and the girls upstairs? You can leave your wraps and freshen up in my room.' She signalled to Denton, the newly acquired butler, to attend the gentlemen who reacted favourably to his portly dignity. When Sander had chosen Denton from the applicants he had known what he was doing.

Upstairs Sybil looked round the bedroom in amazement. 'It's so different from anything I've seen. I just adore the colour scheme, more white than anything, but some green and yellow.'

'I prefer to call them eau-de-nil and primrose,' said Adela.

'Eau-de-nil has something of blue in it,' declared Violet.

'Indeed it has,' Adela agreed.

'Look at the sweet pictures,' said Sybil. 'Who painted them?'

'Margaret Macdonald.'

'I've never heard of her,' said Violet.

'She's Scottish. She married Charles Rennie Mackintosh. They have been one of my chief inspirations.'

'I need the bathroom,' said Sybil, and Adela indicated a door. Sybil came out in further ecstasies. 'My dears, it's all pink marble with *huge* towels. It's so lovely. I would so love a pink marble bathroom.'

'You must speak to Giles,' said Adela.

Sybil looked disconsolate. 'He'd never agree. I'm sure Ralph would have. I used to picture you and him—' She stopped, her face flaming.

Adela said, 'Lady Somers, your hair has become a trifle dishevelled. May I call my maid to attend you?'

Lady Somers sat at the dressing table and looked into the mirror. She smoothed her hands over her hair and put her feathered head-dress straight. 'No thank you, my dear, I'm all right.' She looked round. 'Where are the other ladies' cloaks and mantles?'

'They were shown to a different room. I thought, since we were once so close . . .'

'That was sweet of you, my dear.' She sighed as she got up. 'Unfortunately, those days are gone. Your dress is very pretty, though' – she smiled – 'it leaves quite a lot of skin showing. Well, fashions change. Seeing the young women of today often makes me regret the constraints of my own youth.'

'I don't feel the need to display so much of myself,' said Violet primly.

'I must keep up with the times,' said Adela, keeping her tone mild for Lady Somers' sake. 'I need to impress people.'

'Ah, yes,' said Violet. 'You are in business. I wonder at your husband permitting it.'

Adela only smiled, though it took an effort.

Downstairs Sir Wilfred, Desmond and Giles had congregated in the morning room with several men of their acquaintance. The door was open and Sir Wilfred's voice could be heard booming above the others. 'The country is going to the dogs! There were over five thousand divorce petitions filed last year and the rise in income tax is outrageous. The government takes anything up to six shillings in the pound and one has to

458

work all hours to ensure a proper standard of living. I tell you, when a man like the Duke of Portland needs to tell his tenants he may have to leave Welbeck Abbey because of financial problems, it bodes ill for the rest of us. And where does the money go? I'll tell you. On good for nothing men who won't work!'

Adela thought of Jack and Bert and others like them and burned with fury. Then she heard Sander's voice. '*Can't* work, would be more correct, Sir Wilfred.'

'Can't? Can't? There are jobs for those who seek them.'

'Skilled jobs for healthy men,' said Sander. 'So many of our returning servicemen were boys when they joined up. They have no skills and many have lost their health.'

'If the government stopped paying them uncovenanted benefit, they'd soon have to find work!'

Adela swept into the morning room. 'No politics, if you please, gentlemen,' she said, smiling sweetly. 'This is a housewarming party and must not be marred by sordid talk of money.'

Sir Wilfred glared at her, but when the men drifted out he followed them into the drawing room where there was a temporary lull in the music.

He glared again at the band. 'That man who plays the drums,' he said. 'He appears to be surrounded by motor horns and bells and other noisy implements. Is it all really necessary?'

At that moment the band struck up again and Sir Wilfred took his wife's arm. 'Come, my dear, this is no place for us. I trust you'll excuse us old fogies for not remaining at your party,' he said to Adela.

'Oh, must we go?' Lady Somers pleaded.

'We certainly must, unless you want another of your headaches.'

Lady Somers' hand went to her forehead automatically. 'No. No, I wouldn't want that to happen.'

'Then come along. Don't be too late,' he boomed at his sons and their wives. 'Too much of this cacophony will make you deaf.'

Lady Somers looked longingly at Adela, but she obeyed.

Sybil was jigging in time to the music. 'Let's dance,' she said to her husband.

'Dance! To that row?' cried Giles. 'There isn't even any tune.'

'Of course there is,' said Sybil. 'It's *Hawaiian Jazz*, a foxtrot. I heard it at Bobbie's house. Do let's dance, Giles.'

'I wouldn't demean myself, and neither should—'

He got no further. Sander had bowed formally to Sybil and asked her for the pleasure of a dance, and Giles's wife went capering off around the floor.

Giles went red. 'Well, really! He must have heard what I said and known that I am opposed to this kind of thing.'

'Supper is about to be served,' said Adela. 'Afterwards, perhaps you would like to make up a table for whist or bridge?'

Giles looked happier, though Desmond still frowned. 'I am glad that Violet has too much dignity to wish to take part in this unseemly spectacle.'

Adela crept away and in a moment was dancing with Freddy Stanton.

As supper was announced Millie arrived with Algy, Douglas and Jane Fairfield, and a woman whom Adela didn't know.

'Sorry I'm late,' cried Millie gaily. 'I heard the band from outside. Splendid music, darling. *Divine* musicians. May I present Lady Margaret Purcell?'

Adela held out her hand and Lady Margaret shook it with a firm grip. She had grey eyes and soft fair hair. 'How do you do, Mrs Bennett? I'm afraid I'm partly to blame for our tardiness.'

'*Sweet* of you to take the blame,' laughed Millie, 'but Adela knows I'm never on time. Come on, Algy, I'm starving. How about you others?'

She was followed into the dining room by all except Lady Margaret. 'It's true I was partly to blame. I was fascinated by the decor of Millie's house. I'm getting married next year.' She looked around. 'This hall is utterly delightful. So original. Would you care to have a look at the place my future husband has bought in London, with a view to doing the interior decorating? I haven't been able to decide what I want. Now, after seeing your work, I know.'

Adela's heart beat fast. This could be her big chance to extend her business outside Bristol. 'Will your future husband be as enthusiastic about my ideas?'

'Terence? Oh, yes, he's a perfect lamb. We agree on everything.'

'That must be a unique state of affairs.'

Lady Margaret laughed. 'Perhaps. It makes for a peaceful life. Will you come to London? I'm returning tomorrow and could meet you in two days' time.'

Adela was delighted to accept and her ladyship went into the dining room where tables were laden with food and there were small tables and chairs for those who wanted them. Many preferred to stand, holding plates of oyster patties, plovers' eggs, chicken, lamb cutlets in aspic, and a variety of salads and cheese and fruit. For the sweet-toothed there were jellies and creams, chocolate mousse and icecream. Servants carried trays of champagne cocktails and wine.

'What will you have, Lady Margaret?' asked Adela.

'Make it plain "Margaret" and I'd love a couple of plovers' eggs while I browse. It all looks perfectly lovely. And champagne cocktails. Wonderful!'

Adela was too excited and nervous to eat. She wandered round the rooms, checking that ash trays were being emptied, pots of flowers were safely out of reach of careless guests, that forgotten stoles and scarves were carefully folded and left where their owners would find them. Sander came upon her. 'You've eaten nothing.'

'I can't. Is the party a success? It's so difficult to tell when you're the hostess.'

'It's a one hundred per cent humdinger.'

'What's that when it's at home?'

'A success, darling. Here, I've brought you some chicken.' He unwrapped a napkin and insisted that she take a few mouthfuls and a little wine.

'I've got a London commission,' said Adela.

'From Lady Margaret? Congratulations.' Sander sounded pleased, but there was doubt in his eyes. 'You'll be spending time away from home.'

461

'No more than I must. I want to see Harry as often as possible.'

'Harry. Yes, I see.'

Adela was standing alone in the hall when she heard a knock at the front door. She answered it and was surprised to see Lady Somers hurry in.

'Sir Wilfred is at home, Adela. He went straight to his room and doesn't know I'm here. Where can we talk? I don't want Desmond or Giles to see me. Or Violet, for that matter. Sybil's a sweet child for all her gaucherie. She wouldn't betray me.'

'That sounds very dramatic.'

Lady Somers didn't return her smile. Adela led the way upstairs and took her into her bedroom. Lady Somers looked round. 'How pretty you've made your house. It's light and airy, so different from mine. You won't have forgotten the heavy furniture and the dark wallpaper. I wish that Sir Wilfred – but I didn't come to discuss him.' She stopped and sat down, twisting her hands in her lap. 'Adela, I've heard about the little boy you are caring for.'

'It would be amazing if you hadn't.'

'Don't joke, my dear. It isn't funny.'

'No, it isn't.'

'How old is he?'

Adela stared at Lady Somers. 'Why do you want to know?'

'Please, indulge me, Adela.'

'Harry is two.'

'Is he yours?'

Adela gasped. 'What a question!'

'Please, my dear, tell me the truth. It will go no further. He is the reason I persuaded my husband to accept your invitation. I might have known he would ruin the occasion.' She hurried on, trying to cover her lapse of loyalty. 'Adela, I know that you and Mr Bennett are about to adopt this boy. Is he your son? Please, *please*, tell me the truth.'

Adela said quietly, 'Yes, he's mine.'

'Then he was born before you married Mr Bennett. Is he the father?'

'I'm sorry, Lady Somers,' said Adela gently, 'but you have no right to question me like this.'

'I accept that.' She was silent for a moment. 'Forgive me, Adela, but I know what the boy looks like. There have been rumours.'

'About Harry?'

'About you, my dear. You were absent from society for so long that there was bound to be talk. I even heard that you were living in St Pauls with an odd little man.'

'I had a friend in St Pauls, that's true.'

'Is the child his?'

'You're going too far,' cried Adela.

'I know, I know. I am afraid to ask what I really want to know, but from what I've heard he must have been born only months after Ralph was killed.'

Adela remained silent.

'May I see Harry?'

'I don't think any useful purpose would be served. In any case, he's asleep. His nursery will be darkened.'

'Does he not have a night light?'

'Of course he does. He dislikes complete darkness.'

'Ralph always needed a night light. My poor boy! I accepted his sacrifice as my duty to my king and country, but I've since learned something of what our young soldiers suffered and I've had no peace of mind.'

'It's all in the past, Lady Somers.'

'I think perhaps it is not. Please, Adela, may I just peep at your son?'

Adela was silent. The strains of the band starting up again rose faintly. She looked at Ralph's mother whose lined face was a mask of anguished pleading and knew she couldn't keep her from Ralph's child. She nodded once and Lady Somers followed her up to the third floor and into the nursery suite. Nora the nursery maid was sitting near an open window, knitting. She sprang to her feet when the two women entered.

'It's all right, Nora. This is Lady Somers. She just wants to look at Harry.'

Adela led the way into the night nursery. She closed the door. The two women looked at the sleeping child. His long blond lashes feathered his pink and white cheeks, his light hair was tousled. Even in repose the likeness to Ralph was unmistakable to one who was seeking it.

Lady Somers gave a stifled cry, then held her hand to her mouth. She followed Adela back into the day nursery as Bill opened the outer door.

'Mrs Bennett,' he said, 'I was just gettin' a bite of supper.'

Lady Somers tried to speak and failed.

'Is the lady ill? Nora, fetch her a chair.'

'No! No, thank you,' said Adela. 'I'll take care of her.'

She managed to get Lady Somers into a storage room where she sank on to an old chest. 'The boy,' she said, 'your son, Harry. He's Ralph's, isn't he?'

There was no point in lying and Adela didn't.

'So that's why you went away! How did you manage? Your mother said she had sent you to your grandmother, but I know that Lady Sutton would not have countenanced such a birth. You bore him out of wedlock! Were you alone? Where was he born? Is he strong? Why do you have a man to care for him? Is that wise?' Lady Somers paused, her mouth trembling. When she recovered herself a little she said, 'I am so sorry, Adela. I should not be asking these questions, but I cannot help it.'

Adela felt shaky. She knelt on the floor on a pile of old velvet curtains. 'Lady Somers, no good can come of discussing this. I beg you to go home and forget Harry.'

'Forget my grandson!'

'He is illegitimate, he always will be, but once the adoption goes through he will be as safe as we can make him.'

'You didn't feel you could come to us?'

'No. Mother and Father said you'd be horrified and refuse to acknowledge him. I think they might have been right. At the time.'

'At the time, yes, they were right. At the time.' Lady Somers held her handkerchief to her moist eyes. 'I am different now. I was once upheld by duty, but duty is a cold comfort and easily displaced by reality.'

'I'm sorry you're so unhappy, but I must ask you to keep this to yourself.'

'Others may put two and two together.'

'Maybe, but Ralph was hardly known outside the family. He was at school, and went away and died so young.'

Lady Somers let out a sob and Adela put her arms about her. 'Go home, please. You'll get over this in time.'

'You'll stay in Bristol? I can see him from time to time? I will see him, won't I?'

'That will be inevitable. I certainly won't stand in your way.'

When Lady Somers had left, Adela felt exhausted. The work of the past months, the strain of finding Harry and the pain of his rejection, the nervous tension of the evening and the lack of food, were making her dizzy. She went downstairs where the noise was at its height.

'*Lovely* party, darling,' cried Bobbie.

'Great fun,' agreed Millie, as she dragged Algy on to the floor for yet another frenzied dance.

Adela peeped into the small drawing room where those who didn't dance were talking and saw Blanche and Georgie, side by side, laughing together. They were attracting prurient glances which didn't trouble them in the least.

Sander came and put his arm round Adela's shoulders. 'You look as if you need a drink.'

Adela nodded. 'I'll have a cocktail. It should fizz me up.'

'Has something happened?'

'I'll tell you later. I think I'm mostly tired.'

She sat in the hall with her drink. The evening was turning mild and muggy and Sander propped the front door ajar to gain what air there was. He stood beside her. Someone came up the steps leading to the door and stepped inside. Adela gasped and choked on her drink. Standing in the hall beneath the Tiffany lamp was Jack! Her heart raced so fast she felt ill, then in the next instant her brain corrected the false impression. Of course he wasn't Jack. The man was as tall as Sander, his hair dark, as were the eyes regarding her curiously. But they could have been Jack's eyes. Then she remembered. She had seen this man before in a photograph. He had been younger, of course, but she recognised him.

He came to her. 'Mrs Bennett?'

'Yes.'

'I apologise if I've startled you.' He had an American accent.

'Startled me?'

'Forgive me, but you looked at me as if I were a ghost.'

'For a moment I thought you were. You're Jack's son, aren't you? I saw a picture of you.'

The man said, 'And I've seen one of you. My aunt showed me your photograph and told me of your kindness to them. I decided to thank you. Sorry I barged in on a party. I'll just say hello and go.'

Adela shook her head. 'I thought you were in America.'

'I was. I arrived in Bristol a few days ago.' He smiled. 'Your photograph doesn't do you credit.'

'Neither does yours.'

Michael looked inquiringly at Sander.

'Sorry,' said Adela. 'I was so taken aback I forgot. This is my husband, Sander Bennett.'

Sander shook hands. 'You resemble your father in many ways. Jack was one of the most courageous fellows I've known. He's a great loss to the movement.'

'The movement?' Michael looked quizzical in the way his father had so often. 'Ah, I take it you mean the socialist movement? Yes, he stood up for his class.'

'You don't speak like a Bristolian,' said Adela.

'Neither do you,' said Michael.

Adela smiled. '*Touché*. That sounded gauche.'

Michael relented. 'Not at all. I know you're one of the nobs – that's Gran's term for you – and I was born in St Philips and grew up there, but I changed my accent when I went to the States. Most of the people I met couldn't understand Bristolian.'

'I like your accent,' said Adela. She realised she was talking to him as if she'd known him for years. She glanced at Sander who was frowning.

'I certainly picked the wrong night,' said Michael. 'Shall I come back tomorrow? I should like to hear about my father from all those who knew him.' He turned to Sander. 'You were one of Dad's friends, weren't you?'

'I was. It's a great pity you postponed your return for so many years. Jack always missed you.'

Michael's good humour vanished for an instant and he gave Sander an angry frown. It was gone in a second.

'Do stay,' said Adela. 'Have you eaten? I'm sure there is still some food, or I can have something made up for you.'

'I'm not hungry.' Michael took out a gold cigarette case and offered it to Sander who refused and to Adela who accepted. He lit their cigarettes.

'It must have been a very sad homecoming for you,' said Adela, throwing Sander a glance which dared him to make another derogatory remark.

Michael nodded. 'I was deeply disappointed not to be able to tell Dad that I'd made good.'

Sander, disregarding his wife's silent warning, said, 'Jack didn't know if you were dead or alive. It grieved him.'

Adela felt furious. Sander had clearly taken an instant dislike to Michael. He was judging him harshly on the little he knew.

Michael gave him a cool, calculating look. 'I've been busy. I'm sorry as hell now I didn't write, but it's too late to worry. I couldn't expect Dad to die in his forties.' He turned to Adela. 'Aunt Ida thinks the world of you. She says you've changed her life for the better.'

'That's kind of her. She's a darling. What does Mrs Webster say?'

Michael laughed. 'Gran's tongue hasn't grown smoother with the years.' He looked her up and down. 'She didn't tell me how beautiful you were.'

'Are all Americans as forthright as you?'

'Hell, yes! Well, most of them are. They're in a hurry to get somewhere and make something of themselves.'

Sander said smoothly, 'If you wish to talk, shall we find a place to sit?'

'Sure, I'd like that if Mrs Bennett has time. You've got a lot of guests.'

467

'They're perfectly happy amusing themselves,' said Adela. 'They won't miss me for a while.'

'Great little band you've got. I had no idea that Britain was so up to date.'

'Oh, yes,' said Sander, 'we gave up the minuet some time ago.'

Michael stared at him. 'Say, if I'm in the way I can leave and call another day.'

Sander had the grace to say, if a little stiffly, 'You're not in the way. Adela is interested in you because of Jack.'

Adela and the two men went into the breakfast parlour and she rang for coffee. Sander seated himself a little out of the range of the light where Adela knew he would watch and listen like a cat. She felt irritated, as if he was intruding upon a private family matter. She would prefer to be alone with Michael. The thought in itself was not alarming. What made her agitated was the realisation that she found this young man with his handsome looks, his dynamic personality, maybe even his superficial likeness to his father, very attractive.

'You cared a hell of a lot for Dad, didn't you?' he said to Adela.

'A hell of a lot,' she agreed.

'Aunt Ida told me that you worked on the barrow to keep him after his accident.'

A dozen answers went through Adela's head. It still hurt her to remember Jack and his suffering. 'I repaid only a little of what he gave me. He looked after me when I needed him.'

'That's like Dad.'

'What's brought you to England now?' asked Sander.

'A wish to see my family again,' said Michael blandly.

'What have you been doing all the years you've been away?'

'Sander,' said Adela, 'Michael doesn't expect to be put through an inquisition.'

'I'm interested.'

'Sure you are. That's fine by me.' Michael lit another cigarette. His consumption of tobacco seemed to be as heavy as Jack's, though his cigarettes were gold-tipped and obviously expensive. In fact, everything about him was expensive. His suit was made of grey silk and he wore a matching tie with a pearl stickpin, his shirt was of fine linen and his shoes the same grey as his suit. Father would have taken one look at him and called him 'a damn pansy'.

Coffee was brought and Michael took his black, unsweetened. Adela added cream for herself and Sander, then fitted one of Michael's cigarettes into her rhinestone holder. She inhaled and blew out a stream of smoke.

'You won't have to give money to my folks any longer,' said Michael. 'I'm making myself responsible for them.'

Adela said, 'Your gran will appreciate that. She hated taking money from me, but it was either that or poor relief. However, I shall go on paying Ida for the work she does.'

'Gran will never go on the parish if I can help it,' said Michael. 'And I don't think she'll want Aunt Ida to go on working when she needn't.'

'Ida loves what she's doing,' said Adela. 'She's an expert in her field.'

Michael's eyes opened wide. 'Aunt Ida an expert? That little mouse? What does she do?'

Adela explained and Michael whistled. 'Well, fancy Aunt Ida being so clever! That's just dandy. I guess she'll have to go on working if she wants to, but I'll still give the old girls an allowance.'

'You've hit it rich in the States?' Sander asked. Did he have to sound so belligerent?

'I've hit it rich; big and rich,' said Michael.

'May I ask how?'

'Sure you may. There's no secret about it. When I landed in the good old USA I was penniless and did any job I could find. I was making a fair wage, though not spectacular, not enough to buy my passage back to Britain—'

'A stamp costs little,' said Sander.

Adela clenched her fists. She wanted to yell at him to stop baiting Michael.

Michael frowned briefly again, then continued, 'The

government bowed to a bunch of crazy people and brought in the Eighteenth Amendment.'

'Prohibition,' said Sander.

'That's the banning of all alcoholic drink, isn't it?' said Adela.

'Sure is, ma'am, and boy, oh boy, what opportunities it's giving to men who know how to make best use of the situation.'

'Translated,' said Sander, 'it means that it's a money-making proposition for people who don't mind flouting the law.'

'From what I've heard of you, in America you'd be right in there with the money-makers.'

'I think not,' said Sander, and again Adela was annoyed. Why on earth should he be so unpleasant to Jack's son?

'And I say you would. When you hear how much dough it brings in, no man with an eye to business could afford to pass it up. Folks want drink and no loony law is going to stop them getting it. Any man who knows the ropes can get his hands on the stuff, and it sells and sells.'

'Not all of it is good,' said Sander. 'In fact, some of it is criminally bad.'

Michael's expression didn't change, but there was something in his eyes which jolted Adela. A wary, suspicious look mingled with resentment.

'Some of it is,' he agreed, 'but folks who buy from cheapjacks get what they deserve.'

'Blindness and death?' Sander's voice was icy now.

'I heard about that,' said Michael, 'but I help run a respectable business.'

'Which is still against the law.'

Michael sighed. 'I guess I should leave, Mrs Bennett. I don't think I'm welcome here.'

Adela was angry. 'Of course you are. This is my house, too. I want to talk to you. Sander, please!'

He lit a cigar and leaned back in his chair. 'I'll shut up. Go ahead, Mr Webster.'

'For Pete's sake, "Mr Webster"! "Mr and Mrs Bennett"! I'm Michael, and I'd appreciate it if you use my name and allow me to use yours.'

'Of course,' said Adela quickly before Sander could intervene.

'I work for a guy who's cornered the market in hooch in part of New York. Each boss works his own particular patch and we don't trespass on one another. At least, we try not to or there's trouble.'

'I can understand that,' said Adela, 'business in Bristol is sharp.'

There was a curious snorting sound from Sander which Adela identified as a laugh. She saw nothing funny in what was being said. 'Did you speak, Sander?' she asked coolly.

'No, I'm staying out of it.'

'Go ahead,' said Michael. 'I think you've got something to say.'

'I was amused by Adela's comparison of ordinary business methods with the ones followed by American hoodlums.'

'Are you suggesting I'm a hoodlum?' said Michael. 'Say, that's going too far.'

'Sander, how could you?' Adela protested.

'I was asked for my opinion and I gave it.'

'I'm no hoodlum,' said Michael. 'Oh, yes, I grant you, Prohibition has stirred things up for people, but I just take advantage of the money that's flowing as fast as the prohibitionists pour whisky down the drains. Is that so wrong?'

'Of course it isn't,' cried Adela. 'Go on with what you were telling us, Michael.'

'I'm by way of being the boss's right-hand man. The pay is terrific. As fast as the Feds close down a club, we open six more. Speakeasies, they're called, and they're always filled with people, society guys and dolls who never agreed with Prohibition and don't care about the risk of being raided.'

'Being raided?' Adela was bemused yet fascinated by Michael. His face was animated, his gestures expansive, his eyes alight with enthusiasm.

'The Feds break down a door somewhere every night. No one minds about being arrested for drinking because they don't see Prohibition as a sensible law. In fact, more people drink now than ever before. That's human nature, I guess. In the

471

clubs we install alarms and stash the liquor in different places, in a different joint behind secret doors that can only be opened by electric switches, and we've always got other exits. I tell you, Adela, it's the business to be in. Long live Prohibition!'

Adela caught most of the gist of Michael's account, but asked, 'What are Feds?'

'A kind of police, but lots of them are on the payroll of the speakeasy bosses and the liquor merchants.'

'That's sounds rather dishonest,' she said.

'Is it so dishonest to break a stupid law that shouldn't have been passed in the first place? I aim to be a bootlegger – that's a liquor boss – in my own right one day.'

'Shouldn't you be there now, making sure that no one muscles in on your territory?' said Sander.

'Say, your old man really does know the ropes,' grinned Michael.

'As Adela said, we have our business battles, too, though we draw the line at violence.'

'Yeah, there is some violence, I guess, but we don't provoke it and it's mostly petty crooks who don't think straight who get hurt. It's easy to defend yourself. You can get a gun anywhere in the States.'

'Do you carry one?' Adela asked.

'Out there, sure, but not here.'

Millie suddenly erupted into the room. 'Adela, darling, there you are. People are asking for you.'

She jumped to her feet. 'Heavens, I was forgetting my guests.' Michael was on his feet instantly, looking admiringly at Millie who was extremely pretty in her dance frock of pink satin and chiffon, beaded with Ciro pearls. She returned his look with open interest.

'This is Michael Webster from America. Michael, Millie Norton.'

He held Millie's hand a little too long and she gave him a cool smile and drew back, deliberately putting up her left hand with its engagement and wedding rings to pat her hair. Michael glanced at them and grinned ruefully at her, then at Adela. 'Why are all the best gals spoken for?'

'Not all, surely?' said Sander drily. 'There are many women without husbands after the carnage of the war.'

'Yeah, it was terrible,' said Michael. 'I'm lucky that I never got involved.'

'Won't you join our guests at the party?' suggested Adela.

Sander said nothing but Michael, who was clearly impervious to his unwelcoming attitude, said, 'Sure, I'd like that a lot. Will you dance with me, Adela?'

'I suppose you know all the latest dances?'

'Sure do, though I prefer a slow number when I hold a beautiful woman in my arms.'

'The band is about due to play one,' said Millie. She glanced at Sander who had risen to his feet at her entrance. He said nothing.

As they all walked into the large drawing room the band, as if to order, went into a slow foxtrot and Adela slid into Michael's arms. He moved gracefully and together they circled the room. He bent his head to hers and whispered, 'No wonder Dad was so fond of you. I've never seen a lovelier woman.' All banter was gone from his tone.

Adela was shocked. 'Our relationship was that of father and daughter,' she protested.

'Sure it was,' agreed Michael. 'Still, he was a man and must have seen what a swell looker you are.'

Adela disliked the trend of the conversation. 'I'm sure you pay extravagant compliments to all the girls.'

'I do not! I'm pretty picky about the women I favour.'

'Have there been many?'

'Sure. Women like to have a man who's got plenty of dough. That's money to you.'

'Has no one loved you for yourself alone?' she asked, trying to keep the atmosphere light.

Michael's arms tightened around her. 'I don't think so,' he murmured. 'Maybe my luck will change.'

She looked up. There was no mistaking the expression in his eyes. He desired her.

'You're gorgeous. The loveliest woman I've met in years,' he murmured.

473

'And I'm married, remember?'

'We all make mistakes.'

Adela didn't reply. Whatever she said this smooth talker had an answer which carried her deeper into a conversation which shouldn't be taking place at all.

That night she lay beside Sander, listening to his even breathing. He had made love to her and Michael's image had floated into her mind. Afterwards Sander had stared down into her face. He seemed about to speak but changed his mind. Michael's name hadn't been mentioned since he said his good-byes at the end of the party, promising to accept the many invitations that were extended to him by other guests.

Lady Margaret met Adela at the station in a big red Austin. 'Welcome to London, Adela. Oh, but of course you know the city well, don't you? I'm surprised we haven't met before.'

'The war stopped our visits,' said Adela. 'Father said it wasn't patriotic to go gallivanting about.'

'He sounds a perfect pet. Lots of people tried to carry on as usual, though a good many town houses were closed all through the war. I went to parties, but I didn't enjoy them much. So many casualties. Half the chaps one grew up with gone or maimed.' She stopped speaking abruptly. 'Oh, hell! Millie told me about your fiancé. Damn my chatter. Sorry, Adela.'

'It's all right. I have Sander now.'

'Yes, he's such a darling man. I would like to get to know both of you better. You'll be receiving invitations when I have my own house.'

She applied the brakes and swerved as an old lady stepped off the path. 'Sorry about that! The old folks still don't understand motor cars, do they? Daddy hates me driving. He says it's too technical for a woman, and dangerous, but he still gave me this beautiful vehicle because I begged for it so hard. Do you drive? Does your father mind?'

'I do, and I don't think Father minds. I see little of him. I came up by train because it's less wearing and I can work while I'm travelling.'

'What a conscientious girl you are. I'm so looking forward to hearing your ideas for my house.'

Margaret pulled up in front of a tall terraced house in Upper Grosvenor Street. 'It's such a sweet place, isn't it? And much larger than you'd expect from seeing the outside, though you'll know that.' She unlocked the door. 'Isn't the decor absolutely ghastly! Terence bought it from an ancient lady who kept the Edwardian decorations. Imagine living with purple and green and red. They must have had stronger stomachs than I have. I find it most dreadfully oppressive.

'Make it light, Adela, like your own lovely house. Give me an overall impression of space and air. I feel closed in in London. And I want central heating, and a practical kitchen, and bathrooms and lavatories on all floors, including the attics. Mummy has always insisted on taking care of the servants and I quite agree with her. And I want electricity installed, too.'

'I'll need to call in contractors for that kind of work.'

'Call in anyone you like. If I have to live in London for part of the year, I intend to have everything as perfect as possible.'

Adela got busy with her tape measure. 'Don't you care for the season?'

'Up to a point. I prefer the country. Fortunately Terence feels the same way. He has a darling old house in Gloucestershire where we can hide sometimes. It was used as a hospital during the war and needs a good deal of refurbishment. I'm sure Terence will consult you when he knows how clever you are. However, we need a town house, too, where we can entertain. When will you be ready with your suggestions?'

'I'll call on you quite soon with patterns and ideas.'

Adela worked for two days in the empty echoing rooms, then visited Margaret in her father's house in Berkeley Square and expounded her proposals which her ladyship loved.

'For your boudoir,' said Adela, 'I have designed something entirely feminine which I hope you agree suits your personality.'

Margaret laughed. 'You hardly know me!'

'No, that's true, but an interior decorator must be able to sum up people quickly.'

Adela heard her own words with a certain amount of

amusement, but Margaret looked at the drawings and colour swatches and said, 'Oh, it's utterly lovely and so absolutely *me*. Adela, you're so *clever*. The colours are subtle. What do you call them?'

'Oyster, mushroom, ivory, with rose and linden green. For your boudoir, I thought magnolia with delicate Regency rosewood furniture and pale pink silk drapes and cushions.'

'Lovely! Enchanting! Do you manage it all yourself, buying the stuff and that kind of thing, or should I do something?'

'Only write the cheques at the end,' said Adela with a smile.

Lady Margaret laughed. 'Oh, Daddy will do that. He's giving us all the new decoration and the furniture for our wedding present. Isn't he a pet?'

'Indeed he is,' said Adela. Margaret had her life so neatly planned.

Adela was staying in a small hotel in Bloomsbury. She retired early each night to work on the new designs and draft instructions to her various workers. Margaret was much taken with the idea of small pieces of stained glass, and after a solitary dinner Adela was busy working out the quantities of materials which would be needed for the house when there was a light tap on the door. She was very tired and needed rest. She called impatiently, 'Come in.'

The door opened.

'Yes?' she said, without looking round.

There was no answer, but the door clicked shut. She whirled round to see Michael standing with his back to it, a broad smile on his face. He was carrying a paper bag.

She sprang to her feet. 'You! What are you doing here? How did you know where to find me?'

'It was easy to discover your address. A helpful girl called Esther gave it to me. I said I needed to contact you on an important matter of business.'

'What kind of business?'

'I came to see you.'

'So what business do you have with me?'

'Need you ask?'

Michael advanced and came close, closer than was necessary. She was nervous and angry.

'I'm busy,' she said, 'so you've had a wasted journey.'

'I hope not.' He produced a bottle of wine and two glasses, placed them carefully on the table covered with Adela's drawings, then put out his hands and rested them lightly on her shoulders. There was no constraint, but she felt imprisoned.

'Leave me alone,' she said, denying the attraction she felt.

'You don't mean that.' He bent his head and kissed her on the lips. For a brief instant she returned his kiss before she pushed him away.

'What in hell do you think you're playing at?' she demanded. 'If my husband knew—'

'You don't love him.'

'That's a disgraceful remark.'

'It's true though, isn't it?'

She felt her will being slowly submerged in his and was scared. 'Of course it isn't true, but even if it were, it would be no concern of yours.'

'Adela, I fell in love with you from the moment I saw you.'

'This is crazy! You must leave and take your wine with you. I'm busy.'

'You want me, don't you?'

'You're impertinent, and you're vain. I dare say you've had a good many easy conquests and think all women fall for your charms.'

'Don't you find me attractive, darling?'

'I find you bloody irritating at the moment. I have work to do. If you leave at once, I'll forget this ever happened.'

Michael took off his coat and hat and threw them into a chair. He opened the tall, green bottle and poured wine into two glasses. He handed her one. 'To us, Adela.'

When she didn't drink he smiled. 'I shall stay here until you drink my wine. You can't refuse a present and it's a vintage Mosel.'

'Then you promise to leave?'

He raised his right hand in the air. His dark eyes were mischievous. 'You bet!'

Adela drank. 'It's delicious,' she admitted. 'So refreshing.' She had eaten little and the wine went quickly to her head. 'Now you must go.'

'We have to finish the bottle.'

'You promised you'd leave if I drank.'

'I didn't say how much. We can't waste good wine.'

Adela held out her glass resignedly. The more she humoured him, the quicker he would leave. She knew he was dangerous to be near. In spite of her denials she was drawn to him. Michael poured more wine and seated himself on a low sofa.

'Sit down, Adela. You look rather tired.'

'I am.'

'You work too hard.'

She said nothing, but sipped the wine. Michael filled the glass again. 'Drink up.'

'If you think I'm going to share a whole bottle with you, you're very much mistaken. I've had quite enough. Now, go!'

Michael took the glass from her and put it carefully on the table. 'I want you, darling. It's the same for you, isn't it?'

'Don't be so silly!'

He reached out and caught her arms and pulled her gently towards him. For an instant she felt it would be pleasant to succumb, then she jerked her arms free and said angrily, 'If you refuse to leave, I shall summon assistance. Your behaviour is outrageous!'

Michael stood away from her. He looked mutinous, like an angry boy, and she was tempted to laugh.

He was quick, too quick to comprehend her moods. 'You think I'm funny!' His voice was harsh and grated on her nerves. It also frightened her a little. What kind of man was he? One moment he attracted her, the next he scared her. For a man as good looking as he was it was a dangerous mix, calculated to attract a woman prepared to take chances. Adela assured herself she was past that. She had taken too many in the past and now she had too much to lose.

'I don't think you are at all funny, Michael,' she said placatingly. 'I just wish you would understand that I must work if I'm to get back to Bristol for other appointments. My

478

business is still in its infancy and I can't afford to offend anyone.'

He smiled in a resigned way, then his lips turned down at the corners. 'Sorry, Adela. I think I've had too much to drink. I stopped off and had a couple of beers on my way over. It's such a temptation when there are so many open pubs.'

'I suppose it is.'

'Adela, you do like me, don't you?'

'Yes.'

'Even though your husband hates me.' Again there was an odd, significant timbre to his voice.

'Sander doesn't hate people,' she said. 'That's not his way.' She recalled, even as she spoke, Sander's unforgiving attitude to the aunt and uncle who had treated him so badly, yet he had been so wonderfully kind to Harry. How well did she really know him? 'Sander doesn't hate you,' she said.

'You don't sound at all sure. Is he jealous of me?'

She was genuinely surprised. 'Jealous? Of course not. He—' She stopped. She had been about to say that Sander didn't love her so there were no grounds for jealousy, but she wasn't any too sure. Sander liked to keep what he had won.

'He doesn't like the way I do business,' said Michael.

She smiled. 'If that was a basis for hating you, he'd have a very long hate list.'

'I guess so. I'll have to take your word for it.' He gave her a mock salute. 'I'll be seeing you.'

She watched him leave and flopped on to the bed, her heart racing. Michael had a devastating effect on her. If he had tried any harder she might have given way and that was a terrifying thought, but not as terrifying as the realisation that, for the first time in her life, she had felt basic, carnal desire, and it was for a man she could never possess.

Chapter Twenty-Five

Adela completed the arrangements for Lady Margaret's house and returned to Bristol. Michael had visited her again before she left and this time she had found it more difficult to make him go, not only because of his insistence but also because of her increasing wish to yield to him.

Sander met her at Temple Meads Station and greeted her warmly. 'I've missed you.'

'Have you?' Adela knew she sounded stilted, but she felt guilty. Sander looked searchingly at her and she managed a smile. 'Sorry, I'm awfully tired.'

'Did you go to many parties?'

'No, I was too busy. But Margaret invited me to dinner and I met several friends from the past.'

'Maybe the trip was too much for you. I think you'd better see the doctor again. Perhaps you're overdoing the work; you might need a tonic.'

Adela wanted to shout, 'To hell with the doctor and his tonics.' Then she felt another surge of guilt, knowing that her weariness was partly because she hadn't slept. She had lain awake for hours wondering what it would be like to make love to Michael. Sander tucked a rug about her in his solicitous way and she knew she was lucky to have him for a husband. Harry was already asleep, so she had to make do with leaning over his cot, looking forward to tomorrow when she could kiss and cuddle him.

That night she dreamt of Michael. She couldn't remember what the dream had been about, but she woke with a cry. Sander slept like a cat and was awake instantly. He pulled her into his arms. 'What is it? A bad dream?'

'Yes! Yes, a bad dream.'

'You're trembling. My poor girl.' He smoothed her hair back from her forehead. 'I missed you. Did you miss me?'

'Of course,' she said, guilt swamping her.

His hands began to roam over her body. Sander was hungry for love and she responded to him. In an odd way it was as if wanting Michael had loosened a barrier in her mind. Sander sensed her response and it excited him. He caressed her until he aroused her and brought her to a happy climax. He held her afterwards; Adela expected him to speak, but he said nothing. When he slept, she lay awake, torn by conflicting emotions. Michael was dishonourable, a cheat, but she was powerfully attracted to him. Why? If only he hadn't decided to come home!

In the morning, she went up to see Harry who had had his bath and was eating his breakfast. At least, observed Adela, Bill was coaxing him to take cereal and Harry was pretending to swallow, then spitting it out. They both looked round at her entrance, Bill with a dour nod, Harry with an air of mild interest. Her vision of holding her son close faded and, as always, regrets swamped Adela at the child's indifference to her. She advanced towards the pair and bent to kiss Harry on his corn-silk hair. He did not shrink away. For the first time he looked at her with the glimmer of a smile. Her joy was out of all proportion. She went on her way to work feeling quite light-hearted.

The staff were pleased to see her back. In Adela's office Esther kissed her. 'We've been doing marvellous business while you were away. Mrs Norton has sent lots of customers to us, and it seems that Mrs Cornell and Miss Wethered have been saying nice things about you, too.'

'Bobbie and Vita? Saying nice things about me? Didn't the sky fall in?'

Esther grinned. 'They're in a dilemma. If they give you praise, you think it's false; if they don't, they're admitting to having their houses done by someone not worth talking about.'

'Serves them right,' said Ida's voice.

Adela turned, delighted. 'Ida! You're here! Didn't your mother order you to stay at home.'

'She certainly did, but now I can pay a good neighbour to

keep an eye on her for a few hours a day. Our Michael's turned out well. Our Jack would have been proud of him.' Ida's eyes filled with tears and she hurried away.

'Thank heavens she did come back,' said Esther. 'She's teaching Mattie Hobbs to drape. That kid's got a real artistic streak in her. She's going to be useful and I think it might be a good idea to raise her wages. We don't want to lose her.'

'Is there any chance of that?'

Esther went red. 'I don't know. Perhaps.'

'Out with it! Who's been after her.'

'No one, Adela, but Mr Bennett—'

'What!'

'He had a look round the other day. He said he just wanted to check that everything was running smoothly while you were away. He was very impressed by Mattie's work and said something about her bettering herself.'

'Right. In that case give her half a crown more.' Sander's the limit, she thought. I really believe he'd steal Mattie as easily as he took Elsa. The memory still had the power to wound and shame her. She had seen Elsa a few times since her marriage, but stayed away from her as much as possible. 'How's Bertha settling in?' she asked.

'Pretty well. Her sewing is neat and she never needs supervision.'

There was a doubtful note in Esther's voice and Adela said, 'But—'

'But she's not happy. I think she misses the freedom of her former job. I think she misses your mother.'

Adela nodded. 'I daresay you're right.'

Back at home Adela faced Sander accusingly. 'Why did you go snooping around my showroom? Have you plans to tempt my staff away?'

'Snooping!' he said angrily. 'That's an ugly word. I went merely to see if everything was all right.'

'I neither asked nor needed you to go. My staff are carefully selected and perfectly capable of running my business. And just how do you think Mattie should better herself? By coming to your Castle Street shop, I suppose! You've got no scruples about filching other people's employees, have you? You've done it before and you'll do it again, given half a chance.'

'Oh my God, are we back to Elsa Maitland again? If people are not paid the rate for the job, they should look elsewhere.'

Adela's anger mounted. 'I'll issue a directive. Anyone who tells me they've had an offer of higher wages from Mr Bennett should let me know so that I can match it.'

Sander looked furious but said evenly, 'You must please yourself about that. You'll lay yourself open to exploitation, but that's your affair.'

The quarrel sent her mind winging to Michael. She was disgusted with herself, but her body seemed to be out of her control. She thought of Sander's love-making and her response, and her confusion grew greater. She felt she must have time to herself, time to think and to subdue her flesh. She had her things moved into the guest room.

Sander was late home that night. When he arrived she was already in bed. He came bursting in, angry, as she had known he would be, as he had a right to be. 'What in hell's this about?'

'I get extremely tired, Sander. I thought, just for the present, I'd sleep alone.'

'I told you to see the doctor. You do too damned much and have too many worries.'

Was he truly concerned, or just frustrated?

He leaned over her. 'If you need to be on your own, Adela, I won't argue, but you should have told me.' He straightened, but his eyes stayed on her face. 'Last night, I thought you felt something more for me.'

He waited and she said, 'I am very fond of you, Sander, you must know that. You've been so good to me.'

'Fond of me! Goddamn it, Adela, I want more than that! I want—' He stopped. 'Don't stay away from me for too long. We must each keep our side of our bargain.'

A few days later Michael turned up in the showroom. She saw him first from behind as he was chatting to Esther. She stood still, admiration flooding her as she drank in the details of his appearance: the way his dark hair curled into the nape of his

484

neck, his strong back, his natural elegance. He turned and saw her and his smile transformed his face. He was handsome in a way that Sander could never be. With an effort she greeted him politely in front of the staff and took him to her office.

'You shouldn't have come here. What do you want?' she asked.

He sat down. Her office was small and their knees almost touched. 'You're very unwelcoming,' he said.

'What else do you expect me to be? If for no other reason than that my staff have constant access to me here. As you may have noticed, I am surrounded by glass panels.'

'No need for sarcasm,' said Michael in hurt tones. 'Have you missed me?'

'Of course not. Why should I?'

'You know why.'

'Why have you come?' She gestured to a heap of drawings. 'As you can see, I have little time to spare.'

'You know why. I love you, Adela.'

'No! No, you don't. People don't fall in love so quickly. And even if you are, it's no use. I'm a happily married woman.'

'That's not the tale I hear.'

'What?'

'I hear that you married Bennett because he's rich.'

'Who says such a thing?'

'Gran.'

'She would.'

'I questioned her, and when she told me about Harry, and how ill you were, I understood. Poor girl. You married Bennett because you were desperate.'

'Your gran's tongue should have been cropped at birth.'

'Now is that a nice thing to say about a sweet old lady?' Michael was laughing, his eyes teasing, and she wanted to throw aside her work and say she'd go anywhere with him. 'Why not leave all this and come and have a coffee with me?' he coaxed. 'I'll not keep you long. We can talk. There's no harm in that, is there?'

'There is if you keep saying foolish things to me.'

'Not one foolish thing shall pass my lips.'

485

Adela was tempted. She looked again at the pile of work which awaited her. Her hesitation sapped her willpower and she stood up. 'Just a little while,' she said. She told Freddy and Esther she wouldn't be long.

Michael had a car waiting and drove her to a hotel on the outskirts of town. The receptionist gave him a key and Adela drew back. Then, realising she would provoke curiosity by protesting, she allowed Michael to lead her up the stairs. On a half landing she stopped and hissed furiously, 'Where are we going? A coffee and a talk was what you said.'

'And that's what I'm offering you. Oh, the key. Yes, I'm taking you to my room. It's pleasant there and we can talk in peace.'

Adela hesitated. She knew she should turn back and walk away from this man, but she couldn't.

The room was large and well-appointed and she sank into an armchair. A tray of coffee was brought to the door and Michael poured them a cup each and sat opposite her.

'Now isn't this cosy?' he said. 'Much better than a noisy café, and secluded, too. No one will see you here and there won't be any gossip.'

'There had better not be. As far as I'm concerned, you're Jack's son and therefore a friend.'

Michael laughed softly. 'You're being deliberately naive. Here we are, alone together, and you're young and beautiful and I'm young and not bad looking.'

Adela raised an eyebrow.

'I never said I was modest.' He grinned. His attitude disarmed her and she felt more comfortable. When she had finished her coffee he took her cup and, without warning, seized her hands and pulled her to her feet. Then his mouth was on hers, his lips searching, demanding, and her resistance flared briefly and crumbled.

'I want you,' he murmured against her mouth. 'Darling, sweet Adela, I adore you. And you want me, don't you?'

'I can't! I mustn't!'

'No, but you do.'

'Yes, I do. God help me, I do.'

His hands began to roam over her body. 'No,' she gasped. 'Let me go. Please!'

'You don't want to leave me. You knew when we came here what I wanted.'

'No!'

'Liar,' he said softly. 'You knew. You can't help yourself, can you?'

He drew her towards the bed. She trembled as he undressed her, touching his lips to each part of her body until she lay naked before him.

'Now for me,' he said, laughing down at her.

She couldn't take her eyes off him as he removed his clothes. Then they lay together, hands and lips exploring one another. He was muscular, perfectly proportioned, his body smooth – so unlike Sander's. Sander! In the midst of her fever he floated into her consciousness and the dishonour of what she was doing swept over her. Then Michael was upon her and she forgot everything as she gave herself wholly to him.

He loved her. And she loved him. It was as simple as that. But it wasn't simple at all. As the memory of her husband and son came flooding back, she was consumed with the horror of what had happened. Michael pulled the covers over them and lit two cigarettes, handing her one. She smoked silently for a while, trying to gather her thoughts, striving for calm.

Then Michael said softly, 'Adela, my love, I'm so thankful I came home. Not to have known you would have been a sin.'

'Would it?'

He leaned on an elbow, looking down at her. 'Aren't you glad you met me?'

'Glad! How can I be? I've dishonoured my husband, my child, myself. How can I be glad?'

'Darling, we've made love, that's all. We haven't done anyone any harm, have we?'

'Haven't we? Oh, God, Michael, I wish we'd never met. I wish I had been stronger. This is all wrong.'

'Wrong? Nonsense! You know it's about as right as love can be.'

'What are we going to do?' she cried.

'Do about what? Stop getting so agitated, my love.'

'I mean, what am I going to do about Sander, about Harry?'

Michael seemed amused. 'For heaven's sake, Adela, there's no rush, is there? We've only just met.'

'No one would think so to see us now.'

'That's true.' Michael lit another cigarette from his stub. He laughed. 'Adela, I adore you. You're blazing with passion one minute, and the next you're wondering about practicalities.'

'I have to. How can I go back to Sander after this?'

Michael sat up straight. 'That's crazy talk! Of course you'll go back.'

'Don't you mind?'

'Why should I? I knew you were married when I brought you here.'

'You sound as if that isn't important. How can you be so callous? I can't. I must tell Sander.'

'No!' Michael yelled, making her jump. 'No, don't do that, sweetheart,' he said in quieter tones. 'He's already got it in for me.'

'Why do you persist in thinking that?'

'He's been making inquiries about me. I got a cable this morning from a pal in New York. Your husband is snooping into my business.'

'I can't believe it. Why should he? And what does it matter, anyway? What have you to hide? You said that selling illicit drink was tolerated, that the police turn a blind eye.'

'Not all of them, and in a business like mine you can't help treading on a few toes. If Sander came to the States and asked questions, he'd very soon be dealt with. He can get away with it while he stays here, but he could make things awkward for me back home, very awkward indeed.'

Michael's voice had become granite hard, his whole body tense. He jumped out of bed and began throwing on his clothes. 'Come on, Adela, I've got things to do, letters to write. And you'll be missed if you stay away too long. People will wonder. Sander will wonder.'

Adela dressed quickly. She was tormented by the idea that they would never again enjoy time alone together. Michael, who appeared to have no qualms or doubts, drove her back to a street near the showroom and bade her a brief goodbye before he roared off in his car.

The weeks leading up to Christmas were busy, as always. It was surprising how many women decided at the last minute that they wanted new curtains or chair covers.

'It's the thought of all those mothers-in-law seeing the patch where the kids were sick or the dog misbehaved,' said Sander.

She laughed, but the atmosphere between them was uneasy. Adela veered between self-disgust and gratitude that he left her to sleep in peace. He was too kind to her, she realised in a moment of insight.

She saw Michael quite often at social functions, where he was popular, but never alone. Only the mischief in his eyes when he caught her glance betrayed his inner knowledge of her. Adela was frantic with the turbulence of her feelings. She ached to be with him and couldn't understand why he didn't suggest a meeting.

The New Year began with rain and snow, but the Bennetts' big house on Durdham Down, with its central heating and roaring fires, was always warm. Adela's position, both in business and society, meant that she had to accept and issue many invitations. The house had been filled with guests throughout the festive season, ending with a dance on New Year's Eve. She had smiled and talked and played the gracious hostess to Bobbie and Gerard, Vita and her fiancé, Giles and Desmond and their wives, to Millie, expecting her first child, and her husband; to anyone, in fact, who had the remotest claim on her. Everyone except the one guest she most wanted. Michael had elected to spend Christmas and New Year with his family.

She had managed a few quiet words with him a couple of days before Christmas in Vita's house. Because of her business she seldom turned down invitations, even from people she disliked as much as Vita, but she had found the frenetic atmosphere hard to bear and had moved from the drawing room into the conservatory. Michael had followed her. She was tongue-tied for a moment then said haltingly, 'I miss you.'

'No more than I miss you,' he assured her. 'But it's better if we don't meet for a while.'

'It's better if we don't meet at all,' she had said, disappointment making her snappy.

Michael had shrugged. 'We both know you don't mean that. We'll find a way to be together again. At the moment, we're both busy.'

'I have to work, but surely you're at leisure?'

'Not at all. I was given commissions by my employer.'

'I see.' Adela struggled with her conscience before she said, 'I can leave the showroom any time and say I'm visiting customers.'

'I'll remember that. Adela, you're so lovely. I don't know how I keep my hands off you.'

She had been reassured by his passionate tones, then Vita had come into the conservatory. 'Darling,' she had cried to Michael, 'do come out. People want to hear about your exploits in America. Who's that with you?' She had peered into the semi-darkness. 'Adela, where's that husband of yours? I sent the invitation to both of you, of course. Sander's such a refreshing change from most men one meets.' She had successfully drawn them back into the throng. Michael entertained the guests with stories of his life in America, but he said nothing about his business activities. If anyone asked a question about them, he turned it smilingly aside.

Esther came to one party at her employer's house, but spent the rest of the time with her parents. She visited Bert regularly and returned betraying such a depth of sorrow that Adela found it difficult to look into her face. Freddy Stanton, who now managed the workrooms, accompanied her to the party. He didn't try to hide the fact that he was attracted to her but she, loyal to Bert, kept him at an emotional distance.

People were rejoicing at the betrothal of the Lady Elizabeth Bowes-Lyon to the Duke of York. 'A really nice young lady,' pronounced Mrs Monkton, 'just right for a son of the King, though of course he'll never be as popular as our lovely Prince of Wales.'

Skirts had stuck at calf-length, except for evening wear

which revealed much of the legs and body and scandalised many. Clergymen ranted from pulpits and journalists ranted in newsprint about women's bare backs. The *Sunday Express* blamed the lack of men. 'The strange herd-soul of woman', it thundered, 'has taken fright at the sentence of celibacy which has been passed upon her.' It spoke of 'feminine shamelessness and the hysterical eccentricity of feminine attire. Bare backs should be branded in red.' But fashion was impervious to criticism. Women continued to compress their figures into the boyish style now decreed, though materials remained utterly feminine, and from tube-shaped bodies fell waterfalls of silk and satin, georgette and chiffon, silver lamé and silk fringes, while beads were used extravagantly and rhinestones glittered everywhere. Adela's former interest in fashion returned, doubled now that she thought of Michael's eyes on her.

Sander made her a good dress allowance, but since her involvement with Michael she felt reluctant to use more than she must. She bought herself two Doucet evening dresses, one in grey, the other in black, and invested in a Molyneux suit and a Reboux hat in the new helmet style, which was plain enough to be decorated by Sarah for different occasions. Her purchases were completed by a sailor jacket from Chanel, one of her original, amusing creations. Glass beads, fake pearls, rhinestone bracelets, were all a woman needed nowadays to brighten up her basic wardrobe, and these could be had cheaply. Even Woolworths had something to offer. Bertha made day dresses for her from fashion designs. She was delighted to have something more interesting to do than run up curtains and upholstery.

'You look prettier than ever, Miss Adela,' she said. 'You're happy, aren't you?'

'Of course,' Adela assured her, stifling the truth. She had tried and failed to get Bertha to use her first name, like her other senior employees. 'I wish you were happy, too.'

'I like working for you. You're a very good employer.'

'But you'd prefer to be back at your proper job?'

'I can't help it. I miss your mother and the life I've always had.'

'I wish she'd take you back, though I don't want to see you go, you're such a good reliable worker. Have you approached Mother at all?'

Bertha said sadly, 'I tried. She refused even to see me.'

'How was my father when you were last there? Did you get any news?'

'Mr Evans told me he wasn't too well, Miss Adela. He's over-working. Mrs Danby gets quite cross with him at times, but he says he has to go on to beat men like—' Bertha stopped, reddening.

'Men like Mr Bennett?'

'His name came up. Now that Mr Bennett stocks dress materials in the Castle Street shop, he's in even more direct competition with your father. Women are taking to home sewing, especially those who can afford machines, and Mr Bennett is now stocking those, too, and letting them go on easy terms.'

Adela tackled Sander that night. 'Why are you pushing my father so hard? I'm the one who should be punished.'

He looked searchingly at her. 'Oh? And why should I punish you?'

'I'm the one who jilted you.'

'Ah, yes.'

Adela was seated in the breakfast room which she used increasingly as a home base, papers spread on the table in front of her. Sander leaned against the mantelpiece. Leisurely, he lit a cigarette. He stared at her, his eyes hard, uncompromising. 'Your father – your parents, in fact – treated you abominably. Don't you want to punish them a little?'

'Not if it damages my father's health.'

'He knows his heart isn't strong. It isn't my fault if he insists on working. He should retire. He's made his pile.'

'How do you know? Perhaps he's in more need of money than you think.'

'Nonsense!' Sander blew out a couple of smoke rings. 'Did you see that, Adela? That takes real smoking skill.'

'To hell with your stupid games! What makes you think you know so much about Father?'

'Your dear old dad was one of those who hoarded sovereigns

492

during the war and helped to cause a severe gold shortage. That's why, if you recall, the government had to issue paper money. He's still got plenty of gold salted away.'

Adela opened her mouth and closed it again, recalling snippets of conversation between her parents.

She spoke to Blanche about it. 'Hell, yes,' said Blanche, 'Father's still got plenty. He could retire tomorrow.'

'Why doesn't he, if he's unwell?'

'Because he's greedy. Don't look so shocked, sister dear. Father's always been greedy.'

'He paid our bills without grumbling.'

'Why shouldn't he? It was his duty. He abandoned you when you needed him most.'

'What happened wasn't his fault,' said Adela. 'He tried to help me. He was shocked and worried.'

'Worried that you'd be found out! I think there was a time when he'd have rather seen you dead than expecting Ralph's baby.'

'Blanche!'

'Face facts, Adela. For all your success you're still blind to some things. Why should you defend Father? He won't even see you.' Adela was silenced and Blanche asked, 'What do you think of Michael Webster?'

'What?'

'Jack's son. How does he strike you?'

'I meet him here and there. He's getting quite fashionable.'

'A "slick young guy," I think he'd call himself,' said Blanche drily. 'And a wow with the ladies.'

Adela couldn't resist asking, 'What ladies?'

'Any ladies. He likes the company of women. He's quite open about it.'

'That's not a fault, is it?'

'No, but it's very un-English. The men gossip.'

'How do you know what men gossip about?'

'Their wives tell me.'

'How's Georgie?' asked Adela pointedly.

'She's blooming. Fatter than ever, and I adore every inch.'

Adela smiled reluctantly. 'Some people talk about you. You

haven't exactly got a conventional relationship, have you?'

'To hell with public opinion. I'm happier than I've ever been.'

It was impossible to confound Blanche, but her sister's words about Michael kept returning to torment Adela.

Her work took her out more and more in the evenings as well as during the days. Freddy usually accompanied her, taking the measurements, leaving Adela free to discuss colours, patterns and shapes. She was still enamoured by the bright, bold designs and colours of fabrics by Dufy and incorporated them into her austerely beautiful Rennie Mackintosh rooms. London hostesses engaged her services more often and she went gladly.

On an overnight visit, Michael turned up at her hotel. In spite of her longing for him she had tried to assure herself a hundred times that she would be strong enough to resist him, but his insistence, and her desire, wore her down and they made love with even greater passion.

Adela lay back on the pillows after a climax which left them both drained. 'I love you, Michael. I wish I could be with you all the time.'

'I know, darling, but it just isn't possible. You're stuck with so many commitments.'

'I could arrange things so that we'd never need to part again. If that's what you want.'

'Do you?'

'I love you,' she said helplessly.

'You'd be giving up a hell of a lot.'

'I know. It wouldn't matter.'

'What about your workforce? They depend on you.'

'Sander would take them on. I know he would.'

'Sander?' Michael was startled. 'He'd never make it that easy for us!'

'I don't see why not. He doesn't love me.'

'Doesn't he? Why did he marry you, then?'

'I don't really know.'

'He loves you.'

Adela shook her head. 'No, you're mistaken.'

'I think not. I've seen him watching you.'

'I think he may be jealous, but not because he cares for me – because he see me as another of his possessions.'

Michael lit a cigarette. 'You haven't given any hint of our, er, friendship, have you?'

'Of course not!'

'Good,' he said forcefully. 'Sander's a dangerous man. If he got wind of what we're up to, it might prove very awkward.'

'Awkward!'

'For both of us.'

'You've said things like that before. Your business in America – is it as innocent as you claim?'

Michael said coolly, 'Do you take me for a liar?'

'No, but you sound scared of Sander. What can he do?'

'He could turn you against me.'

Adela almost laughed. 'Is that what's worrying you?' She felt dizzy with relief. 'No one could do that, darling. No one.'

He laughed and pulled her close.

Afterwards, unable to relinquish her dream, like a dog worrying at a bone, Adela said, 'Darling, you do know we should be together for good, don't you? Our love-making proves that.'

'That's not all there is to life. In the States I work hard.' He paused. 'This is a vacation. I'll be going back some day.'

'When?'

'When my boss calls me. I'm not needed just now.'

'It must be an odd kind of business when the owner's right-hand man can take such a long holiday.'

'You wouldn't understand, honey. It's a man's world.'

'Surely the others in your firm have sweethearts and wives?'

'Of course they do.'

'So there's no barrier to my going back with you?'

'Adela, be reasonable. You haven't thought this thing through. There's Grandmother Sutton, for instance. You owe her.'

'But you've said you're rich. You could pay her back for me. If our positions were reversed, I'd do it for you.'

'Hold on a minute! I said I had plenty of dough, but a lot's tied up in the States. I might not be able to get my hands on that kind of ready money for a long time.'

'Grandmother would wait, I know she would. She wants me to be happy.'

'What about Harry?'

Adela fell silent. She smoked for a few moments. 'Harry? He doesn't care about me.'

Michael sounded alarmed. 'But you want him! You're his mother.'

Adela kissed Michael's smooth bare shoulder. 'I'm glad you're a family man. Harry will adore you. You must get to know him.'

'Me? A family man?'

'Why, yes, you spent Christmas with your family, didn't you?'

'Oh, that.'

'Yes, that.'

Michael laughed. 'And just what reason could you give Sander for allowing me access to your nursery? No, Adela, leave things as they are at present. Our day will come.'

She returned to Bristol feeling as if she'd been turned inside out. The long hours of work, the obligatory evening engagements, the vigorous love-making, exhausted her.

Sander frowned when he saw her. 'You're taking on too much. Perhaps you should cut out the London jobs.'

'Are you crazy? That's where the biggest money is.'

'What use is money if you ruin your health?'

'None, as my father will unfortunately realise in time.'

'What's that got to do with this conversation?'

'You know quite well what I mean! You're his chief rival.'

'If you look at it another way, he's *my* chief rival.'

'But surely you make enough money without constantly trying to score off my father?'

'For God's sake, Adela, he could retire! It's not my fault if he chooses not to, and while he's on the scene I shall continue to compete. I've not got the kind of money he has.'

'You don't like him, do you?'

'No!'

Adela hadn't expected the bald agreement. 'But why? He was prepared to accept you into the family.'

Sander's face darkened. 'That's an episode I'd rather forget.'

'I'm sorry.'

'Are you? I sometimes wonder if you give a damn about me or what I think.'

'Sander, of course I do.' But Adela knew she sounded unconvincing.

Sander stared at her for a long moment and she had difficulty withstanding his searching eyes with any degree of composure. 'Your father and his kind are still living in the past. I'm successful now, the old society has crumbled. There's a different spirit abroad these days. Money is the key to the new society.'

'Not to all of it.'

'No, there are a few fuddy-duddys like your parents who hold out, but nobody really cares about them.'

'You're being horrible.'

Sander said smoothly, 'We were discussing your London work. I suggested that you should confine your business to Bristol. There's plenty of work here. For some, that is. We don't count the unfortunate unemployed, of course.'

'How sarcastic you are! I thought you cared about the unemployed.'

'I do, which is why I and Blanche and Georgie, and others like us, are using our spare time to try to help them. We don't like to see desperate men, and hungry women and children.'

'Neither do I!' cried Adela. 'I always try to employ someone who really needs a job.'

Sander sighed then said gently, 'Yes, I know you do, and you could join us in the greater work if you stayed in Bristol all the time.'

Adela resented the way he had manipulated the conversation. 'I shall do no such thing,' she snapped. 'London is the place to build my business. There's more than one society woman short of money who's taking up interior decorating. It's become the done thing since the war. I must have my own income. Sander, I do wish you'd leave me alone.'

'Goddamn it, I have left you alone! I've pandered to your whims, but I've some rights over you.'

'Rights! How dare you?'

'Must you yell like a fishwife? Do you want the servants to hear?'

'Hark at *you*, teaching *me* how to behave,' cried Adela.

His face darkened. 'I may not have been reared in high society, but I know how to be kind. That's something you seem to have forgotten.'

Adela turned and marched upstairs to her bedroom. She hadn't realised that Sander was close behind her until she tried to shut her door and he stuck his foot in it. 'This is one night I won't sleep alone.' He pushed her through and kicked the door shut behind them.

Adela said coldly, 'I can't stop you forcing yourself on me.'

'That's something I shall never do. I want to make love to you. You're my wife and I think I've given you enough time alone.'

'No, Sander,' she said stubbornly.

'What the hell's up with you? I know you enjoy sex. How can you keep me away from you for so long?'

'I'm sorry,' she said as mildly as she could, 'I know I'm being unreasonable. It's just that I get so weary. Don't be angry. I must keep my business going successfully. So many people depend on me.'

'They don't have to. I could give you all the money you want.'

'No! Oh, you don't understand, do you? I want always to be my own boss. I must be in a position where no one can dictate to me, ever again!'

'You're obsessed.'

'Yes, I am. I'll never forget what happened to me. I was humiliated, exploited, deprived, and so was Harry. It was degrading.'

'At least it's given you an insight into the lives of the poor.'

'Yes, and that's why I intend to continue to be independent. My own woman.'

'All right, you shall have an area of privacy. Have I ever dictated to you? Have I been unkind?'

'No, never.' Adela fell silent as the extent of her dishonesty struck her.

Sander put his arms round her. 'Don't look so sad. It'll all work out in the end.'

'I hope so, Sander,' she cried. 'I do hope so.'

She submitted to his love-making and his skill gave her pleasure which shamed her. This was crazy. She felt guilty now whichever man she made love to. Tears rained down her face and Sander held her in his arms and kissed her eyelids gently. 'Adela,' he murmured, 'don't be sad. Don't cry. Let me take care of you. Let me shoulder your burdens.'

She turned away without speaking and, after a moment, he let her go and she heard him leave her room.

Ida came to Adela's office looking a little amused, a little scandalised. 'There's a woman to see you,' she said. 'It's a Mrs Barton.'

'Mrs Barton? I know the name. Wasn't it an Andy Barton who was sent to reform school because he took something from Fred Withycombe's barrow? Is she his mother?'

'Yes, that's the one.'

'Do you know what she wants?'

Ida laughed, covering her mouth with her hand. 'She's got a favour to ask you. Oh dear, I don't think you'll grant it.'

'You'd better bring her up,' said Adela drily.

Mrs Barton was tall and thin with grey hair twisted in a knot on top of her head. Her face was lined, her eyes tired, yet she had an air of triumph.

'Please sit down,' said Adela. She called to Janet, the newest of the young apprentices, to bring tea and biscuits.

Mrs Barton said, 'You've come a long way from the barrows, Mrs Bennett. You'm a clever girl. A very clever girl.'

'Thank you, Mrs Barton,' said Adela kindly. 'May I help you in some way?'

'I hope so. It's about my Andy. He's home from the reform school.'

'I'm so glad! I was disgusted when Mr Withycombe had him arrested for so small an offence, especially when you—' She stopped.

'Especially when I was a poverty-stricken widow with too many young 'uns,' finished Mrs Barton.

The door opened and Janet brought in a tray laid with good china. Adela had ordered a pretty set which was used by the whole staff. She poured a cup of tea and handed it to Mrs Barton, who accepted a plate and helped herself to a biscuit.

She exclaimed with pleasure, 'A Jacob's Marie! One of my favourites. I d'like their cream crackers, too. Of course, with eight kids to rear on my own, I never got the money to buy biscuits, but my kids don't go short if I can help it. I d'make them nice things when I can. It takes a bit o' doin', I can tell you. One day, when they've all left home, I'm never goin' to make a biscuit or a cake again. I'll have all boughten stuff, an' I'll sit by the fire with a pot of tea an' just eat an' read a story out of a magazine. I shan't know meself.'

Adela waited sympathetically for Mrs Barton to finish. 'Sorry, Mrs Bennett, I d'ramble on at times, I know. It d'come of hardly ever havin' a grownup to speak to. I d'go out scrubbin' and the ladies are too posh to notice the likes of me. The reason I come was because I wondered if you'd give our Andy a job? He's a good boy. He never stole a thing before in his life, but his sister was ill and she fancied a bit of fruit. That Fred Withycombe needn't have told on him. He's rich with his underhand ways. But I've done him good an' proper.'

'What?'

'I knew he was receivin' stolen goods an' I bided my time. There's plenty got a grudge against Fred Withycombe an' I soon found out that he'd got a load of silver from a job done over Bath way. Anyway, I got Andy to use a telephone and get on to the police. Andy can sound quite posh when he likes, like a regular nob, an' he didn't let on who he was an' the police caught Fred with the stuff an' now he's up for trial an' he'll go to prison! That did ought to please you, Mrs Bennett, after the way he tried to trip you up, an' there's plenty who thinks that Jack needn't have fallen. Even if Fred Withycombe didn't actually shove him, he could have stopped to help him, but he didn't. He's a wicked man an' deserves to suffer.'

Adela was speechless for a moment. 'I can't say I'm sorry he's going to be punished, Mrs Barton. He certainly deserves retribution.'

'What?'

'He deserves to be punished,' said Adela. 'Mrs Barton, I'm not sure what position Andy could fill here. We employ women except for Mr Stanton.'

'Andy'll do anythin', Mrs Bennett. See, although folk round our way d'know he's really a good boy he can't get employers to believe him, an' with there bein' so much unemployment he can't get a job. He's my eldest an' I d'need his wages.'

Adela looked at Mrs Barton's worn face. Andy was now fifteen, Mrs Barton's first born. Probably the woman before her was not yet forty. She looked a good deal older.

'Has Andy ever shown an artistic streak?' she asked.

Mrs Barton looked doubtful. 'I don't know. He's never had much chance. Half the time he was away from school lookin' after one or other of the kids, or tryin' to earn a bob or two.'

'All right. Send him along and I'll have a talk with him.'

Mrs Barton rose regretfully. 'You've been a pleasure to visit, Mrs Bennett. Folks round our way d'respect you. Young Mattie Hobbs is learnin' to speak real nice an' everyone knows you pay for her talkin' lessons, an' that she loves workin' for you.'

After Mrs Barton had left Adela sat still, forgetting her work. Andy would be another responsibility. How could she walk out on them all? But she wanted Michael. How she wanted Michael!

Esther was subdued; the enthusiastic sparkle with which she had begun to work for Adela, had faded. Adela, worried, asked her gently, 'Are you ill?'

'No, thank you. I'm well enough.'

'Is it Bert? Is he worse?'

'It's hard to tell. He's a lot quieter these days. He prefers his own company and sits for hours listening to music. Why all the questions?'

'You don't seem yourself. We've been friends for quite a while and I care about you.'

Esther smiled faintly. 'That's good of you.'

Adela waited, but Esther remained silent.

'You're very pretty. I'm sure you could find someone to dispel your loneliness.'

Esther turned her face away. 'Yes, I suppose I could.'

'Sorry, it isn't any of my business.'

'I'm still married.'

'I know, but—'

'I still love Bert.' Esther paused. 'At least, I love the man he was.' She turned to Adela, her eyes troubled. 'What's happened to my husband? Is he in that cold stranger somewhere? He doesn't really know me now. How can I go on loving an empty shell?' Her pale face reddened. 'That sounds awful. My poor Bert.'

'We all need love. Why should you be denied it?'

Again Esther was silent, then she said, 'You're right, Adela. I'm lonely. I want someone close to me. I want a proper father for my child.'

'Freddy's a good man. He likes you a lot.'

'Freddy?' Esther looked startled. 'Oh, yes, Freddy.' She got up. 'Thanks for your concern, Adela. I'd best get back to work. The consignment of material you designed – the abstract classicism, as you called it – has arrived. I think you mentioned you were inspired by the artist Mondrian.'

'You sound rather doubtful.'

'It's startling. All those cubes and squares in strong colours. It might do for London but Bristol folk are a bit more reserved.'

'We can try. If it isn't popular I'll use it in London. Is the material well made?'

'Perfect. You chose your factory well. The coffee services have come in, too, the yellow Worcester with the black geometric designs. We already have a customer for them. Mrs Sybil Somers has decided to go ultra-modern. I wouldn't be at all surprised if she was after you soon for a visit.'

'Good for Sybil. I wonder if Giles approves.'

'I don't think so. He came with her to buy material the other day and they almost had a public quarrel, but she was adamant. She said she was paying for the stuff. He was furious.'

'He's a priggish fuddy-duddy,' said Adela.

'And another friend of yours is thinking of having her entire house remodelled – Mrs Mildred Smithers. She's a sweet woman. Mum says she remembers her husband working the barrows. The Smitherses made their big money profiteering.'

'Surely you don't approve of that?'

Esther shrugged. 'It all seems unimportant now. I don't suppose our gallant leaders lost money during the war, so why shouldn't a working-class lad make some?'

After Esther had gone Adela began an examination of the books. Freddy was conscientious, but she liked to have a firm idea of where her money was being spent and made. Her mind kept drifting and she pushed the work aside. Her affair with Michael was static. He had said nothing about returning to the States, for which she was grateful; but he had also said nothing to clarify his plans for their future together. She went down to the showroom, hoping to lose her discontent in creative work, but here again she was thwarted. Ida was so brilliant at display and Mattie was learning so fast that they had no need of her. Adela wandered around, looking at the beautiful silks and satins and brocades, the heavier weaves and twills, the new jagged patterns, the colours ranging from deep crimson and royal purple to the delicate, airspun shades of Rennie Mackintosh whose work Adela so loved. There was a collection of stands displaying older designs in chintz which conventional women preferred, and the fruit and flowers and sinuous leaves of a previous generation were there for them too. There was even a revolving stand which Freddy had made over which flowed a river of bright textiles.

Everything was as clean and shining as the charwomen could make it and large vases of flowers and greenery stood wherever there was a convenient surface. Workmen had even discovered an old fireplace hidden behind the lath and plaster and a cheerful fire was now used as the centrepiece of a mock-up room.

The sales staff were efficient. They didn't need her; any good boss would do as well. Harry was content with Bill. Sander wanted her, but he didn't love her. Her parents were indifferent to her. Jack's family, except for Annie and Ida, weren't interested in her, and Annie had never been close. Florrie, much to her annoyance and Adela's relief, had got pregnant and had left Adela's employ. Esther? She had retreated into some secret place of her own where Adela wasn't welcome.

She stood watching the activity in the showroom for a while, nodding and smiling to customers she knew. Every head turned at the sound of a crash, followed by a cry of anger. Adela had installed a black leather and chrome table and chairs near a modern gas fire. Coffee was served there, and Mattie had been carrying a cup to a woman in a grey suit with chinchilla trimming which had clearly originated in Paris. Her grey hat looked almost casually slouch, but into it had gone the experience of some exclusive milliner. Mattie had dropped the cup of coffee and some had splashed over the woman's grey silk stockings and expensive pointed shoes.

She sprang up. 'My God, you stupid girl! You've ruined my shoes.'

Adela hurried forward. 'I'm so sorry—' She paused, inquiringly.

'Lady Kingston,' supplied the woman. She grabbed the cloth which Mattie had run to fetch and dabbed at her damp feet. 'I doubt I'll ever be able to wear these shoes again! I'm here on a short visit to a relative who advised me to come here. My main residence is in London, of course, but I am having a house built in Somerset. I believe you know my relative, Miss Wethered.'

'Yes, indeed.'

'Yes, well, she burbled on about how you try to marry architecture with interior design. I thought I'd come and have a look. But I shall go elsewhere. Inefficiency in one department says little that is good about the others.'

Adela said, 'Do please purchase another pair of shoes and send the account to me.'

'I most certainly intend to do so, though I may have difficulty in finding a pair to suit me as well. If necessary I shall spend a larger sum.' She got up, tossed the cloth to the floor, and stalked out.

Mattie burst into tears and Adela grabbed her and hurried her into the kitchen. 'Control yourself.'

'I c . . . can't! I'm s . . . sorry, Mrs Bennett. I've lost you a customer.'

'She would probably have been hellish to work with,' said Adela. 'I can't stand women who are beastly to their inferiors.' She stopped. Inferiors! If Sander heard her he'd give her a piece of his mind. So would Blanche.

Mattie had no such notions. 'Oh, you're so good. Aren't you going to sack me?'

Adela remembered the Hobbs house, the constant efforts of Mrs Hobbs to rear her family, and she forgot her own problems and handed Mattie a handkerchief. 'Dry your eyes. I'm sure it won't happen again.'

Later Ida came to her in the office. 'I'm sorry about Mattie's accident, Adela. Somethin's botherin' that girl. She's young, but I think it might be boy trouble. Girls from poor homes mature fast.'

'By trouble, you don't mean—'

'A baby? No, I don't think that, but someone's makin' her miserable. I'll see if I can find out more.'

'Esther isn't happy, either.'

Ida shook her head. 'I've heard a rumour that she's met someone – a man, of course. Men seem to bring so much trouble. I wanted to get married once, but now I'm glad I never did.'

Adela sat on in her office, her mind drifting as it always did to Michael. There was a knock on the door which opened at once. Georgie walked in. 'Adela, you're needed at Speede House.'

'What?'

'Your father is ill. You should be with him.'

Adela stood up. 'How ill? Has Mother sent you?'

'No. Blanche. She says you should hurry.'

505

Chapter Twenty-Six

Adela entered her father's room. The curtains were drawn and the only light came from the fire and a shaded bedside lamp. Her mother was sitting by the bed. Blanche was hovering nearby.

'Who's that? Oh, it's you! Who told you?' Mrs Danby's whisper was harsh.

Adela came close to the bed and looked down at her father. His eyes were closed, but he seemed to sense her presence and opened them.

'Adela?'

'Hush, George. The doctor said you shouldn't talk.'

'Doctors! What difference can it make now? Adela, sit by me.'

A nurse stepped out of the shadows with a chair. 'You must stay calm, sir,' she warned.

Adela took her father's hands in hers. They were cold and dry. 'Father, I came as soon as I knew you were ill.'

'I'm dying,' he said.

'Now, Mr Danby,' said the nurse. 'We mustn't have that kind of talk.'

'Go away,' he said wearily. 'I'm not a fool. Adela, I'm glad you came. I wanted to see you. You've done well – your business – I admire that.'

She glanced up at her mother, angry at the knowledge that Mrs Danby would not have sent for her. Her mother met her eyes coldly.

'Adela,' whispered her father, 'how is he? How is the boy?'

Mrs Danby got up and walked to the window. She pulled aside the curtain and a shaft of sunlight fell across the carpet.

'Harry is well, Father.'

'You married that man in the end. Might as well have done it first as last.'

'Yes.'

'Is he good to you?'

'He's a good husband.'

'You don't sound happy.'

'Of course I don't when you are so ill.' Adela felt a flash of resentment. When she had needed her father most he had failed her. Then other feelings were lost in compassion for him as he stirred uneasily.

'Pain.'

The nurse came to him swiftly. 'Could you leave us for a moment, please?'

'Wait, nurse. Adela, I haven't finished—'

'Yes, you have, Mr Danby,' said the nurse. 'You can talk to your daughter later.'

'Now. I want to talk now.' He sounded like a fretful child.

Adela longed for him to speak. For so long he had been a distant figure. Why should she be denied some closeness, some communication, when he might be dying? But Mrs Danby came to her and tugged at her arm. 'He's suffering,' she hissed. 'Don't you care?'

Adela was angry but she wouldn't quarrel at such a time. Outside the bedroom she and her mother stood near one another but apart, each lost in her own world.

Adela tried to bridge the silence. 'Mother—'

Mrs Danby put out her hand. 'No! Not now.'

'May we talk later?'

'Later?' Mrs Danby glanced at the closed door. 'I don't know.'

The nurse opened the door. 'He's asleep.'

Mrs Danby resumed her vigil by the bed and Adela followed her, standing uncertainly by, hating to leave her father at such a time. 'You should go,' said her mother. 'I'm sure you have plenty to do. He won't wake for hours, and while he's drugged it will make no difference to him whether you are here or not.'

'Doesn't it make any difference to you?'

'No.'

'I care about him, you know, and about you.'

Mrs Danby didn't turn her head.

'Will you call me if there's a change?'

The bedroom door had opened and Blanche said, 'I'll telephone.' She followed Adela out of the room and closed the door. 'He hasn't long. Did he speak to you?'

'Yes. He seemed concerned for Harry and me.'

'Bit late!'

Adela looked at her watch. 'I suppose there's no use my staying here. I should like to sit with him, but Mother – I may as well go back to work. I have appointments to keep.'

'Yes, you may as well,' said Blanche.

'You sound so calm.'

'What's the point of being anything else? I'm grieved that Father is dying, but he brought it on himself. He should have stopped work.'

'You do love him, don't you?'

'I feel affection for him. He has never inspired anything else in me. The trouble with you, Adela, is that there are never any half measures. It's always got to be love or nothing. You take things far too much to heart and you suffer for it. Georgie will drive you back.'

Adela tried to concentrate on work. She had planned a visit to London the next day and wondered whether to cancel. That would mean she might lose an opportunity to see Michael. He would come to London, if he was able. But what if Father died while she was away? He had made it clear that he had something else he wished to say to her. She cancelled her London appointments. The telephone rang as the shop was closing for the day.

'Adela,' said Blanche, 'it's over.'

'Over? Not Father—'

'He died peacefully ten minutes ago.'

Adela was silent, trying to assimilate the fact of her father's death. She felt numb. 'Did he ask for me?'

'He didn't wake at all. At least, that's what Mother said.'

'What do you mean? Isn't it true?'

'Simmer down. I wasn't there. I'm sure it is.'

509

Adela put down the receiver and sat staring ahead of her. In spite of Father's attitude in the past, his death left an unexpected yawning abyss in her life. She wished she could weep. She wanted to weep.

Esther came into the office. 'I'm the last,' she said. 'I'll lock the front door. Why, Adela, what's wrong?'

Adela told her in cool, flat tones which kept sympathy at bay. Esther said she was sorry and left. Adela felt lost and desperately in need of comfort. Sander? He would give her sympathy. But Sander was partly to blame for Father's death. How old had he been? Barely sixty. He should have had years of life left to him. Resentment of her husband's behaviour grew until Adela could bear it no longer. Michael would understand. She would go to see him. She sprang to her feet and raced out of the shop. She managed, with an effort, to control her sense of urgency enough to drive safely, and instinctively pulled up outside the house she had shared with Jack. The curtains next door twitched. Adela knocked and the door was opened quickly by Ida.

Adela stared at her, her senses returning. How could she ask for Michael, here, of all places? The enormity of her conduct struck her.

She was saved from speaking by Ida. 'Come in, Adela. Did you forget to tell me somethin'? Mum! It's our Adela.'

Mrs Webster glared at Adela. She sat in her usual place, her plump legs opened to the fire which she demanded, no matter what the weather. A kettle was simmering and Ida had been toasting muffins. 'What do you want?' asked Mrs Webster ungraciously.

'Mum! Adela, sit yourself down an' I'll spread a muffin for you.'

'I came because – my father died.'

Mrs Webster said sonorously, 'God rest his soul. In the midst of life we are in death.'

'Mum!'

'It's true. We all have to die.'

'I know,' said Ida, 'but we can't help feelin' sad.'

'I don't reckon I'm long for this world. Why should I feel sad

510

about Adela's father? I never met him. Nor did you, our Ida. An' while I'm about it, Adela isn't "*our Adela*". She's married to Sander Bennett, remember?' She peered at Adela closely. 'You aren't shedding any tears, I notice. You're the sort that don't cry easy. You've met our Michael, haven't you? I said he'd come back to his old gran. We don't need your money now.'

'Adela only pays me my proper wages,' protested Ida.

'You work hard enough for them. An' that's another thing. I need Ida home here, lookin' after me. She don't need a job now we've got our Michael.' Mrs Webster sank her teeth into a muffin and the thick butter ran down her chin.

Ida opened the front door and Tibs stalked in, her tail up. She was a good mouser and Mrs Webster had asked for her to be left. She jumped on Adela's lap and she stroked her as she sipped her tea. 'You've grown, Tibs,' she murmured. Then, as calmly as she could, she stated, rather than asked, 'Michael lives here, doesn't he?'

'Off an' on,' said Ida.

'But I thought—'

'What's it to you?' demanded Mrs Webster.

'He's our Jack's son,' protested Ida. 'Of course she's interested in him. He stays here sometimes, Adela, but he's got a place of his own, a flat over a shop in Alma Vale Road.'

Adela felt cheated. Michael had said nothing to her about having his own flat. She got up abruptly. 'I must go. Ida, if I'm away, you'll help Freddy and Esther take care of things as usual, I know. I've put off my London engagements. I may be needed at Speede House.'

Ida fussed over her as she left. Adela got into her car and sat there, ignoring the hordes of children who swarmed about it. She felt sick. Michael had allowed her to believe he still lived with his grandmother. He had given that as a reason for their lack of opportunity to meet in Bristol. But maybe he had only just taken the flat. Maybe he was saving it up as a pleasant surprise for her. That was it. She felt better and put the car into gear.

The Websters' front door opened and Ida hurried out. 'Are

511

you sure you're all right, Adela? Mum's gettin' annoyed at you sittin' here. She says the neighbours will talk.'

'Sorry, I'll go. Ida, I've met Michael a few times. I've invited him to a dinner party, but I need to tell him I'm not entertaining for a while.'

'I'll go an' tell him for you. Don't you fret yourself.'

For once Adela wished that Ida was not so eternally obliging. 'I won't put you to the trouble. I have my motor car.'

'Have you got a pencil and a bit of paper? I'll give you his address. Don't take any notice of Mum. Her rheumatics have been playin' her up somethin' cruel.'

'It's all right. I'm glad she has a relative to take care of her now.'

'Yes, she thinks the world of Michael, but—'

Adela waited.

'Our Michael's young,' Ida said. 'Younger than his years, I sometimes think. I've scribbled his address down for you.' Mrs Webster could be heard calling impatiently. 'I'll go in. Next thing I know she'll be strugglin' to the door an' fall over.'

'Has she fallen often?'

'A few times.' Ida grinned. 'So far she's managed to land on somethin' soft. I don't think she's quite as wobbly as she makes out. Well, we might all go a bit funny as we get old.'

Adela thought of Ida's words as she drove towards Clifton. Ida had said that Michael was young for his age. Probably he seemed so to an indulgent aunt, but Adela knew different. He was a man, strong, vital, and he loved her.

She found the address, parked her car, and rang the bell on the side door of the shop. Now she was here she felt suddenly nervous and agitated. Let him be home, she prayed. Let him be glad I've come. There was a long silence and the shop owner came out. 'He takes ages to answer,' he said. 'I think he stops up late and sleeps in the day. A proper young gadabout he is.'

Adela didn't answer. It seemed as if everyone had an opinion about Michael. At last she heard his footsteps. She'd know them anywhere. He opened the door and stared at her. He was wearing a red and gold silk dressing gown and, in spite of herself, Adela felt desire stir in her.

512

'Adela! Good God, what are you doing here?' Michael looked at her with something close to annoyance. 'What do you want?'

Adela felt as if he'd slapped her. 'Shouldn't I have come? Michael, I need you.'

Business was quiet and Michael glanced at the shopkeeper who was still outside, pretending to examine his window display but listening intently. He blew on the window and polished it with his sleeve. 'You'd better come in, now you're here,' Michael muttered.

Adela stood back, hurt piercing her. 'It's all right. I mean, if you don't want me – you weren't expecting me – if you don't want me – I mean, if it's inconvenient—'

Michael reached out and pulled her through the door. He had recovered his equilibrium and as he shut the door he took her in his arms and kissed her. Adela's doubts vanished. She put her arms round him and pressed herself to him. Beneath his dressing gown he was naked.

'Not here,' he said, laughing. 'Come on up.' Adela preceded him through the flat door. 'Don't look too closely at the furnishings or your fingers will be itching to get busy,' said Michael. 'On the flat – or on me.'

Adela felt suddenly weary. 'My father died today.' She heard the words as if a stranger were saying them.

'That's bad news, honey, but you hadn't seen him for a long time, had you? You won't miss him.'

In the face of such indifference she couldn't begin to explain the emotions which were pounding through her. 'When you found that Jack – that your father had died, didn't it sadden you?'

'Hell, yes, of course it did. I would have liked to tell the old man I'd made good.'

'Yes, that's important, isn't it? At least Father knew I could stand on my own feet.'

'Or Sander's.'

'What?'

'It was a joke. I'm trying to cheer you up.'

'I see.'

513

Michael sat beside her on the scratchy horsehair and leather sofa and slid his arm round her. His lips touched her cheek and slid down to her neck.

She pushed him away, all desire gone. 'I didn't come here for that!' Her voice was sharp.

'What did you come for?'

'I don't know. I suppose I wanted you to comfort me a little.'

He tightened his arm round her. 'Make love to me. That'll comfort us both.'

'No, I don't want to. Not now.'

'Why not?' he demanded.

'I told you. My father—'

'—died today, yes, and we agreed you wouldn't miss him.'

'I didn't agree. Being apart from him made no difference to the way I felt about him. I always had the hope that one day we'd be close again – as we were when I was a child.'

Michael looked bored and made little effort to conceal a yawn.

Adela felt angry. 'You don't understand, do you?'

'Honey, I never put the dead above the living.'

'But it happened only today.'

He said in gentler tones, 'Yes, I know. It's always a shock when someone dies, but life has to go on.' He stubbed out his cigarette. 'Come on, honey, let's go to bed.'

She moved out of his reach. 'How long have you had this place?'

'What? Oh – a few days. I was going to make it look a bit better then surprise you.'

Her relief made her weak. 'Oh darling! I'll be able to visit you when I like now.'

Michael leaned back, lighting another cigarette. 'Not any time, honey. I shall need the flat for other purposes. My boss has made a few contacts in Britain and I shall have to entertain them.'

'Here? It's not very suitable for entertaining. I mean, it's rather small.'

'We're not all descended from kings,' said Michael sharply. He blew out a stream of smoke, got up and walked through a small door and Adela heard the rush of water into a kettle. 'Coffee?'

'Yes, please.' She followed him. The kitchen was tiny and she couldn't avoid brushing against him. 'I just thought that you'd take them to a restaurant. You don't have to be descended from kings to do that. Father used to—' She stopped. Her grief hurt her; her unshed tears were still dammed.

Michael glanced at her. 'Calm down, Adela. Go and freshen up in the washroom, such as it is.'

Adela opened the only other door. It led to a bedroom where a double bed was tumbled and Michael's clothes lay heaped around.

Michael carried a tray of coffee into the living room. 'I'm not very tidy,' he called, 'never have been. The washroom's beyond.'

Adela found a washbasin with a cold tap, and a lavatory. She bathed her face and hands.

Michael had poured two cups of coffee and she drank hers, feeling a little calmer. 'I shouldn't have burst in on you. And I don't have the right to criticise you.' I wish I did, she thought, but dared not say it. If she became possessive he would resent it and he could leave her tomorrow, tonight. She watched him as he went to a gramophone and wound it. 'I bought this. I like a bit of music.'

The strains of *Whispering* filled the room. Michael danced slowly on his own, singing in a soft voice, '*Whispering while you cuddle near me*. But you're not cuddling are you, Adela?' He held out his arms. 'Come on, me ole lover, come into my arms.'

His smiling eyes and beckoning arms tempted her and she joined him.

Afterwards she drove home. In the end his persistence had overcome her reluctance and they had made love. It had comforted her only inasmuch as it had absorbed much of her emotion. Deep down she was shocked and dismayed by his inability, or unwillingness, to comprehend her sorrow.

She pushed open her bedroom door, thankful for the prospect of peace for a time. She took off her dress and shoes and sat in an easy chair, smoking a cigarette. June was hot and sunny and she was glad of the breeze which stirred the lace curtains. Her mind was troubled. Her father's death was a catalyst, setting her off in unfamiliar ways of thought. Death had never touched her so deeply before and it bewildered her. Ralph's had seemed unreal. Jack's had shocked her, but even he had not left her with such a sense of frustration and regret. She turned, startled, as the door opened and Sander walked in. 'Blanche telephoned me with the news. Adela, I'm sorry.'

'She called me, too, otherwise I wouldn't have known. Mother is—' She stopped. 'I'm so thankful I saw Father for a few minutes while he could still speak. Sander, he wanted to say more, but the nurse wouldn't let him. That bloody nurse! I wish I knew what it was he wanted to say.'

'She should have let him speak. What difference could it have made?' Sander's words were sympathetic, but his attitude bothered Adela; there was a quality in his voice which disturbed her. 'I thought you would come to me for comfort.'

'There doesn't seem much to be had at a time like this.'

'No? Didn't Michael Webster manage to help?'

Adela felt as if she had been punched in the stomach. 'What did you say?'

'You went to Webster. Did he manage to help you?'

Adela struggled for control. 'I needed to see him. I couldn't telephone. I must cancel invitations to a dinner party.'

'And Ida couldn't have done it?'

'Done what?' asked Adela stupidly.

'Given a message to her nephew?' Sander walked closer and Adela saw that his eyes were dark with suppressed anger.

'How do you know what I did?' she demanded. 'Have you got someone spying on me?'

'I knew how bad you'd feel about your father. As soon as Blanche called me I went straight to the showroom; I pictured you there, lost in grief. That's amusing, isn't it, Adela?'

'Of course it isn't. I was – I am – grieved.'

'So you ran to Mrs Webster? Or was it Ida? Which one of them did you think had the power to soothe you?'

'I – think I went to where I had been happy.'

'Liar! You're a liar! I arrived just after you'd gone and Ida

516

told me where you might be found. I still thought, or maybe by that time I just hoped, that the reason you had given for calling on Webster was true. I arrived in time to see you go into his flat. I waited until you came out.' Sander walked nearer until he was looming over her. 'You stayed there quite a while, didn't you, my dear little wife? And when you came out it was written all over you.'

'What was?' Her voice was a harsh whisper.

'You'd been making love. I've seen that expression on your face before. And it wasn't the only time, was it? He's been after you from that first night, hasn't he? I believed you were trustworthy. Damn you, and damn him! What does he give you that I can't?'

Adela threw back her head. 'Don't try to intimidate me! All right, if you will have it, yes, we made love. And, yes, we've done it before, and I'm not ashamed.'

Sander grasped her arms above the elbow, his fingers digging into her soft flesh. 'How many times? How many?' With each question he shook her.

'Not many times. Not many.'

Adela thought he was going to strike her. She had never imagined such rage as filled his face, his whole being.

'Sander,' she cried, 'Sander, I didn't mean it to happen. I can't help loving him.'

He dropped her arms. 'You love him, do you? And he loves you?'

'Yes.'

'What does he intend doing about it?'

'We haven't discussed that yet.' How she wished she could tell Sander that Michael had plans for her.

'Did you see him in London?'

'Yes.'

'Every time?'

'No.'

'You cheating little bitch!'

'I tried to resist him, but I couldn't. I'm not proud of what I've done, but I am truly sorry. I'll leave and you can divorce me.'

Sander stared at her incredulously. 'You're willing to sacrifice everything you've worked for, abandon everyone who depends on you – Esther, Ida, Freddy Stanton who gave up a safe job for you, all the others, and me – for that piece of scum?'

'Don't say that! He's a good man. The reason he won't make plans is because of Harry, among other things.'

'The reason he won't make plans is because he's a treacherous, evil bugger who gets any woman who's available into his bed.'

Adela leapt to her feet. 'That's a lie. A wicked lie! You're jealous, that's all, and you've no call to be. You don't love me!'

'I'm your husband and that gives me certain rights, and one of them is to be jealous of my wife's honour, if nothing else. I care about all my dependants which is more than you can say. What do you intend to do about your workforce? What plans have you for Harry? Do you mean to wrest him from the only true home he's had?'

'I thought that you'd be willing to take over my business. It's a good one. It should bring us both an income as well as pay back my grandmother. And I thought you'd let me take Bill to look after Harry.'

'You stupid fool! Bill isn't all that's necessary to the boy. It might be years before he settles after what he suffered. You can't take him away.'

'He's mine!'

'No, he's not. If he's anybody's, he's still the gruesome Mrs Prewett's.'

'He was *never* hers!'

'He's still tied to her in bonds of fear. He always will be unless he's properly treated.'

'Michael will be a good father to him.'

'My God, you really do believe that?'

'Yes, I do. Oh, Sander, please don't torment me. Let me go free. I never dreamed that love could be so wonderful. I just want to be with Michael. I'll give up anything for that.'

Sander said deliberately, 'I shall never divorce you, Adela, no matter what you do. And no court will give Harry to you if you go off with that swine.'

'I'll fight you. I'm Harry's mother. That makes a difference.'

518

'Not when I tell them what Webster is really like.'

'What's that supposed to mean?'

'If you oppose me, you'll find out. If you agree to give him up, you need never know.'

Adela tossed her head. 'You're just trying to frighten me, but there's nothing about Michael I would mind. You can do what the hell you like. All I know is that I'm going to leave you and live with Michael.'

She expected another outburst of anger, but Sander said quietly, 'Adela, listen to me. Michael Webster will never really care for you. He'll take whatever you give him and that's all. Believe me, I know.'

'You can't know. You don't understand him.'

'I understand him only too well and he knows it.'

Adela was silenced, remembering Michael's suspicion and anger, his accusation that Sander was spying on him. 'Is it true that you've been making inquiries about him in America?'

'Perfectly true. I suppose one of his bodyguards told him. He should have brought them over with him. They'd have made short work of me.'

'Bodyguards? What are you talking about? He doesn't need to be guarded.'

'Perhaps not here where we still maintain standards of law, but out there Prohibition is causing the most hellish situations and he's in the thick of them. He's up to his neck in—'

'I won't listen. I don't want to hear any more. You're making it up.'

'I am doing nothing of the sort. Adela, don't you feel you owe me something? I'm the man who married you, the man who's always been ready to pick up the pieces.'

'But you don't love me!'

'And he does?'

'Yes.'

He made a sudden movement and pulled Adela to her feet. 'You're mine. Webster shan't have you.'

'That's all you care about. I'm yours! I'm a possession, just like your factories and shops. You don't know how to love.'

Sander grasped her silk petticoat and tore it from neck to

519

hem. His eyes travelled over her slender body in its crepe de Chine step-ins. 'My God, you're beautiful. I can't blame another man for wanting you. But that you should give yourself to him! That you should sink so low!'

Adela held herself straight. 'Go on, use your strength against me. I can't stop you.'

'No, you can't.'

He picked her up and threw her on the bed. His head was thrust forward, his face dark with fury. 'I could take you,' he said, 'and you couldn't stop me. I have every right.'

'Every right,' she agreed, her heart hammering.

'But I don't want a woman who doesn't want me! When I make love it will be with your cooperation.'

'You'll wait a long time.'

'I think not.'

Adela got off the bed and walked into her dressing room. When she returned to her bedroom Sander had gone.

Mr Danby's funeral was well attended. Prominent Bristol businesses and organisations were represented, and relatives, many of whom were only names to Adela, arrived at Speede House and followed the coffin to church in old-fashioned hearses drawn by black horses. Mrs Danby had felt obliged to invite Adela and Sander because not to do so would bring just the kind of speculation she preferred to avoid, but Adela knew she was unwelcome and that her mother still blamed Sander for his father-in-law's illness. Blanche was there and Georgie, though they didn't sit together. Perhaps even the cynical Blanche felt that her father's funeral was no place to flaunt her unconventional relationship. Lady Sutton was as stiff and solemn-faced as Adela remembered her as a child. No wonder she and Blanche had been so awed by her. A stranger would never credit what she was really like. There was a gathering afterwards in Speede House and Adela and Blanche took their parts in playing hostess, but both left as early as possible.

Adela took her leave of Lady Sutton. 'Come and visit me if you can get away.'

'I'll try, darling, but your mother isn't in a very pliable frame of mind. Poor dear, she loved George in her own way.'

Adela tried to speak words of comfort to her mother, but Mrs Danby was locked into a cocoon of grief and resentment and stared at her coldly without answering.

Adela and Sander had driven to Speede House in their own cars and when Adela climbed into hers she was surprised to find Elsa Maitland sitting in it.

Her presence still had the power to take Adela back to a time when she had been unbearably humiliated.

'What do you want?' she asked, then realised that Elsa had been weeping.

'I'm sorry, Mrs Bennett. I just wanted to know how everything went. To tell you – to tell someone – how grieved I am.'

Tears forced themselves beneath Elsa's lids again and Adela thought, with a shock of understanding: she was in love with Father. Probably has been for years. It was he for whom she made her sacrifice, not me at all. Some of the weight was lifted from her heart.

'The funeral was beautiful,' she said gently. 'Mother chose Father's favourite hymns.'

'I know. I was outside.'

'Oh, Elsa!'

'Did he suffer much?'

Adela didn't know, but she said, 'No, he died in his sleep.'

'Thank God!' Elsa was silent for a moment. 'I missed working for him. He understood that, though no one else did.'

'Would you have gone back to Father if he'd asked you?'

'He didn't ask. Why should he? It would have been dishonourable to retract a promise,' she said proudly. 'And even if he had, I couldn't have gone. Mr Bennett had a binding contract drawn up.'

'Do you mean you're tied to Bennett's whether you like it or not?'

Elsa smiled faintly. 'It's not as bad as it sounds. I enjoy my work and get an excellent wage with yearly rises and the promise of a pension. Few people are so lucky. Mr Bennett is a good employer.'

'I'm glad you came to me, Elsa.'

She nodded, then opened the car door.

'Can I drop you somewhere?' Adela offered.

'No, thank you. I'm going to walk for a while.'

Adela sat in her car for a long time just thinking. That brief interlude with Ralph in the autumn woods was still producing agonising repercussions.

Sander had not mentioned Michael to her since the day of Father's death. Adela respected him for his forbearance. Since the ghastly scene in her bedroom he had treated her with consummate courtesy. More than ever Adela wished she could have fallen in love with him. There was no doubt he had the knack of making life comfortable and secure. She had seen Michael only once, in company, and had unwisely tried to tell him all that had happened. They were interrupted and Michael got the impression that all she wanted was to make love. 'Don't worry, darling,' he had promised. 'I'll fix a time and place as soon as possible.'

That evening she went to the nursery. Harry would be three in a few days and he was sturdy and strong. He and Bill were playing a rowdy game with a balloon before bathtime. They both looked round and, as naturally as if he had been doing it all his life, Harry opened his arms to his mother, gave her a wide smile, and ran to her. Adela knelt and he flung himself upon her, kissing her mouth. She hugged him, tears springing to her eyes. 'Harry, my baby, my baby.'

'Not a baby,' he shrieked, pulling himself away. 'Bill, give me the balloon. I'm not a baby. Look, Mummy!' He kicked the balloon into the air.

Adela caught it and patted it back to him, blinded by tears. He had called her Mummy, he had kissed her; the long wait had been worthwhile.

That night at dinner Sander said, 'I understand that Harry has decided he likes you.'

Sander had dispensed with the servants when they brought coffee and dessert and Adela couldn't be morose on this subject. She turned to him eagerly. 'Yes, isn't it wonderful? Oh, Sander, to think of it. He really does love me.'

'I'm delighted for you,' he said.

'Bill has been good for him.'

'I agree, and living in a peaceful atmosphere must have helped.'

'Yes, and I'm grateful to you, Sander, so very grateful.'

'Are you, my dear? I'm glad. I've done everything I could to repair the damage to your son. You must think deeply before you decide to remove him.'

Adela was glad that the subject was once more in the open and that Sander sounded so calm. 'He won't suffer,' she swore. 'He trusts me; his love was clear in his eyes.'

'Can you read love so easily? How about Webster's?'

Adela felt deflated and depressed. She began to peel an apple, carefully keeping the skin intact in long red and white curls.

Sander watched her. Neither of them spoke again.

The next afternoon Ida came to Adela. 'There's somethin' really wrong with Mattie. I think you should speak to her. She was comin' along nicely at the drapin' an' window-dressin', but she's worse than useless at the moment.'

Mattie came into the office warily and seated herself, at Adela's invitation, on the very edge of a chair. Ida followed with a tray of tea and biscuits. Mattie took one and nibbled it, and had a sip of tea. Then she put her cup and saucer and plate back on the tray.

'Are you unwell?' asked Adela gently.

'No, thank you, Mrs Bennett.'

'Ida tells me you are neglecting your work.'

Adela had hoped to shock Mattie into a response and she succeeded. Mattie's face was suffused with a deep flush.

'Don't you like the work you're doing?'

'Yes, but—'

Adela waited.

'I'm sorry, Mrs Bennett. I'll try to do better.' Mattie stood up.

'No, sit down. Mattie, I don't see myself simply as your employer, you know, but also as a friend. It's clear that you are worried. Won't you tell me what's happened? Is it boy trouble?' she asked gently.

'Boy trouble?' Mattie looked startled. 'No, I mean, I've been to the pictures with Andy Barton, but that's all.'

'Do your parents disapprove of him?'

'What? No, why should they?'

'He's been to reform school. I thought—'

'It wasn't Andy's fault. It was all because of that nasty man, Fred Withycombe. He's gettin' his come-uppance,' she finished with relish.

'Then what is the matter? You know, Mattie, all my employees can receive medical treatment under an insurance scheme.'

'I know.'

'If something more is needed, I will willingly help out.'

Mattie stared wide-eyed. 'I never thought of that.' She paused. 'It's not me, it's my sister. Our Mabel.'

'The dancer? She needs medical treatment?'

'Yes, in a way, though I don't think there's any way to get what she wants. Mrs Bennett, our Mabel's gone an' got herself landed. She's havin' a baby. She's sick about it. If she has to have it, it'll ruin her career an' our Frank's mad with her. They were just gettin' successful, you see, with dancin' engagements at private parties an' their agent's promised them theatre work. Now it's all spoilt.'

'I'm truly sorry. What about the child's father? Is Mabel getting married.'

'He don't – doesn't – want to know. He's a man she met at a posh house. He was only after a bit of fun, though our Mabel was serious about him. I reckon she was ready to throw everything away for love. Only he doesn't love her.'

Adela was silent. What fools women were. She and Mabel were caught in the same trap.

'She knows of a woman over Bedminster way who can do somethin' about that sort of thing,' said Mattie.

'Do you mean an abortion? That's terribly dangerous, even with the best doctors and excellent hygiene.'

'I didn't know you could get doctors to do it.'

'It's illegal,' said Adela.

'I know. But are there doctors who do it?' the girl persisted.

'A few, I believe.'

'I dare say it costs pounds. Lots of poor women have to get it done. They just can't keep havin' babies all the time. They haven't got enough money to feed them.'

'There are ways to stop them getting pregnant.' Damn a society which condemned women to the slavery of constant child-bearing when they could be helped!

'Are there? I wonder if Mabel knows that. I don't think she does, do you, Mrs Bennett?'

'I suppose not. And the man – he won't help her at all?'

'Not him. He says it isn't his kid, but it is because our Mabel's never been with another man. She's a good girl.'

'Mattie, you must stop her from going to a quack. She could die.'

Mattie looked scared. 'I know. A woman up our road died a couple of months ago an' Mum says she knows a couple of others who are invalids because of what was done to them. But it's too late to stop Mabel. She's already gone. She left our house early this mornin'. I've been givin' her all my pocket money an' so has Frank an' the others an' Mum an' Dad coughed some up as well.'

'Your parents know of the deaths and disablements and they still helped Mabel with money?'

Mattie was indignant. 'Mabel was goin' to get rid of the baby whatever our Mum said, an' Mum didn't want her to do it to herself. Mum an' Dad are only tryin' to help. They're real proud of Mabel. They want her to get on. An' our Mum couldn't bear Mabel to get landed like she is. Our Mum's havin' another baby.'

'Oh, my God!' Adela leaned her elbows on the table and rested her head in her hands, staring at Mattie.

'Are you all right, Mrs Bennett?'

'Yes, I'm all right.' Adela looked into the girl's troubled eyes. 'Mattie, if Mabel still needs help, ask her to come and see me. I know of a place where she can be operated on safely. As safely as that kind of surgery can be, that is. Promise me.'

'I promise, Mrs Bennett, though it's probably over by now. I expect she'd be all right with the woman in Bedminster. She's done it for hundreds.'

525

Chapter Twenty-Seven

Early next morning Sarah shook Adela awake. 'Mrs Bennett, I'm sorry to disturb you, but there's a girl called Mattie Hobbs at the back door. She says she works for you and she must see you. Cook told her it was impossible this early, but she began to shout that you'd told her to come. She's in the kitchen.'

Adela was fully awake now. 'Bring her up,' she said, getting out of bed and pulling on her dressing gown.

'What's up?' Sander entered, fully dressed. 'Are you all right?'

'Mattie Hobbs wants to see me. Please, Sarah, wait outside.' Adela watched her maid leave reluctantly, then said, 'Sander, I have a horrible fear that Mattie's sister has been to an abortionist and something's gone wrong.'

'What? You knew she was going and you let her go?'

Before Adela could give vent to her indignant denials Mattie came running into the room, pursued by Sarah. 'I'm sorry, Mrs Bennett, I told her to wait behind me.'

'It's all right, Sarah, I'll call you when I need you.' Sarah threw an indignant look at Mattie and left.

'Oh, Mrs Bennett,' Mattie burst out, 'it's our Mabel. She's bleedin' an' no one can stop it! Mum's tried and the neighbours have done everythin' they know, but it won't stop. Even the midwife can't help. Oh, Mrs Bennett, I think our Mabel's dyin'.'

Adela turned instinctively to Sander. 'What should I do? If she goes to hospital they'll know about the abortion and she'll be in serious trouble with the law. But if she doesn't go—'

'Leave it to me,' said Sander. 'Where's Mabel now?' he asked Mattie.

'At home.' Mattie blurted out the address and Sander hurried away. Adela dressed, while Mattie sipped the tea Mrs Monkton brought.

'I'm sorry to hear of your sister's illness,' said Mrs Monkton. 'I do hope it's nothing serious and she'll soon be well. It's a spot of female trouble, isn't it?' There was a note in her voice that displeased Adela.

'That will be all,' she said sharply. 'And please tell Sarah to go down for her breakfast.' When Mrs Monkton had left Adela said, 'I'm sorry, Mattie, she does tend sometimes to say more than she should.'

Sander returned. 'I've located a doctor who'll help. He's on his way to your house, Mattie.'

'Oh, thank you, Mr Bennett,' cried Mattie. 'Thank you!' She turned to go, then paused. 'Do you have to tell the police?'

'Don't worry,' said Sander gently. 'No one will tell. Go home.'

Adela took a coat from her wardrobe and Sander asked, 'Are you going to work so early?'

'To work? Of course not. I'm going to see Mrs Hobbs. She was kind to me when I needed help.'

'No, that won't do at all!'

'Won't do! Why shouldn't I go?'

Sander said quickly, 'Adela, I haven't time to argue with you. There's been an accident in the shoe factory. That's why I was up so early.'

'Another? Don't you take safety precautions?'

Sander was angry. 'If you'd ever bothered to visit you would see that I protect the workers in every way possible, but there are always a few who break the rules. Apparently one of the belts was stopped while the power was still on and someone decided to adjust the knife lines. The operator forgot to give the all clear before he started up the machine and a man is now on his way to Cossham Hospital minus a few fingers. I'm going to see how he is.'

'So you should! And I'm going to see Mabel!'

'For God's sake, Adela, use some sense! Have you thought

what talk it'll cause if you turn up in your big car and your fancy clothes? Doubtless all the neighbours know everything, but the good souls will discuss it in whispers. They'll stick together and pretend it's not happening because no woman knows when it might be her turn, but if you turn up they can no longer pretend and the wrong one may learn what's happened, and where will Mabel be then? What she's done is illegal.'

'What about the doctor's car?'

'He'll park and walk. He's dealt with bungled abortions before. He knows the ropes.'

'Has he been struck off the register? Is he a quack?'

Sander looked at his watch and sighed. 'Adela, why won't you trust me? He's a well qualified man who sympathises with the plight of poor women. So far no one has betrayed him. Blanche and Georgie know him, too. Go to work, my dear. I'll see you tonight. We're dining out, aren't we?'

Sander telephoned during the afternoon. 'I've had Mabel moved to a private clinic. I'm afraid she's extremely ill. I'll tell you more when I see you.'

Adela found it difficult to concentrate on designs for Vita's new house. She seemed in no hurry to get married and Claud remained her humble slave, pandering to her whims, accepting her dictates. They were fellow guests at a dinner party held by Bobbie and her husband.

The food was delicious and the wine good, and Bobbie looked more content than Adela had ever seen her. Marriage evidently suited her.

When the women left the men to their port and cigars, Vita threw herself into a deep chair and lit an Egyptian cigarette in a long amber holder. Since the discovery of the tomb of Tutankhamen everything Egyptian was popular and Vita was dressed in a Desirée Egyptian brocade with a Nile green georgette underskirt. It suited her. She looked round disparagingly. 'I must say I prefer my decor to yours, Bobbie, darling. Isn't this room just a teensy weensy bit old-fashioned with the flowers and fruit? And although the cherubs look perfectly sweet, I can't say I care for them very much.'

'It isn't old-fashioned,' said Bobbie crossly. 'It isn't, is it, Adela?'

'Would I be guilty of perpetrating such a social solecism?' Adela asked lightly. 'There are as many ways to decorate a house as there are to dress a woman.' She examined her fingernails, painted pink to match her lipstick, and said casually, 'My London clients are well satisfied with what I do.'

She knew this would be a putdown for Vita who began to smoke furiously.

Millie had listened to the exchange. 'I simply *adore* my house,' she put in. 'I had guests from Paris the other day and they were very taken with it. They said they'd be contacting you, Adela. They have decided to modernise their Paris flat and they have a grand country house, too – a chateau really. The possibilities are endless.' Her eyes met Adela's and each turned away before they laughed. Their reactions were deliberately snobbish, and Blanche and Georgie would have howled, but between them they had subdued Vita for a while.

Conversation had become general by the time the men joined them. Claud, his expensive suit hanging untidily from his skinny frame, went straight to Vita. 'What an age you've been,' she said. 'Fetch me a cocktail, for God's sake. I'm parched.'

Bobbie looked annoyed as might any hostess who had just served excellent coffee. 'Gerard will mix you one,' she said.

'What'll it be?' asked Gerard.

'What have you got, darling?' Vita flirted with every man and Claud should be used to it, but Adela surprised a flash of annoyance in his eyes. It seemed that the baronet wasn't quite so compliant as he appeared.

'I can mix most things,' said Gerard. 'How about a Manhattan? You can have it sweet or dry.'

'Dry, of course. Syrup does nothing at all for the figure.'

'Yours is perfect,' said Claud.

'And I mean it to stay that way,' snapped Vita.

Claud subsided, and sat smoking morosely by his fiancée's side.

'I feel sorry for the Americans,' said Millie's husband.

'Fancy having to break the law to get a drop of booze.'

'Ghastly,' said Vita. 'But it isn't at all difficult to find something out there. The country has more drinking clubs than ever before and all Prohibition has done is to breed a new kind of lawbreaker and increase violent crime. Murder seems commonplace and some men are coining money.'

'How do you know so much?' asked Claud.

'Everyone knows that,' said Vita.

'I don't,' said her fiancé.

'You never know anything interesting,' sneered Vita. 'It's perfectly easy to pick up information if you keep your ears and eyes open.'

There was a short awkward silence which Gerard broke. 'Come along, who wants to sample my cocktails? I've been practising. If income tax rises any higher, I may need to get a job as a barman.'

There was general laughter in which Vita did not join. She stared at the others through half-closed eyes, smoke writhing from her lips.

'I say,' said Claud, 'you aren't serious, are you? I mean to say, a barman!'

'He's joking, you fool,' said Vita.

Claud smiled uncertainly. It had become the fashion to speak insultingly to one's friends and loved ones but Vita's insults to her fiancé had a deadly ring to them.

'How long will Claud go on knuckling under to her?' Adela asked Sander on their way home.

'I've no idea. He needs her money.'

'And she wants a title. But surely she'll lose her chance if she doesn't behave more kindly towards him.'

'There are other men around with titles and no money, plenty of competition,' said Sander. 'The war and its aftermath has dug deep into many fortunes.'

'Doesn't it embarrass you when Vita constantly humiliates Claud? I hate it when she acts so badly; I feel sorry for him.'

'Do you? More sorry than you feel for me? I mean, you're not rude to me in public, I'll allow that, but you're cheating on me in private. We could hold quite a good debate on the subject.

531

Invite in a few friends. "This house believes that rudeness surpasses adultery in the bad behaviour stakes." '

Adela clenched her fists and sat in silence, staring at the lighted shop windows without seeing them. Finally she said in low tones, 'You're determined to goad me. You never miss an opportunity.'

'Don't I?' Sander's voice was filled with false amazement. 'Well, I call that downright rotten of me. After all, you've only slept with another man.'

'I've explained to you, Sander. I love Michael. I didn't mean to, but nothing can ever change it. I'm truly sorry about it. I almost wish it hadn't happened.'

'Do you, *really*? How *fearfully* good of you to *almost* wish it hadn't happened.'

'For God's sake, stop mimicking society idiots.'

'I bet Michael never does.'

'No! He doesn't! He rather despises them.'

'Does he now? How interesting. What else does he despise? Cuckolded husbands, perhaps.'

'You're determined to quarrel with me!'

'Well, what a nasty husband I am, when you *almost* wish you hadn't gone to bed with another man.'

Adela fell silent again.

'No more to say?'

'No.'

Sander let Adela out before he parked in the garage. She went straight to her room and Sarah ran a hot bath. Adela was reclining gratefully in the steamy fragrance, eyes closed, when the door opened. 'Run some more hot water, Sarah,' she said. 'I need to relax.'

She opened her eyes to see that the hand which reached for the water tap was definitely not Sarah's. It was large and strong.

Adela sat up abruptly. 'Sander! Where's Sarah?'

'I've dismissed her for the night.'

'I've asked you before not to give orders to my maid. What should you say if I ordered Bill around?'

Sander sat on the edge of the bath. He was wearing his dressing gown. 'I must remind you, dear heart, that Bill is now owned exclusively by Harry. As yet, I haven't found a replacement.'

'You should.'

'I dare say you're right, especially if you intend to take Bill with you when you go. Or maybe Harry will recover his trust completely and allow himself to be cared for by a nursemaid.'

'Oh, shut up!' yelled Adela.

Sander raised his brows. 'Once, you used to be honest. Don't you like hearing the truth any more?'

'I don't need you to point it out to me.'

'Is that so? You surprise me. You seem to have forgotten the decencies of life.'

'Sander, please go away.'

'No! Would you like me to scrub your back for you?'

'No!' she cried. 'Pass me a towel.'

'Get it yourself.'

'Damn you, Sander, why can't you act like a gentleman?'

'Because I'm not one. I daresay Claud is perfect in the gentlemanly behaviour department. How's Webster?'

Adela was furious. 'His behaviour is impeccable.'

Sander gave a shout of laughter. 'You really do believe that, don't you?'

He remained where he was, taking another cigarette from his pocket and lighting it from the stub of the first. The bath water grew chilly. Adela could have run more, but she was tired and angry. This was crazy. She stood up, water streaming from her smooth skin, and stepped out on to the soft bath mat. She reached out for a towel, but Sander took it first and wrapped it around her. 'Here you are. Allow your husband the pleasure of drying you.'

'Please, Sander, please leave me alone. I know you forgot yourself the other day—'

Again he laughed, but not pleasantly. 'I didn't forget myself, just as I don't intend to forget myself tonight.'

'Oh, no, Sander! You can't force me. It would be wrong!'

'I've no intention of doing so. I'll make you want me.'

'I won't let you.'

'Are you sure? Are you absolutely sure?' Sander let the towel fall to the floor and pulled her close. His mouth went down on her breasts while his hands began their knowing exploration of her body, moving on her flesh, teasing her. She resisted him until his skill destroyed her defences and she was lost in a wholly physical world. He carried her to the bed.

'You devil,' she breathed. 'Let me go.'

'You little witch. Are you sure you want me to?'

She couldn't answer and he held her so tightly she could feel the thud of his heartbeats. 'Adela.' His voice was suddenly inexpressibly tender. 'Adela.' He put her gently on the bed and his hands began to roam over her body, whispers of touch, but the roving fingers were bringing her a shivery pleasure which was new to her. She wanted it to go on. She was drowned in sensations that crowded upon her, as with hands and lips Sander fondled and caressed her. His skill sprang from a marvel of sensuousness which she couldn't resist. She was filled with an unfamiliar yearning to touch him and ran her hands over him, enjoying the feel of his hair-roughened skin, making him gasp, finding deep satisfaction in her power over him. They explored one another until their mutual need was too great to deny and he slid into her, moving with long strong strokes until she was lost in a vortex of sexuality and cried out in ecstatic release.

Sander stayed still, looking down at her with an expression of immense tenderness. He began to pull away and, instinctively, she tightened her arms around him.

'What's this?' he asked. 'Haven't I made you happy?'

'You know you have. You must know.'

'Yes, darling, I know.'

'And you?'

'Perfectly. You're wonderful to make love to. It's almost worth quarrelling to make up so beautifully.'

Quarrelling? What had they been arguing about? Adela remembered with a deep sense of shock: about Michael. She had completely forgotten him.

Sander released her and as she lay beside him, his arm still round her, holding her in tender captivity, she saw Michael with new eyes. He was prepared to break up a home, seduce her

534

from a husband who had sheltered her and her son in circumstances which he knew about. And she had risked the security of herself and Harry by disregarding the feelings – and the rights – of the husband who had shielded her from her own folly, however little she deserved it. She remembered how Michael had evaded questions about the future, his callous indifference to her grief at her father's death, and small doubts which she had ignored suddenly loomed large. Sander had warned that Michael was not to be trusted and he had spoken the truth.

Sander said softly, 'Are you sleepy, or do you want to talk?'

'I'll sleep, thanks,' she said, knowing she was lying. She needed to talk, to ask Sander just how much he knew about Michael's activities, what kind of man he really was, but she had begun to fear the truth. She needed a little more time. Sander extricated his arm, bent his head to kiss her and was soon asleep.

Adela looked back with increasing disbelief at her own folly. She must have been crazy to encourage the flattering attentions of an immature boy. That's what Michael was but she had mistaken his crude seduction for love. Sander might not love her, but he cared for her enough to try to protect her from her own stupidity. And to shield Harry, too. She could never forget that. She would never leave Sander.

She felt an overwhelming sense of relief as she realised with absolute certainty that she would stay with her husband, that she wanted to. In time, she hoped, he would forgive her.

As the night wore on, Adela listened to Sander's breathing. Twice he murmured in his sleep and she strained to catch the words. Did he dream of her? Once he half woke and slid his arm over her, murmuring her name. Even in half-sleep, where there could be no pretence, he cared about her. As she did him. More than just cared. She understood with a jolt that she loved him! When had her love begun? She couldn't tell. She knew only that she did love him, and that she was bitterly ashamed of the way she had treated him. She cringed to think of Michael now – he was nothing compared to Sander. She ached to tell Sander, to offer him all the love she had, but if she declared her love for him and at the same time said she had decided not to leave him, he might think it was a ploy to placate him; that she had simply decided to hang on to the security he offered.

As dawn broke and light shone through the windows, she looked lovingly at her husband's face. In sleep some of the lines were smoothed away, though he would never be handsome. The marks of his early struggles would stay with him and those same struggles meant that he would always be aggressive, sometimes overbearing. What of it? That was Sander, a good man and an honest one. He had tried before to help her out of a harrowing situation when Ralph had been killed. How arrogantly she had spurned him! How she had hurt him!

'Sander,' she breathed, 'I love you.' She would tell him again, but she must choose her time.

Harry's third birthday arrived and he presided over the children who came to his party. Adela had appointments until four o'clock, but managed to arrive home just as he was blowing out the candles on his cake, his red cheeks shiny and distended. He was wildly over-excited as the nursery maid cut into it. Adela watched him. His face was glowing with pleasure and health, his eyes were brilliant.

'He's a grand little chap,' said Bill by her side.

His voice held pride and Adela said, 'You've done wonders. I can't tell you how grateful I am.'

'You and Mr Bennett supplied the background he needed. He still has his dark moments and wakes up too often, crying. He can't tell me why, but I think he's been dreaming. Only time will cure him completely, and luckily he's got plenty of that. With you and Mr Bennett to help him he'll come through.'

Adela felt cold when she thought of her headstrong intention to remove Harry from this safe place. She would have smashed his sense of security.

Harry looked up and saw her. His face lit up in a smile as he jumped down and ran to her, and she knelt to receive him. He threw his arms round her and gave her a kiss, smearing her face with icing sugar.

'Mummy, come and see my cake. And I've got lots of presents. I'll show you.'

He held her hand and pulled her towards a table where a selection of toys was displayed.

'They're beautiful, darling,' she said, her voice harsh with happy tears. 'You'll have such fun with them.'

Harry seized a clockwork train. 'You have to wind this one. I can't do it yet, but Bill says I'll be able to soon and Daddy will wind it, too. He's very strong, isn't he? Will you come and play with it, Mummy?'

'Of course. But now you must go back to the table,' said Adela gently. 'Your friends need their host.'

'I'm a host,' Harry said proudly, and allowed himself to be led to his chair. Adela stayed while they played noisy games, chasing around the large light room she had made into a day nursery, screaming their pleasure. Adela scarcely noticed the other children. Her eyes were on Harry and it amazed her that he frequently looked to see if she was still there, still watching him, when lately she had played such a small part in his life. When the other children had been collected by mothers or nannies Harry came to her again. He sat on her knee, flushed and happy. It was the first time since his return that he had sought her out like this, climbing on to her knee as if he knew he had a right, happy in their closeness.

'Did you like my party, Mummy?'

'It was beautiful, darling.'

'Daddy didn't come.'

She was disgusted with herself. She hadn't even known that Harry looked upon Sander as his father. He was looking up at her, his clear blue eyes reminding her of Ralph who had given his young life for duty. She had borne Harry because of that. Now she owed it to them both to continue what she had begun.

'Will Daddy be home soon? He said I needn't go to bed until I'd seen him.'

'If he said he's coming home, then he will,' said Adela. Sander always kept his word.

She went to her room and stayed there and when Sander came to see why she hadn't joined him for dinner she told him she felt unwell. The truth was she was so filled with emotion she felt that food would choke her.

'Have you seen Harry?' she asked.

'Yes, I promised him. I gather you have your heart's desire now.'

'What?'

'You have your son back in every sense of the word.'

'Yes.'

'Aren't you pleased?'

'Of course. He called you "Daddy"? Has he done that before?'

'Yes, often. I was happy about it. After all, I've adopted him. I feel a father's love for him.' His words were kind and reasonable, but he sounded grim. He sent Sarah for hot milk and aspirins, but they were no cure for what ailed his wife. She lay in the gathering darkness, struggling with her thoughts. She must tell him what was in her heart, but she wanted a little more time to gather herself together, just a little more.

Mabel would recover but Mattie, with tears in her eyes, told Adela that her sister would never bear another child. 'All her innards are spoilt,' she said in crude but graphic explanation.

'Maybe she won't mind too terribly,' comforted Adela. 'She wants to be a dancer. It's her chief ambition.'

'That's true. Oh, Mrs Bennett, I couldn't bear that to happen to me! I want to get married an' have babies one day. I think our Mabel would have been glad to have the baby if her man hadn't deserted her.'

'Poor Mabel. Have you ever met him?'

'No. She met him in Clevedon. She and Frank were allowed to dance with the guests after their act. She danced with a lot of men an' even Frank doesn't know who it was.' She paused. 'Mrs Bennett, it must have cost you a good bit of money to keep her in that lovely nursing home. She says that one day, when she's rich and famous, she'll pay you back.'

'Mr Bennett insisted on meeting the bill, Mattie. I don't think he wants repayment.'

'Maybe not, but Mabel always does what she says. Always!'

She gave a little shiver. 'She's got an awful strong will, has our Mabel.'

'Ida tells me that your work has returned to normal. I'm so glad.'

'Thank you, Mrs Bennett. It was a good day when you ran across to our house with Harry. Our Mum never looked for a reward, but she got one. She thinks the world of you.'

Brief images sped through Adela's mind. Herself, carrying her son, running from Bert Rawbone. Mrs Hobbs' ramshackle, grubby house filled with love. 'How is your mother?'

'Gettin' big. She hopes this will be the last baby.'

'I'm sure she does.'

Mattie returned to the showroom. Adela wondered if Mrs Hobbs would accept advice on birth control. Blanche had obtained a copy of *Married Love*, the book by Dr Marie Stopes which had caused such a furore in America and Britain. Adela had read it and decided that it was full of good, forthright advice, but she was still shy of discussing the subject openly. Perhaps Blanche or Georgie would help? They seemed to push their way through barriers, oblivious to convention. When she had married Sander he had been understanding, saying that he was willing to wait for children until she was ready. He took care of that side of things.

Sander and Adela were invited to a dinner party by Millie. Michael was there. He sat opposite Adela in the lovely dining room which she had created. The table and high-backed chairs were of stained oak and they ate from delicate white plates decorated with pale blue birds and soft yellow flowers. Twice Adela looked up and saw Sander's eyes on Michael and shuddered at his expression. Michael, not realising that Sander knew him to be Adela's lover, displayed all his usual charm and grace and captivated his neighbours: Vita on one side, and on the other a very young girl who had only recently made her debut in society and to whom he was paying extravagant attention, enjoying her smiles and blushes. Adela ate steadily, tasting nothing, regrets turning the food in her mouth to chaff.

After dinner, when the men joined the women in the drawing room, Millie poured coffee from a silver set with ivory handles, and the butler and a footman handed it round. Adela was desperate to speak to Michael. She must tell him that she had finished with him. Perhaps he sensed her need because he laughingly left the young girl, whose eyes followed him wistfully, and joined Adela on a white-painted wood and leather sofa.

'When can we meet?' he asked. He had his back to Sander, but Adela could see her husband and the way his eyes slanted angrily as he watched the pair.

Adela said to Michael, 'I have something to tell you.'

'That sounds quite ominous.' Adela thought she detected a note of alarm in his playful tones, but there was no time for more because Millie asked him to play the piano. Smiling, Michael agreed and within minutes the sound of jazz hit the room. '*Ain't we got fun,*' Michael sang. '*The rich get rich and the poor get poorer.*' Adela had had no idea that he could play at all, let alone play so well. In fact, she knew very little about him.

Sander came to sit beside her. 'Talented, isn't he?'

The words were innocuous but his voice held menace, and Adela said, 'I'm tired. I'd like to leave.'

'Of course, my dear. We'll stay just a little longer out of courtesy to our host and hostess, then you can remove yourself from the tantalising presence of your lover.'

'Sander, be quiet! Someone will hear.'

'Does that matter? Everyone will know when you abscond with him.'

'Sander, please.'

She had turned to him and for a moment their eyes met. Adela expected to find fury; instead she found grief. It was gone in an instant. Had she imagined it, or was it a reflection of her own agony of spirit?

Sander said nothing as he steered the car skilfully through the almost empty, echoing streets.

In bed he drew her to him, but she was exhausted, mentally more than physically. 'No. Not tonight. I'm tired. Really tired.'

'I'm sure if Webster wanted to go to bed with you your energy would be miraculously revived.'

'No,' she said, 'it would not.'

Sander was silent for a moment. 'You sound as if you actually mean it.'

'I do.' It was easier to talk in the dim light where she couldn't see Sander's face. 'I've finished with Michael.'

Sander sat up. 'Have you? Did you throw him over, or did he throw you?'

'Neither, yet, but I've come to my senses. I shall never be alone with him again, except to tell him that it's over. You're right, Sander, I mustn't leave you. I can't.' Damn! Those weren't the right words. She was making a hash of this and she wasn't surprised when he sounded cool.

'*Mustn't* leave me? *Can't*? Because of Harry?'

'I don't want to go.'

'You really don't? You want to stay with me?'

If only he would show some emotion she might be able to bring her tongue round the words, 'I love you.'

He slid down on to his pillows. 'I'm glad, Adela, for all our sakes. Very glad indeed.' Soon afterwards his even breathing told her he was asleep.

'Not see me again?' Michael was staring at her in disbelief. 'But, why?'

They were sitting in his untidy flat where she had consented to go for the last time.

'I've explained. I shall stay with Sander. My son has been badly hurt and I can't make things worse for him. I deliberately chose to bring him into the world. He's my responsibility.'

'Of course he is,' agreed Michael, looking relieved, 'and I'd never try to persuade you different. But that doesn't change our love. I still want you, and I know you want me. You do, don't you?'

'Have you heard a word of what I've just said?' she asked incredulously.

Michael came and sat beside her. 'Of course I have, honey.' He took her hands in his. 'You're trembling. Poor darling. It's going to be a wrench leaving you when I go back to the States, but let's take what happiness we can while there's time. Let's

541

not deny our love.' He put his arms round her and tried to kiss her, but she turned her head and his lips brushed her ear.

'Hell, Adela, what's got into you? You love me!' His hand moved swiftly to her breasts. She pushed him away.

'No! Stop it! It's all over. I'm going to stay with Sander.'

'I've told you I understand your reasons, but what's that got to do with us, here and now? I can't drag you away from him by force, but we can enjoy our love. It's been great. Don't deny us what happiness we can get. One day we'll be separated by three thousand miles of ocean. Let's take what we can while we're able. God, Adela, you're so beautiful, I can't keep my hands off you. When I see you with other people I go crazy inside with wanting you.'

Adela slid along the sofa away from him and looked at him, young, handsome, his eyes brilliant with desire, and felt nothing for him but revulsion. He was conceited; he thought so well of himself that he couldn't believe she could refuse him. Just hand out enough flattery and no woman could walk out on him. He had fooled her. In fact, if it weren't for Sander's insight and his patience with her, she might still be a willing victim.

Michael lit a cigarette. He didn't offer her one. 'Honey, why do you look at me like that?'

'Like what?'

'As if you didn't even like me. Come on, Adela, I know you too well to believe that. Let's go to bed.'

'I don't like you,' she said distinctly, 'and I certainly don't love you.'

Michael said sulkily, 'I know you do love me. You've proved it. You're settling for security.'

Adela saw that it was futile to try to pierce his vanity. She stood up. 'I'm leaving,' she said. 'I disgust myself.'

'Disgust?' Michael was furious. 'Because I made love to you?'

'Yes, but more because I made love to you.'

She walked out of his flat and down the stairs and out into the street where she breathed deeply of the fresh air.

In the days that followed Adela saw Michael constantly in society. He was always smiling, always with the prettiest women. Her love for Sander was swelling in her until she felt she would

542

explode with it and there were days when she had to struggle to get through her work. If only he would give her an opening! Even during their love-making he never said a word of love. Perhaps he wouldn't welcome a wife who made emotional demands which he couldn't fulfil? She remembered his childhood experiences and wondered if they had destroyed his capacity for true love. She worked harder than ever in her efforts to conquer her frustration. Bolts of material in her latest abstract designs had begun to arrive and she had to make an effort to appear enthusiastic.

'They're lovely,' said Ida. 'Are they intended for Bristol?'

'Yes. The last lot went quite well. Actually, I have a client who's keen already. Lord Charles is getting married at last, to an artist's model. His people are furious, but he's of age and has his own money and they have no say in it. She's all for constructivism and analytical cubism.'

'What does that mean?' asked Mattie.

'Don't pester Mrs Bennett with questions,' said Ida, though kindly. 'She's enough to do. You'll learn when she has time to teach you.'

'It's all right, Ida. She's right to ask. After all, she may one day be chief sales.'

Mattie was amazed. 'Me? I must learn everything, then. What do I say if a customer asks me questions about the stuff?'

Adela smiled. Somehow the sight of her most junior assistant's puzzled but admiring look gave her a lift.

'They're based on the work of artists I admire – Picasso, Braque and Gris – and others who use paint in what seems to some to be a haphazard way, but really with design and form. To me, it's exciting.'

'I wonder if I'd find them exciting,' said Mattie. 'I like the materials you design. Who else do you like?'

'There's Gino Severini, Paul Klee and Piet Mondrian. Many others.'

'Are all the artists foreigners?'

Adela laughed. 'A good question. I hadn't thought about it, but I reckon they are. One day, Mattie, you must travel abroad and visit art galleries.'

'No one in our family has ever been abroad,' said Mattie. 'Except the soldiers. Who started painting such different pictures?'

'I think it all came from a marvellous painter called Cézanne, though not everyone agrees.'

Mattie touched one of the bolts, running her fingers over the splashes of umber, burnt sienna, raw sienna and muted greens. 'Whose colours are these? They're not very bright.'

'No, they're Cézanne's. He painted a marvellous series of pictures of mountains. I've used the grey of his distant hills as a background.'

'Do you think they'll sell?'

'We'll have to wait and see. Britain is still heavily influenced by William Morris, but the continentals have embraced cubism, especially the Viennese.'

'You could hardly call this one subdued,' remarked Ida, unrolling another bolt.

'No, I wouldn't call scarlet subdued, though again I've used a blue-grey background.'

Mattie touched the cloth. 'It's lovely. All lines and bubbles and squares. And here's a blue and black and purple mixture. What big shapes!'

'Reminds me of a bruise,' murmured Ida wickedly.

Mattie looked shocked, but Adela laughed. 'I've ordered small quantities of each – some are only display samples, but I can get them made up quickly. Do your best with the draping, Ida. I've bought some glass for you to use, by the way – a bowl by Simon Gates and a more delicate creation by Edward Hald of the Orrefors company – and we'll be getting some chairs from the Netherlands painted pale fawn and blue which delineates their angular planes.'

Ida and Mattie looked bemused. 'You'll understand when you see them,' Adela assured them. 'All you need say is that they are all the rage in Paris and the customers will buy so that they can boast to their friends.'

'Rich people are Paris-mad since the war,' said Ida, disapprovingly. 'They should stay home an' sort out the muddle their own country's in.'

*　　*　　*

The new materials caught the customers' fancy and Adela was so busy visiting local mills and factories, creating new designs and discussing decor, that she had no time to think of Michael or even Sander. She went to bed dead tired and fell asleep instantly. Sander let her rest. But she made sure she was home at Harry's bedtime. She bathed him, dressed him in his nightgown and read a story to him, each night bringing her more pleasure than the one before. He kissed her and hugged her tight before drifting into peaceful slumber.

'He doesn't have the bad dreams any more,' said Bill. 'I thought he'd never get over them. Some woman must have been very wicked to him.'

Adela made a non-committal sound. She wondered just how much Bill knew. Not that it mattered. Sander had given him work when no one else would and he thought the world of him. He'd never gossip. Sander had finally relinquished him completely to the nursery, another of his uncomplaining sacrifices, saying that it wouldn't do to disrupt Harry's life in any way. Bill had accepted the responsibility and the nursemaid was good at her work, and kind.

Adela often didn't eat at home; frequently she forgot to eat at all, but Sarah was always waiting for her, ready to produce some dainty sandwiches and hot milk.

'You're an angel in disguise,' Adela said.

'I'm glad to do it for you, but it's Mr Bennett you have to thank. He gave me instructions. It's wonderful how much he thinks of you.'

Adela knew how right she was. Sander made love to her infrequently, considerately. Now her chief wonder was why it had taken her so long to recognise her husband's worth. She forced herself to concentrate on building up her business. She could definitely count herself successful with more machinists added to the workroom staff and two very superior ladies in the showroom, which left Ida free to concentrate on her artistic displays while Mattie learned everything she could from everybody. Andy Barton had proved to be excellent at figures and was a real help to Freddy in the office. Adela was negotiating for a shop in Castle Street, quite near Sander's. When she had told him she was setting up in direct competition with him, he had merely grinned infuriatingly. 'May the best man win,' he had said.

Adela lay back in bed thankfully. It was only ten o'clock, but she'd been working since six this morning. Usually she fell asleep immediately, but tonight she couldn't. She felt hot and rather sick and wished she hadn't eaten the sandwiches faithfully produced by Sarah. She drifted into a heavy doze, then awoke, her heart pounding. She sat up in bed. She was pregnant! She knew it as surely as if a doctor had just voiced the fact.

She went over the past few weeks. She had been busy blanking out thoughts that hurt, keeping her mind solely on work, letting all other considerations slide, and along with them had gone her careful checking of dates. How far gone was she? She slumped back on to the pillows, thinking, Dear God, let me be carrying Sander's baby. Don't let it be Michael's. What would Sander say now? What would he do? The nausea passed and she lay still, struggling with this new horror she had brought on herself. Sander would be late tonight and she had the big bed to herself. Eventually she slept.

Adela kept her news to herself. Once she broke it to Sander their situation would change forever and she wasn't ready to cope. First, she must see a doctor, find out exactly how far the pregnancy had progressed, but she kept putting it off, afraid of what she might learn, afraid that the child she carried might not be her husband's. Sander suggested a party, telling her she needed cheering up. The drawing room must be cleared for dancing, of course. Since the war the world had gone dance-mad and a hostess who didn't offer dancing would be considered a failure. Ida was to help decorate the house with flowers and Mattie asked if Mabel and Frank could come and perform an exhibition dance.

'Is Mabel well again, Mattie?' asked Adela.

'Oh, yes, Mrs Bennett. It took a while, but she's already been on three engagements. She gets ever so tired an' Mum grumbles, but Mabel doesn't take any notice. She's goin' to be famous, she says. She will, too. Like I said, she does whatever she makes up her mind for.'

Chapter Twenty-Eight

Adela's house looked beautiful. Ida and Mrs Monkton had arranged creamy yellow and peach roses and white carnations against pale green foliage, which blended with the delicate decor and filled the rooms with perfume. The approaching party had a mercifully numbing effect on Adela. Afterwards, she *must* face reality and talk to Sander.

She wore a green silk-velvet dress, draped and cut deeply to reveal her flawless skin. On her left hip was a waterfall of crystal beads, repeated in her earrings. Her shoes matched her dress. The whole ensemble looked deceptively simple but she had splashed out and bought a model creation by Madeleine et Madeleine. She went to the nursery to say goodnight to Harry who began to run to her then stopped, one finger in his mouth. He moved towards her slowly. 'Pretty Mummy,' he said, pointing to the beads. He seemed to know instinctively that he must not mark her dress. 'Pretty Mummy,' he said again. Adela felt tears pricking her eyes as she bent to kiss him.

'I've come to read you a story before the party begins,' she said.

He chose *Beauty and the Beast*, a story he never tired of. Sander said it was because the dramatic changes in the life of the heroine were similar to those in Harry's own. She was no longer surprised by her husband's perception.

She had sent invitations to everyone and most had accepted. Blanche and Georgie were almost the first to arrive: Georgie in a mannish suit with an eyeglass, Blanche in a brown lace dress.

'You look spiffing,' said Georgie to Adela. Her language was occasionally inclined to take on nursery overtones. 'Doesn't she, Blanche?'

547

'Spiffing,' agreed Blanche laconically. 'I hear you've invited the Hobbs pair to perform a cabaret.'

'That's true. Mattie assures me that Mabel is going to get to the top of her profession and I've had good reports of their dancing.'

'Poor young Mabel's had a rotten time,' said Georgie. 'Bloody men! They wreak their damage and go on their way. I'm glad I'll never be beholden to one.'

The pair drifted on towards the dining room where cocktails were being dispensed. Millie and her husband arrived soon after, followed by Bobbie and Gerard, then the trickle became a flow.

Giles and Sybil Somers came. Sybil gave Adela a swift kiss. 'I really love your house, Adela, and lots of people admire mine since you redecorated it.'

'I'm so glad. Have you grown to like it?' Adela asked Giles.

'Oh, yes,' said Sybil, 'he does, don't you, Giles? Well, at least, he's stopped moaning about it.'

'Good. Do you know if Desmond and Violet intend to be here?'

Giles turned to greet a friend and Sybil leaned forward and said confidentially, 'I shouldn't think so, though I've a suspicion that Violet would like to come. She's pretty stuck up but even she's getting fed up with Desmond's stuffy ways. I'm glad Giles is more biddable.'

'What about Lady Somers?'

'She sends her apologies. She wanted to come, too, but Sir Wilfred had a previous engagement. Well, he said he had. Personally I don't believe him. He's not a very *kind* man, Adela. I don't think you would have cared for him as a father-in-law.' Once again poor Sybil had blundered and she coloured. 'Sorry, I didn't mean, that's to say—'

Adela cut short her embarrassment. 'I'm sorry they won't be here,' she said. 'I'm especially fond of Lady Somers.' Poor soul, she thought, she would be disappointed at not getting another glimpse of Harry. Since her discovery of his parentage she had seen him only once. She was careful. She wanted no scandal attached to Ralph's only child. Adela knew a brief moment of thankfulness that she had decided to remain with Sander, and even more for his generosity of spirit which brightened her days in spite of all her worries.

As Sybil moved on, Sander muttered, 'That swine Somers is probably spending the evening in his club just to spite his wife. What did you do to make that family dislike you so much, Adela?'

'Marry you, I think,' she said. Sander laughed, then they were obliged to welcome more guests. Michael had not been asked and Adela was irritated to see him arrive with Vita and Sir Claud.

'You don't mind, do you, darling?' cried Vita. 'Michael was a dinner guest.'

'Michael is welcome,' said Adela quietly, her composure shaken by the intensity with which he stared at her.

The drawing-room rugs had been lifted, revealing the polished light oak floor, and the band struck up a tango, a dance which had shocked many until Queen Mary had enjoyed watching it in the modified European form. Adela watched the dancers for a while. Several couples had taken the floor and were swaying and dipping to the pulsating beat. Then Michael appeared at her side and bowed and asked her to dance. There were many eyes upon them. She glanced around quickly and saw that Vita, in particular, was watching them closely. If she refused Michael, a discourteous thing to do in any case, Vita's snake tongue would find a reason to gossip.

She moved and swayed to the heady music in Michael's arms. 'You shouldn't have asked me to dance.'

He laughed down at her in a way which would once have melted her heart. 'You don't mean that.'

'I do!'

'No, you don't. I can see it in your face.'

'My God, can't you take the truth?'

'I've missed you, darling. When can we be together again?'

'I've told you, it's finished, over, dead!'

Michael's arm tightened around her. 'You can't deny that you want me.' Adela could think of nothing to say to convince him.

He insisted, 'You want me, don't you? In spite of deciding to go all respectable on me, you *do* want me. Go on, admit it.'

'I do not – and when you behave this way I hate you!'

'Hate can be a powerful aphrodisiac.'

'Will you be quiet! Someone will hear.'

'So what? People discuss all kinds of things these days. Nobody's shocked.'

'Some are, and everyone gossips. It's become a national disease.'

'There have always been gossips, and surely you should be used to it by now?'

'What's that supposed to mean?' she snapped.

They were forced to suspend the argument to concentrate on the exaggerated movements of the tango. When they were able to talk again it was obvious that Michael was annoyed. He no longer smiled as he continued where they had left off: 'There was your mysterious disappearance to Cornwall when you were really in Bristol. Then, when you married Bennett, you suddenly produced a rather elderly child.'

'Harry has been adopted,' said Adela, 'and if I were you I shouldn't let Sander hear you say anything detrimental about him.'

'But Harry is your natural son. Plenty of folk in St Pauls and St Philips know about him. How long do you think you can keep it a secret?'

They were obliged to stop talking again to execute another manoeuvre, then Michael said, 'How long, Adela, before someone throws mud?'

'I don't know,' she said flatly, 'and I don't care. Sander is quite capable of dealing with anyone foolish enough to try to hurt Harry – or me.'

'Sander! Sander! You weren't so damned impressed with him when you made love to me.'

'Be quiet!' she hissed. 'I've a good mind to walk off the floor now.'

Michael laughed. 'You do that, honey, and watch people's faces.' Adela didn't answer and he said, 'Gran says you're a hussy.' Adela looked up angrily to see that he was openly mocking her. 'There's no point in getting your dander up with me, honey. I don't give a cuss what you did in the past. It's only the here and now that interests me.'

'Why won't you leave me in peace?'

Michael bent his head to hers and said softly, 'I want you. I'll do anything to get you back. Anything!'

'What do you mean by anything?'

'Vita loves to dish the dirt.'

Adela's stomach churned. 'Vita? Are you threatening me?'

'I love you, Adela. A guy in love has to do the best he can.'

'You'd tell Vita? About Harry, about me and you? That isn't love – that's blackmail. You don't know the meaning of love.'

'Does your husband?'

'My husband is my business.'

The dance finished and Michael put his hand under Adela's elbow, holding it firmly. 'I might make him my business. I wonder what he'd do if I told him about our little interludes?'

Adela looked up at him. 'I think it's very likely he'd kill you.' She wanted to tell Michael that Sander already knew, but she couldn't. Not here.

He dropped her arm and she walked swiftly away from him. Sander was standing in the doorway and it was obvious that he had been watching. His eyes were stormy. 'Enjoy your tango?' he asked.

'He's a good dancer.' She hurried past him and upstairs to the bedroom. She must have a few moments alone.

The door opened and Sander strode in. 'Come downstairs, you little fool. Do you think your guests can't put two and two together? Vita looks like she's going to explode. She's ready to stick a knife into your back.'

'Damn Vita!' Adela said with a dry sob. 'And why should she be annoyed? Damn her, and damn them all! I don't know why we decided to have this bloody party.'

'Because it's good for our social and business life.'

'If we hadn't, I shouldn't have been obliged to dance with Michael. I didn't enjoy it, whatever you or anyone else might think.'

Sander looked at her closely. 'I believe you're telling the

truth. You really didn't enjoy it. How unflattering for him. Is that why he looks like thunder?'

'Does he? Oh, Sander, he was threatening me, saying he'd tell Vita all about our affair if I refused to see him again, and you know what that means. She'll tell everyone.'

He said grimly, 'If that happens it'll be another thing we must face together, Adela. It can't be helped. But if you don't wish to dance with Webster again, I'll make damn sure it doesn't happen. Now, no more talking. We must return to our guests.'

The evening dragged for Adela, though everyone appeared to be enjoying themselves. She was thankful when the supper break was announced and the revellers flocked to fill plates with small lobster and oyster patties, tiny sandwiches, salads and jellies, creams and icecream, fresh fruit. The meal was deliberately light. Curves were unfashionable; the craze for slimming had taken a hold on everyone who wanted to be able to follow the new slender line.

Afterwards Mabel and Frank Hobbs would be giving their exhibition dances. They had already arrived and Adela had allotted them a small parlour in which to change.

'Are you well now, Mabel?' Adela asked.

'Yes, thanks, Mrs Bennett. Perfectly well.' Mabel's eyes were too brilliant, her movements restive.

'Would you like refreshments before or after your act?'

'Oh, after, thanks,' said Frank. 'We can't dance on full stomachs.' He had grown much taller and was acquiring the polished look of a professional. Both he and his sister wore elegant clothes which had clearly been made to measure.

'You look successful,' said Adela.

'We are that, Mrs Bennett,' said Frank. 'Mabel—' He stopped, reddening.

'Is over the little inconvenience that interfered with her dancin',' said Mabel harshly.

'I'm glad.' Damn, that wasn't the right thing to say, but what *could* one say in the face of such a disaster as had overtaken Mabel? She wanted to add something sympathetic but the girl's attitude didn't invite further comment.

As Adela turned to go, Mabel asked casually, 'Is Vita Wethered here?'

Adela turned, a little annoyed by her tone. 'Miss Wethered is a guest, yes. Why do you ask?'

'I just wondered. I haven't seen her around so much lately. Is Sir Claud with her?'

'Yes.'

'Good.'

Adela felt uneasy as she left the room.

The exhibition dances proved that Frank and Mabel Hobbs possessed immense talent. Their lithe young bodies made even the most crazy jazz dance look both easy and attractive. Frank, strong, graceful in his white tie and tails, was a perfect complement to Mabel who wore scarlet and twisted and leapt like a flame. Adela had no doubt that they would reach the top of their profession. Afterwards, as had become the custom, she invited them to dance with the guests.

'Such a good idea,' Vita said, stifling a yawn. 'God, how weary one gets of parties.'

Claud gave his fiancée a searching look and she scowled. 'Don't glare at me, Claud. I won't have it. What's got into you?'

'If anyone is glaring it is you,' said Claud in a precise voice, quite unlike his usual drawl. 'I cannot think why you are so weary lately. You used to be able to keep up with the crowd. Now you frequently refuse invitations.'

'Are you insinuating I'm getting long in the tooth?' Vita's voice was shrill and several people looked round.

'Certainly not! No such thing,' said Claud, immediately uneasy at the attention he and Vita were receiving.

Adela watched Frank Hobbs bow gracefully to Millie and ask her to join him in a foxtrot. Then, to her irritation, Michael walked over and stopped by her side as she stood in uneasy conversation with Vita and Sir Claud. Vita's blue eyes slanted up at Michael in a provocative smile.

The band were preparing for the next dance when the crowd parted and Mabel appeared. She walked slowly and sinuously up to Michael. 'Dance?' she asked laconically.

He reddened, clearly reluctant.

'Come on, Michael, just a quick turn round the room. I'm allowed to dance with the nobs,' said Mabel.

'Go away!' said Vita. 'No one here wishes to dance with you. We prefer to keep our own company.'

Michael looked uneasily at his companions, then at Mabel. 'You heard Miss Wethered,' he said. 'You must go away. I don't want to dance with you.'

'Is that so?' Mabel raised her voice until it rose easily over the soft music of *A Kiss in the Dark* and reached each member of the small group. 'Michael does want to dance with me, really, don't you, darlin'? No? You used to enjoy holdin' me, and not only for dancin'.'

'What the hell are you talking about?' snapped Vita. She was angrier than Adela had ever seen her, and combined with her anger was a note of fear.

'Michael knows, don't you, lover boy? In case you were wonderin', I lost the baby, but that doesn't bother you, does it? I was very ill. It'll affect my future but not yours, so that's all right, isn't it?'

The atmosphere was so filled with hate it was almost tangible. Vita looked as if she could quite easily kill Mabel and it wouldn't take much more of this to provoke Michael into violence.

Adela was shocked, then filled with a deep sense of disgust. Michael's face told it all. Mabel had been seduced by 'one of the nobs'. Of course! No matter what his family history had been, Mabel and her brother had only met Michael at grand houses, dressed in impeccable clothes. He had swiftly removed himself from his grandmother's house and taken a flat in a better part of Bristol, and his speech, his manners and his friends effectively removed him from any day-to-day connection with the Hobbs' background. He had fathered a child on Mabel who had nearly died as a result.

Pain and regret tore through Adela at her blind stupidity in falling for such a despicable man. Sander had rescued her from her folly. Sander had been instrumental in saving Mabel's life; they had both been embroiled in situations caused by Michael. She wanted to run away, to escape from the images which filled her mind, but she was unable to move.

Vita said to Mabel in a low, furious voice, 'Go away, you stupid little bitch.'

'Oh, I'm goin', I just thought you'd be interested to know that you were sharin' your lover with me. If you wanted, we could get together an' compare notes. Michael's good, isn't he? At makin' love, I mean. He's bad, really. You want to be careful, Vita, in case he lets you down like he did me, though I expect a grand society lady like yourself won't get caught with a kid like I did. An', of course, Sir Claud will want to be in the picture, too, won't you, Sir Claud? I'm sorry for you, I really am. I would have thought you could have done better for yourself than a cow like Vita Wethered.'

Adela had been quite still, riveted by horror and disgust. People were getting wind of something interesting going on and were beginning to drift towards them. She wondered what had already been overheard. She was the hostess and she must do something, anything, to try to defuse the situation. The band struck up and Adela looked up to see Sander approaching, presumably to protect her from Michael. He saw her face and she could tell by his expression that he realised at once that something was very wrong. She meant to wait for him, but abruptly felt horribly ill and hurried from the room.

She was detained by a hand on her arm. 'What's happened?' asked Sander. He was holding her in a firm but gentle grip.

'Let me go, please,' was all she could gasp.

'Are you ill? You don't look so good.'

'I'm all right,' she managed. 'At least, I will be soon.'

'Who's upset you like this?' He dropped her arm, frowning. 'Was it Michael Webster?'

'No! Yes – You don't understand!'

'Come in here.'

Sander drew her into the small parlour used by Frank and Mabel, empty now. 'Tell me why you're running away.'

Adela's torment was too great to stifle. Sander was the only one she could talk to, the only one she would permit to hear her anguished moan. 'I'm running from everyone. I feel dirty. I've been used.'

'By Webster!'

'Yes.'

'But that's nothing new.'

'I know, but I did think he loved me or I would never have yielded to him. What a fool I've been! Sander, I've just discovered that he's also been making love to Vita.'

'My dear, I did warn you. He uses everybody, and he takes from everyone, especially women. No female is safe with him. He never gives anything of value.'

'That's not quite true,' said Adela bitterly. 'He gave Mabel Hobbs her baby.'

'My God! So it was he who fathered her child? That shouldn't surprise me. And he refused to help her. He really is a swine. He nearly killed the poor kid. How old is she? Sixteen? Seventeen? I always knew he was worthless.'

'Yes, you always knew,' Adela said tonelessly.

Sander stared down at her. 'You're feeling horribly humiliated, aren't you?'

'Yes. If you wanted revenge, you've got it in full.'

'I don't want revenge, Adela. I'm truly sorry.'

'What have you to be sorry about? I'm the one who cheated.'

'Nevertheless, I'm still sorry.'

'Are you? I believe you are, a little. I wonder how long that will last.'

'What do you mean?'

'Something has happened. No, I can't tell you now. Later.'

'Tonight!' It was a statement.

'Yes, all right, tonight.'

The door opened and Mabel and Frank came in. Frank looked angry, Mabel sulky but triumphant.

'I'm sorry, Mrs Bennett,' said Frank. 'Our Mabel shouldn't have made a scene at your party.'

'It wasn't so much of a scene,' said Adela. 'Few people heard.'

'Only the right ones,' said Mabel. 'That bugger deserved to be shown up for what he is. I vowed I'd get my own back on him.'

'Mattie told me you always kept your promises.'

'She's right, an' now Sir Claud knows what his precious

fiancée was up to. He's gone home, Mrs Bennett. I don't think Miss Wethered will be Lady Overton after all.'

'You could lose us work,' muttered Frank. 'Just as our act is gettin' off the ground.'

'Oh, hell, I didn't stop to think of that! Well, Michael Webster deserved it. Remember what he did to me. It'll be with me as long as I live.'

Tears filled Mabel's eyes and Frank handed her a handkerchief. 'Don't cry, sis.'

'Try to be brave, Mabel,' Sander said. His voice was immensely gentle. 'Mrs Bennett and I feel sad for you, but no one can alter the past. Make the most of what you have. You and Frank are highly gifted and, if there can be a good side to this wretched business, you'll get more engagements than ever because everyone will want to see the girl who shared a lover with Vita.'

'An' they won't look down on you because you're a show-girl,' said Frank grimly, 'but they'll have their knives in Miss Wethered.'

'She didn't look as if she really cared a bit,' sobbed Mabel. 'I shouldn't have done it. I daresay we'll be the ones to suffer. That sort always get away with things. They've got money.'

'Calm down,' said Adela softly. 'You're probably still not well. My husband is right, you know. You'll get lots of engagements. I promise I'll recommend you here, and in London, too, but don't let any more society lounge lizards tempt you.'

'Don't worry, Mrs Bennett, I've learned my lesson, though it's a bit late in the day.' Tears flowed again.

Frank put his arms round his sister. 'Cheer up, my love. Mr and Mrs Bennett know what they're talkin' about an', like they say, what's past is past.'

'But Michael goes everywhere. I'll have to see him all the time, an' he'll most likely blacken my name. An' so will Vita.'

Sander said firmly, 'I doubt if Vita will say much in the circumstances. If she's really lost Claud, her own reputation will be in the balance and, in spite of the present so-called liberality, a woman's reputation is still important. As for Michael, he'll soon be returning to the States.'

'Will he?' Mabel looked up hopefully. 'How do you know?'

'Just accept that I do know. I doubt if he'll return to Britain again either. At least, not for a very long time. You'll be spared that.'

'I hope so. Oh, Frank—' Mabel wept into her brother's shoulder.

'Cool down,' he said. 'You're ruining my new suit.'

Mabel managed a shaky laugh.

'Blow your nose,' said her brother, 'an' we'll go home.'

Sander and Adela went into the hall to see them off. Vita had just arrived there on her way out. The butler was placing her fur evening wrap about her shoulders. 'Goodnight, madam. I trust you enjoyed the evening.'

'Ah, my host and hostess,' said Vita, ignoring him. 'Thank you so much for a most interesting party. Such a pity that one is laid open these days to insults from one's inferiors. I shall make sure I never engage that poisonous pair.'

Frank nodded affably to her and said, 'May we give you a lift, Miss Wethered? Of course, our car is only a small one – not what you're used to—'

'Go to blazes!' she snapped.

Frank shrugged and put his hand beneath his sister's elbow as they negotiated the front steps with dignity. Sander and Adela watched as he handed his sister courteously into their small, battered car.

'That young man will go far,' said Sander, 'if he can keep control over Mabel.'

'She was wickedly deceived,' said Adela. 'Michael is disgusting.'

Vita had stayed in the hall. She walked up close to Adela, her eyes sending out sparks of fury. 'That's not what you used to say about him, is it? Did you know, Sander, that Michael was Adela's lover as well? Michael covered a lot of ground, didn't he? Oh, by the way, where is he?'

'I've no idea,' said Sander, making no effort to conceal his distaste for her. 'Haven't you?'

Vita hesitated for a moment. 'He'll soon get in touch with me.' She gave Adela a contemptuous look. 'He loves me, you know. He has all along. We used to laugh about you.' She turned and left.

Adela could scarcely bear to look at her husband. 'How vile she is! She's bound to talk.'

'Maybe she won't. She's very vain, and it isn't very flattering to her to know that Michael was paying attention to at least two other women while he was seducing her.'

'None of it is very flattering to me.'

'No. Come on, Adela.'

'Where?'

'Back to the dance, of course.'

'Must I? I feel ghastly.'

'You'll feel a lot worse if you don't face up to our guests now.'

'Do you think anyone else heard Mabel?'

'Possibly, but she didn't say anything to involve you.'

'I shouldn't be surprised if Vita had already talked. She's the most vicious woman I know.'

'All the more reason to face it out with your devoted husband,' he said briskly. 'We'll kill the talk stone dead.' In a softer voice he said, 'Adela, you were kind to Mabel.'

'So were you. She needs kindness after what she's been through.'

'I know, but you'd just learned something which devastated you. What you did was commendable.'

'Was it? I've had an excellent teacher.'

Her meaning was clear and Sander looked pleased.

'Come along, my dear. Back to the dance.'

When they re-entered the drawing room there were curious looks. It was obvious that the guests did know there had been some kind of scene and were having fun trying to guess who, or what, was involved. The band had been swinging a jazz number, but now they broke into a waltz and Sander put his arms round Adela and held her close. Her body moved in unison with his, their steps matched perfectly. She felt safe. Sander's embrace was a haven in the midst of chaos.

'Smile,' he said. 'Look as if you're enjoying a waltz with your husband.'

'I'll try. I mean, I am, truly. You're a good dancer.'

'Good God! If that ghastly smile is all you can manage, you'd do better to scowl.'

'Sorry, I really don't feel at all well.' Adela forced her lips into a happy smile.

'That's better.'

Adela wished the dance would go on forever so that she'd never have to face up to the future, to the possible consequences of her reckless behaviour. She laid her head on Sander's shoulder and smelled the tang of his soap, the scent of his tobacco; she sensed the powerful passions which he was suppressing. He wanted to make love to her. If only he loved her! When the dance ended she was reluctant to move away and he gave her a gentle push then escorted her from the floor.

'Can I get you a drink?' he asked.

'Do I look as if I need it?'

'Yes.'

'A champagne cocktail, then, please.'

He called a servant who brought over the drink. 'Cigarette, Adela?'

'Yes, please.'

Sander snapped his lighter and she took a long drag, then felt her stomach heave and remembered that pregnancy turned her off cigarettes.

'Excuse me,' she gasped, and hurried into the hall for fresh air. She looked at herself in the hall mirror. She was pale, her hair a little dishevelled, and she went to the downstairs cloakroom to tidy herself. The door was solid and the music came to her distantly, the beat of the drum throbbing insistently. There was a tap at the door.

'Are you all right?' asked Sarah. 'Mr Bennett wondered.'

Sander had sent her maid. He hadn't left her alone since Mabel's outburst, in spite of the fact that she had been unfaithful to him, had treated him shamefully. Her emotions felt twisted and jagged as a wave of bitter remorse engulfed her. She had used Sander even more selfishly than Michael had used her, and she had spoiled everything. She had been an immature fool, grabbing at a mirage, wallowing in sexual infatuation, believing it to be love. Now she had to tell Sander that she was pregnant and he might not believe the child to be his. How many chances was he prepared to give her?

'Mrs Bennett! Are you all right in there?' called Sarah more urgently.

'I'm fine. I'll be out soon.'

Sarah was waiting for her. 'My goodness, your hair needs doin' properly an' you look pale. Come upstairs, do, and let me make you presentable again.'

Adela returned to her guests, her hair immaculate, her cheeks slightly rouged.

'There you are, darling,' said Sander. 'Webster has left and we're just in time for the Turkey Trot.'

Even had she wanted to there was no opportunity to talk while following the fast steps of the dance. The musicians blasted out the music in the new approved style, pointing the wind instruments towards the ceiling in movements as exaggerated as the dance itself. It was said that this had been a necessity in the Hammersmith Palais because of the crush of people determined to follow the new dance fashions, and it had caught on and become part of the jazz scene.

Adela danced herself into exhaustion, with Sander, with others, receiving with bright smiles compliments on her vitality, her beauty, the house, the party. When the final guest left in the early hours, she made her way upstairs to her room. Sarah had waited up.

'I told you to go to bed,' said Adela wearily.

'It's a good job I disobeyed,' scolded Sarah. 'You look dreadful.'

'Thanks.'

'If a personal maid can't speak her mind, who can? You work too hard to be stayin' up half the night.' Sarah helped her mistress out of her clothes and led her to a hot bath. 'You'll feel better for it, an' when you're in bed I'll bring you some malted milk. It'll help you sleep.'

'I don't think I need it.'

'Maybe, maybe not. Sometimes a person gets too tired to sleep. You'd best have it.'

Sarah had left and Adela was lying back on her pillows when the door opened and Sander walked in. 'How are you?' he asked.

'Better after Sarah's ministrations,' she said with a smile.

'Good. You have something to tell me, I know, but it can wait. You need rest.'

Later, as she was drifting into sleep, Sander climbed into bed beside her and placed one of his large artisan's hands on her waist. It was warm and strong and promised safety. She slept.

She was up late for work and Sander had already left. She was regretful, wishing he had awakened her. Adela spent most of the day going through accounts with Freddy and talking to customers she knew. As soon as she could slip away she phoned her doctor – not the one in St Pauls, a new fashionable one – and asked for an immediate appointment. It was granted. No one would wish to offend the wealthy Bennetts.

The doctor examined her gently. 'Yes, my dear, you are expecting a child, but it's very early days yet. I'm amazed that you suspected it. I can scarcely trace the difference in your womb.'

'Very early days? How early?'

'Not more than six weeks. Possibly five. It's never possible to predict with absolute accuracy, especially so soon.'

Adela drove to the Downs and sat in her car, under the trees, thinking back. If the doctor was right, the child was Sander's. She wanted to believe it, she longed to bask in the joy of it, but she was still afraid.

That night they dined alone and afterwards, in the small, quiet drawing room, Sander said, 'I've given orders that we shouldn't be disturbed. We can talk now.'

'Yes.' Adela's nerves were jumping.

'Good.' He came to sit beside her on the couch. 'Well then, I'm listening.'

'I saw the doctor today.'

'And?'

'I'm expecting a baby.'

There was silence and Adela's heart began to race. 'Say something, please,' she whispered.

'I'm sorry, I've no wish to hurt you, but I have to ask the obvious question, Adela. Is it mine?'

'The doctor thinks I'm only five or six weeks into the pregnancy and I haven't – I didn't—'

'You haven't slept with Webster in that time.'

'No,' she gasped.

'Yet you sound worried.'

'Doctors can be wrong. And you said you wouldn't dream of giving me a child until I was ready, and we haven't discussed it.'

'No, that's true.'

'Oh, Sander, I pray that it's yours.'

'I'm sure it is. Adela, lately I've not taken a single precaution. I don't really know why. Perhaps I had it in mind to make you pregnant and keep you here. Do you mind?'

'Oh, I'm glad, so glad.'

Sander turned her to face him. 'You really mean that, don't you? You want my baby.'

'Yes, oh, yes! Sander I love you. I love you! I've wanted to tell you before, but I wasn't sure if you'd want me to. Then my pregnancy – I thought – I wondered – if you'd think I was using it just to stay with you. I couldn't bear to be sent away. I love you so.'

Sander had been listening to her, his hands on her shoulders, his watchful dark eyes seeming to probe her mind. 'By God, you do, you really do. Adela!' He pulled her to him. 'My love, if only you knew how I've longed to hear you say those words.'

'You love me?' she asked uncertainly.

'I think I always have.' He gave a little laugh. 'Why do you think I've been so ready to rescue you.'

'I didn't know. I thought you had ulterior motives at first. Then I believed everything you did was for Harry.'

'If I had any other motives, they came a long way second to my love for you. As for Harry, I saw him as the boy I once was. A boy who could end up as wounded as I did. I'll never willingly watch a child suffer like that. The little fellow has already been through hell. I aimed to secure his future.'

They were quiet for a while, then walked up the stairs

together to bed and made love in an untamed way such as Adela had never known before. Her whole body was alive with exquisite sensation as she gave herself, wholly and entirely, for the first time in mutual love.

After all that had occurred it seemed dream-like to return to work. Adela missed Bertha who, after Mr Danby's death, had gone to her former mistress, hoping to comfort her. She had returned only briefly. 'She wants me back, Miss Adela!' Her face was alight with happiness. 'She's forgiven me and she'll take me back. I'm afraid she's lonely. One day she'll want you, too, I just know she will.'

Adela felt well as long as she avoided getting over-fatigued and she continued to produce her designs and to visit the factories and outworkers. One of her favourites was the joiner's shop run by a man and his two sons. When she entered it one afternoon she sniffed at the scents of cut wood, lacquer, paint, and even the glue which was kept hot constantly on a stove. She no longer felt sick as she had with Harry. Perhaps her happiness had something to do with it.

Dan Phipps turned to her as she entered and his sons paused in their work of turning chair legs, to smile. When their country had nothing to offer them after the war, Mrs Bennett had given them employment.

'How are you getting on with the beechwood chairs?' she asked.

'Just fine,' said Dan. 'When we've japanned and gilded them, you'll not know them from Regency.'

Adela smiled. 'Good. Of course my customer will be told that they are reproductions.'

'I wouldn't expect anything else from you, Mrs Bennett, but I dare say some folk will sell them for originals. Some folk got no morals.'

Adela watched the work for a while, then asked them to make her a beechwood cradle. Her child would lie in the sweet-scented wood. Sander's child. She had had time to calculate dates and the doctor was now positive in his diagnosis. She loved Sander more each day; each day was filled with a joy which she often felt she didn't deserve. She saw Michael sometimes, but he held no power over her now. She was cocooned in perfect safety.

Dan smiled. 'It'll be the most beautiful cradle ever made,' he promised.

Esther had grown even more morose and miserable and Adela asked her to wait after hours. Her daughter, Rose, was now too active to leave in the garden room and Esther's mother had taken on her care while Esther was at work. Adela made tea and produced some biscuits.

'What do you want to see me about?' Esther asked distantly.

It wasn't a good beginning and exemplified the gulf which had grown between them. 'Have a little refreshment, Esther. You've been hard at work all day, as usual. In fact, I think you're working too hard.'

Esther allowed herself a small smile. 'That's a strange thing for an employer to say.'

'But I'm more than your employer, I'm your friend. Something is making you miserable. Can't you talk to me about it? We used to share confidences.'

Esther pressed her lips together and shook her head.

'Please, I don't mean to pry, but you look positively ill sometimes. You know whatever you tell me won't go any further.'

Esther took some tea, but refused the biscuits. She sat silently for a while, then said, 'It would be a relief to talk to someone.' She paused. 'I suppose there's no harm in it now it's over. Adela, I've been having a love affair and I'm so ashamed, with Bert as ill as he is.'

Adela pitied her. 'No one could blame you.'

'Plenty would.'

'So many of our soldiers are permanently disabled. There must be other women who get lonely.'

'I know that's true, but it doesn't help. I feel I've let Bert down, but the most awful thing is I feel more miserable about losing the man than I do about deceiving my poor husband.'

'Has he gone away?'

'Not yet, but he soon will and I'll be glad. I'm still tempted to see him, though I know he's no good. I don't understand how I've let myself get into such a state.'

'You need someone to care for,' suggested Adela.

'Yes, but it was wrong all the same. I've never stopped feeling guilty about this affair, not for a single second.'

'I'm so sorry.'

Once having broken her silence, Esther wanted to talk. 'You know the man. He's Jack Webster's son. He's so handsome. He told me he had fallen in love with me and I fell for him completely.'

Adela put down her cup and saucer so hard that the saucer cracked.

'Oh, it's broken,' cried Esther.

'It doesn't matter. So Michael Webster has been making love to you?'

Esther was shocked. 'Oh, no, nothing like that, but he wanted to and once I almost let him, only I knew how wrong that would be. First he got angry with me, then he said he wouldn't see me again because he couldn't bear it unless I let him love me. Oh, God, Adela, I did want to, so much. One night I couldn't stand it and went to his flat – I'm disgusted just hearing myself say this – I don't know what I intended to do, whether I would have gone to bed with him or not, but I was saved from the decision. I saw him open the door to let Miss Wethered in. It was late at night and why would a woman like Vita Wethered call on Michael at that hour? I've been so stupid and I'm so ashamed.'

Adela looked at Esther's sad face. How many more women had Michael tried to seduce? 'I'm sorry you've been hurt,' she said, 'but it could have been worse.'

'Yes, I know. I've heard about poor Mabel Hobbs.'

'How?'

Esther flushed. 'Lots of people know what happened to Mabel, and a couple of customers were talking in the showroom about a scene she made at a party at your house. Thank God I didn't let him take liberties with me!'

'How is Bert?' asked Adela gently.

'His condition is slowly destroying his health and they tell me that he can't live very much longer,' Esther said unhappily. 'Freddy Stanton still wants me. I've promised I may walk out with him one day. He's a good man.'

'I'm glad,' said Adela.

Esther got up. 'Thanks for the tea. I feel better. I couldn't talk to anyone else. You're a good friend, Adela.'

Esther left and Adela heard her light footsteps echoing as they descended the stairs and crossed the showroom. Then the front door opened and closed and she was alone.

Michael had left England for the States. The news reached Adela through Blanche.

'It's rumoured he's left Bristol scattered with broken hearts,' she said. 'However Jack came to have such a ghastly son, I can't imagine.'

Adela asked evenly, 'How did you hear?'

'That's what's so rich! Vita learned of his departure and had a fit of hysterics. Her maid told Georgie's cook and the news went round like wild fire. And as if that weren't enough,' said Blanche, 'Vita's gone to America after him. She took the first possible passage.'

'Has she no pride?'

'Apparently not.'

'What about Claud?'

'He ended the engagement after the scene at your party. Of course, he was a gentleman and allowed people to think it was Vita's idea.'

'Of course. Blanche, do many people know exactly what the scene was about?'

Blanche looked quizzically at her sister. 'There are rumours. No one really knows the truth.'

'Do you?'

'That you had a fling with Michael? Yes. Georgie found out, but we don't talk. Don't worry, Adela, you're not the first woman to be taken in by a scoundrel and you won't be the last.'

* * *

Sander already knew about Vita. 'I can't stand the woman, but I can't help feeling sorry for her this time. I wonder if she's heard of Webster's activities in the States.'

'I don't know. I don't suppose she'll care what he is if she loves him enough. Sander, what exactly *does* he do? It's illegal, isn't it? Though he made it sound almost innocent.'

'Innocent? He's the right-hand man of a gang boss in New York. Ruthless gangsters are taking over the manufacture and sale of alcohol and they'll kill anyone who gets in the way of their making money. They also deal in drugs, manage prostitution on a large scale, and have their hands in any other dirty game they can think of.'

'But Michael couldn't kill! I know he's not worth much, but murder!'

Sander hesitated. 'Adela, you had best hear the truth about him, then never think of him again. He came over here because he had killed two members of a rival gang. His boss sent him away until the coast was clear. The rival boss was gunned down a couple of weeks ago and Michael has gone back to take over his territory.'

'Michael is a *murderer*?'

'Yes, though they don't seem to call it murder over there but "gang warfare". It can impinge fatally on the lives of the innocent. It was a bad day for America when a few fanatics slapped a ban on booze.'

'To think I—' She stopped. 'How long have you known all this?'

'Almost as soon as Webster landed. I'd already heard something about him and I soon discovered the rest. I blame myself, partly, for what happened to you. He'll go for any woman he wants, but he might have given up on you if I hadn't angered him by looking into his background. I'd heard rumours about him, and I wanted to know just how dangerous he was. He revenged himself by going for my wife.'

'Why didn't you tell me about him?'

'He seemed to be behaving himself and I could see no reason for talking. After all, he had no intention of remaining here. When I discovered what had happened to you, it was too late.

You thought anything unpleasant I told you about him was a cheap jibe and I had no proof to offer.'

'I wonder how Vita will fit into his life?'

'She won't. Webster's been engaged since last year to his boss's daughter and only his hasty flight postponed their wedding. Michael won't back out of that, or try to cheat on her, because he knows if he tried he'd be dead. Her father would have him destroyed.'

Adela had never thought she'd feel sorry for Vita. 'What ghastly people,' she said. She fell silent for a while. 'The more you tell me, the more ashamed I am.'

'Forget it, darling. I will. You'd had a tough time and were taken off balance. If I'd had the guts to tell you I loved you it might not have happened, but I was scared of being rejected. I've had enough of that in my life.'

'And I rejected you again. I don't know how you can be so forgiving.'

'Because I love you.'

Adela kissed him, softly, deliberately, before his arms went round her and held her close. 'What do you say to an early night?' she suggested, smiling up at him.

'It's the best idea you've ever had,' he said. 'The very best.'

318
 50
───
268
  80 Aud
───
188
 1 50 Male
─────
  38

Aud   Male
 80   150
 38   118
───   ───
118   268
───
 50
───
168

Aud
260
 38
───
162
  0
───

Male

234
150
───
 84
═══